Critical acclaim for Sundowners

'A very 21st-century bl[...] elements – nailbiting [...] glamorous locations – w[...] Much more than a c[...] glamorous and exciting world that is so contemporary and convincing you'll feel like a special fifth member of their group'   *Cosmopolitan*

'A sort of Blockbuster Plus – in this case, plus a little bit more intelligence and social and political grip than is normal . . . Agreeably glamorous and page-turning'
Daily Mail

'Make way Jackie Collins – there's an exciting new writer on the block . . . [*Sundowners*] has glamour, forbidden love and exotic locations. What more could you ask for?'
Bella

'[A] big-hearted women's read'   *Daily Mirror*

'A novel where Glamour with a capital "G" is the entire raison d'etre . . . It's a good, old-fashioned saga . . . a rattling good read . . . refreshingly, wonderfully unpretentious . . . *Sundowners* sets out to entertain and it does, not least because, unlike many writers of similar sagas, Lokko has the skill to make you care about what happens to the characters . . . Lesley Lokko is a new voice . . . this is her first novel. I'm looking forward to her next one already'
Wendy Holden, *Sunday Express*

'*Sundowners* is an entertaining read with a dollop of intellect'   Sue Leonard, *Irish Examiner* (Cork)

'A "brainy blockbuster", tremendous fun and scarily readable'   *Bookseller*

Lesley Lokko was born in Scotland in 1964 of mixed Ghanaian–Scots parentage. She grew up in Ghana, West Africa, and was educated in Ghana, the US and the UK. She trained as an architect and is currently completing her PhD in Architecture at UCL and working on her second novel.

Sundowners

❦

LESLEY LOKKO

ORION

An Orion paperback

First published in Great Britain in 2003
by Orion
This paperback edition published in 2004
by Orion Books Ltd,
Orion House, 5 Upper St Martin's Lane,
London WC2H 9EA

A CIP catalogue record for this book is
available from the British Library

ISBN 0 75285 921 8

Typeset by Deltatype Ltd, Birkenhead, Merseyside

Printed and bound in Great Britain by
Clays Ltd, St Ives plc

www.orionbooks.co.uk

for Lois

There are so many people to thank in the (long) making of this book – first and absolutely foremost, my agent, Christine Green, whose fierce encouragement and enthusiasm has guided this novel from the beginning; Jeremy Till, who very generously provided the spark that set it off; Antonia Till, who read the manuscript in its earliest form and who sent me Christine's way; Jane Wood and Kate Mills at Orion, who polished and pruned and showed such patience; Annette Sommer, who read it in its fiftieth draft and pronounced it 'actually pretty good'; to the translators, Sonja Petrus-Spaner, Jonathan Manning and Bridget Pickering, Gigi Dupuy-McCalla; to the following people for their 'muse' qualities, even if they were completely unaware at the time – Lori Rose, the original über-model from way, way back; Ilana Landsberg-Lewis for being everything Gabby is and more besides; Lisa Molander for her insider info on the legal world; Nael Evans for unwittingly entering the plot; Sacha Noordin for taking it all in his stride!; Rahesh Ram and Adrian Hallam for trusting me without ever having seen a draft . . .

. . . Another set of heartfelt thanks go to those whose characters miraculously aren't in the novel (well, almost not . . .) – Charles, of course, for all the things that go without saying; my brothers and sisters, for putting up with its ghost for so long and keeping faith; Kay Preston, who took it seriously, right from the start and to whom I owe a special debt of gratitude; my best mates Patrick Ata; Samir Pandya; Victor Sackey; Yaw KanKam-Boadu; Sean Hardcastle; Jonathan Hill; Greig Crysler; Ro Spankie and Caroline Osewe, for such splendid times over the past eight years and more; the 'cover girls' Ana, Anyele, Bridget, Clare, Nadine, Patti, Paz, Sagit and Yael, for their great judgement and aesthetic advice; my best 'girl' Marilí Santos-Munné, Lorenz Wyss and my godson Joán Nii Adom Wyss-Santos, for their constant generosity and their Basel retreat and finally, my darling niece, Lois Innes Lokko, who makes all things possible, and worthwhile.

'We talked, and you have forgotten the words.'
Borges

Note from the author:

While *Sundowners* is clearly a work of fiction, certain historical events and persons have been folded into the story that readers will no doubt recognise. Readers will also note that, in places, slight variations in timing have occurred in favour of sustaining the narrative. It is hoped that these few incidents of artistic licence will be understood.

PROLOGUE

December 1990: Paris

It was already dark at four o'clock in the afternoon and a fine grey mist was falling on the Champs-Élysées. Christmas lights shimmered in the rain, sending rivers of red and gold cascading onto the slick, dark surface of the damp streets. A tall, slender young woman stepped hurriedly off the kerb, wrapping her black woollen coat tightly around her. She looked anxiously at her watch: he would be waiting for her half-way across the city and, as usual, she was late. A black car pulled up in front of her, but she was too busy searching among the headlights for a taxi to pay it any attention. A man emerged from the car, stopping directly in front of her and blocking the road. Impatiently, she tried to move round him, still looking for a cab. He held out his hand to her and called her name.

She looked at him warily. She was used to being recognised, but there was something familiar about his voice. She looked closer, peering at him in the glow from the streetlight.

'What are *you* doing here?' She was surprised to see him. She tried to think where they'd last met. Los Angeles? London? Before he could answer, she heard another car pull up, heard the heavy door slam and the scuffle of shoes behind her. She turned round, wondering what all the commotion was about. She missed the quick nod the man gave to the two standing behind her. One of them lunged forward suddenly and grabbed her by the elbow, dragging her quickly towards him. She began to panic, struggling to release her arm. Before she could do anything, even scream, a gloved hand went over her mouth, the second man opened the car door and she was shoved into the back of the waiting car, banging her head painfully against the car frame as she was pushed inside. No one on the street noticed anything: it was over in a matter of seconds. Someone inside the car pulled her roughly by the hair and pushed her, face down, onto the leather seat. The man who had grabbed her got in beside her and someone else jumped in on the other side. The doors slammed, one after the other and the two cars began to move. She started screaming as the car powered away from the kerb, swerving wildly as the driver cut across several lanes of traffic and disappeared towards the Arc de Triomphe. She felt, rather than saw, the hand coming towards her, felt a crisp, sharp odour flood her senses and then, suddenly, everything went blank.

PART ONE

1

September 1981: Malvern, England

Somewhere along the journey she awoke with a start. For a split second she was at home in the backyard watching Poppie hang the day's washing in the searing white light of a Johannesburg summer. Just for a second she could hear the shrieks of laughter as her cousins Hennie and Marika escaped the heat in the pool at the bottom of the garden. The pool. Tears welled in her eyes almost immediately. She shook her head abruptly, forcing herself out of the past. *That* was South Africa. That was then. She was in England now. She looked out of the window as the Mercedes ate up the miles from Heathrow to Malvern, in the west of the country. Grey skies, grey fields . . . low dense cloud, the persistent threat of rain. It was so different from the light and space she had left behind, a world away from the clear skies of the high veld and the vast, sweeping landscapes of the Western Cape. The rain ran against the car window, a dreary, slow spittle that swallowed the light and blurred the distinction between cloud and sky. *England*. She shuddered. She had never felt so alone. She huddled down in the soft leather seats, hurriedly wiping her tears with the back of her hand. She closed her eyes again.

She could still see their faces as they waited in the departures lounge – Marika's wet with tears; Hennie silent and brooding; her aunt Lisette anxious and guilty. Rianne ignored her, her heart thumping inside her chest. She was being sent away. Lisette was casting her out of the only family she'd known since the death of first her mother, then her father. She was shaking with a mixture of rage and fear. But she was determined not to let it show. She hugged Marika one last time, then picked up her carry-on bag and disappeared through the door of the first-class cabin without looking back, not once. She was damned if she'd let Lisette see her cry.

She walked quickly to her seat, ignoring the sympathetic glance of the stewardesses. Saying goodbye to Marika and Hennie had been hard, but saying goodbye to Poppie had been hardest. Poppie was maid, housekeeper, surrogate mother, keeper of secrets and best friend, all rolled into one soft, dark, comforting figure. She had said goodbye to Poppie hundreds of times before as she left to spend the South African winter in Europe's summer with her mother's relatives, or a month with Aunt Lisette and her business associates in New York. But she had always returned, back home to Poppie and the warm, familiar smell that had been with her for as long as she could remember. It was Poppie who had held her and turned her face away after her mother drowned and they came to take her body out of the pool. It was Poppie she had run to after her father had disappeared and Lisette had told her he was dead. And it was Poppie who had intervened when Lisette told her it would be best for her to leave Vergelegen and the terrible memories that surrounded the house and come to live with her in Johannesburg. Rianne was hysterical and refused to leave, clinging desperately to Poppie and screaming that she would rather *die* than leave Poppie behind. So Poppie moved too, bringing her own children with her to Lisette's elegant, sprawling house in the northern suburbs. There was no *way* Rianne would have gone without her. And now she had left her behind. Just thinking about it hurt. She swallowed her tears.

The chauffeur flicked a quick look backwards at her as she sank below his field of vision. He wondered who she was.

His instructions had simply been to pick up a Miss de Zoete from the Penhaligon Hotel at Heathrow and deliver her to boarding school. Born and bred in East London, the name meant nothing to him. Who was she?

She was Rianne Marie Françoise de Zoete, daughter of disappeared tycoon Marius Tertius de Zoete; niece of South Africa's most powerful businesswoman, Lisette de Zoete-Koestler; and heiress to the vast de Zoete mining fortune. She was sixteen, rich, beautiful and thoroughly spoilt. Tall, slim, with heavy blonde hair that fell to her waist, high, tight cheekbones and, unusually, dark brown, almond-shaped eyes. Her mother's eyes. And her father's temperament.

Her mother, the French socialite Céline de Ribain, was nineteen when she met the young, brash South African at a London ball given by mutual friends. Although his French was atrocious and her English limited, she was intrigued. Her parents were worried. Despite his wealth, they thought him gauche, unsophisticated and rather *nouveau*. When she married him, three months later, they were horrified and more than a little afraid. They had reason to be. Before they realised what had happened, she was gone, heading for a new life they could scarcely imagine at the 'bottom of the world', as they put it. Overnight, it seemed, Céline de Ribain had become Céline de Zoete – and, as Marie-Hélène de Ribain remarked acidly to her husband, not only was he an *africain*, she suspected the family might even be Jewish. *Affreux*.

Claude de Ribain's worried but discreet enquiries bore little fruit. Not much was known in European circles about the *nouveaux riches* families down south. He found out that the man's father – a penniless Jew – had indeed come to South Africa from some Eastern European village, seeking his fortunes in the gold and diamond mines like so many had. He had married into a good, respectable family – again, nothing new there – but other than that, there was

5

surprisingly little information Claude could get his hands on. Marius bought them a large, sunny apartment on the Avenue Foch, just doors away from her parents, but it was clear that she was lost to them: she spoke English at first, then later Afrikaans, that strange and difficult language, to her husband and their beautiful daughter, Rianne. They adored their only grandchild and begged Céline every time she came to Paris to leave her with them for a season, just *one*, to improve her French and get to know her mother's culture. But Céline always refused, laughingly claiming she couldn't bear to spend a night apart from her darling child.

And then the unspeakable happened: she drowned. In the family pool. In front of her daughter on one of those clear, Cape summer days that she had always spoken of. Rianne was ten when it happened but she was old enough to understand what it meant. Her mother was gone. When her father disappeared, only a few weeks later, she understood, too, what that meant. Her life had changed for ever, and for the worse. Her grief-stricken French grandparents, Claude and Marie-Hélène de Ribain, had begged Lisette to allow them to look after Rianne. Claude had flown to Cape Town, to the gracious family home at Vergelegen. He pleaded with Lisette to be allowed to take all that was left to them of their daughter back to Paris, but Lisette was coldly adamant: Rianne was Marius's daughter, a de Zoete. And, as such, she was Lisette's responsibility, not theirs. Claude had returned to Paris empty-handed with a heavy, dull pain in his chest that never fully left him, despite Rianne's visits every other year. Rianne never knew of their attempts to claim her. Her aunt thought it best not to tell her. She would look after Rianne as if she were one of her own. Unfortunately, Rianne didn't see things quite the same way.

Their relationship did not begin well. Rianne shied away from Lisette and her cloying attempts to mother her. She was cold, unreachable, then hostile, prone to mood swings and periodic outbursts of tears. She was unpredictable, flighty, wilful. She and Hennie, close as they were in age, were sworn enemies. They *hated* one another. Lisette feared pulling into the driveway to find her beautiful home turned into a battlefield. She would look at her son's arms in horror – covered in scratches and bruises – the result of days and weeks of fighting between the two of them. Sometimes, coming upon them wrestling each other to the ground in the hallway or pinching each other as they sat together on the floor watching television, she would call in desperation for Poppie.

'Why can't you *stop* fighting, you two?' she would shout exhaustedly, pulling them away from each other and trying to protect her nails in the process. 'Stop it – I said *stop* it, Rianne!' Invariably Rianne would burst into tears and run crying down the corridor to her own room. Then it seemed Poppie was the only one who could comfort her and Lisette would wearily leave her to it. *She* had to comfort Hennie. Those were terrible months. Hell. No other word for it.

Marika would look on in sympathy, unable or unwilling to intervene. She was two years older than Rianne and already somewhat in awe of her looks and her dare-devil attitude towards everyone and everything. The 'good' girl in the family, Marika longed in secret to be more like her younger cousin. She would often take Rianne's side, sending Hennie into fits of rage. Lisette was at her wit's end. She tried everything, every approach she could think of – she was motherly, friendly, strict, sisterly, but nothing worked. The girl remained as aloof and distant as ever.

By the time Rianne was twelve, they had settled into an uneasy truce. They tolerated each other. Rianne was not like most other girls, Lisette would confide worriedly to friends, and certainly nothing like her older cousin. She was popular at school. Everyone wanted to be close to her. Everyone wanted Rianne as a best friend. The phone rang constantly. Curiously, she seemed not to notice or care. She was as happy alone as she was the centre of the crowd. Lisette, whose good looks and trim figure owed more to years of rigorous self-discipline than any natural gifts, remembered with pain beautiful girls just like Rianne at her teenage school who *never* had to try. Being beautiful was enough. People moved towards Rianne, not the other way round. She was used to having things her own way. She simply took what was given or what she wanted *when* she wanted.

She was sent to Glendales, the expensive, co-educational day-school just outside Pretoria. Marika was a model pupil there but it was clear that Rianne had no such ambitions. Marika was responsible and dedicated; Rianne was flighty and undisciplined. Marika was class prefect and routinely came first in exams. Rianne routinely skipped class and was twice caught smoking with a couple of older boys behind the chemistry building, her skirt tucked inside her under-wear as she showed off her long, brown legs. At Glendales, this was nothing short of a scandal. Things quickly got worse. Eventually Rianne was spotted sneaking into a senior boy's car, leaving the school grounds and returning after dark. Where they disappeared to, no one knew: she refused to say. Lisette, called in to pick up her niece, on a temporary suspension order, was at a loss as to what to do, she told Poppie, as she walked through the kitchen to fetch a glass. She desperately needed a drink. Poppie simply shrugged and squeezed Rianne's waist as the girl slipped past, a bored expression on her beautiful face.

Lisette had almost resigned herself to living in a perpet-ual state of war when, just before Rianne's sixteenth birthday, a miracle happened. She and Hennie suddenly stopped fighting and appeared to make peace. A calm descended upon the house. Marika was preparing to sit her matric exams and rarely left her room. Lisette was so grateful for the ceasefire that she paid neither of them any attention – she was fully preoccupied in those days with the family business. She and Hendryk, her and Marius's younger brother, were moving the company into a rapid series of expansions, from diamonds and gold into platinum, titanium and other rare precious metals. She travelled frequently to London, Amsterdam and further afield, to New York and Buenos Aires. The three children – although one could hardly call them children any longer – were used to her long absences and the sight of her neatly monogrammed leather cases standing in the hallway. They were looked after by Poppie, Seni – Poppie's youngest son – two drivers and three security guards.

They were safe in the way young white South African teenagers were safe: rich, pampered, secure. Everything in their world was as it should be, nothing would ever change. On the rare occasions when Rianne was home in the early evening, they would take their plates from the formal dining room and carry them into the den, flopping down on their stomachs to watch TV. For the most part, Rianne enjoyed those evenings, lying sandwiched on the floor between her cousins. It made a change from hanging out at the mall or, lately, in bars where she and her friends looked old enough to pass for eighteen. With Lisette frequently gone, she could do as she pleased, free of her aunt's watchful gaze and the burden of trying to decide how to behave, what to do, how to *be*. She had never figured it out. What was she in this house? Sister, cousin, daughter, friend? She was sixteen: she knew she had to start making some decisions about her life, where she would go, what she would do. Marika would be leaving soon, she wanted to study medicine at Stellenbosch. In a year or so Hennie would go into the army. Rianne had no desire to go to university. She couldn't imagine working. Should she go abroad? But where? She appeared to have no real ambitions yet did not seem disturbed by it. She seemed quite content to drift.

That year, she and Hennie spent hours talking in front of the TV or floating on their backs in the kidney-shaped pool. Things had begun to change between them, subtle changes that both alarmed and excited Rianne. She noticed the way

Hennie looked at her, the way his hands trembled a little when she asked him to tie her bikini straps or put sunblock on her tanned shoulders. At seventeen, almost a year older than her, Hennie was turning into a younger, fair-haired version of his uncle, Rianne's father. He was loud, physically confident, alternately aggressive and insecure. He was handsome, too. He certainly didn't lack admirers – the house was often full of girls from Glendales and other prestigious schools, some of them friends of Rianne who thought she was just the *luckiest* thing in the world to be living with Hennie *all the time*. Rianne laughed at them.

Unfortunately, Rianne was not the only one to notice the changes. Lisette came home late one evening from a business meeting to find Rianne and Hennie lying on the floor of the darkened TV lounge, limbs entwined, her head on his lap as he whispered something to her. She switched on the lights, horrified, although more by what she feared than by what she had actually seen. In a shaking voice, she ordered them to bed. 'It's a school day tomorrow, what on earth are you thinking of? It's past midnight!' Hennie at least had the grace to look embarrassed, his cheeks flushed. He scrambled to his feet and beat a hasty retreat down the corridor. But Rianne simply stood up, wearing only a pair of skimpy shorts and a loose top in which her adolescent breasts swung freely, and calmly walked past her aunt to her room.

Lisette stood in the middle of the room, breathing deeply. That was it. Something had to be done. With Marika gone in a few months, she couldn't leave the two children alone. Although they were hardly children, she kept reminding herself. She had to do *something*. But what?

A few weeks later, as she stood on the patio waiting for Hennie and Rianne to finish their tennis lessons at the bottom of the garden, she thought she had the answer. She would send Rianne overseas, to England, like her father before her. A change of scene would be good for her. Perhaps after she'd done a year or two in England, she could go on to Switzerland – one of those expensive finishing schools where Rianne might learn the rudiments of charm. She had spoken to a few friends in the UK, asking them to help her select a suitable school for her troublesome niece. But first she had to tell her.

She stood there, nervously watching the two of them as they walked slowly up the short hill to the house, arms linked, racquets trailing behind. They were so alike. She did not take a photograph, but kept the image of the two of them, her son and her beloved Marius's daughter, as if it were the last time she would see them so. Hennie was almost a head taller than his cousin, but she was easily as strong. She had inherited Marius's love of the outdoors, his passion for sport and physical challenge, as well as her mother's more delicate beauty. At sixteen, she was stunning. Lisette was worried, not only for her son but for all the other young men who had taken to hanging around the house lately, just as Rianne's friends hung hopefully around Hennie. Yet despite her beauty, there was something in the girl that was ... *damaged*, something fragile and brittle and painful. Of course it was to do with the loss of her parents, Lisette knew that. But Rianne had lacked nothing ... love, security, warmth. Lisette had seen to it that the girl was brought straight into the heart of her own family ... and yet, somehow, it was not enough. There was a kind of hunger in the girl, although for what exactly, Lisette couldn't say. There was a fearlessness about her, a recklessness that worried her. Rianne behaved as though she were accountable to no one, not even to what was left of her family. And this worried Lisette.

She smiled at them as they came up to the patio. They were both sweaty and tired from an hour's game in the late autumn sun.

'Darling,' she said to Rianne, as she handed her a cold glass of lemonade, 'won't you come here and sit with me for a minute? I have some important news ... for you both.'

Rianne looked at her suspiciously. Whenever Lisette addressed her as 'darling', she usually had bad news. She was not wrong.

'England?' Rianne looked at her aunt, alarmed. '*England?*' she repeated. 'Why?'

'Well, your . . . father would have wanted it, darling,' Lisette said quickly. 'He was educated among them, you know. He would have wanted you to have the same.'

Rianne's dark eyes flashed dangerously. 'But I don't *want* to go to England,' she burst out angrily. 'I like it here. I don't want to go. I—'

'It'll be good for you, *skatjie*,' Lisette interrupted her. 'You'll enjoy it, you'll see. I would have given *anything* to go, at your age, you know.'

'I don't care about *you*,' Rianne shouted. 'I'm not going. I'm *not*!'

'Can't she go to Ellersby, Mum?' Hennie mentioned the exclusive all-girls boarding school near Cape Town. It wouldn't be Johannesburg but it wouldn't be England either.

'No, it's decided.' Lisette was firm. 'Uncle Hendryk and I have agreed, Rianne, that you'll be going in September when the school year starts over there.'

'I won't. I *won't*. I'm not going, d'you hear me? You won't *make* me!' Rianne threw her racquet angrily onto the ground and raced indoors.

Hennie immediately started after her but Lisette stopped him. 'Leave her alone for a while, darling, she's upset.'

'Of *course* she's upset. Wouldn't you be? Why do you always have to decide everything *for* her?'

'Me?' Lisette was alarmed. Hennie had never spoken to her like that before. 'Everything I – *we* – do for Rianne is for the best, you know that.'

'No, everything you do is the best for *you*, best for what suits *you*, not for her. Why can't you just leave her alone?'

'Hennie!' Lisette was furious now. 'Hennie! Come back

here this minute!' But he was gone. Lisette sat down on the wicker patio chair, her hands trembling and her heart racing. She needed a cigarette. Her angry exchange with Hennie had upset her. She was not used to talking to her children in that way. But she was also sure she was doing the right thing. Although she thought that nothing had 'happened' between her son and her niece, it would be no bad thing to put a bit of distance between them. She sighed. For about the hundredth time that year, she missed Marius dreadfully. What was she to do with his daughter?

'Are you all right, miss?' the chauffeur enquired gently, breaking in on her thoughts and forcing Rianne back to the present.

'I'm fine,' Rianne replied tightly. She rubbed her eyes fiercely.

'Would you like to stop for a bit, get something to eat?'

'No.' She wished he would leave her alone. He was paid to drive, not talk. Who did he think he was? All the drivers she'd known back home were black and knew their place. They hardly ever spoke to her. She preferred it that way.

'Well, we won't be much longer. Another hour, I'd say. Miserable weather, isn't it? Mind you, that's England for you,' he added.

Rianne ignored him. The weather outside just about matched her mood inside. Grey. Sad and grey. She watched the windscreen wipers through tear-soaked lashes. Swish-wish, swish-wish, swish-wish . . . She was lost again in thought.

2

She was dimly aware that the car had come to a halt. She opened her eyes. They were outside an enormous dark building. She struggled to sit upright as the chauffeur opened his door and ran round the car to open hers. It was still raining, a fine misty spray that stung her cheeks as she swung her legs out – as Lisette had repeatedly taught her to do – and emerged onto the empty forecourt. She looked about her. A large brass plaque on one of the gate pillars announced the building as '*St Anne's and the Abbey Independent School for Girls*'. She mouthed the words silently feeling her stomach contract. So this was it. She looked in dismay at the forbidding building in front of her. Even in the mist, it appeared cold and austere. It resembled nothing so much as an ancient fortress, complete with heavy oak and iron door and dozens of barred windows. She could just make out the two wings that flanked the main building, and the formal, very English gardens that ran around the side of the forecourt, sloping down the hill.

The front door swung open and in the light that spilled out she could see someone coming through the vestibule, moving rapidly towards her. Her stomach began to churn. She hoisted her bag onto her shoulder and walked reluctantly towards the door. The figure stopped in the doorway, waiting.

'Rianne!' a woman cried out. 'Welcome to St Anne's, my dear! Come in out of the rain!' She opened her arms and Rianne suddenly found herself pressed against a matronly chest. She caught the scent of lilies, faint and sweet, then she was held at arm's length as the woman looked at her approvingly. Rianne pushed her away rudely, squirming. She *hated* being hugged. Especially by strangers.

'I'm Miss Matthews, the housemistress of Gordon House,' the woman said, smiling. 'Was it a long trip?'

Rianne nodded sullenly, looking past her to the hallway

beyond. It was everything she'd imagined an English boarding school to be – dark, with gloomily reflective floors and heavy wood panelling. Endless trophies and washed-out watercolour portraits of past headmistresses and head girls adorned the walls. A wide staircase wound its way up past several landings. She could see a few girls glancing curiously at her as they leaned over the banisters to see who the new arrival was and why she was arriving almost a month late – *and* why she'd arrived in a chauffeur-driven Mercedes.

'It's nearly supper-time,' Miss Matthews said briskly. 'You must be *famished* after that dreadful journey. I'll take you along to your room and introduce you to the girls you're sharing with. They can show you the way to the dining hall after you've had a chance to settle in. You'll be with three girls, all *very* nice. I'm sure you'll all get along famously. Gabrielle Francis will be in charge of helping you settle in.'

The butterflies in her stomach were fluttering again. *Three* girls? She was going to share a room with *three* girls? She had never shared a room with *anyone* in her life. She couldn't imagine sharing her space with three complete strangers. They would be best friends already, of course, and they would hate her. The latecomer. The odd one out. She followed Miss Matthews out of the hallway, trying to ignore the thudding in her chest.

3

Upstairs, in room twelve on the third floor of Gordon House, Charmaine Hunter and Gabrielle Francis were rearranging the furniture, trying to make space for a fourth bed in the already crowded room.

'Why do *we* have to have her?' Charmaine complained, pushing her narrow bed closer to the wall. 'It's not bloody fair. Everyone else has three to a room . . . and we're *fine* with just us.' She kicked her trunk under her bed and flopped down. Enough exertion for the time being.

'Because,' Gabby muttered, 'Matthie decided . . . and that's that. No use moaning about it. She can change rooms at Christmas, Matthie said.'

'But it's so *cramped* in here. Look, there's no room for an extra dressing-table.'

'She can share mine. Will you shut up and *get* up? She'll be here any minute. Come on! Matthie'll be livid if it's not organised when she comes in.'

'Hello, what's going on in here?' Nathalie Maréchal, the third member of room twelve, bounced into the room, red-faced and sweaty from lacrosse practice.

'Can you *imagine*?' Charmaine squawked. 'We've got someone else moving in.'

'What? In *here*? When?'

'Yes, in about five minutes. I mean, it's not as if we're not already living like sardines.'

'Charmaine, will you *stop* whining?' Gabby said crossly, lugging a pile of sheets, pillows and a duvet. 'It's only for a few months. Come on, help me make the bed up, will you? Nat, why are you just standing there? Why am *I* doing all the work?'

'Cos you always do.' Charmaine smiled at her sweetly.

'Who is she?' Nathalie shoved her lacrosse stick under her bed.

'She's South African . . . Rina something or other. She'll be here any minute. Matthie wants us to look after her, be nice. I think her mother died. She's *loaded*, apparently.' Gabby began to stuff the duvet into its cover.

'God, that's all we need.' Charmaine rolled her eyes. 'Some spoilt little rich kid. She'll have a *fit* when she sees this place. I bet she's used to servants running around after her. Don't they all have servants in Africa?'

'Not everyone, you idiot.' Gabby laughed at her. 'Although I suppose she does – oh, come on, it won't be that bad—' She stopped. They all heard footsteps outside. 'Quick! It's Matthie!'

Miss Matthews walked in and cast a quick eye around her. The three of them were lined up to meet Rianne and the room, thankfully, was tidy. She gave Gabby a grateful smile and turned to Rianne, who hung back reluctantly in the doorway.

'Come in, my dear, they won't bite!'

Rianne paused, drawing a deep breath, and walked into the room. All three girls stared at her, dumbstruck. Not only was she rich, she was absolutely *beautiful*.

4

There was an awkward silence. Rianne ignored the girls and looked around the room in dismay. Four of them, in this tiny room? She looked at the narrow beds lined up so close to each other that they practically *touched*. Impossible. She turned to Miss Matthews, her eyes narrowing. 'I am *not* staying here,' she announced firmly, holding on to her overnight case. 'I want my own room.'

'Now, Rianne,' Miss Matthews said, 'there are no single rooms at St Anne's. Sharing a room is part of the whole experience of boarding school. I know it's a little more cramped than you're probably used to—'

Rianne cut her off mid-sentence. 'I don't care. I'm *not* staying here. You'd better find me my own room or I'm going straight home.' The three girls were staring open-mouthed at her, then at Miss Matthews.

Miss Matthews pursed her lips. 'I'm afraid that's the rule, Rianne. Everyone shares. You'll just have to manage. You may change rooms at Christmas, not before. Now, I'll leave you to settle in. Gabby, make sure Rianne finds her way to the dining room in time for supper. Please don't be late.' She quickly turned on her heel and walked out.

Rianne looked angrily at Miss Matthews's disappearing back. The woman was walking away? What the hell was she supposed to do now? She was used to stamping her foot and getting her own way.

'Um, it's not *that* bad,' a voice said.

Rianne turned. A large, overweight redhead with thick, ugly glasses had spoken, and now smiled rather shyly. 'It's a bit of a squeeze but it's only till Christmas. We can all change rooms then, if we want.'

Rianne stared at her, unsmiling. 'I don't care *how* long it's for. I'm not staying here.'

'Well, where are you going to go?' A small, voluptuous blonde girl piped up. Her uniform skirt looked at least four inches shorter than anyone else's.

'Home,' Rianne said curtly.

'Where's that?'

'What do you care?' Rianne retorted. The girl blushed angrily.

'Look, it's a bit late to go back tonight. Why don't you just put your bag down and come with us to supper? You can ring your parents when we get back and they can sort it out.' The overweight girl spoke.

'They're dead.' Rianne looked at her coldly. Gabby grimaced. She'd forgotten.

'Oh . . . I'm really sorry, I forgot. Well, your . . . is it your aunt? You can ring *her* tomorrow. Look, why don't I introduce everyone, just in the meantime? I'm Gabby. This is Charmaine, and that's Nathalie.' All four of them stared at each other.

There was another short silence.

'We'll show you where supper is,' Gabby offered. 'It starts in about ten minutes.'

'I'm not hungry.' Rianne was dismissive, determined not to give an inch. She would phone Lisette that very evening and demand to be sent back home.

'But you have to go. We're not allowed to miss it.' Nathalie looked worried.

'I don't care if I'm allowed or not. I'm not going.'

'OK. I'll tell Matthie you're not feeling well.' Gabby spoke again. She could see there was no point in arguing with her. She beckoned to the others to follow her.

'Tell her what you like.' Rianne shrugged. She didn't give a damn what Gabby said to Miss Matthews. She wasn't going to be around long enough for it to matter. The others looked at each other quickly and headed for the door.

'Bloody *hell*,' Nathalie said, as soon as the door shut behind them. 'She's a *night*mare.'

'What a *bitch*!' Charmaine hissed. Her cheeks were still red with anger. Gabby nodded.

'But awfully pretty,' Nathalie added, sighing. All three nodded. '*Really* pretty,' she repeated glumly.

Alone in the room, Rianne sat on the edge of one of the beds. Apart from the four beds, there were three dressing-tables, two large ungainly wardrobes and dozens of pop posters stuck to the walls. Piles of clothes, discarded shoes, books and papers lay everywhere. It was all so ugly. There were hundreds of little stains where the posters of previous occupants had been ripped off the walls, and everything looked like it needed a good scrub. It was so different from the cool, spacious bedroom and bathroom she'd left behind. She thought of her room with its warm terracotta tiles and french patio doors that opened onto her own balcony; her pretty mosaic-tiled bathroom with its shower, fluffy white towels and fresh flowers that Seni brought in from the garden every day. *That* was home. Suddenly her eyes filled with tears. Her new sweater and horrible corduroy skirt – items that Lisette had been so careful to buy according to the list they'd been given – scratched terribly. She wanted nothing more than to strip them off and take a long hot shower. She wondered where the showers were.

Five minutes later, having looked in all the rooms on the floor, she gave up. There were no showers. She couldn't believe it. There was a bathroom at the end of the corridor, a damp, musty-smelling room with several cubicles and a row of washbasins. She'd never taken a bath in her life. Utterly miserable, she walked back to the room, collected her nightdress and toothbrush and made her way back to the bathroom. The taps creaked and hissed as the tub filled with water. She watched the steam rising from the hot tap as she stripped off the sweater, unbuttoned the starchy shirt and stiff skirt and kicked off the clumpy brown shoes. She peeled off the woollen stockings and hideous underwear and, shivering, climbed into the bath. The water was warm and soothing. She hugged her knees to her chest and closed her eyes. She longed to be at home with Hennie and Marika. She scrubbed herself fiercely, trying to wash away the events of the past two days and the feel of the prickly new clothes.

Her eyes were red and swollen by the time she got out of the tub and started to brush her teeth. She would put a call through to Aunt Lisette immediately. There was no *way* she was going to stay here. No way. She made her way back to the room. She would find that woman, Matthie or whatever her name was, and call home immediately.

But Miss Matthews found her first. When Rianne opened her bedroom door and saw her standing by the window, her heart sank.

'Rianne,' Miss Matthews began, in a firm but kindly voice, 'Gabby said you weren't feeling well.'

'I'm fine,' Rianne replied. Her heart was thumping.

'Well, then, why aren't you at supper? I'm afraid you're not allowed to miss meals. That was pointed out to you.'

'I'm not hungry.' She was defiant.

'That's not the point. You are required to attend all meals in the dining room, except Saturday supper.' Rianne said nothing. 'I realise you're tired and probably a little upset, but you do have to comply with school rules. Have you eaten anything?'

'No. I said I'm not hungry. And I don't *care* about your stupid rules. I'm going home tomorrow,' Rianne retorted rudely.

'We'll see about that,' Miss Matthews replied calmly. 'In the meantime, I'd like you to come down to my flat and have something to eat before you go to bed. You can't sleep on an empty stomach. And I won't take no for an answer. Come along, dear. Put your dressing-gown on.' Rianne had no option but to follow the woman out of the room. She *was* hungry, it was true. She followed Miss Matthews, close to tears again. But there was no way she was going to cry. She was a de Zoete, for God's sake. As Lisette was always reminding her.

5

Rianne woke with a jolt. An alarm clock had gone off, rudely interrupting her sleep. It was still pitch dark and, for a moment, she lay still in her narrow bed, confused. Where was she? England, she remembered suddenly. She closed her eyes. All around her, the other three were stirring grumpily. She could hear doors opening all down the corridor and the sound of the bathroom taps being turned on. She lay still for a minute. She would get up when they'd all left and phone Lisette. With any luck, she'd be gone by lunchtime.

'Bloody hell,' Charmaine groaned, yawning. 'It's freezing in here!'

Rianne snuggled down further in her bed.

'What time is it?' came Nathalie's sleepy voice.

'Time to get up.' Gabby began to surface. She struggled to sit upright, looking at the sleeping figure beside her.

'Come on.' She prodded at Rianne's figure under the covers with her leg. 'Time to get up. Breakfast's in half an hour.'

'I don't want any,' Rianne muttered. She was too tired and cosy in her little nest to even think about moving.

'Well, don't say I didn't warn you.' Gabby swung her legs out of bed. 'Coming, you lot?' She tugged at Charmaine's duvet as Nathalie sleep-walked her way to the bathrooms.

Rianne burrowed even further into her bed. Within minutes the room was empty, leaving her alone with her thoughts. She'd been having such a pleasant dream ... back home, of course, riding or swimming ... something energetic and in the sun. She drifted off.

'Rianne, get up!' A voice penetrated her sleep. Rianne looked up from beneath her tousled mane. It was Miss Matthews and she looked furious.

'You have approximately seven minutes to get dressed and make your way to the dining room. I've asked that breakfast be put on hold for the lower sixth until you get there. You'll keep twenty-three of your classmates waiting until you present yourself so I suggest you hurry.' Miss Matthews closed the door.

Rianne stared at the closed door in disbelief. She had no other option but to get up. And quickly.

Five minutes later, having pulled the horrible school sweater over her head and buttoned up her skirt, she rushed into the hall, her cheeks burning. Twenty-three pairs of eyes stared accusingly at her as she made her way towards the lower-sixth table. All the other years in the school were finishing breakfast and the Lower Sixth hadn't even started. She did her best to ignore everyone but Miss Matthews was determined to make her point.

'Breakfast starts at seven-thirty, Rianne. Please make sure you're here on time from now on.' Rianne was about to inform her that she would be gone by the following morning but she recognised the tone of the woman's voice:

it brooked no argument. She bent her head as nonchalantly as she could, grimaced at the cold scrambled eggs and reached for a piece of toast.

As Rianne concentrated on her toast, the chatter around her slowly resumed. She took the opportunity to cast a quick look at the other girls. Apart from Gabby, Charmaine and Nathalie, they were pretty dull, mostly thin, wan girls with mousy brown hair and spotty skin. At one end, much to her surprise, there were four *native* girls, including one who looked at her superciliously. They were wearing uniforms – it wasn't possible! They were pupils? Surely not.

Assembly took place as it did every morning in the large hall half-way down the short hill from Gordon to the Big House. It was mercifully short – prayers, announcements and a short reading for the day. To Rianne's irritation, Miss Caruthers, the headmistress, insisted on welcoming her publicly to the school. Three hundred pairs of eyes turned to look at her and Gabby nudged her to stand up. Miss Caruthers even mentioned that 'Rianne comes to us from somewhere considerably warmer, from South Africa, and we welcome her most heartily into our school community. I hope you will settle in splendidly among us, my dear,' she finished, beaming. Rianne nodded impatiently. It was a complete waste of time, welcoming her to the school. She'd be gone in a couple of days.

As they stood up to leave, she was aware of the black girl she'd seen glaring at her at breakfast looking at her with the same hostile expression again. She glared straight back. Who the hell did she think she was? Rianne was shocked. It had never occurred to her that there would be native or even Indian girls at a school in England and yet, looking around the assembly hall, there were quite a number of them. Rianne had never had any encounter with blacks in any capacity other than as servants.

'Who the hell is that?' she asked the others, as the girl

gave her a final, dismissive glance. Rianne narrowed her eyes. How dare she look at her in that way?

'Oh, that's Jumoke Olalade,' Gabby whispered. 'She's awfully clever – she's sitting Oxbridge next year. She's really nice.'

'Oh, yeah?' Rianne snorted. 'Why's she staring at me?'

'Oh, you know,' Gabby said, suddenly conscious of Jumoke's sneer, 'she's from Nigeria – she probably doesn't like South Africans.'

'Well, you'd better tell her to stop. I'll report her.'

'Who to?' The other two looked at Rianne in surprise.

'I don't know. To whoever. I mean, at home she wouldn't even be allowed to *speak* to me.' Rianne was arrogantly dismissive. Another reason to call Lisette. She would have a *fit* if she knew Rianne had to share her classes – or, even worse, a *bathroom* – with natives and Indians.

'Well, you're not at home now,' Gabby replied tartly, 'and we do things differently in England. Just stay out of her way. Anyhow, look, we've got to get to class.' She tried to change the subject. 'What subjects are you taking? I've got history first.'

'Subjects?' Rianne looked at her uncomprehendingly. No one had said anything to her about choosing subjects.

Gabby fished in her bag and produced a rather dog-eared timetable. 'Yes, for your A levels. You have to choose at least two. That's if you're doing them. Charmaine's not. She's doing secretarial training.'

'I don't know and I don't care,' Rianne said. 'I'll be leaving soon.'

'You'd better come with us for today, though,' said Nathalie. 'You can talk to Matthie later on about what subjects you want to do.'

'I *told* you,' Rianne repeated, irritated. 'I don't *care* about choosing subjects. I'm not staying.'

Gabby and Nathalie looked at each other. 'Just *take* it, Rianne. If you can't leave until the weekend, you might as well know where you're supposed to be each day. Go on.' Gabby proffered the timetable.

Rianne took it reluctantly and stared at it. She'd never seen so many subjects – chemistry, maths, history, geography – good God, how the hell was she supposed to choose at least two? Or even one? She wasn't much good at any of them, unless you counted French. Which was hardly fair since it was her mother tongue. Her *mother*'s tongue. Her mother. She shut her eyes immediately, a trick she'd used ever since that awful day. When she opened them a second later, the image of her mother's body, covered in blue tarpaulin, dripping water, was gone. She reluctantly followed Gabby to the English classroom.

The day dragged by. The monotony of lessons was interrupted only by 'elevenses', a short break that involved running back to Gordon House and stuffing one's face with as many slices of thickly buttered toast as possible. Gabby ate more toast than Rianne had ever thought possible for one person and she had to hide her shock when one of the Indian girls took *her* empty mug, rinsed it out and poured herself a cup of tea. Back home, people of different races *never* shared utensils. Never. It was unthinkable. Lisette would be horrified. Rianne was confident of her response: come home *immediately*.

But unfortunately for Rianne, after a long, tedious afternoon of classes and yet more toast at four o'clock, when she finally rang home, Lisette wasn't there. Unknown to her, Miss Matthews had taken the precaution of phoning her aunt that morning. They had decided to force Rianne to spend at least a fortnight at St Anne's by pretending Lisette was away on business and unreachable. That way, they had reasoned, she would have to give the school a chance . . . and then, who knew? She might even enjoy it. Her aunt was away on a business trip, a maid told her. She'd be back in about three weeks' time. Whatever it was, Miss Rianne would have to call back then. Rianne nearly wept with frustration. She slammed down the phone in Miss Matthews's little flat and, ignoring the sympathetic look, ran upstairs to her bedroom and flung herself down on her bed, sobbing. Nathalie was the only one in the room but, after a couple of attempts to find out what was wrong with Rianne and getting no answer, she gave up and left the room to find the others. Let her stew in her own misery. She'd have to snap out of it sooner or later.

6

But she didn't. By the end of the second week, even Miss Matthews was worried. Rianne was as unhappy as she had been on her first evening. She withdrew into herself, rebuffing everyone's efforts to draw her into school life. She was rude, sulky and, on the odd occasion when she condescended to speak to anyone, she was sarcastic, arrogant or both. She spent every evening alone in the shared bedroom, writing in her diary or listening to her Walkman, counting the days until Lisette's return.

Her room-mates were annoyed. Rianne made them feel uncomfortable, even in their own space. She would hum loudly to herself, her Walkman turned up full blast, which made it almost impossible for the other three to have a normal conversation. Gabby spent more and more time in the library, away from the tension in the room; Nathalie suddenly became an avid sports enthusiast, signing up for extra lacrosse and hockey practice almost daily. In that way, she managed to spend most of her day outside the room. It was left to Charmaine, who was unfortunately interested in neither books nor sport, to brave the awkward silences. She was still in awe of the beautiful newcomer.

'What're you doing tomorrow?' she enquired casually on the Friday evening at the end of Rianne's second week. She was sitting on the floor, carefully painting her toenails.

Rianne was lying on her bed, eyes closed. For once, she had forgotten to put on her headphones.

'Nothing.' Rianne was uncommunicative.

'D'you want to come into town with me?'

'Where?'

'Town – you know, Malvern. There's a group of us – we meet every other Saturday at a tea-shop in town. It's fun.'

'What? Drinking *tea*?' Rianne sounded faintly contemptuous. 'No thanks.'

'Oh, come on,' Charmaine insisted. 'I mean, it's not like you're doing anything here, right?'

'I'd rather do nothing than sit in a room full of girls drinking tea.'

'Oh, suit yourself,' Charmaine said crossly. She was only trying to be nice.

There was silence for a few minutes.

'OK,' Rianne said suddenly.

'What?'

'OK. I suppose I *could* go. There's nothing else to do.'

'Oh, good! It'll be fun, I promise. We'll go after lunch.' Charmaine was rather pleased with herself. She'd cracked Rianne's frosty exterior. She looked up, smiling, but Rianne was rummaging around for her Walkman.

If Charmaine thought it was the start of something approaching friendship, Rianne thought to herself, she was sadly mistaken. Going into town with someone once meant nothing. She ignored Charmaine and put on her headphones. She was surprised at herself. Why on earth had she agreed to spend an afternoon with a bunch of silly girls drinking tea? Back home . . . Well, that was another matter altogether. Saturday mornings the phone would start ringing at eight o'clock, everyone desperate to get her approval for their plans or, even better, her company. In the summer, she'd get up, pull back the sliding doors of her bedroom and walk across the lawn to the swimming pool, watching the early morning sun slither across the still-wet grass. She loved the silky feel of the water, warmer than the air outside, chasing the sleep from her eyes. Then it was breakfast with Hennie and Marika in the enormous, sunny kitchen – a slow start to the day as they discussed their options and Poppie bustled about filling coffee cups, spooning egg onto their plates . . . another piece of bread? And there were always options: horse-riding, swimming, hanging out at the mall, someone stealing an older brother or sister's car and heading out of the city . . . back home there was always something to do and someone interesting or fun to do it with . . . but here? Look at her, stuck in the middle of nowhere, contemplating a day's outing *drinking tea*? What the hell had happened?

She was bored. She'd been cooped up indoors with a bunch of noisy, weird girls for almost a fortnight. For someone accustomed to living in the sun, this was confinement at its worst. She turned onto her back and lay listening to music until Charmaine had finished painting her nails and waddled off to the bathroom, bits of cotton-wool sticking out from between her toes.

'You must be joking,' Nathalie said, cramming the last piece of toast into her mouth. They were sitting in the kitchen at Gordon, gossiping. 'She's going to town with you? Tomorrow?'

'Yes. We're going in after lunch.' Charmaine looked at her and Gabby.

'Well, good luck. I hope you get more than a word out of her, sulky cow. And you'd better get her to change her clothes. Did you *see* what she was wearing last week? Those awful trousers?'

'Oh, God – they were awful.' Nathalie grimaced. 'So baggy and . . . *yuk*!'

'Doesn't she know corduroys are *so* out?'

'Maybe they don't have any fashion where she comes from.'

'They're probably just a few years behind,' Gabby said mildly. 'Besides, she'd look good in anything.'

'Not brown cords!' Charmaine laughed. 'Specially not with white tennis shoes! Did you see them?' The three of them nodded and laughed.

The kitchen door opened loudly and they fell silent. Rianne walked past them and opened the fridge. Her cheeks were unusually red.

Gabby blushed too: she was sure Rianne had heard them talking about her. The others were staring into their mugs. 'Hi, Rianne.' She rushed to fill the awkward silence. 'I heard you're going into town with Char tomorrow. It'll be fun.'

'Don't bet on it,' Rianne said tightly. She collected a pint of milk from the fridge and walked out of the kitchen.

The three looked at each other.

'Shit! She probably heard us.' Charmaine looked a little worried.

'Who cares? Serves her right. We've been nothing but friendly to her and she's been a bloody cow,' Nathalie said defensively.

'Now she won't come,' Charmaine said gloomily.

'Don't be silly, she's probably bored to tears sitting on her bed every night,' Gabby said calmly. She knew, even if the others didn't, that Rianne cried herself to sleep almost every night. She reached for another piece of toast.

Charmaine nodded. Gabby was always right.

'You're not going in like *that*, are you?' It was just after lunch the following afternoon. Charmaine looked at Rianne's outfit in horror. She was wearing a blue cotton skirt, a thick patterned jumper, brown tights – and, horror of horrors, bright green leg-warmers.

'What's wrong with what I'm wearing?' Rianne demanded, immediately defensive. She'd actually thought quite hard about what to wear. She'd been a bit unsure about the leg-warmers – on the list they'd been under 'bedwear' – but everyone seemed to wear them.

'Well, everything, really.' Charmaine was thrilled at the

opportunity to wax lyrical on her favourite subject, which was style. 'You can't mix your fabrics,' she said sternly. 'Cotton and wool. Your skirt's cotton, that's mistake number one. It's October and you shouldn't be wearing cotton unless it's a shirt. Mistake number two, it's blue and those awful leg-warmers are green. Don't you know the rule? Blue and green should *never* be seen. Your jumper doesn't go with anything and your tights are *completely* the wrong colour. And leg-warmers only go with trousers.'

'Jesus. We're only going into some stupid little village,' Rianne said, in exasperation. 'It's not a fashion show, for Christ's sakes.' What was the girl twittering on about?

'Fine. Suit yourself. You'll see,' Charmaine muttered. Ungrateful cow. She was squeezing into her denim skirt when Rianne pulled off the leg-warmers and skirt and put on a pair of jeans. Charmaine smiled to herself. So she had been listening, after all.

Rianne looked at Charmaine out of the corner of her eye. In a denim miniskirt, red tights and a black sweater, she looked far better than Rianne did. It was something of a shock to her to realise that she wasn't leading the pack in terms of what she wore, looked like or said, the way she did at home. Here everything was topsy-turvy: *she* had to follow the others, figure out from watching them what to wear, say, do . . . She *hated* it. She watched Charmaine run a brush through her short blonde hair and she was ready. Almost. As an afterthought, she reached into her drawer, pulled out a stick of lip gloss, ran a practised finger round her mouth and dabbed a bit of the gloss on her eyelids. They were forbidden to use make-up, she explained as she turned to Rianne. 'D'you want some of this?' She held out the little tube. Rianne took it ungraciously and put some on her own lips. 'Shall we go?' Charmaine said, checking herself one last time in the mirror.

'Suppose so.' Rianne was careful not to be too enthusiastic although she was looking forward to leaving the school grounds. She hadn't been outside the stone walls since she'd arrived.

'Look, there's the bus! We'll have to run for it!' Charmaine broke into as elegant a run as she could manage in her tight skirt as they neared the bottom of the hill. Rianne had no idea where they were running to. She overtook Charmaine and reached the corner a good minute ahead of her. She could see the bus – an ancient blue thing – trundling up the hill towards them but she'd no idea what to do next.

'Stand at the stop, Rianne!' Charmaine shouted, struggling along behind her. 'At the stop! The *stop*, you idiot!' Rianne looked around her, confused. The stop? She had no idea what a bus stop looked like. Fortunately, the driver saw them, chugged to a halt and waited obligingly.

Charmaine caught up with her, out of breath. 'Didn't you see the stop?' she panted, as she fished out money for their fares. 'You've got to stand next to it otherwise they just drive past.'

'Where?' Rianne looked around. They were standing next to a pole. A small red sign at the top proclaimed 'Bus Stop'. She rolled her eyes. 'How'm I supposed to know it's a stop? There was no one else here.' She'd never taken a bus in her life. She'd seen people waiting for them – natives, of course – but there were always hundreds of them queuing at the side of the road . . . it was hard to miss them.

'Don't tell me you've never been on a bus!' Charmaine exclaimed disbelievingly. They got on. It was almost empty. It was a little early for the afternoon rush when all the girls in the sixth form descended on the town.

'We have drivers at home,' Rianne said haughtily. 'Only natives take buses.'

'Really? You have a driver to take you everywhere? What about when you go out with your friends? Do *they* have drivers too?'

'Everyone has a driver. They just drive you and bring you back. That's what they're supposed to do.'

'Really?' Charmaine was intrigued. 'Anywhere you want to go?'

'Of course. How do *you* get around?'

'At home in London? Oh, on the tube. Or sometimes in a taxi, if I'm with a boy. But taxis are awfully expensive.' Rianne said nothing. Back home, no one talked about money: everyone simply had plenty of it. She sat back in her seat and looked out of the window.

It was really quite pretty, she had to admit. In Malvern the leaves were turning from a dark, mossy green to burnt orange and fiery gold. The bus creaked and groaned its way down the hill towards the town, slipping past stone cottages, some with thatched roofs and gardens full of tea roses. They stopped a couple of times at more funny poles with red placards to pick up a handful of people. Rianne looked at them out of the corner of her eye. There were little old ladies, heads in scarves, with shopping-bags and sensible walking-shoes. She'd never seen an old lady carry her own shopping, let alone stand by the side of the road to wait for a bus. An old white lady, that was. She wondered where all the servants were. She looked at the houses on the way down – tiny little places, hardly bigger than those in the townships. And with such funny names – Five Elms, Riverbrook, Sweet Charity, though there wasn't an elm or a river in sight. She thought of the homes in her neighbourhood in Bryanston, enormous, every single one, with sprawling gardens, pools, tennis courts, and with protective walls, some with bits of jagged glass on top to prevent anyone climbing or even peeking over. Almost everyone she knew had a little sentry post at the front gate, with an armed guard who lived, ate and slept in it as the first line of defence against *them*. Aunt Lisette's guard was an elderly Zulu – she couldn't remember his name – but he'd been there for ever. He had a large wooden stick he called a *knobkerrie*, and his gun was always propped against his chair. He was afraid to use it. Hennie sometimes joked that Festus – *that* was his name – thought the gun was simply a heavier *knobkerrie*. He'd no idea how to use it and probably wasn't aware even that it fired bullets. She giggled suddenly.

'What's funny?' Charmaine asked. It was almost the first time she'd seen Rianne smile. She looked enviously at the perfect, pearly white teeth and wide, generous smile which completely transformed the otherwise tense and unhappy face.

'Oh, nothing. I was just thinking about my cousin.'

'What's her name?'

'He. Hennie. He's really nice.'

'Is he here too? In England?' Charmaine was interested. Rianne's life, with its chauffeurs and natives – whatever *they* were – sounded so much more glamorous than a two-bedroom flat in Pimlico.

'No, he's going into the army.'

'The army?' Charmaine sounded impressed.

'Yeah. He doesn't want to go.'

'Why's he going, then?'

'Well, all the boys back home have to go to the army when they're eighteen.'

'Oh.' Charmaine vaguely remembered a Swiss boy at the Boys' College who had done the same. She'd thought it terribly unfair. 'That must be awful – having to do it, I mean.'

'Yeah. There's a war at the moment, somewhere, but I don't think Hennie'll have to fight.' Rianne supposed he'd crack enemy codes or command troops from an air-conditioned office, something like that.

'Really? How thrilling.' Charmaine was captivated. It all sounded so much more romantic than anything that was happening in her little circle of friends.

'Suppose so,' Rianne shrugged, uninterested. She couldn't have cared less about wars.

Charmaine was suddenly aware of the young man sitting in the seat opposite staring incredulously at the two of them. She looked away. She tried not to speak to the village 'yokels' as they were known. They were ever so rude. Thankfully, the bus was coming to a stop.

'Come on, this is where we get off.' She beckoned to Rianne.

The young man also got up. Charmaine stopped to let him pass. 'Fuckin' toffs,' he said loudly, and she blushed.

'What did he say?' Rianne asked, as they descended from the bus.

'Oh, don't take any notice. He's just jealous,' Charmaine whispered.

'Of what?'

'You know. Of us. Well, he's poor.' Rianne gazed after the disappearing back, confused again. Poor? How could a white person be poor? Then she remembered. She'd once driven through the northern Transvaal with Lisette and Uncle Simon, her aunt's financial adviser. They'd passed some farms, Rianne remembered, and she'd asked about the dirty little white children running barefoot at the side of the road, playing with the pot-bellied native children. Her aunt had murmured something about poor Afrikaner families. It was terrible what the – what word had she used? – *boycott*, that was it. It was *terrible* what it was doing to their farms. So there *were* poor white people in the world. But what were they doing in Malvern?

Charmaine was walking purposefully towards the end of the road. 'Come on – Serendipity's is on that corner. I want to get a good seat.'

'What for? It's a tea-shop!' Rianne was puzzled.

'To get a good *view*,' Charmaine replied. Rianne followed her across the road. View of what?

The tea-shop was packed. The little bell above the door tinkled as they entered. Inside was noisy and smoky. There was a short lull in the conversation as all the girls in the room simultaneously sized up the newcomer, noted she was with sexy Charmaine Hunter and groaned inwardly. Double assault.

Rianne looked around her. The room was packed and the girls outnumbered the boys by about ten to one. She was surprised the little shop could hold so many tables.

'Char, darling!' someone called from the back of the room. Charmaine and Rianne struggled through. *Mwah!* Charmaine and three other girls who'd called them over did the English schoolgirl version of the French welcome kiss – two loud kisses on either side, mostly in the air – and smiled rather superciliously at her new – and beautiful – friend. Unlike Charmaine and Rianne, the others wore uniform – 'Ledbury School for Girls', Rianne read from the stitching on their jackets. Where the hell was Ledbury?

'Darlings,' Charmaine cried, 'this is Rianne. She's from South Africa. Her family own all the diamond mines or something.'

'Really?' One of the girls arched an eyebrow. Beautiful *and* rich.

Rianne gave a tiny smile. Why was everyone suddenly called 'darling'? Charmaine was acting *very* strangely.

'Have you met Ree?' one of the girls asked Rianne. 'He's from South Africa too.' Rianne shook her head.

'No,' Charmaine interrupted. 'I don't think he's here today.' Rianne glanced at her – she'd sounded like she wanted to get her claim for him in first.

'Shall we have some scones?' Charmaine asked Rianne, as they sat down and pushed their bags under the table.

'If you like.' Rianne shrugged. She opened her new bag and pulled out a packet of cigarettes. Charmaine, she could see, was watching with ill-concealed admiration as she lit up, drawing smoke expertly into her mouth and exhaling through her nose. Everyone knew that Charmaine had been practising for months but somehow, no matter how hard she tried, she always wound up spluttering and coughing. Lately, she'd developed the habit of barely inhaling, but it still looked fake. Rianne, on the other hand, knew she looked cool.

A minute later, a couple of boys from the upper sixth at

the Boys' College strolled casually over. 'Hi, Charmaine,' one said, looking not at Charmaine at all, but at Rianne. She slowly and deliberately blew a cloud of smoke in his direction. He coughed and reddened.

'Hi, Michael.' Charmaine smiled engagingly. It was Michael Rhys-Walker, the deputy head boy. He'd never so much as *looked* at her before.

'I don't think we've met,' he said to Rianne, ignoring Charmaine.

'No, we haven't.' Rianne looked at him through half-closed eyes. The girls at the table looked at her admiringly. She was just too cool for words! Michael Rhys-Walker seemed unsure what to do next.

'Oh, Rianne, this is Michael, and Michael, this is Rianne de Zoete,' Charmaine said quickly. Rianne had almost finished her cigarette and certainly seemed in no hurry to respond.

'Well, hello, Rianne.' Michael gave a half-bow. Rianne nodded. The other boy grinned at her too, inanely. Rianne looked bored. There was a short silence. Charmaine and the other girls rushed to fill it, chattering nervously.

It was all rather silly, Rianne thought. A couple of pasty-faced boys in the whole tea-shop and fifty girls fighting for their attention. She looked at the two in front of her. Ugh! What was wrong with English boys? One looked like he needed a good haircut and the other a bath. Thankfully, after they had realised she wasn't going to join in the conversation – it was all about people and places she'd never heard of – they sloped off, receiving a warmer welcome at the next table. Charmaine and her friends were now analysing the brief encounter, and Rianne found herself gazing out of the window. It was all a bit childish. She wondered what her crowd back home were doing . . . what Hennie was doing. She hadn't allowed herself to think about him very much since she'd arrived. She missed him. She missed his easy laughter, the way his eyes crinkled at the corners when he smiled. She even missed their arguments. Only another few days to go until Lisette was back, she thought. Then she'd see them all again. She even missed Lisette. Well, not that much, but she would be a *little* nicer to her when she got home.

'What?' Charmaine had asked her something.

'What're you wearing to the ball? It's in three weeks, you know.' The four were on their favourite topic – the Half-term Ball.

'I won't be here,' Rianne said firmly.

One of the others looked at her in surprise. 'Why? Where are you going?' she asked.

'Home. Next week. I *hate* this place.' Rianne's voice was a little louder than necessary. A couple of girls at the next table looked up.

'Oh, you can't miss the ball! It's such *enormous* fun.' This came from the rather horsy-looking girl who had shouted to catch Charmaine's attention when they first came in.

Rianne raised her eyebrows. Enormous fun? With boys like these? She shrugged her shoulders and looked at her watch. It was nearly five o'clock. It would soon be time to go back to school. She lit another cigarette. *God*, she was bored.

In the library at St Anne's, sitting in her usual spot beside the tall, elegant windows, Gabby closed her books with a snap and watched the late-afternoon sun dance across the manicured lawn. She was restless. She'd read the same paragraph through almost three times and she still couldn't remember what she'd read. She was sitting in her favourite seat, studying her favourite subject – history. She'd even managed to resist buying a KitKat to go with her afternoon tea – no mean feat – but she was still miserable. She kept thinking about the ball and what she would wear. Last year's dress, she already knew, simply wouldn't go over this year's hips. She'd tried it on secretly one night in the bathroom when everyone else was asleep. It wouldn't go past her thighs.

She chewed the end of her pencil. There was no way she'd get anything out of her parents for a new one. That was problem number one. She didn't want to go to the ball but she knew – just *knew* – that Matthie would be counting on her to patrol the corridors and the patio outside the dining room to make sure no one slipped off into the bushes or, *quelle horreur*, was found doing anything other than dancing a respectable foot apart – rumour had it that Miss Caruthers actually came round with a ruler. However, no one would be dancing with *her*, that was problem number two. Or was it three? She made a quick mental calculation; the ball was three weeks away. How much weight could she lose in three weeks if she hardly ate anything? Enough to squeeze into last year's dress? Fortunately it was navy blue – the practical Charmaine had seen to that. Perhaps she could do something with her hair. She stared at her reflection in the window. Fat, frumpy, foolish. That was what she'd look like on the night. Who'd want to dance with *that*?

Reluctantly Charmaine turned to Rianne. It was almost six and they'd have to run to catch the last bus. 'I suppose we'd better get a move on,' she said, with a rueful smile.

Rianne had never dreamed she'd be pleased to go back to St Anne's, but hanging around in a tea-shop was not her idea of fun. They both got up.

'See you in a fortnight.' Charmaine bent down to kiss everyone ostentatiously. It seemed to be part of the silly game.

''Bye, darling,' the others chorused. ''Bye, Rianne, see you next time.'

'Not bloody likely,' Rianne muttered to herself, and gave a half-hearted wave. She walked to the door.

Charmaine was still busy kissing the air, giggling and fluttering her fingers at different tables as she made her exit.

Rianne rolled her eyes and reached for the doorknob, but the door opened suddenly and she almost lost her balance. She stumbled against the step but was immediately caught by a pair of strong hands. She caught a glimpse of a navy blazer and grey flannel trousers as she straightened.

'Ree!' she heard Charmaine squeal excitedly behind her. She looked up. Straight into the face of a young black man. She jumped back, snatching her arm away, but before she could do or say anything else, Charmaine had practically shoved her aside. There were cries of welcome as he walked inside the shop. Charmaine quickly staked her claim.

'Ree!' she exclaimed again. Evidently she wanted *everyone* to see her standing next to him. 'We're just going – what a *pity*.' Rianne looked on in amazement as Charmaine and the native boy exchanged kisses – a peck on each cheek.

'Hi, Charmaine,' he said, giving her the briefest of smiles. He didn't seem quite as enthused to see her as Charmaine obviously was to see him. He straightened up. He was a good head taller than Rianne. He looked at her, a faintly amused expression on his face. Rianne's cheeks burned. How dare he look her in the face?

'Oh, Ree, this is Rianne. She's just arrived. She's from South Africa too.' Charmaine reluctantly made the introductions.

Ree looked at her again, more closely. 'I didn't catch your name,' he said, sounding just like any one of the well-spoken English boys she'd met that afternoon.

Rianne looked at him in confusion. Charmaine had said he was South African but he certainly didn't sound it. Who the hell was he? And what was he doing in the Boys' College uniform? He even had a little gold badge pinned to his immaculate lapel – 'Head Boy', it read. What was a head boy? She stared at him. 'What?' she said, as coldly as she could.

'Your name?' he said again, a little more slowly this time.

'Rianne de Zoete,' she said imperiously. If he really was from South Africa he'd know to show her a little more respect.

His eyes narrowed. He looked at her insolently for a second and then, to her complete shock – and Charmaine's – he brushed past them both and walked away.

'Ree!' Charmaine called. Everyone was watching them curiously. 'Wh-what's the matter?'

'Nothing. Nothing wrong with *you* – I'm just fussy about the company I keep.' He joined Michael Rhys-Walker and his sidekick. There was a stunned silence. It was the most monumental snub. Someone giggled. Charmaine hurriedly opened the door and stepped outside, pulling Rianne with her. She closed it firmly behind them.

'Oh, my God!' she said dramatically, putting a hand to her face. 'Oh, my *God*!' she repeated. She looked at Rianne. Rianne's face was flushed.

'What an asshole!' Rianne said angrily, close to tears. She had never, ever been spoken to that way – and by a *native*!

'What on earth – does he know you?'

'Of *course* not! He's a *native*, you idiot. How *dare* he speak to me like that?' Rianne was furious.

'What's a native?'

'An African – a black person, you idiot.' Rianne marched up the road, wanting to put as much distance between her and the damned tea-shop as possible.

Charmaine trotted after her. 'Look, stop calling me an idiot, all right? I'm not *stupid*. I *know* he's black! But Ree's not a *native*, he's Riitho Modise!' Charmaine said indignantly.

'What's his name?' Rianne stopped in her tracks. Modise? Where had she heard that name before? 'What did you call him?' she repeated.

'Riitho. Except none of us can pronounce it properly so we call him Ree. Don't you *know* who his father is?'

'Who?'

'Livingstone Modise!' Charmaine said triumphantly.

'Who's Livingstone Modise?' Rianne said, puzzled. She knew the name . . . but why?

'Eh?' Charmaine stared at her. 'You've never heard of Livingstone Modise?'

'No. Why should I? Who is he?'

'I don't believe you! He's just about the most famous person in the world! He's in jail. You're the idiot! He's *much* more famous than you are.'

'Well, I don't care how famous he is, or how famous his *father* is, he's just a native and he'd no right to look at me. No right at all. I'll—'

'Oh, don't tell me, you're going to *report* him,' Charmaine said crossly. Rianne was beginning to get on her nerves. Ree was gorgeous, he wasn't a *native*! What the hell was wrong with her? 'Go ahead, see if anyone listens to you. You're not at home now, you know. It's different here.'

Rianne resisted the temptation to slap Charmaine. She was *so* ignorant. She had no idea how the world worked. Just look at her, kissing a native boy. Rianne couldn't get over the stab of revulsion she'd felt watching them. Although, much as she hated to admit it, he'd seemed a lot better than the native boys she'd met back home. Not that she'd met very many. He was tall, broad-shouldered and well dressed . . . and he spoke so nicely. But *still*. What was it Charmaine had said? His father was in jail? He was practically a *criminal*. She would phone Marika as soon as she got back. She'd know who his damned father was.

7

An hour later, having picked at the disgusting plate of corned beef and chips – it looked and tasted like something you'd feed the cat, Rianne complained – Rianne knocked on Miss Matthews's door and asked permission to use the phone. It was a Saturday and Miss Matthews agreed. She left Rianne alone in her sitting room and went into the kitchen to make them both a cup of tea. Rianne dialled the familiar number. It was Poppie who answered. Neither Hennie nor Marika ever picked up the phone.

'*Ay*, Rianne, *hou gaan det?*' Poppie asked her excitedly, in Afrikaans.

'Oh, Poppie, *ek saal nie bly hier nie, aseblief. Ek kaan nie kom nie*,' Rianne answered, her lower lip trembling. I can't stay here, not a moment longer.

'*Ag, Tannie Lisette saal moêre kom*, Rianne,' Poppie said comfortingly. Lisette will be back tomorrow. '*Jou kaan med Tannie Lisette praat. Sy kan alles te rekening maak.*'

'OK, Poppie.' Rianne sniffed. '*Waar's* Marika?' She heard Poppie shout for her cousin and Marika's '*Ek kom!*' in the hallway.

'Hey.' Marika grabbed the phone, excited. 'Rianne! How's it?'

'It's awful, Marika, just awful. I can't wait till Aunt Lisette comes back. When's she back? Tomorrow?'

'Er, yes – tomorrow.' Marika sounded uneasy. They'd all been instructed not to let Rianne talk to Lisette for the first three weeks. 'It's for her own good,' Lisette had instructed firmly. Marika bit her lip. She hated lying. 'What's up?'

'Nothing. Well, just . . .' Rianne hesitated for a moment.

'What? What's the matter?'

'Do you know who Livingstone Modise is?' Rianne asked, in a rush. Her cheeks burned again as she recalled Ree's insolent stare.

'Livingstone Modise?' Marika sounded surprised. Both

at the fact that her cousin had never heard of him and the fact that she was asking.

'Er . . . yes, the one in jail. Who is he?' Rianne lowered her voice.

'He's a political prisoner. Why?'

'Oh.' Rianne was momentarily taken aback. A political prisoner. What was *that* supposed to mean? 'Well, you'll never believe it,' she continued, after a moment's hesitation, 'but his *son* is here. In my school. Well, not *my* school but the school next door. Can you *believe* it? It's disgusting!' Rianne's voice rose indignantly. Matthie put her head round the door. Rianne turned her back. 'Just wait till Aunt Lisette finds out. I'll be home tomorrow, I can tell you!' she whispered.

'You met him?' Marika seemed impressed. '*Wow!*'

'There's no "wow" about it! It's just *awful*! There's *all* kinds of people here. I have to share a bath with *you-know-whats*,' she whispered fiercely. Rianne was disappointed. Marika sounded more like Charmaine!

'Er, what shall I tell Mom?' Marika asked hurriedly.

'Tell her to call me as soon as she gets in. She can call the housemistress.'

It was almost lights out by the time Rianne returned to her room. She'd wandered down into the gardens at the bottom of the school grounds and sat on the stone wall, smoking. There was someone else in the room – Rianne recognised her vaguely, Rebecca something or other. She slept in the room next door with two others and often popped into their room. Gabby was reading, Nathalie was towel-drying her hair. Charmaine and the new girl were studying the clothes in the style section of her favourite magazine, *Tatler*. They were looking for useful tips on what to wear – or, more importantly, what *not* to wear – at the ball. They looked up as Rianne entered.

'Did you have fun today?' Rebecca asked.

Gabby put down her book and gave her a warning glance. Rianne wondered why.

'No.' Rianne was curt.

'Oh? Why not?' Rebecca persisted. Gabby looked up sharply. She'd been afraid something like this would happen.

'I just didn't.' Rianne started for the door.

'I hear you met Ree Modise. Did you two know each other? From back *home*, I mean?'

'Becky,' Gabby said warningly.

'No. Of course not. Don't be stupid,' Rianne said arrogantly. She'd almost reached the door.

'What d'you mean?' Rebecca ignored Gabby's warning tone.

'He's a native. Of *course* he doesn't know me. Where I'm from, they know their place.'

'Ooh! Do they?' Rebecca's eyes were wide. She turned to the others for support. 'Do they really?'

'Yes, they do. And so should you.' Rianne was losing her temper.

'And what's *my* place?'

'Rebecca!' Gabby raised her voice. 'That's enough. Just leave her alone.'

'Why don't you mind your own business?' Rianne said angrily to Gabby. She was perfectly capable of fighting her own battles.

'Why don't you just fuck off, Rianne?' Nathalie burst out suddenly. She looked at Rianne. Two bright red spots stood out on her cheeks. The others turned to stare at Nat. It was years since anyone had seen her that angry.

'Why don't *you*?' Rianne retorted. 'All of you.' She looked at them, her eyes glittering with tears. 'Just fuck off.' She yanked open the door and slammed it behind her.

'*God!*' Rebecca looked at the others in shock.

'You really didn't have to start that, Becky,' Gabby said

44

crossly. It was ages since she'd seen Nathalie so wound up. 'She's *our* room-mate, not yours.'

'*Me*? *She* started it!' Rebecca protested angrily. 'Did you hear what she said about Ree? I mean, everyone knows where she's from but—'

'Don't start,' Gabby said. 'I know she asked for it, but still . . . I know loads of South Africans – well, one, anyway – and she's *nothing* like Rianne. Nothing at all.'

'Well, I think we should ignore her and not talk to her at all. She'll soon learn. Maybe she can talk like that where's she's from, but not here.' No one said anything, but Gabby was uncomfortable. Much as she agreed that Rianne was a pain, she didn't like the idea of ignoring her. It would only make the atmosphere in the room worse. She sighed. Keeping the peace between the four of them was just about manageable but keeping it between Rianne and the rest of the house would be impossible.

'Why don't you go back to your room, Becky, just for now? I'll talk to Rianne tomorrow,' she said. 'Give her a bit of time. She's new – no excuse, I know, but let's leave it till tomorrow.'

Rebecca got up and flounced out of the room. Gabby switched off the light abruptly. Time for everyone to simmer down.

Rianne sat in the bath for what seemed like an eternity. At first she was simply too angry to cry. She stared at her legs under the water, now losing their golden tan, then slid further down in the tub. The lines of her body blurred, sliding, and she wept. Again. Today was positively the last straw. She was leaving, whether Lisette agreed to it or not. Stuff them and their silly schoolgirl ways. She'd find somewhere else to go.

The following morning, as soon as she was awake, she knocked on Miss Matthews's door. The housemistress let her in without a word and Rianne rang home. Lisette was firm. Rianne was to stay at St Anne's until Christmas. That was all there was to it. Then the whole family would be flying to Sans Soucis, the de Zoete family home on Martinique in the Antilles, and Rianne was to stay put until then. End of discussion. If she tried to run away, Lisette would call the police. And that was no idle threat. Although Lisette was horrified – *horrified* – to hear that Rianne was sharing her living space with native and Indian girls, Rianne would just have to ignore them.

She listened to Rianne's tearfully indignant story. 'Don't pay any attention to the other girls, Rianne, and stay well away from the native girls, darling,' she said briskly. 'Make sure you don't use the same cups. And clean the bath before you use it. You know.' That was the plan. *Period*.

Rianne listened to her aunt in silence. She slammed down the phone and rushed upstairs, ignoring the look of exasperation on Miss Matthews's face.

'Look!' Nathalie walked over to Charmaine's bed with the previous month's *Vogue*. 'What d'you think of this?' She pointed to a simple black evening gown with a wide, flared skirt and an off-the-shoulder neckline.

'Mmm. It's OK.' Charmaine looked up from her own magazine. It was two weeks to the Half-term Ball and both girls were preoccupied with what to wear. 'A bit plain, though, don't you think?'

'Not if I wear one of Mama's necklaces,' Nathalie said, grinning. Along with perfume, bath oil and the occasional ten-pound note, she'd acquired a few pieces of her mother's jewellery to supplement her own modest collection. 'I nicked this one in the summer.' She opened the small leather case on her dressing-table.

'God, it's *gorgeous*! Didn't she notice?' Charmaine asked, admiring the white gold necklace with the single square diamond encased in gold.

'Nope. She's got so many. My stepfather spoils her rotten. D'you think I'll ever find someone who'll spoil me?'

Nathalie said, fingering the necklace. Her stepfather was simply too generous – to all of them.

'Course you will. Try it on.' Charmaine said. Nathalie held up the necklace against her throat. The diamond caught the light, sending brilliant flashes this way and that, as Nathalie gazed at herself in the mirror.

'Up or down?' she asked, pulling her hair off her neck.

'Oh, up. Definitely,' Charmaine advised. She was playing her favourite role – stylist. 'Where are you going to get the dress from?'

'Mama'll send it. I'll write to her this evening. I just have to tell her where to get it from in London.'

Charmaine sighed enviously. 'I don't think my mum will let me get something new, and I'm broke. I just can't wear the dress I wore last year.'

'Can't you alter it?' Nathalie suggested. Her own mother simply handed over wads of cash as compensation for the time she never spent with her two children.

'I suppose I'll have to,' Charmaine mumbled. 'I just hope I get asked to dance.'

'Of course you will,' Nathalie said soothingly. 'You always do.'

Gabby pulled on a sweater as she made her way to the library. It was freezing. St Anne's held fast to the ridiculous tradition of not switching on the central heating until half-term, regardless of the temperature. She pushed open the heavy wooden doors and wound her way through the reading carousels to her usual spot by the window. She wrapped her scarf round her neck and dumped books on the table. Gabby had a secret, something she hadn't told anyone – yet. She was planning to sit Oxbridge the following year. Jumoke Olalade wasn't the only girl at St Anne's with academic ambitions. The only person who knew she was thinking about it was Miss Featherstone, the English teacher, a graduate of Magdalen College. In fact she had put the idea into Gabby's head. Gabby had gone pink with embarrassment when Miss Featherstone had suggested she sit for the exam and had tried to laugh it off.

'Oh no!' she'd giggled. 'Me? You need *brains* to sit Oxbridge. I'd probably fail.'

'You *have* brains, Gabrielle,' Miss Featherstone said earnestly. 'You should really think about it. Whether you choose to read English or not.'

'Well, it's really nice of you to say so, Miss Featherstone. I will think about it,' Gabby said, smiling shyly. She didn't quite believe her, but still . . . it was nice to be thought of in that way.

'Nothing to do with being nice, Gabrielle. You have talent. You should use it.'

Gabby was too pleased to do anything other than nod. She'd always had difficulty accepting praise – she wasn't used to it. Although few people at St Anne's knew much about it, Gabby's home life was one in which compliments were rarely, if ever, voiced. In fact, nothing much was ever voiced. Her father, Geoffrey – third-rate solicitor and domestic bully – hated noise, hated raised voices, hated conversations he did not dominate. In fact, Gabby thought, he much pretty hated everything. She and her mother lived in his shadow, speaking only when spoken to, attuned to his overbearing presence. It was a pretty stultifying environment for a lively, naturally curious child.

Gabby knew she had been a mistake. She had learned from her grandmother, whom she adored, that her mother, on finding herself pregnant at the age of forty-one, had sunk into a post-natal depression from which she had never fully recovered. Rearing a child, as far as Ellen Francis was concerned, wasn't something she'd planned. And as everyone knew, Geoffrey was a careful planner. Geoffrey's public persona, that of a pompous and patronising lawyer, masked his true nature: he was a weak and vain man who traded on his privileged upbringing – Harrow, Cambridge, the City. He was desperate to conceal the truth – he'd failed the Bar so many times even Ellen had dared suggest he give it up. Predictably, he'd reacted badly to the timid suggestion.

After that, things in the house rapidly got worse. The more apparent the failings in his professional life, the more domineering he became in his little domestic world. And it *was* little – just Gabby and Ellen. To make matters worse, Gabby was neither a pretty nor a quiet child – in Geoffrey's eyes, essential qualities in a woman. He had managed to tame his wife; Ellen Francis was a timid, dreamy woman – given to secret gin tippling and whispering her words. But Gabby was another matter altogether. She was loud and boisterous, the result, no doubt, of having to scream for attention. Geoffrey was outraged by her.

By the time Gabby was six, Ellen contemplated sending the clumsy, overweight child to boarding school but Gabby's grandmother, who adored her grandchild, intervened. It was out of the question that the child should be sent away at six. From then on, Gabby had spent most of her time in the big, comfortable house in Hereford, reading the hundreds of books her grandfather had left in his enormous study under the eaves, amusing herself and asking endless questions about the world – most of which her delighted grandmother couldn't answer.

When she was nine, things came to an abrupt stop. Geoffrey insisted on sending her to boarding school and her grandmother reluctantly agreed. She couldn't live deep in the Herefordshire countryside with only an elderly woman for company. So, dressed uncomfortably in her new uniform and shoes that pinched, Gabby boarded the train for St Anne's, along with a dozen other girls of her age, and was welcomed by a large, smiling woman whose expression told Gabby everything she needed to know: this home was going to be a vast improvement on her own. Every holiday she went back to her grandmother, returning only to the stifling London house before the start of each term for a short ceremony she had grown to hate: the handing over of her allowance. Geoffrey would dole out her pocket money for the coming term, ceremoniously holding out a cheque for almost the same amount he had been given at Harrow, some forty years earlier. That times had changed, and inflation with them, had barely made any impression on him. What had been good for him, he would pompously assert, was good for her, and bloody lucky she was, too.

Geoffrey was unnerved by his daughter . . . there was something in her expression . . . was it contempt? He couldn't be sure. Whatever it was, it infuriated him. Gabby would take the cheque, fold it once, twice, and ask to be excused. Once, she'd forgotten to say thank you and had earned herself a quick slap. She remembered from then on – and hated it all the more.

She looked at the books in front of her and smiled to herself. They were reading Daphne du Maurier's *Jamaica Inn* this term and Gabby was enthralled by the story of Mary Yellan and the strange family into which she was suddenly thrust. She was fascinated by the relationships in the story; by Patience Merlyn's private hell, governed largely by her fear of her husband. Perhaps there was something in the balance of power between the protagonists that Gabby recognised from her own home and her troubled relationship with her parents; perhaps there was something about Mary Yellan's relationship with Jem Merlyn, Joss's younger brother, that spoke directly to her, to her loneliness as an only child – she didn't know and couldn't tell. The story fascinated her, that was all. She looked again at the question they had all been set: *Despite her own misgivings, what reasons did Mary Yellan have for staying at Jamaica Inn?*

She chewed her pencil thoughtfully. She thought she understood only too well the dreadful impasse in which Aunt Patience found herself but it was the relationship with

Jem that intrigued her. Gabby had never had a boyfriend, never been in love, never even contemplated it. Love – at least the heart-stopping, panic-inducing, appetite-suppressing version of it as experienced by Charmaine and Nathalie – didn't happen to girls like her. She had male friends, yes – one or two, but that was different.

Nael Hughes was a friend. He was at the Boys' College and was in her history class. Over the past few years, as the popularity of history at St Anne's had declined, a decision had been made to send the one or two students still interested in it to the Boys' College, rather than pay for a part-time teacher. At first Gabby had been terrified – dropped in among all those loud, confident boys – but as soon as it had been established that she was every bit as good as the best of them, if not better, things were fine. Nael was one of the brightest pupils, and although it had taken him a while, he had come to respect Gabby and like her. Theirs was a real friendship, albeit one tinged sometimes with rivalry. Nael was sitting Oxbridge – of course – and he wanted to read politics and philosophy at Cambridge. Gabby just loved the sound of the different combinations: PPE – Politics, Philosophy, Economics; PPP – Politics, Philosophy, Psychology. She was unsure as to what *exactly* one studied under the umbrella of the various Ps, but they *sounded* impressive. Her only problem was that she enjoyed English too much to give it up. A new combination was needed: PHE – Politics, History, English, now *that* was something to wish for.

She was sure Nael would get in, he was so clever. And funny. Handsome, too, if you thought about it. He was half something – Italian or Spanish, Gabby couldn't remember exactly, and half English – or Welsh. His dad was Welsh. He didn't talk about his parents much. Gabby had the feeling there was something not quite . . . *right* about his background. She couldn't say what . . . just a feeling. And then there was that thing about his name. Nael: it was pronounced Neil. Gabby asked why it was spelled funny. He'd told her his mother had got it wrong on his birth certificate but when Charmaine had asked him, a year later, he'd told her it was an old family name . . . an old Welsh name. It had been on the tip of Gabby's tongue to accuse him of making up stories to make himself sound exotic, but something about the way he'd blushed made her keep quiet.

He was unusual-looking for an English boy . . . olive-skinned, dark glossy brown hair and hazel eyes. Last summer, just after they'd sat their O levels, the lower and upper fifth history class had taken a picnic onto the hills. It had been boiling hot and Gabby, with her pale skin and red hair, had had to sit under the shade of a large parasol that Mr Rosenthal, the history teacher, had thought to bring along. She sat underneath it, feeling large, ungainly and uncomfortable in her long skirt and baggy T-shirt, and envious of Nael and the other boys who'd unbuttoned their shirts and were lying in the grass. By the end of the afternoon Nael had turned almost nut-brown. Gabby was amazed: she'd never seen anyone tan so quickly – and so well.

He smiled and said his mother was Mediterranean – *that* was it – he always tanned easily. She liked looking at him, at his strong, well-drawn features and square, determined jaw. But he was just a friend. He already had a girlfriend, a perfectly nice girl called Mandy, who was at the Ladies' College. Gabby had seen her once, holding Nael's hand as they walked around Malvern. She'd quickly ducked into a shop before Nael had seen her. She wasn't sure why. If she sometimes experienced a strange, fluttering sensation in her stomach when he turned to her in class and gave her one of his slow, sure smiles or winked at her when Rosenthal asked her a question and she answered it correctly, she put it down to nervousness. After all, it wasn't easy being the only girl in a class of fifteen boys. She sighed and turned back to her essay.

What reasons did Mary Yellan ... She looked at the question for the third time. What was she doing? She'd wasted almost fifteen minutes day-dreaming ... and about nothing useful either. She had to concentrate. She stopped chewing her pencil and began to make notes. It was odd, though. Whenever she thought about Jem Merlyn or pictured him in her mind's eye, he looked an awful lot like Nael.

8

To her surprise, Rianne found the weeks beginning to slip by. Since she'd given up – at least for the time being – the thought of leaving the very next day, she found that the school routine asserted itself almost immediately and before she had had time to think about it, another weekend had arrived and gone. She'd been forced to choose her subjects, winding up with French, German and English – easy, if uninspired choices. There was no way she could have done history. She knew nothing of world events and the long lists of dates simply terrified her. For her, languages would be the easiest choice and the path of least effort. So it was. She was bored to tears in French and German although English seemed to involve an awful lot of reading. Gabby and Nathalie took English and Nathalie took French. She hardly ever saw Charmaine.

Aside from one or two cursory remarks, the girls in her room more or less ignored her. She was fine with that. She didn't want to speak to them either. She spent most of her lessons looking out of the window or doodling in her notebook. She'd started a letter to Hennie when she'd arrived at the school and she was no closer to finishing now than she had been three weeks ago. As the bell sounded, signalling the last class of the week, she gathered her books in relief and headed for the door. She would finish Hennie's letter after supper. Two weeks to go until half-term, she thought, as she climbed the hill to Gordon. Then five weeks after that until the Christmas holidays. Could she last that long?

Lisette put down the phone, frowning. Rianne had just rung, demanding a dress for a school dance . . . a ball. A dress? What kind of dress? Lisette had asked. Rianne had no idea: she didn't know what to buy so she'd rung home to ask Lisette to send something. *She* ought to know – she went to enough damn balls. Lisette frowned, then hurriedly reached up with a forefinger to smooth away the wrinkle. No more frowning – her new rule. Frowns caused wrinkles. She sighed. If Rianne needed a frock she would have to organise it immediately, but she was far too busy to do it herself; she had back-to-back meetings scheduled all week and her personal assistant was ill – blast Rianne! Why did she leave everything so damned late? It was typical of the girl, she thought crossly. Everything had to be done on *her* schedule, according to *her* needs. She stubbed out her cigarette in a thick crystal ashtray that Clara had brought her and, despite her irritation, smiled her thanks. She prided herself on being courteous to her staff. Just then, Marika wafted past, on her way to the pool.

'Marika, darling,' Lisette called, 'come here for a minute, *skatjie*, will you?' Marika stuck her head round the door. 'Darling, I need a favour,' Lisette began, smiling at her daughter.

Ten minutes later, it was done. Marika would find a suitable dress for her cousin. Marika was thrilled. 'Not too frilly, hmm?' Lisette cautioned, as she stood up and smoothed her skirt. She knew Marika's tastes sometimes ran to the . . . well, ever so slightly *gaudy*. She supposed it was a reaction against her own aesthetic regime. She checked her reflection in the hallway mirror. As always, she was elegant, groomed, not a hair out of place. Her lilac suit fitted her to perfection and the colour was offset nicely by the discreet gold jewellery she favoured. Her short blonde hair had been expertly cut to frame her face. Her eyes were touched at the corners with her favourite black pencil, just a little smudge to give them depth. She disliked the overdone *faux*-glamour of many of her countrywomen: too much gloss, too much red, too much of everything. Hers was discreet. As she herself was. One last glance at her perfectly toned, lightly tanned bare legs and smart court shoes, and she disappeared down the cool, air-conditioned hallway.

'Seni!' she called out. '*Waar's my kar?*' She'd asked for the car to be washed and brought round to the front door. She had a meeting in Pretoria in an hour's time and today, unusually, she felt like driving herself. Moments later, she heard the soft purr of the Mercedes' engine and she picked up her handbag.

Six thousand miles away, Rianne consulted her watch. It was only ten o'clock. She'd managed to miss breakfast by pretending she had period cramps, not that there was anything to miss – except cereal, lukewarm scrambled eggs and burnt toast – but she was restless and didn't feel like going for a walk. In a week it seemed as though autumn had given way to winter. Almost all the leaves were gone and the countryside was shrouded in a damp fog. What to do now? Gabby was in the library, Charmaine and Nathalie were involved in some complicated beauty ritual in preparation for the following week. She blew out her cheeks. Well, at least Lisette was organising her dress for the ball. She thought for a moment.

Perhaps she should go into Worcester and buy a pair of shoes – there was no way she'd wear those awful black lace-ups or even the flat-heeled pumps Lisette had bought. Yes, that's what she'd do all afternoon. She'd go shopping this afternoon. She wouldn't tell anyone, just slip off after lunch and be back before tea. She knew it was a school rule that they had to go out in pairs but she'd seen Charmaine coming back by herself the previous week and no one had said anything. Miss Matthews hadn't even known. She grinned. She might even go to the movies.

It was all so easy. At half past one, just as everyone was either getting ready to go into town or setting off for the playing-fields, Rianne put on her duffel coat, laced up her shoes and left Gordon by the back entrance. She walked a short way up the hill and then, as soon as she was out of sight of Miss Matthews's flat, she cut across the hill and ran down the other side. She only had to wait about ten minutes at the bus stop and the Malvern bus came rumbling into view. There were three sets of juniors on the bus; they smiled shyly at the beautiful sixth-former but she ignored them. She'd grown accustomed to everyone staring at her.

She got off at Malvern Link – Charmaine and Nathalie had mentioned that the station was there – and bought a ticket, ignoring the questioning look that the middle-aged woman behind the screen gave her. 'Just going for the afternoon, are you?' She looked at Rianne's gold credit card in amusement. 'That'll be three pounds. Haven't you got any change?'

'Oh.' Rianne fished in her pockets. She'd no idea how much a train ticket cost. She pulled out a crumpled five-pound note.

'Lovely. From the Ladies' College, are you?' the woman asked.

'No.' Rianne was irritated. What business was it of hers where she was from?

'Only you're not in uniform. Head girl, are you?'

'Yes.' Rianne guessed correctly that only head girls were allowed into Worcester without uniform. But how did the woman know she was a schoolgirl? She smiled briefly at her as she collected her ticket.

'Enjoy yourself, love. Mind how you go.'

Rianne nodded, impatient to get on the train. She was excited at the prospect of leaving Malvern and going to the city – the city! She'd never been to Worcester but at least it was a *city*. The train creaked its way slowly into the tiny station. There were only two other people on the platform. The doors slammed, one after the other, the guard blew his whistle and they pulled out of the station. Rianne found a window-seat and sat down, delighted with her adventure. She pulled her Walkman out of her bag and put on the headphones. This was *fun*!

Worcester turned out to be the biggest disappointment ever. It was barely bigger than Malvern, Rianne thought in disgust as she looked around the Shambles. Three clothes shops, all selling more or less the same brands of cheap, badly made clothes; two shoe shops for old ladies, a biggish but nondescript department store and a bakery. She thought longingly of Sandton Mall in Johannesburg with its eight floors of shops, its cinemas, hairdressers, cafés, beautiful people, cars, bars – what the hell was this? There wasn't a cinema in sight! She was hungry too and nothing looked even remotely tempting. She might as well have stayed in Malvern.

She wandered off in the direction of the station, wondering if the real shops were somewhere else, where the real city began perhaps, but after a couple of attempts to ask passers-by she gave up. To begin with, she could barely understand what people said. Why didn't anyone at school speak like them? And they seemed to have as much difficulty understanding her. 'Weyre yew lookin' fer?' someone asked her, for the third time. Rianne shook her head.

'I don't understand,' Rianne said, exasperated. The man repeated himself. Rianne shrugged her shoulders helplessly and walked off. So much for an afternoon in the city, she thought angrily.

She arrived on the platform and looked around for the Malvern train. A woman's voice came over the loud-speaker: the Paddington train was about to depart from platform one, 'calling at Didcot, Swindon, Reading and London Paddington.'

Rianne didn't stop to think. She simply walked up to the train, opened the door and boarded. As simple as that. A second later, the whistle blew and the Paddington train moved out of the station. Rianne stood for a minute at the door, watching the station blur as the train picked up speed. She smiled slowly to herself. Why hadn't she thought of it before? She would go to the de Zoete apartment in Knightsbridge – there was always a housekeeper there. She would go shopping, she'd call Matthew Hillman or Pearl Fraser, Hennie's friends who lived in London, and she'd go back to St Anne's tomorrow afternoon. Her room-mates wouldn't even notice she wasn't there. Or if they did, they wouldn't care. It was a brilliant plan! She walked down the train until she came to a first-class compartment. Might as well start her adventure in style.

'Have you seen Rianne?' Gabby asked Nathalie. It was nearly supper-time and there was no sign of her.

'Not since this morning,' Nathalie said, looking up from her book. 'Why?'

'Well, it's nearly supper and I haven't seen her all day.'

'I saw her going up the hill,' Charmaine said. 'She sometimes goes for a walk in the afternoons.'

'Well, I hope she doesn't get lost,' Gabby said, sounding worried. It was already pitch dark outside.

'She won't,' Nathalie said reassuringly. 'Coming?'

The three made their way to the dining room. It was a Saturday and although they didn't have to go in to supper, none of them was a particularly keen cook and they were hungry.

Miss Featherstone was on duty that evening. She smiled at them as they came in. 'Rianne not with you?' she asked, as they walked over to the buffet table.

'She's not feeling well,' Charmaine lied quickly. The last thing they wanted was to draw attention to her absence: all sorts of things might happen – a nine o'clock curfew, for one. That had happened the year before. 'We'll take her some fruit,' she added. Miss Featherstone nodded approvingly.

'Stupid!' Nathalie whispered to Charmaine, as they took their seats. 'You didn't *have* to lie!'

'Well, what else should I have done? I don't want Matthie flying off the handle just because Rianne can't keep track of time,' Charmaine said, aggrieved.

'Well, if she's not back by nine, I say we tell Matthie,' Gabby said. Curfew or no, it wasn't safe to be on the hills alone in the dark. The others agreed.

By nine there was no sign of Rianne. Gabby began to panic. What if she'd fallen and hurt herself on the hills? What if she was lost? There was nothing for it but to report her to Miss Matthews.

'What do you mean "missing"?' Miss Matthews said, looking even more concerned than Gabby. 'When did you last see her?'

'This morning, I think. I mean, I didn't see her – I've been in the library all day – but Nathalie saw her at lunchtime. She said she was on her way up the hill.'

'By *herself*?'

'Yes.'

'But why didn't Nathalie go with her?' Miss Matthews asked. Really, how could they have let the poor girl go on her own?

'Umm . . . well, you know . . .' Gabby was embarrassed.

'No, I *don't* know. Honestly, Gabby, I'm surprised at you,' Miss Matthews said sternly.

Gabby looked at the floor. She knew it wasn't her fault but Matthie was right – perhaps they ought to have tried harder with Rianne.

'Well, I'd better phone Miss Caruthers. You go back upstairs. I'll come up in a minute.' She closed the door and bit her lip. Oh dear. This was serious. Where had Rianne disappeared to?

'Well, we'd better organise a search party,' Miss Caruthers said. She, too, was worried. The de Zoete girl was worth millions – God forbid that anything should have happened to her. She pulled on a coat, then went to call Mr Collins, the maths teacher, and two of the caretakers. Between them, they would organise a group of men to go up on the hills. She stepped outside. Blast! It was chilly *and* it was raining. She practically ran from her office to the care-takers' quarters. It took the men half an hour to get the search party together and, followed by an anxious Miss Caruthers and Miss Matthews, they set off. 'Not to worry,' one of the men kept saying cheerfully. 'We'll find her soon. Can't have gone very far.'

By midnight they were no closer to finding Rianne or figuring out where she might have gone. The party of six men had combed a four-mile radius, and to search any further they would have to call the local police. Miss Caruthers was reluctant to involve them so early in the search: she could not afford the negative publicity. If Rianne was on the hills, she knew, they would have found her. That left only one possibility: the wretched girl had run away.

She disbanded the search party until morning, and the two women went wearily to Miss Matthews's kitchen. Rianne's room-mates were still wide awake although they were under strict instructions not to leave their room. There was no point in everyone becoming hysterical, which was what tended to happen in such situations. None of Rianne's clothes had gone, Gabby confirmed. She hadn't even taken a toothbrush. Miss Caruthers wasn't sure what *that* proved but she said nothing. She was worried but experience told her it was far more likely that the girl had bolted rather than wandered up onto the hills and fallen down a ravine. The difficult bit would be explaining to her aunt how she had remained undetected for almost a day. In the morning she would make a few discreet enquiries at the railway station and with the Malvern taxi drivers. Everyone in the small town knew that such situations could – and often did – occur.

In London, her evening not having gone quite as planned, Rianne was watching TV in the large, comfortable sitting room at Wilton Crescent. She'd arrived just before five o'clock by taxi from Paddington and – thank God – Dinah, the housekeeper, was in. If she was surprised to see Rianne emerging from a black cab with no bags, no cash and wearing a school-regulation duffel coat, she said nothing. She paid the taxi driver and ushered her in out of the cold. Was she staying long?

'No, I've got to go back to school tomorrow,' Rianne said, thinking how nice it was to be back in a proper home. Although the flat at Wilton Crescent – more like a house, really – was only occupied for short periods by Lisette and the family, no expense was spared to keep it functioning as a year-round home. Fresh flowers were delivered every week, and a maid came every Friday to clean, polish and dust as though her life depended on it. Which, in the case of the stream of young girls who came through the maid service, it probably did. Dinah had her cosy flat on the second floor and the de Zoete family owned the entire third floor. It was a very nice arrangement.

Since Lisette's business activities now included London on almost every overseas trip, Dinah had the arrangements down pat. A quick call from Lisette, often just as she was about to leave Jan Smuts International airport and Dinah would set things in motion. The flight from Johannesburg to London took twelve hours and she would arrange for a car to pick up Lisette the following morning at Heathrow. Then she would call the maid service and have the place dusted, fresh flowers brought in, including the lilies that Lisette favoured and tiny yellow roses for the three bathrooms. She would phone Harrods' food hall, and place the usual order for fresh coffee, croissants, a selection of ripe vegetables, fruit and meat. She would spend the afternoon cooking something delicious, transfer it to a plastic carton and leave it in the fridge for Lisette's lunch the following day. If Lisette ate out, as she often did, Dinah would eat what she had prepared or – occasionally – give it to the maid with the proviso that the carton was to be brought back clean. Lisette always brought a couple of bottles of excellent South African wine with her, but Dinah would check that the stock in the larder was replenished and that several excellent bottles were on hand in case Lisette entertained at home.

'Shall I make you supper, Rianne?' Dinah popped her head round the door.

'No.' Rianne was cross – and it showed. She was lying on the enormous cream sofa, and although the TV was on, she wasn't really watching it. She'd given up trying to find Matthew Hillman's number and a call to Hennie at Bryanston had yielded nothing. Poppie had said he and Marika were in Cape Town, Lisette was out and no, she didn't know who Matthew Hillman was. Or Pearl Fisher. Rianne put down the phone, almost in tears. Her *one* night of freedom and she couldn't find anyone to spend it with!

At about eight o'clock she put on her coat and went out. It was horrible walking along Old Brompton Road, enduring the lewd stares of middle-aged men as they cruised the streets. She did her best to ignore them but there was hardly anyone else walking along at that time, and especially not tall, beautiful young women. When a police car slowed down and watched her walk along Beauchamp Place, she turned round and quickly went home. What did they think she was? A prostitute?

She stopped outside Harrods to look at the clothes in the windows. She would come back the next day. No, the next day was Sunday. Well, she'd wait until Monday to go back to that . . . that place. There was no way she was going back without at least half a new wardrobe! Although she'd sooner die than admit it, she'd spent the past fortnight looking carefully at what everyone else wore. She had a good idea of what she needed to buy. She was sick of feeling badly dressed or, worse, unfashionable. She laughed. *Her?* Unfashionable? Back home, everyone struggled to copy her! She ignored the businessman in a grey suit waiting at a restaurant door who had evidently thought her smile had been for him.

Despite Rianne's refusal, Dinah had cooked something for supper, she noticed as she wandered into the kitchen when she got back. She lifted the lid on one of the pots on the stove. It was still warm; she found a spoon and tasted it. It was lovely. Something spicy, just like the meals Maria made at home. She spooned some into a bowl, added some rice and found a beer in the fridge, then carried it into the living room and switched on the enormous TV. What a difference it made, she thought, settling herself comfortably on the sofa. A bit of space, a giant TV and a beer. Why couldn't St Anne's provide the same comforts?

An hour later, she was bored again. It was nearly eleven. What else was there to do except go to bed? She *was* tired, it was true. But still . . . a whole weekend in London, on her own? Dinah's head appeared round the door. What did *she* want? No, she didn't need her bed turning down. No, she didn't know yet what she wanted for breakfast. No, no, *no* . . . Dinah disappeared. Rianne turned back to the TV.

9

By the time Gabby and the others surfaced the following morning, Miss Caruthers was already one step ahead in finding out what had happened to Rianne. She had telephoned Margaret Simpson, the manager at Malvern Link station.

'Oh, yes,' Margaret said. 'Very pretty girl, blonde. She said she was the head girl . . . What? Really? Oh, the cheek of these girls.'

'But where did she buy the ticket to?' Miss Caruthers asked, relieved.

'Only to Worcester, but I'm quite sure she didn't come back. Probably in London, if you ask me. She had a credit card, I remember. A fancy gold one. Tsk. Spoilt rotten, half of them.' Margaret Simpson had little sympathy for the rich, wayward girls who came to her part of the world – and looked down on her own children.

'Thank you, Margaret,' Miss Caruthers said, wondering what the next move would be. Perhaps she ought to phone Lisette de Zoete-Koestler. 'You've been most helpful. As usual.' She put down the phone and turned to Miss Matthews. 'I suppose we'd better telephone the aunt. They have a house in London, I know. Perhaps she's gone there.'

Miss Matthews nodded. 'More than likely. Would you like me to call Mrs Koestler?'

'No, I'd better do it. I'll ring her from my office. I'll let you know what we decide.' Miss Caruthers got up. South Africa was two hours ahead of the UK. It was already late morning. Hopefully, she'd catch Lisette at home.

Twenty minutes later, she put down the phone and breathed a sigh of relief. Rianne was indeed tucked up in bed at the flat in Wilton Crescent. Lisette had called the housekeeper. They decided not to confront the girl until she was safely back in Malvern. Apparently the housekeeper had confirmed that Rianne intended to come back the following day. She wanted to go shopping on Monday morning. Lisette knew from past experience that confrontations didn't work with her niece. There would be a time and place for her to account for her actions but the main thing was to keep her at St Anne's until Christmas, at least. If she needed to spend the odd weekend in London, well, Miss Caruthers would just have to arrange it.

'Typical,' Miss Caruthers said to Miss Matthews. 'No

thought as to how this will impact on the other girls. How do I explain to them that *they* aren't allowed weekends in London?'

'Well, we've not got much choice, have we?' Miss Matthews said. She too was relieved. At least the girl was safe and sound. She hurried upstairs to tell the girls.

'Unbelievable!' Charmaine said, as Miss Matthews closed the door. 'She went to London – just like that?' She sounded half admiring.

'Pretty cool,' Nathalie mumbled, yawning. 'She has a flat in London? She's too cool for words.'

'She could have left a note or something,' Gabby said crossly. She'd slept badly, thinking guiltily about Rianne lying on the Malvern Hills with a broken neck. 'I was worried sick. Maybe we've been a bit hard on her.' She looked at the others.

Nathalie nodded. 'Yeah, maybe we have. I mean, she's a real bitch and everything, but maybe we should have made a bit more effort, you know ... What d'you think Matthie'll say when she gets back? Bet she gets away with it.'

'Yeah,' Charmaine agreed. 'She's probably under orders from Miss Caruthers to act as if nothing's happened. Some people have *all* the luck.'

She was right. When Rianne returned on Monday at tea-time, Miss Matthews simply told her to make sure she let them know in future when she planned to leave Malvern. They'd been a *little* worried.

Rianne looked at her, surprised. She'd heard Dinah talking to Lisette that morning and figured someone at the school had reported her absence, not that she was afraid. On the contrary, she didn't give a damn what they thought. If anything, the mild rebuke was a little disappointing – she'd hoped for a more dramatic reaction. It was nearly lights-out by the time she hauled her parcels upstairs.

*

'Hel-*lo*,' Nathalie said, as Rianne entered the room. They were in their pyjamas, getting ready for bed. Rianne nodded cautiously. Gabby and Charmaine smiled.

'Had a good time?' Gabby asked, hoping she didn't sound *too* friendly.

'Yeah.' Rianne put down her bags. The dark green and gold Harrods bags looked a little ostentatious in the rather drab room.

'What did you do?' Charmaine asked. 'Heard you went to London.'

'Oh, I just went shopping,' Rianne replied. She pushed the bags under her bed.

'Ooh, let's see! What did you buy? Did you get a ballgown?' Nathalie was really trying hard; Gabby suppressed a smile.

'No, nothing, really.' Rianne didn't feel like examining her purchases in front of them. She took off her coat, then picked up her sponge-bag and towel.

'Where did you stay?' Charmaine asked enviously. She wished she could have popped home for the weekend.

'In our flat.' Rianne made for the door.

Charmaine rolled her eyes as it shut behind her. 'Well, the trip hasn't improved *her* nature,' she said, aggrieved. 'I was only asking.'

'I wish she *had* dropped off the edge of a cliff,' Nathalie agreed.

Gabby had noticed something the others hadn't: there had been a hint of pride in Rianne's voice . . . along with the usual arrogance, of course. She thought about it. What was Rianne up to? What was she trying to do? Ah, confidence.

That was it! She was slowly trying to build back her confidence. Although the others only saw her rudeness, aloofness and downright arrogance, Gabby had detected fear in her . . . No, not fear exactly, something more like irritation. Irritation at not being the most popular, or the best-dressed, or the person everyone wanted to be friends with. At St Anne's, Rianne had been assigned a role she was unaccustomed to playing: second, or even third, fiddle. Sauntering off to London, going shopping without even talking about what she'd bought, keeping quiet about her little adventure . . . Gabby suddenly understood. These were the strategies Rianne was using to win back her place at the top of the pile. Well, it was working. Whatever else she managed to provoke, she now had their attention.

At eleven on the dot, Rianne ran up the hill and into her room before anyone else had made it into the kitchen. No one would come up, she knew. She sat cross-legged on the floor and opened the box that had just arrived. She couldn't wait to see the dress. Marika had spent days looking for the perfect ballgown – it had taken her ages to find it, she had told Rianne on the phone, and she knew Rianne would love it. She'd rung twice that week to find out if it had arrived. As she pulled away the wrapping tape and paper, Rianne's excitement rose, despite herself. She'd sooner have *died* than admit it but she was looking forward to the ball – just as a break in the routine, she told herself sternly. She pulled impatiently at the strings and began unwrapping. The parcel was securely wrapped with yards of tape, and bubble-wrap.

At last she peeled off the remaining piece of tape and lifted the lid. Her jaw dropped. Inside, nestled among the tissue paper, was a white and pink silk dress with more lace, frills, bows and ribbons than she'd ever seen on anything, wedding cakes included. She looked at it in horror. It looked like something she'd worn as a child bridesmaid. What on earth was Marika thinking? She pulled the dress free of its gold tissue paper. It was floor-length with a tight, fitted bodice and puffy, lacy sleeves. The skirt was of a stiffer, thicker silk and – horror of horrors – the waist was surrounded by an enormous pink silk ribbon that tied into an elaborate ruffle at the back. Rianne groaned. There was no way she could wear *that* to the ball. No *way*. But what the hell was she supposed to do? She had nothing else in her wardrobe that was even remotely appropriate . . . nothing. She looked again at the silk extravaganza in despair.

Just then the door opened and Gabby swept into the room. 'Oh, sorry, I didn't realise . . . What on *earth* have you got there?' she asked, dropping her books.

Rianne coloured. 'Nothing. Just a . . . my dress. For the ball,' she added quickly. She began shoving the pink and white confection back into the box.

There was an awkward silence.

'It's awfully . . . you know, *frilly*,' Gabby said finally.

'Yeah. My cousin chose it. I don't think she's been to one of these silly . . . balls . . . before.'

'Well, maybe Charmaine can do something with it. She's a whizz with scissors and a needle,' Gabby said, trying to sound encouraging. She could sense Rianne's discomfort.

'Oh, no, I probably won't go. It sounds pretty stupid,' Rianne said quickly. She hated the idea of having to ask any of the others for anything.

'Don't be silly, you *must* go to the ball. Everyone does. Even *I* have to, worse luck.'

'What d'you mean?'

'Well, it's not really my cup of tea, you know. I'd rather read a good book. And it's not like I'll have a queue of dancing partners.' Gabby gave a short, embarrassed laugh.

Rianne said nothing. Although she was beginning to like Gabby – or, at least, thought her the lesser of the three evils – she had to admit it was true: Gabby was the most ungainly person Rianne had ever encountered. Her carefully chosen social circle at home did not contain overweight, bookish redheads with zero style and a motherly sense of responsibility. Another silence.

'Well, I'd better get going,' Gabby said eventually. 'Boys' College this afternoon.'

'Yeah . . . I've got French in a minute.' The little extra bit of information had somehow slipped out. Rianne shoved the box under her bed and got up. 'Well, see you . . . later,' she said, and made her exit, leaving Gabby standing in the middle of the room.

'Honestly, you should see it, Char,' Gabby said earnestly. The three, Gabby, Charmaine and Nathalie, were walking up the road to the sweetshop. Rianne was struggling with English homework – probably the first essay she'd deigned to do all term.

'What's it like?' Nathalie giggled.

'All ruffles and bows . . . She'll look an absolute fright. Like a pink meringue.'

'Well, what do we care what she looks like? It's her own fault. If she'd been a bit nicer we could have helped her out. Why didn't she buy one when she bought out the rest of Harrods?'

'I don't know. Her cousin chose it, apparently. But she'll be the laughing stock. Couldn't you just offer to do something with it?'

'Gabby Francis, you'd better stop thinking about how to help Rianne out and start thinking about what you're going to wear. What *are* you going to wear?' Charmaine said.

'God, I dunno. I've got that skirt, the black one. I might have to let the zip out a bit . . .'

'You mean Charmaine might have to do it. You can't even thread a needle!' Nathalie laughed.

'Well, yes . . . I don't know what to wear on top, though.'

'You could wear my green jacket – the long one Mummy bought me last term. It'll fit – it's *huge*.'

'Thanks, Charmaine,' Gabby said drily.

'I didn't mean it like that. I mean it's huge on *me*,' Charmaine said hurriedly.

'Well, I'll try it on . . . thanks,' Gabby said. If she could let out the zip on her skirt, which was a kind of black, slightly shiny material – not silk, but close enough – and if she could get into Charmaine's jacket, well, perhaps all wasn't lost. At least she wouldn't look ridiculous. 'So,' she said cheerfully, turning to the other two, 'now that we're all sorted out, what about Rianne?'

Friday seemed to rush past in a blur. By the end of the day, exhausted by the boredom of classes and the fact that she'd been forced to stay up late the previous night doing homework, Rianne climbed the hill to Gordon. She was dreading the ball, she realised. She'd seen Nathalie and Charmaine twirling about the room in their sophisticated, grown-up dresses and was worried. She'd shoved her dress under her bed and tried not to think about it. But now, with less than a day to go, something had to be done. But what? Much as she was dreading standing among the others in her Alice-in-Wonderland frock, she didn't want to sit upstairs all night by herself either. Even Gabby looked nice. The emerald green jacket brought out the colour in her hair, and without her glasses she was actually quite pretty.

Gordon was full of girls rushing between rooms, trying on shoes, discarding jewellery, adding an accessory here or there, everyone in a state of panic. There were disasters – Marianne Simpson who shared the room opposite them with Gillian Hemmings had burned her fringe to a crisp with curling tongs. She'd howled with rage as well as pain as Gillian and Gabby had pulled the offending appliance off her head, together with most of her fringe. She was now wearing a wide satin Alice-type headband but bits of singed hair kept creeping out. On the other hand, some girls were transformed for the better. Chantal Laurent, a quiet, mousy-haired French girl who shared a room with two equally quiet girls, had shocked everyone by appearing in a red and black figure-hugging dress with a padded bra and the most spectacular cleavage – and she'd had something done to her hair. It was blonde. Sparkly, golden blonde. When she'd come into the TV room the night before, everyone's eyes had almost popped out of their heads. Charmaine had narrowed her eyes and resolved to increase the length of the split in her skirt. She wasn't about to be outdone by some silly little French twit, even if she did have a cleavage to die for and highlights.

Rianne sighed. As far as she could tell, she was the only one with a problem – a major problem. And, unlike Charmaine and Nathalie, she could barely tell one end of the needle from the other. She looked angrily at her unfinished essay. She had no idea who the characters were in the question they'd been set – she hadn't read that far.

10

Even Rianne was impressed. The dining room, the site of so many awful school dinners and cold breakfasts, had been transformed. Mrs Smith and her team had spent the whole afternoon hanging white balloons and silver streamers, and emptying the space of almost all its furniture. The long, barrack-like tables had been pushed to one side and covered with fine white linen. There were small vases of white lilies and blush-pink carnations on every table, and the whole place was lit with flickering candles. On the stage at the end of the room, where the High Table normally stood, a sound system had been set up. Mrs Smith's eldest son, Neil, was the DJ and he was already flirting with some of the upper-sixth girls under the nervous, watchful eye of his mother.

The fifth-form home-economics group had been in charge of the evening's catering – from the amount of food arranged artfully on the tables, it seemed as if they'd been cooking all week. Plates of plump, flaky sausage rolls; little skewers of gherkins, cherry tomatoes and feta cheese; dark green vine leaves stuffed with coarsely chopped lamb, pine nuts and seasoned rice; delicate filo-pastry parcels of spiced, grilled vegetables; and wafer-thin slices of roast chicken.

They had outdone themselves. Pity they wouldn't get to taste it.

At one end of the room, presided over by Mr Collins and Miss Featherstone, was the evening's prize: the punch bowl. It contained less than 0.5 per cent alcohol but all the girls – and Mr Collins – knew that the boys would arrive with little silver hip flasks of vodka. Even the plastic cups Mrs Smith had laid out looked magical, glinting in the soft candlelit glow.

'Ooh, will you *look* at Chantal Laurent!' an upper-sixth girl exclaimed, as the lower sixth made their way into the hall. The older girls were standing around in small groups, scrutinising them. Among themselves, they could count on one another not to run off with each other's boyfriends – prospective or otherwise. The risk of being named and shamed was too great. Everyone within the year cautiously observed the rules as they were laid down in the weeks before the dance. Unfortunately you couldn't count on the lower sixth to comply. Worse, this year the lower sixth had a number of absolute *tarts*, Charmaine Hunter for one and that new girl Rianne whatever-her-name-was as well as Chantal Laurent! She was practically falling out of her dress!

'Where'd she get those tits from all of a sudden?' Madeleine Blythe-Stanton asked crossly.

'Socks,' Justine Scott said drily. All the girls back home in Australia knew *that* little trick. Problem was, back home, you eventually had to go swimming, and there was no way you could do that with socks stuffed down your chest. They glared at Chantal and Gillian as they passed.

'Wow!' Gabby breathed. 'What a transformation!'

'Chantal looks amazing,' Charmaine moaned, nervously smoothing her own dress.

'So do you,' Nathalie assured her. She, too, was sizing up the room. Not too many pretty girls, she noted with relief. For some reason, the girls in the upper sixth that year were almost uniformly dull. Justine Scott and Madeleine Blythe-

Stanton were the only sparks of interest in a swotty year and, thankfully, neither of them outshone Charmaine or herself – or Rianne, for that matter. She cast a quick look sideways at Rianne. Her dress had been transformed at lightning speed – and, unfortunately, not terribly well. There just hadn't been time. Rianne had surprised them both by asking for help at the eleventh hour. They'd hacked off the sleeves and the high neckline, ripped off the pink sash and removed two layers of lace from beneath the skirt. It was now a sleeveless, strapless white satin dress with a rather loose skirt of indeterminate length. The bodice had been pinned back and stitched together so that Rianne would have to rip it apart to get out of it – but, as Charmaine said when she sewed the two sides together, that would happen after midnight and no one would see.

Now Rianne's hair hung almost to her waist, a thick, golden cascade, and luckily hid some of the more haphazard stitching. She had used Nathalie's mascara – or, rather, Nathalie's mother's mascara – to thicken and lengthen her already long lashes and Charmaine had quickly pulled a few hairs out of her sleek, glossy eyebrows, which lengthened and framed her face beautifully. Her almond-shaped, dark brown eyes had regained something of their sparkle as she looked around the room and ran a tongue over her lips. Charmaine had insisted on lending her some lip gloss and they were sticky. She couldn't believe it – she was nervous!

Suddenly the doors at the end of the room were thrown open and Miss Caruthers walked in, resplendent in a gold evening dress with a black silk shawl. Her rather horsy features had been softened by the addition of a little lipstick and she smiled serenely at Mrs Smith and her staff, then walked up to the High Table. She gave a five-minute speech about the *importance* of social occasions between St Anne's and the Boys' College, about the *importance* of acceptable and respectable behaviour at all times, about the *extreme importance* of restraint, particularly in respect of the punch. She was *absolutely* sure none of the girls present would embarrass the school or let them down *in any way*. '*Do* enjoy yourselves, young ladies, and remember, that is what you are. Young ladies.' Everyone tittered politely. They could hear footsteps coming down the corridor. The boys had arrived.

'Would you . . . um, like to . . . er, dance?' A tall, rather thin young man had approached Rianne almost as soon as the music began. She looked around. Charmaine had been waltzed away by Thierry Pasquier, even before the music started.

He, along with Ree Modise, Michael Rhys-Walker and Nael Hughes, was now in the upper sixth and he only had two chances to 'make it' with Charmaine: this ball, and the summer one, almost nine months away. His eyes had travelled over Charmaine in seconds: she looked good enough to eat in her narrow silk dress with its black waistband and her black velvet choker. He wanted nothing more than to slide a hand down her cleavage . . . her breasts looked wonderfully large and soft. Her hair was slicked back with gel and she'd done something to her eyes – they were all dark and smoky. She had that fantastic combination of being slightly . . . *coquette* and yet really classy. He felt his pulse quicken as she smiled up at him. He would find a way to sneak out with her before the evening was over! *Merde*, he *had* to!

Nathalie was surrounded by a group of besotted lower sixth boys, determined to stake their claim before the seniors did. She looked so pretty, with her diamond catching the candlelight. Her black velvet dress fitted her perfectly, elegant, yet sexy, in an understated, sophisticated way. She seemed to bring out the protector in boys – they looked like they wanted to hold her, slip a hand round that slight waist, tilt her little chin, kiss those perfectly formed lips. Martin Pickering kicked Stuart Graves, one of the boys

74

who had formed a half-circle around Nathalie, sharply on the heel. He was gazing down at Nathalie, moonstruck.

Rianne looked at her would-be suitor again. She nodded, although she didn't much like the look of him. Too thin, she decided, as he led the way to the dance floor.

'What's your name?' he shouted above the noise.

He couldn't dance either, she noticed. 'Rianne.'

'That's a pretty name. *You*'re awfully pretty, too,' he blurted out.

'What?' She couldn't hear him. Duran Duran's 'Girls on Film' was thumping from the loudspeakers. At least the music was good.

'You're really pretty,' he shouted again. 'Are you new here?' he asked. His knees kept bumping into hers.

She moved away slightly. She was a good dancer. She had a natural, supple sense of rhythm and several boys were watching her from across the room. She'd make her escape as soon as the song was over. 'Yes,' she mouthed.

'I thought I hadn't seen you before. Where were you before this?' He kept shouting in her ear.

'At home.' She wished he would shut up.

'Where's that?'

'South Africa.'

'Oh. You don't *sound* South African.'

'Oh? How'm I supposed to sound?' she asked, bored. Not the most interesting line of conversation.

'I don't know . . . Different, I suppose. Have you met Ree? He's South African, though he doesn't much sound it either.'

Rianne stiffened. He was the last person she wanted to meet that evening. The memory of his insult the last time they'd met still rankled.

'Yes, thanks, we've met,' she said quickly. Just then, a gentle tap at her elbow announced the presence of someone else. She turned and looked up. It was another young man, *much* better-looking. This one was tall, broad-shouldered and tanned. He had curly brown hair, lovely hazel eyes and a wide, rather sexy smile. Was he going to ask her to dance?

'Parker . . . may I?' he said smoothly. The young man who'd been dancing with Rianne shrugged ruefully. Nothing he could do about it. Nael Hughes was in the upper sixth. His *droit de seigneur*, or whatever the hell it was they called it. He reluctantly turned away. 'Hi, I'm Nael,' the newcomer introduced himself. Soft Cell's 'Tainted Love' began and the beat changed. This one was a much better dancer, too. He matched her own body movements perfectly and fluidly. *Much* better.

Across the room, Gabby ate one sausage roll after another. She felt like crying. She'd seen Nael almost immediately. He'd come in with Ree Modise, whom Gabby liked but always felt a little awkward with. Ree made her shy – he was so good-looking, so confident, so sharp, and beside his chiselled, dark good looks, she felt like a fat, pale, mumbling idiot. She never *quite* knew what to say to him. I'm awfully sorry about your father? Don't you hate being here? I think you're so brave? None seemed appropriate, although that was mostly what went through her mind on the odd occasion they met. He wasn't in her history class, but he sometimes waited for Nael.

She watched them walk across the room. They stood out from the rest of the crowd of boys. They were both tall, well over six foot, and both were rugby players with the build to match. Ree had that fluid, sexy swagger – he seemed to dance rather than walk. Although he was finding it hard to move anywhere in the room, with girls practically swooning at his feet. He was immediately swallowed into a group of upper sixths, including Justine and Madeleine. They looked as though they wanted to eat him alive. She watched Nael look around, then catch sight of her. He smiled at her and walked over. Something tightened in her chest and suddenly it was hard to breathe.

'Hey, you,' Nael said, squeezing her arm as he came up

beside her. Gabby felt a sharp stab where his fingers had touched her.

'Hi,' she croaked.

'You all right?' he asked. 'You look like you've seen a ghost.'

Gabby swallowed. 'No . . . no, I'm fine. You look really nice,' she said. It was true. The starched white of his dress shirt brought out the sun-kissed colour of his face – she wanted to reach out and touch him.

'You too,' he replied automatically, but he wasn't looking at her. 'Who's that?' he asked, and touched her arm again.

Gabby followed the direction of his eyes. Her heart sank. 'Oh, that's Rianne. She's new.' She watched him run a hand through his curly hair.

'Right. She's gorgeous.' He whistled softly. Gabby looked at him in panic. 'What's the matter?' He noticed her stare.

'Oh, nothing . . . I mean, what about . . . you know, Mandy?'

'Mandy?' He laughed. 'That's what I like about you, Gabs, you're so straight! No, Mandy and me, it's not going too well at the moment.' Impulsively Gabby put a hand on his arm. He covered it with his own. 'But, hey, lots of fish in the ocean. Like that one!' He jerked his head in Rianne's direction. Gabby left her hand in his for a second, savouring the feel of his fingers against her own. Her hand felt small in his, she closed her eyes briefly. She remembered something . . . faintly . . . the unfamiliar physical sensation of being held . . . When he removed it, she experienced an aching sense of loss. 'Wish me luck!' he whispered against her ear, and then he was gone. Gabby put up a hand to her ear . . . it felt hot, where his breath had touched it. What the hell was wrong with her?

She watched miserably as Nael moved towards Rianne and her partner. Despite the silly dress, Rianne looked fantastic. Her neck and bare shoulders glowed in the candlelight – all firm, toned muscle and smooth, faintly tanned skin. Nael was a terrific dancer. Just looking at the way the two moved together made her feel all funny inside. Apart from the odd shimmy in front of the mirror in their bedroom, Gabby hadn't danced with anyone since she'd been a bridesmaid at an aunt's wedding – when she was eleven. She looked at Rianne and Nael again. The sun-kissed couple. She frowned. What was she thinking? He was her friend. She ought to be *pleased* he was having a good time, not frowning at him from across the room like some lovesick puppy. She stopped. Lovesick? Oh, no, don't tell me you're falling in love, Gabby Francis, she said to herself sternly. Don't be ridiculous! Her eye fell on the buffet table. She chose a sausage roll. She could always count on food to make her feel better. She reached for another one.

'Ah, slowing down . . .' Nael smiled at Rianne as the music changed to a slow dance. All across the floor young men sighed with relief as the tempo changed. It was nearly ten o'clock. Now they could get down to business.

Rianne smiled back at him. They'd been dancing together almost all evening, apart from a short break when Michael Rhys-Walker had practically dragged her away. Now Nael pulled her close to him. She could feel the heat of his body through his shirt. 'So, you're Gabby's new room-mate,' he said, his voice close against her hair. She nodded. He reminded her of Hennie. Rianne felt herself move in closer, moulding her body to fit his. He tightened his hand against her back. 'And you're South African?' he murmured. 'Have you met Ree?'

Rianne pulled back a fraction. What was wrong with everyone? Why did everyone keep asking her the same question? 'Yes. And no, we don't know each other. OK?' she said sharply.

He pulled his face away from her hair and looked at her questioningly. 'What's the matter?' he asked.

'Nothing. It's just that everyone keeps asking me the same silly question.'

'Why's it silly? It's a fair question.' Nael was puzzled.

'No, it's not. Why should I know him? It's a big country.' She could feel Nael's hesitation. Perhaps they were friends. In which case . . .

'Oh. Well, you should get to know him. He's a great guy.'

Rianne said nothing. She didn't want to think about Ree Modise, great guy or no. Suddenly, Nael leaned forward, his mouth close to her ear. 'Aren't you hot?' he asked, his arm tightening round her again. She nodded. 'Come on, let's see if we can slip outside for a bit. Follow me.' He let go of her and moved slowly towards the door. Mr Collins's eyes were on the punch bowl and so many people were going in and out that Miss Featherstone, who was standing sentry, had simply lost track.

'I have to go to the loo,' Nael said to her as they made their way across the floor. 'Give me five minutes and then follow me. There's a little side door just before you get to the library. I'll be waiting outside.'

Rianne nodded. Whatever else Nael had in mind, she was dying for a cigarette. He gave her arm a quick squeeze and disappeared. Rianne looked round for Gabby. She could just make out Charmaine, her arms locked around the neck of some lucky boy, tangled and half hidden behind the curtains in the far corner. Nathalie was nowhere to be seen.

She turned back to the door, waited until Miss Featherstone was distracted for a moment and slipped out expertly. There was no one about. After the noise and chatter of the hall, it was suddenly quiet and cool in the wide corridor. She walked quickly, the heels of her new shoes making a sharp, clicking sound on the flagged stone floor. She wanted a cigarette and she wanted to be back in the warm, comforting embrace of Nael's arms. His young, strong body against hers had reminded her – pleasurably – of home, *vrying*, as they called it, with the boys in their group. None of them, Rianne included, had yet gone *all the way*, but Rianne, of course, had come pretty damned close. She would. If there was ever a limit to be reached, a line to be crossed, Rianne would be the first. It was more her confusion over her feelings for Hennie, who desperately wanted to be the *first*, as he blurted out once, that had stopped her. Unlike most of the other girls, she wasn't afraid of the consequences, whatever these might be. Lisette, sensible as always, had explained things to Rianne and Marika, and what Lisette hadn't told her, Rianne had figured out for herself.

She reached the little side door. She looked around. No one about. She put out a hand to push it just as it was opened from the other side. She caught herself in time and stepped back, leaning against the jamb. It was just as well. For who else should emerge from the other side but the one person she'd been only too happy to avoid the entire evening. She looked up in disbelief.

Ree Modise walked through the door and, for a second, their eyes met and held. She had time to take in his height, the way his presence filled the doorway and the astonishing intensity of his gaze. His ebony skin stood out in sharp contrast to the snowy-white of his shirt and his eyes, behind silver-framed glasses, burned straight into hers. For a split second they stared at each other and then, for the second time, he looked her up and down with that same insolent, contemptuous gaze and walked off, without saying a word. She stared after him furiously. He'd done it again! He'd snubbed her again, the arrogant jerk! She felt the familiar prick of tears behind her eyes. She always cried when she was angry.

'Hey, Rianne,' someone called softly. She looked up. Nael was coming towards her across the grass. She drew a deep breath and walked outside. The night air was cold and sharp. She shivered. 'Here,' Nael came up to her, holding his jacket over one arm, 'put this on – you'll freeze in that half-dress!'

The air was cooling her cheeks. She took the jacket gratefully and slipped it on. It was huge, warm, and smelled of him, a faint, sensuous blend of cologne and cigarettes.

'D'you have a cigarette?' she asked, trying to regain her composure.

'Yeah . . . here . . .' He fished in the jacket pocket and produced a packet. They both took one and lit up. Rianne inhaled gratefully. They smoked in silence for a couple of minutes.

Rianne looked at him from under her lashes. He was good-looking – no, make that *very* good-looking. Warm, dark brown eyes, dark curly hair, a bit longer than all the other boys', a strong, well-turned jaw. She liked the tanned, olive skin. He didn't look English exactly, more Italian or Spanish. She'd liked the way his body felt as they danced. He was bold, sexy . . . strong.

'Come on,' he said suddenly, stubbing out his cigarette. 'Let's go to the cloisters – it's a bit warmer down there.'

'How d'you know all these places?' she asked, as they walked through the garden.

'Been here a few times, you know,' he said, laughing slightly.

'With different girls, you mean?' Rianne laughed too.

'Well, that too. But I've been at the Boys' College for ages.'

'What is it with you English?' Rianne asked. 'You send your kids away to school as soon as they can walk.'

'Wouldn't know. I'm not English.'

'No?'

'No.'

'Well, what are you?' It felt odd to be the one asking the question. She'd heard it directed at her so many times.

'My dad's Welsh.'

'Same thing,' she laughed again. 'What about your mother?'

'What about her?'

'Well, where's she from?' Rianne was curious.

'Oh . . . she's . . . Mediterranean.' He sounded vague.

'What does that mean? Italian? Spanish?' she asked.

He stopped and turned to her. 'Something like that. Here, see that door?' He pointed to a small wooden one up ahead. Rianne nodded. 'That's the door to the cloisters. We paid one of the gardeners last week to leave it unlocked.' Rianne shook her head in disbelief. 'Yeah, the same bloke does our gardens. Come on, mind your head.' He led the way. The door opened onto an underground corridor, an exact replica of the corridor overhead that led from the dining room to Big House. The arched openings had been filled in with glass panes and although it wasn't exactly warm, it was bearable. Nael shut the door. It was dark inside. Rianne was glad she wasn't alone. '*Are* we alone?' she whispered.

Nael nodded. 'Yeah, for the minute. But there's four of us.'

'What d'you mean?' Rianne couldn't see anyone else.

'Well, there's me and Ree and two others. We paid Jimmy to leave it open. You must have just missed Ree – he left a few minutes ago. He's got about ten girls on the go.' Nael laughed admiringly. 'There's no one here now. Come on, let's go down the other end. You can see the dining room from there.' He held her hand and their footsteps echoed loudly in the underground space. 'See? You'll hear anyone coming in,' he said. 'You don't have to whisper.' They reached the corner. Rianne looked out of the dusty windows and, sure enough, the view led directly onto the dining room and the west façade, it looked beautiful: the candlelit windows cast a soft glow in the darkness. Nael stood behind her and slipped his hands round her waist.

She leaned into him and felt him tense. He buried his face in her hair. Slowly, she turned in his arms until they were facing each other. He bent his head and kissed her, gently, tentatively. Rianne surprised him by parting her lips and letting her tongue slide against his. He groaned and tightened his arms round her, kissing her hungrily and—

'Yeow!' He jerked his hand away. He'd been stabbed by something. Rianne stopped, her knees trembling.

'What's the matter? What happened?'

'I don't know . . . ow! There's something in your back . . . Look! Shit, it's a needle or something!' Nael hissed, nursing his finger. 'I'm bleeding . . . what the hell is it?'

Rianne started to laugh. 'Oh, God, it's my dress . . . Charmaine altered it this evening, just before the ball began. She must have left a pin in it.' She squinted in the dim light. His finger was indeed bleeding. 'It's only a scratch. Just suck it – it'll stop in a minute.' She lifted her arms and pulled his head towards her again. She wanted more. He obliged.

Sitting miserably in front of the empty sausage-roll plate, Gabby watched Miss Matthews look at her watch and begin the round-up routine with the rest of the staff. It had been the most miserable evening – no one had asked her to dance, not once. She'd stood chatting to her *friends*, the boys she'd known since her first year at St Anne's, then watched them saunter off to try their luck with girls like Nathalie and Charmaine. And Nael had gone off with none other than Rianne. There they were now, coming back into the hall together. It was more than she could bear.

'Hey.' He had come over and was smiling at her. He cuffed her affectionately. 'Danced your toes off, I bet,' he said, as they watched Rianne glide across the floor. Gabby just nodded. She couldn't look at either of them.

The lower sixth were counted, discharged and escorted

back to Gordon by Miss Matthews and Miss Featherstone. No major incidents, no drunken displays, no one found hiding in the cloisters this year. Thank goodness someone had had the foresight to lock the cloisters' side door the week before. Last year's ball had been *dreadful*. A dozen drunken couples in various states of undress, lying on the stone floor among the old tennis nets and desks. Dreadful.

Gabby pushed open the door to their room, tears running down her cheeks, thankful that no one was there to witness her distress. Rianne had gone to the bathroom with Nathalie and Charmaine to unpick her way out of her dress. Gabby had been unable even to speak to her on the way back. And it wasn't *her* fault: Rianne had no idea how Gabby felt about Nael. In fact, Nael didn't know how Gabby felt about him. The only person who had any inkling was Charmaine – and even she thought it was a bit of a joke. She pulled off her skirt and jacket, rummaged under her pillow for her pyjamas, then climbed into bed. Things couldn't possibly get any worse.

Nael was puzzled. Ree had hardly spoken to him on the way back to college. They shared a large, comfortable, sunny room with an adjacent study on the top floor of Plymouth House, one of the privileges of sharing with the head boy.

'What's wrong with *you*?' he asked, as they made their way upstairs.

'Nothing.' Ree was curt.

Nael sighed. Ree could be a moody bastard at times. 'Bullshit. You've been in a stink all evening. What's up?' If there was one thing he'd learned since he and Ree had first met, some six years ago, it was to be direct with him.

Ree was silent. He started unbuttoning his shirt. Nael shrugged. He'd say something sooner or later. He, too, peeled off his shirt and began to hang up his dinner-jacket.

He grabbed his sponge-bag and made his way to the bathroom.

'What were you doing with that de Zoete girl?' Ree asked, as he came into the bathroom a minute later.

Nael was brushing his teeth. 'Why?' he asked, through a mouthful of foam.

'Just wondered.' Ree's voice was unusually quiet.

'You know, usual stuff. She's hot.' Nael grinned. He felt a sharp stab of arousal as he thought about the evening.

'You should stay away from her.' Ree bent down to brush his own teeth.

'Why? You keen on her or something?' Nael met Ree's eyes in the mirror. Without his glasses, they looked even more intense.

'Don't be stupid. Don't you know who she is?'

'Well, I know she's South African ... Oh, you mean ... ? But you go out with white girls all the time. What's wrong with her?' Nael was puzzled. As for her being South African, the previous year Ree had slept with Francine du Toit, a South African girl at the nearby Wychwood School for Ladies. What was different about Rianne?

'She's Marius de Zoete's little girl. You know, the mining family. They practically run the country.' Ree was brushing his teeth vigorously. He was angry. Nael could tell by the way the muscles in his forearm moved.

'So ... who's he?'

'Come on, Nael, those bastards are propping the whole country up.' Ree spat into the basin. He straightened up. 'I don't need to give *you* a lesson in political expediency.' Nael was silent. Ree turned to face him. 'It'd be like you fucking Menachem Begin's daughter,' Ree added bitterly.

The two boys looked at each other. Nael's face darkened. There was a tense silence. Nael broke it first. 'Sure,' he said at last. 'I get you. I'm sorry. I didn't think.' He picked up his bag and left the room.

Ree turned back to the mirror and stared at his reflection. He had hated saying that. But he'd had to. It was their secret, his and Nael's, the thing that bound them together – the thing he'd found out by accident. Nael had sworn him to absolute secrecy. His mother's life depended on it. Nael's mother wasn't Mediterranean, at least not in the European sense of the term. She was Palestinian. And she was also in jail.

11

In Johannesburg, Marika looked at her mother, a huge smile on her face. 'Really?' she squealed. 'You mean it?' Lisette nodded.

They were sitting on the veranda at home, and Hennie was thrashing around in the pool. It was a warm spring evening and the scent of jasmine and lilies filled the air. Poppie had just served a light salad and a crisp, dry white wine.

Lisette poured them a glass each. '*Ja*. You'll fly out next Friday, arrive in London on Saturday morning and Rianne will be there on Saturday evening.' She looked fondly at her daughter. She had done so well in her exams and deserved a little treat – a week in London, a bit of shopping, the theatre, the kind of things Lisette loved to do whenever she went overseas. The kind of things you couldn't really do at home any more, she complained.

'Ma, you're just the *best*.' Marika hugged her mother.

Lisette smiled. She loved making her children happy.

'Can I tell Hennie? Now?' Marika jumped up.

'*Ja*, of course you can. Just don't fall in, *skatjie*. We've just done your hair.' Lisette had just paid a fortune to have Marika's curly hair straightened and cut. Apparently, it was all the rage. Marika nodded, too excited to speak. She jumped off the veranda and ran down the garden to the pool.

Lisette saw Hennie's face light up, even from where she was sitting. She sighed, relieved. He'd been an absolute *beast* since his cousin had departed. He moped around the house, swore at Seni unnecessarily and he'd even scraped the fender on Lisette's new Mercedes as he'd backed out of the driveway at top speed. As unhappy as she was at the thought of him going into the army in December, she secretly wondered if it wasn't perhaps the best thing for him. She watched him haul himself swiftly out of the water. He came running up the garden, still dripping. He had a good physique, his mother noted. Tall, strong and muscular. More like Marius than her husband, she thought, with a sudden lump in her throat. She squealed as he bounded up to her, cold drops of water flying everywhere.

'*Ag*, Hennie!' she cried. 'Go away! Dry yourself first – *ag*! It's *cold* !'

Hennie grabbed her arm. 'Mom, that's fantastic! Really? Next week?'

'Yes, yes! Now go away, dry yourself, then come and sit down. Look, Poppie's laid the table – come on, settle down!' Lisette shooed him away. She was pleased: both of them seemed so happy. Hennie ran back inside the house, whooping.

Poppie stuck her head round the patio doors. 'Missus?' she asked, wondering what all the commotion was about.

'*Nie*, Poppie.' Lisette shook her head, still laughing. 'It's all right. They're going to London next week to see Rianne.' Poppie smiled widely, happy for them. Lisette knew that she, too, missed Rianne, but she would have to wait until Rianne came back to them at Easter. Poppie had never been abroad. In fact, moving from Cape Town to Johannesburg after Missus Céline's death had been the longest trip she'd taken since childhood. And she could scarcely remember the other. Her family were originally from Natal and had been moved off their ancestral land by one government resettlement scheme or another, Poppie couldn't remember which. One minute she'd lived in a traditional thatched hut in a *kraal* at the foot of the Drakensberg mountains and the next minute she was in a squatters' camp in Khayalitsha. Moving into the de Zoete household at Vergelegen when she was ten had seemed like a dream. She couldn't remember how it had come about . . . her father had somehow met Rianne's father, Marius de Zoete. How? She had no idea. *Meneer* Marius and his beautiful wife were really the only family she knew. Lisette was okay but she was not like her brother Marius. She missed Marius. And at Easter her favourite child Rianne would be coming home. Poppie clapped her hands excitedly.

Rianne was puzzled. It was now Wednesday afternoon and she hadn't heard from Nael since the boys had disappeared on Saturday night. She'd been sure he would call. As was the custom following any social event that involved the Boys' College, the phone on the second floor had been ringing almost non-stop since Sunday afternoon. But none of the calls had been for her. She couldn't understand it – he'd seemed so keen. She and Gabby were making a cup of tea in the kitchen when someone shouted for Gabby.

'Gabby! Phone call!'

Gabby looked up. For her? She couldn't remember the last time she'd had a phone call at Gordon. She put down her toast, grabbed a tea-towel to wipe her buttery fingers and went to see who it was.

'Hello?' she said, wondering who it could be.

'Gabs, it's me, Nael.'

She felt something cold run through her. Nael? 'Oh . . . hi,' she said. Her heart was suddenly hammering in her chest.

'Gabs, can you do me a favour? Can you meet me at Serendipity's in about an hour?'

Gabby looked at her watch. It was a quarter to four. 'Um

. . . sure. Why? What's wrong?' Her heart was racing. He wanted to see her?

'I'll explain when I see you. It's about Rianne – it's a bit awkward over the phone.'

Gabby suddenly felt utterly deflated. 'Oh. Sure. I'll catch the four-fifteen bus down.' She hung up. Of course it was to do with Rianne. Why had she thought for a second that he might want to see her? She walked upstairs. She'd even forgotten her toast. She pulled her navy coat off the back of the door, found a pair of boots and pulled on her woollen socks.

When she got there Serendipity's was almost empty. Nael was sitting alone at the back of the café. He waved as she walked in, but he seemed tired and a little sad. His hazel eyes had lost some of their sparkle. He smiled as she came up to the table.

'Thanks, Gabs . . . you're a real sport. Thanks for coming. It's freezing outside.'

Gabby unwound the scarf from her neck. Her face was red from the cold. She nodded.

'What's the matter?' she asked, as she sat down.

Nael stirred his tea slowly. 'Well . . . it's Ree – Riitho, not Rianne,' he began, taking a sip. 'You know we've been friends since . . . well, since for ever.' Gabby nodded. The two of them were almost inseparable. 'He's pretty upset about me going off with Rianne. For his own reasons. Her being, you know, white South African and all that,' he continued carefully. 'The thing is, I completely understand him. I'd be the same if the situation were reversed. We talked about it the other night and, well, I just think it's best if I don't see her again.'

'Oh. Right. Well, d'you want me to tell her then?' Gabby asked. She assumed that was what she was there for, that that was why he'd called.

Nael looked at her, surprised. 'Tell Rianne? No . . . I just

89

wanted to talk to you about it,' he said. 'I didn't want you to think I was a complete jerk.'

Gabby was unsure what to say. He cared about what she thought? 'Oh.'

'I mean, she's pretty and all that, but . . . I'd feel the same way if I were Ree—'

'But you're not,' Gabby pointed out.

'I know. Still, I can't do that to him. He hates her. I mean, *really* hates her.'

'God, these friendships – it's all a bit complicated for me,' Gabby said. Suddenly it didn't matter any more that he'd called her to talk about Rianne. It felt nice sitting with him, smiling together, being . . . well, friends. That was what they were.

An hour later, as Serendipity's was about to close, he leaned across the table and touched her arm. 'Thanks for coming, Gabs, I really mean it. I feel heaps better just talking to you.'

Gabby went pink with delight. She smiled at him. Her friendship with Nael was something special, she thought to herself as she waved goodbye through the bus window. Boyfriends came and went – that much she'd observed from everyone else – but real friends stayed. She hoped they'd always be friends.

12

Nathalie was mooching around upstairs. Philippe wasn't coming until five and he'd phoned to say he was bringing a university friend with him. She was cross. She'd hardly seen him all summer – he'd gone off travelling round Europe with his university friends and now she would have to share him with one of them. At least it wasn't anyone she knew. His friends were usually so boring. This one was from Malaysia or some other God-forsaken place. Sacha, his name was. She pulled a face and opened her wardrobe to start packing. No point in taking anything even remotely fashionable back to Malmesbury, she thought. Two pairs of jeans, a few jumpers. Her mother dressed each evening as though she were expecting royalty – black cocktail dresses and gold jewellery. In *Malmesbury*! Nathalie grimaced – she secretly liked annoying her mother by appearing at dinner in jeans and an old cardigan.

A whole ten days with her mother. She wasn't sure how she would manage. Their relationship was complicated: Nathalie feared and adored her in equal measure. She longed to be like her, but somehow always fell short: where Cordelia Sutton-Farris, formerly Maréchal, then Bates, née Weissberg, was beautiful, Nathalie was pretty; where Cordelia was interesting, Nathalie was sensible; where Cordelia was exotic, Nathalie was plain and boring. And Cordelia was certainly exotic. Although Philippe and Nathalie knew little about their mother's past, she was careful to let fall certain charmingly intriguing hints.

They knew she'd been born to Czech-Jewish parents somewhere close to the Austrian border and that she'd been adopted by friends of her parents to escape the Holocaust. They knew that she'd grown up in Vienna – you could hear it in her carefully cultivated accent – and that she'd moved to Paris, then London, making good marriages, as she put it, along the way. Nathalie and Philippe's father, Claude Maréchal, had died in a car accident, which had left Cordelia with a handsome allowance and a house somewhere in the Loire valley. But provincial France was *not* where the young and vivacious Cordelia intended to spend her days: London was *the* place to be in the sixties, and Cordelia Weissberg-Maréchal was *the* person to be with. She had married Nick Bates, a British rock star who unfortunately had a penchant for white powder and teenage groupies. His early and rather sordid death had left her with another house, in Chelsea this time, and a middle-aged accountant telling her as gently as he could that she was close to broke.

Her third marriage, to the accountant, proved a surprising success. Clive Sutton-Farris adored Cordelia and, perhaps more importantly from Nathalie's point of view, her two children too. Nathalie had never met a man as patient, kind and loving as Clive. Nothing was too much trouble for him, especially where Cordelia was concerned. He waited on her, hand and foot. Nathalie often found herself wondering what Clive got out of it all – Cordelia was forever complaining, and especially that she *hated* life in the countryside. Clive had persuaded her to sell her London house and move to Malmesbury with him, to his country mansion. Although he continued to work from the Hanover Square offices in London during the week, he loved nothing better than to return to Rosebud Cottage on Thursday evenings, looking forward to the peace and calm of the Wiltshire countryside and golf on Saturday mornings. Cordelia, however, found Malmesbury just a *trifle* parochial.

She was twelve years his junior; she worried constantly about her looks and was always on a diet even though her measurements were almost exactly the same as they had been twenty years earlier, when she was twenty-one. Her glossy blonde hair was still thick and shiny, her face unlined, save for a few tiny creases around her mouth that all men found irresistible.

But in Malmesbury she was frustrated, and it showed. Nathalie had been on the sharp end of her mother's edginess during the summer holidays and she was dreading half-term. She hoped Cordelia was still riding every day: it seemed to calm her down. That way, she'd have Philippe to herself when the house was quiet for a couple of hours.

She could hear Charmaine and Gabby getting ready to leave. She ran downstairs to say goodbye. Rianne was also ready and the three agreed to share a taxi to the station. Nathalie waved them off. There were only a couple of girls staying behind until the afternoon. She yawned. Another couple of hours' sleep would suit her just fine.

Just before five she heard a car horn outside and pulled back the curtains in their bedroom. It was already dark. She peered out – yes! It was the familiar dark blue Jaguar, a wedding gift from her stepfather to her mother. She grabbed her bag and coat and flew downstairs, yanked open the front door and jumped on her brother, who staggered under the sudden assault and nearly toppled backwards on the steps.

'Gnat!' He laughed as he straightened up. It was his childhood name for her.

'Peewee!' she grinned back. They hugged.

He took her bags and stowed them in the boot. 'You look wrecked.' He opened the door for her. 'What've you been up to?'

'I've been asleep all afternoon,' she protested, climbing into the back seat. 'It's taken you ages to get here. Everyone else has gone.' She looked at the person sitting in the passenger seat.

'Gnat, this is Sacha. Sacha, my baby sis.' He got into the driver's seat: he'd passed his test in the summer and had probably had to twist their mother's arm to borrow the car that day, Nathalie thought.

'Hello, Baby Sis.' The young man in the front turned and smiled at Nathalie, who blushed. In the dark, she couldn't make out more than a row of perfect, pearly white teeth and lots of curly black hair. His accent was unusual, a bit of American, English, and something else she couldn't place.

'Hi,' she said casually. 'And my name's Nathalie, not Gnat. Or Baby Sis.'

'I know. Philippe's told me a lot about you.' His voice sounded as though he was smiling.

'Oi,' Philippe protested, starting the engine. 'We haven't

even got there yet and already I'm in trouble.' They all laughed.

Nathalie looked back at the receding Gordon. Too bad there hadn't been anyone present to see her rather glamorous departure. She looked at Sacha's profile as Philippe swung the big car round and started down the hill. He was tall, that much she could tell from the way his head almost touched the roof. His hair was swept back from his forehead and he had a straight, perfectly shaped nose and a wide square chin – a rather determined chin, she guessed as she looked at him surreptitiously from the back seat. She couldn't see his eyes properly – she'd caught a flash of dark, almost jet-black eyes and straight, heavy brows . . . Stuart Graves suddenly seemed awfully short and inconsequential beside this rather exotic stranger.

'Are you at Reading with Philippe?' she asked, leaning forward between the two front seats. She wanted to hear that strange, soft accent again. How come she'd not met him before?

'Yep. We were in halls together in the first year but I didn't really know him then. We shared a house last year.'

'Sacha's from KL,' Philippe supplied.

'Oh.' Where was KL?

'Malaysia.' Sacha had read her mind. 'My father's Malaysian and my mother's Finnish.'

'Really?' Nathalie was impressed. He was the first Malaysian *and* the first Finn she had met.

'Yes. I grew up in Malaysia, though. My parents are divorced.'

Nathalie smiled happily. They had something in common. He also came from a family that had suffered a loss. 'Our mother has remarried, but our stepdad is great!'

'Yes, we met them this morning. Your mother's really beautiful.'

Nathalie pulled a face. Yes, her mother *was* really beautiful. And she knew it.

'How's Charmaine?' Philippe asked, his eyes meeting

Nathalie's in the rear-view mirror. Charmaine had spent a few days at Rosebud Cottage at the beginning of the Easter holidays and it was no secret that Philippe had been rather taken with the voluptuous fifteen-year-old.

'Oh, fine. She's off to London to meet Thierry,' Nathalie answered gloomily. 'She's so lucky.'

'Who's Thierry?'

'Her new boyfriend. He's at the Boys' College. They're meeting up tonight. Imagine! Her mum lets her do anything. Mama won't even let me go into Cheltenham,' she grumbled.

'It'll be different this time, Nat. I'll teach you to drive if you like.'

'Oh! Can I? Really?' Nathalie said, delighted. Learn to drive! Just wait till she told the others!

'Sure,' Sacha turned around, smiling. 'We'll both teach you. It's easy.'

Nathalie's stomach fluttered. The thought of sitting next to Sacha as he guided her through the complexities of learning to drive was almost too exciting to contemplate. The car sped along, eating up the miles of undulating Worcestershire countryside. She leaned back in the soft leather seats. Perhaps it wouldn't be such a bad half-term, after all. Curled up in the back, listening with half an ear to Sacha and Philippe, she dozed off.

It was completely dark by the time the car nosed into the driveway at Rosebud Cottage. Philippe brought it gently to a halt and pulled up the handbrake.

'Look at that,' he said, turning round to look at Nathalie. 'Out like a light.'

'I'll wake her up,' Sacha said, getting out of the car. 'My dad showed me this great trick – he does it on his patients. Watch.' He opened the back door and, leaning over the sleeping Nathalie, gently rubbed her earlobe between his thumb and forefinger.

She woke slowly, his light touch pulling her slowly from

her dreams. It was a rather delicious way to wake up. She was dimly aware of the musky aroma of his aftershave as he moved away. She stretched.

'Sorry . . . I couldn't hear what you were talking about.' She smiled sleepily at the two of them. 'It got boring . . .'

'Us? Boring?' Philippe ruffled her curls affectionately. 'Come on, supper'll be ready. Gimme your bag.' She handed over her things and followed the two young men into the house.

'Nathalie!' her mother cried, all smiles as she came to meet them. 'But you look so tired, darling! And what have you done to your hair? It's *terrible*!' She hugged her exasperated daughter briefly before turning to the other two. 'Come in, come in!' she welcomed them, taking Sacha and Philippe by the arm. She had met his charming friend earlier that morning. She turned back to her daughter. 'Nathalie, ask Janice to take your bags to your room. Is that all you brought with you? What's happened to that lovely coat we bought last winter? What's this you're wearing?'

'Oh, Mama,' Nathalie said, irritated. She'd only been home five minutes! 'I prefer this one. It's warmer.'

'But it's so drab, darling.' Cordelia frowned. 'We'll go shopping on Monday, *hein*?'

'Yeah, whatever,' Nathalie muttered and looked away. Why did her mother always – but *always* – succeed in making her feel about as attractive as – as a gnat? Cordelia's glamorous continental ways – the little *heins* and the *Schätzles* she dropped into her speech – sounded so charming, so cultured. Nathalie on the other hand felt like a provincial schoolgirl every time her mother opened her mouth. It just wasn't fair. Philippe turned and winked.

'Hello, darling.' Clive Sutton-Farris had come into the hallway. 'I thought I heard your dulcet tones.'

'Clive!' Nathalie hugged her stepfather. 'I'm *so* glad you're here. I thought you'd be coming up tomorrow!'

'Couldn't miss seeing you two,' he said. He was

genuinely fond of his stepchildren, having missed his own children's teenage years. 'Drink, anyone?' He turned to greet Philippe and Sacha. He and Philippe exchanged the Gallic kisses he had always found so charming in Cordelia, with her German background, and her children. He picked up a heavy crystal decanter. It was a special occasion – the family at home together. He and Philippe clinked glasses. 'Glad to see you made it back. Car still in one piece?'

'He's a *great* driver, Clive.' Nathalie beamed at her brother. 'He's going to teach me!'

'Dear God, *no*?' Clive teased her. Philippe and Sacha grinned at one another.

'Darling, don't you think you should have a bath or something before dinner, and put something nice on?' Cordelia interrupted, looking pointedly at Nathalie.

'Why? I'm fine, Mama.'

'Well, I mean . . . jeans, darling? Really, *mein Schatz*. Janice will be serving dinner at eight, you've got an hour.'

'Let her finish her drink, Cordy,' Clive said gently. 'The poor girl's barely had time to get in.'

Cordelia frowned. He was always so quick to jump to Nathalie's defence.

'I'll go in a minute.' Nathalie capitulated suddenly. She looked at her mother – a simple knee-length black evening dress with sheer stockings, black high heels and perfectly coiffed hair . . . Perhaps she ought to put on a dress. There'd be something hanging in her wardrobe. God, her mother got on her nerves. She took a gulp of sherry.

'Lovely, darling.' Cordelia smiled at her. 'I'll go and see how Janice is getting on.' She moved gracefully towards the kitchen. Clive took Philippe and Sacha into the drawing room.

Nathalie downed her drink and ran upstairs to draw a bath.

She poured in plenty of Cordelia's favourite scent – Chanel No. 19. It was the one thing she liked about her mother – her dressing-table. She stripped off her clothes and stepped gingerly into the perfumed bubbles. She lay submerged for a minute or two and closed her eyes. She thought briefly of Stuart Graves, his rather fumbling attempts to kiss her the week before. And then, rather dreamily, of Sacha. Ten whole days . . .

'Nathalie!' Cordelia shouted, from the bottom of the stairs, breaking her reverie. Guiltily she clambered out of the bath and wrapped herself in a huge towel. She hurried down the corridor and into her room. She tugged open the wardrobe door and quickly scanned its contents. She picked a lemon-coloured knit dress and a pair of plain black pumps – nothing too fancy. She dressed quickly, pausing only to run a brush through her curls. She looked at herself in the mirror. Better . . . if not beautiful. She added a dab of perfume behind her ears and hurried downstairs.

'That's better, *mein Schatz*.' Cordelia smiled graciously as Nathalie joined them in the drawing room. A fire was burning in the grate and Philippe and Sacha were admiring Clive's collection of antique naval paintings. Nathalie sat next to Clive on the large pale blue sofa and looked across at her mother. For the umpteenth time, she wondered how it was that her mother never seemed to age. Cordelia looked wonderful – every inch the gracious, sophisticated hostess. She adjusted her delicate gold necklace with a long, scarlet-tipped finger. 'Shall we?' she enquired of the young men. The two of them turned round, a little bashfully – naval artistry was not Cordelia's forte. She stood up and again slipped an arm through Sacha's. Clive smiled at Nathalie and held out his arm. The five of them walked through to the elegant dining room.

Dinner was an elaborate, rather fussy affair: five courses and endless plate changes. Poor Janice ran to and fro from the kitchen, trying to make sure everything went smoothly under Cordelia's sharp eyes. Thankfully, there was plenty of wine. Cordelia kept everyone entertained with her usual dinner-party repartee: charming little stories about people and places she'd known. Her blonde hair shone in the firelight, a sleek, glossy frame around her oval-shaped face. She ate little – 'Watching my figure,' she said archly. Clive smiled and patted her arm. He would have preferred just a *little* more flesh on her – all those sharp bones and tummy exercises. He found it exhausting just watching her.

They retired to the drawing room for an after-dinner drink. Philippe and Sacha excused themselves: they'd been up early that morning to catch the train to Malmesbury and what with the drive to pick up Nathalie . . .

'I do hope you'll enjoy your stay with us,' Cordelia said to Sacha, standing up and leading the boys to the door. 'Malmesbury can be a bit quiet, you know, but perhaps you ride.'

Nathalie looked at her mother crossly. At the age of nine, Nathalie had fallen off Midget, her pony, and had refused to mount a horse ever since, and neither Philippe nor Clive were keen riders.

'Yes, yes I do,' said Sacha, turning his perfect smile on Cordelia. 'I didn't know you had horses.'

'Oh, my dear,' Cordelia's laugh had a sharp edge to it, 'that's all we have. We *must* go riding together. Perhaps tomorrow? The countryside is at its loveliest early in the morning.'

'I'd love to,' Sacha agreed. Philippe looked pleased: his mother usually ignored his friends. Nathalie sat on the sofa beside Clive, suddenly and furiously jealous. She was almost tempted to break her seven-year ban and join them. Almost, but not quite. She was uncharacteristically quiet for the rest of the evening and escaped to her room as soon as it was decent.

'Are you sure you want to get up so early, darling?' Clive asked his wife anxiously, as they prepared for bed. 'I mean, it's the first day of the holidays . . .'

'Of course I'm sure,' Cordelia replied, creaming her face and neck. 'You never come with me and you know how I love the early morning. Don't worry, we won't go far.'

'Well, if you're sure . . .' Clive picked up his trousers and neatly folded them as he had every night for the past eleven years.

'I am.' Cordelia got up from the dressing-table. She smiled winningly at him as she walked to the bathroom. 'You worry too much.' He smiled back and reached for his pyjamas as she disappeared through the door.

In the bathroom, Cordelia drew the bolt on the door quietly and slipped out of her peach-satin robe. Naked, she stood in front of the gilt-framed mirror and drew the scales from under the chair. She stepped on and looked anxiously at the dial. Perfect. Not an ounce heavier than the day before, or the day before that. She looked at herself in the full-length mirror, pleased with what she saw. Her stomach was perfectly flat, even in profile, and her breasts were still rounded and firm.

She smiled at her reflection and raised a red-tipped finger to her breasts and started stroking. As the nipples stiffened she lowered herself into the antique chair beside the bath and spread her thighs. With swift, practised strokes she brought herself to a quick, sweet climax – as she had done every evening for the past eleven years. She allowed herself the tiniest of sighs. Sacha. She smiled to herself and reached for her robe. She glanced at her watch. The nightly ritual had taken less than ten minutes. With any luck, Clive would be asleep.

13

Nathalie was sulking. Hard. The holiday was not living up to its promise. It was mid-week. Clive spent every day in Cheltenham, returning only for dinner, then leaving again early in the morning. He was working on some big case – he looked tired. Philippe and Sacha were always out, she'd no idea where. Apart from on Sunday evening in the local pub, they'd pretty much ignored her. Her mother – after the early morning ride with Sacha, which had become a daily fixture – spent most of the day in bed. She descended at dinner-time, dressed ever more elegantly, and flirted *outrageously* with their good-looking guest. And Sacha *was* good-looking. Nathalie was fascinated by him – she thought he was the most exotic and sophisticated person she'd ever met. On the rare occasion that he and Philippe stayed at home long enough to chat to her, she found herself hungry for more. His life seemed so interesting, compared to theirs. A Finnish mother – never mind that she'd fled back to Finland almost as soon as he was born – a Malaysian father, rich, privileged, the American school in Kuala Lumpur, then boarding school in England, a year spent travelling around the world before university . . . it was exactly what she imagined a glamorous, adventurous life to be. He seemed not to notice . . . that was just his life.

She kicked at a pebble. It was eleven o'clock on a damp, blustery morning. She wandered across the courtyard and into the kitchen. No one was about, not even Janice. Something was simmering on the Aga. It was quiet. She opened the cupboard and found a packet of biscuits. She'd find something to read. She wandered into the drawing room, picked up one of her mother's endless romance novels, then went out again, across the pebble courtyard to the second row of empty stables. The high loft above the abandoned row of stalls had long been a favourite place to hide. When Clive had first brought them to Rosebud Cottage, she had spent hours in the loft with an old duvet and a good book. It was her escape from her mother's unbearably high spirits. Over the years, she had dragged an old sofa and a small heater up to the little nest, despite Cordelia's dire predictions of fire. Munching steadily, she settled herself in the sofa, wrapped the duvet round her legs and picked up her book. Before long, she was transported from the mundane present to an exciting world of passion, intrigue and betrayal.

At first the soft moans and sighs that penetrated her subconscious appeared to her to be part of her own imagination. She put down the book, distracted by faint rustling noises beneath her. The light from the skylight was fading fast – darkness was on its way. She peered at her watch. It was almost four o'clock. She'd been reading for hours. As a groan echoed through the empty stables she scrambled to her knees and peered over the edge of the loft.

She nearly lost her balance. Lying almost directly below her, bathed in the dying light, was her mother. Her tousled blonde hair was spread over the blanket upon which she lay, half naked. With a gasp, Nathalie recognised the jet-black curls beside her. Sacha. She perched above them, unable to move or to tear her eyes away. Cordelia smiled luxuriously, grabbing Sacha's hand and placing it on her stomach . . . lower . . . lower. Nathalie gulped.

'Oh, *ja*,' Cordelia whispered lazily, turning to face him. Sacha laughed softly.

Suddenly her mother's body was obliterated by his muscular back as he pushed her knees apart and entered her. It was terribly quiet. Nathalie tore her eyes away and scrambled to her knees. She could hear Sacha's ragged breathing and her mother's gasps. She put her hands over her ears. She was trembling. She was trapped upstairs. The only ladder down was right in front of them. She stood there, absolutely still, her palms pressed tight against her ears. She could hear the thud of her racing heart as the minutes ticked by.

'*Kom, Schatz*,' she heard her mother say at last. 'Philippe will be home soon and I can't *think* where Nathalie has got to. We'd better go in. I'll go first and you can slip in through that door over there. Wait a few seconds, hmm?' There was a rustle of clothes and the sound of a zip. Nathalie heard the heavy oak door creak open, then the sound of

Cordelia's heels tapping across the courtyard. Sacha let out a deep breath and, seconds later, he too was gone.

Nathalie felt her legs give way. She needed to sit down. Her face was burning. Her heart was racing and her hands felt clammy – with shame and embarrassment. She could scarcely believe what she'd seen. Sacha? Doing *it* to her *mother*? Tears welled behind her eyes. How could she face either of them ever again? She began to sob, her chest heaving. A mixture of shame and fear swept over her, making her nauseous and weak at the same time. She sat on the couch for what seemed like an eternity, tears running down her cheeks, her mind unable to grasp what her eyes had seen.

The evening was torture. She found herself staring constantly at her mother, marvelling at how normal Cordelia appeared, fussing over Clive, sipping her wine, slowly asking how Nathalie's day had gone. She was her usual seductive, charming self. At times Nathalie wondered if she had simply imagined the whole episode. She watched Sacha intently, but his dark eyes gave nothing away. Was she going mad?

'She's here!' Marika gave a shout from her position at the window where she'd been waiting for the past hour. Darkness had closed in and Dinah had just switched on the lamps. The large, double-height sitting room, with its enormous sofas and deep leather armchairs, was warm and elegant. Marika looked around it with pleasure. She loved the way you could be in the clear, bright light of Johannesburg one minute, then emerge into the sombre gloom of London the next. Except that it was cold. She was dressed in a pair of jeans, two T-shirts and a burgundy cardigan, a pair of woollen socks and one of Lisette's cashmere shawls – not that it was cold inside. On the contrary: the first thing Hennie had done on arrival was locate the thermostat and turn it up. He walked around the house as though he were still at home, in a rugby shirt and a pair of cotton trousers. He came running down the corridor. Rianne had arrived.

'Ssh!' Marika warned him, pulling him into the alcove behind the curtains. They could hear Dinah greeting Rianne and the sound of her bag as she dragged it up the stairs.

'Any messages for me?' Rianne asked, heaving her bag into the hall. Dinah would pick it up and carry it through to her room.

'No, but there's a letter. It's in the drawing room on the coffee table,' Dinah said, as Marika had told her to say.

'Oh?' Rianne couldn't imagine who would write to her at Wilton Crescent.

Behind the curtains, Marika could barely suppress a giggle. It was all a bit childish. Then, 'Sur*prise*!' she shrieked, as Rianne walked towards the coffee table.

Rianne jumped and, for a second, was speechless. She and Marika hugged tightly, and then she turned to Hennie.

He hung back a little, diffident. 'Hey,' he shrugged, his cheeks reddening, 'the letter thing was her idea.' He pointed at his sister.

Rianne laughed. She didn't care whose idea it was, it was the *best* surprise ever! 'How long are you here for? When did you come? Where's Lisette?' The questions tumbled from her lips.

'She's in New York. She gets back to Jo'burg a week after we do. We've got nearly three weeks of freedom!' Marika said smiling widely. 'It's a going-away present for Hennie.'

Hennie scowled: he hated being reminded that he was on his way to the army.

'What'll we do – what d'you want to do?' Rianne said, looking at her watch. It was nearly six o'clock. She couldn't wait to go out with them, somewhere nice, somewhere grown-up, after being cooped up in that prison. 'Let's go to a bar!'

Marika looked a little doubtful. Bars were not really her scene. But the sight of her cousin's beautiful face lighting up with pleasure when Hennie agreed convinced her. She didn't care where they went ... she wanted to hear all about Rianne's 'adventure', as she called it, amongst all those English girls and, of course, to hear about the ball. She hoped Rianne had taken a picture or two of the beautiful ball dress. In her mind, her cousin's life had suddenly transplanted itself into one of those frightfully nice Enid Blyton stories about boarding school that she remembered from about age twelve. The three wandered into the kitchen. Luckily, Dinah had a teenage daughter and seemed to know all the right places – and how to get to them.

At home in Pimlico, in the pretty, somewhat frilly flat she shared with her mother, Charmaine paced up and down in her room, anxiously listening for signs that her mother's conversation, which had lasted over an hour, was nearing the end. 'Get off the phone,' Charmaine longed to yell. 'Thierry might call!' She bit her lip. What if he'd given up? She could hear her mother chattering away and rolled her eyes heavenwards. Mary Hunter could talk for England. Charmaine stuck her head round the door, unable to bear it any longer. 'Mum?' she pleaded. '*Please!*'

Mary covered the mouthpiece with her hand. 'Just a minute, Charmaine,' she whispered. 'I've nearly finished.'

'You said that an *hour* ago,' Charmaine complained. 'I'm waiting for a call.'

'Well, she'll just have to ring back,' Mary said, and returned to her conversation.

'Mum! It might be Thierry!' Charmaine wailed. 'He might not!'

'Oh, for goodness' sake, Charmaine,' Mary said, exasperated. She flapped her hand at her daughter. 'Betty, I'd better go,' she said. '*Madam* here's waiting for a call. Prince Charming *might* just ring,' she said meaningfully. Charmaine scowled at her behind her back. 'I'll phone you later. *If* he calls.'

'He *will* ring. Not like *your* boyfriend,' Charmaine said pointedly, and Mary's cheeks reddened.

Charmaine flounced back into her room. Men were a touchy subject between her and Mary. Charmaine had never stopped blaming her mother for her father having walked out on them some nine years previously. Charmaine still dreamed about him. Charlie Hunter had simply gone to work one morning and never come back. No note, no explanation, nothing. A month later, Mary received a letter. Charlie was in New Zealand, making a new life for himself. He was sorry but he couldn't stand it any longer. He had seen to it that Mary and Charmaine were generously provided for: on the first of every month, a cheque arrived, drawn on a Swiss account and posted from Zurich without fail or explanation, with no trace of the sender. Also, Mary's own father, whom Charmaine barely remembered, had left his only daughter a sizeable inheritance, so she could go on living pretty much in the manner to which she'd become accustomed. But it meant little. Charlie Hunter, whom she'd married at eighteen, had left her.

A new life. Charmaine, who had been seven at the time, couldn't grasp what it meant. She was full of questions to which Mary had few answers. A new life? How could you decide to have a new life? What had happened to the old one? Did he have another family? Another pretty little girl? Someone else to tell bedtime stories to and hoist up on his knee when he came home from work? She was Daddy's little girl – he loved her, he told her so, a dozen times a day. What had Mary done to him?

It was easy to blame her mother – the weeping, distraught Mary was an easy target. But deep down, somewhere in the back of her mind late at night when the lights were off and her imagination ran wild, Charmaine couldn't help but wonder . . . was it *her*? Had she said or done something? Perhaps she hadn't been enough for her father – she wasn't pretty enough, she didn't smile enough

. . . or was she too heavy? In the months before he left, Charlie had complained that Charmaine was getting too heavy to sit on his knee – my little Heffalump, he had called her. Charmaine often turned her face into her pillow and wept.

By the time Charmaine was in her teens, Mary had been through a string of unsuitable men – Uncle Justin, Uncle Henry, Uncle Peregrine – who had all vanished, bored by Mary's insufferable *niceness* and irritated by the maudlin conversations that somehow always ended with Charlie, the husband who'd left. The lesson, as far as Charmaine was concerned, could not have been clearer. Her mother was going about it all wrong. In her demure twin-sets and pearls, her hair carefully lacquered into place and her sensible, flat shoes with gold buckles, she oozed motherly charm tinged with a *hint* of desperation.

Charm and desperation got you nowhere, Charmaine decided. Sex and bored indifference were where it was at. And she'd proved it. The summer she'd turned fourteen, two years ago, she'd been rewarded with a look of confusion by one of her mother's suitors as she'd sat with them, sipping a glass of wine. Charmaine had run the tip of her tongue across her lips – not on purpose, mind – and the man had blushed a fierce red as her eyes caught his. From then on, it was easy. Every holiday, her skirts were that bit shorter, her blouses unbuttoned to the third buttonhole, not the second; her T-shirts a little too tight. She knew from the hungry look in their eyes that the men who came to take Mary out to dinner or the theatre wished they could stay behind on the Laura Ashley sofa where Charmaine was curled up.

Yes, sex was the weapon, and at sixteen Charmaine knew how to use it. She could get men – and get *back* at them – with ease. She wasn't the prettiest girl at St Anne's, especially not since Rianne had arrived, but she was certainly the sexiest. At Serendipity's, boys from the college were always falling over themselves to sit at her table.

'Darling,' Mary Hunter called, interrupting Charmaine's reverie. 'There's someone on the phone for you – Thierry someone-or-other.'

Charmaine leaped out of her room and tore the receiver from her mother's hand. She held it against her chest for a second – she didn't want to sound breathless. Two minutes later, she hung up, her face beaming with happiness. Thierry had asked her to meet him in Chelsea, as he had said he would, but there was more. He was going to meet Ree and Nael and a couple of others from the Boys' College. They were all in London for the half-term holiday. Did she mind? Charmaine squeezed her eyes shut in excitement. Mind? Was he mad? She rushed into her room and threw open her wardrobe doors. What could she wear? Something low-cut and clingy, she decided, hurriedly pulling clothes off the rails.

Ten minutes later, she was ready. She'd squeezed into a tight black jersey dress that barely did up across her breasts – she'd had to slip a safety-pin between the buttons directly over her cleavage. She rummaged under her bed for her favourite suede Chelsea boots. Then, with a blue and white striped scarf wound round her neck, she thought she looked fantastic. She grabbed her coat and headed for the sitting room.

Mary grimaced as she noted Charmaine's outfit. 'Darling,' she began, hesitantly, 'your dress . . . Don't you think it's a *little* tight? Your bra's showing—'

'Mummy, it's *supposed* to. That's the fashion nowadays,' Charmaine replied breezily, pulling on her gloves. 'I'll be back before midnight, I promise.'

'Well, all right – but do take a taxi home, won't you? Make sure Thierry comes all the way to the door. There're all *sorts* of people in the streets at that time.'

'Yes, Mummy,' Charmaine said.

'Uncle Justin might drop by for a drink,' Mary called, as Charmaine disappeared, 'so we'll probably still be up when you get in,' she added.

Charmaine grinned. She'd make sure she was back *long* after midnight. She'd no desire to see Uncle Justin's shaky hands tremble as he handed her a drink. She hailed a cab.

If I die now, at this very minute, Charmaine thought, as she watched Thierry, Ree and Nael cross the King's Road and make their way towards her, I'll be happy. Nothing can top this. She was sitting by the window of Blushes, her favourite café on her favourite road in the whole world. Not that she had seen much of the world. She waved at them from her seat. Thierry saw her first and waved back enthusiastically. Ree and Nael were being their usual too-cool-for-words selves. Another man was following them. Charmaine frowned. Oh, it was Ree's bodyguard. Was he coming too?

'Charmaine, hi,' Thierry said, unwinding his scarf. He kissed her twice, once on each cheek. 'Have you been here long?' he asked.

'No, just got here. Hi, Ree,' she said. Everyone in the café was looking at them, Charmaine noted happily. They made a striking group. The three young men couldn't have been more different – pale, almost blond Thierry with his Parisian affectations, a Paisley scarf round his neck, a dark blue trench-coat; Ree, with his jet-black skin and eyes, tight-cropped hair and trademark black jeans and black coat; and Nael, golden-skinned with curly brown hair and hazel eyes. All three looked good enough to—

'Hi.' Nael lowered his head to kiss her. Ree made no move. Disappointed, Charmaine sat down. Ree's body-guard sat at a nearby table. It was all too thrilling for words. A waiter glided over. Yes, she would have a drink, thank you, a Bloody Mary. She'd heard other girls order it and it sounded so worldly. Ree and Nael had beer and Thierry a glass of wine. The bodyguard drank water.

'Doesn't it feel a bit strange,' Charmaine asked Ree, as the waiter served their drinks, 'having him around all the time?' She indicated the bodyguard.

Ree shrugged. 'You get used to it.'

'Have you ever been . . . you know, shot at or anything?'

'No.' Ree didn't look as though he wanted to be drawn on the subject.

She turned to Nael. 'Are you going to see Rianne?' she asked brightly, remembering the ball.

'Er, no.' Nael blushed. There was a short silence. Charmaine took a sip of her drink. Ugh. The conversation wasn't flowing quite as smoothly as she'd hoped. Thierry sat next to her, his arm draped casually over the back of her chair. She smiled at him, and was rewarded with a grin. He looked like he appreciated her, even if the other two didn't. She moved a little closer.

By eleven o'clock Charmaine was feeling rather drunk. She'd had two Bloody Marys, a glass of wine, a shot of tequila, followed by another glass of wine. Nael's gentle warnings not to mix her drinks went unheeded. He and Ree had disappeared at about ten o'clock, bodyguard in tow. The evening hadn't been the unbridled success that she'd hoped it would be. In fact, Ree and Nael spent most of the time talking between themselves, leaving Thierry free to nuzzle her ear, slide a tentative hand up and down her thigh and watch delightedly as she knocked back one drink after another.

'Shall we go, *chérie*?' he asked, as the bell sounded for last orders.

'What? To my house?' she asked, her words slurring slightly.

Thierry thought quickly. *Merde*. His aunt and uncle were at home – couldn't go back there. Charmaine lived with her mother, he knew that. A hotel? Not around here – he couldn't afford it. 'Well, perhaps not. Would you like to go somewhere else?'

Charmaine brightened. 'Ooh . . . where? A party?'

'Mmm. Not exactly. We could have our own little party, just the two of us . . .'

'Yes, but where? My mum's at my house – but she's probably asleep by now.'

'How about a hotel?' Thierry hardly dared say it.

'A hotel? Sure . . . but which one?'

Charmaine was having difficulty standing up. He held her by the waist and helped her with her coat. 'We'll see. Let's get a taxi.' He helped her outside, where the cold air stung after the fug and warmth of the bar. He hailed a black cab, and they got in. Where could they go? He remembered there were tons of cheap hotels around Victoria station.

Ten minutes later, the cab pulled up in front of Belgravia Gardens, a reasonable-looking hotel near Eaton Square. Charmaine was snoring gently. Unable to believe his luck, Thierry paid the driver and staggered up the steps with Charmaine. He sat her in the chair beside the receptionist's desk and hurriedly paid for a room. The bored receptionist took one look at the sleeping girl and the nervous young man in front of her and snorted. He'd be lucky. He'd just paid £49.99 for a long night's kip on a hard and lumpy mattress. Thierry turned to help Charmaine to her feet.

'Come on, Charmaine, we're here. *Viens* . . . up we go.' Charmaine groaned. The room was beginning to swim. Where the hell was she? They climbed the stairs slowly. The lift was broken, the receptionist told them. She didn't appear at all apologetic. Thierry struggled with Charmaine as they made their way slowly down the corridor. *Dieu*, she was small but she was no lightweight.

Ten, eleven, twelve . . . ah, there: room thirteen. He put the key in the lock and opened the door. Well, he'd seen worse, he thought, as he deposited her on the bed. At least it looked clean. He took off his coat and scarf. Charmaine had slumped onto the bed and was snoring. He dug a hand into his coat pocket – yes, *merci, Dieu*, he had them. He'd nipped into Boots and bought a packet of condoms, as he'd heard the other boys do. Thierry – like the sleeping girl on the bed – was that terrible thing . . . a virgin. But no one knew. Living in Paris, he was able to invent a steady stream of conquests, including the maid, her mother, her cousins and her sister. Luckily for him most of his friends were too inexperienced to recognise a fantasy when they heard one – since most of them had never done it either, his descriptions sounded *most* convincing.

'Charmaine,' he whispered, as he sat down beside her. She stirred. Her lipstick was smudged and her mascara had smeared – she must have rubbed her eyes. He'd have to help her get undressed. He bent down and tugged at a boot, slipped it off, then the other. Charmaine murmured something and, annoyingly, rolled over.

'Charmaine,' he murmured, 'come on, turn over. You've got to get undressed.' She made no response. He swore. She was lying on her side now and he could see the red lacy bra that had been driving him mad all evening through the thin material of her dress. He tried to prise open the buttons. His fingers were a little clumsy and her necklace caught between the buttons. There was a faint tearing sound as the material gave way. *Merde!* He'd ripped it. He stared at her in panic. She rolled over again. Ah, that was better. He managed to pull her dress down, past her lacy white panties – he almost choked – to her knees. His heart was hammering so hard he thought it would burst. Something else was ready to burst too. He pulled her dress off, then stripped off his own clothes. He left his socks on – it was cold – and climbed onto the bed beside her.

Her wonderfully soft, full breasts were cupped splendidly in the red bra. He swallowed. Charmaine stirred sleepily. She was cold, she murmured. He pulled up the blanket that was lying at the foot of the bed and reluctantly covered her. Now he'd have to feel his way around. He started on her breasts. Slowly, he caressed the mounds made by her underwire bra and stroked the soft skin. Charmaine moaned softly. He slipped a finger underneath the lace and felt for her nipple. She moaned again, louder. He had to put a hand on his own trembling stomach to stop himself from ejaculating. She rolled over on her side again, away from him. He pressed himself against her lace-covered buttocks and unfastened her bra. It worked easily. He slipped a hand round her, and felt her breasts spring free. He couldn't help it . . . he lifted the blanket and craned his head to look – oh, *merde*! He started rubbing himself hard against her – he just couldn't stop – *merde* – *merde*! '*Charmaine!*' he cried out, unable to stop himself.

Charmaine dimly felt something wet against her back, felt a hand clutch her breast so hard she woke up. And promptly vomited.

Gabby stared at the mountain of food on her plate. Her grandmother served herself a fraction of what she'd put on Gabby's plate, and walked slowly round the kitchen table to her place. She smiled fondly at her granddaughter. Then she frowned.

'What's wrong, darling? Don't you like venison?' she asked anxiously.

'No, Granny, it's not that.' She stared at her plate, then looked up at her grandmother. 'Granny,' she began, 'd'you think I'm . . . *fat*?' Gabby looked at her anxiously.

'Oh, darling,' Clarissa murmured, 'you're *fine* the way you are. What brought this on?'

'I don't know . . . Everyone at school's really thin and there's this new girl – she's South African. She's awfully pretty and, well, there's someone I like, you know, but he likes her and I just thought . . .' Gabby trailed off.

Her grandmother reached across the table and patted her arm. 'I know, darling, it's awfully hard. Tell you what – I think you're beautiful just the way you are, you know that. But if you want to make yourself even *more* beautiful, well, let's do it together.' Gabby smiled at her grandmother gratefully. She really did know how to phrase things. 'We'll devise a little *plan*, shall we? A little eating plan, not a diet. No potatoes, no bread, no puddings. Instead we'll have lots of vegetables, lots of fruit and lots of water. I was quite . . .

curvy in my day, you know.' Gabby looked at her grandmother in surprise. She'd been elegantly slender as long as Gabby could remember. 'Oh, yes,' she continued. 'I know quite a lot about *planning* – you'd be surprised.'

'You? But you hardly eat anything, Granny,' Gabby protested. 'I don't think I could live on what you eat.'

'That's because I'm old, darling, and I walk everywhere. I'll bet you don't, what with all those taxis you take!' Her eyes twinkled. Gabby had taken a taxi for the quarter-mile journey from the station to the gates at Windmere.

'What'll I do with all this?' Gabby indicated the pile on her plate. 'I feel ill already.'

'Well, start by eating half of everything except the mashed potatoes. Drink lots of water in between mouthfuls and chew slowly. You'll see, darling. If you can stick to it you'll be positively svelte, by Christmas. And then you and I will go shopping. How about that?'

Gabby felt better already. She scraped away the potatoes, half of the delicious venison stew and added some more carrots. Her grandmother nodded approvingly. It was true, she adored her only granddaughter just as she was. But she could see it might be a *little* difficult for her to find a nice young man . . . She was so tall and she was intelligent – Clarissa knew from experience that the combination didn't always go down well. So, if Gabby wanted to lose a little weight, feel a little more confident about herself, well, she'd do everything she could to encourage her. She was *so* special . . . she deserved to be treated as such.

14

All too soon, it seemed, half-term was over. Marika and Hennie saw Rianne off at the station and watched, amused, as she lugged two enormous suitcases across the platform. She'd been shopping. She'd show them back at St Anne's, she told a wide-eyed Marika. She'd show them what South African girls were made of. Somehow, and without realising it, she no longer thought of running away. She was now considering how to regain her position at the top of the tree, starting with the one thing that had knocked her out of it: her clothes. She'd replaced almost everything in her dull 'regulation' wardrobe with something stylish. The salesgirl at Harrods had been beside herself.

She found the right train almost at the same time as Charmaine and a couple of the other girls in their house found her. She followed them into the compartment and folded her new navy blue coat, with its belted waist, over her knees and looked out of the window as the train pulled out of Paddington.

Charmaine chattered non-stop about what she'd done in the holiday, where she'd been, Thierry Pasquier, something about a hotel and wet sheets. Rianne couldn't work out what had happened. Whatever it was, Charmaine looked exceedingly pleased with herself. Rianne sighed. Another three hours of prattle. She dozed off, and in no time at all they were pulling into the now familiar station at Malvern.

'Hi,' Rianne said guardedly, as Gabby came into the room. She still wasn't used to the drama surrounding arrivals and departures at this place.

Gabby grinned at her. 'Had a good half-term?' she asked, flinging her bag on to her bed.

Rianne nodded. She was hanging up her new clothes.

'Cor, someone's been shopping!' Gabby laughed.

Rianne reddened. 'Just a few things. I was a bit fed up with the stuff my aunt got for me.'

'Wow.' Gabby looked at the purchases. 'These are really cool.' She picked up a pair of knee-length black leather boots. 'Where d'you get all this stuff?'

'Harrods. They have these personal shoppers, you know. You tell them what you want and they go and find it for you. It's easy.'

'Hmm. Well, can't say I've ever used one but . . . maybe one day.' Gabby felt good. She'd stuck to her 'plan' all week, and she and her grandmother had gone for long walks in the gentle Hereford countryside. She was drinking a large bottle of water a day and she felt great. She loved the feeling of control and calm that came over her when she'd had a 'good' day. She loved feeling 'good' and disciplined, not frantic and depressed. She couldn't yet see a difference, despite staring at herself in the mirror every evening before going to bed but she *felt* thinner.

She looked on enviously as Rianne unfolded a dark brown tweed skirt with a single large pleat mid-thigh and a black cashmere sweater, which she slipped onto the hanger over the skirt. She looked down at her own navy blue skirt and jumper, large, shapeless items, and grimaced. Although she'd never be thin enough to fit into anything Rianne owned, perhaps it wasn't too daring to imagine that soon she'd look for things that suited her, rather than just fitted.

Just then the door opened and Charmaine walked in, dragging her bag. 'Gabby,' she squealed, flinging her arms around Gabby and nearly knocking her off the bed. 'Oh, I'm so pleased to see you – you'll never *guess* what happened . . .' Without even bothering to take off her coat, she sat on the bed next to Gabby and was off again, recounting the half-term drama. This time, Rianne listened with more than half an ear. Ah, so that was what the fuss was about: she had done 'it'.

'Did it hurt?' Gabby asked eventually, suitably impressed.

Charmaine shook her head. She was a little vague about the details. Actually, she couldn't remember very much. 'No, not at all. I didn't feel anything. Well, of course, I did . . . a bit. It was rather . . . nice.'

Rianne lifted an eyebrow as she continued hanging clothes. Nice? Not likely. Everyone knew the first time it bloody hurt!

'So, are you going out with him, then?' Gabby asked.

Charmaine's half-term seemed an awfully long way from walking with her grandmother and the two Labradors.

Charmaine nodded vigorously. Oh, yes. Practically engaged.

Rianne snorted to herself. For all their air of sophistication, some of these English girls were clueless. She supposed it came from spending half their lives locked up in places like St Anne's – deprived of male company, they spent their time imagining it. And as everyone knew, especially when it came to boys, the imagination was not always the most reliable tool.

'God, you bought a lot of stuff,' Charmaine said suddenly, eyeing the pile of clothes on Rianne's bed. She picked up a long grey woollen skirt with mustard yellow embroidery at the hem. 'Pretty. Where d'you get it?'

'She's got a personal shopper at Harrods,' Gabby told her.

Rianne blushed. 'Everyone can have one – they're just there, in the store. You just have to go and get one.' It wasn't strictly true. You had to have an account at Harrods. Which Lisette, of course, did.

'Well, she certainly knows what to pick. Oh, these are *really* nice.' She picked up a pair of stone-washed jeans with a custom-made rip in the knees – the absolute latest. 'Shit, you'll be the best-dressed person in Malvern at this rate.'

'Yeah, well, from the worst to the best in ten days,' Rianne said drily. The others laughed.

Rianne looked at them, surprised at herself. For the first time since she'd arrived at St Anne's, she felt something like warmth. It was strange. She'd spent the first month dying to get away. She'd never been so miserable in all her life. Now, although she still hated the *idea* of being at an all-girls' school in the middle of cold, wet England, she had to admit there were things about it that she was learning – albeit grudgingly – to like. Slowly. Sitting around the room on a cold, damp evening, looking at clothes and talking about boys for one thing. Choosing what to wear for that all-important first evening back after half-term for another. She pulled the jeans out of the wardrobe. 'Shall I wear these?' she asked Gabby and Charmaine. They both nodded vigorously. Charmaine was wondering how and when to broach the subject of sharing . . . there were one or two things in there that she would look absolutely stunning in. Even if they were a bit long on her, and possibly a little tight?

'I wonder where Nat is,' Gabby said, watching Rianne slither into her new jeans. Was it possible to be *that* thin?

'Her brother's bringing her back,' Charmaine said. She was fingering one of Rianne's new Benetton sweaters. She'd bought six – they lay on top of each another, like an enormous liquorice all-sort. Black, cream, orange, green . . .

Nathalie was sitting miserably beside Philippe as he negotiated the bends along the hill leading to St Anne's. He couldn't understand what was wrong with her. At some point during half-term, she'd simply closed up. Stopped speaking. Stopped eating, practically. All attempts to draw her out of herself had failed. She spent hours in her room, reading and – judging by her red nose and swollen eyes – crying, too. At dinner last night Cordelia, fed up with her daughter's sulky behaviour, asked her if she was mooning over some boy. Nathalie had burst into fresh tears and run upstairs to her room. But half-terms and holidays usually ended this way – Cordelia needling Nathalie and Nathalie bursting into tears, Philippe recalled.

'Nat, you know you can tell me if something's wrong, don't you?' he said as they rounded the last bend.

Nathalie nodded. She looked out of the window into the darkness.

How *could* she tell him? That very afternoon, as Nathalie prepared to return to St Anne's, Clive had gone off to meet a business partner in Bristol and Sacha had opted to stay behind. A headache, he claimed. Nathalie blushed fiercely beside Philippe . . . she knew *exactly* what he and Cordelia were doing . . . right this very minute. They were probably doing it . . . in Cordelia's bedroom, in the same bed that . . .

'Nat?' Philippe couldn't let it drop. 'Come on, what is it?'

'Nothing,' Nathalie said, in a small voice. 'I'm just . . . not feeling well.'

Philippe bit his lip. Not feeling well? He didn't like the sound of that. A girl at Reading had had to have an abortion a few weeks after term started. She'd gone about the place alternately weeping and running up to her room just like Nathalie was doing. But, no, it wasn't possible, not his little sister Gnat? He stole a quick look at her. He couldn't bring himself to broach *that* possibility. He pulled the car up in front of St Anne's. Perhaps he ought to leave it for a while. She'd talk to him when she was ready. Maybe his mother had it right – a bloke or something. He got out, opened the boot to retrieve her bag and hugged her. She looked so forlorn standing there. But then she turned and walked up the steps. Whatever it was, it would have to wait until the Christmas holidays.

'Nat!' Charmaine jumped up as Nathalie pushed open the door. 'Nat! Whatever's the matter?'

Nathalie burst into tears as soon as she saw them. Everyone stopped and hurried over.

'What happened, Nat?' Gabby asked, putting an arm round her slender shoulders. Nathalie couldn't stop sobbing. She allowed Gabby to lead her to her bed and relieve her of her bag and coat. Between sobs and gasps, the story emerged. The others, even Rianne, listened in horror. The *thought* of it!

'Well,' Gabby said eventually, as Nathalie's sobs died down, 'horrid as it is, there's nothing you can do about it. If your mother—'

'I don't care about *her*!' Nathalie burst out. 'What about *me*?'

'What d'you mean?' Gabby was puzzled.

'I mean, how can I – I can't – I don't want to—' She was unable to continue.

'It's not *your* fault,' Charmaine said indignantly. 'It's hers. And his.'

'I don't care about *that*.' Nathalie wailed even louder. The others looked at each other. What was she getting at?

'Darling,' Gabby began, 'it's their business – I mean, they're both adults. Even if Sacha is the same age as your brother. You don't imagine he's never, you know, done it before, do you?'

'You don't understand!' Nathalie sobbed. 'I feel all – *funny* when I think about it—' She covered her face with her hands. Gabby made an alarmed *help-me* face at Charmaine. She was out of her depth. Perhaps Nathalie ought to talk to . . . someone?

'Nat,' she began again, hesitantly. 'I think you'd better try to put the picture out of your mind. It's no good thinking about it. Honestly. Just try to forget it ever happened.'

'I can't. I can't face them – I can't face my mother. Whenever I see her, I think of—'

'Why don't you come to the Caribbean with me? All of you, why don't you come?' Rianne broke in suddenly. The others stared at her. She reddened immediately. Whatever had made her say that? she wondered.

'What?' Gabby said, not sure if she'd heard right. 'The Caribbean?'

'Yeah, we go there every Christmas. It's no big deal. You'll have a good time and, Nathalie, you'll forget about *it*,' Rianne said quickly, trying to sound offhand. She went back to hanging her clothes. What the hell had she done? She'd just invited three friends – if you could call them that – to spend Christmas with her. Was she mad? She wanted to get *away* from them, not bring them along!

'Really?' Nathalie looked at Rianne through her tears. 'At Christmas?'

'Yeah, we're leaving from London the day after term breaks up.'

'But won't it cost an awful lot?' Gabby asked.

'I've no idea.' Rianne lifted her shoulders. 'It can't be *that* expensive. All you'll need is a plane ticket.' Perhaps it would be fun. At least Lisette couldn't accuse her of not *trying* . . .

'Are you sure, Rianne? I mean, three of us? It's a bit of an imposition,' Gabby said anxiously.

'Yeah, sure, it's no problem. My aunt won't care. There's plenty of space.' Rianne made a face. 'She won't even notice we're there.' A *bit* of an exaggeration, she thought, but probably true. And Nathalie had stopped crying.

'Oh, gosh,' Nathalie said, smiling shakily, 'it's really nice of you, Rianne. I'd love to come – I can't bear the thought of going home.'

'Yeah, me neither,' Charmaine added, for no apparent reason.

'Come on, Nat, dry your eyes,' said Gabby. She looked at her watch. 'We may be going to the Caribbean for Christmas,' she said, half jokingly, 'but we're due in the dining room in ten minutes. Let's go.' They got up reluctantly. Nathalie went off to wash her face, Charmaine following.

'It's really nice of you, Rianne,' Gabby said, as they waited outside the door for them, 'but don't feel obliged. I mean, Nathalie can always come home with me.'

'It's no problem.' Rianne shrugged. 'It'll be fun.'

'I'm sure it will, but I don't think I'll be coming somehow,' Gabby said, a little despondently. 'I doubt *my* father will spring for an air ticket to the sun.' She couldn't imagine asking her father for the money to go off on a Caribbean jaunt – coughing up the school fees each term was hard enough.

'Why don't you ask your grandmother?' Charmaine said, overhearing. Gabby bit her lip. Now *that* was a possibility. Her grandmother would be thrilled to hear her grand-daughter was going on holiday. She doubled her resolve to stick to her 'plan' . . . just in case she had to appear on a beach in a swimsuit.

'OK. I feel a bit better now,' Nathalie came out of the freshly painted bathroom. She did look better. The colour was back in her cheeks and she'd stopped sniffling. They walked down the hill together to the dining room.

The Caribbean! It was almost too good to be true.

Of course, it was impossible to keep their Christmas plans secret for any length of time. By the end of the week, everyone, including the kitchen staff – though God knows how they found out – knew that the four girls in the lower sixth were going to Rianne de Zoete's private Caribbean island for the Christmas break. Despite Rianne's protests that no, it wasn't a private island – Martinique was a French colony, not a South African one! – the girls were the envy of the entire school, including several teachers.

Suddenly it seemed that from being the outsider whom everyone laughed at, Rianne had become someone people envied. She would never shine in the classroom like Gabby, it was true, or on the lacrosse pitch like Nathalie, and she wasn't regarded as admirably sexy like Charmaine, but she wasn't *quite* the social and style disaster that she had been at the beginning. She hadn't yet managed to get over the shock of sharing her living space with the four African girls. She and Jumoke still occasionally caught one another's eyes . . . Rianne usually looked the other way. Jumoke's glare reminded her of Ree Modise and her cheeks burned fiercely over that memory.

Nathalie found that by concentrating on her lessons, playing hockey and lacrosse vigorously at weekends and daydreaming about Sans Soucis – just the name sounded perfect – the image of Sacha making love to her mother began to fade, although the feelings of shame and disgust didn't – but at least the image itself began to disappear. She'd lost interest in poor Stuart Graves and practically had to be dragged out by the others on their Saturday-afternoon excursions into town.

'Mind you,' Gabby said, 'to think of seeing your *mother* like that – it would be enough to drive anyone mad.'

Rianne shrugged. She'd no idea what to do or even how to think about it. Her memory of her own mother had faded to the point she could hardly remember what she looked like. She could remember bits of her – her smile, the way she moved, for example . . . The way she would suddenly bury her face in her daughter's neck, as if she couldn't quite believe how special, how fortunate she was. Little things like that, she remembered. But she couldn't recall the whole of her face, or even the sound of her voice. Rianne had also buried the memory somewhere deep inside her. It was the only way she knew how to survive the shock and pain of losing her. She never talked about her with anyone. In the weeks following her death, she had wanted to talk about her, she longed to go to her father and tell him how it was hurting her, but Marius was beside himself with grief – even as a ten-year-old she could see that – and unable even to look at her. She had come upon him one evening, on his knees in the study, howling like an animal in pain. She'd backed away, too frightened to speak. And she'd never told anyone. A week later, when he disappeared, she knew why. The loss was simply too great to bear.

Nathalie had easily extracted a promise from her mother to pay. She'd put off ringing her at first, hoping she would be able to talk to Clive privately, but getting hold of him without going through Cordelia was impossible. She finally rang one wintry evening and Cordelia picked up the phone. She had no idea why Nathalie was so hostile. She'd heard nothing from her since half-term when she'd behaved *so* strangely.

'No, you *can't* go, Nathalie. It's out of the question. Clive and I will be away over Christmas and you and Philippe are to stay with Uncle Robin,' Cordelia said firmly. An island in the Caribbean? Had she lost her senses?

'Uncle Robin? Why? Where are you going?' Nathalie demanded belligerently.

'To Singapore. Clive has business to attend to and I'm going to do some shopping—'

'In Singapore!' Nathalie flushed angrily. 'What, via Kuala Lumpur?' she asked sarcastically. In Malmesbury, Cordelia also flushed. What on earth could the child mean? Surely she hadn't noticed anything . . .

'What are you talking about?' Cordelia asked sharply.

'You know exactly what I'm talking about – or is Sacha going to Singapore too? *That* should be fun – the three of you!'

'Nathalie!' Cordelia almost shouted. 'Stop it immediately. Immediately! How *dare* you speak to me like that?'

'Well, should I speak to Clive, then?' Nathalie interrupted her recklessly. 'I'm sure he'd enjoy it – his wife with—'

'That's enough, Nathalie! H-how much is the airfare?' Two very bright spots stood out on Cordelia's cheeks. She must have seen something. But where? She felt faint.

'About six hundred pounds.'

'I'll put a cheque in the post.' Cordelia hung up.

On the last Saturday before term ended, the four of them went down to Serendipity's for the last time. Rianne's wardrobe had been shared out between them – even Gabby had borrowed a new scarf. They walked into the tea-room and the conversation immediately stopped.

Oh shit, Nael thought, as he saw the four girls approaching. He hadn't seen Rianne since the Half-term Ball and had managed pretty much to blot her out of his thoughts. He watched them come through the door. Rianne was taller than the rest – she stood out immediately. The long blonde hair he remembered so vividly was hidden under a colourful hat and scarf combination. She didn't see him at first, for which he was thankful. It gave him a couple of seconds to compose himself. He tried to ignore the lurch in his stomach. She was so beautiful it almost hurt.

'Look what the cat's dragged in,' Ree said, as he joined Nael at the table. Nael grimaced. He had given up thinking about Rianne the minute Ree had voiced his objections. But seeing her now unlocked all sorts of feelings that he knew he should suppress. It didn't help that Ree was with him, probably watching him closely. He bent his head – he hoped Gabby would be a sport and lead them to another table. She did. If Rianne noticed either of them, she made no sign. You had to hand it to her, Nael thought, as he watched her. She had nerve. And class. God, she would be hard to forget.

Gabby and the others watched Rianne admiringly. She calmly smoked one cigarette after another, drank a cup of tea and simply pretended Ree and Nael weren't there. When it was time to leave, she sauntered past their table and flashed the sweetest smile at a bewildered Michael Rhys-Walker. There wasn't even the *tiniest* possibility of Ree Modise snubbing her ever again. On impulse as they reached the door, Rianne put an arm through Gabby's as they stepped out into the street. Gabby smiled at the others. Yes, Rianne was settling in, joining the group. The four walked to the bus stop, laughing together.

PART TWO

15

December 1981: Sans Soucis, Martinique

The Air France 747 circled the island of Martinique lazily. Charmaine and Nathalie, noses pressed flat against the glass, could only stare open-mouthed at the perfect crescents of white sand and azure sea. Rianne and Gabby were still dozing. It had been a long journey, from Malvern to the flat in Wilton Crescent – which, Charmaine whispered as they prepared for bed, was the biggest flat she had seen in London – *ever* – and the next morning to Heathrow. And, of course, they'd stayed up practically half the night talking. Breakfast was served by Dinah – fresh fruit, orange juice, muesli and scrambled eggs. The three of them simply stared at the feast too excited to eat. Rianne was on the phone talking to Marika. Lisette, Marika and Hennie were already on the island. It was two o'clock in the morning at Sans Soucis but Marika couldn't sleep. She was also excited – and a little nervous at the prospect of meeting three of Rianne's friends.

'Look!' Nathalie said, in awe, to no one in particular as the plane dipped and banked, preparing to land at Fort-de-France. The others leaned over and silently contemplated the tropical paradise unfolding below them. It was the kind of panorama only seen in glossy travel brochures – high-walled white villas with ochre-tiled roofs, gently waving palm trees; every now and then the turquoise flash of a swimming pool. Paradise. The stewardess came through the first-class cabin, checking safety-belts and clearing the last of the Buck's Fizz glasses. Minutes later, they touched down on the tarmac at Fort-de-France with a gentle bump. They'd arrived.

Clearing Customs was easy. All the staff seemed to recognise Rianne and within half an hour they were walking through the 'Nothing to Declare' channel and stepping outside into the blinding brightness of the Caribbean afternoon.

'Hey, Rianne!' someone shouted.

It was Hennie, and next to him Marika was waving frantically. She rushed up to Rianne and, suddenly, everyone was kissing and hugging – even Hennie. He led the way outside to the waiting Jeep, which he'd parked illegally at the kerb – there were no policemen about. Someone had silently taken their suitcases which were being stowed in another Jeep, also illegally parked behind Hennie's. A tall, lithe, brown-skinned young man stood beside it, keys in hand.

'It's going to be a bit of a squeeze,' Hennie said, clearing some space on the back seat of his vehicle. He picked up a couple of bags and threw them in the general direction of the young man, who bent down silently and picked them up. Gabby glanced at him. No one had said anything to him, not even 'Hello'. He began loading the passenger seat of the second Jeep. He wore shorts and a faded white T-shirt with 'Sans Soucis' emblazoned across the back. Obviously an employee.

'Come on, jump in,' Hennie said, as he slid into the driver's seat. 'It'll be a bit tight but it's not far. Marika, d'you want to go with Joules?' He jerked his thumb backwards. 'I don't think we'll all fit.' Marika nodded reluctantly: she wanted to be with Rianne.

'I'll go with Marika,' Rianne said. They got into the Jeep behind. Charmaine slipped in beside Hennie, smiling while Gabby and Nathalie arranged themselves in the back seat and looked around, open-mouthed. It really was a tropical paradise. The little airport was thoroughly modern, all steel and glass and blue and yellow signs – in French, of course. The cars pulling up in the drop-off lane were the latest European and American models – Mercedes, BMWs, countless convertibles and Jeeps, much like the one they were riding in. Although it was hot, a cool breeze wafted in off the ocean, sending the tops of the palm trees into a frenetic dance. There were flowers everywhere. Enormous, blood-red flame trees provided shade at almost every corner and even the tiniest buildings were covered in a dense riot of purple, orange and pink bougainvillaea. Every now and then, as they sped along the main high road leading into Fort-de-France, the aquamarine blue of the sea came into view.

'We're heading to Le Marin,' Hennie shouted, above the noise of the Jeep. The girls looked at the road signs. La Savane, Les Trois-Illets, Anse d'Arlets ... The names tripped off the tongue. They were spellbound. In the back seat, Nathalie and Gabby held on to the roll bar above their heads, enjoying the rush of wind on their arms. 'The house is on the south beaches – the white ones,' Hennie continued. '*Much* nicer.'

'What does he mean?' Gabby whispered to Nathalie. 'The people?'

Hennie caught her eye in the rear-view mirror. 'The sand. The ones in the north are all volcanic ash,' he said coldly.

Gabby reddened. She'd taken an immediate dislike to the tall, over-confident young man. She hadn't liked the way he had tossed the bags down on the pavement for Joules, not even bothering to look where they fell.

'What do they speak here?' she asked, trying to change the subject.

'Only French and English,' Hennie said arrogantly. '*They* have some funny kind of dialect, Creole, but it's not really a language. And none of *us* speaks it, of course.'

'Of course,' Gabby murmured. Creole ... she loved the sound of the name.

They were climbing, following the winding road round

the southern peninsula. In the distance, the blue folds of the mountains could just be seen through the hazy afternoon sun. It was cooler now and Gabby leaned back against the seat, allowing the breeze to lick at the back of her damp neck. She was looking forward to getting to Sans Soucis. A long, cool shower was what she needed.

'What's that?' Nathalie pointed to a small rock nestling at the mouth of the bay. Perched on top of it was a British flag, of all things.

Hennie laughed. 'That's the Rocher du Diamont – it was part of the British Empire once, I can't remember when. Some British soldiers took possession of it . . . something about controlling the channel between Martinique and St Lucia. I think they lived on it for over a year. Can you imagine?' Nathalie shook her head. It was hard to believe they'd left St Anne's only a day or so ago. And even harder to recall the reason why they'd come to Martinique in the first place. Sacha and her mother. It seemed so long ago. She turned to smile at Gabby.

At a small hand-painted signpost that read 'Trinité-Tartâne-Sans Soucis', Hennie made a turn. They bumped down a sandy road, through palm trees, pink and yellow hibiscus and bamboo until at last they stopped outside a gate almost completely hidden by bougainvillaea and ferns. A small brass plaque set into the white walls read, 'Sans Soucis. Bienvenue.'

'We're here,' Hennie announced. He honked once, loudly, and jumped down from his seat. The wooden gates opened and a dark-skinned couple, both in white uniforms, came forward to meet them. Hennie tossed them the car keys and strode off. He was obviously used to an army of servants clearing up behind him. Just then, Joules pulled up behind them and Rianne and Marika jumped out. Gabby walked over to the second Jeep and started to unload her bag but Joules was beside her in a flash. With a quick shake of his head, he lifted it for her. 'My job,' he said, in good, if accented English. She smiled her thanks. He ignored her.

'Come on, let's go inside. I'll introduce you to Aunt Lisette,' Rianne said, leading the way through the gates. 'They'll take care of the luggage.' She turned to the woman and rattled off a string of instructions, whose bag should go where, who was sharing a room with whom. Gabby felt more than a little uncomfortable. Rianne hadn't even said 'hello' to the couple. She smiled at them, but the woman lowered her eyes.

The girls walked through the gate and down the path. The foliage suddenly cleared and there, in front of them, stood the villa, and beyond it the sea. Gabby gasped. It was a white-washed, two-storey house with wide, deep verandas running along the ground and first floors. The arched windows, dark mahogany shutters and terracotta tiles were perfectly off-set by the cool white elegance of the building. The garden was a riot of colour – every imaginable shade of red, orange, yellow and pink – but the grass was soft, thick and cool. She could feel it through her sandals. There was a row of dark green trees at the bottom of the garden which shielded the house from the beach. They swayed gently in the breeze and through them, there was the sea, the clear, turquoise sea. The property was set in a half-moon bay – she could see a small boat tethered to a wooden jetty and the fence on either side of the quarter-mile stretch of beach that marked the end of private land. She turned to the others, who were equally dumbstruck.

'*Crikey*,' she said. She couldn't think of anything more to say. Nathalie and Charmaine nodded in agreement. They were speechless.

'Darlings.' A woman's voice floated out over the veranda. They turned. A slim, elegantly dressed woman in a white linen shift dress with a pale coral scarf hanging loosely around her neck came down the steps to meet them. It had to be Aunt Lisette. She kissed Rianne first, then each of her niece's friends. Perfectly charming, she thought, as Rianne presented Nathalie and Charmaine. Pretty, well-mannered young ladies, and suitably impressed by Sans

Soucis. The third one, Gabrielle, seemed an odd choice of friend for Rianne: *most* ungainly.

She instructed Marie, the woman who had been at the gates, to show the girls to their rooms, and Joules to deliver their bags. Lisette spoke about ten words of French but somehow, over the years, Marie had apparently picked up enough English to understand her employer.

'There're two rooms – split them any way you want,' Rianne said, as Joules delivered their bags to the first-floor landing. 'Mine's just down the hall. That's Hennie's across the way and Marika's is next to mine.'

'God, how many rooms *are* there?' Charmaine said, looking around the spacious, airy room in delight. It was beautiful. The two beds had mosquito nets hanging about them, gauzy diaphanous veils that floated in the breeze, crisp white linen sheets. There was a large wicker sofa, with plump white cushions, and a small coffee table at one end of the room, and a console with a TV and video at the other. It was more like a luxury hotel than someone's home.

'There're eight in this villa, and then there's the smaller guesthouse just across the path. There're usually loads of people at New Year. You'll see, it'll get pretty full.' Rianne opened the french windows that led onto the veranda. 'You can sit out here in the morning. Marie brings breakfast upstairs if you don't feel like coming down.' She turned to Joules, who was waiting patiently with their bags. '*Tu peux les deposer ici . . . et là,*' she said. Joules followed her instructions silently. 'I'm going to take a shower,' she told the others, 'and then go for a swim. It's the best thing. If you go to sleep now, you'll have really bad jet-lag for days, I promise. I'll come and get you in about ten minutes.' The others nodded, still too impressed by their rooms to speak. Rianne left them, followed silently by Joules.

'OK. I give up. I've died and gone to heaven!' Nathalie flung herself onto the sofa. 'Can you believe this?'

'I'll go next door,' Gabby said, hoisting her bag onto her shoulder. The thought of a cool shower and the chance to lie down for five minutes on one of those crisp beds was just too tempting.

The next bedroom was identical, but with pale green cushions on the wicker sofa instead of white ones. She closed the door and peeked into the all-white bathroom. Gorgeous. Simply gorgeous. Suddenly she had a little more sympathy for Rianne's initial reaction to St Anne's: if she'd been born into such wealth and luxury, she'd also have been a little put out by an English boarding-school. Still, that only excused some of her behaviour. Although judging from their treatment of the servants, there was plenty more where that came from. And she didn't like Hennie. Didn't like him at all.

Ten minutes later, after tying her blue sarong in ten different ways to hide the stubborn roll of fat round her midriff, Gabby was ready. That her black school swimsuit fitted was a major triumph: six weeks previously it had been too small. But compared to the other three, no, four – she kept forgetting Marika – she looked about as appealing as a marshmallow. She met them in the corridor. Charmaine had on a yellow bikini that barely contained or covered her breasts, a matching yellow sarong and a pair of purple flip-flops. Nathalie looked pretty in a flowered bikini with a pair of white denim shorts and plimsolls and her wide-brimmed straw hat. She and Charmaine had visited Miss Selfridge in Worcester a week before they left. Rianne was walking towards them, in a white string bikini and denim shorts. She was barefoot and her hair was tied back in a pony-tail. For someone who never seemed to do any exercise other than walk up the hills occasionally, Rianne had the physique of a dancer – strong, long limbs and taut skin stretched smooth over well-defined muscles in her arms, back and stomach. Muscles in her *stomach*? The others looked at her enviously.

They walked through the garden, opened the little gate at the end and stepped onto the soft, white sand. It was still hot: the sun was only just beginning its descent towards the horizon. Marika and Hennie were already there. Hennie's eyes nearly popped out of his head as he watched Charmaine bounce towards them.

Rianne looked at him, eyes narrowed. She hated him staring at Charmaine, his mouth hanging open.

But Charmaine seemed to love it. She couldn't stop giggling.

They spread their towels on the sand, kicked off their shoes and ran, squealing with pleasure, into the clear blue water. There was a whoop from the shore as Hennie ran to catch up with them. He raced into the shallows, all thrashing limbs and spraying water, then dived suddenly, his body a light blur as he looked around underwater for someone's feet to grab.

'There aren't any sharks, are there?' Charmaine asked, standing nervously at the water's edge.

'Not at this time of the evening,' Hennie called to her, as he broke the surface of the water.

'You're joking,' said Charmaine, stopping dead in her tracks. 'I'm not going in.'

'Don't listen to him,' Marika said calmly, and walked past her into the water. Her brother was behaving most oddly. 'He's full of shit.'

Charmaine hesitated.

'*Ag*, come on, there are no sharks or jellyfish or snakes – I swear it,' Hennie said. 'The water's absolutely clear here. Only thing you'll ever see are fish and even they don't come close.'

'How do you know?' she wailed.

'I know. That's all. Don't you trust me?' Hennie said, staring openly at Charmaine's breasts.

Rianne was shaking slightly. She hadn't expected to feel so strongly about Hennie. At half-term, things had been fine. They'd grown apart, of course, but she had started a new life, albeit one she hated, and he was starting another. Ever since they'd arrived that afternoon, she'd been aware of a hot, tight pain in her chest whenever she saw

Charmaine flirt with her cousin – and it was even worse when he responded. She dived into the water, feeling rather than hearing the water fill her ears, her body perfectly attuned to the gentle tug of the current. She came up for air. The late-afternoon breeze was wonderfully cooling on her skin. The sun was almost touching the horizon – amazing how quickly it set in this part of the world. All around her, the sky was changing colour – flaming yellow dying to gold, then burnt orange. She turned and floated on her back. By the time the others had dried off and collected their towels and shoes, the sky was purple, the colour of raisins. She came out reluctantly as darkness fell.

In the enormous study inside the villa, Lisette was poring over a sheaf of papers. She had replaced her sunglasses with black-framed reading glasses. With a pencil and notepad beside her, she could have passed for an attractive English professor, marking essays, but she was a businesswoman and these were no essays. Being in charge of the formidable business empire that was de Zoete Inc. was no small task. Apart from the enormous mining operations in South Africa, which made up the bulk of their wealth, they were seeing huge returns in the property markets in which their subsidiary company, Kalen de Zoete Koestler, had invested. KdZK now owned commercial premises in London, New York and Frankfurt, the business capitals of the world. As CEO of both companies, Lisette operated on myriad levels simultaneously. She was owner, investor, speculator, and nothing went ahead without her authority, which meant an ever-increasing number of details requiring her constant attention. It was exhausting, flying round the world at half a day's notice, overseeing the mines and their Byzantine management structure, reading reports, analysing the information, making decisions. No wonder she was so thin. She barely had time to eat. And then there were the children: although she hated to admit it – with Rianne gone, Hennie on his way to the army and Marika scheduled to leave for

Stellenbosch in a few months' time – she was looking forward to an empty house and a release from the day-to-day demands of parenting single-handed.

But she wouldn't have changed a thing. She loved it. Especially the parts that *she* controlled. She, Simon Kalen, the vice-president of de Zoete Inc., and her late husband, Axel Koestler, had formed KdZK to handle the other areas of business enterprise that de Zoete Inc. was able to fund but not pursue directly. The mines – well, she left those to Hendryk. All that in-fighting among senior management, the rocky relationship with the trade unions, whom she loathed, the dirty, hot mining sites with all those native workers and that terrible language they spoke, Fanagalo, was not what she intended to spend the rest of her life watching over.

The mining operations had been going for half a century. Now, with Hendryk at the helm, Hennie and Hendryk's two sons, Piet and Coen, soon to join him, it would run for another half-century without disruption. Or so she hoped. The latest reports of labour unrest were *most* upsetting. The native problem, of course. She sighed. Didn't they know how lucky they were? One only had to look at conditions in the rest of the God-forsaken continent to see where they would be had the whites in South Africa not stepped in to save them. No famines, no tribal wars, no dreadful political turmoil. Three meals a day and housing thrown in. What the hell else did they want? She tapped her teeth with her pencil and turned back to the report.

Speculative Development. Portfolio of Interests. Investment Risks. She scanned the headlines. Property was her thing and KdZK had been smart enough – or lucky enough – to invest in some of the most interesting places in the world. She loved New York, with its raw energy and optimism – the view from Carlton Towers, the eighty-storey skyscraper they owned on Fourth Avenue, had no rival. Sometimes, when the cloud cover floated at the fiftieth floor, she would stand at the floor-to-ceiling windows in her office on the seventeenth and look out at the world, trapped between the sky above and the white, dense cloud below. On those days, when the ground was obscured, floating there, surrounded by other skyscrapers, she felt as though the world were at her feet. It was awe-inspiring. And Frankfurt, too, she loved, the solid, European, old-money feel of the place with its serious, *cultured* inhabitants and their calm, measured pace. But it was currently London that interested her most.

She and Simon, whose business advice she depended on and trusted, had recently spent a week in London looking at an area into which Lisette, under normal circumstances, would not have ventured. For her, the East End of London was as unlikely a place to visit as any of the black townships at home. She'd lived in South Africa all of her forty-six years and had never once set foot in Soweto or Katlehong or Langa or any of the other townships built to house South Africa's poor.

The East End? She'd looked at Simon and frowned, puzzled. But she spent a week walking through the vast, deserted dock areas with Simon and a couple of their London associates, looking sceptically at the place Simon dubbed the New Manhattan. It was hard to believe that the deserted patch on which they were standing would one day host Europe's tallest building. Regent's Wharf, he called it. Simon's dream. She looked around. Nothing but flat, empty docks, crying seagulls and a handful of resentful locals who made rude signs at them as they passed in their chauffeur-driven car. A wasteland. But Simon was convinced. This was where KdZK should be: this was where the smart, visionary money would go. And although she was initially sceptical, the picture he painted was compelling. A new business centre for London, for Europe, for the world.

She reached for the phone. It was midnight in London but she knew he would be awake.

'Lisette, how are you?' Simon was indeed awake.

Lisette wasted no time in getting down to business. 'Looking through the paperwork.'

Simon smiled. It was one of the things he loved about her. That and all the rest. Among the more senior management of de Zoete Inc., it was well known that Simon Kalen had for years been in love with the unattainable. Probably the only person who didn't know it was Lisette.

'What d'you think?' he asked her.

'It looks good enough on paper. What's the government's position?' Lisette was careful. As Simon knew, it was a lesson she'd learned from her father, Anton de Zoete. Watch where the political winds blow, he had said. But steer clear; don't do business *with* governments, do it around them. Carefully.

'They're behind it, a hundred per cent.' Simon had been at a dinner the previous month where one of the guest speakers, the Environment Secretary Michael Heseltine, had impressed him with his vision for the London Docklands. It was imperative, Heseltine had said, running a hand through his hallmark blond mane, that entrepreneurs grabbed the opportunity to give London what it needed – new housing, new environments, new industrial developments, new architecture. Everything that could be used to bring the barren area into valuable use.

It was the word *valuable* that had caught Simon's attention. A number of factors made it attractive: the rapid urban decline and the flight of industry from the area; the fact that the area was so close to the established and somewhat overcrowded financial heart of the capital; and the opportunity to kick-start a moribund domestic economy by promoting what would eventually become one of Europe's largest urban-regeneration schemes was irresistible. The government designated the management of the London Docklands Urban Development Area to the London Docklands Development Corporation and a new era in property speculation was born.

'Ten years, Lisette,' Simon said, his deep voice booming excitedly. 'We get a ten-year tax break. They're pushing the Private Bill for the transport extension and the new airport's due to open in 1985. That's four years away. If we hit the ground running now, we'll be well under way by then. Just in time for the air and rail links to be fully functioning. What more can we ask for?' Lisette nodded.

Transport was the key. If the government was putting the infrastructure in place then, as Simon predicted, they would be sitting on a goldmine.

'OK. Let's do it.' Lisette said decisively. 'Let's do it. When can you get here? Can you call Mike Ruesch? He's in New York – get him and the rest of his team to come down here for New Year. We need to discuss this together. Let me know when your flight gets in and I'll send Joules over. Will you bring Stella and the kids? Rianne's here with some friends from her new school – nice girls.'

'Sure thing, boss,' Simon laughed quietly. He felt a surge of something powerful flow through him – fear? Excitement? This would be their biggest venture yet. Could they handle it? He thought so. He wanted to see Lisette, see her face break into one of her rare smiles. 'I'll see you in about a week's time,' he said. He hung up and walked to the window.

It was raining in London, and the road was a slick, shimmering surface on which the headlights of the odd car danced. He watched a couple cross the street. The man was carrying an umbrella, a large, colourful one with a company logo sprayed across it, the woman hanging onto his arm as they ran across the tarmac. From the way the man held the brolly above her head and the way she clung to him, they were obviously in love. Middle-aged, too, he noted, as they passed directly beneath him. He sighed, thinking of his own emotionless marriage. Stella was asleep in the guest bedroom, at Wilton Crescent, their two teenage children were fast asleep in one of the other rooms. He used Wilton Crescent when he was in town. It was Lisette's house, it was true, and in one way, at least, he was in her life. But not in the way he wanted.

'*Bann beke salop*,' Joules spat.

Marie was busy shelling peas. She was worried about him. Ever since he'd come back to Sans Soucis from the six months he'd spent in the capital, he'd been different. '*Pouki foc ce mwen ki poci pote say yo a? Yonira pote safe ya yo men*,' he'd demanded angrily. Why should he fetch and carry for them?

'*Se kon sa baguay-la yé.*' Because. Marie continued shelling. Because that was the way things were in Martinique, no matter what Joules and his new-found friends might like to think. She looked at her son. '*Calmé cou*,' she told him. Take it easy. '*Sonje bien . . . si yo paté-la. Pa te ke ni lecol, pa te ke ni travay, ni la jan.*' Just think. If it wasn't for them, there'd be no school, no jobs, no money.

'*Ki moun ki bizouin vye lajan yo a?*' he retorted. Who needs their damned money? He got up suddenly and kicked at the tin basin of peas. There was a moment's silence. '*Souple eskize mwen. Mwen pa te le diw sa*,' he said at last. He rummaged in his pocket for a cigarette. She nodded. His apology was accepted. Whatever was eating at him, he had no reason to speak like that in front of her. She watched him leave.

16

'Have you thought about what you'd like to do?' Lisette asked Rianne as they sat over breakfast together on the veranda. Unusually, they were alone. Hennie was already in the water and the four other girls were still fast asleep.

'Do?' Rianne repeated crossly. 'What d'you mean? Why should I do anything?'

'Oh, for goodness' sake, Rianne. You can't *not* think

about your future. What do you want to do? It's a simple question.' Lisette took a sip of espresso.

'I don't know. I don't care. I'm stuck in that awful place, I hate it. You *know* I hate it. I don't *care* what I do. I just want to get out of there.' Rianne was exaggerating, but Lisette's questioning had set her teeth on edge. She knew her aunt was *pretending* to care what she did. Deep down, Lisette didn't give a toss.

'But, *skatjie*, look – you've made some friends, they seem really nice girls—'

'They're all right,' Rianne said, 'but they're not like my friends at home. I *told* you. There's even natives at the school. I have to eat with them. And that man Modise, his son is at the Boys' College and he was rude to me and—'

'Whose son? Who are you talking about?' Lisette looked at her niece sharply. Surely not Livingstone Modise?

'You know, the one who's in jail. Livingstone Modise. His son is at the Boys' College and he's a complete asshole. He was so rude to me, in public, too—'

'Now look, *skatjie*, you must just stay away from him – from them, d'you hear me? Just *ignore* them. Livingstone Modise? What are they *thinking* of? Why – how does *his* son come to be in England? Oh, this is *too* much!' Lisette was outraged. Modise? The Communist? The banned leader of that terrorist organisation, whatever it was called . . . African Freedom Party? How had *his* son wound up in the same place as her niece? She would call Francine van Gelderen as soon as she got back to Johannesburg. *She*'d suggested St Anne's. Did she have any *idea* who else was in the neighbourhood?

'What's all the fuss about, Ma?' Marika asked, yawning. She'd heard Lisette's raised voice from upstairs. She plopped herself down in one of the wicker chairs and reached for a croissant.

'*Skatjie*, I'm sorry, I shouldn't have raised my voice. Did I wake you up, hmm?' Lisette's cheeks were flushed.

'Why, what's the matter?'

'Nothing darling,' Lisette said quickly. She didn't want Marika worrying about Rianne just before leaving for university.

'I just told your mum about Ree Modise at the Boys' College,' Rianne said sarcastically before Lisette could change the subject. She was furious. Lisette didn't seem to care about her, how she felt – she was more worried about that *kaffir* Ree than she was about her own niece!

'I know. I think it's pretty cool,' Marika said innocently, helping herself to jam. 'He's really good-looking, too. I read that article in the *Weekly Mail* about him the other—'

'*Marika!*' Lisette nearly fell off her chair. 'Marika, darling, what are you saying? Don't be ridiculous! He could be *dangerous*!' Her face had gone unnaturally pale.

Marika looked at her in surprise. What had she said? 'I only said—'

'*Enough!* I won't hear another word about it. Enough, both of you.' Lisette got up from the table, her hands shaking. The *Weekly Mail*! Her daughter was reading that Communist filth? She walked into the study, closed the door and sat down on the arm of one of the leather chairs. Her report from the previous night was on the floor. To steady her trembling hands, she picked it up. She was breathing deeply, unevenly. No one, not even Simon, could know how the conversation between her daughter and her niece had upset her.

The image of the last time she'd seen Marius, her beloved brother, floated into her mind. It was almost three weeks after Céline's death, and Marius had been inconsolable. Lisette'd flown from Johannesburg the minute she'd heard, but Marius was already gone from them. She could hear him at night, pacing around downstairs, unable to sleep, think, eat. One night, in the early hours of the morning, she'd been woken by a sound – the sound of a man crying. She pulled on her dressing-gown and hurried out of bed. She'd found him in the elegant dining room, on his knees on the floor, the portraits of the last generation of successful de Zoete men staring, unseeing, down at him.

'Marius?' she called, worried to see him kneeling in the dark. 'Marius? Are you all right?' She moved towards him, her heart reaching out to her younger brother. The tragedy had devastated them all, even the servants. She touched his arm and he started, not having heard her come in.

'How long?' he turned red-rimmed, exhausted eyes towards her. She looked down at him questioningly.

'How long?' she repeated. 'What do you mean, how long?'

'How long, Lisi?' He called her by her childhood name. 'How long can we go on getting away scot-free?' He shook his head, as if in wonder. He sat back on his heels. He was fully dressed. He obviously hadn't been to bed.

'What are you saying, Marius? Who? Who is getting away scot-free?' She was alarmed by the look in his eyes – and by the question.

'Us! *Us*, Lisette! How long can we go on?' He grabbed her forearm, pulling her roughly down to the ground beside him. His grip was crushing. 'It'll soon be over for us, Lisi, for all of us.' His fingers tightened.

'Marius, *please*, you're hurting me!' Lisette cried, struggling to break free. She was frightened. He let go of her arm abruptly and got to his feet. Without looking at her he walked out of the room. It was the last time she saw her brother. The following morning, he had disappeared.

Now Lisette shook herself, suddenly cold. She breathed deeply. She reached for a tissue and dabbed her eyes. She couldn't go back out to the children now. She needed a few moments to compose herself. She got up and walked quickly upstairs. She would go for a swim. It would clear her head.

After Lisette had practically run from the veranda, Rianne and Marika sat in uncomfortable silence. Both girls were shocked. Marika got up and went in search of her mother.

She felt it was somehow her fault. Rianne sat on her own for a few minutes and then decided to go for a walk. She didn't feel like talking to Hennie any more. She walked down the garden and out onto the beach. She could see him, miles out, swimming powerfully past the edge of the bay to where the water was deeper, colder . . . dark blue. She walked to the edge of the de Zoete property and onto the public beach, not that there was ever anyone down here. Between them, the three properties, Trinité, Tartâne and Sans Soucis had gobbled up most of the beachfront. She walked under the colonnade of palms, kicking desultorily at the odd coconut husk that had fallen from the great, wavering height. It was getting hotter by the minute. Through the soles of her plimsolls she could feel the sand beginning to burn.

She walked on. Strange to think she'd done the same thing only a month or so before, along the vastly different Malvern Hills. She stared out to sea. The shimmering blue surface yawned in front of her eyes, like a tough, glittering skin. There was no one about. She'd walked round the bend of their own little bay and she could no longer see Hennie. She moved closer to the water's edge, feeling with pleasure the lick and curl of the gentle waves as they caressed and cooled her feet. She bent down and peeled off her plimsolls, dangling them from her fingers. She watched the way her feet sank into the soft sand and released with a faint *plop!* as she put one foot in front of the other. Tiny silver-backed fish crowded around her feet, darting this way and that. She wondered how they sensed her presence. She was beginning to feel a little better.

Perhaps it had been a mistake to invite all of them to Sans Soucis. It wasn't as if she knew them well. Gabby was all right: she'd struck up a friendship with Marika – they were both swots. And at least she wasn't trying to steal Marika from her. Rianne was surprised at herself. The realisation that she was afraid of seeing the only two people she cared about – except Poppie, of course, and now she didn't really count, somehow – being drawn to others had come to her slowly. She was afraid of losing them, of being left behind. She hadn't realised how much she cared about Hennie and Marika. But they were all she had. She didn't feel the same way about Lisette, unfortunately. At times she positively *hated* her.

She stopped walking and squinted up at the sun. It was nearly directly overhead – it was close to noon and the light was blinding. The heat rose in waves all around her and she could feel her shoulders tightening. She looked back at her solitary footsteps in the white sand. It was time to go back. Any more, and she'd be seriously burned.

'He's got lovely eyes, don't you think?' Nathalie said to Charmaine, as they lay in bed, the fan above their heads rotating gently. 'Especially when he smiles. Not that he smiles often,' she added. But he'd smiled at her the day before, suddenly, unexpectedly. She'd bumped into him as she ran out of the bedroom, the forgotten sunblock in hand. He cleaned their rooms at eleven on the dot every morning. 'Oops . . . *pardon*,' she said, in French, smiling at him. He smiled back. She blushed furiously and ran back down the stairs.

'He's a *servant*, Nat,' Charmaine said firmly. 'Doesn't matter if he's got lovely eyes, you can't fancy a servant. It would be like – like . . . Well, you just *can't*,' she concluded, somewhat lamely, unable to think of a suitable comparison.

'Who says?' Nathalie asked defiantly. After seeing her mother underneath Sacha, her view of the way things ought to be had been horribly, irrevocably changed. 'Anyhow, I don't *fancy* him, I just said he had nice eyes,' she added, annoyed.

'Yeah, right.' Charmaine threw back the sheet and swung her legs out of bed. 'Shall we go for a swim?' she asked, walking across the room to open the shutters. The room was flooded with brilliant light. Another gorgeous day in Paradise. She couldn't imagine going back to St Anne's.

Nathalie shielded her eyes. 'No, I'm going to stay in bed. I'm feeling lazy today.'

'Suit yourself. I'm off.' Charmaine pulled a bikini out of her suitcase. She hadn't bothered to unpack. She'd discovered that, in this house, when you wanted something washed or ironed you simply left it on the table outside the room. An hour or so later it came back pristine. She slipped off her pyjamas, squeezed herself into the pink gingham bikini and inspected her tan. With the exception of Gabby, they'd all gone golden brown. Then she grabbed a towel, waved at Nathalie and ran off in search of Gabby. And Hennie, of course.

After she'd left, Nathalie got up and closed the shutters. The room sank mercifully back into darkness. She left the fan on, climbed back into bed and glanced at her watch. The heat of the day was building, even in the darkened room. She could feel the familiar trickle of sweat forming between her breasts. She pulled off her cotton pyjama top and lay naked from the waist up on top of the crumpled linen sheets. It was lovely to feel the air play over her damp skin.

She closed her eyes. A week to go until Christmas. She'd already sent a postcard to Philippe and one to Clive, even though they were away. Philippe was in Rotterdam with a group of friends, and Clive and Cordelia were in Singapore, she thought.

For almost a week now, she'd managed not to think about Sacha. But lying there in the dim light, her thoughts wandered. She recalled his face, the burnished colour of his skin, his thick dark hair. The way he ran a hand through it when he talked or searched for a word. His voice . . . that strange mixture of accents. She liked the way his eyes crinkled at the corners when he smiled, or the way . . . She realised suddenly that she was no longer picturing Sacha's face. Joules's had floated into view.

She turned her head sleepily into the soft down pillow. Joules . . . Sacha . . . they weren't all that different. Dark gold skin, black curly hair . . . She smiled to herself. Her body felt hotter than usual, and there was a warm, wet feeling in the pit of her stomach. She turned onto her back. The air fanned her hardening nipples. Everything seemed suddenly vivid, urgent. She slipped a hand under the waistband of her pyjamas and, for the first time in her life, touched herself. There was a clamouring sound in her head as she slipped her hand lower, fingers trembling. It was as if the pitch in her ears had changed. Her fingers found something – so pleasurable she gasped. She heard a movement in the room . . . but it seemed so far away. She closed her eyes and her whole body tensed, poised deliciously on the edge of something she'd never felt before. Sacha. Joules. Suddenly, it was over. She lay quivering in the gloom, her heart hammering. And then, unmistakably, she heard the door close. She sat bolt upright, terrified. Had someone been in the room?

At supper that evening everyone was subdued. They were in the phase of the holiday where everyone was getting on everyone else's nerves. Nathalie was quiet and withdrawn. She was excruciatingly embarrassed. Who had seen her that morning? She eyed the others nervously.

Charmaine was in love. She had spent the day swimming and snorkelling with Hennie, bumping up against him, allowing him to carry her further out to sea than she would have dared to go. Nothing had 'happened' yet, but she was sure it would. His eyes told her so.

Gabby and Marika were tired. They'd been discussing politics all afternoon and had almost had an argument.

Lisette was preoccupied with reports and phone calls: she was assembling the group who would come to Sans Soucis for New Year's Eve – and not only to celebrate the New Year. It would be one of the biggest KdZK business meetings they'd ever had. She was quiet, eating little and reaching up every now and again to smooth away the frown that appeared between her eyes. A quiet Christmas, that was what they needed. A few days of rest, swimming, walks, picnics and perhaps a video or two before the excitement of the party. She would speak to Marie in the morning about the catering. There was a lot to be done.

In the cool of the air-conditioned hotel room, Cordelia Sutton-Farris tried for the third time to pick up the phone and dial. Her hands were shaking. She took a deep breath. Pick up the phone. Dial his number. She hesitated and put it down again. Not yet. She sat on her hands on the edge of the silk-covered bed and looked around the room. The suite she and Clive had booked at the legendary Raffles Hotel in Singapore was everything she had dreamed of. From the enormous marble foyer with its liveried bell-boys, trickling waterfalls and fountains to the discreet but pleasant tinkle of the piano in the corner, this was luxury Far Eastern-style. Even the white lilies in their huge crystal vases were larger and more fragrant than the ones for which she paid a fortune back home. It was perfect. That morning Clive had left on a three-day business trip to Hong Kong. She had kissed him goodbye, her heart thudding. Now she was alone in the splendid comfort of one of the world's grandest hotels. But not for long.

She picked up the receiver for the fourth time. Quickly, she dialled the unfamiliar number. There was a short 'beep' as the international call went through and then, unbelievably, his voice was on the line.

'Hello, this is Sacha.'

'Sacha,' she said, her stomach churning, 'it's Cordelia.'

In his bedroom in his grandmother's house, Sacha Nilam put down the phone slowly. He didn't know what to think. Cordelia was in Singapore? What the hell was she doing there? And without her husband. He'd be gone for three days. And she wanted *him* there. She wanted him to drive to Singapore immediately. He ran a hand through his hair. His mouth was dry.

'Sacha?' his grandmother called.

'*Nek*, I'll be out in a minute,' he called. He looked around his room. He'd only just arrived. His bags weren't even unpacked. Leave for Singapore now? How was he going to explain *that* to her?

'But you've only just arrived!' she repeated, frowning in bewilderment.

'I'll be back on Monday, Mai, don't worry. Tell Aunt Nuria I've borrowed her car. I'll call you when I get there.' He had a bag in his hand. Before she could stage any further protests, he bent down, kissed her soundly on both cheeks and disappeared.

As he started his aunt's silver BMW, he reflected that there would be hell to pay on Monday. He'd deal with it then, he thought grimly. Despite his unease, he wanted to see Cordelia. As he collected his ticket at the Shah Alam toll gate, he felt a rush of desire that lasted almost the whole three-and-a-half-hour drive until he handed over his passport at the Malaysia–Singapore border.

He rang her from the lobby and ran up the stairs, two at a time. Cordelia jumped at the sound of his knock. She hurried across the floor, her heels clicking on the marble. She opened the door. For a second they stood in the dimmed light, staring at each other. She was wearing a black sheer silk robe and, through the thin fabric, he could see her nipples harden as he stared at her. Tentatively, he reached for her, his hand slipping beneath her robe to touch her. She moaned softly.

He kicked the door shut behind him and pulled her to him. His hands moved around her back, stroking the soft skin between her shoulder blades and running down the length of her back. She felt even better than he remembered. His tongue pushed into her mouth, hard and insistent. Cordelia closed her eyes, running her fingers

through his thick black curls and opening her mouth wide
. . . wider. Slowly, they sank to the carpet. He pushed her
backwards until she was lying beneath him, then rose long
enough to strip off his shirt, not bothering to undo the
buttons.

Her eyes were on him – his golden-brown chest, with the
faintest smattering of curly dark hair that tapered to a V
and disappeared into his jeans. He followed her eyes, then
slid his long, muscular legs out of his jeans. Suddenly he
was lying naked beside her . . . on top of her . . . inside her.
She moaned again, louder this time. His dark eyes were on
her as he brought them both to a fast, furious climax. He
buried his face in her neck and bit her gently as his own
intense pleasure subsided. For a few minutes they lay
together, their ragged breathing the only sound in the quiet,
air-conditioned room.

'I'm so glad you came,' she said, breaking the silence.

Sacha rolled over and looked at her, a smile playing
around his mouth. 'I'm glad *you* came,' he said mischievously. 'Would you like to come again?' Cordelia laughed
with delight. She put out a hand and touched his taut
stomach, then let her eyes wander slowly over him. He was
breathing fast, unevenly, and she began to tease him,
brushing against his erection and stroking him with the tip
of her finger.

'Me?' she whispered, as she lowered her head. 'I think
you might get there before me . . .'

Two days later, they were sitting on the balcony outside the
room, the closest either of them had come to leaving the
room. They had made love on and off all the time, pausing
only to order room service or take a bath together. Cordelia
had never experienced anything like it. She was forty-one
years old, she'd been married three times, she had two
children . . . she'd done it all: she'd escaped the war,
married a rock star, declared herself bankrupt, fled from

one country to another. Whatever else one could say about her, she had *lived*.

'I have to see you again. I *have* to.' She looked at him from behind her Dior sunglasses and took a sip of coffee. They were having breakfast. Or, at least, Sacha was having breakfast. He'd eaten everything on her plate as well.

'How?' He looked at her calmly, his dark eyes expressionless. 'You can't come to KL – your husband is coming back tomorrow.'

'I'll think of something.' Cordelia sounded firmer than she felt. What on earth had she got herself into? She thought of Clive coming back from Hong Kong the following morning and shuddered. How could she bear his staid conversation and folded trousers? Sacha reached across her for the last croissant. He held it up. She shook her head. She'd eaten almost nothing in the past two days. She glanced at his strong, muscular forearm and felt a stab of pleasure, longing, somewhere deep inside her. She *had* to see him again. That's all there was to it. She would find a way. It was that simple.

Cordelia looked at the date on her Piaget wristwatch again: 26 December. Her period was two months late. She closed her eyes. It was a week since she'd watched Sacha climb into his BMW at the crack of dawn and begin the 400-kilometre drive back to Kuala Lumpur. Clive's plane had landed at seven thirty a.m., and by eight thirty he had been back at the hotel. She'd pleaded a migraine brought on by shopping in the heat the previous day. Clive had said nothing, but he was puzzled; he'd been gone for three days and Cordelia had bought nothing. No shopping bags, no new shoes, no jewellery. Cordelia loved to shop – she *lived* to shop. It was the one thing that was guaranteed to turn her on, even if he couldn't.

'Another drink, my darling?' he asked, as they sat beside the hotel pool, watching the sun go down. She shook her head, her eyes staring blankly into the distance. Her fingernails tapped nervously on the arm of her chair. She was wondering how to slip away from him and phone Sacha. She got up abruptly, slipped her feet into her high-heeled sandals, gathering her bag. 'I'm just going in for a moment – I've forgotten something,' she said hurriedly. He watched her clip her way across the poolside patio and disappear into the hotel. He frowned, concerned. Something was definitely wrong with her. Perhaps it was the food.

Inside, she took the lift to the penthouse. But instead of going directly to her room, she hurried down the emergency stairs to the floor below where there was a wall of public telephones. She ran to the nearest, inserted a few coins and dialled Sacha's number. The phone rang for what seemed like an eternity before an old woman's voice came crackling down the line.

'Hello? Hello?' Cordelia shouted, straining to hear above the static. 'Can I speak to Sacha, please?' she asked. She felt sick.

'Sacha?' the old lady asked, then let forth a torrent of incomprehensible words.

'Sacha. Sacha Nilam?' Cordelia shouted again. 'Do you speak English? English?' She was close to tears with frustration. 'Can I speak to Sacha?' The woman answered in her own language. Cordelia gave up and replaced the receiver. She bit her lip, suddenly aware of an elderly Singaporean couple staring at her. She smoothed back her hair, straightened her skirt and walked as calmly as she could to the emergency exit. Opening the door, she escaped into the stairwell and leaned against the wall. What was she to do next?

Sacha had been right. There had been hell to pay. His aunt and grandmother had stared at him in disbelief. To disappear for three days – *three days* – was so unlike him. And, to make matters worse, he'd forgotten to call either of them from Singapore. What the hell was he doing in

Singapore with his aunt's car? Had he taken leave of his senses? His aunt was furious. She suspected the worst – a girl, some pretty English or American girl, no doubt about it. She dismissed his story of a schoolfriend in need with an abrupt wave of her plump hand. Speaking to him in English, so that his grandmother – who could not, *would* not believe her darling Sacha could do *anything* as disrespectful – could not understand, she said quickly, 'All right, I'm prepared to accept your excuses this once. If it happens again, make no mistake, I'll inform your father. Do I make myself clear?'

Sacha had nodded curtly and walked into his room. His father was the last person he wanted to know about the affair. It wasn't just that he wouldn't approve: his father would be furious if he knew Cordelia was European. The day Sacha's mother had left her infant son in the care of her mother-in-law and boarded a plane at Kuala Lumpur International Airport bound for Helsinki Dr Yusef Nilam had forbidden everyone in the household, including the tiny Sacha who couldn't yet speak, ever to mention her name. His hatred for his ex-wife extended to all European women – all white women. When Sacha reached his teens, the message was clear. Girlfriends, yes; European girlfriends, no. Never. Sacha learned to hide.

His bewildered grandmother turned to her daughter in despair. '*Apa yang telah terjadi?*' she asked. What could have happened? She looked at Sacha's closed bedroom door sorrowfully. It was the first time in a long while that she'd had occasion to raise her voice to her darling grandson.

'It's probably some friends of his from university,' Nuria said soothingly. 'You know what these young men are like, *Emak. Jangan khuatir, ianya tak akan berlaku lagi.*' Don't worry, it won't happen again.

The older woman looked at her daughter thoughtfully. No one knew Sacha like she did. She said nothing. When Sacha was ready, he would tell her what had happened. For the moment, Allah be praised, he was back home and safe. That was what was important.

But then she received a phone call in the afternoon from someone – a woman, a hysterical *woman*, not a girl – asking for Sacha, and she was worried.

'Karadia ... Cabodia ... Cameelia?' She recounted the unfamiliar names to him.

Sacha suppressed the urge to laugh. 'Cordelia?' he offered, his eyes narrowing. Oh God, not again, surely? Jamila nodded vigorously. 'Cordeelya,' she repeated. '*Siapakah perempuan itu?*' Who is that woman?

'She's my friend Philippe's mother,' Sacha replied truthfully. 'Perhaps something's happened to him.'

'You'd better phone him, then,' his grandmother said. She got up heavily and brought him the phone.

'I – I've lost his number.' Sacha answered evasively. He hated lying to his grandmother, but he couldn't speak to Cordelia in front of her. Even if she didn't understand English, she was no fool. And where was he supposed to call Cordelia? At the hotel? In front of her husband? 'I'll call her later,' he said, and got up.

Jamila watched him go. She noticed his sudden flush and his agitation. She decided it was high time he told her the truth. 'Sacha,' she called, as he disappeared into his room. '*Ada sesuatu yang Nek hendak bincangkan.*' I want to talk to you. She settled herself on the settee and patted the space next to her. '*Mari. Duduklah di sini, disebelah Nek.*' Come. Sit beside me.

'I can't. *Nek ... maafkanlah saya.*' I'm sorry. He gave her an almost pleading look and closed the door. She gazed after him, more worried than ever.

In the safety of his room, Sacha switched on the air-conditioner and lay on his bed. He closed his eyes. He had a headache. How had he got into this mess? He liked Cordelia well enough – she was beautiful and charming and experienced, and he liked the way he made her feel. It had started when they'd gone riding, and she'd made a pass at him at the top of the hill. She'd got off her horse, pulled a rug from her neat leather side-saddle and spread it on the ground. It was cold at that hour of the morning, but they were both hot from the gallop.

They sat on the blanket, resting and watching the horses recover. She pulled out a small silver hip flask, and they shared the whisky. He tasted it on her tongue as she drew his head down to hers and pushed his hand between her legs. He was shocked by her boldness, but was excited too. They didn't make love then – it was too cold – but they did every day after that, sometimes twice, when they could. It was risky. He couldn't remember how he'd managed to sit there every evening, eating calmly, chatting to her husband, smiling at Nathalie and Philippe.

Cordelia was the most demanding woman he'd been with. Not that he'd been with many. Sweet little Emily Baker, a good girl. She was English, in his class at the International School. God, just getting his hands inside her blouse was a major event. Eventually he had tired of her girl-next-door freshness and her outright refusal even to contemplate sleeping with him. She had been replaced by Toril, a dark-haired Swede, also in his class. She'd been fun, but short-lived. After a few clumsy but enthusiastic sessions, they'd both lost their virginity and he'd promptly lost her. She had moved on to better things, an older boy who ran track. A jock.

Sacha had already had his eye on the next, Samantha Donaldson, an American exchange student, as Californian as they came. But before their relationship could progress any further, his father had announced, out of the blue, that he was to enrol immediately at Eton. He was to live among the English, the better to beat them at their own game. Quite what Dr Nilam thought the 'game' was, he never made clear to Sacha. No matter. Living out of the reach of his domineering father appealed to him.

There were no girls at Eton, although they met a few of

the more adventurous ones from the girls' school half an hour's walk away. But apart from a few Saturday afternoons spent wasting precious pocket money in the village café, where would you take a girl even if you could get her to agree to it? It wasn't until he arrived at Reading University that he realised just how devastating the combination of good looks and just the right amount of foreignness was. For the first time in his life, girls practically threw themselves at him – and he was enjoying it. Being away from home, in all senses of the word, was liberating. He was free to do as he pleased, when and with whom he liked. There had been pretty girls and dull girls, all inexperienced. But Cordelia was different.

He opened his eyes. Despite his youth, he knew he wasn't in love with her. In lust, perhaps, but not love. Cordelia demanded too much. She treated him as if he were both child and father, a confused tangle of her own insecurities. She wanted his attention all the time. Making love to her, he recognised the hunger in her eyes: she wanted him to love her, adore her, worship her – *stay* with her. And he had no intention of doing that.

But how to tell her? That was the problem. How to tell her without *her* telling everyone else? He knew he'd done the unthinkable – Philippe would never forgive him. And now that she had his telephone number . . . His scalp tightened. He would ignore her for a few days. Perhaps she'd take the hint, back off a little. He'd see her when they were back in England and explain things to her. He was young, just finishing university, his whole life lay ahead of him. He couldn't afford to be involved with someone like her, beautiful and desirable though she was. He couldn't afford to lose his friendship with her son. Surely she would understand?

17

Nathalie slipped through the gate at the bottom of the garden and peered anxiously into the darkness. Where was he? The New Year's Eve party was in full swing behind her. A jazz band was playing softly on the veranda, the music floating out into the black-velvet night, mingling with the sound of laughter and the chink of champagne glasses as Marie, Joseph and two other helpers from the village – wherever it was – looked after the guests. She glanced around her again. It was pitch black. The moon was only a quarter full and it shone weakly on the surface of the sea, casting a pale watery light.

'Hey.' A man's voice floated up through the darkness.

She looked again. He was sitting on the sand, a little to the left of where she was. She could see him pull on his cigarette: it glowed orange in the dark. 'Joules?' she called softly.

'*Way.*' She loved the sound of his language. Creole. She moved carefully over to him, feeling the warmth of the sand under her bare soles. He stood up as she reached him. 'Come. Let's go 'way from 'ere. We can find someplace else.' She slipped her hand into his. It all felt so easy.

The tension between them had been building all week. She knew, somehow, that it was he who'd seen her that morning. She knew it from the way he looked at her, and it excited her. They'd done nothing but smile at each other when no one was looking. And once he'd touched her as she came out of the bedroom on her way to the beach. The house was empty – everyone was already in the water. He touched her shoulder lightly . . . the softest caress. She stared at him, her heart beating fast. And then he had disappeared.

When she had seen him that evening, dressed in a white shirt and black trousers, his skin suffused with a deep gold glow – he'd been working outdoors all day, hanging lights, decorating the garden – she'd experienced a sharp pull in her stomach and caught her breath. He had come over, a tray of champagne glasses in his hand.

'*À boire?*' he asked, smiling at her.

She looked into his laughing brown eyes, then glanced around quickly. No one was watching them. '*Oui,*' she answered. '*Merci.*'

'*Ah, tu parles bien le français.*' He offered her a glass. Their fingers touched for one electrifying moment. Then, with another quick smile, he was gone.

Her fingers tingled from their brief contact. She drained her glass, feeling the bubbles go straight to her head. She wandered about the garden, her whole body suffused with a kind of erotic energy she had never felt before. She accepted a glass of wine, nibbled at one of Marie's delicious canapés, sipped Rianne's whisky and Coke. She laughed louder than anyone else at Hennie's awful jokes and smiled widely at Gabby, her blue eyes shining with a secret, sensual excitement. And when Joules whispered to her, just after eleven when dinner had been served and everyone was dancing, to meet him on the beach, she moved towards him dreamily, placing a hand boldly on his forearm. *Dix minutes?* She nodded. He disappeared again. She looked around carefully. No one was watching. She waited until the band began a new set, then walked quickly through the rhododendron bushes towards the beach. She disappeared into the darkness. No one saw her. It was as easy as that.

'Where shall we go?' she whispered as they walked down the beach, away from the house.

'There is a place . . . a – 'ow you say? For swimming? You know, to put your clothes,' Joules answered, not looking at her.

'A cabin?' Nathalie asked. She could feel the tightness in her groin spread through her body.

'*Way. Une cabine.*' He knew the way, even in the pitch dark. It was a simple thatched structure, not even a cabin, three walls and a roof that gave some shade during the burning heat of the day. Now, in the middle of the warm, humid night, it was damp and cool.

'No snakes?' Nathalie asked, apprehensive. Joules laughed. '*Non.*' He spread out the sisal matting, brushing off the sand. 'Come. You sit with me. *Ou pa bezwen pè. M'pap fè-w anyen.*' Don't be afraid. I won't hurt you.

Nathalie knelt down. Her heart was beating fast. He leaned forward and pulled her to him. For a second they stared at each other in the dark. Nathalie could just make out his dark, shining eyes and the white of his teeth as he bent his head towards hers. They kissed, softly at first, and then she felt his tongue move into her mouth, thick, warm and wet. It was all happening so fast. She felt his hand move beneath her dress, felt his fingers fumble with the elastic of her panties and then he touched her, right there, where she had touched herself the other day. She had been so shaken by the powerful wave of feeling that had swept over her she'd been afraid to do it again. But now, lying next to him and feeling his hands moving over her as her own had done, the wave was beginning again, rising swiftly through her body, causing her to arch against him. She felt him move away from her for a second, felt him unbuckle his trousers and shift his weight as he undressed. Then he was on top of her, pressing her into the damp sand, his hands and mouth swallowing her greedily, stroking her, pulling her towards him.

All of a sudden, she felt a chill run through her, a moment where her excitement and longing turned to fear. She could hear him grunting as he probed her wetness with his fingers. In a flash she was back in the loft at Malmesbury, hearing Sacha's moans as he caressed her mother. She looked at Joules, but all she could see was Sacha's curly head as he too began to make love. To her mother. She felt dizzy, as though she couldn't breathe . . . His mouth was on hers, his tongue pushing inside her as something hard and warm pressed between her legs. She panicked, trying to move away – she wasn't ready – it was happening too fast. She moaned, twisting her head away from his, pushing at him. But he was too far gone in his own pleasure.

With one hand he pinned her struggling arm and with the other he forced open her legs and thrust inside her, urgently. Nathalie was crying. He was hurting her, banging her head against the hard sand. He was heavy, too heavy – she felt something sharp and hot burst inside her and he gasped, his body tensed and, with a final, savage thrust, he climaxed, shuddering and shivering on top of her. Nathalie pressed her face into the sand, away from him. She could feel the salty tears trickle into her bruised mouth, feel grains of sand on her teeth. She choked back a sob.

'*C'était bien?*' she heard Joules ask, as if from a great distance. He was lying beside her now, reaching for a cigarette. He stroked her face.

Nathalie lay beside him, her mind a swirl of emotions, fear and shame among them.

'*Ça va?*' he asked. She nodded, not trusting her voice. It was all over so quickly . . . and, God, it had hurt. She hugged her knees to her chest and closed her eyes.

Fifteen minutes later, a trembling Nathalie slipped back into the garden and made her way to the bathroom. Inside, she switched on the light and gasped. Her lips were swollen and bruised, and one side of her face was still covered in sand. She turned on the tap and searched for a towel. Carefully, she wiped her face and hands. She lifted her white skirt, which was covered in sand and mud, and did her best to remove the stains. She closed her eyes and wiped at the stickiness between her legs. When she pulled away the towel it was bloody. The short, sharp pain she'd felt as Joules entered her – she knew now what it had been. She began to cry again. That wasn't how it was supposed to be. She heard shouts as fireworks exploded, and looked out of the window. The sky was lit up in flashes – green, red, gold. It was 1982.

To 1982! Lisette lifted her glass. The dozen or so guests followed suit. Lisette looked at the group of men – she was the only woman – standing on the veranda: 1982 would be a good year for them, she was sure, bringing new challenges, new opportunities. She looked fondly at her brother Hendryk, a younger, perhaps less handsome, less charismatic version of Marius, but family. That was the important thing. She and Hendryk were alone now. With their father and mother dead – and Marius? Well, no one knew: his body had never been found. No note had been left, no call, no trace. Nothing. One day he was there, the next he was gone. But there were the children, and for that she was for ever grateful.

She looked around the gardens: Hennie, with his arms wrapped round that little tramp Charmaine; Rianne, alone as usual, looking uncannily like her mother in a long white evening dress, her hair swept off her beautiful face; Marika, watching the fireworks with an expression of pure delight on her pretty face. Lisette's eyes moistened. She loved seeing her children happy and contented.

Hendryk's sons, Piet and Coen, were with their mother in Pretoria. She hated family gatherings: Renata van Wyk was a simple girl, from a simple Afrikaner farming family. Marrying into the de Zoete clan was as unlikely a step as she'd ever imagined taking. God knew where they had met – Hendryk had never said. Lisette had her suspicions, but kept them to herself. On balance, Anton's three children, Marius, Lisette, Hendryk, had not done exceptionally well with their marriages: Céline dead at the age of thirty-three; Lisette's husband, Axel, dead at forty-one in the terrible car accident; and Renata, sequestering herself in the family estate near Pretoria. She might as well be dead for all one saw of her.

Lisette turned back to the group on the veranda. For three days, they'd been going over the figures, analysing the information and planning, planning, planning. They were ready. Over the next couple of days, they would fly back to their respective bases and prepare to put KdZK firmly on the financial map.

18

It was five o'clock. Marie and Joseph watched the cars disappear round the bend and turned to go inside. After the noise and bustle of the previous three weeks, an eerie silence had descended on the house. Marie breathed a sigh of relief and followed her husband into the villa that, though they planned to spend all their lives in it, was off-limits to them. Having been through the routine every year for the past decade, they worked quickly, pulling out the dust covers, stripping the beds, locking cupboards. They were looking forward to eleven months of peace and quiet. The arrangement whereby they watched over the property, tended the gardens and worked twelve-hour days at Christmas suited them just fine. Their eldest child, Martine, was already at the École Supérieure on the proceeds of that salary.

Marie wondered where Joules was – she knew what had passed between him and the little brunette. Well, she reasoned, at least he hadn't tried to take mademoiselle Rianne down to the beach at midnight – God knows what sort of tensions *that* would have produced. It was hard for him, she knew, watching Hennie, Rianne, Marika, and their friends come and go as they pleased while he was stuck at Sans Soucis, with no means of escape. Still, she reminded herself again, she was relieved it had been *la p'tite Anglaise* and not Rianne.

The enormous bunch of keys jangled against her hip as she and Joseph walked from room to room, locking doors and windows. Another Christmas gone, another year's salary in.

19

As soon as he heard Philippe's voice on the other end of the long-distance line, Sacha knew something was seriously wrong. His grandmother watched anxiously as he nodded slowly. She couldn't understand what was happening. He listened for a few minutes and replaced the receiver. He stood with his back to her for several minutes, breathing heavily.

'What is it, Sacha?' She touched him gently on the shoulder.

He started and turned to face her. '*Nenek*,' he began, looking her straight in the eye with the clear, honest gaze she had always known. People always remarked on how dark his eyes were. To her, they had always been light. Light, clear eyes – the colour of aubergines. She looked at him tenderly, waiting for his explanation. When it came, she was quiet. Nothing she had ever been through, either with him or his father, could have prepared her for the shame and horror that swept through her as his voice died away. She folded her hands in her lap and stared at them, twisting the ring she wore on her index finger – her only piece of jewellery. 'When did it start?' she asked, not knowing what words to use.

'About four months ago, *Nek*. I went to stay with them. She started it—' He stopped.

She was shaking her head: traditional Malay family relationships such as theirs did not allow for discussions of this nature between the generations. To talk about it with her son would have been hard enough, with her grandchild it was impossible. 'But why? Why did you . . . ?' She forced herself to speak. 'She's old, Sacha, old enough to be your mother.' She raised a hand to her mouth. Perhaps that was it. She and Sacha had never talked about his mother. Yusef had seen to that. Jamila worried about what to say when the time came for Sacha to ask. So far he never had. It wasn't possible to know what he thought. He turned his silent, inscrutable eyes on her, not saying anything.

'Sacha,' she began gently, 'I . . . It is not for me to decide what to do. This is for you to decide. If there is . . . a child, you must go to her. Help her. I will tell your father.'

'No.' Sacha turned to her. There was a strange look in his eyes. 'This is not his business. He has no right to know.'

'How can you say that?' his grandmother cried. 'He supports you. It is through him that you are there . . . in that place. You may be grown enough to father a child, Sacha, but you are still his child.'

'No! I'm sorry, *Nenek*, you can't – you *mustn't* tell him. If you do—' He stopped, aware they were skirting uncharted territory between them. She looked at him soundlessly. 'I'll go back to London tomorrow. Tell Papa that there was an emergency. One of my friends.' He looked at her, pleading. She sighed. Nuria would be furious, she knew. Well, she would just have to stall her. She watched him get up, open the door to his room and close it again, quietly. Tears came to her eyes as she thought of what he must be going through. Damn that woman, she thought angrily. Damn her! And the child.

Cordelia was dimly aware of people moving around her. Her limbs felt heavy, leaden and floppy. She struggled to open her eyes. The effort exhausted her and she closed them again, sliding back into darkness. She felt someone take her arm, then a prick . . . then nothing. Deep oblivion. And silence. Velvety, thick silence. She slept.

At her bedside, Clive watched her anxiously, his face drawn and tired. It had been almost twelve hours since they had rushed Cordelia to hospital. He closed his eyes briefly, reliving the terrible scene.

She had come through from the lavatory, looking wan, and slipped into the seat beside him, her hands trembling slightly.

'What's the matter, darling?' he asked. She hadn't looked

well since they had left Singapore, some ten hours earlier. She had refused food or drink and had slept only fitfully. Now, in the last hour, she had been to the toilet every ten minutes.

'I feel a little dizzy,' she murmured, her eyes closing. 'I feel . . . funny.'

'Shall I call one of the stewardesses, darling?' he asked, and stared around the first-class cabin. They were always on hand.

'I'll be all right once we land,' she murmured.

But she wasn't all right. As their plane touched down at Heathrow, he struggled to wake her. It was only when one of the efficient British Airways staff bent down to help him that he noticed the bright red stain on her Karl Lagerfeld trouser suit. He drew away in horror and then, suddenly, all hell broke loose. Within seconds, a doctor had been summoned, and an ambulance rolled up on the tarmac outside.

'Is she pregnant?' the doctor asked, placing a stethoscope on her stomach.

Clive shook his head. They hadn't made love in months.

The doctor gave him a quick glance and lowered his eyes.

Cordelia was lifted gently onto a stretcher and into the waiting ambulance. Luckily, their private health insurance speeded things up. They were whisked to the Portland Hospital and Cordelia was taken straight to the operating theatre. He waited anxiously in the private room . . .

A nurse woke him, shaking him gently. 'Would you care for a cup of tea, sir? We've given her a sedative, and she'll sleep now.' Clive stared at her for a second, momentarily confused, then nodded. He hadn't eaten anything since their arrival. He stood up. He had to call Philippe. Luckily Nathalie was on holiday and would be spared the trauma. The nurse returned, bearing a cup of tea and an assortment of sandwiches. He smiled at her gratefully. 'I'd like to make a phone call to our son. He's in Somerset,' he said.

'Of course,' the nurse answered, and brought the telephone round from the other side of the bed. 'Would that be Sacha? It's such a lovely name, a bit unusual.'

'Sacha?' asked Clive, feeling cold.

'Yes, she kept mentioning his name. "Our son", she kept saying. Are you all right, sir?' she asked. Clive had gone as white as a sheet.

At that moment, the door opened and two men walked in, still partially dressed in operating-theatre scrubs. 'Mr Sutton-Farris?' One offered his hand to Clive. 'Semple. I'm the consultant gynaecologist and this is Dr Banks – he assisted me during the operation.' Clive shook hands with both doctors and turned his blank, numb face to them. He knew, with a certainty approaching dread, what he was about to hear.

'I'm so sorry, Mr Sutton-Farris,' the consultant began, 'but we weren't able to save the baby. Your wife will recover, rest assured, but I'm afraid there won't be any more children. We had to remove her womb.' Clive was struggling to focus on what they were saying. Ignoring the worried looks of the two doctors and the suddenly quiet nurse, he walked out of the room.

Cordelia woke suddenly, as if from a fright. She opened her eyes wide and made out, in the corner of the room, a figure slumped awkwardly in a chair. She recognised Clive, obviously exhausted from his bedside vigil, and closed her eyes again in pain. All she could think about was the searing pain in her abdomen – and Sacha. Where was he? Where was *she*? She opened her eyes again cautiously and tried to move her head from side to side, seeking to establish where she was and why.

A nurse popped her head round the door, then came in. 'Hello, love.' She stroked Cordelia's arm soothingly. 'How are you feeling?' Cordelia shook her head, tears filling her eyes. The nurse nodded sympathetically, going to the foot of the bed and checking the chart. 'You had a dose almost an hour ago,' she said, noting the time on her chain watch. 'I can't give you anything else for at least another hour. Can you make it that long?' Cordelia shook her head.

At that moment, Clive jerked awake, disturbed by the voices. Cordelia closed her eyes quickly. She couldn't bear to meet Clive's. He knew – he knew everything. He *had* to know. There was no way he couldn't . . . The thoughts spun around in her pounding head until she felt herself sinking again. Blackness. I'm drowning in blackness, she thought, as she sank deeper and deeper. Then silence. She slept.

Sacha hugged his grandmother unusually tightly. His cab was waiting. He ran a hand through his curls. 'Don't worry, *Nek*, it'll be all right. I'll phone as soon as I get to London. Philippe will meet me.'

She snorted. What kind of world was it where the son of the man Sacha had wronged – no other word for it – would offer to meet him, pretend nothing had happened? It had all been so different in her day. But the world was changing, she reminded herself, as she watched him stow his bags in the back of the cab – and Sacha was changing with it. She sighed. When Yusef had told her Sacha was to go to Europe, where Anna-Mikka had come from, she had known that there would be trouble. Still no one could have foreseen this. She watched the cab roll down the driveway and splutter into life just before the gate. For a long time she remained standing there, Sacha's beautiful Persian cats rubbing themselves around her ankles.

Sacha slept almost all the way to London. When they touched down at eight in the morning, there was a cold sensation in the pit of his stomach. He shook himself awake, ignoring the rumbling in his stomach. He collected his hand luggage and waited impatiently for disembarkation to begin.

'Philippe.' He said it quietly. Philippe turned. The two

young men looked at each other. Neither knew what to say. 'Thanks for coming to get me.' Sacha gripped his bags. They stood for a moment, facing each other. 'Philippe, I'm sorry about this,' he began. 'I don't know what to say. I . . . never meant for this to happen—'

'Please don't talk about it,' Philippe interrupted him. 'I don't want to know.'

Sacha understood. He didn't want to talk about it either.

Philippe motioned with his head. 'Come on, I'm parked outside.' He led the way.

They drove back to London in silence, each preoccupied with his own thoughts.

When Clive saw Sacha enter with Philippe, he quelled the urge to get up and hit the good-looking young man. He's only twenty-two, he reminded himself. This must be as hard for him as it is for all of us. And Clive knew Cordelia well. If he'd been Sacha, he doubted whether he would have found the strength to resist her, married or not. He beckoned to Philippe, and they left Sacha and Cordelia alone. But not for too long, he thought, as they went together to the cafeteria. Just long enough to be decent about it all.

'Sacha,' Cordelia whispered weakly. He gazed at her wordlessly. She looked so different: her sparkle and her glittery, flirtatious manner were gone. She looked haggard and old. 'Sacha, I . . . lost it . . . I lost the baby, our baby.' She began to cry, her shoulders heaving with the effort. He remained motionless at the foot of her bed. She closed her eyes, tears trickling down her cheeks.

At that moment a nurse poked her head round the door, saw Cordelia's distress and took charge. 'Are you the son?' she asked crossly. 'She's supposed to be resting, not crying. Come on, out. I think your father's downstairs in the cafeteria. I'm sorry, but you really must leave. Your mother needs all the rest she can get.' Cordelia was still sobbing.

He looked at her again, his dark eyes giving away nothing, and left the room. As quickly as his feelings had turned four months ago, from admiration to lust for the attractive, vivacious woman, they had now turned to disgust. He wanted never to see her again.

PART THREE

20

August 1983: New York

'Rianne?' A woman's voice rang out in the cramped waiting room at Face!.

Rianne looked up from where she was perched uncomfortably on the edge of a sofa alongside a dozen desperately hopeful girls, fanning herself ineffectually with a magazine she'd picked up off the glass-topped coffee table. New York in August was unbearable: a muggy, oppressive heat enveloped the room and the single air-conditioner struggled noisily to keep the temperature down. A woman was standing in the doorway, holding a clipboard and beckoning impatiently. Twelve pairs of eyes watched her enviously as she walked across the room. They turned anxious faces towards one another as soon as the door closed – how come she'd been picked? Why didn't she have to wait? What did she have that they didn't?

Rianne followed the woman down the long corridor. She tapped lightly on a door at the end of it and ushered Rianne inside. Rianne paused awkwardly on the threshold of a large, sunny office, which was cooler than the waiting room. She looked around. It was marvellously chaotic. There were lights, enormous white photographer's blinds, props, wires and cables running everywhere, pictures tacked onto the walls, negatives and contact sheets strewn across the floor, and magazine covers on almost every surface. Face! was one of the hottest new modelling agencies in town and its owner, the South African-born Ross Carter, was one of the best in the business.

'Rianne!' A diminutive grey-haired woman got up from behind the enormous glass desk. She waved Rianne over. 'My dear, how nice to see you again.' She held her by the shoulders and kissed her quickly on each cheek. 'My God, darling, the last time I saw you, you were *so* high!' she said, holding a hand at her own height and chuckling delightedly.

Rianne smiled vaguely. When would that have been? She had no recollection of ever meeting Ross Carter, despite Lisette's insistence. The woman continued to study her appraisingly. 'Turn around for me, darling, please,' she said suddenly. 'Let me see you walk . . . That's it . . . Good. Just walk to the door and back, slowly, and now turn. Good.' She went back to her desk, settled herself comfortably in the leather swivel chair and pressed a button on her phone. 'Gina, come in for a second, will you?'

Seconds later, the door opened and a young woman, dressed stylishly in black despite the heat, walked in.

'Gina, this is Rianne de Zoete, an old family connection. What d'you think?'

'How old are you?' Gina asked, crossing the floor to join Ross. The two women looked at the file that the secretary had left open for them.

'Eighteen,' Rianne replied.

Ross pulled a face. 'A little late to *start* modelling,' she murmured. 'Well, we'll see.'

Rianne stared at them. Late? At eighteen?

'Have you done any modelling before?'

Rianne shook her head. It had been Lisette's idea, not hers. 'Why not?' Lisette had asked her a month ago, as Rianne moped around the house in Johannesburg. 'What else would you like to do?' Rianne had shrugged moodily, as she always did. What would she like to do? It was Lisette's favourite question. She had no bloody idea.

Gina turned to her. 'OK. Well, you're certainly very

pretty, Rianne, but that doesn't necessarily mean anything. We get lots of pretty girls in here. It all depends on how you come out in print, how you move, whether you can walk down a runway, all sorts of things. We'll take a few test shots with our in-house photographer this afternoon and see how you do.'

It was on the tip of Rianne's tongue to tell both women to take a hike – they were acting as though she was desperate for a modelling career and, actually, nothing could have been further from the truth. As usual, she'd gone along with Lisette's plan simply because she couldn't come up with a better one. Lisette's other suggestion, interior design, sounded far too much like hard work. She looked at the ground.

'Have you had breakfast?' Ross asked.

Rianne nodded.

'What did you have?'

'Um . . . a bagel and coffee. Why?'

'Well, that'll have to change. No wheat in the morning, darling. Bloats the stomach. Just coffee . . . and maybe a little fruit.' Ross smiled briefly. 'Don't look so worried! You've gotta do what's necessary. Follow Gina, sweetie. I'll see you later.' She waved her plump little hand and turned back to studying the prints of the last gorgeous young thing who'd come into her office. It was the month before the spring/summer collections in Milan, Paris and New York, the busiest time of the year.

Rianne followed Gina, who rushed along at breakneck speed through the converted factory, up stairs, along corridors, into offices where Gina paused to bark orders. By the time they finally arrived in what she assumed was the hairdressers' studio, she was exhausted.

'Gina, darling, what's *this*?'

A man had come up behind Rianne and lifted her mane of hair. She pulled a face. It was horrible the way they stared at her, touched her, ordered her to walk around. She felt like a piece of merchandise. She was pushed into a chair and swivelled round to face a wall of mirrors. The man ran his fingers through her hair, piled it on top of her head, then let it tumble down her back. He stepped back, sizing her up.

'Who is she?' he demanded.

'This is Rianne . . . de Zoete? Did I say that correctly?' Gina looked at her clipboard. Rianne nodded. 'Orders from the boss. Tidy it up but no real cutting – it needs a bit of volume. She's having tests done with Steven at one.' The man nodded, running his professional hands through the golden mass of hair, lifting it a fraction, judging where and how he would cut. He gazed at her reflection in the mirror. Mmm . . . lovely face – perhaps a tad too lovely? But the combination of dark blonde hair, brown eyes and slightly sullen expression was rather refreshing after the decade of smiling blonde blue-eyed perfection they'd just gone through. He liked this one's rather haughty, aloof look. Like she could throw a tantrum or two. He swivelled her round to face him. 'I'm Martin,' he said, holding out his hand. 'From Manchester. That's Manchester, *England*, not Manchester, Illinois. Style director. Follow my directions and we'll get along *famously*, me love. Cross me and you'll – well, just *don't*. Right, we'll get you washed, bit of conditioner . . . Ling!' he screamed, at the top of his voice. A tiny Asian girl appeared from behind the wall of mirrors. 'Shampoo! Conditioner! *Now!* The girl darted forward and wheeled Rianne off. She didn't even have to get out of her chair.

An hour later, her eyebrows stinging, she was turned yet again to face the mirror. The team who had worked on her stood around, admiring their efforts. Her hair had been trimmed and shaped: it now fell away in heavy waves from her forehead, curling just a little around her face, cascading in swirls over her shoulders and down her back. It was thick and silky and moved when she did. She reached up to feel it – Martin slapped her hand. 'No fiddling!' he said sternly.

Rianne studied her face. Her eyebrows had been shaped with a piece of thread. Jenny, the make-up artist, had extracted it from her case and before Rianne could see what she was doing, there was a faint sting as she twisted the cotton round a hair – and yanked. 'Ancient Indian technique – a *bitch* to learn but the best,' Jenny breathed, in her Southern drawl. Twenty minutes later, it was done. The transformation was subtle, but dramatic. Her eyes were wider, clearer, the new, neatly elegant lines of her brows had opened up her face, polished it somehow. She looked older, sleeker – a more sophisticated version of herself.

'Fab, darling,' Martin crooned.

'Didn't really have to do much,' Jenny said, as the three looked at Rianne's reflection. 'Little base, touch of blusher – looks pretty good, dontcha think?' The others nodded. Martin was pleased. He turned round and yelled for yet another assistant. A young man came running forward this time and whisked Rianne off again. 'To the photographer's studio,' he panted, and they ran up another flight of stairs.

'Great! Look at me, keep looking . . . hold it! Fabulous, darling. Now, turn slightly . . . *slightly* . . . That's it, darling, keep turning . . . OK, *hold it*! Great!' Steven murmured to Rianne, as he trained his lens on her. 'Hold that – no, don't smile, raise your head . . . Great!' His old-fashioned camera clicked and wound on, clicked and wound on. It wasn't as embarrassing as she'd feared. Steven gave good directions so he was easy to work with. Thank God he didn't ask her to pout, smile, or laugh the way she'd seen other girls do. That would have been too embarrassing for words. He seemed to like her reserved manner and faint air of boredom.

For the next two hours they worked almost without a break. Profile shots, straight-ons, three-quarter angles, sitting, standing, moving, lost in thought, every pose and every angle he could think of. Finally, just when she had decided she couldn't hold it a minute longer, he announced he was satisfied with the session and she was allowed to relax. Christ, if this was what modelling was all about, she thought, as she took a sip of water, it was a hell of a lot harder than it looked. She watched, bemused, as Steven rushed off with the film to have the contact sheet processed.

The studio door opened. Gina beckoned to her. 'OK, honey. We're all done for today. Get some rest and we'll call you in the morning. Where are you staying?'

'We have a house in New York,' Rianne said, 'I have the address somewhere.' She fished out a card: fifty-nine Mulberry Place. Gina couldn't resist a smile. An elegant townhouse in the heart of Greenwich Village. Modelling, Ross had explained to her whilst Rianne's shots were being done, might actually be something of a step *down* for the young heiress.

'OK. I'll get a car to take you home. Ross has your number, right?' Rianne nodded. 'You'll hear from us tomorrow. And you did good today,' she added unexpectedly.

Rianne wondered what that meant. She picked up her bag and walked back through the building to the front office. The same girls were still waiting, still looking hopeful. She glanced at them pityingly. They had no idea how much work it was.

'Miss de Zoete?' It was the chauffeur. Rianne followed him to the sleek black car waiting at the kerb. She climbed in watching the world outside disappear behind the tinted window as it silently rolled up. She closed her eyes. She hadn't quite recovered from the twenty-two-hour flight from Johannesburg via London, and suddenly her bed in Lisette's townhouse seemed the most natural place in the world to be.

Later that afternoon, Ross stood at her desk admiring the contact sheets and photos that had just been delivered. 'Well, what do you think?' she asked the small group of bookers who'd assembled in her office.

Stefano Pilla, the creative director at Face!, was scrutinising them carefully. 'She's got something,' he said slowly.

Ross nodded. She saw thousands of beautiful girls every year. And, yes, Rianne was beautiful, but there was something just below the surface of her face that was more interesting than beauty. Anger or pain ... or maybe boredom? When she turned it on for the camera – something about the way she lifted her chin, flared her nostrils, the knowing, almost patronising look in her eyes – she was magnetic. The question was, could she turn it on and off? Ross couldn't tell yet.

Stefano straightened up, a slow smile playing at the corners of his mouth. 'Odd. She's that rare thing, you know, all qualities rolled into one – strong, sexy, vulnerable, fragile, yet none. Completely blank. She *could* be fantastic.'

Ross had to think carefully about the next moves. Rianne was good, that much was clear. She was graceful, confident, arrogant – exactly the kind of girl the big fashion houses were always after for their seasonal collections. No doubt she'd earn well on the catwalk.

But there was something else about her ... If they marketed her carefully, placed her with the right clients, advertising the right products, she might just do better in print. The next Diandra, or Tiffany West, models whose earnings outstripped the rest of the pack combined. And, significantly, both of them worked for the competition. Diandra had come in to see Ross two years previously, and the memory still rankled. She had been a skinny, lank-haired teenager – barely sixteen – and Ross had hesitated. Diandra was different from the rest of the girls at that time – maybe a bit too different. She took the photographs home with her over the weekend to mull over. On Monday Ford had signed her. She was now the face of Lancôme and had signed the biggest endorsement deal to date. Ross still lost sleep over that one. She knew from her inside sources that Lovell, the cosmetics giant, were looking for the new face of the eighties. While landing an endorsement deal was about as fabulous – and rare – as winning the pools, it was every model's dream. To be the face of one of the big players, Revlon, Estée Lauder, was a million-dollar contract and one that the best agents were always seeking. A million dollars or more for a couple of weeks' work a year. Not bad. And that excluded what the agency made. She looked again at the shots on the table in front of her. 'OK, let's get her composite cards ready. I'll book Steven again on Friday and we'll do a full day's shooting. Gina, will you set it up?'

Back at Mulberry Place, Rianne opened the front door and put her bag down in the cool hallway. She was hot and sticky from the afternoon's work. Elise, the pretty young housekeeper from Guatemala, was moving around in the kitchen. She hurried upstairs. A cool shower and a nap was what she needed. Elise had made her bed and put a fresh spray of wild roses in the vase beside her bed. Peace. Everything looked so tranquil.

She peeled off her shirt and jeans and walked into the bathroom. She had to hand it to Lisette. Now that KdZK were truly global players in the property market, with Regency Wharf taking shape, they'd invested in houses in London, New York, Los Angeles and Frankfurt so that they could conduct their business in the '*minimum* of comfort', as Lisette described it. Looking around the bathroom, it occurred to Rianne, not for the first time, that Lisette's minimum standards were pretty damned high. The three-storey townhouse in one of the most elegantly fashionable New York neighbourhoods had been renovated at enormous cost – and it showed. The two bedrooms on the top floor, where Rianne had chosen to sleep, shared a pale mint-green bathroom with an enormous porcelain tub and shower. Both rooms were decorated in a rich mixture of deep burgundy red, dark mahogany wood and pale grey. The wonderfully thick carpet was soft enough to sleep on but it was the high, firm beds, with their snowy white Irish linen and grey silk counterpanes, that Rianne loved most. Lisette's New York decorator had done a fantastic job.

She walked through to the shower and stood for ten minutes under its powerful stream, feeling the stickiness of the day disappear. She finished with a blast of tepid water – a trick her mother had shown her when they spent the Christmas holidays in tropical Durban, 'Bathing in tepid water keeps you cool,' she had told the eight-year-old child – and stepped onto the luxuriously fluffy bathroom mat. She patted herself dry and walked back into the bedroom. She glanced at her watch. She had a date – of sorts – that evening and needed a nap before he arrived. She sighed. A date engineered by Lisette was the last thing she wanted. Lisette had somehow found out that Bruce Eastman, the eldest son of Ron and Deirdre, her neighbours in Bryanston, was studying in New York and she'd arranged for the two of them to meet.

'But it's *years* since I've seen him!' Rianne protested. 'I hardly know him.'

'It doesn't matter, *skatjie*. They're neighbours. It must be a bit lonely for him all on his own in New York. It's just an evening, darling.'

'How do *you* know he's lonely?'

'Don't be difficult, Rianne. He'll take you out to dinner. I've given Deirdre a list of good restaurants. Please be nice to him, just this once, hmm?'

'Christ, OK. But only this once. I'm old enough to organise my own social life!'

'I know, darling,' Lisette said, lighting a cigarette. Jesus, Rianne could be difficult. 'How did it go today?'

'I don't know. I don't care.'

'All right. I'll speak to Ross tomorrow. And wear something pretty, won't you? He's *such* a nice boy,' Lisette instructed as she rang off.

Rianne rolled her eyes. Wear something pretty! Honestly, Lisette could be such a nuisance. She glanced at her watch again. At least three hours until he arrived. She knelt down on the floor and rummaged through her luggage. She pulled out a knee-length floral chiffon dress with tiny straps. That would do. It was rather crumpled. She ran downstairs in her towel and handed it to Elise. Since Elise could barely speak English and Rianne couldn't speak a word of Spanish, a quick ironing mime sufficed.

Rianne hurried back upstairs. She pulled out a loose cotton nightdress, tied her hair back and slipped it on. At last. Peace and quiet. She lay down on the crisp white sheets and feather pillows to go over the day's events. It was hard to believe it was only six weeks since she'd left St Anne's. Six weeks since she'd boarded the train at Malvern Link for the last time. She'd cast a single glance back at the imposing skyline of the Malvern Hills and turned away. After two years, she was finally going home.

She'd flown to Johannesburg immediately. That tedious flight from Europe heading west over the Atlantic since none of the African countries over which South African Airways could have passed would grant them airspace. They flew out into the ocean, around the bulge of West Africa, stopped to refuel at the tiny Cape Verde islands just off the coast of Senegal, then down over the Atlantic, across South West Province and finally into Johannesburg. An eighteen-hour flight. It was exhausting. She longed to be home.

But home had changed. It wasn't the same city she'd left, and she wasn't the same girl. She didn't know why, but her friends were different. She found them boring, provincial, narrow-minded. They were obsessed with leaving South Africa – they talked endlessly about who was going overseas, who was planning to go, who had just come back. They wanted to know all about the latest fashions in London, New York, Paris, what people did in London, New York and Paris, where they hung out and who with. They saw South Africa as backward, behind the times, lagging behind Europe and America. They despaired of ever getting to see the latest films, read the latest magazines. They hated being 'stuck here', as they called it. You're lucky to *be* here, Rianne wanted to say angrily, but couldn't. They thought she was the luckiest person alive. To have been 'overseas' was the pinnacle of young adulthood achievement. In their eyes, Rianne was a sophisticated, polished version of themselves, and they couldn't – or wouldn't – see it otherwise. For them Europe – and London in particular – was the centre of the universe, and wasn't it just typical of Rianne de Zoete to pretend it wasn't? For Rianne, half-longing to tell them how lonely and cold it was, how petty and mean the English could be, and what a horrid shock it had been to have to share with native girls, coming home was the biggest anticlimax ever. She couldn't tell them, not only because they wouldn't listen but because her pride wouldn't allow it. So she fell silent and tried instead to summon up the enthusiasm to follow the twists and turns of local plots – who was going out with whom, who'd cheated on whom, who *would* cheat on whom, given half the chance. It was all too boring for words.

She missed Hennie. He was still in the army, at some godforsaken camp near the Zimbabwean border. She called him once, but it was clear, from their rather stilted conversation, that there was now a greater distance than ever between them. His army experiences had changed and hardened him, and he had little time for small talk. She'd hung up, stung to tears. Marika was staying in Cape Town with her new boyfriend from university and wouldn't be back until the end of the summer. Rianne was alone in the house with Poppie. And now that she was eighteen even her relationship with Poppie had changed. She no longer thought of her as her best friend. And, besides, Poppie was distracted by the disappearance of Seni, her eldest son. It seemed he'd left Bryanston one morning to visit a friend in Alexandria, the nearby township, and never returned. There'd been all sorts of police and security officers at the house but no one knew anything. Poppie spent her days alternately crying and cleaning.

At first Rianne escaped the atmosphere by swimming every morning, although it was really too cold, and playing tennis or riding in the afternoons, mostly alone. She felt as ill-equipped in Johannesburg to deal with her future as she had in Malvern. After two years at St Anne's she had almost nothing to show for the enormous effort it had taken her just to stay there. So when Lisette had cornered her one afternoon a month or so after she'd been back, it was with a sneaking sense of relief that Rianne answered her questions and allowed her the satisfaction of plotting the next moves. Which was how she had come to be in the house on Mulberry Place, dropping off to sleep on a humid mid-week afternoon in early August.

When Elise came up fifteen minutes later to return the dress to the señorita, Rianne was fast asleep. Señora Lisette's daughter was *muy, muy guapa*, she thought, as she tiptoed into the room. She should be a model or something. She hung the dress carefully on the wardrobe handles, picked up the clothes that were strewn around the room and tiptoed out. She would wake her in a couple of hours. She knew she had come from somewhere far away. From Africa, Señora Lisette had told her. Funny. Elise thought Africans were black.

'Señorita, señorita . . . *andalé*.' Elise was shaking her gently. There was a young man downstairs, asking for her.

Rianne opened her eyes groggily, struggling to focus.

'*Hay un hombre*, señorita . . . *bajo en la casa*. Meester Eastman.'

Rianne struggled to sit upright. 'Bruce?' she asked, peering at her watch. Shit! It was almost eight o'clock. She'd slept for nearly five hours!

'*Sí, sí!*' Elise said excitedly. 'Meester Bruce Eastman – *quieres usted algo màs?*'

'I don't speak Spanish, Elise,' Rianne said, getting out of bed. How the hell did Lisette manage? She gesticulated: the señor should wait. 'Show him into the drawing room. Tell him to sit and wait.' She motioned with her hands. Elise nodded and hurried downstairs. Amazing what you could communicate without words, Rianne thought, as she walked into the bathroom.

Her dress was hanging up, neatly pressed, and she'd already had a shower. It would take her ten minutes to get ready. She couldn't really remember Bruce Eastman. He was a couple of years older than her and, for some reason, had gone to school in Swaziland or somewhere weird. She couldn't think why. She couldn't remember what he looked like – medium height, medium build, spotty, fair hair? Or was she mixing him up with someone else? She slipped the dress off the hanger and slid it on, inspecting herself in the enormous bathroom mirrors. It would do.

'Oh, hi,' she said casually, when she spotted him standing in the hallway, inspecting the family photographs that Lisette insisted on displaying in each of their homes – rather ridiculously, Rianne thought, especially when they never seemed to spend more than a month of each year in any of them. She'd grown used to the heavy silver frames in Wilton Crescent, Sans Soucis, Avenue Foch and, now, Mulberry Place. Thankfully, there wasn't one of her mother on display. In Wilton Crescent, she and Lisette had waged silent war over the photograph that showed Céline, Marius and the baby Rianne. Every time Rianne came in, she'd shove it in the drawer of the elegant console on which the whole display rested. She wanted no reminders of her mother and father in that place. And every morning, Lisette would instruct Dinah or the current housekeeper to put it out. And then Rianne would put it away again. And so it went.

'Hey, Rianne!' Bruce said, as she came down the stairs. He wasn't the medium-height, medium-build boy-next-door Rianne remembered. Bruce was tall, dark-haired and *very* well built. Rugby-well-built. He was wearing a light blue shirt and tan chinos. And his shirt was out, rather than in. Rather hip, she thought, for a Jo'burg boy. 'How're you?' he asked, kissing her cheek as she joined him in the cool hallway. 'Long time no see.'

'Yeah, fine. You?'

'Oh, good. Hot, you know. Can't get used to the humidity.'

'Yeah, it's pretty bad. Would you like a drink?' Rianne was pleasantly surprised by him.

'Sure.' He followed her into the kitchen where Elise was packing an assortment of delicious meals into Tupperware boxes and putting them into the enormous fridge. Rianne slid past her and took out a couple of beers. They walked through the drawing room to the rear of the house. It was still light, still warm. The patio was softly lit with outdoor citronella candles and standing lamps. A heady mixture of jasmine, frangipani and summer roses wafted in from the garden. Bruce pulled out one of the upholstered teak chairs that Lisette's decorator had spent months searching for.

'Cheers.' They clinked bottles. Rianne pulled out a packet of cigarettes.

'So, what're you doing in New York?' he asked, as she lit one. He'd declined – he'd given up.

'Oh, you know . . . stuff. I'm modelling a bit. I don't know if I really want to do it,' Rianne said.

'Well, you're beautiful enough,' he said, smiling at her. She shrugged, blushing a little. It felt nice to be sitting here with him. She liked the sound of his voice: the flattened South African vowels reminded her of Hennie. 'What about you?'

'I'm at film school. At NYU. It's my second year. It's good. I like it. I like the people.'

'Have you been home recently?' Rianne asked, stubbing out her cigarette. 'Seen Hennie or any of the old gang?'

'Nope.' He was suddenly quiet. There was a silence for a few minutes. Rianne wasn't sure how to fill it. Eventually he broke it. 'Hey, we'd better get going,' he said. 'Your aunt faxed Mom a list of restaurants but I thought you might like to try something new. There's this really great place midtown, Cheech 'n' Chu's. It's a Cuban–Chinese place. Great food. You interested?' Rianne nodded – it sounded fun. They walked back through the house.

'How long have you lived here?' Bruce asked, as she collected a set of keys off the kitchen table.

'Oh, no one lives here. My aunt stays sometimes and I got here on Saturday. She uses it when she's in town, I guess. It's quite new.'

'You mean you keep it running even when no one's here?'

'Yeah . . . I suppose it's better than a hotel.' Rianne pulled a face. 'You know my aunt.'

'Guess so.'

'Shall we take a cab?' Rianne asked, as they walked down the steps to the tree-lined avenue.

'Yeah. It's a bit far to walk – in those pretty shoes,' he added, with a glance at her strappy sandals.

She blushed. It had been a while since she'd been on a date.

They caught a cab easily and, within half an hour, were squeezed into the entrance at Cheech 'n' Chu's, alongside thirty other couples waiting for a table. It was obviously a popular place.

'You barely ate anything,' Bruce complained, as they finished their meal.

'Oh, come on, I'm stuffed! I've got a photo shoot on Friday and I've already been told not to eat bread for breakfast,' Rianne protested. It wasn't strictly true. She'd drunk more than she'd eaten. It was almost midnight and her head was spinning. She giggled.

'Well, I guess I'd better get you home,' Bruce said, sounding reluctant. 'Shall we?' He pushed back his chair and walked round to help her up.

Rianne couldn't remember the last time a young man had done that. 'Where do you live?' she asked him. Not that she'd know: New York was a mystery to her.

'Other side of the river in Brooklyn.'

'Where's that?'

'Sort of south – you cross the Brooklyn Bridge. I don't think you can see it from your neighbourhood but maybe some other time.' Rianne's stomach fluttered. Some other time! Did that mean . . . ? 'When do you go back?' he asked, as if reading her mind.

'I don't know. Depends what happens.'

'Are you always this . . . ambivalent?' Bruce asked, tucking her arm firmly into his as they left the restaurant. Rianne's steps were not the steadiest.

'What d'you mean?' She wasn't sure what it meant.

'You don't seem to care what you do. You're not working to any schedule, not even your own.'

'Well, not really. I mean, it doesn't matter what I do. I can do anything or nothing.'

'Not true.' Bruce was frowning. She struggled to follow what he was saying but her head felt incredibly thick. He flagged down a cab and they both got into the back. She leaned into his shirt as he gave the driver directions and felt his arm tighten round her shoulders. He smelled good. She closed her eyes.

The cab sped silently downtown, bumping and flying over the appalling New York roads. She didn't mind. Every jolt sent her snuggling into Bruce's chest and she liked the warm, solid feel of him. Was that a kiss he had planted on top of her head?

'Hey, sleepyhead,' he whispered, nudging her. 'You're home.'

Rianne opened her eyes. Despite the nap, she was

exhausted. And drunk. He kept the cab waiting and helped her up the stairs. Before she could scrabble in her bag for the keys, Elise opened the door and helped her in.

'*Gracias*, Meester Eastman.' She smiled at Bruce as she relieved Rianne of her bag and keys. '*Gracias. Valle.*'

'Night, Rianne,' Bruce said softly. 'See you around.' He turned and ran quickly down the steps. She sleepwalked her way upstairs. See you around. She hoped he meant it.

21

In London, in the splendid comfort of yet another of Lisette's homes, Gabby was stretched out on the sofa in the living room. She fished for the remote control. It was almost midnight. She was staying there over the summer, working to earn some money before going up to Oxford in October. She'd taken Oxbridge entrance a term early, under Miss Featherstone's gentle encouragement, and to no one's surprise but her own she'd gained a Commoner's place to read English – which she'd always longed to do. And after his own gap year Nael was going to Christ's, Cambridge, reading what he'd always longed to do, PPE. She'd long ago forgotten the silly 'thing' she'd had about Nael: he was her best friend now, which he always should have been. She doubted he'd even noticed her three months of agony after That Ball. And he'd never spoken to Rianne again. Now, despite her grandmother's promise of help, she needed to earn some pocket money before beginning life as an impoverished student. Staying at Wilton Crescent, rent-free, was an absolute blessing.

She had found a job at the Dillon's bookstore on Gower Street and spent her days lugging books around the five-storey shop. It was full of students, about-to-be students, wish-they-were students and wish-they-could-have-been students. There were more of them crammed into the bookshop than across the road at UCL. In the strange code of public-school young men and women, working in a bookstore wasn't really *working*. It was more like a paid hobby, which made it OK. Rianne's invitation to stay at Wilton Crescent couldn't have come at a better time. Gabby was thrilled to be living in London by herself, with Charmaine and Nathalie for company. It was a pity Rianne wasn't there: in the last year, they'd grown closer – or as near as it was possible for Rianne to be close to anyone – and she missed her. But her days began so early – at nine o'clock on the dot, which meant getting up at seven – and she rarely finished before eight in the evening. She didn't really have time to miss anyone.

But, still, it was a difficult time: she was in a strange, suspended state between two halves of her life. There was the old St Anne's part – and, actually, working at Dillon's was like being back at St Anne's, same people, same jokes, same names – and then there was the part that was yet to come: university and all that that would bring. She was both terrified and impatient. It was unsettling. She'd begun eating again, partly in response to the stress of the changes in her life and partly out of hunger – lifting books, running up and down the stairs to find customer orders, stacking the shelves were all rather taxing. So if she found herself buying not one but *two* sandwiches at lunch-time, not one but *two* after-sandwich 'treats' – a Mars Bar, a packet of crisps – well, she'd earned them. She'd work it off. Once she started at Magdalen it would be easy to stick to a routine. Or so she told herself as she reached for the last digestive on the coffee table.

In the unglamorous location of Stoke Newington, north London, Charmaine was having the time of her life. She wasn't working – *God*, no! – and, thank God, she wasn't at home, living under her mother's nervously watchful eye. She was independent – well, almost: Mary's monthly allowance hardly seemed worth mentioning, although without it she had to admit, she'd have been scuppered. She'd left St Anne's without a single – not *one*! – qualification to her name. 'Not even a certificate in *typing*! How could you fail *typing*, Charmaine?' Mary Hunter had looked at her daughter in despair. Charmaine bit her lip. Typing was difficult. 'What on earth are you going to do now?'

Charmaine smiled. That was easy. 'I'm moving in with Baz,' Charmaine announced. Mary Hunter rolled her eyes. *Baz!* She despised Charmaine's latest beau, a loafer of the highest order . . . even his name . . . Baz? What kind of a name was Baz?

'Bartholomew, Mummy, but no one calls him that. Would *you*?'

'It's not the point, Charmaine. What does he do?'

'He doesn't "do" anything, Mummy. People don't always have to *do* something, you know.' Charmaine lit a cigarette and blew a cloud of smoke in her mother's direction.

Mary waved it away crossly. 'And what would *you* know about that, young lady?' she snapped.

'Anyhow, he's already got a place. In Stoke Newington. We're going to share it with one of his friends.'

'Stoke *Newington*?' Mary was almost in tears. 'It's not even in London!'

'Don't be so old-fashioned, Mummy. It's very fashionable, you know.'

'Oh, please! It's dangerous, Charmaine. There's all *sorts* of people living up there. Why can't you stay at home and just *visit* him?'

'Because.' Charmaine was unmoved. She had only just escaped the narrow confines of St Anne's and was in no hurry to replace them with her mother's Pimlico flat, even if it was rather more comfortable.

The following Saturday, to Mary's dismay, Baz came to pick her up. Two suitcases and a fresh set of tears later, she was gone. She'd be back at weekends – '*Promise!*' – she called from the car window, as they began the drive back to north London. North London? Mary scarcely knew where it was. She wrapped her cardigan around her and walked heavily back into the quiet flat. This wasn't how she'd planned Charmaine's homecoming. She missed her already.

By the time they pulled into Windus Road, Charmaine was in seventh heaven. Baz shared the tiny semi-detached house with Richard, a taciturn New Zealander who was teaching in a local primary school. There was a large living room with barely any furniture but an impressive record-player and several speakers, a small, cosy kitchen with an oven and little else. And upstairs, a bathroom and two bedrooms, one of which was where she and Baz spent most of their time.

At first she'd thrown herself into the role of the 'woman' in the house. Richard was less than amused to come home from work to Charmaine's ill-fated attempts at home-making – burnt lasagne one night, soggy rice and watery vegetables the next. When she nearly set the kitchen on fire trying to fry sausages Richard suggested they might share the cooking duties. 'You know, set up a rota?' he suggested.

Whatever. Baz had shrugged, concentrating on the far more important task at hand: rolling a spliff. Charmaine had discovered to her delight that smoking a joint in the evenings produced two phenomena, closely related. Spliffs took the edge off her appetite – she lost weight – and made her horny. Baz was delighted with the latter discovery, which was why rolling them had become something of a nightly ritual. After a month of living with two men, St Anne's – where she'd spent the better part of her childhood – seemed like another planet. Which, in many ways, it was.

Nathalie was also doing nothing, but she was fretting about it. On the other side of town, closer to Gabby and Mary Hunter and in an infinitely preferable postcode, Nathalie surveyed the empty flat with a mixture of trepidation, guilt and pleasure. Clive had bought her and Philippe – who had just started working for Bloomberg's – a two-bedroomed flat in the almost-trendy part of Notting Hill. It was on Elgin Crescent, a stone's throw from the Portobello market and the flower shop, in an elegant-but-faded period house and it was perfect.

After the terrible events with Sacha and Cordelia the previous year and Philippe's desire to end his friendship, Nathalie and her brother had grown close. Neither wanted to return for any length of time to Rosebud Cottage and its strained atmosphere. They had both jumped at Clive's unbelievably generous offer. Nathalie didn't want to go to university – at least, not yet. She wasn't quite sure what she wanted to do – something in fashion, she thought, or maybe retail. She had a good eye for detail, fabric, furniture, loved displays, window-dressing, that sort of thing.

After the initial excitement of moving into Elgin Crescent and the task of stripping, painting and decorating the place on their rather tight budget had been completed, she was restless. Philippe had his friends and his job. He was out a lot – and he had a new girlfriend. A month out of school, Nathalie had neither work nor a boyfriend. 'It'll come,' Philippe had explained to her patiently. 'Took me a year to find my feet. London's pretty hard sometimes.' Nathalie knew he was right. In time, she'd find herself here, just as she'd done at St Anne's. But she hoped it would be soon.

22

It was the end of August. The thick, close heat of summer had given way to frequent thunderstorms, which lasted only an hour or so but cleared the air. The humidity was finally beginning to break. For Rianne, it was a blessing. When she'd first arrived in New York at the end of July, she'd had no idea how long she would be staying. Now, after the remarkable events of the past three weeks, it seemed as though she'd be here for a while.

Not that everything was great. Bruce Eastman had been a major disappointment. They'd gone out again, once, about a week after their first date, but inexplicably he'd stopped calling. She had no idea why. Their second date had been great fun. They'd gone to see a film – she couldn't remember the title, something to do with basketball – they'd had coffee near the agency and she'd shown Bruce where she spent most days working.

They'd walked back along Broadway and he'd held her hand and it seemed so easy and, well, really nice. He'd promised to call her again in a couple of days – he had a lot of work to do, some documentary he was working on, and then nothing. She was surprised to find that the memory of Nael's behaviour still hurt. She wondered if it was always going to be like this. Hennie, Nael, Bruce: they had come after her and done their best to impress her, but when she responded they disappeared.

'What do you think?' Ross asked her as her comp cards were spread across the table. Rianne looked at them, unable to believe that the cool, arrogantly aloof face was hers. She picked up one of the cards. Eight shots in all, and on the back, her least favourite, the full body shot. Not that there was anything wrong with her body, it was just the concept. She still winced when she remembered the shoot. Ross had been insistent: Rianne was South African with a particular angle – diamonds, gold, wealth. She wanted a shot that reflected it. Gina disagreed: 'She's not black. It's ridiculous. It won't wash.'

'I'm not saying we dress her up as *black*, Gina, don't be silly. I'm saying use your imagination and create something that links her to Africa. It's her home too, after all. I don't know – animal prints, gold, bold patterns, that sort of thing. Here, Stefano, *you* think of something. That's why I pay you a damned fortune.'

Stefano rolled his eyes. Exotic, that was it: Rianne had that tawny, feline look. With the right make-up and lighting, she could look exotic, not ethnic but exotic, he told them. With her unusual name and the fact that they could add 'South African' to her vital-stats list, it might bring another dimension to her appeal.

Two hours later, covered in a light gold body make-up, which made her skin shimmer, and heavy black eye make-up, she looked stunning. 'A white Sheba.' Stefano grinned, pleased with the result.

Rianne grimaced. She hated the references to South Africa. Why couldn't they see she was just like the rest of them? Ever since she'd left Johannesburg her nationality had followed her around like a dead weight. She didn't want to have to think about it.

'You're flying to Paris on Monday, Rianne,' Ross said, as Rianne walked into her office on Friday morning. 'We're sending you on your first "go-and-see" at Yves Saint Laurent. They're looking for a fittings model but we think they'll like you and confirm you for the show. We'll put you on the morning flight, arrange the hotel, get someone to pick you up—'

'I don't need a hotel. We have an apartment in Paris,' Rianne interrupted. She was relieved to be leaving New York. She hated being in the house at Mulberry Place and her stomach lurching every time the phone rang.

Ross laughed shortly. Of course. Homes all over the world. She kept forgetting. 'Of course. Well, give Gina the address so that she can send the car round for you on Tuesday morning. Now, our Paris booker is Anne Clochard. Here's her number. After the fitting, call her. You got that? Make sure you get your voucher signed and let her know how it went.'

*

'It's always a bit nerve-racking,' Gina said, taking a sip of espresso. She and Rianne were having breakfast in Joel's, the popular diner-restaurant across the street from Face!. At least, Gina was having breakfast: Rianne was having lemon-scented water and three mango slices. 'Call your parents – er, your aunt the night before for a bit of a pep talk. It really helps, especially when it's your first job. Don't call your friends. They'll just make you more excited and you need to be calm.'

'You don't know my aunt,' Rianne said drily.

'Well, try to relax as much as you can. Anneline can organise a massage or something if you're feeling really stressed in the morning. It's important to come across as confident and professional. I mean, I know you always look incredibly confident but just watch out for nerves. You know Diandra? First time she went on a go-and-see at Dior, she threw up all over the seamstress. She nearly *died*.'

Rianne was unimpressed. Nervous? Not her. She was made of sterner stuff.

On Tuesday morning, however, standing in front of the YSL mansion on rue Rambuteau, she wasn't quite so sure. She looked up at the impressive stone façade and swallowed. It looked rather forbidding. She pressed the discreet gold buzzer and waited. A second later the wrought-iron gates opened with a little click and she went into the courtyard. Another buzzer sounded to her left. She could see a glass-fronted doorway and, beyond that, what looked like a reception area. She crossed the cobblestones and pushed open the door. It led into a magnificent white marble entrance hall, with an enormous theatrical staircase sweeping up to the floor above, gold balustrades, a dark mahogany reception desk and the requisite intimidating receptionist.

'*Bonjour*,' she said nervously. The woman looked her up and down. Gina's instructions had been clear: a go-and-see uniform – slim black Capri pants and a slim-fitting black short-sleeved shirt. 'Black always makes you look more professional,' she advised. Rianne's hair was tied back and she carried the trademark enormous black leather tote in which everything she could possibly need was stored.

'*Oui*?'

'Um . . . a fitting? You . . . I have an appointment?'

'Ah. *Suivez-moi*.' The receptionist led her briskly across the hallway to a side room.

Rianne's eyes widened, and she looked around for a seat. She'd never been in the company of quite so many beautiful girls. There were icy blondes, brunettes, one or two redheads, a coal-black girl with a shaved head, two girls – twins? – the colour of coffee with almost white-blonde ringlets, an Asian girl with long blue-black hair. She swallowed. What the hell was she doing here?

'*Mettez ça*.' The receptionist handed her a neatly folded housecoat, a pair of stockings and a pair of high-heeled shoes. She was told to get dressed right there, *sans brassière*, in front of everyone, and wait until she was called. The receptionist turned and clacked her way across the floor. Rianne looked around her. Take off her bra in front of all those girls? But many of them were stripping to their underwear – and less – quite unselfconsciously. She had no choice but to follow. Everyone was studiously ignoring everyone else. She took off her clothes, including the little white lace bra, and stepped into the white housecoat dress. She smoothed on the stockings and tried on the shoes. Everything fitted perfectly. She sat down, palms sweating, and tried not to look at the specimens of female perfection all around her. She understood why Ross and Gina thought eighteen might be a little old to start. Some of the girls in the room couldn't have been a day over fourteen! She'd forgotten to bring a book with her. Another of Gina's must-haves.

Half an hour passed. Then another. Every so often, the receptionist would summon one of the girls. No one talked. Some of the more experienced ones simply sat in their white housecoats, reading or filing their nails, rifling through magazines. One girl was knitting! The younger ones looked slyly at each other, comparing legs, breasts, buttocks, skin, hair. It was a veritable cattle-market. An hour passed. And another. Rianne's stomach whined. She took a swig of bottled water. Finally, just when she was on the verge of standing up, stripping off the ridiculous nurse's uniform and walking out, the receptionist called her name.

An exceptionally handsome young male assistant led her upstairs to the second floor, which, in stark contrast to the studied air of indifference below, was a hive of activity. Assistants rushed around trailing armloads of fabric, hats, shoes. There were several dressmakers' dummies, and seamstresses were frantically pinning and tucking, measuring and cutting. Rianne had never seen anything like it. She was led through the atelier into a quiet side room. The assistant closed the door and, suddenly, Rianne was alone with the great man. He said nothing, simply indicated with a wave of his fingers that she should walk up and down in front of him. He motioned her to continue as he moved with her, his trademark black-framed glasses glinting as he surveyed her from almost every angle. Five minutes later, he murmured, 'Thank you,' and the go-and-see was over. Rianne had no idea what he thought. The door opened and the gorgeous male assistant escorted her out. That was it.

'Wait here,' the assistant said, and disappeared. Fifteen minutes later, an elderly seamstress and her assistant appeared, carrying a number of dummy outfits in white muslin. The woman asked Rianne to take off her clothes and they began to pin a facsimile of a long, strapless evening gown onto her. The copy would be pinned to fit exactly, she told Rianne, then used as the pattern for the garment. Rianne was puzzled – did that mean she'd got the job? The woman shrugged: she'd been told to measure her up, that was all she knew. They worked quickly. Rianne was measured for six different outfits – the whole thing took almost two hours. Finally, just before four o'clock when she thought she'd faint with hunger and fatigue, she was done. She got dressed for the last time, dropped off her housecoat, stockings and shoes, and was asked to bring her voucher to Reception. They would contact Madame Clochard about the show. It was all rather bewildering.

She walked out into the bright Paris sunshine, crossed the road, went into the nearest café and ordered a hamburger with a glass of wine. She was ravenous. She sat outside, wondering if she'd made the right decision. So far, a modelling career seemed to involve standing around all day being eyed up jealously by the competition and having pins stuck into her. It was a far cry from the glamorous world she'd imagined when Lisette first made the suggestion. She was even wondering whether or not to have crêpes Suzette for dessert. Bugger them, she thought, and ordered another glass of wine. She didn't care if she wasn't chosen.

To Gabby, listening eagerly on the phone the following evening, Rianne's life seemed to glide from one exciting event to the next. Somehow it wasn't surprising. When you were rich, beautiful *and* bored, things were guaranteed to happen. When you were none of those things, they didn't. Simple as that. She wished her life were even a *hundredth* as interesting. Apart from the flutter she felt in her stomach every time she thought about Magdalen College and how her life would be once she got there, there was little to distract her from the daily routine of trudging to and from Tottenham Court Road. In fact, the only thing that broke the monotony was meeting Nael in one of the Covent Garden cafés and occasionally seeing a film with him.

'When d'you think you'll be in London again?' Gabby asked her, wielding the remote control like a weapon. There was nothing on TV.

'I don't know. I've got another fitting tomorrow morning, then it's back to New York. It's hard work, you know.'

'You don't say,' Gabby said, half laughing. 'I'd give my back teeth—'

'You wouldn't, believe me. You just wait around all the

time. It's incredible. You wait four hours for something that's over in ten minutes.'

'Well, it sounds more glam than lugging *The History of the World in Ten and a Half Chapters* around.' Gabby was unsympathetic. 'I hope you get here before I leave. Oh, God, did you hear about Charmaine?' she asked, clapping her hand to her forehead.

'No. What's happened?'

'You know she's with that awful guy, Baz? Well, he wants them to go to LA – he's going to join a band or something. Charmaine's thinking about going with him. She's *mad*! What'll she do out there? Can you imagine?'

Rianne was astonished. Silly, love-struck Charmaine running off to LA? She'd thought *she* was the adventurous one. Of them all, it hadn't been Charmaine she'd pictured getting up and doing something out of the ordinary.

As Gabby filled her in on what had been happening to everyone, she realised that she missed them. That, too, was a surprise.

Slowly, the weekend rolled around. Gina had flown to Paris to be with Rianne on her first major assignment. They were sitting in a café near Bastille métro station, Gina's favourite area. She was attempting to teach Rianne a thing or two about the industry to which she now belonged. Rianne was having difficulty staying awake. It was nine in the morning, far too early for her.

In the ready-to-wear – *prêt-à-porter*, to Europeans – category, she explained to the yawning girl, there were only three places that counted: Milan, Paris and New York. The collections took place twice a year, in early September/ October and again in February/March. The shows ran on tight schedules – a week at the beginning of September for the Milan-based designers, then, a fortnight later, the Paris shows with the Parisian designers, and finally, towards the middle of October, the Americans close the season in New York. 'Are you listening, Rianne?' Gina asked. Rianne nodded sleepily. 'Then stop yawning,' Gina told her sternly. She'd seen too many beautiful girls come into the business and crash straight out of it. To stay in, you needed more than looks – brains and attention to detail helped.

An hour later, Rianne was eyeing the half-eaten croissant that lay on Gina's plate. She was *starving*. 'It's not about the mass-market in Paris,' Gina finished, munching away, 'it's about luxury. Just think of the names – Chanel, Yves Saint Laurent, Dior, Givenchy. Paris probably has the highest concentration of magazines, fashion editors, cosmetics companies and, of course, designers – all of whom are damn picky about the girls they use. But once you've made it onto the Paris runways, everything else pretty much falls into place. So, you're in a really good position, honey. If you can pull it off on Monday, New York is the next stop. And that's where the big bucks are made, darling. It's that simple. You build your name in Europe, and *then* you come back to the States and cash in. New York's where you earn the most for advertising, plus you get the longest contracts. And, of course, if you're *really* lucky, you get an endorsement. But we'll talk about those another time.' Rianne lit a cigarette. Jesus, it was a lot to take in. And she still hadn't had breakfast.

23

'Hey Gabs, sorry I'm late.' Nael came walking into the café. He bent down to kiss her, then sat down, dropping his bag of books on the floor. She peeked at the titles. Philosophy. Politics. That was all he ever read.

'How's work?' he asked, signalled to a waitress and ordered a beer. He frowned at Gabby's drink – a glass of water with what looked like soggy lemons floating in it.

She hesitated, unsure whether to tell him about Rianne's exciting news. She decided against it. Somehow they had agreed without saying anything that they wouldn't talk about her. 'Crap,' she said cheerfully. 'Customers are so rude most of the time. They're lazy too. They come into the shop, read the store directions and can't be bothered to climb the stairs. So they ask *me* to get their books for them – and there's no lift! How's yours?'

Nael grimaced. He'd found what he called the most boring job on the planet, processing film at Boots. He complained that the smell of chemicals never left his hair or his clothes. Gabby nodded sympathetically. Only days really, for both of them. She was going to Hereford to see her grandmother, and then it was the beginning of term. She got butterflies in her stomach every time she imagined herself walking through the lush quadrant to her new rooms.

'Mine take the most God-awful pictures, then try to blame us for developing them,' Nael went on. 'Anyhow, I don't want to talk about work. When are you going up?'

Gabby thrilled to the words. Going up. Going up to Oxford.

'Next week. You?'

'Same. My dad's picking me up from Ben's.' Nael was staying in Earls Court with his cousin.

'What about your mum? Won't she come too?'

'No.' Nael was suddenly curt.

Gabby looked at him. In all the time she'd known Nael, he'd never talked about his mother. She heard plenty about his father, a Harley Street doctor, and his two sisters – even his cousin. But nothing about his mother.

'What d'you fancy seeing?' He changed the subject quickly.

They'd arranged to see a film together. Something foreign, with subtitles, Gabby had requested. Foreign films always made her feel so grown-up. He pulled a rather battered *Evening Standard* out of his bag. They looked at the offerings.

'*Sophie's Choice*?' Gabby asked. It wasn't foreign, but it was certainly grown-up.

'Only if you promise not to cry,' Nael said sternly. They'd seen *E.T.* together at the beginning of the summer and Gabby'd cried all the way through the last fifteen minutes.

'I won't. I promise.' She laughed.

'You said that last time and you ruined my hanky. OK, *Sophie's Choice*. What time's it showing?'

'Twenty minutes. We'd better get a move on.' Gabby made a face as she drained her *citron pressé*. It had *sounded* glamorous, but in reality it was an expensive glass of bitter water. Probably tap, too. They got up to leave.

In Paris, backstage at YSL, Rianne was waiting for the make-up team to arrive. The rehearsal for the show had taken place early in the morning and she'd arrived even earlier: she hadn't wanted to be late on her first day so she'd ordered a car to pick her up from Avenue Foch at seven thirty. Her fitting wasn't until nine and, to her irritation, the address turned out to be a five-minute ride from the apartment. Thank God she'd remembered to bring a book this time. She pulled it out of her bag and settled down in a corner of the large hall to read until the first members of the team arrived.

By eight thirty, the backstage area was abuzz. Rianne found that watching what was going on around her was ten times more interesting than what was happening in her book. She'd never seen anything like it. The models started arriving, each one more cranky and petulant than the last. Even she, who was no lightweight when it came to bad behaviour, was shocked. Some refused point blank to try on the outfits until someone had gone out and bought them a cappuccino, a packet of cigarettes, headache tablets, some flowers for the dressing-table, *chérie*. One stunning redhead demanded that she be given somewhere private to change –

the hall was too stuffy, there were too many people, too many photographers, too much light.

The show team rushed around placating their fragile charges, soothing this one, gently chiding that one, sending some poor gofer out for coffee, cigarettes, tablets. There were people around whose sole job, it seemed, was to stroke their over-inflated egos.

Rianne couldn't believe her eyes. And she'd thought she was spoilt! The rehearsal ought to have been straightforward: try on the clothes, run through the order, make sure the new models fitted in well with the regulars. Instead, it degenerated into a kind of circus where no one spoke to anyone, some girls walked out half-way through, claiming they knew everything they had to know, and others looked as though they were still asleep. When one of the girls stumbled in front of Rianne as she was about to step onto the catwalk, Rianne realised she was stoned. She suppressed the urge to giggle.

It was her turn. She walked a little unsteadily down the catwalk, focusing as she'd done in ballet classes on a spot in the distance, swinging her hips provocatively as she'd seen the girls before her do. Simple. She could see Gina sitting at the back of the hall, watching her. She pivoted at the end, stopped with one leg placed in front of the other, then swung round fluidly. Easy. She sashayed her way back to the curtain, paused one last time, then disappeared. No one looked at her as she walked down the steps.

Five girls, wearing nothing but their underwear, some with rollers in their hair, were huddled together in a corner. She wondered what they were doing. Then she saw that they were downing shots of whisky and smoking joints. At ten o'clock in the morning. She looked the other way.

Finally, almost an hour later, it was over. No one had spoken to her apart from the controller, the man who lined the girls up backstage and made sure they went out in order. And even he had only barked solitary commands. She looked at Mora, girl of the moment, whose face was in every magazine and on every billboard. Even half dressed she looked smart and professional. Gina had told Rianne not to expect the big names at the rehearsal. Really famous models, she said, rarely attended rehearsals. They were professionals: they were expected to show up and know what to do. Mora was the exception. She attended every rehearsal, every run-through, every meeting. More professional than the professionals, she liked to have her finger on the pulse of every aspect of the business.

Laden with bags, having dashed out for a quick shop after the morning's rehearsals, Rianne only just got back in time. She'd forgotten what rush-hour Paris was like. The taxi driver dropped her as close as he could get to the entrance of the disused gymnasium where YSL was showing his spring/summer collections. Rianne paid and struggled out.

Inside, everything was transformed. The ugly concrete interior had been swathed in cream and white toile, and over five hundred seats were lined up neatly on either side of the catwalk. Enormous potted plants had been arriving all afternoon and formed a kind of indoor hedge at the back of the hall, obscuring the ugly windows and bare concrete walls. The lighting was dramatic: a single row of spotlights was trained on the catwalk and the rest of the room was in semi-darkness. Loud disco music was pumping from the enormous speakers dotted around the hall – the atmosphere was more nightclub than fashion show.

'Rianne!' someone called.

It was her make-up artist – Rianne couldn't remember her name. They'd met only briefly that morning. 'Over here. Come on, we need to get started.'

She joined a row of models sitting in directors' chairs. She recognised some from the morning's rehearsal – several looked rather the worse for wear – but no one said hello. It was horribly like being back at St Anne's. Her stomach tightened.

'OK.' The make-up artist pulled over a chair and turned

Rianne to face the mirror. She studied the sketches in front of her. Rianne was modelling six evening gowns – a richly coloured collection, with a shimmering emerald silk sheath, a white body-hugging jersey-knit in the sheerest, lightest wool, and a layered platinum, silver and dark grey cocktail dress among them, plus absurdly high, strappy heels. Rianne swallowed. She needed more practice in the shoes before she stepped onto the catwalk. Two girls went to work on her hair while Mina – that was her name – did her face.

All around her, the pace was picking up. A champagne and buffet table had been laid out behind them and everyone was helping themselves, except the models who smoked cigarette after cigarette until the air backstage was thick with fumes. The make-up teams were in a state of near-panic, powdering, polishing, pencilling in lips, brows, beauty spots. The hair crew darted about, looking for a hairdryer, a brush, a comb.

Rianne was pinched, pulled, teased and twisted into shape. Her hair was parted and twisted until it fell in heavy ringlets around her face and down her back. Her eyes were outlined in smoky black kohl and her lashes tipped at the ends with gold mascara. Her lips were a deep red, the liner drawn lightly around the outside, making them appear even fuller.

At last the make-up artist stepped back to admire her work. A light dusting of a gold powder across her cheeks and Rianne was ready. Her reflection stared back at her from the mirror: it was almost impossible to recognise herself under the serene, beautiful mask. Her dresser helped her into the first outfit – the emerald silk gown, held up by tiny diamond-encrusted straps and flowing in slinky curls around her legs. She wasn't wearing anything under it, not even stockings. The silk clung to her like a second skin. She stepped into the high heels and the dresser fastened the tiny straps.

'*Che bella!*' the Italian dresser cried, and Rianne walked

unsteadily to join the queue of girls waiting behind the curtain. She could hear the music thumping and the applause as Mora hit the runway first, all golden-brown legs, orange silk and spectacular heels. One by one, the models disappeared through the curtain to roars of applause. Rianne could barely breathe she was so nervous. The girl in front of her vanished through the curtains. Someone gave her a shove and she stepped out blindly into the spotlight. She was dimly aware of a hundred flashbulbs exploding, a roar of applause and the beat of the music – and then, suddenly, she was backstage again, being tugged along impatiently by her dresser. Before she had time to think about how she felt, she was off again, one foot in front of the other, swaying, turning, hand on hip, turning again. She felt as though she'd been doing it all her life.

An hour and a half and five garment changes later, she was dripping with sweat, despite the cold, and surrounded by screaming models, excited bookers, photographers and hangers-on. Backstage, it was pandemonium. Mora had just come through the curtains with Yves, and the rest of the models crowded around him, holding glasses of champagne and smiling widely for the cameras. No one paid her any attention. She was unsure what to do. She wanted to get out of her last outfit, a fantastic concoction of grey lace, taffeta and white raw silk, but her dresser had disappeared and she needed help to unhook it. She bit her lip. None of the other girls looked even remotely approachable.

She spotted a female photographer and motioned to her – can you help me? The girl walked over. Just as she had undone the hooks Rianne overheard another model hiss to her companion, 'Will you *look* at that new girl? She's been here barely five minutes and she's already sucking up to the press!' Rianne was outraged. *Bitches!* She couldn't run after them holding on to her dress so she had to settle for shooting a look of hatred at them.

She was wrong – it was worse than St Anne's, much worse.

'Rianne! Over here!' she heard Gina shout over the din. 'Well *done*,' she said, pushing her way through the crowd. 'That was great. You *looked* great. *Gorgeous* clothes. To *die* for!' She was wearing a fitted burgundy-velvet coat with pearl buttons and a high neck. Her short black hair was swept off her face and she wore a pair of heavy antique-looking glass and ruby earrings – completely different from her smart but pared-down black work suits and spiky hair. 'Come on, get changed. We're going to Byblos – there's the after-show party. Did you get something to wear?'

'Yes.'

'Then get dressed and let's get out of here. I wanna introduce you to some people and I can't do it with you half-naked. *Move* it, girl!' She grinned, and turned to talk to someone else.

Rianne took a quick look around her at the girls slipping casually in and out of outfits, and did the same.

24

Nathalie looked in despair at the boxes stacked to the ceiling. It was her first week at TopGirl on Oxford Street and already she was feeling like the store skivvy. Management, for reasons known only to themselves, had suddenly insisted on relabelling all their lingerie, including their bras, in metric. Julie, Nathalie's buxom supervisor – although in truth she hardly looked older than Nathalie – gave the orders. In her thick Geordie accent, she told Nathalie where to find the stock, still in boxes, and where to find the new labels. She was to go through every single hanger, carefully peel off the old designations – 34B, 36A, 38C and so on – and replace them with the new labels: 95D, 105C, 100B. Same for the panties.

Nathalie stared at her. Had she gone mad? 'This is silly,'

she protested, as Julie showed her to the warehouse at the back of the store. 'No one's going to understand the sizes. I'll just spend all day explaining that 95C is the same as 36C. It'll be like the fishmongers all over again – little old ladies wanting a pound of haddock and getting it wrong.'

Julie looked at her crossly. Stuck-up, rich little slip of a girl. Who was she to question management decisions? She'd only been here a day!

'Well, s'gotta be done, thass all I know,' she said frostily. 'An' we need it done quick, like. Mr Byrd's comin' in on Monday.' She marched out, her nose stuck firmly in the air.

Nathalie sighed. She cast a quick eye over the stacks of boxes. Twenty, maybe thirty, perhaps twenty bras to a box . . . Work it out . . . Four hundred labels to peel and stick. Ugh! It would take her *days*. She looked around for the little ladder she'd seen the day before. She would need it to get to the boxes on top.

By lunch-time, the sheer boredom of the job had nearly killed her. It was unending. Slit open the box with a penknife, lift out the plastic packet inside. Open that and stack the little hangers in front of her. Pull off the labels, replace them with new ones, pack the hangers back into the box, fold the plastic cover, seal it. Open the next. This was not what she'd imagined a career in fashion retail to be: there was nothing glamorous about being stuck in a hot warehouse with thirty cardboard boxes. She slit the next box viciously.

She'd spoken to Gabby the night before and listened in envious disbelief to her news about Rianne. Now *that* was glamour. Although she agreed with Gabby that if you were born with a silver spoon in your mouth, it rarely fell out, it was still a bit galling to hear. Nathalie had worked so much harder in the last six months at St Anne's than Rianne – who had barely passed French *and* it was her mother tongue! – and here she was, with three A levels under her belt and a flat in Notting Hill, sticking labels on bras. Rianne had waltzed straight onto the catwalk.

Later that evening, after she'd come back to an empty flat with no food in the fridge and no sign of Philippe, she phoned Charmaine. Gabby was at the cinema with Nael. 'It's not fair,' Charmaine agreed. She was holding the phone with one hand while she painted her toes with the other. Since Baz had announced casually that they 'might go somewhere . . . dunno . . . LA or something', she had been in a frenzy of excitement. 'Anyway, it was probably her aunt or someone who opened the door for her. You know what modelling's like – you need to know someone.'

It was probably true, Nathalie thought. Although Rianne was awfully pretty.

'Anyhow, enough of Rianne, what about *me*? What should I do about Baz?' Charmaine asked happily.

Baz was her favourite topic of conversation, and Nathalie sometimes worried about her. The speed with which Charmaine moved from one boyfriend to the next was alarming, as was the extent to which her personality changed each time she moved. With Thierry Pasquier she'd been sassy, confident, flirty. It was clear to everyone that he adored her. But for some reason, Charmaine attached herself to boys who didn't want or need her attachment . . . and then she spent all her time trying to win it. Thierry had been far too easy . . . far too available. She tired of him almost immediately. She had dumped him, rather publicly, in Serendipity's. Then it was *that* holiday in Martinique – much as it pained Nathalie to think about it – and Hennie. Overnight Charmaine had become edgy, unsure of herself. She had simpered and giggled, she hung on his every word. Hennie had had her at his beck and call. After their return to St Anne's, Charmaine had moped around for months. Hennie hardly ever wrote to her, never called, and on the rare occasion when he did send a card, she'd driven everyone mad, poring over the scrappy sentences for evidence of his 'love'. Even Rianne had been forced to admit her cousin was a cad. Nathalie prayed that she'd move on to someone else before long. Which, of course, she did.

Next in line was Jonathan Hamilton-Butler, one of the 'posh boys' at the Boys' College. With him, Charmaine was desperate to appear sophisticated, worldly, loaded – which, of course, she wasn't. Everyone had suffered through yet another character transformation and in the end he'd dumped her, although not publicly: he'd simply stopped calling, leaving Charmaine and the rest of them in charge of the post-mortem which lasted months. And now this one, Bartholomew Howell, Baz to his friends. A tall good-looking, rangy charmer with dirty blond hair and blue eyes, he'd been expelled from school for selling drugs. Ironically, he was a friend of Thierry's, and Charmaine had met him at a party in London the Easter before they'd finished. Baz was a creep – everyone said it, everyone knew it. Everyone except Charmaine, of course. She loved his *insouciance* – which Gabby said wasn't insouciance at all but a dope-induced stupor. For Charmaine, he was everything her life at St Anne's wasn't: undisciplined, unregulated, unorthodox. Baz didn't work – he didn't need to. His father owned a chain of pharmacies, 'somewhere up north', he said vaguely, and he lived, reasonably well, off his family stipend. He liked to think of himself as a poet and a singer. In truth he was neither, scribbling odd bits of verse to Charmaine when the mood took him.

'Plus he listens to an awful lot of music,' Charmaine added earnestly. Nathalie snorted. She'd had the full story. Music, not to mention beaches and bikinis, were on his stated agenda for LA. He had a friend out there, Touch – what kind of name was that? – who was in 'the business'. Baz was eager to get out there and 'get into the scene. Man.' At first, when he began talking about going 'out there', he'd made it clear he was going alone for a couple of months. When he'd sorted himself out, Charmaine could follow. He'd been adamant. Charmaine had sulked, pouted, cried, the usual. But Baz had been firm. Then one day – she had no idea why or how – he'd suddenly changed his mind. Charmaine would love it out there. She'd *love* it. They'd have a great time. Plus she could help him get his band started – talk to agents, help them find the right venues, that sort of thing. Charmaine was overjoyed.

'We're going to stay with Touch in some place called Thousand Oaks – isn't that a lovely name? Baz says it's in the Valley somewhere. I meant to get a map of LA this morning, but I forgot.'

'Yes, but what are *you* going to do out there, Charmaine?' Nathalie asked. Following Baz was one thing but being stuck out there on her own with nothing to do was another.

'I don't know – we'll see. I might even do some singing with the band or something.'

'The band?' Suddenly Baz had gone from vaguely knowing someone in LA to having a fully fledged band.

Nathalie sighed. Charmaine was *so* impractical.

'Well, just make sure you've got a return ticket,' she cautioned. 'That way, if it doesn't work out, you can always come back.' Charmaine nodded impatiently. Typical Nathalie – no sense of adventure. Of course it would all work out.

The black Mercedes pulled up at the kerbside at Charles de Gaulle. The driver jumped out to open the doors. Rianne and Gina staggered out under the weight of their luggage. Gina tipped the driver generously and hoisted her bag onto her shoulder. She held their tickets. It was drizzling slightly, the sky heavy and overcast. 'Got everything?' she asked Rianne, as the car pulled away.

Rianne nodded. She was looking forward to going back to New York, a silent Bruce Eastman or no. It had been the most exhausting week of shows, rehearsals, post-show parties, even a pre-show dinner. She'd drunk more alcohol in a week than she had in the previous six months and she hadn't made a single friend. Compared to the models she met backstage, the girls at St Anne's had been a walkover. She followed Gina through the revolving doors to the Air

France desk. They had almost an hour to kill. Ever organised, Gina hated being late for a flight. She hated rushing. Especially with a hangover.

They checked in, collected their boarding cards and made their way to the first-class lounge. A waiter glided over with champagne. Both women declined. Orange juice, perhaps? Rianne had run out of anything to read – she'd spent so much time in the past week just hanging around, waiting for something to happen, that she'd finished everything she'd brought with her. She remembered there was a bookstore on the second or third floor of Charles de Gaulle's excellent duty-free shopping area. 'I'm just going to get a magazine or something,' she said to Gina as the waiter reappeared with two tall glasses of juice.

'Sure, we have plenty of time.' Gina took one gratefully.

Rianne walked out of the lounge and into the inner atrium – she loved the glass-covered moving escalators. She went over to the bookstore, which was almost deserted, picked up *Vogue* and *Time*, then browsed through the paperbacks, looking for something long and juicy to read on the flight. After ten minutes, she had about six titles in her hands. She paused to look at one more. Then someone moved opposite her on the other side of the rack, blocking the light. She looked up, irritated. Her eyes widened. She squinted . . . no, no . . . it couldn't be.

She couldn't believe her eyes. Standing less than a metre away from her, separated only by the shoulder-height pyramid book rack, was Ree Modise. She stared. It *was* him: the same height, the broad shoulders underneath a grey jacket, the hair cut close to the scalp. He was looking at books, his lower lip caught between his teeth. His glasses were different, black-rimmed instead of silver, and rectangular, not round. She was amazed she remembered the details. Suddenly, as if he was aware of her gaze, he looked up. And froze. They stared at each other. This time, it was she who broke the stare. She couldn't look at him for a second longer. She saw his bodyguard move imperceptibly closer, wondering discreetly what his charge was looking at. She whirled round and had almost walked out of the store without paying for the pile of magazines and books in her hands when the attendant shouted at her. In confusion and embarrassment, she slid them hurriedly back across the counter towards him and fled.

'What's the matter?' Gina looked up, as Rianne joined her in the lounge.

'Nothing.'

'You sure? You look like you've seen a ghost.'

'I'm fine. When do we leave?' Rianne was agitated, her cheeks bright red.

Gina stared at her. 'Didn't you find anything?'

'Huh?'

'To read. I thought you went to get a book,' Gina said.

'Oh . . . no, no . . . there wasn't anything.'

'Not even *Vogue*? Although you won't be in this month's, probably next.'

'Er, no.'

'You sure you're OK? D'you want something to drink?'

'No. No. I'm fine. Really.' Rianne looked at her hands. Her cheeks were still burning. She'd been unable to hold his stare. Everything about him was the same. His smooth jet-black skin, the intense dark eyes behind the glasses, the full dark lips with sharply defined edges, his height and powerful bodily presence. Even hidden by the bookshelf she could feel it.

25

It was October. In Johannesburg, it was late spring. The air was desiccated, unbearably dry. Everything was still, waiting breathlessly for the summer rains. The veld was yellowed, the tall willowy grasses bleached of all colour by the cold, dry winter. Lisette broke off speaking and turned to look out of her fifteenth-floor office window across the cityscape. It was nearly dusk. She had called a meeting of top management to discuss the latest outbreak of strikes in the mines. She turned back to the group of men seated around the boardroom table. She looked at her younger brother angrily. 'I am not – I repeat, *not* – dealing with them. We will not bow to union pressure. It's out of the question. And I *forbid* you to consider it.'

'*Ag*, Lisette, come on,' Hendryk complained. 'We're going to have to do something. It can't go on like this. Since the *vuilege* commission, we're under pressure, man. I tell you, I'm at my wit's end.' He sat in a chair by the window, his shoulders slumped.

Lisette blew out her cheeks. Hendryk had no stomach for conflict, that was the problem. And they certainly had a conflict on their hands. From the report in front of her, Lisette had been horrified to learn that the average South African worker now cost almost five dollars an hour – double what they were worth in Brazil or Mexico, and more than five times the amount in China. It was disastrous. Big investment would simply look elsewhere – where de Zoete *wasn't*. She was furious. KdZK required so much of her time and energy and it was just *too irritating* that Hendryk couldn't be trusted to manage the mines on his own. 'Well, we've got to do *something*,' she repeated, looking around the table. 'I'm all ears.' She leaned back.

Eventually, Kapie Vorster spoke. He was the ex-police chief Hendryk had hired to clear up the recurring security 'issues' at their most profitable mine, Deep Kloof. '*Ja*. Give me a month. I'll clear out the scum from hostels one and two. If you don't ask me any questions, and you don't get in my way, I guarantee it.' He looked at Lisette directly, his hooded eyes giving nothing away.

Lisette shuddered inwardly. Much as she longed to see profits rise to pre-'trouble' levels and much as she wished to rule with a firm grip, there was something about the crop-headed, paunchy ex-cop that disgusted her. Despite his designer suits, which barely fastened over his enormous gut, he looked like a red-necked thug from the *platteland*. He could barely speak English. Was there no more creative way to bring the compounds under control? 'OK, Meneer Vorster. You have my permission.'

'*Dankie*.' Vorster inclined his head, then left the room without another word.

Lisette knew Vorster resented having to thank her, a woman, and that he was excited by her 'permission' to run things the way he pleased. She'd heard him talk about the *vuilege kaffirs* a million times before – they and the Commie-bastards who'd been infiltrating their property and poisoning his 'boys'. She wasn't sure she'd done the right thing in giving it over to him, but what else could she do? They had to stifle the unrest. And Hendryk couldn't, or wouldn't, do it. That left Vorster. She shuddered again.

'You did *what*?' Justin Groenewald looked at Bruce Eastman uncomprehendingly. They were standing in Justin's tiny one-bedroomed apartment on 143rd Street and Houston, deep in the heart of Harlem. 'When?'

'God, I don't know – about a month ago. Why?' Bruce was nervous: somehow, word of his date with Rianne had found its way to Justin.

'Fuck it, Eastman. Are you kidding me?'

'It was harmless. She's harmless. I took her out to dinner. We went to a movie. She's harmless, I swear it.'

'What do you mean, she's harmless? She's a *de Zoete*, for Christ's sake! She's Hendryk's *niece*!' Justin drew on his cigarette. He stared angrily at the over-confident young white man in his home.

Bruce sighed. 'I'm sorry, Justin. I know – I haven't called her since. It won't happen again, trust me.'

'Trust you? How the fuck am I supposed to trust you? You're new to this, Eastman – you have no idea. We've got months – *years* – to go . . . All I ask is that you keep your fucking nose clean. Is that so hard? Just stay out of trouble.

You're no use to us if you're identified *in any way*. You got that? *In any way*.' Justin ground out his cigarette on the floor and stood up. He walked over to the desk where he kept an old typewriter and drew up a chair. 'Look, forget it. I'm not going to report it – you just stick to making the contacts we send you and avoid getting involved with anyone else. You got that?'

'But I'm not involved! All I did was take her to dinner,' Bruce protested.

'Just *don't*!' Justin told him. 'I'm prepared to forget it ever happened and you'd better do the same. Now, clear out, Eastman, I've got work to do.' He pulled the chair up to the desk and turned his back.

Bruce sighed and got up from the window-sill. He walked towards the door and stopped, listening intently as he had been taught. Then he opened it and stepped out into the corridor. He ignored the lift and ran down the stairs onto the street. He resisted the temptation to look up to see if Justin was watching him and walked away.

Upstairs, Justin watched him leave and turned back to the desk. Putting a fresh sheet of paper into the old typewriter, he typed out the date, the title of his weekly report and outlined exactly what Bruce had just told him. It wasn't in his power to decide what got reported and what didn't. But Bruce Eastman didn't know that – and, as far as Justin was concerned, he didn't need to.

26

Gabby's first week at Oxford was everything she had dreamed of – and more. At first it wasn't all that different from St Anne's. There was something about the routine, the people she met at supper the first night, the cosy atmosphere in halls that was all surprisingly familiar. She had a small but pretty little room to herself in the south quadrant of the college. It had a crooked doorway and the walls weren't quite straight. 'Sinking.' Mary from across the corridor smirked with satisfaction as she dropped in to borrow some sugar. 'The whole place has been sinking into the Cherwell for centuries. You'll notice the doorway – we have to stoop to enter – not conquer, no pun intended – people were a lot smaller back then.'

Gabby smiled. She liked Mary. She was reading French. In fact, Gabby liked most people she'd met. Everyone was so friendly, always inviting each other – and her – into their rooms for coffee. She rushed out and bought the requisite kettle, storage jars and mugs so that she, too, could make coffee and tea and offer packets of biscuits around. Soon, Mary assured her, she'd be able to use the window-ledge as a pretty efficient fridge. 'The rooms are freezing in winter,' she said gloomily. She was in her final year. 'First year you live in,' she explained to Gabby, as they made their way to supper. 'Second year you have to live out – I was in Cowley. God, what a dump! Third year, if you're lucky, you get a place back in college. I got one. I'm going to get a First. I think they thought I deserved it.' Mary was also extremely confident.

At the end of the week there was the matriculation ceremony, Gabby's first taste of the pomp and circumstance that went along with admission to one of the world's finest institutions. From the minute she put the mortar-board on her head, with trembling fingers, she was hooked. All the Magdalen students were gathered in the Junior Common Room, doing their best not to appear excited or nervous. Mary and some of the second- and third-year students watched them, doing their best not to appear patronising. Matriculation and graduation were the two most important ceremonies at Oxford.

'Why have they got different gowns?' she whispered to Suzy Menzies, also reading English, as she tried to secure her mortar-board more firmly on her head.

'Well, there's basically three types of place at Oxford.

Commoner – that's you and me. We've got shorter gowns. Then there's Exhibition, a kind of lesser scholarship, can't remember why. And then there's Scholarship places. I think they used to be given to the . . . you know, the *poor*.'

'That's why they've got longer gowns – more room to hide the leftovers at mealtimes,' Dominic Fraser quipped, as he joined them. 'Silly distinctions, really. We're all students – lowest form of life around here. Though some aspire to greater things.'

Gabby laughed. Dominic was also reading English. She loved his dry sense of humour and his wit. She longed to be as quick off the mark as he was.

'Ready?' he asked, offering an arm to both girls. The procession, headed by the college dons in their elaborate academic gowns and hats, wound its way slowly up the high street, past the Bodleian Library and through New Cattle Lane to the Sheldonian where they were joined by all the other first-year students from the thirty-odd colleges dotted around the city. Inside, the atmosphere was measured and stately, contrasted only by the wide-eyed enthusiasm of students like Gabby who couldn't quite believe the formality of the occasion. The entire ceremony, which lasted over three hours, was conducted in Latin and was incomprehensible. Gabby loved every precious second.

'It's just like St Anne's,' she told Nathalie, over the phone the following weekend, 'except they're all really brainy.'

'Well, not like St Anne's, then.' Nathalie laughed. 'What are the boys like?'

'Boys? What boys?' Gabby asked, a touch nervously. Apart from Dominic, she'd hardly spoken to any. 'They're mostly girls, specially round here. I'm in the female quadrant, silly.'

'Oh. Well, I'll check back with you soon. Have you heard from Rianne?'

'Not since last week. She's in New York, I think.'

'It must be amazing, flying all over the world, having people do your hair and make-up every day and all you have to do is stand there and smile into a camera,' Nathalie said enviously.

'Oh I don't think it's that easy,' Gabby said. 'Just think of the pressure to stay thin and all that – I'd *hate* it.'

'Well, of course you would!' Nathalie laughed. 'Speaking of which . . . ?'

'I know, I know. I'm starting on Monday.' Gabby grimaced. The last time she'd seen Nathalie, she'd spent the evening explaining why she'd begun putting on weight again. After the hard-fought battle at St Anne's to drop nearly two stone, she'd regained one in just over a month.

'Yeah? You'd better. I'm coming up to see you in a month so you'd better have started.'

'Promise. Now, what about you?' Gabby was keen to change the subject. 'What's new in your life?' She would start her diet on Monday. In the meantime, she might as well stock up on all the forbidden fruit she could find. A picture of a Mars Bar floated into her head.

'Me?' Nathalie sighed. 'How long have you got?'

'Charmaine!' Baz yelled from the bedroom. 'Where's the fucking lighter?'

'I don't know. Isn't it on the bed?' Charmaine answered. She was brushing her teeth.

'If it was, I'd hardly be asking, would I?' Baz threw off the duvet and searched under the pillows. 'Where the fuck did you leave it?'

'I haven't seen it!' Charmaine protested, then rinsed and spat. Honestly, Baz got worked up over the slightest things these days.

'Where the *fuck* is it?' Baz's voice grew louder.

'Shut it, will ya?' Richard shouted from the adjoining room. 'Some of us have to get up tomorrow, you know. Some of us *work*.'

Charmaine sighed. Baz was turning into a nightmare. His dope consumption had more than doubled since they'd moved into Windus Road. She was worried about him, and so was Richard. The only person who wasn't was Baz. He simply lit up another joint and leaned back. And he was doing an awful lot of that these days. Especially during sex. Charmaine couldn't remember the last time he'd roused himself sufficiently to take part.

She hoped things would straighten themselves out once they got to LA. She'd finally got him to book their tickets. Another month and they'd be swapping dull, dreary London for the brilliant sunshine of southern California. She couldn't wait.

'*Char!*' Baz yelled.

'I'm *coming*. Keep your voice down – Richard's trying to sleep!' she hissed, as she switched off the bathroom light and walked into their room. He was lying back on the pillows – he'd taken all four – with an erection under his boxer shorts. Charmaine knew exactly what he wanted.

'What are you doing for Christmas?' Rianne asked Gabby over the phone. She had just come back to New York from a week on location in Thailand for *Elle*. New York was crisp and cold, a refreshing change from the damp humidity of the Andaman Seas. Much to Ross's annoyance, she'd also gone golden brown.

'I've got to work,' Gabby said, pulling a face. 'I'm going to Granny's for three days but I've got a job pulling pints in the Fox and Hounds.'

'The Fox and Hounds?'

'The local pub. It's just round the corner. I'm working the evening shifts. It's crap money but apparently loads of Americans come in and they always tip, it's supposed to be good fun. Mary's working there – so's Dom.'

'Oh.' Rianne couldn't *quite* picture working in a pub. She felt guilty. She probably earned more in an hour than Gabby would all holiday. But she envied her, too. She seemed so happy at Oxford, surrounded by bright, interesting people. It was the perfect environment for her. She was *bien dans sa peau*, as Rianne's mother would have said:

right at the centre of her group of friends at Magdalen and right at the centre of student life.

'Yes, it'll be fun, not like working at all. Especially with Mary and Dom around. You must meet Mary, Rianne, you'll love her. She's so funny and sharp.' Rianne had never met any of them – Mary, Suzy, Dominic – but with a pang she felt an old fear resurface. Was Gabby, too, slipping away? Suddenly she missed her. New York seemed awfully lonely. 'Why don't you come here for Christmas?' she said impulsively.

'I *wish*!' Gabby giggled. 'I can't, silly. I'm working – remember?'

'Oh. Well, how about if I buy you the ticket – as a Christmas present?'

'Still can't. Who's going to do my shifts at the pub? Why don't you come here instead? You can stay over in my room, come to the pub and watch me pulling pints. Come on, it'll be fun! We break up next week, you can come on the Monday after that and stay until I go up to Hereford – why not? Maybe we can get Nat to come as well. Charmaine'll be gone by then but it'll be great with the three of us. Say you'll come. *Please!*'

'OK. Yes, I'll come!' Rianne was excited now. Somewhere deep in the back of her mind, her recent encounter with Ree Modise had disturbed her and she wanted to . . . What? Tell Gabby? She didn't know. All she knew was that the sight of him had stirred something inside her. And she couldn't get his face out of her mind. 'I've got a dinner to go to tomorrow night, a celebration-type thing, you know, signing the contract with Lovell and all that, then there's something else at the weekend. I'll come on Sunday night. I'll get into London on Monday and come up to Oxford straight away.'

'Deal!' Gabby said, laughing gleefully.

Nathalie was thrilled. Visiting Gabby would be fun, and seeing Rianne at the same time would be even better! She was still slaving away at TopGirl, hating every moment. Even the 25 per cent staff discount on clothes couldn't compensate for the boredom of the job. She'd recently graduated to being on the floor in the lingerie section, which essentially meant standing around making sure no one stuffed a pair of knickers down their shirt or walked into the changing rooms with more than three items. She'd never thought standing around all day could be so tiring. By the time she walked out at six o'clock, having had her bag checked by their friendly security guard, and climbed onto the number-fifteen bus, she was shattered. Some days she fell asleep, which, as the bus terminated in Kensal Rise, was not the quickest way to get home.

'What shall I bring to wear?' she asked Gabby on the phone.

'Wear? What d'you mean?'

'Well, will we go out for dinner – you know, to one of those black-tie dinners?'

'You must be kidding. I'm a student, Nat. I'm broke all the time!' Gabby shook her head. She'd not really thought about it before but of the four of them, she was the only one who actually had to work for a living. Nathalie was working in that clothing shop, it was true, but she certainly wasn't doing it for the money. She had some vague notion of being a businesswoman – she wasn't yet sure how – and was basically working for the experience. Her paltry salary did little more than pay her weekly bus fare and provide her with a growing wardrobe of TopGirl clothes.

'You still have to eat,' Nathalie pointed out.

'Sure. But not at black-tie events!'

'Well, we'll treat you, for your Christmas present.' Gabby began to laugh. A plane ticket to New York, a posh dinner . . . no one could say her friends weren't inventive!

'OK, you win,' Gabby said. 'We'll think of somewhere to go when you get here. Anyway, I'd better get back to my books. We've got a seminar tomorrow morning and I'd better do some work. See you next week?'

'See you. I can't *wait*!' Nathalie put down the phone.

The limousine waited discreetly, if that were possible for a mile-long, snow-white vehicle, just outside the front door at Mulberry Place. Elise, who had been peeking through the blinds every five minutes, gave a whoop and then gasped at Rianne as she walked down the stairs.

'*Ay, que bélla!*' she breathed, as Rianne checked her reflection in the mirror one last time. She was going to the party at Lovell, which was being held to celebrate the Christmas season and – far more importantly, according to Ross – the signing of her contract. She had spent the afternoon at one of the luxury spas on Fifth Avenue, a pre-party indulgence on which Ross and Gina had insisted, where she'd been massaged, pampered, indulged, groomed to perfection, then whisked back to the flat with barely an hour to spare before the limo arrived. Not that she needed more than an hour – she'd slithered into the white silk dress that Gina had pulled off the racks at Dior and, with a white cashmere stole trimmed with grey fur and sparkly, strappy sandals, she looked like a million dollars. Elise gaped at her as Rianne pressed her lips together one last time before heading out the front door.

The limo driver, resplendent in his black uniform, whistled under his breath as she descended the steps. He opened the door for her and carefully helped her in. The tinted windows glided smoothly shut as the car powered slowly away from the kerb. A glass of champagne and a single red rose were waiting for her on the table inside the car, which was more like a small room than a vehicle. She picked up the flower and opened the little white card attached. 'Sky's the limit. Well done, *skatjie*. Ross'. Rianne smiled. Not bad going for someone who'd had to ask for permission to visit Serendipity's six months ago. She took a sip of champagne and glanced at her watch: 10 p.m. It was going to be one hell of a party.

The limo pulled up outside the restaurant on Sixth

Avenue and the driver leaped out. He opened the door for Rianne and she stepped out onto the kerb. She looked up and down the length of the street. Christmas in New York: there was nothing like it. The trees that lined the shopping avenues were sparkling with a thousand fairy-lights and overhead, suspended perilously between the buildings, the fantastically ornate Christmas lights shone down: rows of glittering gold and yellow five-pointed stars in one street, hundreds of miniature red and silver Santas in the next, then huge holly wreaths, glittering cones and tiny red bulbs further away.

It was magical. It had just snowed – an unexpected storm which blew out of nowhere and lasted half an hour. A thin blanket of pristine white powder covered the city. Everything looked clean, pure, untouched, despite the crowds. Cars were crawling along. The shops were still open, and people were walking arm in arm, glancing curiously at her as she pulled her wrap round her and disappeared through the enormous steel doors.

Inside, the party was in full swing. Scores of beautiful people wandered around, champagne glasses in hand, squealing their hellos and lovely-to-see-you-darlings as they passed one another. The entire restaurant had been taken over by the Lovell crowd and an A-list selection of models, bookers and *fashionistas*. To Rianne's amazement, she was everywhere: enormous black and white silkscreen banners of her face hung from the walls, billowing gently. The celebrations were for her. As she walked down the steps to join Ross and Gina, who were beaming at her, the crowd burst into applause. Blushing furiously, she made it down the steps without stumbling and accepted congratulatory kisses from the team assembled at the foot. Dean Prescott, Lovell's director of marketing, held their newest acquisition by the arm and propelled her towards the other players in the deal: Martine Turner, international commercial director, Sylvia Hammond, something in public relations, Nicola, José, Stefano – the names and faces blurred as she was paraded around the crowded room. Everyone wanted to meet her, everyone wanted to be photographed next to her and flashbulbs went off continuously.

To the Lovell team, she was a find, a major asset to their marketing plans. As Ross had explained to them, not only was she beautiful, graceful, sophisticated – *just* the look they'd been waiting for – she had a pedigree for which most of them would give their right arm. Rich, privileged, touched by tragedy, the de Zoete family, she had announced, at their first meeting, were to South Africans what the Kennedys were to Americans. They were duly impressed. As they watched her glide from one set of hands to the next, they could see for themselves: pure class. 'Nothing like it,' Dean Prescott murmured to Martine Turner. 'Good breeding . . . it shows, doesn't it?'

Ross, within earshot, went pink with delight. As she'd said to Rianne in her congratulatory note, this was just the beginning. She watched her protégée handle the crowds like a pro – she made a mental note to have a word with her as soon after the party as possible. Rianne had made a stunning debut into the modelling world . . . she'd gone in almost at the top. It was important she stayed there.

It had been a week of press, press, press. Rianne had handled it well but her exasperation at being asked the same dumb questions – as she put it – fifty times a day was beginning to show.

'Things are changing in the industry, Rianne,' Ross said, reaching for a cigarette at the end of their dinner. In all the celebrations surrounding the deal, she hadn't had time to explain to Rianne exactly what her strategy had been and exactly what type of contract she'd just signed. Typical of Rianne, she didn't seem all that interested. Rather than go for an exclusive endorsement, Rianne would be the face of Lovell in their new spring collections campaign, with an option to renew once the season had changed.

Estelle Lovell had made a comment about Rianne that

had made Ross sit up and take notice. 'Funny – she's not WASPy, y'know?' Estelle had been studying a series of shots. 'I mean, she's white and all that . . . but she could be anything – Spanish, Italian, Brazilian. She's darker, more sultry than you think, especially when you meet her. And that's good for us. She's not exactly a woman of colour, but she's not lily-white, either. She's no Christie Brinkley. She'll appeal to a whole lot of women.' Ross nodded emphatically. Estelle, as usual, had her finger exactly on the pulse . . .

Rianne looked up from her coffee. She'd had a plate of pasta, sun-dried tomatoes and a sprinkling of olive oil. She was *still* starving. What on earth was Ross going on about now? She'd had just about enough of the peptalks, the approving – or disapproving – glances, the fussing with her hair and make-up. Ross was beginning to resemble a shorter, rounder Lisette. She frowned. 'What d'you mean? What's changing?'

'Well, models come with their own . . . *baggage* nowadays. The public don't only want to see you, they want to *know* you, too.'

'So?'

'So . . . everything. Models used to be just models. Their job was to look good, sashay down the runway, model the clothes, make-up, whatever. Nowadays everyone wants to know who you are, where you're from, what you're like, what you think. It's no longer enough to be beautiful.'

'Your point is . . . ?' Rianne enquired, a touch impatiently. Ross always took forever to make hers.

'My point, as you so charmingly put it, Rianne, is that there's going to be an intense amount of media interest in you, the details of your life, who you *are*.'

'So?' Rianne repeated.

'There will be a fair amount of prying, from journalists particularly. I don't need to tell you what coming from your background will mean.'

'I *still* don't understand.' Rianne was impatient.

'Well,' Ross began as delicately as she could. After all, she herself was South African and had had to deal with the most unpleasant allegations when Face! had started out. 'Being South African, coming from a family like yours, there'll be lots of stories, you know. Stories about your family, the tragedy, your position in South Africa ... maybe even your *political* position – if you have one. There'll be all sorts of things made up about you, some true, some not. We're not only here to help you win contracts and make money, we're also here to help you through these – and other – difficulties. I promised your aunt that we'd look after you, and we intend to. But you must also help us.'

'I'm not sure I know what you mean. Who cares what I think about anything?'

'The public will. And it all helps. Look at Mora, Diandra, Tiffany. Everyone wants them, *Vogue, Elle, Marie Claire*, they're hot properties. And it's not just because they're beautiful. They're interesting – they have lives, they go to parties, clubs, they date famous men. They're glamorous and they're a commodity that everyone wants. That's going to happen to you too and I want to make sure you can cope with it. This can be a really rotten business, Rianne, but you're lucky, you came to us first. I can't tell you how many girls don't even make it that far. For every success story, there's a hundred failures.'

'I still don't see what that's got to do with me,' Rianne interrupted. 'I mean, I'm here in New York. You've promised Aunt Lisette you'll look after me. Fine. If it gets to the point where I don't want to do it any more, I won't. It's simple. You're making a big fuss over nothing.'

Ross sighed. Rianne could be a real pain in the ass. 'Let me spell it out for you then,' she said, fingers tapping. 'No late nights, no missing appointments, no tantrums, no alcohol, no drugs, no scandals. This is a big contract we've landed and I intend to keep it. That means promoting

Lovell products at all times. That means being on time, polite, *professional*. Do I make myself clear?'

Rianne nodded. At last, Ross had got to the point. She needn't have worried. Cigarettes were about her only vice, and the occasional glass of wine. She wasn't about to go overboard. Ross had misunderstood one thing: she'd been rich all her life. Winning the Lovell contract was great but she hadn't done it for the money. In fact, she wasn't sure why she'd done it at all.

27

Charmaine swore under her breath. LAX was just about the ugliest damned airport she'd ever seen. That was her first impression after getting off the thirteen-hour flight. It was obviously still under construction – there were ugly hoardings everywhere – but really! The arrivals hall was little more than a glorified Portakabin! Thanks to the time difference, they'd taken off at ten in the morning and it was only two o'clock in the afternoon. She looked around for Baz. He was staggering towards her. He'd been drinking almost non-stop from Heathrow and now that they were back at sea level, he was looking distinctly the worse for wear.

'Where's our luggage?' she asked him. There were no monitors, no signs, no airline officials, nothing.

'Fuck knows,' Baz said. He needed a cigarette. It had been a full flight and, somehow, the stupid travel agent had given them non-smoking seats. He'd had to get up and go to the back of the plane every time he wanted a fag. Right now, he wanted more than a fag but even he didn't dare. He hoped Touch would be outside. If they ever made it outside.

'Look . . . I think the bags are coming on over there . . . see?' Charmaine pointed to a makeshift carousel. She recognised some of their fellow passengers. Baz shrugged. She was Little Miss Bossy Boots. Let her sort the damned luggage out. Could he sneak a toke in the toilets?

Half an hour later, having sweated their way through Immigration, they were let out into the blinding California sunshine.

'What is the purpose of your visit to the *Yeew*-nited States?' the moustachioed official had asked Charmaine, looking sceptically at her passport photo. She'd been twelve when it was taken.

'Um . . . we're on holiday?' she ventured. She didn't really know what to say.

'And how long do *yew* intend to stay?'

'Um . . . a couple of months? I'm not sure. My boyfriend's a singer.' The official looked at her chest, coughed and let her through. She was wearing a white T-shirt with a low-scooped neck and the bold words 'RELAX' on the front, and 'Don't Do It' on the back. The Frankie Goes To Hollywood-inspired T-shirts were all the rage that year. She grabbed her passport and went in search of Baz.

Typically, he'd left the queue, gone to the toilet to see if he could take a puff and when he came out, he'd somehow mis-read the Immigration signs thinking there was no way 'Aliens' could possibly refer to him. Half an hour later, having been thrown out of the 'US Citizens Only' line, he finally made it to the desk. The young Hispanic officer who looked at his documents was charmed by his accent and quickly let him through. 'He looks like David Bowie!' she whispered to her colleague. He snorted. Looked nothing like him.

'Yo! Baz! *Yo!* Over here!' They both turned round. A man was standing in front of them, shouting.

'Hey, Touch!' Baz dropped his suitcase on Charmaine's toes. He walked over and gave the shorter, older – God, *much* older, Charmaine thought – man a bear-hug.

'How're *you*? Great to see you, man. And who's the little

lady?' Touch leered at Charmaine, his arm draped round Baz, smiling in his gap-toothed way.

She stared at him. He was fifty, if he was a day . . . Short, wiry, unshaven, his grin was nothing short of disgusting: there were several large holes where his teeth should have been. She nearly passed out.

'Oh. This is Charmaine. You can call her Char,' Baz said. He seemed suddenly agitated, hopping from one foot to the other, tapping his watch. Charmaine frowned. What was wrong with him? 'Um, Touch, you got the car?' he asked.

'Yep, sure do. Out in the parking lot. You got *every-thing*?' There seemed to be special significance attached to the 'everything'.

Baz nodded. 'Come on, let's get out of here,' he said. He snapped his fingers at Charmaine, who was still gaping at Touch. 'Come on, Char, move it. Let's get these cases to the car.' He took the two lighter ones, leaving Charmaine and Touch to struggle with the heavy one. Charmaine wondered, not for the first time since they'd left Stoke Newington, why the hell he'd needed such an enormous suitcase. It wasn't like Baz had *that* many clothes. In fact, he had very few. And the cases were heavy. 'Records,' he'd said to her in London. 'I've got to take my records along.' She rolled her eyes. What the heck did he need records for? She thought he was going to play music in LA, not listen to it.

Ten minutes later, the cases safely stowed away in the back of Touch's huge, ugly bubble car – 'A Pacer, honey, best car Ford ever made!' – they roared out of the parking lot and headed for the 405 freeway. Charmaine forgot her earlier irritation as the city unfolded before her. Baz seemed to have calmed down. As they hit Century Boulevard, he gave a great whoop and turned in the front seat to grab her face and kiss her hard. She blushed. It was ages since he'd done anything so nice.

'I've got a little place for you in Redondo,' Touch shouted, above the roar of the engine.

'Where's that?' Charmaine asked. 'I thought we were going to Thousand Oaks.'

'No, honey, that's where *I* live. Redondo's *way* better. By the beach. It's a condo. Belongs to a friend of mine. He's gone for a couple of months – you'll love it. Pity it's winter – coulda had you walkin' around in your itsy-bitsy all day. Huh?' He roared with laughter.

Disgusting old man. Charmaine looked out of the window. LA was gigantic – it seemed to stretch on in all directions for ever. And it was all single-storey, too. Thousands and thousands of little box-like houses, mostly white, with their own neat patches of front lawn. The roads were enormous, huge wide streets to accommodate the huge wide cars. She grinned. This was *America*! Everything was bigger, brighter, better. Just think what the girls at home were missing.

She fished around in her bag for her Ray-Ban sunglasses, a leaving gift from her mother. 'I'm only going for a couple of months, Mummy!' Charmaine had said, the night before they left. 'It's not like I'm going for ever. Come on! Cheer up. Anyone would think I'd never been away from home!' But Mary had only cried harder. Charmaine couldn't figure out why, not when she'd spent most of her life away from home. She found them – the cool, black Wayfarers Tom Cruise had worn in *Risky Business* – and put them on.

Touch was preparing to exit the freeway. 'Redondo Beach,' she read. 'Manhattan Beach. Hermosa Beach.' The names were fantastic. They were heading towards their own place, a – what did he call it? A condo? – on the beach. They could sit in the living room, watch the sun set on the waves, get up early for a morning swim, walk for hours along the white sand. She felt a sudden rush of feeling for Baz – he was fantastic, just the coolest guy in the world. OK, Touch was a creepy old man but the rest of Baz's friends would be great, she knew it. She couldn't wait until they got 'home'. They could have a cold beer and a spliff – bliss.

'Well, it's not *exactly* on the beach, honey, but it's real close. And it has its own pool – it's pretty cool. You gotta see it.' Charmaine looked at the apartment complex dubiously. A huge signboard announced the address: Camino Village Apartments. 10921 Camino Real, Redondo Beach, CA 92045. She followed Baz out of the car. There must be three hundred apartments crammed into the little plot of land about a mile from the beach, she thought to herself.

They lugged their cases up the stairs and a security guard opened the lobby door for them. Touch had the keys to Apartment 226, he told the guard, and they were waved through. She looked around curiously. It was clean, there were potted plants in the lobby and some sort of reception desk. Was it a hotel? They walked through landscaped gardens – and, yes, she could see the pool, a decent-sized flash of turquoise among the greenery. There were enormous lush plants and neatly trimmed patches of lawn everywhere. It wasn't bad. In fact, if you forgot that it was a mile away from the beach, it was quite nice. Touch stopped outside a ground-floor apartment and, after a few minutes of fumbling, managed to open the front door. Charmaine left the suitcase standing on the step and walked inside. It was empty.

'But what are we supposed to sleep on?' she whispered to Baz, as they walked through the rooms.

'Don't you worry,' Touch said, coming up behind them. 'I'll be back later on tonight with a mattress and a coupla things. We'll have you sorted out in no time, honey, just you watch. Now, if you'll excuse us, me and your man here got some business to take care of.'

Charmaine looked at Baz, confused. 'But—' she began, wondering what kind of business he was talking about, and why she had to be excluded.

'Char, give us a minute, will you?' Baz said, irritated. He and Touch pulled the heavy suitcase from the centre of the living room and dragged it into the first bedroom. They shut the door.

Charmaine could hear the sound of the zips being opened and then a low, long whistle from Touch. What the fuck was going on? She tiptoed over to the closed door. They had gone silent. She put her ear against the door. Big mistake. The door swung open and Charmaine practically fell into the room. She caught sight of Baz's face – surprised and livid with rage – and the open suitcase, full of bulky Sainsbury's bags and a few flat brown packages, wrapped in masking tape.

Dope.

She couldn't believe she hadn't realised what was going on. She picked herself up and ran out of the room. She paused only to thrust her feet into her flip-flops and yank open the front door. Stupid! *Stupid!* She could hear Baz running after her. Which way was the pool? He caught up with her easily, grabbed her by the upper arm and almost lifted her into the air. 'Char, get back inside. Now!'

'Ow – ow! Baz, you're *hurting* me. Ouch!' She started to cry.

'Sssh! Shut *up*, will you? Everyone's going to hear you. Just get back inside the house. Come on, let's go.' He held her arm tightly, dragging her back inside the flat.

Touch was standing nervously at the front door. 'Look, man, I'm gonna run. You take care of business. Give me a call later on tonight. Cool?'

'No prob,' Baz said, propelling Charmaine towards the other bedroom. 'Give me a couple of hours. Sorry about this.'

'Hey, no sweat. You do what you gotta do. I'll see ya later.' He vanished.

'Char . . .' Baz began, looking at the weeping girl. Her arm was red where he'd grabbed her.

'Why didn't you *tell* me?' Charmaine sobbed, rubbing her bruised arm. 'I thought you were coming here to play in a band,' she wailed. 'What if I'd got caught?' She realised that the heavy case was the one she'd checked in. She wailed even louder.

'Ssh, baby.' Baz held her head against his chest. He was thinking fast. He needed to placate her, stop the tears, get her back on his side and then figure out what to do. He had a whole game plan, one that he and Touch had worked out over the past couple of months. And he needed Charmaine. 'Ssh . . . come on, Char, come on . . .' He kissed her tears gently, stroking her wet cheeks. 'I need you. *We* need you, me and Touch.' He could feel her body beginning to relax. He warmed to his theme. 'I would've told you, honestly, but I was worried you wouldn't come.'

'Of course I'd have come,' Charmaine sobbed, a little less forcefully. She liked his arms round her, his mouth resting just above her ear. He continued his soft, slow whisper . . . He sounded so sure of himself, and of her . . . so sure of her place in the scheme of things . . . He *needed* her. He'd said so.

28

Nathalie sat on the edge of her bed and eyed the drawerful of underwear with exasperation. Why was it that every goddamn piece of lingerie she owned turned grey in the wash within a couple of weeks? She picked up a bra. What had been wispy white lace a week or two ago was now bedraggled grey – even the label was falling off. She sighed. She was going out that evening and she was *trying* to look her best. Philippe had grown tired of seeing her mooching around the house and had invited her to come out with him, Jenny and a friend of his called Marcus.

'And put on something decent. Marcus is a nice bloke and you look like a bloody housewife!' He laughed.

'Piss off! I *am* a housewife!' Nathalie grinned at him. It was a joke between them. Every morning Nathalie set off for Oxford Street in the latest, trendiest outfits. Every evening, by the time Philippe came home, she was slopping around in sweatpants and baggy jumpers. 'I'm comfortable,' she protested. 'I have to dress up every day. Leave me alone!'

'You're like those girls who wait until they've caught a husband, then suddenly stop putting on make-up and shaving under their arms. What if I bring a friend back here and he sees you, Old Mother Hubbard, in your grandfather's jumpers?' Philippe teased her.

'They're *your* jumpers, stupid,' Nathalie shot back. 'And bring a friend back – I don't care. It's not like I'm going to go out with them. And I *always* shave under my arms.'

'Why? You never go out with *anyone*!'

'Piss off,' she repeated.

'Bye. Have a nice day at work, dearest.' Philippe grabbed his briefcase and ran to catch the bus.

She picked up a pair of panties that had been part of a matching set. Because panties were washed even more frequently, they lost their shape and colour faster. After a couple of weeks, you could guarantee that the sets no longer matched. Such a waste of money, she thought, exasperated. She pulled out another pair and inspected the lace. It was coming away from the seams.

She glanced down at her bedspread, suddenly noticing the fabric. She and Cordelia had chosen it in Heal's the last time Cordelia had been in London. It was gorgeous, a riot of delicate pink, red and white roses splashed over a pale cream silk background. Now, why couldn't someone make underwear like that? Bras, panties, slips, teddies, basques, in a multitude of colours, fabrics, styles. She was now the lingerie specialist at TopGirl – she knew more about lingerie than anyone else in the store. In fact, she knew more about it than she'd ever thought possible.

Suddenly she sat bolt upright. Somebody? Why couldn't *somebody* make underwear like that? Why couldn't she? She almost fell off the bed. Of course! Underwear! That was it! Why hadn't she thought of it before? Why couldn't she do it? She would go into business making and selling underwear. Her hands were trembling. That was it! She'd found it. She'd found what she wanted to do. Suddenly, everything seemed absolutely clear. Underwear. It was perfect.

'I think it's a *great* idea, Nat,' Philippe said slowly, blowing his cigarette smoke away from the table. The four of them – Philippe, Jenny, Marcus and Nathalie – were sitting at Flame, the trendy new restaurant on Westbourne Grove, just round the corner from the flat. Nathalie's eyes were shining. She'd been unable to keep it to herself.

'What'll you call it?' Marcus asked, looking at her admiringly.

'Oh, I don't know, I haven't thought that far ahead, yet.' Nathalie liked him, and the fact that they were taking her seriously.

'Undie Heaven!' Jenny suggested, smiling at Philippe. She was a trainee solicitor in a large City firm. Nathalie liked her too, but she was a trifle dull.

Philippe snorted. 'Christ, Jen, needs a bit more panache than that. Stick to your day job, love.' Jenny laughed, unembarrassed.

'Lily White's?' Marcus hazarded.

Nathalie pursed her lips. No, too . . . *plain*. She wanted something funny, something witty. 'I don't know . . . It's funny, I have the whole thing in my head already. I know what I want the shop to look like – really sumptuous, with velvet curtains, nice carpets, baskets instead of drawers, elegant, not seedy. I want it to be an experience – luxurious. With assistants running around, getting different sizes, making suggestions. Posh. That's it. I want it to be posh.'

'Oh, yeah? What, like *Upstairs Downstairs*, with assistants doffing their caps and touching their forelocks?' Philippe teased her.

'That's it! *Upstairs Downstairs*!' Nathalie laughed. 'That's perfect.'

'No! Absolutely not!' Marcus and Philippe both howled. 'That's terrible!'

'No, it's not,' Jenny broke in. 'It's funny. *Up*stairs . . .' She put her hands under her breasts.

'*Down*stairs, don't tell me.' Philippe rolled his eyes. 'It's corny.'

'Yeah, you'd never catch a bloke dead in a shop with that name. Especially selling knickers,' Marcus confirmed.

'I don't care if men don't come in. Women need a shop of their own. Somewhere they can be free to try things on, look at other women, talk about underwear and . . .' Nathalie blushed.

'*Sex?*' Jenny giggled. 'Cor, yes! You could sell sex toys.'

'Stop!' Philippe had started to laugh. 'Enough. I don't need to hear any more. Jenny, stop, you're corrupting my sister. Or, Nat, you're corrupting her. Come on, let's get the bill. Time to go home.'

Nathalie agreed, her face reddening. Sex was still a difficult subject for her. Especially in front of her brother. Ever since the disastrous encounter on Martinique when she'd realised it would never be right for her, not after Sacha, not after Joules, she'd avoided it, not even daring to think about it. On the surface she seemed fine, same old Nathalie, pretty, charming, flirtatious. At school dances, she'd danced with almost everyone, even Ree, much to Rianne's disgust. But she'd refused to slip outside with anyone, even Ree – whom no girl had turned down, *ever* – and she'd never gone further than a first tentative kiss. Pretty soon the word was out around Malvern that Nathalie Maréchal was sweet but limited. Charmaine Hunter – now *there* was a safer bet.

'OK. I guess I'd better get going.' Marcus got up and pulled out Nathalie's chair for her. 'Thanks for the evening. I really enjoyed it.'

Nathalie smiled prettily at him. He was kind and thoughtful. Actually, most of Philippe's friends were kind and thoughtful. Except one. She shook her head suddenly.

'You all right?' Philippe asked, as they waved goodbye to Marcus. He lived in South Kensington and was off to look for a taxi.

'Yes, fine. Just a bit tired. And I drank too much.'

'Well, you certainly talked enough. I think Marcus really likes you.'

'Yes, he seems keen.' Jenny joined them. 'He kept smiling at you.'

'Oh, stop it. We've only just met!' Nathalie was embarrassed. They reached home. 'And, besides, I'm going to be too busy to have a boyfriend. I'm going to be *really* famous and *really* rich.'

Philippe ruffled her curly hair. 'Sure. Upstairs Downstairs. Come on, I'll show thee upstairs . . . Get to bed!'

'I will. You'll see.' Nathalie climbed the stairs and pushed open her bedroom door. Now, that was a silly thing to say, she thought, as she got undressed. She sounded like a little girl. I *will* be rich. I *will* be famous. She giggled again.

29

'That is *so* cool.' The leggy blonde looked at Riitho Modise in awe. He rolled his eyes. It was almost two in the morning and he was tired. They were standing in the kitchen at a party in her parents' enormous home in St John's Wood. He'd somehow wound up there after going to a party somewhere down the road with two friends – brothers – from UCL, Kunlé and Bayo. Riitho liked them. He liked the fact that they were African and he especially liked the fact that they were proud of it. Unlike the few African boys at the Boys' College, who immediately adopted English names – or versions thereof, like Ree, in place of the more 'difficult' Riitho – these young men were different and defiant. They didn't give a damn how difficult the English found it. Learn my name. Speak my language. And, surprisingly, people did. Girls learned to get their tongues round all three names – or, more frequently, all three young men. Riitho had always been popular with women, but these guys? This was something else. He turned his attention back to the girl. Lebohang, his bodyguard with the patience of a saint, was waiting downstairs, nursing a Diet Coke. 'Come on, it's a name.' Riitho looked at her, wondering whether or not she was drunk.

'How do you say it? *Reethoo*?'

'Ree-tho. Simple. Riitho.'

'Where's it from? I mean, where are *you* from?' she asked breathlessly, moving closer.

She *was* drunk. 'Where d'you think?' He always enjoyed this bit. Colonial geography. Surprising how much they *didn't* know.

'Um, Africa. Well, that's obvious.' She giggled.

'Is it?'

'Well, you could be from Jamaica or something but you don't look Jamaican.'

'And how do Jamaicans look?' He knew where this was going.

'Oh, I don't know . . . I mean, they have . . . you know, *gold teeth* and things.'

He smiled, shaking his head. Stupid little bitch. 'No, I'm not Jamaican. No gold teeth. Look.' He opened his mouth. She stared at him, mesmerised. He kissed her. She kissed him back, sliding her tongue around his teeth. He could taste the alcohol in her mouth. Whisky. Johnnie Walker.

Someone nudged him. It was Kunlé, on his way to one of the bedrooms, an identical girl in tow. He winked. 'First on the left,' he mouthed, propping up the blonde lolling against him. 'Take the second bedroom. It's hers.' Riitho nodded.

'What's he saying?' the girl slurred, her hands moving towards his buckle.

'Nothing. Which one's your room?'

'Second on the left.'

'Lead the way.'

An hour later, he lay back, winded. She might have been drunk, but she was energetic. She lay sprawled across the double bed, asleep. He looked around. The room was a mess. Clothes everywhere, shopping-bags, shoes, boots, make-up, toilet paper, sweet wrappers, magazines – you name it. What had his housemaster said to him his first week at the Boys' College? Keep your room tidy. No girls here. He propped himself up on an elbow and pulled a stack of magazines towards him. Usual stuff. *Elle, Marie Claire . . . Vogue.*

He frowned. He stared at the picture. It couldn't be . . . He fumbled for the bedside light and switched it on. The girl mumbled, disturbed by the light. He ignored her and held the magazine up to the light. British *Vogue*. March 1984. He flipped to the inside page. It *was* Rianne de Zoete. He put the magazine down slowly. Christ, she looked good. Something about her picture disturbed him, he was damned if he could work out what it was.

Gabby had reverted to an old habit. She was chewing the end of her pen. It was Mods week and she was struggling through her first set of exams. The hall was full of freshers doing the same thing. Out of nowhere, it seemed, Trinity Term had ended and, with it, her first year. She was going back to London – she'd found a job as secretary to two young property developers, Rianne had insisted she stay at Wilton Crescent, Nael was coming to visit – but first she had to get through the exams. All of a sudden she, who had never flinched before an exam question, was finding it very hard to concentrate.

Dominic was sitting in front of her; Suzy was somewhere at the back of the hall. She was staring at the back of Dominic's head. Unbelievable, she thought. They'd been best friends for almost the entire year. She was as used to the sight of his lanky frame lying sprawled on her narrow bed as she was to her toothbrush propped up in its plastic cup on her wash-basin. And now wherever he appeared, she lost the ability to concentrate and spent inordinate amounts of time gazing at him or at the nearest patch of sky. She still wasn't sure what had happened, or why.

They'd been cramming for the exams, lying on the grass in the Parks. It was hot, and Gabby had wandered off to buy ice creams for everyone. When she came back, she noticed Dominic's face was flushed and Suzy was grinning at him in a strange, almost embarrassed way.

'What's going on, you two?' she asked, handing over the dripping cones and flopping down on the grass.

'Nothing.' Dominic was short. He turned back to his books. Gabby looked at Suzy, who fluttered her eyelashes and shook her head. Gabby was puzzled.

'Christ,' he said suddenly, rolling over onto his stomach and looking at the two girls. 'What's the bloody point? It's a gorgeous day, I want to go punting with my favourite girls and here we are reading bloody *Beowulf*. What's the world coming to?' Suzy giggled. He rolled onto his back and looked at the sky. 'Besides,' he continued, 'I'm aiming for a fourth. I think they still give them out. First or a fourth – anything in between's a waste of time.' Suzy giggled again.

Gabby looked at them. Oh. Oh, no. Dominic was keen on Suzy. She stared at him, disappointed beyond belief. Well, of course, who wouldn't be? Suzy was pretty – long, dark brown hair, huge dark eyes, even if she did savage her eyebrows – and, most importantly, of course, she was slim. Gabby looked at the grass and at her open copy of

Beowulf. Tears pricked at the back of her eyes. It was Nael all over again. She wasn't going to cry. *Please*, no. She struggled to keep her voice under control.

'Well, why don't you?' she said, as calmly as she could. *Beowulf* lurched and blurred dangerously in front of her eyes.

'Will you?' Dominic reached out and grabbed her ankle. In surprise, she jerked, and kicked his face. 'Ouch! Gabs!'

'Oh, shit, I'm sorry – honestly, you gave me such a fright! Oh, Dom, did I hurt you?' Gabby was mortified.

'Honestly, you two, you're like a couple of kids. Everyone's staring.' Suzy laughed.

Gabby and Dominic looked up. There was no one about.

'Suzy – you little cow!' Dominic punched her playfully.

She stood up, brushing the grass off her skirt. 'Look, I've got to go. I'm meeting . . . Lisa in a few minutes. You go off punting if you want. I'll get a first, don't you worry your pretty little heads about me. See you at supper?' She picked up her books.

Gabby felt disappointed for Dominic. She should have taken the hint and offered to leave them.

'Sure,' he said easily. 'See you later. Give our love to . . . Lisa.'

Gabby wondered who Lisa was.

'So, Frankie, coming?'

He never called her Gabby, always Frankie. He liked it better than Gabrielle, Gabby or Francis, he said.

She smiled, suddenly shy. She'd never punted before. 'Well, OK. But *I* should have scarpered. Sorry.'

'What d'you mean?' He stood up and held out a hand.

'Oh, well, I mean, if you wanted to go with Suzy, it would've been OK, you know. I—'

'What are you talking about?' Dominic looked surprised.

'Er . . . nothing.' Gabby wasn't quite sure how to say it. He looked at her. 'I wanted to go with you,' he blurted. 'Me?'

'Yes. *You.*'

'Oh.' She didn't know what to say. Surely he didn't mean . . . no, he couldn't . . . *What* did he just say? They walked along in silence towards the river.

'Why—'

'Do—' They spoke at once, then laughed nervously.

Gabby's hand went up to the thin gold chain she wore round her neck. Her grandmother had given it to her, years before. She fingered it, wondering what the hell she was supposed to do next. It was ridiculous. Dominic was her best friend. She'd never felt awkward around him, or struggled for words or – or anything. He was as easy to be with as – as . . . well, anyone.

'Ladies first,' Dominic said, as they reached the river. 'What were you going to say?' A dozen empty punts were moored to the small jetty. He paid the boy a fiver and helped him untie the boat as Gabby stood on the bank, watching.

'Well, I just wondered . . . I mean, why did you . . . Oh, God, Dom, this is really silly. *I* feel silly. What were you going to say?'

'Oh, nothing, really. I was just going to ask you if you minded. You know.'

'Minded? Me?'

'Yeah, you. Look, we're not going to go through that pantomime again, are we?'

'What pantomime?'

'Who me? Yes, you. Me? You.' Gabby giggled. Suddenly, it was beginning to feel easier. He always made her laugh. He'd untied the boat and it was floating a little unsteadily off the jetty. He held out a hand. For the second time that day, Gabby took it and now stepped gingerly onto the rocking punt. His hand was warm and firm. He felt steady and solid as she tried to sit down without capsizing them. She leaned back as she'd seen other girls do while their boyfriends struggled with poles. She was sure it was a heck of a lot harder than it looked. They were quiet for a few minutes as Dominic steered them away from the bank and out into the middle of the river. They passed under Magdalen Bridge, past the playing fields and out towards Summertown.

'Where d'you want to go?' Dominic asked her, smiling at her. She was lying back with her eyes closed, a warm smile on her face. She looked amazing, he thought to himself, watching her. He'd always liked Gabby, right from the very first day he'd met her. She was funny, warm, clever as hell – she made him feel like a complete novice with her comments and perceptions. She had a particular way of seeing things. When they were arguing a point – which they frequently did – and she turned the full force of her intelligence on him, he had the strange feeling of being led somewhere he'd never get to on his own. He was bright, everyone who knew him would have said that about him, but he'd never met a mind like Gabby's before. It was disconcerting. He knew she was shy with boys, but he couldn't understand why. She was just as pretty as anyone else. She was tall, soft and curvy, with the most fantastic curly red hair. She should let it grow. She was always scrunching it up into a knot or pulling it off her face. It had escaped the clip now and was curling round her face. 'So?' he repeated, his heart suddenly beating faster.

'Vicky Arms?' she suggested. The Victoria Arms pub was a favourite stop on the punting trail.

'Roger.'

An hour later – she couldn't believe it had taken them an hour to float two miles down the Cherwell – they landed at the Vicky Arms and rocked their way to the river's edge. Gabby took off her shoes and leaped as gracefully as she could onto the bank. It was muddy and cold. They squelched their way through the grass and up to the pub. Ten minutes later, sitting side by side under a large parasol with a beer in hand, they congratulated each other.

'Splendid effort,' Gabby said, raising her glass.

'Thank you, m'lady.' Dominic turned to face her. He looked at her for a moment and then, ever so slowly, bent his head and kissed her. It was Gabby's first kiss.

And now she was sitting in Exam Schools, staring blankly at the question, chewing her pen as if her life depended on it, and gazing at the back of his curly dark head.

30

Charmaine sat bolt upright as the coke hit her brain. She felt giddy, as though she were floating. Through half-closed eyes she could just make out Baz, across the room, as he picked up the remains of the coke on his finger and ran it across his front teeth.

She'd been terrified the first time she'd tried it – somehow coke really was, you know, a *drug*. Spliffs weren't, not really. Smoking a spliff was like smoking a cigarette. Coke, though – well, you had to snort it. But she liked it. It made her feel great – powerful, confident and sexy. Spliffs made her lazy. Coke made her strong. It was almost two months since Baz had first introduced her to the stuff and although she wasn't hooked – of course not – she had to admit that no day really went anywhere until and unless she'd had her hit.

She got up rather unsteadily and made her way to the kitchen. Touch had managed to find two mattresses, a sofa, a TV and a dining-table with four mismatched chairs, but the place still looked half empty. At least they could sit down on something, though, instead of leaning on pillows against the wall. They'd done that for a couple of weeks when they'd first arrived. Charmaine thought about that for a second. How long had they been in LA? Three months? Time was flying by.

She opened the fridge. What had she come for? Ah, beer. She grabbed a couple of ice-cold bottles and walked back to the bedroom where Baz was oblivious to the world.

'Here.' She knelt down and handed one to him. 'They're cold.'

'Sit on me.' Baz didn't even open his eyes.

'Stop it.' She slapped away his hand. She knew from past experience that she'd get half-way there and he'd fall asleep or roll over. 'Baz,' she said, trying to wake him up. 'Baz.'

'What?'

'How long have we been here?'

'What?'

'In LA. How long have we been here?'

'Dunno. Couple of months – why?'

'How long are we allowed to be here?'

'What d'you mean? In this apartment?'

'No. Immigration. I can't remember how long my visa lasts.'

Baz opened his eyes. 'Where's your passport? Where's mine?'

'I don't know. I can't remember where I put them.' Charmaine was worried.

'Are you fucking kidding me?' Baz leaped out of bed. Naked, he ran to their suitcase. Charmaine began to giggle. 'It's not funny, you silly cunt. If the Immigration police come looking for us, we're fucked. D'you know how much coke is in this flat?'

Charmaine stopped laughing. 'Oh, God, I remember seeing them the first couple of days – but after the furniture came . . . I don't know.'

'Will you give me a hand?' Baz was shouting now. Coke, Charmaine had heard, made you paranoid. Well, Baz was certainly paranoid. She got up and started looking through their things.

An hour later, she gave a triumphant shout. 'Here! In the kitchen! I've found them!' Baz came stumbling through, still naked, and snatched them from her. For some bizarre reason, Charmaine had wrapped both passports in a ZipLock bag and stored them in the cereal jar. He opened the bag and flipped through his dark blue passport. 'We've overstayed by a week,' he said. 'Fuck.'

'No sweat. Just means you might not be able to come back for a while.' Touch rolled a spliff and looked at Baz. 'Thing is,' he continued, 'they're too busy lookin' for wetbacks and spics even to think about lookin' for the two of you. We need more Anglos in California, man. Don't worry about it.'

'But what d'you mean, we won't be able to come back? You mean we can't leave?' Baz sounded worried.

'No, nothin' like that, man. Just means they ain't gonna come lookin' for you. See this thing?' Touch pointed to the white I-94 card stapled inside Baz's passport. 'When you leave the US you hand it in. You give it to the airline, they pass it on to the INS. That way, they have a record of you leavin' the country. If you don't give it in, if you throw it away, say you lost it, whatever, they'll just say it might be difficult for you comin' back in the next time . . . if the INS don't believe you. Don't mean nothin'. You're English. You'll get back in. Anyways, how long you all plannin' on stayin' anyway? How much stuff you got left?' Touch looked at him. He knew Baz and Charmaine had been working their way through the stash. He could tell.

'Oh, enough. Dunno. Might stay another couple of months. See how it goes, you know.' Touch nodded. The stuff he'd brought from England was Grade A. First class. Tip-top. He couldn't wait for Baz to go back and get another batch.

'Baz.' Charmaine shook him. 'Baz. Wake up.' He grunted and rolled over. Charmaine looked at her watch. It was almost noon. 'Baz.' She shook him again, harder.

'Charmaine . . . what the *fuck*?' He opened his eyes.

'I need some money.' He'd been gone for almost two days. She was used to his bizarre comings and goings, but two days? He'd left her without any money, and their stash was finished. She felt terrible.

'I don't have any. Now shut the fuck up.'

'But what am I supposed to do?' She began to cry. 'You've been gone for days – you don't phone, you don't tell me where you've been. I've been here since Thursday on my own and there's no food in the house. What am I supposed to do?'

'Jesus, Charmaine, I don't know. I can't find Touch. We've got a cash-flow problem on our hands and we're out of blow. In fact, we're out of luck. I don't know what we're going to do. OK?' Baz was awake now.

Charmaine stopped snivelling. 'Shall I call my mother?' she asked nervously. She hated lying to Mary, and it had been almost a month since she'd last called.

'Sure.' He sighed.

'She could send us some money – you know, Western Union or whatever they call it. It'll be here in fifteen minutes.' She didn't tell him she'd already asked Mary for money twice.

She scrambled out of bed. It was past noon. Nine o'clock in the evening in London. If they wanted to eat that day, she'd better call her quickly. There was a twenty-four-hour *bureau de change* at Victoria station that her mother had used the last time. She pulled on her jeans.

'I know, Mummy. It's the last time, I promise. Baz hasn't been paid by the band manager yet, I don't know why. Everything just takes so long over here. It's complicated.'

'But, darling, Baz hasn't been paid since you got there. It's been more than three months. Why don't you just come home?' Mary Hunter was in tears.

'I will, Mummy. Soon. I'm going to stick it out for another month and then I'll come back, I promise.'

Charmaine wiped away her own tears with the back of her hand.

'Charmaine, if something's happened to you, you'd tell me, wouldn't you, darling? I don't care what it is.'

'Of course I would, Mummy. Nothing's happened. Honestly. I'm just . . .'

'Just what, darling?'

'Nothing. Look, I'll be home in a month. Promise. And thanks for sending the money.'

'Don't worry, darling. Just come back soon. I miss you.'

'I miss you too.' Charmaine hung up. In fact, she missed her mother so much it hurt. But she couldn't leave Baz. What would he do in LA without her? He needed her. She *knew* he needed her. She blew her nose and walked slowly to the supermarket on the corner of Camino Real and Baxter. The guys at the Western Union counter already knew her name.

'Well,' Clive said, leaning back against the cushions. 'It seems reasonably sound.' Nathalie looked at him gratefully.

'But, darling, I don't understand,' Cordelia said. 'It's so much *work*. Why don't you do something else? Find a boyfriend or something normal.'

'What – like you?' Nathalie said sharply. Cordelia shot her a wounded look. There were certain areas in which her relationship with her daughter would never be the same again. She sighed.

'Darling, it's a very nice idea,' Clive, ever the peace-maker, spoke, 'but your mother's right. It's an awful lot of work. Manufacturing, retail, management – you're only nineteen.'

'I know, but we've got a whole team planned. Philippe will help. And Marcus. And we've got a friend, Juliette, who's studying fashion – she's nearly finished. We'd all work together. Share the profits.'

'Marcus?'

'He's . . . a friend of Philippe's. He's really nice.' Cordelia looked sharply at her daughter. Nathalie reddened. 'But it would be a proper business partnership,' she said quickly. 'We'd get a lawyer and everything.'

'In principle, it's never a good idea to go into business with a spouse or a friend,' Clive added, 'but there are legal measures—'

'Clive!' Cordelia protested. 'She's far too young. It's too much responsibility. We can't let her do this.'

'Cordy,' Clive said gently, 'think of what you'd done by the time you were nineteen.'

'Well, yes. But those were different times, you know.'

'Not really,' Nathalie contradicted her. 'And, besides, I'm good at what I do at TopGirl. I know I am. And they know it. But I'm tired of using my talents to make money for someone else. How hard can it be?'

She'd asked Juliette the exact same question. How hard can it be? Juliette had picked up a bra off the kitchen table and examined it with an expert eye. 'Not much to it,' she'd said, turning the material over in her hands. 'Underwiring, straps, fasteners – a doddle.'

'We'd need a reliable manufacturing source. Somewhere cheap, English-speaking. Steve at college says Malaysia's a good bet.'

'Malaysia?' Nathalie was startled. 'Why Malaysia?' There was a sudden silence. She looked at her brother, then at Juliette, who was reporting on a conversation with her tutor.

'He says it's absolutely the best place,' she said. 'They speak good English – it's an ex-British colony. Their labour costs are almost a quarter of Hong Kong or Taiwan, good workers, good work ethic. And they're looking for foreign investment. He says you can't go wrong.'

'Well, we don't know anyone in Malaysia. How would we go about it?' Philippe interjected.

Nathalie was chewing the end of her pencil.

'Steve can get us a list of contacts, small-scale seamstresses,' Juliette told him. 'We'd have to go there – or, at least, one of us. Kuala Lumpur is where most of the industry's located. I can't go. I've got my final show in about a month, but what about you, Nathalie? It'd be so cool!'

'Er, well, let's think about it. I mean, maybe Malaysia's not the only place. Might be others.' Nathalie's cheeks were flushed.

'Yeah, but it's definitely the *best* place. What's wrong with it? Have you been there?'

'No,' Philippe said briskly. 'Let's think this one over. Nice work, Jule.' He got up to fill the kettle.

Nathalie watched Juliette gather the drawings into a neat pile. She had a pattern-cutting class to go to and she was already late. They'd been sitting all afternoon looking at fabric samples and brainstorming. Marcus was coming over that evening and Nathalie wanted something concrete to show him. She had great taste but a complete inability to draw a straight line. Or a curved one, come to that. She talked, cut things out, drew with her hands, and Juliette sketched. Juliette was amazing. Nathalie picked up one of the designs she'd been working on – TootieFrootie, she'd named it. The sketches showed bras and panties with graphic fruit prints, sliced oranges, apples, tangerines, lemons, in bold black and orange, black and green, black and yellow prints. Even as sketches they looked tempting.

'See ya later!' Juliette called. The front door slammed behind her.

There was a sudden silence.

'Nat?' Philippe's voice was gentle.

Ever since the dreadful accident – as everyone liked to call it – with Sacha, Philippe and Nathalie had hardly mentioned him. 'Nat?' he said again. 'You OK?'

Nathalie turned to look at him. 'It doesn't mean we'll see him or anything,' she said, in a low voice. 'KL's a big city.'

'I suppose so.'

'And it sounds like it's the best place – right?'

'I guess. Are you really OK with it, Nat?' he said. 'I'll come with you, if you like. If you're worried about bumping into him. Or Marcus could go with you . . .'

'Don't be daft. You're at work, remember? It'll be fine. I won't run into him. I'll set up a tight schedule. I'm sure Juliette's tutor will put us in touch with someone reliable to show us round and stuff. It'll be fine.' Nathalie sounded firmer than she felt.

'OK. I suppose so. I'm just being over-protective, I expect.'

'You don't have to protect me from Sacha, Philippe. He means nothing to me. Or to you. Come on, it's all over, that silly fuss. It's finished. Let's forget about it.'

'Wait till Mum hears about it,' Philippe predicted gloomily.

'You can't let her go alone!' Cordelia shouted at Clive. 'It's out of the question. Half-way round the world? Have you lost your senses? One of us had better go with her. *I'll* go with her.' Cordelia was shaking. Kuala Lumpur? Nathalie was going to Kuala Lumpur – *alone*? Her heart was beating fast. She had put Sacha out of her mind – hadn't thought about him in months. Now Clive was standing there telling her Nathalie was about to take off for a ten-day business trip to the city in which he lived? He *had* to be joking.

'Now, Cordy,' Clive began placatingly, as always, 'she's a big girl, we agreed that—'

'She's *my* little girl!' Cordelia shouted. 'And if *you* don't care about what happens to her, *I* do!' She flung the cruel accusation at him. Completely unfounded, she knew, even as the words left her mouth, but the thought of Nathalie being in the same hemisphere as Sacha – it was enough to make her go mad.

'*Cordelia*!' Clive yelled. She stopped in mid-sentence.

She'd never heard him yell before. Her mouth hung open. 'Will you shut *up*? Nathalie's going over there alone, she's on a business trip. I will arrange for her to stay with some business associates of mine. They'll provide her with a driver, make sure she knows where she's going, and that's the end of it. I won't hear another word about it.' He walked out of the room.

Cordelia stared after him. She'd never seen him so angry.

31

It took Nathalie almost a week to decide. The questions swam round and round in her head. Should she call Sacha? Should she open up those old wounds? She and Marcus were getting on so well, and she liked him. He was kind and patient and didn't rush her into . . . well, into *any*thing. With him, it wasn't the nerve-racking, exquisitely painful emotional state she felt whenever she thought of Sacha, and she managed – almost – to kiss him without that awful vision of her mother and Sacha floating into her head. And it wasn't the horrid feeling she got when she thought about Joules. No, Marcus was easy. He was *exactly* like Clive. Kind, patient, gentle. So why didn't she want him in *that* way? In Marcus she had everything any sane young woman would want, a nice, decent young man, so why did she find it so hard? She had no answers. When she felt his arms around her, or the gentle pressure of his lips, her mind drifted away from him. It was as if he were too . . . *nice*.

A month later, Nathalie walked into a small bar in Bangsar, the hippest part of KL. She was surprisingly calm. She saw him almost as soon as she entered. He was sitting by the window, reading a paper, and he was every bit as gorgeous as she remembered. His hair was still dark and curly, but shorter now, and he wore glasses. She stopped, her heart in her mouth.

Then, as if he sensed someone watching, he lifted his head from the paper and their eyes met. He got up slowly and walked towards her. 'Nathalie.' He kissed her on both cheeks.

'Sacha.'

'Long time.' She couldn't read his face. He was making her nervous. 'Would you like something to drink?' he said. She'd have swallowed a bottle of gin, if she could. They walked towards the bar. 'What would you like?'

'A gin and tonic, please,' she said, fiddling with her watch-strap. The calm that had descended upon her ever since she'd called him the day before had deserted her. He said something in Malay to the bartender.

'Here you go. D'you want to sit down?'

She nodded. Her legs were wobbly. He led her to a table by the window. They sat down, and Nathalie took a gulp of her drink. She wished she'd taken a couple of gulps of something before coming out.

'Philippe sends his regards,' she began brightly. Untruthfully.

'Really?' His dark eyes looked straight through her.

She blushed. 'Well, not really. He'd probably have a fit if he knew I was here.' Sacha said nothing. Nathalie chewed her lip. This wasn't going very well.

'What're you doing in KL?' he asked.

'Well, we're thinking of opening a business,' she began. He raised his eyebrows. 'And?' He took a sip of his drink.

'And KL was recommended by one of our . . . consultants as a possible manufacturing base.' She took another gulp, and outlined their business plans, described the set-up, the concept, their search for premises. Sacha seemed impressed. 'So,' she concluded, almost half an hour later, 'that's why I'm here. Lim Soon have been fantastic.' She'd met with the small garment manufacturers several times over the past few days. They were perfect. Teresa Soon, a smiling, middle-aged woman and the brains behind the factory, Nathalie guessed, was in charge of operations and she ran a pretty tight ship. Nathalie had liked her the minute they met. She hadn't patronised her, which, when you were nineteen and starting out in the business world, meant a lot.

'Hmm. Didn't know you were a businesswoman, Nathalie,' Sacha said quietly.

Nathalie was pleased. 'Oh, I'm not. At least not yet . . . We're only just starting.'

'Still. It's pretty impressive. Where did you go to university?'

'Oh, I haven't. I'm not sure I want to.'

'Right. You were in school when we last met.'

'Yes. I was in the lower sixth. You and Philippe were just finishing at Reading, I think.' Sacha nodded. 'Enough about me,' Nathalie said. 'What are you doing now?' She drained her gin and tonic.

Sacha signalled to the bartender for another. 'Me? I'm an accountant – almost. I'm doing my final set of exams this year. It's boring, for the most part, but it's hard work. Lots of exams. Hey, have you had dinner?' He glanced at his watch. It was almost ten.

'No, I forgot. I was really busy this afternoon,' Nathalie said, lying through her teeth. She'd spent the entire afternoon trying on different outfits. She'd been through her suitcase almost ten times by the time eight o'clock rolled round. She'd finally settled on a pair of black silk palazzo pants and a silver lamé top with silver hoop earrings and flat black pumps. She'd caught a little sun since she'd been in KL and her cheeks were prettily pink. Especially now, after a drink. 'Do the restaurants close early round here?' she asked, looking around the bar. It didn't look as though they served food.

'Are you kidding? This is KL-*la*.' He smiled suddenly, for almost the first time that evening.

Nathalie felt her heart lift. Ridiculous! She couldn't help staring at his smile, his perfect white teeth and the faint shadow of beard under his tanned skin.

'What does that mean?' She laughed, relaxing.

'Which part? The KL bit or the "*la*"?'

'Both.' She was intrigued.

'Well, KL doesn't sleep. It's like New York. You can get anything you want, anytime you want. We work, we Malaysians. Not like you lazy Brits.'

'Come on, we work hard!' Nathalie protested.

'Sure. Teabreak-*la* . . . every five minutes. I used to work on a building site.'

'No! Really? And what about the "*la*" bit?'

'Oh, that's just what we put on the end of everything we say. OK-*la*. You come now-*la*. What's your name-*la*? Doesn't mean anything. It's just typical Malaysian.'

'And are you just typical Malaysian?' Nathalie felt bold enough to ask.

'Sure. Joe Bloggs. Just your average guy.'

'Come on. Not all Malaysians are like you. Even *I* can see that. But isn't your mother German or something?' Nathalie pretended not to remember.

'Finnish. But she left a long time ago. Come on, you want to see KL-*la*?' He finished his drink. Nathalie followed suit, and they got up to leave.

It was pleasantly cool outside, not as muggy as it had been during the day. They turned left, away from the main strip.

'Where are we going?'

'Oh, we'll just drive around for a bit. Show you the sights. Have you ever eaten satay?' He stopped in front of a silver BMW and opened the door for her.

'No. What is it?'

'It's good. Now, stop talking. You ask too many questions.' Nathalie giggled as he slid a CD into the player and started the car.

Three hours later, they were drinking something called

tea-tarée, a kind of sweet, milky tea, at a junction on the outskirts of KL. It was well after one in the morning and the place was full.

'Everyone comes here for tea-tarée,' Sacha explained. 'It's what we do before we go out to a club or whatever and it's what we do afterwards. You come back here at five and it'll still be packed.'

Nathalie was entranced. She loved KL. It was so vibrant, so optimistic. The people were friendly and charming and outgoing – she'd never been in a country where so many people were 'in business'. The whole country was on the move. Everyone was striking a deal, making a contact, signing a contract. Malaysia was building itself up, slowly but surely, and everyone was part of it. To Nathalie, coming from Britain, it was magical. No one seemed to think it odd that a petite nineteen-year-old girl had the *chutzpah* to come up with a business idea, find a team of willing partners and fly half-way round the world to make it work. The fact that her trip was made easier and more comfortable by her stepfather's connections? Well, that was business. Didn't all great trading dynasties start the same way? The Malaysians had centuries of trade and a mercantile culture behind them. So did the British.

'Let's go,' Sacha said quietly. They'd driven high up into the hills above KL and were sitting in the car, looking out over the twinkling lights of the city. It was nearly three o'clock. Nathalie couldn't believe she was still awake, still sitting next to Sacha, still hanging on his every word. All evening, she'd been aware of a hot, trembling feeling in the pit of her stomach. Every time he looked at her, opened the door for her, passed her a drink or a glass of tea-tarée, she'd felt her insides quiver, a rush of emotion. He started the engine. He drove quickly in silence, stopping only once to buy a packet of cigarettes from a roadside vendor. Nathalie didn't dare say a word until he pulled into the driveway of a small bungalow and killed the engine. He turned to face her.

'Is this your—' she began.

'Ssh. I've told you already – you ask too many questions. Come on.' He opened the car door quietly and slid out.

As if in a trance, Nathalie followed him, her stomach contracting with nerves and excitement. He stopped at the front door and removed his shoes. She did the same. Malaysians never walked into a house with shoes on. He opened the door quietly and pulled her inside.

It was pitch black and hot, and she felt his hands on her shoulders as he steered her towards his room. He shut the door, turned on the air-conditioning and pulled back the curtains. The streetlamp cast a pale yellow light into the room. He leaned against the door and stared at her.

Nathalie swallowed, not trusting herself to speak. In the dim light, she watched him take off his glasses, unbutton his shirt and tug it off with the white T-shirt he was wearing underneath. She saw the dark patches of hair under her arms. Then he unbuckled his jeans, slid out of them . . . and waited for her.

And she came to him, tears prickling behind her eyes. He slid his hands under her top, feeling for the softness of her breasts, touching each little nipple until she moaned softly. The intense pleasure coursing through her body was almost painful. He bent his head and kissed her playfully. His hands slid down her stomach, resting just below the waistband of her trousers, stroking her belly-button lazily, erotically. She was tense, so tense. She ran a hand over his arms, revelling in the feel of hard muscles and taut skin. His own breathing was ragged as he undid her trousers and let them fall in a crumpled heap at her feet. He pushed her top up over her breasts, not even bothering to take it off and expertly unfastened the lacy bra.

'Sacha,' she whispered as he pushed her backwards towards his bed. She could no more stop him than she could stop herself. She held her breath, waiting for the moment when her body would turn against her, revolt against the feelings flooding her . . . but it didn't. It just got better and better. And when he moved inside her, she couldn't think of anything other than the waves of pleasure that shuddered through her as they both exploded and she closed her eyes against the storm. 'I love you,' she whispered against his neck. 'I love you.'

Sacha did not reply.

Some time just before dawn Sacha awoke and gently disengaged Nathalie's arm from round his neck. He slipped out of bed, picked up the discarded T-shirt and a clean pair of boxer shorts. He opened the bedroom door quietly. The house was silent as he pulled on his clothes, then padded across the living room.

He opened the front door. It was still and warm outside, away from the cool of the air-conditioning, and he stood in the darkness, listening to the crickets. He remembered the packet of cigarettes he'd bought and walked out to the car to find them. He lit a cigarette and sat down on the steps of the veranda, shaking his head in disbelief at what he had just done. He had just slept with Cordelia's daughter. She was lying there, in his bed, in his grandmother's house. Why hadn't he taken her to a hotel? What would happen if his grandmother found out?

He finished his cigarette quickly and peered at his watch – he had to get Nathalie out of his bed before Nek woke up. It was five thirty. She'd sleep until six thirty or so. And she wouldn't wake up. Aunt Nuria used to joke she'd sleep through an earthquake. He got up and walked quietly back into the bedroom. To his surprise, Nathalie was standing by the window. She turned as he came into the room, wrapped in the bedsheet, and gave a small, quick smile.

'I . . . noticed you were gone,' she began, walking towards him.

He put up his hands as if to stop her from coming closer. Nathalie stopped, her heart sinking. 'Look,' he said quickly, 'I'm sorry about what happened, Nathalie. I didn't mean for it to happen. I don't want to hurt your feelings.'

'What d'you mean?' Nathalie whispered. She had a dreadful feeling she knew what was coming.

'Nathalie, I – I have a girlfriend. She's someone I – I'll eventually marry. It's been decided between our families for ages. I should have told you, I know. I – I'm sorry.'

'Oh.' Nathalie didn't know what to say. Suddenly she felt very young and very stupid. Her eyes filled with tears and she turned away. 'You'd better take me back to the hotel,' she whispered.

'I guess so.' Sacha picked up his jeans.

'Do you mind waiting outside while I get dressed?' she asked, tears rolling down her cheeks.

'Sure.' He picked up the rest of his clothing and dressed in the living room.

Twenty minutes later, she got out of the car in front of the Marriott and walked into the lobby without saying a word. Not even goodbye. She pushed open the door to her room and sank down onto the floor.

She couldn't have said how long she sat there, staring into space. She got up when her legs had lost all feeling and stumbled to the bathroom. As dawn broke over the city, she showered away every last trace of Sacha, watching the soapy water curl around her feet and disappear down the drain.

32

Charmaine struggled to open her eyes, which felt as though they were glued shut. When she succeeded she looked around for Baz. He wasn't there. She sat up, trying and failing to remember what they'd been doing the night before. She dimly recalled going out with Touch and one or two of his friends to a club somewhere near the airport – Blue something-or-other. It had been hot, dark and smoky, and she'd had a drink, done a few lines in the bathroom – usual Friday-night activities. But that was it. She couldn't remember how they'd got home or why she was still fully clothed.

She swung her legs gingerly off the bed and tried to stand up. Her head was pounding and she felt nauseous. She pushed open the door and stumbled into the bathroom, trying to control her breathing. The last thing she wanted was to start the day vomiting.

She fumbled for the switch and winced as the tiny bathroom flooded with light. She looked at herself in the mirror as she turned on the tap to clean her teeth. Skin, blotchy, flaking and dull; eyes, dimmed, smudged make-up and tired; hair, lank and lifeless, her roots showing. She stared at herself, too tired even to register how awful she looked. Mechanically she bent down and started brushing. As she spat and rinsed, she noticed her gums were bleeding. A horrible cold feeling moved up the back of her neck.

Only days before Touch had showed off the disgusting gaps in his mouth where his teeth ought to have been. 'Yep,' he said, with satisfaction, noting Baz and Charmaine's horror. 'Gum disease. This shit eats away at your gums,' he said, crumbling a tiny piece of cocaine between his fingers. 'Gotta be careful. Visit the dentist. Don't do what I did and put more on to numb the pain.'

Charmaine had picked up the habit of rubbing a little coke on her gums before doing a line – both Baz and Touch swore it entered the bloodstream directly through the saliva and made for a better buzz. She stared at the pinkish-red foam in the sink. Suddenly, there was a knock at the door. She was puzzled. Baz never knocked. The door wasn't even shut properly. She rinsed her mouth.

'Baz?' she called, washing away the blood. 'What d'you want?'

'It's not Baz, it's me, Lindy. Can I come in? I'm busting for a pee.'

Charmaine yanked open the door. Who on earth was Lindy? A near-naked, small dark-haired girl ran in and plonked herself on the toilet. She didn't seem to register Charmaine's presence.

Charmaine stared at her. 'Who're you?' she asked. 'How did you get in?'

'I came with Baz,' the girl said brightly, reaching for the toilet roll. 'Dontcha remember? We all came back together.'

'What d'you mean? Who's we? Me and Baz?'

'Yeah. Last night ... Whassa matter with you?' She flushed the toilet and got up. She was wearing what looked like a pair of Baz's boxer shorts and little else. 'God, I look *fucked*.' She examined her face critically. She was young, perhaps no more than eighteen, with pale skin, large blue eyes and long, dark brown hair. Charmaine had never seen her before in her life.

'I'm sorry, but why are you wearing Baz's underwear?' Charmaine asked. 'Did you come with Touch? I mean, are you one of his friends?'

'No, I told you. I'm *Baz*'s friend. Look, are you gonna stand here all morning asking dumb questions or what?' She picked up Charmaine's toothbrush and rinsed it in preparation for use.

'That's *my* toothbrush!' Charmaine snapped, and snatched it out of her hand.

'Ow!' the girl squealed, as Charmaine's nails scratched her. 'Watch where you put your fucking hands!' she snapped.

'Just get out of my bathroom,' Charmaine ordered, her voice trembling with rage.

'Oh, *excuse* me!' The girl laughed nastily. 'I thought this was Baz's place.'

'Just get out!' Charmaine was shouting now. She had no

idea who Lindy was – and she didn't care to find out. She wanted her out of the flat – fast.

'What the fuck's going on?' Baz yelled sleepily, from the sitting room.

Both girls turned. Charmaine pulled open the sitting-room door. Baz was lying on the sofa cushions, which were spread out on the ground, making a sort of bed. A double bed. Lindy's clothes were tangled in the sheets – black bra, tank top, leopard-print miniskirt. Charmaine stared at the mess in disbelief. 'Char, get off her case, will you?' He pulled a pillow over his head.

Charmaine turned to the girl, her eyes blazing. Something inside her had snapped. It was the last straw. 'Get the fuck out of my house before I call the police. Go on, pick up your shit and *get out*,' she said, as calmly as she could. She walked over to the makeshift bed, bent down and picked up the girl's clothing. 'Go *on*,' she shouted, flinging the items at her. 'Get moving. *Now*.' The girl glared at her. She began to get dressed.

'For fuck's sake, Char,' Baz moaned, from under the pillow.

Charmaine looked at him coldly. 'Just say one more word to me, Baz, and I swear I'll pick up the phone. I'm sure the LAPD would love to know what you've been up to since your visa ran out. That's two strikes against you.' Charmaine looked at the pair contemptuously, then went back into the bathroom.

She sat down on the toilet seat, the blood ringing in her ears. Her hands were shaking. Through the thin walls she could hear them whispering. Somehow the enormity of what Baz had done – brought another girl home while Charmaine was knocked out on a combination of alcohol and coke – paled in comparison to the mess she now recognised she was in. She had to get out of there. She had to clean up her act. It was the end of the road for her – and for Baz. Terrified as she was at the thought of staying in LA alone, she knew she had to leave him. She would have to get a job, make some money, save enough for a ticket back to Britain.

Baz was in way over his head, she thought, and she saw now that he wanted to drag her down with him. He'd come out to LA full of ideas – although she couldn't quite remember what they were – and had got himself mixed up with the wrong crowd. Touch was an asshole. He'd led Baz astray with his promises and wild fantasies about making it big. Two tears splotched onto her hands. Seeing that stupid little girl in *her* bathroom cleaning her teeth with *her* toothbrush, after having done God knows what to *her* boyfriend . . . She couldn't take it any more. Not another day. But what the hell could she do? She reached for the toilet roll. She felt sick. Her mind was racing. She had no money, nothing . . . $20 in change . . . nowhere to live, unless you counted this flea-pit, which she shared with Baz, and she *had* to get out. But where to? She couldn't ask her mother for another penny. All she needed was enough money for another few weeks and a plane ticket to London. But how? In her position, finding the cab fare to get downtown seemed impossible.

Suddenly she remembered talking to one of the girls Touch picked up and brought home with alarming ease. Jessica was her name. She was a dancer, of sorts. She worked in a club somewhere downtown, some sort of dance club where men paid you to dance with them – that was *all* – and maybe chat a little. She worked the late shift, from midnight to four and made tons of money. I could do that, Charmaine thought blowing her nose. You didn't need too many skills to dance and make inane conversation with a bunch of middle-aged businessmen which was how she'd heard Jessica describe it. It wasn't like she'd be *stripping* or anything like that.

She heard the front door slam. The little bitch had gone. She got up. She would get Jessica's number and call her. The first step towards getting out of there. She was unsure of herself, scared, lonely, but seeing that little tramp in her bathroom had jolted something in her. She needed to get away from Baz – fast. Why the hell had she stayed so long?

33

It was one of those fantastically clear, sunny days in late September that sometimes occur after the Santa Ana winds have blown across LA, chasing the smog out to sea. Everything was sharp, in focus, even the shadows. The sky was egg-shell blue, the clouds floated wispily white and high. It was perfect. The sea shimmered to his left, a deeper blue mirror of the expanse overhead, and the shadowy folds of the Sierra Madre mountains followed the curve of the snaking road as it wound its way up the coast. Bruce Eastman sped down the Pacific Coast Highway towards Santa Barbara, nudging his ancient convertible Karmann Ghia to just above 75 m.p.h., the fastest she'd ever gone. He'd been in California for six weeks and this was his first trip outside LA, the ugly, sprawling city he'd been sent to. *Exiled* to, he thought grimly. He hated it.

He thought of Cape Town, the deep blue ocean and the wide, pale skies. The widest skies in the world. Nowhere did the sky seem so distant as in Cape Town. He felt a pang of homesickness and shook himself. He was on his way to the most important meeting of his life. It was not a time for nostalgia. He shifted his gaze from the sea and tried to concentrate on the task ahead. He'd spent months cultivating this latest contact, a young student from Bahrain whose father had the kind of access to arms they so desperately needed. Now he, Abdul and Justin were to meet at a college bar in Santa Barbara and talk money. It would be the first time he'd been to such a meeting, although Justin was an old hand. Justin had been around. He'd even been in Algeria when MK first went underground. Or so he said.

He nudged the car up the long hill north of Malibu. In a

couple of hours, with a bit of luck, he would hit Santa Barbara. He went over the checks in his head. All the phone numbers he had been given had checked out. He had the telegram from Paul in London; the confirmations from Bahrain and Abu Dhabi were in his pocket. His stomach tightened. He'd been waiting for this moment for a very long time.

PART FOUR

34

November 1986: London

Two years later, at a glittering reception held at the Grosvenor House Hotel on Park Lane, Nathalie received an honourable mention in the Young British Entrepreneur of the Year awards from a beaming Liz Brown, editor of *Cosmopolitan* and a co-sponsor of the event. She posed for photographs with her three partners, Philippe, Marcus and Juliette, then went out and got blindingly drunk.

The following morning, she woke up next to Marcus with cotton-wool in her mouth and a spongy, liquid feeling behind her eyes. She lay still, watching the long muslin curtains billow in the morning breeze. It had been a surprisingly mild autumn and the sun peeked through the cloud every now and then, causing myriad variations in tone in the all-white room. Marcus was on his back, snoring gently. It was unbelievable to Nathalie that she'd managed to put Sacha out of her mind and come back to Marcus, knowing deep down that she would never feel for him anything close to what she felt for Sacha. Sometimes she thought he knew her heart was elsewhere, but he never said. He was happy to have her any way he could, he told her.

She sighed. She knew she couldn't force herself to feel something she didn't, but Marcus's easy acceptance, the fact that he was prepared to put up with her mood swings, her temper, the fact that she hated sex – with him, at least

. . . Sometimes she thought his willingness to accept her as she was only made her worse. She could feel his bare leg next to hers . . . she must have managed it last night. She was relieved. It was the only way she could do it – get absolutely plastered and close her eyes. Unfortunately, as she wasn't much of a drinker, it didn't happen often. Still, Marcus never said anything. He loved her so much, he told her over and over again, it wouldn't matter if she didn't really enjoy it. She wondered if she would ever again feel anything like the pleasure Sacha had somehow managed to wring from her.

Her stomach lurched. She was going to be sick. She lifted the heavy duvet, slid out of bed and only just made it to the bathroom before bringing up the caviar, Tiger prawns and cherry tomatoes she'd picked at during the reception. She clambered up and looked at herself in the mirror. Pale, her hair needed cutting . . . She could do with a holiday. She looked around the bathroom, which always lifted her spirits. Cordelia had taken charge of decorating the flat she and Marcus had bought at the beginning of the summer. Jenny, Philippe's girlfriend, was pregnant and Nathalie had thought it only fair that she and Marcus should move out.

They'd found the one-bedroomed flat in the Chelsea Studios, a charming little hideaway just off the Fulham Road. Originally an iron foundry, it had been transformed in the sixties by a private developer, with a passion for all things Italian, into a series of artists' studios and lofts, complete with a tinkling fountain in the middle of the pretty, shared courtyard. It was perfect. A thick blackened-oak door set in a nondescript wall off the main road opened onto a different world: gently drooping willow trees in a little courtyard, trailing wisteria and the sound of running water gave the little development a *Secret Garden* atmosphere. They'd fallen in love with it on the spot.

Cordelia had been magnificent. She was about to become a grandmother and was bathed in maternal warmth. No one, least of all her children, would have predicted it. She threw herself into the role of Principal Helper with abandon. Nothing was too much trouble for her. She would drive to London at the drop of a hat. She helped in the shops, the new flat, she took Jenny on extravagant shopping trips, treated Nathalie and Marcus to tea, to the opera. She had suddenly discovered a passion for interior design, spending hours poring over magazines, a large pair of scissors in hand as she cut out things that caught her eye and pasted them into a large, leatherbound scrapbook. When Nathalie and Juliette had a spare moment, she would bear down on them, sketches and ideas in hand.

In the bathroom, she had chosen an off-white stone floor tile. The walls were a chalky white, the wooden accessories dark teak. At one end, an enormous mirror with an elaborately carved Indonesian wood frame rested at a flattering angle against the wall. The bath was deep and wide, with a recessed shower-head above it. Woven baskets were dotted around the floor containing towels, soaps, fragrance – 'Anything and everything for the Complete Bathing Experience,' Cordelia had laughed, reading yet another one of her interior design books. She'd become quite an expert. Nathalie smiled to herself. Just looking around at the home she and Marcus had managed to make was calming.

'Nat?' Marcus called. 'You OK?'

'I'm fine,' she said, coming through to the bedroom. 'I'm going to take a shower. What d'you feel like doing this morning?' she asked, lifting her dressing-gown off the floor. He paused for a moment. Truth was, he'd like nothing better than to make love to her again – he thought of himself as something of a morning man – but it was out of the question. He sighed.

'Breakfast?' He looked at her enquiringly. 'Can you face it?'

'Sure. Gimme half an hour.' She disappeared into the

bathroom. He peeked at himself under the duvet. It was getting harder, not easier. And he wasn't referring to his cock.

Rianne looked across the kitchen table at Gabby. She had lost so much weight it was scary: her collarbones were standing out. *Collarbones?* Gabby?

'What's happening to you, Gabby? You're wasting away.'

'Oh, don't be silly. I'm not. I'm just working hard. I don't have time to eat.'

'Rubbish. You've never been so thin before. I'm worried about you.'

'I should be worried about *you*,' Gabby said drily, getting up to put the kettle on. 'There's practically nothing of you.' It was true. Rianne had grown even leaner, and looked fantastic. She and her new Spanish boyfriend, Olivier – possibly the most drop-dead gorgeous man Gabby had ever seen – were in town doing shows for London Fashion Week. Olivier was also a model.

'Look, stop trying to change the subject,' Rianne said firmly. 'How's Dominic?'

Gabby smiled brightly. A little too brightly. 'He's great.'

Rianne frowned. Great? The expression wasn't one Gabby used. Something odd was going on. Gabby was outwardly cheerful, brisk. She looked well, if thin. Her hair was long and curly and . . . had she coloured it?

'What have you done to your hair? It looks great.' Now *that* was the proper use of the word.

'Oh, d'you like it?' Gabby blushed suddenly. 'I had a henna rinse. I don't know . . . I . . . well, it's a bit different.' She touched her curls self-consciously.

'No, it's lovely. I've never seen you with your hair so long, that's all. It really suits you.' Gabby blushed again.

What was wrong with her? Rianne wondered. She was acting as though no one ever paid her a compliment. Was that it? Rianne hadn't seen Dominic in over a year. They weren't living together – he had his flat in Clapham, which he shared with a few other people, and Gabby had moved into a shared house in Bloomsbury. She'd absolutely refused to stay at Wilton Crescent while she did the law conversion course. 'Don't be silly,' she'd said to Rianne firmly. 'I've sponged off you every year since I started at Oxford. Enough's enough.' Rianne had protested loud and long, but Gabby was firm. Besides, she had added, the opulence of Wilton Crescent was just a little at odds with her current lifestyle. Not that she had much of one.

'Anyhow,' Gabby said suddenly, 'you know who I'm really worried about?'

Rianne nodded. They were all worried about Charmaine. 'Did you manage to get through to her?'

'No. Her mum gave me a number but there's never anyone at home . . . and there's no answering-machine. I don't know what's going on.'

'What d'you think we should do?' It seemed so unfair, Rianne thought. Life was going so well for the three of them, but not for Charmaine. In the three years since she'd left St Anne's, Rianne had come to realise not only what each of the others meant to her, she had learned what they meant to each other. If anything, their friendship had deepened since they'd left. In the shallow, fickle world of modelling and short-term celebrity, she'd come to understand how much she depended on them. Apart from Lisette, whose support was more nagging than genuine, the three were the most constant and dependable source of affection in her life. Hard as it had been to trust them at first, she now trusted them utterly, especially Gabby. They were more like sisters to her now than friends. For Rianne, whose sense of family was shaky, at best, this last was a complete revelation.

'I don't know,' Gabby said, stirring her coffee slowly. 'Maybe one of us should go out there.'

'But we don't know where she is. LA's a big place,' Rianne said slowly, feeling a pang of guilt. She'd been in LA six months previously – horrible place. She hadn't tried to find Charmaine – she wouldn't have known where to start.

'I know. It's a silly thought. I'm just so worried. It seems so unfair. I mean, look at you, look at Nat – you've got everything sorted out. You've both done so well.'

'And you, Gabs,' Rianne pointed out, and frowned. Something was *definitely* wrong with Gabby, never mind Charmaine. 'Everything's . . . OK with you, isn't it?' There was silence. 'Gabby?' Rianne looked at her closely. She had gone very still and quiet. 'Gabby?' she said again.

'Oh, I'm fine,' Gabby said suddenly. She stood up and walked over to the sink. She made a great show of washing her mug, drying it, wiping the sink clean.

Rianne watched her anxiously. Something was definitely up with Gabs – it wasn't only her appearance . . . something was wrong. Don't worry about Charmaine, she wanted to say to her, worry about yourself.

On the other side of the world, the object of their concern was getting ready for work. It was 10.30 p.m., half an hour before her shift would begin. Hurriedly, she finished applying mascara and slapped on some concealer. A quick squirt of hairspray and she was ready. At exactly ten thirty-five she heard the taxi's horn, opened the motel-room door and ran down the stairs.

'Hey, Lady Charming,' Joe, the driver said, as she got in. 'How you doin', girl?'

'Fine, Joe. Bit tired tonight.' Charmaine smiled at him. He always called her Lady Charming – on account of her lovely voice, he said. Just like Lady Di. Joe was the nicest person she'd met since she'd been working at Club Flamingo. He was from the Deep South – Louisiana – with a booming voice and a laugh to match. He looked like

Barry White, sang 'a whole lot better', or so he claimed, but still hadn't cut a record deal. Still, as he was wont to say, fame was 'just around the corner'. And *that* was where he was headed.

'You sure don't *look* tired. That's a pretty dress you got on tonight.'

'Thanks, Joe.'

The fifteen minutes it took to drive to Vermont and Third, where the club was, kept her sane. She looked out of the window at Pico Boulevard. Full of hustlers, drug-pushers and prostitutes. There was a cop car on every corner – and a doughnut shop – and this wasn't even the worst part of town. She opened her bag – forty dollars, some loose change and a lipstick. She owed Joe twenty-five and Jessica ten. That left her with five dollars to last until Monday. She pulled out Joe's twenty-five and snapped her purse shut angrily.

'Here we are, Lady Charming. You take it easy, now. See you tomorrow morning.' Joe got out and opened the door for her. It was almost eleven o'clock. She gave him her weekly cab fare and hurried up the stairs. This neighbour-hood – Club Flamingo, in particular – was not a place you wanted to hang around.

'Charmaine?' Sharkey, the manager, glowered at her as she walked past the dance floor. It was already full. Middle-aged men were eyeing the row of girls at the back of the hall. She spotted a few of the girls who were now her best friends. Tanja, a tall, striking Russian blonde – she'd been at Flamingo's almost as long as Charmaine, nearly a year and a half. *A year and a half?* Time had just slipped by. She'd only ever intended to work at Flamingo's for two months. She spotted Shanique, spectacularly kitted out in shocking pink Lycra, already stepping onto the dance floor with her 'regular', a short, balding man named Johnny. Johnny? Yeah, right. They were all called Johnny. None of Charmaine's regulars had arrived yet. She disappeared into the cloakroom to touch up her lipstick and stow away her bag.

Tina Turner's hit – a favourite at Flamingo's – was blaring over the loudspeakers. 'Private Dancer . . .' A couple of the men gave a little cheer as Charmaine took her place in the line-up, waiting for someone to ask her to dance.

Within seconds, a short, perspiring Korean had singled her out, given her number to the controller and they were moving onto the dance floor. 'Where you from?' he asked, as they did a half-waltz across the floor.

Charmaine sighed. It was always the same question in LA. Where are you from? Didn't *anyone* come from LA? 'Moscow,' she replied, bored.

'Ah.' He didn't smile. Charmaine didn't care. He'd already paid the fifteen dollars for a dance – five of which she kept. She waited impatiently for the ten-minute slot to finish.

'Charmaine.' It was Jessica's voice. 'You in there?'

'Yeah, I won't be a moment.' Charmaine flushed the toilet. She'd been taking a nap.

'You got my ten dollars?' Jessica asked, when she came out.

Charmaine nodded. 'In my bag. What're you smoking?'

'Grass. Want some?'

'I'd love some,' Charmaine said truthfully, 'but I didn't bring enough money with me tonight,' she lied. 'Can I pay you for it on Monday?'

'Jee-*sus*, Charmaine! How come you *always* owing me?' Jessica grumbled. She adjusted her wig in the cracked mirror. 'OK – but this is the last time, you hear me?' She fished in her purse for a small plastic bag. 'This is the *last* time, I swear it! Now gimme my ten dollars!'

Charmaine handed over the money, took the bag gratefully and slipped it under her bra. Time to get back on the dance floor. She glanced at the clock on the wall – only another two hours to go.

By four she was tired. Only two of her regulars had shown up, which meant she had had to spend time sitting at the bar, waiting for someone to approach her. She'd drunk almost a gallon of lemonade. Sharkey didn't like his girls getting drunk – made them depressed, he said. She finished the last dance of the evening and made her way to the cloakroom. Joe would be outside and she hated making him wait. She grabbed her bag, squeezed past Sharkey and felt his horrible pudgy hands on her hips. Having to endure Sharkey's pawing was simply part of the job – one of its many 'perks', as the girls joked. Fortunately, he had never tried anything with her.

''Bye!' she yelled, as she hurried down the steps. She wanted nothing more than to take a hot shower, lie in bed and smoke herself to sleep.

'Evenin', Lady Charming!' Joe opened the door. 'Busy night?'

'Too busy. I want my bed!'

'I heard *that*!' Joe walked around and got in. He worked the graveyard shift as well as the morning, afternoon and early evening shifts – he seemed to do nothing other than work, Charmaine thought. He lived somewhere near Compton, he'd said once, not that she knew where that was. In the two years since she'd moved out of Baz's grubby little apartment, she'd seen downtown, where she lived in the Blue Anchor Motel, Beverly Hills and a beautiful beach called Pacific Palisades where she and a bunch of the girls had once gone for the day. She'd been in LA two years and had never once left it.

She opened the door to room 301, kicked off her white high-heeled shoes and walked barefoot to the bathroom. Inside, she stripped off, turned on the tap and thanked God for America: even the scummiest places had good showers. She washed her hair, rinsing the cigarette smoke from her bleached tresses – gentlemen preferred blondes, or so

Sharkey said. She opened her bag, pulled out the grass, and quickly rolled herself a joint. Five minutes later she crawled into bed, somewhat more relaxed. Just before she drifted off to sleep she thought longingly of London, and wondered what Rianne, Nathalie and Gabby were doing. She remembered seeing Rianne's face on the cover of a magazine a few months ago. She thought about her mother. Luckily, before the tears could begin, she'd fallen asleep.

35

'You've done well, again, Eastman,' Justin said, pulling on his cigarette. Together, they watched Abdul al-Rasani get into his convertible Porsche and roar off down the street.

'Thanks.' Bruce tried not to show his delight. 'When do they deliver?'

'Some time in the next week or so. Mzima will call to confirm. Well done,' he repeated. 'If this goes through smoothly, we could be in business in less than a year.'

Bruce was silent. He had no idea what being 'in business' meant. Justin wouldn't tell him. It was one of the unwritten rules. Although he'd heard of whites who'd risen above the rank-and-file, he'd never met one. For the moment, he was content to serve in whatever small way he could. Strange times, he mused, as they sipped their beers, looking for all the world like a couple of college friends. Back home there was no way they'd have met, let alone planned to overthrow a government together. Not that he was anywhere near the decision-making centre. He didn't even know how many members MK had, where their operations were concentrated, who was in charge. In a funny way, he didn't want to know. He was content to take orders from someone his father would sooner have shot than allowed to sit in his living room. Or drink from the same cup. That was the paradox: he loved his family, he loved his country, and he loved his new life and the tiny part he was playing in it.

'So, *boertjie*,' Justin was saying, 'where to now?'

'Dunno. Back to LA, I suppose.'

'Keep in touch. We may have something else in the pipeline for you. I'll let you know.' Justin stood up and drained his beer. For the first time, he gave Bruce the triple handshake and disappeared.

Bruce fought back tears as he watched him go. In three years of working with him this was the first time he'd seen Justin display any emotion. It felt good.

36

'*Unjani, mfana?*' How are you, young man? The four men had looked up as Riitho entered the elegant, book-lined study.

He walked slowly round the group, shaking hands, bowing, answering respectfully when addressed. '*Ndiphilile, enkosi mhlekazi.*' Fine, thank you, sir.

Lebohang looked on proudly. Whatever else had happened to his young charge since they'd first arrived in Britain almost fifteen years ago, he hadn't forgotten his Xhosa, or the appropriate behaviour. The bodyguards moved quickly among the small group, pouring drinks, proffering little bowls of peanuts. Some warm tap water for Dyani – he complained that the cold water in England ate away at his throat.

It was the most important gathering of top Movement officials that Lebohang had witnessed in the past few years. With the state of emergency still in force back home, most of the important leaders were now scattered around the world in exile. It was safer that way. When everyone was settled, they left the room to wait in the kitchen under the nervous gaze of the wife of the prominent British Labour politician who had offered them his home. Riitho remained standing, as he was supposed to, until one of the older men invited him to sit down. Then sat facing them, his face impassive.

'It gladdens and pains me to see you here,' one of the men began, clearing his throat as he spoke. He was powerfully built, in his late fifties.

Riitho was struggling a little to follow the words. It was his father's language. His mother wasn't South African but Kenyan, although she'd never returned to Kenya after meeting Livingstone in London in the early sixties. It had been her decision to learn Xhosa and to make their children learn it, rather than her own language, kiKuyu. But she'd been adamant about his name: as her first son, she wanted to give him one that spoke of her heritage. Livingstone, amused at his wife's insistence, agreed. But neither had foreseen a life spent in exile, away from either culture. Apart from the odd conversation with Lebohang, it had been years since Riitho had spoken Xhosa.

He frowned, concentrating on what the man in front of him was saying. Riitho, we want you at home. Your people need you, they need your skills. But not now. Not just yet.' Riitho swallowed. What was he going to say? 'We've decided London is no longer safe. We want you in Paris. You should finish your studies, then we'll see. There's so much work to be done.'

Riitho puzzled over the precise meaning of the word 'work'. In Xhosa, the term wasn't clear – did they mean as an architect, or in some more overtly political capacity? Had the Movement claimed him back, or were they preparing him to make the choice? He looked at the men in front of him. They were the closest he had been to his father – or, indeed, his family – in almost twenty years.

In 1968, some four years after the arrest of the ANC leader Nelson Mandela, the South African secret service had tracked down Livingstone Modise to the house where he and his associates were hiding in Mbare, the Salisbury township in Ian Smith's Rhodesia. News of their arrest immediately reached Njeri Modise in South Africa where she was single-handedly raising their four children. She had the presence of mind to take the two eldest, Riitho and his sister Mpho, hand them over to Moses Dyani – the man who now sat facing him – and entrust him with their lives. When BOSS finally arrived at her door in Soweto to place her under what would become a twelve-year house arrest, the children were long gone.

They had been smuggled across the border into neighbouring Malawi and from there it was a series of night-time car journeys to Zambia. Then six-year-old Mpho went on to Oslo and two-year-old Riitho to Geneva to live with a junior member of the command in exile and her Swiss lawyer husband. At the age of twelve, Mpho had been sent to the US to live with relatives of Njeri's brother-in-law. There were no exiled command members in Oslo. Mpho had been brought up by a Norwegian family and it hadn't always been easy. The Movement acknowledged that a closer family atmosphere would be more appropriate for the twelve-year-old girl. When Riitho was twelve he had gone to the exclusive Malvern College. The Movement had their connections to call upon on behalf of their leader's son.

He looked at his hands. He had anticipated this for so long. In many ways, his life and the choices it contained were not his to make. He understood only too well the importance of the meeting. It was the direct expression of his father's wishes, a measure of how highly he was held in his esteem. These men, his father's deputies, they didn't need to be here. They could have sent the message through any number of their own deputies. They had come to London at considerable risk – Dyani from Stockholm, Nokwe from Moscow, Chikama from Algiers. But he understood why they had come, out of respect for Livingstone's eldest son. His heir. He looked up.

'*Kakade*,' he said calmly. '*Mhlekazi ndizakwenza noba*

yinoni oyicebisayo.' He would do whatever they decided was best. The men looked at each other and smiled. He was his father's son. Everyone could see that.

The meeting over, the men embraced each other and Riitho: first the traditional way, shaking with the right hand while holding the right elbow with the left hand, indicating their openness and honesty – nothing to hide – then the political embrace, the triple handshake, the murmuring of '*Amandhla! Ngawethu!*' Freedom. Justice. Then it was the emotional embrace, each man hugging Modise's son to their barrel chests. The end will come. Your father will walk free. One by one, they left the house in the leafy Hampstead road, each shadowed by a body-guard. The cars were waiting and, within minutes, they had disappeared into the fog. Riitho's eyes were unusually bright as he and Lebohang stepped out into the wintry afternoon. The familiar black Mercedes was waiting and he got into the back seat, deep in thought.

Olivier was still up when Rianne got back to the flat they had borrowed for the week. It belonged to one of Olivier's friends, she couldn't remember who. It made a change from staying in hotels. Lisette was in London and Rianne hated staying at Wilton Crescent when she was around. She fumbled with the unfamiliar key and then the door opened. He stood there in his bathrobe, his hair still damp from the shower.

'*Salut, toi,*' he said, pulling her into the doorway.

'*Holá, tú,*' she replied. It was their private greeting. His mother was French and he spoke it badly. She spoke about three words of Spanish. She looked up at him – she never tired of looking at him: he was perfect, six foot two of tanned, muscular perfection. When he turned his brown-flecked, hazel eyes on you and flicked his shoulder-length dark hair out of his eyes, you melted. Simple as that. 'You must have been the most devilish child,' Rianne told him, hours after they'd met for the first time, backstage at a charity fashion show. He'd been sitting in a dark corner of the dressing room in an armchair, boxer shorts and a Calvin Klein T-shirt, Gameboy in hand. She'd peeled off down to her underwear before she noticed him sitting there. 'I bet you drove your mother mad.' He smiled, his slow, sexy smile. He'd heard the same comment a thousand times before.

'Where've you been?' he asked, shaking his finger playfully in front of her nose.

'With a friend.' She grabbed the finger and bit it. He kissed her, then pulled her into the living room and was just lifting her shirt over her head when the phone rang. He swore and walked over to it. It was midnight. It was probably one of her friends. He'd never met anyone with quite so many friends. Acquaintances, Rianne reminded him constantly. I only have three *real* friends. And you.

Rianne rolled her eyes and tugged her shirt down again.

Olivier picked up the phone. '*Holá . . . acquí* Vasquéz.' He listened for a minute, nodding slowly. He looked at Rianne. '*Para tí.*' He held out the receiver to her, his eyes troubled.

'Who is it?' she mouthed, as she walked over.

'Hello?' She felt suddenly cold and put a hand to her cheek. 'When?' she whispered. There was fear in her face. 'Does Lisette know?' she asked. Her face crumpled and the tears came. 'I'll be there tomorrow, Marikije. I'll be there as soon as I can.' She put down the phone and turned to him. 'My uncle's been killed. He was shot this afternoon.' Olivier pulled her closer. 'I have to go to my aunt's in Jo'burg tomorrow. This will nearly kill her. It's the second one.'

'¿*Qué?* What do you mean?'

'The second brother. My father was the first.'

Olivier squeezed her tightly. 'Your father was shot? *Por qué no me dijíste?* Why didn't you tell me, *mi amor?* You told me that he died.'

'No one knows how he died. They never found his body. He could have been shot – we just don't know.'

'*Ay, mí* . . . Rianne. *Que história.* You want me to come with you?'

She shook her head. 'No. I'll go alone. I'll be fine.' She looked around for her coat.

'No. I'm coming with you. Don't argue. *Me voy* . . . I put on some clothes and I'm coming with you.'

Rianne nodded tearfully. She was dreading seeing Lisette. She had never seen her aunt cry.

'Come on, *mi corazón.* I'll get a taxi.' Olivier had reappeared. She put on her coat and followed him out of the front door.

37

It was impossible to keep the press out. Hendryk de Zoete's funeral took place the following weekend at a private, non-denominational cemetery at Kyalami, just outside the city. The headlines said it all. 'A BLOW TO THE HEART!' screamed the *Allgemeente Zeiten.* 'LOSS OF A BELOVED SON' – the *Cape Times.* The *Daily Mail* was more circumspect: 'STRIKING BACK: DE ZOETE BROUGHT LOW'.

It was disgusting the way they behaved, Lisette complained. Even the foreign press. Getting into the cemetery had descended into a rugby scrum. The BBC had seemed more interested in getting footage of Rianne than they had in the funeral cortège. There had been some confusion – how were they to bury him? As a Jew? Hendryk's distraught wife was horrified. No! He was *not* Jewish. Fine, maybe the *father,* old Anton de Zoete, but not Hendryk. He was an Afrikaner and a God-fearing Christian as she was, Nederlandse Gereformeerde Kerk, the Dutch Reformed Church. That was where he belonged.

Lisette was uncertain. With both her brothers dead, she was the last of Anton's three children. She had never given it a thought. So what if their father had been Jewish? Their mother was not. She, Hendryk – even Marius – they had never talked about their ancestry. They knew the barest facts: their father had arrived in South Africa from Russia – the Ukraine, perhaps, they weren't sure. It had been difficult for him, at first – Anton Lubinsky was from the wrong side of the line that divided Ashkenazi Jewry, poor, a *shtetl* Jew, not an upper-middle-class German Jew, of whom several had emigrated to South Africa – but it hadn't mattered. Anton had changed his name, married into a good but cash-poor Afrikaner family and slowly shed those parts of his identity that did not fit with his newly prosperous and increasingly influential persona. In time, no one remembered where he'd come from: the de Zoetes were South African, first and foremost. When he died, Anton was buried at the family plot in Highfields. But Hendryk was different: he'd supported Jewish causes, planted trees in Israel – he'd been curious about their background in a way that Lisette or even Marius never had.

'I don't know what to do.' Lisette bit her lip and looked at Simon Kalen. 'I mean, it never meant much to any of us. But now I don't know. I feel I should do something in tribute . . .'

'Lisette,' Simon began hesitantly. Stella was present, for once. They were sitting on the patio in Bryanston, watching the children – he had to keep reminding himself that they were no longer children – talking to each other on the grass below. He could scarcely believe it. Rianne – just look at her! She was on the cover of magazines around the world – there was hardly an airport he passed through where her face wasn't featured on something. Her boyfriend too, the exceptionally good-looking young man who had turned up at the airport with her. The press had been in paroxysms of delight, not knowing where to focus, whom to train their lenses on. And Hennie, so tall, so handsome – and so hard.

The army had toughened him. And then there was poor Marika. She couldn't stop crying. It was as if Hendryk was her father. Simon remembered her at her own father's funeral, a quiet little girl, stoically looking after her mother and younger brother. Perhaps that was it: a delayed reaction.

Simon patted Lisette's hand, wanting nothing more than to take her in his arms, but his wife was there. 'You must do what your heart tells you, Lisette,' he continued. 'We all should. We waste so much time on the things that don't matter. In the end, death comes to us all. The final frontier.' He winced. He was sounding trite, he knew it.

'*Ja*, I know. I feel that Papa . . . he would have wanted it. To return Hendryk, you know. He should be buried at Evenside.'

Simon checked himself. This was for the family to decide. Not him.

Hennie looked at Olivier from under his lashes. Little prick. Or, rather, tall, good-looking prick. What the hell was he doing here? It wasn't his place. The cousins were sitting on the grass, not talking much. It was early summer, a cloudless, still day. They should have been anywhere but here, at home, mourning the death of their uncle. He clenched his fists. The police were worse than useless. Everyone knew who'd done it. The PFP. The People's Freedom Party. Freedom. That was a joke. Fucking *kaffirs* wouldn't know what to do with freedom if it slapped them between the eyes. It was a revenge killing, pure and simple. Revenge for the latest bust-up of one of their cells in Lusaka. The army were making progress in the neighbouring countries, the so-called front-line states. They had invaded Angola and were launching attacks on Lesotho, Mozambique, Zimbabwe and Zambia. In return, the ANC and the PFP – and their armed branch, MK, a bunch of guerrilla thugs— He gave a short laugh. Guerrillas, gorillas.

He became aware of Rianne's eyes on him. He flushed and got up abruptly.

'I'm going in. I'm hot.' He stalked off.

Rianne looked at Marika and shrugged. He was getting worse. He'd barely spoken to Olivier . . . hadn't even said hello. She turned to look at Olivier. He was lying in the sun, his eyes closed. She was grateful he'd come. She bent her head and kissed him, suddenly overcome with tears.

38

Charmaine struggled with the zip on her white jeans, almost catching her skin and breaking a nail in the process. She glanced at herself in the mirror. This was the second pair of jeans she'd had to abandon in the last couple of months – she was getting too large. She pulled in her stomach, held her breath and forced the zip up. She picked up her handbag, felt for the familiar plastic bag at the bottom, then grabbed her car keys. It was already eight and she was supposed to be in Huntingdon Beach by nine. She locked the motel door and ran down the steps. Her little yellow Rabbit was parked in its usual place in front of the Blue Anchor Motel, freshly cleaned and valeted. Safer, Drew had warned her. Drive something cheap, but clean – not the sort of car the cops are on the lookout for. She pulled out of the driveway, pushed a Bruce Springsteen cassette into the tape deck, and joined the 405 freeway heading south. Club Flamingo seemed a million miles away.

She was now running errands for Drew, a guy she'd bumped into in the local supermarket. Drew ran a small courier service on Wilshire Boulevard. She liked him. He was hard, ambitious and driven, not like the slackers who hung around Baz and Touch and the rest of their sorry gang. She sometimes wondered what had happened to Baz.

Not that she missed him. Hanging around with Drew was exciting – not the do-nothing, say-nothing, feel-nothingness that hung like a low cloud over Baz and everything he did – or didn't. In the beginning, she had wondered how on earth Drew managed to drive a red BMW, a black Porsche and a white Jeep on the proceeds of the rather shabby agency he ran, but no one in LA was straightforward. Underneath all the hype and buzz, everyone had some kind of 'story' to tell. She'd simply wondered what his was.

It didn't take her long to find out – or, rather, for Drew to tell her. Drugs. Of course. Or, more specifically, the LA 'party' drug of choice. Cocaine. Everyone was doing it. At times Charmaine wondered if there was *anyone* left in LA who wasn't either selling or doing drugs – or both.

She'd started off doing small deliveries, packages to Drew's clients in Orange County and then, closer to home, small deliveries to the college kids, whose appetite for 'snow' outdid even Baz's. There was money to be made, especially if you didn't sniff the profits. She didn't – had cleaned up her act. She'd quit sniffing, if not smoking.

It had been hard. At first she'd been terrified, like the Gloria Gaynor song everyone at Flamingo loved, but after the first week when she'd made enough money to pay two weeks' rent up front at the Blue Anchor, with plenty of change left over, she realised she was better off without it. And it hadn't taken her long to make a few new friends, get a few regulars at the club . . . Before she knew it, she'd slipped into her new life and its new rhythms with ease.

She'd been hanging out with Drew for almost two months and he'd introduced her to a whole new set of people. She knew she ought to leave – her mother cried every time she phoned home. And she would, soon. Of course she missed London, and Gabs and Nat and Rianne, but they seemed awfully far away, as though they belonged to another life. And the quicker the months slid by, the faster they disappeared. But, as she kept saying to herself, she'd pick things up with them once she'd made it back to

London, hopefully two stone lighter with a bit more of a story to tell. She couldn't face the thought of meeting them all with nothing to show for her three-year exile other than the spare roll of flesh that hung over her jeans. The question was, how to make enough money to be able to save some.

Meeting Drew, learning how he did it, watching how he operated, was the first ray of hope. She studied him discreetly. She was the ideal runner – a pretty girl, driving a clean car, never staying out past midnight, never with a man in the car – the perfect cover. In a month she had doubled her Flamingo salary and – to Sharkey's annoyance – had danced her last dance and walked off without a week's wages. As if on cue, Springsteen began singing 'These Are Better Days, Baby'.

She turned into the driveway of her pick-up address a couple of minutes late. Raoul, a Haitian accountant and long-term client of Drew's, met her at the door with a drink and a kiss. She spent half an hour making small talk and watching Raoul expertly cut and bag a pound of cocaine, offering her a quick line, which she declined. Stay clean on the job, Drew had warned her. Never drive drunk or drugged. It was 1987, and the heat in Los Angeles was on. If she was caught, he explained, they wouldn't be looking for her, they would come after him. After nearly ten years, the LAPD had figured out that chasing the petty street pushers was a waste of taxpayers' money. They offered the small fry freedom in exchange for information about the big fish. It was an offer few turned down.

'*D'accord.*' Raoul smiled. He stowed the bag in the freezer and pulled out a briefcase. He counted out a thousand dollars and pushed the bundle across the smoked-glass coffee table. '*Merci*, baby,' he said.

'Thank *you.*' Charmaine smiled prettily. She counted the money, holding one of the fifty-dollar bills to the light and checking for the tell-tale red thread that would authenticate it and satisfy Drew. A thousand dollars – two hundred and fifty for her trouble, the rest to him. She drained her glass of orange juice and picked up her keys. 'See you next week.' She gave him a Gallic kiss.

'See you.' Raoul nodded, thinking how pleasant it was to have his weekly order delivered by a pretty young girl like Charmaine. Some of the thugs who'd come around in previous months were more frightening than the thought of being busted. He waved goodbye, closed the door behind her and thought about his profits: 28 grams of cocaine for $1,000 with a street value of $2,800. Not bad for half an hour's work.

Driving back north, Charmaine was thinking exactly the same. She was thinking ahead. Delivering small amounts here and there was all very well but it would take her ages to make enough money to pay off her debts and get the hell out of LA. She could, if she worked hard enough, make between two and three hundred dollars a week, but she wanted more. She wanted to *be* like Drew. He was only twenty-one, but when he snapped his fingers people jumped. She ought to think about building up her own clientele. That way she could start selling to people directly, rather than delivering. She knew she could work out a good enough deal for herself from Drew: it would simply be a matter of negotiation.

'So . . . you wanna strike out, huh?' Drew inhaled deeply, blowing cigarette smoke over her head. Charmaine tried to look casual. Drew smiled suddenly. 'OK. Here's the deal. Number one, you buy from me direct. I don't know who you sell to and I don't care. You buy from me. From no one else, I don't care *how* good a deal you think you can get somewhere else. Number two, you get busted, you're on your own. I don't care what you say, who you say it about, you don't name *me*. Three, I'll tell you when you get a price break – you don't come asking for it. You treat me right . . . and likewise. Good enough?'

'Good enough.' Charmaine was thrilled. She didn't know

whether to shake his hand or not. She had concluded her first business deal and, boy, it felt good!

'Feel like a drive?' Drew asked, getting up. Butcher, his enormous black Rottweiler, growled. Charmaine looked at him uncertainly. Apart from business-talk, she'd spent barely five minutes in his company.

'Sure,' she said casually.

'I've just taken delivery,' he said, and reached for a set of keys.

'Delivery?' Charmaine was puzzled.

'A Porsche. Bitchin' machine. Let's take it up to Malibu.'

Charmaine needed no second invitation. Driving a Porsche sounded far more exciting than driving her Rabbit. She grabbed her bag, carefully avoiding Butcher's dripping mouth, and followed Drew to the underground parking area. He even held the door open for her and she remembered to keep her knees together. St Anne's had had its uses. It was certainly a far cry from sitting in the back of Joe's cab *en route* to the Flamingo she thought, as they shot out of the garage and hit Sunset Boulevard.

Drew handled the car expertly and half an hour later they were in the canyons high above Malibu. As they whipped round one hairpin corner after another, she felt herself relax and enjoy herself for the first time in months. The sun was hot, despite it being only February, and she luxuriated in its warmth. They stopped at Fatburgers just south of Redondo Beach where she surprised herself by declining one of their infamous cheeseburgers, and sipped a Diet Coke. Drew demolished two burgers, a large plate of cheese fries and a butterscotch milkshake – all of which Charmaine could easily have polished off.

Later he dropped her at the Blue Anchor. 'Get an apartment, Charmaine,' Drew said to her, as she thanked him for the ride. 'This dump ain't safe. You can afford it now. If you want me to hook you up someplace, say the word.'

'I guess so.' Charmaine had been thinking about moving for a while. 'I'll look around.'

'You do that,' Drew said, and roared out of the parking lot.

Charmaine watched him disappear then walked upstairs and opened the door. She surveyed the room with distaste. Drew was right – she had to move out. She was going up in the world and getting somewhere decent to live was priority number one. She rummaged around in her bag and found a pen. She pulled one of the chairs over to the window, lit a cigarette, sat down and wrote down everyone she could think of who might be a potential client. Half an hour later, she had a list of fifteen names – not bad, she thought admiringly. Even if only half came through as regular customers, she'd be in business. Suddenly she felt hungry. She'd walk over to Denny's on 1st and Spring. That was the nice thing about Denny's. You could get breakfast at any time, day or night. Eggs Benedict. Her favourite.

39

Nathalie looked around the small shop in Camden Passage, eyes narrowed, concentrating. Marcus had been scouting for additional properties for weeks now. This would be their third shop and, so far, things were looking good. She had some reservations about the area – Islington was a little out of the way. Their other two stores, U/d 1 and U/d 2 were in the Notting Hill/Bayswater area – convenient for her to get to in the mornings – but their research indicated that Islington was smart, up-and-coming, full of young professional women and couples. The kind of women who'd spend ten pounds on a bra, but not twenty, as Marcus had put it.

It had been an antiques dealer's, she noted, from the estate agent's handout, and had the potential for something different. They could go the opposite way: high-tech, lots of steel and glass, make it stand out.

They'd used the same tactics in the other two shops. At U/d 1 on Portobello Road, theirs was an oasis of luxury among the minimalist designer stores with their single-cake windows and the one pair of shoes on display. U/d 1 was luxurious, opulent, sensual: stepping inside was like stepping into a velvet, cushioned boudoir, complete with heavy carpeting, thick silk curtains and wrought-iron *faux*-Louis XIV furniture. The slightly older clientele loved it. U/d 2 was similar, but less formal, more Laura Ashley than Marie Antoinette. Lots of bold florals, cream walls and a cream carpet that was an absolute bitch to keep clean. Both stores were a terrific success.

It had been Juliette's idea to change the names from Upstairs Downstairs to U/d 1 and 2, respectively. 'It'll give us room to expand,' she explained, 'and the freedom to try different things in each one.' It worked. It allowed them to tailor-make the in-store selections to their locations, something that both Nathalie and Juliette understood instinctively. They hired SoftCore, a young, frighteningly hip and savvy advertising company to co-ordinate the packaging and branding of the stores. To Cordelia's dismay they had been keen to get involved with the interiors too.

She nodded to Marcus. Philippe was in Kuala Lumpur, searching out new manufacturing opportunities. Lim Soon couldn't keep up with demand. Nathalie had suggested keeping them on as principal contractors and giving them the responsibility for sub-contracting what they couldn't manage, but Philippe had been wary. 'No one's going to look after your business as well as you'd look after it,' he'd said. Nathalie could never understand his reservations: she was as headstrong in business as she was nervous in private. So Philippe had gone, leaving a six-months pregnant Jenny behind. 'You'd better pray it's not premature.' She'd grinned. 'I'd kill you if you miss this.'

'I'll kill him.' Cordelia had looked up from the kitchen

table. She was knitting a shawl for the baby. *Knitting!* Nathalie could hardly believe it.

'It's just about the right size, darling,' Marcus said cautiously. It irritated Nathalie that he never voiced his opinion before she had divulged hers.

'I like it,' Nathalie said firmly. 'I like the neighbourhood, I like the other shops . . . I really like it.'

'We could concentrate on getting the interior done well this time.'

Nathalie nodded, a little impatiently. Marcus always stated the obvious. She checked her watch. They had one more property to view, in Camden Town, but she had practically made up her mind. And she was toying with an idea she'd had in the bath a couple of weeks previously: a catalogue. If they managed to pull off this latest store, a catalogue would be in the works. That way, she reasoned correctly, they would be able to expand their network at a fraction of the cost. She opened her crocodile-skin handbag and took out a small compact. She checked her lipstick quickly and smiled reassuringly at the estate agent. 'I like it,' she said briskly, 'but I've got a couple more to see. Can I get back to you later on this afternoon?'

'Of *course*,' the young man replied, and held open the door.

It was pissing down with rain, and Marcus brought the car round to the shopfront. 'One more to go,' he said, as he turned into the traffic along Upper Street, 'but I'm really keen on that one.'

'Me too,' Nathalie confirmed. 'But let's wait until we've seen them all.'

At three o'clock that same afternoon, a decision had been reached. Juliette had dropped by to look at it and they had made up their minds. Philippe and Marcus were less involved in the day-to-day running of the shops – they trusted the 'girls', as Marcus sometimes teasingly called them, to make the right decisions on that score. With the success of U/d 2, both Philippe and Marcus had been able to give up their day jobs to concentrate on the business. The timing was good. Britain was clawing its way back out of the recession of the early eighties and confidence was high. Money was being made in the City, in the property sector and in IT. As a result two things were happening: as both girls knew, men with money liked to *spend* it. On women. Women liked having money spent on them. One way of reciprocating was to spend that money on things that men appreciated: great lingerie, for one. It was a clever way of spending *and* giving at the same time. Second, they'd noticed a marked increase in the number of *women* making money, and spending it on themselves. Pretty, sexy, flirty lingerie hit the right note with these newly independent women, who had considerable financial clout. Whatever the sociology of the times, U/d 1 and 2 seemed to have got it right.

Now, as Nathalie sipped her espresso at the tiny Italian coffee shop just across from the tube station, she reeled off instructions for Marcus to follow. Juliette had rushed back to the shop. They hadn't yet hired a full-time manager and she was reluctant to leave the assistants alone. Juliette still thought of the shops the way you might think of a small child. It was probably why she didn't have a social life.

Nathalie was excited: with two shops under her belt, she felt confident enough to think about the future. The first year or so had been rushed, all four of them doing everything for the first time. They'd made as many mistakes as they had good decisions. She was excited about the new shop. She could see it already – sleek, edgy, cool colours, lots of stainless steel and glass. Juliette had talked about turning over one of the collections to a friend of hers from St Martin's, a Dutch designer. Camille Jespersen would design a pricier, slightly sexier range for sale exclusively in U/d 3 and they'd see how it went. Camille had struck her with her witty reworking of casual, everyday underwear for both work and play, and her meticulous attention to cut and detail. She also looked like she'd be fun to work with – her chaotic social life sometimes made Nathalie, three years her junior, feel positively ancient. She'd call her as soon as she got back to the shop. Showing Camille the new premises and talking about the ambience they wanted to create would help her in sketching out the new collection.

'Nat,' Marcus said, breaking into her thoughts.

Nathalie looked up from her notebook. 'Mmm?'

'Have ... have you thought any more about it?' he asked, sounding nervous.

'About what?'

'About us. Getting married.'

'Oh, Marcus. Do we have to talk about it now?' Nathalie was irritated. She didn't want to talk about the wedding. She had other things on her mind, much more *important* things. The business was going so well. She loved the buzz, the thrill, the hard work, the late nights, and the meetings that lasted all day. She loved the shops and sorting out the stock, hiring the assistants, supervising the new lines. She hated thinking about the other thing – about her and Marcus. She couldn't describe how she felt about him. All she could say was that he was kind. And nice. And that that, for her, was enough. As far as she was concerned, they were getting along just fine. They had the business and their beautiful home – what more did he want? He was always trying to pin down her commitment to him. He wanted to know that she was with him, that she would always be with him. It was exhausting. The last time they'd spoken about weddings had been almost a month ago.

'Yes. Why not? Why not now?'

'Marcus, this really isn't the place to talk about it. Can't it wait till later?' She looked around the busy coffee bar.

'I know it's not the place, but we never seem to have time to talk about it anywhere else. I just want to be sure.'

'Sure about what?'

'I want to be sure that you still want to.'

Nathalie put down her cup carefully. 'Of course I want

to, but we're so busy at the moment. Let's wait until after we've finished Camden Passage. We'll talk about it again in a couple of months.'

'But—'

'Marcus, *please*,' Nathalie interrupted. 'We'll talk about it later.' She opened her briefcase.

Charmaine looked around the apartment. It was in the Valley, Van Nuys, close to the freeway and the Sherman Oaks mall. It was light and airy, with high vaulted cathedral ceilings, a generous bedroom and a small study leading off the sitting room. She peeked into the bathroom again – yes, nice and clean.

'OK. I like it and I'll take it,' she said firmly, to the manager. 'When can I move in?'

'Just as soon as I've done a credit check and you gimme a cashier's cheque for a thousand dollars,' the manager said, closing the sliding doors to the small balcony.

'Fine. I've got the deposit right here,' Charmaine said confidently. Drew had provided her with the requisite California driver's licence, a social-security number and two sterling references. Yet more evidence of the way the incredibly well-connected young man was able to get things done. She followed the manager down the stairs to her car.

'What did you say you did?' he asked her, as she opened the door.

'I'm in sales.' Charmaine smiled. 'It's been a good year,' she said truthfully.

'I'm sure you'll like it here,' he said. 'There's some real nice people movin' in. The couple across the way are dentists and there's an English lady on the ground floor. She's a dancer or an actress, something like that. Real nice. I'm sure you'll get along just fine.'

'I'm sure we will, Mr Kozak,' Charmaine said. 'I'll hear from you later on today?'

'You bet. Have a nice day!' Charmaine headed back to downtown. She would pop in on Drew, pick up a couple of bags at the same time and see if there were any deliveries to be made. She really ought to get a beeper – everyone had one, these days. Drew had two.

'Hey, Char. How's it goin'?' Keith, one of Drew's sidekicks, greeted her as she pulled up outside his West Hollywood apartment. It was his fifth apartment in less than a year. 'Gotta keep movin',' he said continually.

'Hey, Keith.' Charmaine struggled out from her seat. She *had* to do something about the pounds she'd been piling on. Go to a gym or something. 'Is Drew home?'

'Yep, go on up. I'm outta here.' He gave her a friendly wave and climbed into his own car, a gleaming dark blue sports affair. Two seconds later, she heard his tyres squeal as he hit Sunset. Idiot, she thought – no better way to attract attention.

'Drew?' she called, at his door. She could hear Butcher growling on the other side.

'Come on in. Butcher's cool. He won't hurt you.'

Charmaine opened the door, hurried past the snarling canine and flopped into one of the enormous leather couches. 'How's things?' she asked, surprised to see Drew still in what looked like his pyjamas. It was almost six thirty in the evening.

'Things are shit.' Drew was channel-surfing on the wide-screen TV. 'I've done something to my back. It's fuckin' killing me. Can't sleep, can't sit still, can't *drive*, man.'

'What did you do?' Charmaine peeked at Drew's broad shoulders and lean, tanned stomach. His pyjama top was open, showing a smooth stomach with the faintest smattering of brown hair below the navel. She blushed and looked away. It had been a while since she'd seen anything so attractive.

'I don't know. I was at the gym yesterday, pressing two twenty, everything was cool. Then I must've pulled a muscle or something on the rebound. Fuck, it hurts.' Drew spoke in the *lingua franca* of LA – gymtalk, beachtalk, drugtalk.

'D'you want me to take a look?' she asked quickly. 'I could . . . I mean, I'm pretty good at massage.' The thought of touching his back was making her feel rather breathless.

'Oh, yeah?' Drew looked up from the TV. 'But you gotta be careful, this thing is *killing* me.'

'Cross my heart,' Charmaine said. 'Just show me where the pain is.'

Drew sat up awkwardly, pulled off his top and turned his back to her. It was every bit as muscled as she'd imagined. 'There, in the lower back, just to the right,' he said, as she ran her fingers lightly over the smooth flesh. 'There, exactly *there*.'

She could feel a slight inflammation, just above the waistband of his pyjama shorts. 'Why don't you lie down on the couch?' she offered, kneeling beside him. 'I'll start and you tell me if it's hurting.'

'Cool. But be *careful*.' He grimaced as he lay face down on the cool black leather.

'Just relax,' Charmaine said. It was making her feel quite giddy. She switched off the TV and gently pressed the flesh around the swollen area, kneading the small of his back. He gave a small groan of pleasure and settled deeper into the couch. She worked quickly and expertly, gradually getting closer to the source of pain and warming the skin beneath her fingers. 'Have you got anything to put on it? Deep Heat or something?' she asked.

'Maybe in the bathroom – in the cabinet.'

Charmaine got up reluctantly. A minute later she was back with a small tube in her hand. She smoothed on the cool white cream and went back to work. Within seconds, Drew's regular breathing told her he was asleep. She worked on, luxuriating in the feel of his skin beneath her fingers, daydreaming as she rubbed the pain away. Half an hour later, when the pain in her knees was unbearable, she got up. Drew was fast asleep, and even the disgusting Butcher was somnolent beside the front door. She sat down next to Drew and switched the TV back on.

It was growing dusk outside. The room slowly filled with the purple-gold colours of the LA sunset – pollution in the air, someone had told her. She glanced back at the young man beside her and felt the unmistakable urge to run her fingers through the tousled brown hair. She dragged her eyes away and tried to concentrate on her favourite sitcom – *Three's Company* – with the sound turned down.

'Charmaine.' Drew startled her. The show was nearly over. 'Baby girl.' He yawned languorously, sending a shiver through her as he stretched. 'You are *the* absolute best. Where'd you learn to do that?' He sat upright, smiling at her.

'Oh, picked it up, here and there. Lots of things I know how to do.' She tried not to look too pleased.

'I could *hug* you. I feel great.' He got up and walked towards the bathroom.

Charmaine winced. Well, why don't you? she wondered. He kicked the door shut. She got up, mindful of Butcher, and switched on one of the table lamps.

'Leave it off,' came Drew's voice, as he walked back into the sitting room. 'Come out on the balcony – you can see the sun going down.' He opened the sliding door and beckoned her over. She squeezed past him, her heart thudding uncontrollably. It was still warm outside, early spring, not too hot but warm enough to stand outside naked at midnight. The thought made her blush.

'Damn, that was some massage,' Drew murmured, against her ear, as they watched the fiery orange globe sink beyond the horizon. 'Been workin' too hard lately . . . Need to take a rest.'

'Business too good?' Charmaine said brightly.

'Too damn good.' Drew slipped an arm round her shoulders and turned her to face him. Her legs turned to jelly as her blue eyes met his.

His lips were so soft, she thought in surprise, as he kissed her. He ran his hands over her hips and pulled her towards him. Her arms reached up round his neck.

'Come inside.' Drew broke the silence. Charmaine allowed herself to be guided back through the doors, past the leather couches and into his bedroom. It was sparsely furnished, with a low futon and a leather swivel chair in one corner. He pulled her towards the bed, stopping only to switch on a tiny paper lantern on the floor beside them. The room was filled with a delicate glow. Shit, she hoped he wouldn't see the stretch marks that had appeared, as if by magic, on the tops of her thighs. He sat down, cross-legged, while she remained standing, rather awkwardly, in front of him. He pushed her long white skirt up past her knees and looked at her.

'What're you staring at?' she asked, embarrassed. She wished he would pull her down beside him.

'You,' Drew said, his hands travelling further up her skirt. His fingers touched her lace panties and gently peeled away the material. Charmaine gasped as he reached for her and she sank to the futon beside him.

It was past midnight when they both fell into an exhausted sleep. He was good – better than good.

40

'Can you handle it?' Two months later, Drew looked at Charmaine questioningly. 'It's a pretty big deal.'

'No problem.' Charmaine's smile belied her inner panic. She went over the instructions for the umpteenth time. Pick up from Hermosa Beach. Bring the bag over to Drew's and divide it in two. Leave half in the apartment. Take the other half over to Frank and Mike in West Hollywood and wait for their contact to arrive. Pick up the cash. Drive home. Hand over the cash, minus her share, to Keith, and wait for Drew to call. Simple. 'I'll be fine. Honestly.'

'OK, baby girl, if you're sure.' Drew squeezed her arm quickly and stood up. 'I'll call you tonight.'

Charmaine picked up her purse. It was a long drive to Hermosa Beach and the traffic would be murderous. She tried to suppress the butterflies in her stomach. She had a bad feeling about the evening ahead.

It took over an hour to drive from West Hollywood to Hermosa Beach but, to her relief, everything went like clockwork. If Jimmy, the man who answered her knock, was surprised to see a pretty young girl, he gave no sign of it. They went into the kitchen where he weighed out five kilos of cocaine and Charmaine handed over almost ten thousand dollars. She unzipped the false bottom of her handbag and stowed the flat package beneath the lining. Then she shook hands with Jimmy, ran down the stairs and was on her way to the car.

'Charmaine.' She jumped. It was almost dark outside and she couldn't see where the voice had come from. She paused, her keys in her hand. 'Where the fuck have you been?' Baz appeared around the side of the car. She stared at him, shocked that he'd found her. It had been more than two years and she'd heard nothing from him. She should have known it wouldn't last.

'Baz,' she said, holding her bag close to her chest. 'What the hell are you doing here? Where the hell have *you* been?'

He stared at her for a moment, his face full of rage. 'Bloody bitch.' He spat the word. Charmaine looked anxiously around her. The street was quiet. 'Bloody fucking *bitch*,' he repeated, moving even closer. She tried to put her keys into the car door, hoping to put it between them, but he blocked her with one arm and grabbed her by the hair. She staggered as he pulled her towards him. 'I've been watching you,' he growled, twisting her head. 'I've been watching you for *weeks*. I know where you've been, I know where you live. You fucking *ruined* me, you bitch. What the fuck were you trying to do?'

'I wasn't trying to do anything, Baz,' she shouted, angry now. 'You're the fucking loser – what the hell did you think? You brought me here, you fucked up – what the hell was I supposed to do?'

'Wait for me, you cunt!' Baz shouted at her. 'Sit tight and wait. I'm out there, taking care of business—'

'Taking *care* of business?' Charmaine interrupted him angrily. 'You weren't taking care of anything. *I* had to. I was the one taking care of things. You never did anything. I'm the one—'

'The one who's been screwing me over!' Baz was screaming now. 'I've been watching you – watching you and that guy you've been screwing! I *know* what you've been doing. Here, give me that!' Baz made a grab for her. Charmaine wheeled around, shielding the precious bag. She was trembling now, with rage as well as fear.

'Get away from me, Baz!' she yelled, panicking. 'Get off me – get *off*!'

'What the fuck's going on here?' Jimmy's voice broke in on the scuffle. He descended the stairs at a run.

Baz was still holding her by the hair and had almost prised the bag out of her grasp. 'Mind your own fucking business,' Baz growled, tugging at the bag. Suddenly he stopped, his eyes widening. The cold steel of a handgun had appeared at his temple.

'Let her go and let go of the bag. I don't want to do anything stupid, man, so just be cool.' Jimmy spoke quietly, but with deadly intent. 'You OK?' He glanced at Charmaine. She nodded, too terrified to speak. 'Get in the car and get the hell outta here before someone calls the cops. I'll deal with this jerk. Go on, get outta here.' She started the engine and pulled away from the kerb, not daring to look back. Trembling from head to foot, she made it back to Hollywood in less than thirty minutes, breaking all the safety rules. She didn't dare think about what had happened – or what might happen – to Baz. All she wanted to do was curl up in the safety of Drew's arms and cry.

'Can you believe it?' Rianne was almost yelling down the

phone. Gabby held the receiver away from her ear. She'd never heard Rianne so upset. Never.

'But what happened?' she asked.

'Those *bastards*!' Rianne shouted, banging her wine glass angrily on the glass coffee table. In the kitchen in Mulberry Place, Elise jumped nervously. 'The filthy lying *scum*!'

'Who?' Gabby was mystified. Who was she talking about?

'The fucking foreign press! They have it in for us. They always have. It's those *terrorists* who need boycotting, not *us*! The *assholes*! Who *cares* where I'm from?'

'Rianne, hey, calm down,' Gabby said, soothingly. 'Start at the beginning. What happened?'

'They cancelled my contract, can you believe it? There was this piece in the *New Yorker*—'

'Who cancelled your contract?' Gabby interrupted.

'Lovell. The *bastards*! There was this piece—'

'Why? What piece? What happened?'

'It wasn't *my* fault!' Rianne yelled. 'This guy – this idiot – at the Ralph Lester show, he jumped at me from nowhere. He was carrying this bloody great sign – I slapped him. He was sticking it in my face!'

Gabby groaned. She could picture the scene. Rianne was an easy target for protesters. There had been that article, Rianne had said something stupid, something about not really caring to know how Africans in her country lived, it wasn't her business. Gabby had read it and winced. Now this.

'So, calm down, tell me what happened. Who did you slap?'

'I don't know! Some fucking jerk was jabbing this sign in my face. I thought he was going to hit me. So I hit *him*.'

'And then?'

'Then – then the police came and some stupid journalist started taking pictures and I—'

'Hit him too?'

'Well, no, not really – there was a policeman in the way and then Ross grabbed me. My arm still hurts.'

'Oh, Rianne.' Gabby sighed. 'You shouldn't have—'

'You don't know what it's like, Gabby,' Rianne said angrily. 'It's like that every single day. I can't go out of my house now. Ross said just to lie low for a bit, you know, let it blow over. And then this! I got a call from Gina this morning. They've cancelled my contract! Too risky, they said. I can't *fucking* believe it. They're afraid that me being South African's going to impact on their precious sales. They're full of *shit*.'

'Hey, take it easy.' Gabby tried to be practical. 'Look, it's not the end of the world. There'll be other contracts. It'll blow over. Come on, you know it will. You've still got plenty of other work.'

'I don't give a shit about the work!' Rianne yelled. 'I don't *need* to work. I don't care about it. I don't care if I never set foot on another bloody catwalk again in my life!'

'You don't mean that, Rianne,' Gabby said carefully. It was tricky. Gabby knew more about the economic boycotting of South Africa and South African goods than Rianne did, that was for sure. And she supported the boycotts. 'You know you don't. Look at it from their perspective—'

'Don't *you* start, Gabby!' Rianne shouted. Gabby flinched. 'I don't need to hear it, not another bloody word! I'm sick to *death* of hearing about South Africa – sick to bloody death! Ross and Gina are acting like it's the end of my career. It's stupid, stupid, *stupid*! I don't want to hear another word! Not from anyone!'

'OK,' Gabby said mildly. 'I won't.' There was silence for a few minutes. She could hear Rianne struggling to control herself. It struck her that she'd hardly ever seen Rianne cry. Not since those first few weeks at St Anne's. She normally kept her emotions tightly under control.

'I'd better go,' she heard Rianne say. Someone had come into the room, probably Olivier. Gabby could hear his plaintive voice in the background.

'Call me later,' Gabby said. In her own delicate state, she wasn't sure she could handle Rianne's temper at that moment.

'I can't say I blame them, actually,' Gabby said to Nathalie, the following month. Rianne had stopped in London at the weekend *en route* to a fashion shoot somewhere in Scandinavia and she and Gabby had met for lunch. Rianne was so wrapped up in what she melodramatically called Lovell's act of blatant discrimination that she'd failed to notice Gabby's distress, or the fact that it wasn't directed at her. Nathalie hadn't, which was why she'd gone over to Gabby's new flat in Earls Court.

Nathalie stirred her tea. It was a miserable, rainy late-autumn day. Gabby's mood matched the weather outside. She took a sip. 'Problem with Rianne is she doesn't need to work, you know. She's always had everything, she doesn't have to struggle.'

'Well, that's not quite true. She's had different sorts of struggles. Her family and all that,' Gabby said, anxious as ever to be fair.

'Still, with all that money you can do what you like when you like. Not like us.'

'I suppose so.'

'You're OK, Gabs, aren't you?' Nathalie turned to look at Gabby.

Gabby fiddled nervously with her hair. 'Course I am. I'm fine.'

'Sure? How's work? You still enjoy it, don't you?'

'Yes, it's fine. It's a lot of reading – boring stuff, mostly. Case law, precedents, that kind of thing.'

'But is it what you wanted?' Nathalie loved what she did. She couldn't imagine doing anything else. And she was lucky enough to work with a team of people who felt the same.

'I don't know, Nat. It seemed like a good idea at the

time. Law, I mean. What was I going to do with a useless degree in English?'

'You mean a first in English from Oxford, don't forget,' Nathalie reminded her. Gabby reddened. Nathalie frowned. 'Gabs, what's wrong?' she asked. Gabby looked at the floor. There was a short silence. 'Gabs?'

'I'm fine, Nat. Really. I'm fine. Just a bit tired, that's all.' Nathalie looked at her doubtfully. She was more worried than ever, but if Gabby didn't want to talk about it, what could she do? She reached out and squeezed her friend's arm. Her rather thin arm. Gabby got up and refilled the kettle.

Nathalie looked at her watch. It was almost four. She had to stop by U/d 3 on the way home. 'I'd better run, Gabs,' she said, collecting her bags. 'When're you going to drop by the shop? We've almost finished decorating and you haven't seen it.'

'I know. I'll come soon,' Gabby promised.

'Well, you said you'd come for the opening night. Rianne's promised to do the ad campaign and get some of her modelling pals in for the party. Should be a laugh.' Gabby nodded distantly. The idea of a glamorous underwear party couldn't have been further from her mind.

She sighed and turned to face Nathalie. She looked so happy – the business was taking off, she was running things the way she wanted . . . it was fantastic. She shook her head sharply. Now wasn't the time to wallow in self-pity. She hugged Nathalie quickly, before the temptation to burst into tears overwhelmed her. Nathalie departed, leaving behind a lipstick-stained mug and a cloud of expensive perfume.

The flat seemed cold and lonely. Gabby wondered what Dominic was doing. It was four o'clock. Would it be a good time to call? She hesitated. If – and it was a big if – she caught him in a good mood, it would be fine. He might suggest going out, seeing a film, visiting friends. If he wasn't, he'd be curt, leaving Gabby to wonder all evening what she'd done, why he was angry, where he was . . . It was killing her, this relationship. *Killing* her. She didn't know what to do or how to make it better. She sat down at the kitchen table, overcome with despair. She didn't know who to turn to. Admitting to herself that there was something seriously wrong between them had been hard enough, but she couldn't bear the thought of telling Nathalie or Rianne, both of whom seemed to have perfect partners and perfect relationships. Dominic was so unpredictable and so weird – she had no way of judging whether there was something wrong with him or with her. She found herself comparing every moment they spent together with her memories of other people's relationships, desperate for something to compare him to. How did he talk to her? What had he said? How had he said it? Did Marcus ever call Nathalie just to say hello? Did Olivier ever smile at Rianne for the sake of it? It hadn't always been that way. She thought back to when they had first met, as freshers, almost four years ago. The first two years had been almost perfect. He'd seemed genuinely to *like* her, finding her funny and beautiful, clever and perceptive – all the things she'd wanted to be but never thought she was. With him, she was confident, sure of herself . . . secure. He made the world safe for her; he was someone she could depend on, always. And he didn't seem to mind that she did better than he did, both in class and in exams. He would ruffle her red curls when the results were announced and she racked up a first, then another.

It didn't matter to her that they appeared more like best mates than lovers. It was a role in which she felt comfortable. She and Nael had been like that, and even though they were no longer in touch, she still thought of him as her best friend, even referred to him in that way, which irritated Dominic. Sex . . . well, she had nothing to compare it with. She had liked it in the beginning. It was thrilling to her to think she was finally like almost everyone else in the world, and it was especially thrilling to close the door of her room at Magdalen when Dominic stayed over and know that on the other side of the corridor Mary was doing the same thing. She felt as pretty and wanted and loved as every other girl she knew. She didn't know whether she was any good at it – Dominic never said much. He was a little quick, and a little rough, sometimes, but she would sooner have died than admit it and, anyhow, they didn't do it that often. Not like Suzy, who seemed hell-bent on sleeping with every eligible young man – and some not so young – in Oxford. There were weeks when Suzy did it every night. Gabby couldn't imagine that – she'd have been *exhausted*. At the end of the first year, they had moved out of Magdalen into rented accommodation but Dominic hadn't wanted to share with Gabby. She was a little disappointed but understood his explanation. He would be too distracted to study. And he'd failed his first-year exams – he'd had to resit them in the autumn of his second year. He needed to buck up a bit: it would be better if they stayed a little bit apart. And it was fine, really it was. They saw each other at weekends, sometimes he stayed over. She was sharing a large house in Summertown with four other girls. She kept the place clean and tidy, stocked up with food and did the laundry every fortnight, including Dominic's. She was meticulous: she had a routine which she stuck to, rain or shine. Tutorials three times a week, enough time for her reading, preparation for her seminars. She was always one step ahead, always prepared.

There had been just one little thing, an incident, nothing to worry about, at first. It happened during one of their seminar groups. Mr Simmons had addressed a question to the group and Dominic had answered. Then Gabby had added to his comments. Added to, not challenged – but Dominic didn't see it that way. He'd sulked for hours, claiming she'd made him look a fool. She was mortified – she hadn't meant to, she was sorry, she wouldn't do it again. Eventually he calmed down. It was months before he did it again, the next time over an equally innocuous comment she'd made in the pub. They were there with Suzy, Suzy's new boyfriend, the three guys with whom Dominic shared a house and their girlfriends – she couldn't remember what they were talking about. Gabby had contradicted something Dominic had said. He hadn't retaliated, but he was cold to her, standing apart from her and turning rudely to talk to someone else when she spoke. She was hurt and upset, especially in front of Suzy. When they walked out at closing time, he gripped her upper arm, painfully, and told her he was going home, alone. He needed time to think.

It was almost a week before he rang her, late on Friday evening, to say he was coming over. He sounded slightly drunk. She was so relieved to hear from him and so delighted that he wanted to see her again that she made no comment when, almost as soon as they were lying on her futon mattress, he asked her to do something for him . . . something rather unpleasant. She hesitated, then saw the hard look come back into his eyes. She swallowed and turned round. And, actually, it wasn't all *that* bad. It hurt, but he seemed so pleased. He cuddled her afterwards, stroking her hair and whispering how special she was. She closed her eyes and basked in his warmth. She was being silly – of course he loved her. He was just under pressure. She knew he'd been clever and popular at school: she supposed being in Oxford, where everyone was clever and popular, was difficult for him. She made excuse after excuse. Suzy was worried about her but Gabby wouldn't – or couldn't – admit to anything being wrong.

'He's a moody bastard, Gabs,' Suzy said, one evening as they sat in Gabby's room. It was a month before finals and everyone was sick with nerves. Dominic hadn't been round in almost a fortnight and Gabby was more worried about him than she was about her exams.

'Mmm.' She sighed, looking longingly at the door. Please call. Please. *Please*. Suddenly it seemed as though it had been *months* since someone had yelled, 'Gabby! Phone!' up the stairs. She and Suzy had been lucky enough to find places back in halls for their final year. Dominic was living on a houseboat just outside Oxford with a friend. It had no phone, which added to her stress. 'He's not always like this. It's just the exams.'

'God, you sound like a battered wife,' Suzy said. ' "He's not always like this, he loves me, he doesn't mean it." Come *on*, what's the matter with you? Don't let him get away with it.'

'Oh, it's not that bad' Gabby laughed it off, trying not to show how deeply Suzy's comments had struck her. 'I do give him hell. Everyone's just worked up about finals, that's all.' She tried to be her usual, cheery self.

'Well, he's your boyfriend,' Suzy said. 'If it were me, I'd probably strangle him.' She giggled. Gabby smiled absently. Please ring. *Please*.

Eventually, of course, he did ring. And, she was so relieved to hear his voice that any complaint she might have voiced was forgotten. It was a week to exams, and she was just relieved he'd called. Not hearing from him, not knowing where he was or with whom, she'd found it impossible to revise. But, in the end, it probably wouldn't have mattered. Gabby got a first. Dominic got a third. Just after the results were announced, he made a little announcement all of his own.

'Where?' She was appalled by the tears that suddenly burned behind her eyes.

'America. Just for the summer. Simon's parents have some friends who own a house in the Hamptons. They need someone to house-sit. I'll be back in September.' Gabby looked down at her drink. They were getting ready to leave

Oxford for ever. Dominic wasn't sure what he was going to do. A third hadn't been on the cards.

'Oh.'

'Come on, Gabs, don't look so miserable. Cheer up . . . you've got what you wanted.' His voice was hard.

'Me? I – don't care about the first, Dom. I – I just want to be with you.' There. She'd said it. He hated it when she got all 'clingy', as he described it.

'You *are* with me. I'm just going away for a bit. I need some space, Gabby. I need to sort my life out.'

Gabby looked at him, alarmed. What on earth did he mean? 'But your life *is* sorted out, Dom. I mean, OK, you didn't get what you wanted, but you still got your degree. Come on, you used to joke about it – remember? First or a fourth – anything else is a waste of time.'

'Easy for you to say.'

'I didn't mean it like that. Dom, please don't go. Please.'

'Stop it, Gabby. I'm going and that's the end of it. I'll be back in September.' Gabby struggled to control the tears. They finished their drinks in silence.

He did leave. And he did come back. For Gabby, the summer months were unbearable. For the first time in her life, she was unable to eat, think or sleep. She lost even more weight. She left Oxford to work for Jonathan and Stephen Cope, the property developers she'd worked for the summer before. They were only too delighted to have her back. A secretary with a first from Oxford!

She stayed at Wilton Crescent over the summer and she tried to figure out what to do next. A degree in English – even a first from Oxford – didn't immediately point out a career path. But she couldn't make a decision until Dominic got back. What if he wanted to do something different? Move to another country? Live together? Marry? She could barely think about it. She spent each day at work practically counting the minutes, wondering how she was going to get through the month of July, then August and then September.

He returned in the third week of September and Gabby was so relieved she thought she would die. He still wanted her.

Except not just yet. He was going to move in with some friends he'd met in New York. They owned a large house in Englewood Road, near Clapham Common. Gabby went round with him. Two girls and two guys. It was a large, comfortable house with a garden and a large, sunny kitchen where everyone congregated each evening. They were all very friendly, the two girls, Jemima and Mandy, had boyfriends of their own, so why was she making such a big deal out of it? She needed to get her own life together.

She spent a few weeks thinking about what to do. Should she continue with English, do an MA? She loved it but it wasn't enough. Law? Like her father? The idea of spending the rest of her life in commercial law as he had done did not appeal but, as someone pointed out in the pub one night, there was more to law than mergers and acquisitions. She made a decision. Human-rights law. The following week she enrolled on the conversion course at Store Street in London. The first year, taken up largely by case law and precedent studies, was easy, if boring. She shared a flat with Becky, an earnest, timid girl on her course. For the first time since leaving Oxford, Gabby found she was too busy to think most of the time. Which was just as well. Dominic's mood swings were more unpredictable than ever and he wasn't working. He was 'signing on', but somehow managed to pay his rent and half-attempting to write a *major* novel. Where before he'd needed space and time to 'find himself', he now required vast amounts of solitude to write. By the time Gabby entered the second year, which was marginally more interesting, the relationship was almost wholly controlled by Dominic and his – increasingly – bizarre demands.

Somehow she stuck it out. She didn't tell anyone. Not even Nathalie. If her flatmates, Becky at first, then Annie, thought her boyfriend was a little odd with his intense, glowering eyes, well, she was a sensible girl and she looked like she could cope with anything. In fact, she was pretty amazing. She was a great listener, always giving sensible, practical advice – if you had a problem, you went to Gabby . . . it was that simple. Somehow she always knew what to do. It was inconceivable that she'd put up with Dominic if there was something really wrong.

41

Rianne walked straight past the magazine rack in the departures lounge at Charles de Gaulle without noticing. Olivier was ahead of her, searching desperately for a bottle of Evian – it had to be Evian, God only knew why. She stopped. Something had caught her eye. She turned back to the rack. There it was. *L'Observateur*. Not the kind of magazine she normally flicked through. Riitho Modise. It was his face on the cover. She hesitated, then ran back and snatched it off the stand, she couldn't have said why. She fished money out of her pocket, slapped it on the counter and rushed off.

In the club lounge, with Olivier still hunting for his bottled water, Rianne flipped open the magazine to the cover story, heart racing although she didn't know why. '*Modise . . . l'architecture et l'avenir de l'Afrique du Sud*.' She chewed her lip, searching through the index for the cover story. '*Interview exclusive avec Riitho Modise, architecte et fils de Livingstone Modise, maître du PFP (de l'Afrique du Sud). Page 48*.' She skimmed through hurriedly.

'*¿Qué cosa es?*' Olivier interrupted her. He stood above her, triumphantly holding not one but two bottles.

She closed the magazine hurriedly. 'Oh, nothing. Just bought something to read on the plane.' She flushed.

Just then their flight was announced, Air France to JFK. She jumped up. 'Come on, we'll miss the flight.' She gathered her bags and strode off. Olivier looked after her, puzzled. Rianne was always the last one on board. She never worried about missing a plane.

Almost as soon as they took off, Olivier fell asleep. She loved watching the effect he had on people. Women's eyes widened ever so slightly as they looked at him – it didn't matter how young or old they were. The stewardesses stared as he arranged himself in the wide, comfortable seats, rested his head against her shoulder and closed his eyes. 'Aw, bless,' one said, quite carried away by the sight of him – glossy dark brown hair with its golden sun-bleached ends, thick, jet black lashes that stood out against his lightly tanned skin, his perfect lips, parted ever so slightly.

Rianne turned to page forty-eight. It was a long interview, held in Paris the month before. It made little mention of his work, just that he now worked for an award-winning architect in Paris. In fact, it wasn't really about him, or his work. It was an attack ... a blistering attack on the situation in South Africa. Absolutely damning. She was aware of a faint hammering in her ears as she read his description of living conditions for the 35 million blacks – his people, in his own country – she'd had no idea there were *that* many – and the near-total state of military and political crackdown.

She put the magazine down and stared out of the window. It was a clear, bright day as the plane hurtled towards New York. She watched the world below her – first the outer edges of what she supposed must be Scotland, all tiny islets and a ragged, rocky coastline, then the deep, wide blue of the Atlantic. She could see tiny flecks of white bobbing unsteadily in the shifting, heaving blue mass. One or two clouds drifted by below them casting dark blue, almost black shadows on the ocean's surface.

Something was happening inside her as she read his

words – she couldn't say what. Something like anger – hot, heart-racing, but no, not anger. Something else, some other emotion, just as strong. Her pulse was racing. She read on. He was articulate, clear, concise. He attacked the mining industry, the big family-owned mines – de Zoetes, de Beers – and the conglomerations, like Anglo-American. He talked about the rising strength of the now-politicised black unions, their resolve, and how this was one battle that the landlords – as he called the mining families – would eventually lose. He criticised de Zoete particularly for their handling of the Vlakfontein Six.

Rianne frowned. The Vlakfontein Six? What was that? The next paragraph told her: the brutal murder of six black union workers – their mutilated bodies had been dumped outside the hostels at de Zoete's largest mine, Vlakfontein, part of their East Rand Proprietary Mines. Rianne stared at the page. She'd never heard of Vlakfontein or the Proprietary whatever-they-were-called Mines. Lisette never talked to Rianne or her own children about the family businesses. Marika and Hennie weren't interested. None of them knew – or cared to know – where their money came from.

She turned to stare out of the window again. They were passing over Greenland, the captain announced. She looked down. A bizarre landscape unfolded below – strange, irregular patterns of ice-floes and glaciers. From this height, it looked surreal, a bleak expanse of a thousand shades of white, the earth falling away to its own, curved horizon. The article had stirred many things in her, memories of home, loss, childhood, and another landscape, far away, the calm fullness of an early spring morning somewhere in the high veld, outside the city. A holiday, perhaps? Walking in the fields with her parents, Céline on one side, Marius on the other, balancing her between them. The child kicking and swinging against them, legs flying in front of her. The earth sloping towards the river, the blue, hazy range of hills to the north, a plane flying overhead on its way to Europe or America. Where was it?

She picked up the article again. '*C'était quand la dernière fois que vous avez vu l'Afrique?*' When was the last time you saw Africa? Nineteen years ago. He'd left South Africa in 1968 as a child and had never been back. '*Et est-ce que vous pensez à retourner?*' Did he wish to go back? 'Every minute of every day.' She swallowed. She couldn't read any more. She was shaking. She leaned her head back against the seat and closed her eyes. His face floated in front of her. She shook her head, trying to clear her thoughts. Why was she so upset? She slipped a hand into Olivier's, and he mumbled in his sleep, then nuzzled her neck, reminding her of his safe, solid presence. She was grateful. Why had she picked up the blasted magazine? It had stirred up all kinds of unpleasant memories. Things she tried to forget.

But she couldn't. She walked off the plane with a strange sense of foreboding. Something in the magazine article had stirred up in her emotions she couldn't identify or understand. She ought to be angry – as angry as she had been with those Lovell people – but she wasn't. No, it was something else. The bit about him wanting to go home every single minute of every single day had opened up something inside her, though she was damned if she could understand why. What did she care whether or not the arrogant asshole she remembered from schooldays could go back to South Africa?

From JFK she and Olivier went straight to Mulberry Place. She was quiet on the journey, lost in her own thoughts. She kept to herself over the next few days, cancelling two bookings. Gina tried to explain to Rianne that her star was waning and this wasn't the time to start playing up, but Rianne shrugged. She was tired. She wanted to go to London for a couple of weeks. By herself. She'd be back in time for the summer shows at the beginning of March. She declined Olivier's offer of a weekend somewhere sunny, just the two of them. No, no, she was fine. Just a couple of weeks on her own – maybe see her old schoolfriends. He nodded: it had been a hard year for her, with the murder, then the Lovell contract thing.

But when she arrived at Heathrow the following morning she didn't go to see her old friends. She didn't even call. She walked through Customs, out through Terminal Three and back into the airport again at Terminal One. She walked calmly up to the BA desk and bought a ticket to Paris on the next flight – just as she had boarded a train for London, years earlier, after a disappointing afternoon in Worcester. She was nothing if not impetuous.

She stood, her heart hammering, in front of an anonymous-looking building in the Bastille district of Paris and wondered for the hundredth time that day what the hell she was doing. Her hair was hidden by a silk Hermès scarf and she was wearing a pair of black, wraparound sunglasses. The taxi driver who had dropped her off had looked at her curiously but Paris was full of beautiful women who hid behind scarves and sunglasses. He grinned with surprise at her generous tip and roared off, leaving Rianne standing outside a doorway with a single, discreet plaque: 'J. Neumann et Assocs. Architectes'. Twice she brought a finger up to the buzzer and twice she dropped it. On the third try, the buzzer sounded, alarmingly loud. She jumped.

'*Oui?*' a woman's voice barked out at her.

'I . . . I'm looking for Riitho Modise,' she began, in English. 'Ree Modise?'

'Who shall I say is calling?' the voice replied, switching smoothly to English.

'Um . . . an old friend,' Rianne said.

'One moment, please.'

Rianne chewed her lip while she waited.

'I'm sorry,' the voice came back. 'Mr Modise does not see unannounced visitors.'

Rianne was stung. She hadn't come all the way from New York to be turned away so easily. She rang the buzzer again.

'*Oui?*'

'*Bonjour*,' she began again, this time in French. '*C'est* Gabrielle Francis *pour* Riitho Modise.'

'*Moment, s'il vous plaît.*' Seconds later, the buzzer sounded and the door opened. Rianne walked in, heart thudding. She shook her hair loose from her scarf, then stowed scarf and glasses inside her bag. She followed the signs to the second floor and was met there by an immaculate woman in black. She looked Rianne up and down, expertly sizing her up.

'M'selle Francis?' she enquired frostily.

'*Oui*,' Rianne said, unsmiling. Her heart was thudding so loudly she was sure it could be heard. She was shown into an austere waiting room and offered a cup of coffee. She declined. She sat down on one of the black leather and chrome chairs. She felt sick. She had no idea what she was doing. Then she heard footsteps coming towards her. She stood up, the door opened and, suddenly, there he was.

There was silence as they stared at each other. Riitho's face was blank. If he'd expected to see Gabby – even if he'd remembered who she was – he gave no sign. Rianne felt a slow, steady blush come over her. He was the same as she remembered, yet different. His presence was the same: a strong, powerful physical presence – it seemed to fill the small space. He had the same broad shoulders, the same tense, athletic body. She could sense, rather than see, the curve of his thighs in his black trousers and the bulge of his biceps in his black polo-neck sweater. But his face was different: it was older, harder. She could see a muscle clench and unclench at the side of his jaw. She shivered, suddenly cold.

'De Zoete.' He looked at her without smiling.

'Hi ... I – I was just passing through,' she began nervously, as he quietly closed the door behind him. 'Paris. I saw – in the article – I saw that you were working here and I—'

'De Zoete,' he interrupted. 'This is a surprise.' He shook

his head, as if he couldn't quite believe it. He gestured with his hand. 'D'you want to sit down?'

She nodded gratefully. Her legs had gone jelly-like. 'I'm sorry,' she began, as they sat facing each other. 'I feel like a complete idiot – I shouldn't have come. I read an article about you in some magazine or other and I'm in Paris for the week and—'

'How did you find this place?' Riitho interrupted.

She swallowed nervously.

'From the article . . . I looked in the phone book for Neumann's address. Look, I didn't mean to—'

'Rianne de Zoete. Well, well.' Riitho smiled very slightly for the first time. Rianne was unable to take her eyes off his face. 'So, what are you doing in Paris?' he asked, his eyes unreadable.

'I'm . . . a model,' she answered slowly. She had never before felt ashamed of what she did for a living, but she did now. For all sorts of reasons.

'Right.' He stared at her.

She wished the ground would open up and swallow her. She felt a complete fool. There was silence.

'I'm sorry,' she said suddenly, getting to her feet. 'I shouldn't have come. I – I don't know why I did. I'm sorry I bothered you.' She picked up her bag and smoothed down her black woollen skirt. Riitho stood up with her. He said nothing. Her cheeks were burning.

'Wait,' Riitho said quietly, reaching for the door handle before she did. 'Wait here for a minute.' He opened the door and disappeared. She was fighting to control herself. She was an idiot. Why the hell had she come? The door opened again and he walked in, holding a piece of paper. She took it. It was a small business card with a name and address written on it. 'Meet me there tonight, seven-thirtyish. Wear something over your hair, if you can,' he said. She blinked and looked up at him. He touched her shoulder lightly. 'I *am* glad you came.' Then he was gone, with that same walk, the confident, arrogant swing of the thighs. She looked down at the card. 'Chez Marie. 18 rue Neuve de la Chardonnière. 18ème.' She had no idea where it was.

At seven o'clock that evening, she hailed a cab outside the apartment. The taxi driver looked at her in surprise. 'Barbès?' he asked her, astonished. Pretty white girls generally did not go to Barbès on a Wednesday evening. Or any other evening, for that matter. '*Vous êtes certaine?*'

'Yes, I'm sure.' Rianne had answered firmly. She found retreating into English a useful ruse – particularly as her South African accent was difficult for the French to place. '*Australienne?*' they would always ask. She settled back into the taxi. They were early. Rue Neuve de la Chardonnière was a tiny one-way alley just off the main boulevard. It took the taxi driver half an hour to find it.

She was frantic with nerves by the time they pulled up outside the hole-in-the-wall restaurant. What if he'd come and gone? What if he'd changed his mind? She paid the man, and walked into a small restaurant that looked more like someone's living room. There were several tables, an odd assortment of chairs, a sideboard, a large sofa and an enormous TV, around which all six people were gathered. The conversation stopped as soon as she entered and everyone stared at her. She had hidden her hair under a baseball cap. Although she'd sworn not to as she left Neumann's earlier, she'd spent the rest of the afternoon in an agony of indecision about what to wear. She had finally decided on something simple – a pair of jeans, black high-heeled boots, a fitted black shirt and an oversized sheepskin coat. With her hair in a knot at the back of her head and the cap pulled low, she was pretty unrecognisable. Perhaps *he* didn't want to be seen with *her*. A stereo played calypso music softly in the corner. She checked her watch. She was only fifteen minutes late . . .

'M'selle?' a dark-skinned woman with long, plaited braids looked questioningly at her. '*Vous cherchez . . . ?*'

'I'm meeting someone.' Rianne assured her. '*J'attends quelqu'un*,' she repeated. The woman looked at her dubiously. Rianne nodded firmly. The woman exchanged a glance with the man sitting on the sofa behind her and shrugged. She indicated an empty table. Rianne sank into a chair and ordered a glass of wine. She needed something to calm her nerves. She was concentrating on the paintings hanging on the walls when a telephone rang.

'*Excusez-moi*.' The proprietress came towards her, trailing a telephone cord. '*Pour vous*.'

'*Moi?*' Rianne was surprised. The arrangements were becoming more complicated by the second. She took the receiver. 'Hello?'

'De Zoete.' He never seemed to call her anything else. A thrill ran through her at the sound of his voice. 'Ask Marissa – that's the lady beside you – to take you through to the back of the house. Wait for me there.' He hung up before she could ask any further questions. She got up and followed Marissa out into a tiny courtyard.

'*Je vous laisse*, m'selle,' Marissa said quietly, and closed the back door behind her. Rianne listened to her departing footsteps and waited in the darkness for someone – or something – to move. It was chilly outside and she wrapped her coat closely around her. She could hear the domestic sounds of the houses around the courtyard: a door closing, a woman complaining, the static crackle of a TV being switched on somewhere; out of the darkness a child began to wail. She heard a car pull up, then the creak of a side door as a man entered.

'Hi.' It was Riitho. 'You're alone?' he asked.

'Yes,' she whispered. Why was she whispering?

'Come on, my car's outside. Ready?'

'Er, yes . . . sure. But I had a glass of wine – should I go back and pay for it?'

'No.' He smiled faintly. 'Let's go. I'll settle with Marissa some other time. Come on.' He led the way out and opened the door of the parked car. He slid in beside her, checked the rear-view mirror and started the engine.

'Where are you taking me?' she asked, as he swung into the traffic heading towards Porte de Clignancourt.

'How well do you know Paris?' he asked, checking the rear-view mirror again.

'Well enough. I used to come here as a kid.'

'Why?'

'Well, my grandparents live here. My mother's family. I used to spend holidays with them.'

'Ah, yes. Your mother's French, I remember now.'

'Was.' Rianne corrected him. Why did he remember? She watched his profile carefully.

'Was?'

'Yes, she died. A long time ago.'

'I'm sorry. I'd forgotten. It's your father who gets all the attention.' He stopped at the traffic lights.

'And yours.' Rianne met his gaze squarely. They stared at one another for a second as the lights changed. She could hardly breathe: the tension inside her was unbearable.

'*Touché.*' He smiled briefly. 'Well, we're heading out towards St Denis. Sarcelles. You know it?'

'No. I've never been this far north of the city before.'

'Doesn't surprise me. You strike me as more of a Rive Gauche type, *non*? Sarcelles is a bit different from the *quartier Latin*. It's a housing estate. One of the worst.'

'So why are we going there?' She was puzzled. And not a little nervous.

'I have friends there. It's safe.'

'Safe?'

'De Zoete. Don't be naïve. I can't be seen walking around Paris with you. Just as you probably shouldn't be seen with me. It took me half an hour to give my bodyguards the slip tonight.'

'Oh,' she said, embarrassed. 'How many d'you have?'

'Two. Officially. And that's not counting the BOSS unofficial ones.' Rianne raised an eyebrow. The South

African Secret Service. No wonder he didn't want to be seen walking around with her. He exited the *périphérique* and turned onto a main boulevard. The street lamps cast a yellow, eerie glow over the unfamiliar streets. This wasn't the Paris Rianne knew: street after street of ugly, badly maintained tower blocks, graffiti, rubbish, broken-down cars.

Where the hell were they going? She was experiencing a slow, fluttering sensation in the pit of her stomach. She stole a look at his hands gripping the wheel. Strong, wide fingers. The line where the blackness of the skin on the back met the pale, yellowish-pink of his palms was pronounced. She had never seen hands like his before. And except for when he'd steadied her outside Serendipity's, all those years before, she had never been so close to a black man. She noted the thick silver ring on his index finger and the slim silver bracelet just beneath his shirt sleeve. He had changed since she saw him that morning: he was wearing a light blue shirt, a black blazer and black jeans. He had style, she thought. She remembered that from Malvern.

'Don't stare. It's rude.' He looked at her briefly, a slow smile playing around the corner of his mouth.

She blushed and looked away. He was pulling up at the side of a row of shops – all closed – and preparing to park the car. She looked out in the darkness, confused. Someone's home?

He opened the door for her. As she put her hand in his, a rush of emotion ran through her, leaving her breathless. She could smell his cologne, feel the heat of his body as he helped her out and reached behind her to lock the car. Just standing next to him made her feel dizzy. He seemed not to notice. He walked ahead and pressed a buzzer on one of the shop doors. To her surprise, he spoke French as well as any Parisian.

Rianne followed him through the dim hallway to an as-yet-undiscovered location at the back of the house. Suddenly the realisation that there were things about him she longed to know hit her like a blow between the eyes. It seemed inconceivable that twelve hours previously the man striding down the corridor in front of her had been simply an image, a face she'd seen a number of times in the past few years and a humiliating memory of a teenage snub. Walking behind him, she was aware of a faint but persistent clamour in her head. She had no idea what she was doing or what she wanted – or even why she'd come. All she knew was that after today, whether or not she saw him again, things in her world would never be the same. She thought fleetingly, briefly, of Olivier. *She* would not be the same.

It was nearly midnight. Riitho signalled to the man in the corner of the room that they were leaving. They'd drunk a bottle of wine between them, and Rianne had ordered a whisky sour. They'd eaten something – she couldn't remember what – and they'd talked. And talked. She was conscious throughout of his intense dark eyes upon her as she answered first this question and then that. He didn't talk much, just listened to her, probing thoughtfully, making a comment, asking a question. As the evening wore on and the bottle slowly emptied – more by her than by him, 'I'm driving, remember?' – she ventured deeper into unfamiliar territories of intimacy, memory. She was afraid – of him and of herself. She couldn't help it. Suddenly, it was the most natural thing in the world to tell him things that she wouldn't have told anyone else. At some point, she stopped, self-conscious. Had she said too much? She looked at him uncertainly as he got up and paid the young man – from Zaïre, he told her – and pulled on his jacket. She slipped into her coat.

'*Merci*, Dumi,' Riitho gave the man a triple handshake. Rianne looked at them silently. '*À bientôt.*' They turned and walked back through the corridor into the cold night.

'Where are you staying?' he asked, as he started the car.

'We have a place on Avenue Foch. It was my mother's.'

'Alone?'

'Yes. My grandparents live a couple of doors down. It's better that way. They can be a little over-protective.'

'Probably have reason to be.' It was more of a statement than a question.

'Not really. It's not true, what you read about models – wild parties, hundreds of boyfriends. We get eight hours' sleep, no alcohol, no drugs – you can't afford to.'

'No men?' He looked at her quickly.

'No, not really,' she said softly. It was true – it had been the minute she'd set eyes on him that morning. She blushed. 'You?'

'Men? No. Prefer women.' He smiled suddenly. She caught her breath.

He slid a CD into the player and they both fell silent. He drove fast – there was little traffic about at that hour. The music was haunting, and she knew it was South African. The rhythmic cadence of the language rose and fell around her, familiar as the sound of her own voice inside her head, speaking, breathing, laughing. It was the sonorous back-drop of South African daily life, familiar to whites and black alike.

'How long are you in town for?' Riitho asked her, as he turned onto Avenue Foch.

'Another week or so.' She was due back in New York in ten days' time – she had a Calvin Klein shoot and she knew Ross would personally kill her if she didn't show.

'What are you doing on Friday?' He pulled up the handbrake.

'I haven't planned anything.'

He took a quick look around the quiet street. A couple of solitary cars passed them. 'I'd get out, but . . .' he said, watching a car turn into a side-street in the side mirror. 'I'm sure you can open your own door, de Zoete,' he said.

'Why do you call me that?' she asked.

'De Zoete? It's your name, isn't it?'

'Well, yes, but most people call me Rianne.'

'I prefer it. Reminds me of who you are.' There was a short silence. Rianne didn't know what to say. 'So . . . you want to go somewhere on Friday?' he asked, after a moment. She nodded. 'Meet me outside the Métro at Alésia, four o'clock. Look it up on the map. Wait for me at the entrance on rue Duvernet.'

'Why there?' she asked, opening the door.

'Why not?' He waited for her to get out. 'Don't be late. And wear the cap. It suits you.' Then he was gone. She stood in front of the apartment for a minute or two, watching his tail-lights as he sped down the road. She put up a hand to touch her face. It was still hot. She felt strange, almost breathless. She wasn't sure *what* to feel. He was the most enigmatic, compelling and terrifying person she'd ever met. He was black. It was everything – and nothing.

42

'So, what do you feel like eating?' Marcus asked Nathalie patiently.

She stood by the window, tapping her finger against her teeth, holding an envelope in her hand. She seemed distracted. But then again, these days Nathalie was usually distracted.

'Italian? Thai? D'you want to go out for dinner?' He tried again.

'Oh I don't know.' Nathalie was barely listening. She wished Marcus would go away. She needed to be alone. She'd spent almost the whole day arguing with Camille, who was determined to push U/d 3 in a different more *risqué* direction, with more sexy lingerie and less of the pretty back-to-basics underwear that Nathalie favoured. They'd been arguing since the morning. Nathalie had had a couple of meetings to attend and had escaped just after lunch. She'd missed the morning post, which Angie, their secretary, had opened for her and she'd only managed to go through it when she returned, just after the shop had closed.

She poured herself a drink, sat down at her desk and pulled the pile towards her. The thick cream envelope was lying on top. She picked it up, admiring the calligraphy. 'Nathalie and Philippe Maréchal.' She wondered who it was from. She opened it. It took her a minute to work it out. 'Mr and Mrs Neil Ellingham request the pleasure of the company of . . . at the marriage of their daughter, Siena Julia, to Sacha Karponen Nilam.'

As she stared at it, the print blurred. Clearly Sacha's father had overcome his aversion to European girls, Nathalie thought bitterly. Why had Sacha invited them? She had tried so hard to forget him, to put his face out of her mind, never to think of what had happened – either between them or between him and her mother. For the most part, she'd succeeded. Throwing herself into the company had helped. She worked harder, longer, faster than anyone she knew. It was part of what had made U/d so successful: Nathalie was always prepared to go the extra mile, stay open longer, take bigger risks, experiment, plan ahead. She was twenty-three, she had three shops, a flat in one of London's more fashionable neighbourhoods, a loving boyfriend – so why was she feeling as if everything was about to disappear down the drain?

'Nat?' It was Marcus again. 'Well? What do you want to eat?' he asked.

'Marcus, I don't care. Just get yourself something. I'm not hungry.'

'But,' Marcus began worriedly, 'you should eat something. You haven't eaten anything—'

'I'm not *hungry*!' Nathalie interrupted. 'Just go! Get something for yourself.' She didn't want to turn around: tears were spilling down her cheeks.

Marcus grabbed his coat and headed for the lift. Nathalie

was always so touchy. He fished in his pocket for the car keys. They had just bought a new company car, a silver BMW, out of this year's profits and driving it would cheer him up. He pressed the key-ring and the 'pip' of the alarm sounded. As he pulled out of the underground garage, he noticed someone in a striking, *faux* zebra-skin coat. It was Camille. She was hurrying away from her car, an ancient Volkswagen.

He pulled up beside her. 'Hi, Camille. What's the matter? Something wrong with the car?' She looked amazing, with her long black hair cascading down the stunning coat.

'Oh, hi, Marcus.' She slowed down. 'Yes, the stupid thing won't start. I have to get to Soho – I'm meeting some friends and I'm already half an hour late.'

'Well, hop in, I'll give you a lift. It'll take twenty minutes.' Marcus needed to hear the voice of someone who wasn't perpetually tired, irritated or moody. A twenty-minute drive through London with the vivacious Camille seemed inviting. She opened the door gratefully and sank into the plush leather seats.

An hour later, he was sitting in a bar in Soho with four Dutch women, starting on his second gin and tonic and beginning to unwind. Not only was he enjoying being out with someone as pretty and lively as Camille, her friends were great company too. He caught Camille's eye and smiled. Perhaps this evening would be fun. With Nathalie usually working late, either in the office or in one of their shops or, even more frequently, in her attic studio at home, he'd grown used to watching TV on his own or going to the local pub with Philippe – although fatherhood had cur-tailed Philippe's evening activities. He ordered a third drink, forgetting that his – *their* – brand new car was parked outside and that he was well on the way to being over the limit. As the drink, laughter and cigarette smoke swirled around him, he moved closer to Camille. He was acutely aware of her perfume as she reached across him to accept a light from one of the other girls. He couldn't help but notice her cleavage; she was wearing a tight, black jersey-style dress with a red bra underneath – the lacy straps peeked out when her dress slipped from her tanned shoulders. He had forgotten all about Nathalie and her funny mood. With Camille so close to him, and her occasional hand on his arm as she talked and laughed, he was, for the moment, blissfully content.

It was only when they got up to leave, almost three hours later, that he realised two things: one, he was *completely* drunk; and two, he was *completely* in lust. Fortunately for him, Camille's alcohol consumption had been far more moderate. She took one look at him and ordered him to hand over the keys. He allowed himself to be led, smiling sheepishly at her amused friends, towards his car.

'Where do you live?' Camille asked, as she opened the door for him. 'I'll drop you off, then take a cab back to mine.'

'Fulham,' Marcus mumbled. The idea of going home to Nathalie – particularly in this state – was most unappealing. He turned to look at Camille sitting in the driver's seat. 'I don't really want to go home. D'you want to go somewhere else for another drink?' he asked.

'Not really. But you could come round to my place . . . *for another drink*,' she said, in a stage whisper. 'I have some very good Dutch beer . . .'

'Sounds great to me,' Marcus replied happily. Although he wasn't particularly keen on Dutch beer, he was particularly keen on spending more time with Camille.

She leaned across him to fasten his seatbelt and he caught a glimpse of her wonderfully firm cleavage. Almost without thinking, he caught her arm as she moved back into her seat.

She hesitated for a second. Then, with a low, throaty laugh, she placed her hand between his legs and squeezed gently. 'Hmm,' she laughed, 'I think it's not only Dutch *beer* you'll be wanting . . .' and started the car.

Marcus was stunned. At that moment, he wanted

nothing more than to feel her hand there, between his legs, anywhere. He closed his eyes as Camille pulled out into the late-night traffic.

Nathalie lit a cigarette, her hands shaking. It was well after midnight and Marcus was still not home. She had no idea where he had gone but she had seen him and Camille – that unmistakable long black hair – drive away from the office together, almost six hours ago. He wasn't at home – she'd been trying the phone almost every half-hour. She paced up and down the office, fuming.

All around her were the signs and trappings of their success: batches of their latest line in underwear, still in its clear Cellophane wrapping; dressmaker's dummies with swatches of pretty fabric and lace pinned to their svelte forms; sketches and drawings piled high on trestle tables. She had worked so hard to make U/d a success. And it *was* a success. Everyone who was anyone in London came into one of their three shops on a daily basis. Nathalie loved the feeling that they had created something out of nothing. She loved the buzz and the adrenalin, the bigger picture and the detail.

Her emotional life, however, was another story. Marcus was just *there*, part of the company, part of the furniture, part of her life. In the beginning, she'd relied on him, on his business acumen, his ability to deal with difficult suppliers and tradesmen. She'd needed him to be there. They'd made a great team, the four of them, she, Marcus, Juliette and Philippe. But somewhere along the way she'd found out she could handle things on her own. In fact, she could handle things better when he wasn't around. Philippe was almost a sleeping partner now that he was a family man, and he was moving into other things, property and such, which suited Nathalie. Juliette was hinting that she'd like to design more than bras and knickers and that, too, was fine. Nathalie had half expected, half hoped that Marcus would find other diversions and start expanding into other areas as Philippe and Juliette had done. But it hadn't happened. He mooned about the offices, bugging her about tiny little things, wondering about the wedding that hadn't yet happened. Their conversations were only about the business. At home she found ways to escape his sad eyes, shutting herself in her little sanctuary, her attic, while he stayed downstairs and did whatever. She had learned to survive on little affection, preferring to be admired by her co-workers and others with whom she came into contact every day.

Except Camille. In the beginning she'd enjoyed the energy and sensuality Camille projected. She had graduated at the top of her year from Central St Martin's and both Nathalie and Juliette had been bowled over by her quick, witty designs and bold ideas. At first, things had worked well. She had an eye for detail and for the unusual that Nathalie liked, even though some of the designs were a little too ... well, *sexy* for Nathalie's taste. It had been Camille's idea to run the series of different lines within U/d 3 – 'from the naughty to the nice', as she'd put it. But Nathalie disagreed – partly because the idea had come from Camille, not from her, but also because the raw, open sexuality of the lingerie had embarrassed her.

Now, however, she had even more reason to be annoyed with Camille. She looked at her wristwatch. It was almost half past one. Where the hell was he?

At that moment, he was lying on Camille's bed, oblivious to everything except Camille's mouth on his cock and the spread of her hair round his thighs. She held his wrists as her head moved back and forth, back and forth. He groaned, every nerve-ending in his body concentrated between his legs as she sucked him, gently at first, then harder and harder – until he exploded into her mouth, breaking free of her hands and burying his hands in her hair. They lay together for a moment, her hot mouth still on him.

'Camille,' he mumbled, stroking her hair and shoulders, 'that was—'

'Shh. Don't say anything.' She raised her eyes mischievously. 'Ready for more?' Marcus closed his eyes. This was better than anything he'd experienced in the last few years. This was what it should be like with Nathalie. *This* was what he was missing.

It was nearly dawn by the time he had sobered up sufficiently to drive home. He parked the car in his usual spot and looked up at the flat. Thankfully, all the lights were off. He pushed open the main door and fumbled for his keys. He bent down, trying to find the lock so as to make as little noise as possible.

The flat door opened and Nathalie stood on the threshold. 'You bastard!' she hissed, as he stood up. 'You absolute *bastard*!' She had been crying – all night, by the look of things. 'How *could* you?' She was blocking his way into the flat.

'Nat,' he began, trying to edge her aside so that he could enter, 'look, I'm sorry, I know it's late and—'

'And what?' She refused to budge.

'Can I at least come in? I don't want to talk about this in the hallway. We'll wake the neighbours.'

'*Fuck* the neighbours! Or isn't that what you've been doing all night?' She wrapped her arms round herself, protectively. Her nails dug into her flesh. He could see her whitened knuckles.

'Nat! We can discuss this inside.'

'No! I want you to tell me where you've been.' Her voice rose. 'I want you to tell me what you've been doing – I want you to—'

'Nat! Stop it! Let's get inside.' Marcus pushed her out of the way as firmly as he could and shut the door behind him. 'I was out with Philippe, we had a few drinks and – *ouch*!' Nathalie was hitting him with considerable force, crying hysterically. He grabbed her arm.

'You're *lying*!' she screamed. 'I saw you – I *saw* you! You were with – *her*,' she choked. He had both her arms now, not caring if he hurt her. She was struggling against him, her face contorted with rage. He'd never seen her so angry. She tried to wrestle her arms away but he held her fast. She was sobbing, choking on her tears and rage. How *dare* he lie to her? She'd seen him, she'd seen them together, she even *smelled* him. He stank of cigarettes and her fucking perfume. She tried to free her arms again but couldn't.

'OK, OK, I'm sorry. I lied.' Marcus said, trying to calm her down, holding her at arms' length. 'I went out with Camille. I'm sorry, Nat. We went for a drink. I was – I got drunk. I'm sorry. I wanted to go out with *you*, but you seemed so . . . angry. I don't know what's got into you lately. You—'

'*You*'re what's got into me. *You!*' She wrenched her arms free and stood there, chest heaving. They looked at each other for a moment. Then the words tumbled out of her mouth: 'I'm sick and tired of you, Marcus. I'm sick and tired of you hanging around with nothing to do. I'm sick of seeing you in my life every bloody day. I don't need you in the office, I don't need you to run my life. I don't *need* you.' She walked into the centre of the room. 'I'm *through* with you, Marcus – don't you understand? I don't care if you slept with Camille. Our relationship has been over for years. I just want you out. We'll settle the business issues later.' She looked straight at him. Marcus stared back at her, wordless. 'Get out.'

The door closed behind him. Nathalie couldn't believe that four years of her life had suddenly ended. She looked around her uncertainly. This was her life. This was her home – their home. The flat was full of *their* things – Marcus's things . . . his clothes, his books, his shoes, his stuff. She felt exhausted. She had been awake all night, sitting in the Eames armchair by the front window.

She walked to the mantelpiece and fished about for her cigarettes, sat down on the couch and lit one. She inhaled deeply. She'd been up all night thinking, she realised, but not about Marcus. She'd been thinking about Sacha and what *he* might be doing with Siena, his future wife. With a shock she discovered that her rage had not been directed against Marcus, but against Sacha. When she had hit Marcus, she'd really been hitting Sacha. Now that Marcus had gone, all she felt was relief.

She drew her knees up under her and lay back. Her mind was fully alert now, despite her exhaustion. Deep inside herself, since her trip to Kuala Lumpur, she'd buried her feelings about Marcus, Sacha and herself. She'd been too afraid to think about Sacha – about him and her mother particularly – so she hadn't. Instead she'd thrown herself into the business, Philippe, even her shaky relationship with Marcus. But she was still competing with Cordelia for Sacha.

The tears ran down her cheeks as she smoked and remembered. The guilt and shame she felt every time she made love to anyone, Joules, Marcus, *anyone*, could only be washed away by him and that was not likely to happen. He was about to get married to someone else. And even that hadn't removed him from her life. If anything, it made it worse.

43

Rianne pushed open the door to the study cautiously. It had been years since she'd been inside the oak-panelled room with its books, family mementoes and Marius's enormous, leather-topped desk. She paused in the doorway, the hairs standing up on the back of her neck as she looked around, half expecting to see her father sitting at the desk, his dark head bent as he worked. She had never understood exactly what he did. He travelled, went to meetings, went to the mines. In the last few years he was away a lot, like Lisette.

She supposed that was what happened when you ran a company. On the few occasions that they had all been together in Avenue Foch, he'd spent most of his time in here.

She walked across the soft carpet to the desk. Aïcha, the maid, kept the place spotless and she supposed her grandparents visited often. They had their own Parisian apartment nearby, but she knew her grandmother still came in sometimes and wandered slowly among her daughter's possessions. She looked at the desk, polished daily by Aïcha and her predecessors, the gold filigree pattern at the edges faded now. She sat down, feeling in its soft leather surface the ghost of her father's hands as he wrote letters, studied reports or read aloud to Céline while their baby girl slept. There were pictures of him, of Céline . . . and of her. She picked up one of the heavy silver frames – the same ones Lisette favoured, although she never came to Avenue Foch. By some unwritten agreement the apartment belonged to the French side of the family and she was careful to keep her distance. Claude and Marie-Hélène, polite as they were, had made it clear that this was Céline's home. A de Ribain household. Rianne had free use of the apartment – they both hoped she would come back one day to live there – but that was it. Lisette had been uncharacteristically gracious in defeat.

Rianne stared at the picture of her parents in her hands. She had no idea where or when it was taken. It had been years since she'd studied their faces. She had kept a picture of them taken the year before they died, on holiday in the south of France – Céline with her slim, tanned arms wrapped round Marius, he clasping her forearm, his strong, determined features softened with love. Rianne had no idea who had taken it. She had found it in one of the drawers in his desk at Vergelegen, an almost near-perfect replica of the one at which she now sat. She didn't know what had happened to it. It had probably dissolved in her tears during the months after his disappearance.

It was quiet in the study. The late morning sun came to rest tentatively on the carpet. Rianne got up from the desk and began to move among the shelves. Books. Hundreds of books. She wasn't sure what she was looking for. She had never before wondered what her father read, what he thought. She ran a finger along the spines. They were in alphabetical order. Aïcha, perhaps? There was little else to do all day in the empty flat. Berger, N., *Chapters from South African History, Jewish and General*. Biko, S., *I Write What I Like*. Bundy, C., *The Rise and Fall of the South African Peasantry*. Her fingers followed the trail. Guy, J., *The Destruction of the Zulu Kingdom: The Civil War in Zululand, 1879–1884*. She hadn't known there'd been one. Hanlon, J., *Apartheid's Second Front: South Africa's War Against Its Neighbours*. She stopped. Horriel, M., *Laws Affecting Race Relations in South Africa*. She moved on. Mandela, N., *No Easy Walk to Freedom*. Modise, L., *My People, My Life*. She stared at it for a second, aware of the blood rushing to her head. She tugged it out gently. It was a slim volume, published by the Heinemann African Writers Series, London. She turned it over and read the description on the back: 'Livingstone Sandilé Modise, together with Nelson Rohlilala Mandela, has been in prison for over twenty years. For twenty years, the international campaign for their release has been gathering strength. This collection of essays, speeches and articles from underground, brought together for the first time since his imprisonment, powerfully illustrates the arguments of one of Africa's most talented and forceful champions of justice, freedom and human rights.' The book fell open – someone had marked a page by folding the top right-hand corner . . . Marius? She read: '"South Africa belongs to all who live in it, black and white." – ANC Freedom Charter.' Another corner had been turned back. Someone had underlined a sentence on the page. 'Why is it that no black man has ever had the right of answering,

335

before a black prosecutor, a black judge, to laws in whose drafting my own people, blacks, have had any say?'

She closed the book. She couldn't read any further. This was *his* father – those were his words. She looked at the book-covered walls. This was what *her* father read? She had never heard of most of the writers, or their subjects. She was not sophisticated enough – or educated – yes, that was the word – to understand what it meant. He read widely, she could see that. But she had never expected to find Mandela and Modise, Nkrumah and Khumalo among the Kriges, van der Merwes and Robertsons that she had somehow – but why? – expected to find on the shelves of his study, his life. She turned and walked to the leather sofa that stood opposite his desk. She lay, face down, on the soft, worn leather, inhaling deeply. Tears came to her eyes, easily. She'd heard somewhere, no recollection where, that the sense of smell brings back memories more acutely than any of the other senses. It was true. The scent and presence of her father came to her, only for her. She lay there, unmoving, for hours.

Riitho looked at his watch and frowned. She was late. It was a quarter past four. Quite apart from the fact that he loathed people who were late, he was agitated. And worried. Rianne had unnerved him. He couldn't say why but he'd been expecting her. When Marcelle had buzzed to say first that there was an 'old friend', then Gabrielle Francis to see him, he'd known it was her. But knowing it was one thing: walking into the waiting room and seeing her there was another.

It wasn't that she was beautiful or sexy or famous, or even all three. Since that first time, at that girl's flat in London, he'd seen her face everywhere. For a couple of months she'd been on a billboard at the end of his street in the Marais. He was aware of her long before she came to him. And it wasn't that she was white, or even South African. He'd slept with – *been* with – too many beautiful, sexy white girls to remember, including a couple of South Africans. No, it wasn't that. When he saw her sitting there, her habitual haughty arrogance replaced by something he had never seen in her . . . a vulnerable, lost look, as if she didn't know what she was doing or who she was, the rush of desire and rage – such a strange combination – that had flowed over him had rendered him speechless. He hadn't expected that. He remembered only too well the anger that had flooded through him the first time they'd met in that awful tea-shop. She'd stumbled and almost fallen against the door. He hadn't forgotten the look in her eyes when he – a *native*! – had reached out to steady her. He'd walked away from her, his hatred flowing over him in waves. When he saw her next, he had pretended she didn't exist. That part was easy. Then he'd forced Nael to give her up, even before anything had happened. At the thought of Nael, his own face burned. They were still close. What was he going to tell him? That he'd met Rianne de Zoete in Paris by accident and taken her to dinner?

He looked up. It was nearly four-thirty. There was no sign of Rianne. He blew out his cheeks. She had decided not to come. He gripped the steering wheel. Perhaps it was for the best. He had been mad to think – well, he didn't know what he thought. He'd wanted to see her again, that was all.

He started the car, checking the rear-view mirror automatically. It had been a while since BOSS had followed him. They were lazy, these days. Gone soft. Content to check up on him at Neumann's every Friday, occasionally driving past his flat. He checked one last time, switched on his indicator and – she was running out of the Métro station, her hair flying behind her, baseball cap in hand. He watched her look anxiously at the street sign – *oui*, rue Duvernet. He was aware of a great tension slowly seeping away, out of his body.

He pulled away from the kerb. She hadn't seen him. He joined the traffic and circled the block. If anyone *had* been watching it would have been too obvious. He pulled back into rue Duvernet and parked the car a few hundred yards down the road. He watched her walk to the bus stop, tie up her hair and stuff it under the cap. She checked her watch. He would wait ten minutes and move forward. For the time being, he was enjoying watching her.

Rianne cursed as she struggled through the crowd to get to the top of the escalator. Why were there so many people about? It wasn't yet rush hour. She couldn't believe it. She'd thought about nothing else all week, she'd hardly been able to eat or sleep, and here she was – *late*. Half an hour late! It was hardly her fault. She'd been stuck in the Métro for almost thirty minutes as they cleared something – someone? – off the tracks. It was suffocatingly hot in the carriage. She hated taking public transport but couldn't think of any other reliable way to get to Alésia. When they finally did get moving, it was already four fifteen and the journey wasn't even half over.

She elbowed someone out of the way and rushed through the barriers, up the steps, two at a time. She felt her hair come loose but couldn't stop to fix it. Please be here, she whispered to herself as she raced up the second flight. She emerged onto the street, looking frantically around. Yes, it was rue Duvernet and no, there was no waiting car. Someone was pulling away ahead but she couldn't see . . . no, no . . . it didn't look like him. She looked around. Nothing. She felt utterly deflated. She pulled her hair back into its knot and pushed it under her cap. She checked her watch again: 4.30 p.m. Perhaps he was late too? She walked slowly over to the bus stop, not knowing quite what to do. She would wait until 5 p.m. If he had come and gone, she'd go back to his office on Monday and explain.

He gave a short hoot, twice. He watched her jump and turn in his direction, then come towards the car, relief evident on her face. He leaned across and pushed open the door. It was cold outside.

'Oh, God, I'm so sorry,' she began immediately, sliding gracefully into the passenger seat. 'There was a fuck-up on the train – it stopped for ages. I thought you'd given up and—'

'De Zoete. Relax.' He was calm.

'Yeah. Sorry. I – I was just – I hate being late.'

'You're here.'

'Yes. I'm here.' She let out a deep breath. He waited for her to calm down. She pulled off her cap and ran a hand through her hair. They drove in silence for a few minutes. He watched her out of the corner of his eye. 'So, where are you taking me?' she asked, her voice steadier. He turned onto the A6 heading south out of Paris.

'Vaux-le-Vicomte. Ever been there?' He was brief. She was beginning to recognise his short, precise way of talking.

'No. What is it? Where is it?'

'Wait and see.' He turned to look at her as they stopped in the toll queue. She was wearing a black, knee-length leather coat and a woollen dress with high black flat-heeled boots. 'Been hanging out with any architects lately?' he asked. She turned, confused by the question. He was smiling slightly, his sensuous, perfectly chiselled lips parting to reveal a flash of white against his flawless, jet-black skin.

'Huh?'

'You're wearing black. It's what architects wear all the time. Myself included.'

'Oh.'

'Nice boots.'

'Oh.'

'Is that all you ever say? Oh?'

'No.' She blushed. She suddenly felt quite tongue-tied.

'Then say something else.'

'Like what?'

'Like what you've been doing.' He glanced at her sideways. Rianne started. How would she explain it? That she'd spent the week walking through the ghost of her father's past? That she'd been reading what his father had written twenty years earlier when the regime her father supported had put his away? It was hardly light conversation. She swallowed nervously.

'Oh . . . this and that. Went shopping, the movies. You know. Usual stuff.'

'Liar.' He laughed at her.

She grinned. 'OK. So I didn't do anything. I lazed around the whole time. What did *you* do?'

'I work for a living, de Zoete.'

'So do *I*,' she protested. 'Modelling's hard work, you know.'

'Oh, yeah?'

'Yeah.'

'If you say so.'

'It *is*,' she said, with a flash of temper.

'I know, de Zoete. I'm teasing.'

'Oh.'

'Ever listen to this?' He changed the subject suddenly, taking a CD out of the middle compartment and passing it to her. She looked at it. Dollarbrand and Abdullah Ibrahim. She shook her head. Never heard of them. The corners of his mouth lifted as he slid it into the player. It was a pianist, a simple, slow, haunting melody. She turned to look out of the window, watching the slowly darkening suburbs disappear and give way to countryside. Where were they going? She leaned back and let the quiet music wash over her.

'*Voilà*.' Riitho broke the silence and swung the car into a long, tree-lined driveway.

Rianne looked about her curiously. 'Where are we?'

He killed the engine and turned to look at her. 'Vaux-le-Vicomte. Built by Nicholas Fouquet and his architect, Louis le Vau. When Louis XIV came to the opening, he was so furious at its beauty that he imprisoned Fouquet. Rumour has it that he beheaded the architect. I've never been able to find out if that part is true.'

Rianne stared at him. It was possibly the longest speech she'd heard him give. 'And I'm supposed to remember the details?'

'*Mais oui.* Short test afterwards.' He locked the car doors. 'Coming?' She followed him through the gates. 'There's a candle-lighting ceremony every evening at six. It's quite something.' He paid the entrance fee and they walked into the grounds. It was almost deserted. They walked slowly, the gravel crunching under their feet. Riitho led the way up to a small château, surrounded by its own moat. They went up the steps to the main entrance and waited while the grounds staff brought out the candles and prepared to start the evening ritual. They followed the candle-bearers into the reception rooms. A few visitors stood around, watching spellbound as the lights were dimmed and the hallways filled with the flickering yellow light from the thick candles. The procession moved slowly up the stairs.

Rianne glanced at Riitho in the dancing light. He was looking straight ahead, his glasses shining in the light. In the shadow, she studied his profile – the short, tight black hair, just slightly fuller at the crown, the short, flat slope of his forehead and the small, straight nose with the flared nostrils, which gave his features a proud, arrogant slant. His lips . . . sensuous, full lips with the darker outer ribbon that edged and gave sharp definition to his mouth. Chin: square, determined. And the skin: ink-black, silky smooth . . . She could see the faint beginnings of a beard under the chiselled slant of his jaw. He was handsome – no, beautiful – in a way she had never before encountered. He attracted her in a way that was beyond desire, beyond concentration – beyond anything she had known. When he turned to look at her, his black eyes focusing on her, she was taken aback by the sensations that the sight of him could wring from her.

'Worth his head?' Riitho murmured, as they watched the candle-bearers climb the steps in front of them. Rianne looked at him. Head? Whose head? 'Le Vau. The architect. I told you I'd test you.'

Her mind was swirling and she stared at him blankly. 'I . . .'

'What's up, de Zoete?' He frowned. 'You OK?' He bent his head towards her.

'Yes, I – I'm a bit . . . hot.' The candlelight and his proximity were making her feel faint.

'Hot? It's freezing in here.' He looked down at her, her golden blonde hair falling over her face. 'Come on, let's go outside. Fresh air might do you good.' He took her by the elbow and took her through the salon, with its elaborate Jardins de Vauxhall wall coverings and plush, ornate furnishings. There was no one about. He opened a set of french windows and they stepped out onto a small balcony.

The air was cold and crisp and she drew a deep breath. It was almost completely dark. Overhead, an owl hooted on its way to the stables. The balcony was only just big enough for both of them and he was disturbingly close. She wanted nothing more than to reach up and touch the nape of his neck, then run her fingers down the side of his face. She felt dizzy just standing next to him. But she also wanted to turn and run. Suddenly, as if reading her thoughts, he turned towards her. For a moment, neither spoke. Her heart began to thud.

'De Zoete,' he said softly. 'I . . .' he seemed almost hesitant. 'I . . . are you OK?' She nodded, not trusting her voice. She looked up at him, afraid to breathe or move for fear of breaking something, she had no idea what. 'Sure?' he asked. He reached forward and caught a lock of hair, twisting it between his fingers. His face was inches from hers. Then his arms moved round her so gently she wasn't sure if she'd imagined it. He leaned forward and, without warning, kissed her.

She felt the gentle pressure of his lips on hers and stood

still for a second, hardly breathing, wanting to catch hold of the moment for ever. Her arms reached up round his neck. The sensation she'd been thinking about – the nape of his neck beneath her fingers – suddenly it was there, real . . . his tongue parted her lips tentatively, and she felt his heart pounding as he drew her closer. His hands moved down her back, slipped inside her jacket and came to rest on her waist. She gripped his lapel, pulling him towards her, her tongue finding its own way inside his mouth. He was the first to break away, his breathing uneven. Oh, Christ. What had he done?

'Leave it to me, de Zoete,' Riitho said, staring at the traffic streaming down the Champs-Élysées. The enormity of what had just happened lay heavily between them.

Rianne's heart was in her mouth. 'I go back on Wednesday,' she said softly, looking down at her hands and twisting the heavy gold ring she wore on her index finger.

'I'll figure something out.' He started the engine. 'Give me your number in New York.'

'Riitho, there's something I ought to tell you . . . In New York, there's someone . . .' she began hesitantly. Olivier hadn't crossed her mind in four days.

'I know,' he said shortly. He pulled down the sides of his beautiful mouth. '*Peu importe.*' No matter.

She looked at him. It was true. Nothing mattered. She fished a piece of paper out of her bag and scribbled down her number. 'Wednesday's almost a week away,' she said, not looking at him. How would she manage sitting in the empty apartment on Avenue Foch every day, knowing he was halfway across the city.

'I know.' He nodded. 'But it's risky. I need to figure a few things out.' He gripped her forearm tightly, a clasp, not a caress. He drew a deep breath. 'Go back to New York, concentrate on your job, and leave the rest to me. I need to think about this, de Zoete. I have to be very, very careful.'

He touched her cheek. 'And so do you. Understand?' He saw that she did.

'Call me.' She slid out of the passenger seat. If she stayed a minute longer, she would start to cry. She closed the door and walked away. She heard the soft squeal of tyres as he joined the Friday-night traffic. Too risky to drop her at Avenue Foch, he'd said on the way back. She flagged down a taxi.

44

Charmaine swore to herself that as soon as the deal was over she was going to give it up. That was it. Out. No more dealing. She'd take the money she'd made and head back to London, Drew or no. She was waiting in Mike's apartment for a man to appear, check the goods and give her the cash. She tried to appear calm. Since the last fiasco, with Baz appearing out of the blue, Drew had been somewhat cool. He'd been angry at first, mostly because she hadn't made it to Frank and Mike's and he'd had five kilos of cocaine sitting in his apartment – which he *hated* having to do – for almost two weeks until he could calm Mike down and set another date. Charmaine knew she couldn't fuck this one up, so she sat on his 'pleather' couch, sipping a warm soda, and waited.

Thirty minutes later, there was a knock at the door. Frank jumped up to answer it. He appeared to be as nervous as she was. She could hear their voices, speaking a language she didn't recognise. Frank and Mike were their 'American' names, but beyond that, Charmaine knew little about them. The living-room door opened and Frank beckoned her. She picked up the bag containing the coke and walked over to the doorway where the three men stood. She handed over the small sample package and watched as one expertly sliced through the plastic bag with a flick-knife and extracted a small amount of the white dust. He snorted it through his right nostril, leaned his head back and smiled. Frank and Mike relaxed visibly.

Within minutes, the deal was done, the bag weighed, and Charmaine had three and a half thousand dollars in her hand. For a second as the stranger bent down to replace the knife in his sock, she thought he was going to pull out a gun – but no. Thank God. She pocketed the money, left Drew's beeper number with Frank and ran down the stairs. Her dress was soaking under the arms.

She reached her car, looked nervously around her, jumped in and sped away. Unfortunately, she didn't notice the dark blue sedan parked across the road. Neither did she see it pull out after her and tail her back to West Hollywood.

'Everything cool, baby doll?' Drew asked, she walked through the patio doors. Charmaine nodded, relieved that it had gone well. He gave her a laconic smile.

'I gave Frank the beeper number. He'll be in touch soon. I think he liked it.' She began to hand over the cash. Two and a half thousand for Drew, a thousand for her. She had just put the last fifty dollars into her purse when Butcher barked.

'Anyone follow you?' Drew asked, and reached into his waistband.

Charmaine looked at him uncertainly. 'I don't think so,' she said. Butcher was still barking.

'You don't *think* so? What the fuck do you mean, you don't *think* so?'

And that was when it all started to go wrong.

To Charmaine's horror, he pulled a gun from behind his back. She stared at it, paralysed by fear. He motioned for her to get away from the patio doors. She could hear the sound of running feet, could hear Butcher barking furiously and then, 'Crack!', a loud shot, followed by silence.

Drew gestured for her to get down on the ground,

jumped forward and slammed the heavy patio door shut. Then he ran through the apartment, locking the doors.

All hell broke loose. Footsteps pounded up the steps towards the patio and she could hear cars screeching to a halt outside. There were more footsteps, a shout, more cars and tyres squealing. Sirens wailed. There was a bang, like a thunderclap, and Charmaine screamed: someone had fired a shot at the patio door, which had shattered. There was another crack, more shouts, and three men burst into the room. There was gunfire from the direction of the bedroom, then more glass breaking. Something thudded, as though someone had fallen or jumped out of the window.

'LAPD!' a man screamed above the noise. 'Hold your fire! *Hold* your fire! LAPD!'

Charmaine covered her ears as someone let off a round of bullets into the hallway door, which splintered and nearly disintegrated.

She was still screaming as one of the men yanked her upright. There was blood on her arm and, for a second, she thought she'd been shot. More men burst through the broken patio door and raced through the apartment. The man holding her shook her and pushed her outside. One of her sandals had come off and she was being propelled over broken glass. She was still screaming when she saw that there were ten or fifteen policemen outside, including a policewoman in what looked to be a bulletproof vest. Charmaine had never been so scared in her life. The man still had her by the upper arm and was marching her down the front stairs. Her foot was bleeding and she was aware of an acute pain in her ankle.

'Get her into the car, the front car,' he shouted to the policewoman, who grabbed Charmaine's wrist and began to read her her rights, as Charmaine had seen on countless TV shows.

'Name?' the policewoman barked, as she handcuffed her. 'Date of birth?' A second policewoman was writing down the details.

'My shoe.' Charmaine was crying. 'I've lost my shoe – and my leg is hurt.'

'Shut the fuck up,' the policewoman said brusquely, snapping the handcuffs into place. 'Get in the car. Get *in*!' She pushed Charmaine's head down roughly, shoved her into the back seat, and got in beside her. The door opposite opened and the other policewoman climbed in on Charmaine's other side.

The driver barked a series of commands into the police radio, then the car screeched away from the kerb and sped up Sunset Boulevard.

'What's happening?' Charmaine asked the policewoman tearfully. 'Where are you taking me?'

'Sybil Brand,' the policewoman replied.

'What's that?' she asked, afraid to hear the answer.

'You'll find out soon enough.' And neither policewoman said any more. Charmaine sat between them, tears rolling down her cheeks. What was going on? And where was Drew? She was too afraid to contemplate what might have happened to him.

An hour later, her ankle, wrists and head were throbbing. She was waiting in the booking 'cage' of the Sybil Brand LA County Correctional Facility for Women. She looked around her tearfully. There were about a dozen other women, a couple of whom were manacled at the ankle as well as the wrist. Most looked high, drunk, or both. On the other side of the bars were police, including the two who had brought her in, warders and social workers. There was a wooden bench along one side of the wall but there was no space to sit. Two women were lying down on it and Charmaine didn't dare ask them to move. She stood to one side, wishing that the pain coursing through her would subside, frightened about what was going to happen to her. A wave of despair washed over her, and she stifled a sob.

'Hunter!' A female warder, holding a clipboard, was

looking through the bars of the room. 'Hunter?' she repeated.

'Yes . . . yes,' Charmaine looked up uncertainly. She inched her way forward.

The woman pulled out an enormous bunch of keys and unlocked the sliding door. 'Time to check in. No, not *you*.' She pushed one of the other women aside. 'Come on, I ain't got all night! Move it! *Move* it!' Charmaine slipped through the door and waited as the warder slammed it shut again.

Half an hour later, she was standing under a lukewarm shower, and her clothes, jewellery and other possessions had been confiscated. She'd been fingerprinted, thumb-printed, photographed and recorded, according to LAPD procedures. Her ankle had been taped up by a prison medic and she had an appointment to visit the prison clinic the next morning. She had never felt so humiliated, afraid and alone. She turned off the taps, shivering, and gathered up the pale green pyjama-like outfit that the prison provided. She dressed quickly, wanting only to disappear somewhere in this vast factory of women, warders and watchful eyes. Wasn't she entitled to a phone call? That was what happened on TV. But even if she was, who would she call? She had no idea where Drew was – maybe in an adjoining prison. Her mother? She could hardly call London from a prison cell and say, 'Mummy, I'm in jail.' Rianne? She'd no idea where she was. Gabby? No. It had been over two years since she'd spoken to any of them. Nathalie . . . Wait a minute . . . She knew how to find Nathalie. All she had to do was get the number for that shop of hers – her mother had told her about it. Shit, what was it called. Upstairs/ Downstairs – U/d 1. She'd call Nathalie – Nathalie would know what to do. Where was the bloody warder? She *had* to make that call.

It took Charmaine two days to track down Nathalie. It was only after her arraignment, at which she'd been appointed a public defender – a morose man named Clifton – that some of her rights were restored to her. He was *outraged* that his client – pretty little English thing that she was – had been denied a phone call for so long. As he pointed out to her later, the shock of being in prison often made prisoners forget their rights and the LAPD were in no hurry to remind them. Particularly when those rights involved a phone call to London.

When Charmaine heard Nathalie's voice, she broke down. Within an hour, Nathalie had phoned Rianne in New York and set off a chain of calls that eventually culminated in the arrival of Daniel Friedman at Sybil Brand. He was the classmate of a boyfriend of the best friend of a girl who worked with Rianne. Charmaine was too distraught to follow the trail, but relieved to see him sitting across the table from her in his sharp suit with an expensive-looking briefcase. A hearing was arranged for the following day and, almost four days after she had been led into the correctional facility, she was allowed out on a five-thousand-dollar bail. Rianne wired the money to the offices of Friedman, Capriati and Schwann and Charmaine was let out of the cell at exactly 3.15 p.m. the following day. She had spent a total of four days in prison. But a release on bail did not mean she could leave the country. Her trial date was set for 15 March. That was quick, Daniel assured her. Sometimes it took months.

'I'm catching a flight on Tuesday morning, Char,' Nathalie promised over the phone. 'Don't cry, it'll be OK. Whatever's happened, we'll sort it out, all right? No, don't call your mum, not just yet. I'll be there soon.' She put down the phone and turned to Gabby. The three had decided it would be best for one of them to go to LA and rescue Charmaine. Rianne was due to leave for the Bahamas shortly, and Nathalie had more money than Gabby.

'Jesus Christ. How could this have happened?' She looked at Gabby as she put down the phone. 'Drugs?

Charmaine? How the hell did she get mixed up in this?'
Nathalie was of the opinion it was all some ghastly mistake
– there was no way Charmaine would ever – would she?
She looked at Gabby uncertainly.

'I don't know.' Gabby shook her head slowly. She was in
shock. 'She's been gone for a long time. *Anything* could
have happened – LA's a dangerous place. God, why didn't
she call us and tell us what was happening? I feel terrible.'

'Don't you *dare* start, Gabby,' Nathalie warned her. 'It's
not your fault. It's no one's fault. The best we can do is be
there for her and help her get out of it. She needs all the
support we can give right now. No use blaming ourselves.'

'I know. I know. But, still . . . D'you want me to come
with you?' Gabby looked at Nathalie.

'There's no point. You can't afford it right now . . . I'll
see if I can bring her back to London. I've no idea what's
going to happen. Rianne's friend says she'll get off lightly if
she agrees to testify against . . . what's his name? Drew? I
hope she will, but you know what she's like with men.'

Nathalie landed at LAX on the afternoon of the same day
she left London. Despite having flown business class, she
hadn't slept a wink on the twelve-hour flight. She had no
idea how serious Charmaine's situation was – it had been
difficult to grasp Daniel Friedman's explanation of events –
but a five-thousand-dollar bail did not sound promising.
She was also exhausted. Between calling Rianne to arrange
the transfer of funds, organising the office for her absence
and catching the flight, she'd had barely any sleep. It *would*
happen at a time like this, Nathalie thought grimly, as her
cab pulled away from the terminal. Charmaine's timing
was shit.

She hadn't seen or heard from Marcus since he'd left over
a fortnight ago. His belongings were all packed, ready to be
picked up. No one at the office had spoken to him, and that
bitch Camille was nowhere to be seen either. She was sure
everyone at U/d was speculating wildly, but she didn't care.

At the moment, she had other things to worry about. She directed the driver to the Biltmore in Beverly Hills, where Charmaine was waiting. Daniel had taken her there on her release. He hoped, he'd said, that a night in the charming old hotel would calm her down.

It took almost two hours to get to the hotel. It was Nathalie's first trip to LA but, even in mid-winter, it was warm. The traffic was solid and she was almost asleep by the time they pulled up outside. She crawled out of the cab, paid the driver and gave her suitcase to the waiting bell-boy. Yes, Miss Hunter was there, the receptionist told her, smiling and showing off impossibly perfect teeth. 'You have a message.' She handed Nathalie a slip of paper. 'Go straight up – she's expecting you. Have a *wonderful* day.'

'Oh, Charmaine,' Nathalie was crying as well, 'why didn't you call us? We would have done anything – *anything*. I can't believe you've been through all this and you didn't say a word.'

'I couldn't,' Charmaine sobbed. 'I felt so *stupid*, Nat. I mean, everyone warned me about Baz. It was supposed to be this great big adventure – come here, play in a band, meet interesting people – but it's just been *awful*. I had to borrow money from my mum, Baz's friends – I didn't know how to pay it back. It was drugs, he was selling drugs. He didn't know what he was doing – oh, God, I feel such an *idiot*.' She buried her face in her hands.

Nathalie reached out and stroked her hair. It was so sad: while everyone else had been getting on with their lives, Charmaine had been falling through the cracks – and none of them had known about it. She shuddered. Charmaine had to come home. But first she had to get her out of LA.

'Char,' Nathalie said, 'listen to me. We've got to get you out of here. Your trial's in March and I can't stay here that long, but let's talk to Daniel tomorrow and get his advice. If we have to find you another lawyer, we will, and a place to stay until the trial's over. And, believe me, if you have to testify against Drew, you will. You're coming home. End of story.'

'But what if—'

'What if what?' Nathalie refused to consider the possibility of Charmaine going to jail.

'What if I lose?' Charmaine was crying again.

'You won't,' Nathalie said firmly. 'It's the bigger fish they're after. Not you.'

'But what if Drew's dead?' Charmaine wailed. 'I don't know what happened!'

'He's not dead.' Nathalie held out Daniel's message, which read, 'Drew gone. Charmaine at risk of prosecution. Call me.' 'He got away – and left you to take the shit.' Charmaine looked at the piece of paper. 'So if you have to testify against him, you will. Now, dry your eyes and let's start thinking about how you're going to get out of here.'

Suddenly things took an unexpected turn for the better. Daniel Friedman was worth every penny of the $4,325 plus expenses retainer that Nathalie and Rianne had paid him. Less than a week later, a deal had been struck: Charmaine had testified in a closed session with the district attorney against Drew, Mike, Frank, Keith – all the characters with whom she'd come into contact in the past six months; in return, the charges against her had been dropped and she was given a plane ticket to London. From contemplating weeks of waiting fearfully for her trial, she was sitting next to Nathálie on a BA flight to London.

'Nat, what would I have done without you?' she said to Nathalie, as the plane was readied for take-off. 'I owe you everything.'

'Don't be silly. We're friends, Char, and that's what friends are for. You'd do the same for any of us.'

Charmaine nodded. It was true. But what did she have to offer? Nathalie had her wildly successful business, Gabby was well on her way to becoming a lawyer, and Rianne . . .

well, Rianne had everything. What could any of the three of them possibly need from her?

45

Olivier and Rianne were sitting facing each other at Jay's, Olivier's favourite East Village hangout. The paparazzi were usually close at hand, which was mostly why he liked it.

'*¿Como?*' He looked puzzled. '*¿Qué dices?*'

'I – I – It's just not working, Olivier. I'm sorry. I don't know what else to say.' Rianne was impatient. It wasn't that she felt badly about telling him that their relationship was over. On the contrary, from the minute Riitho had asked her to meet him in Barbès it had been over and she wanted out as quickly as possible. Had she been prone to self-reflection, she'd have noted this as one of her worst qualities: once she'd gone off someone, she was gone. The shutters came down and the unfortunate friend, lover or cousin would find themselves on the outside. 'It's not you. It's me,' she said, hoping he wouldn't cause a scene. Riitho hadn't called and she'd been back for over a week. She was due to leave for the Bahamas on Saturday for a three-day shoot and couldn't bear the thought of leaving without speaking to him.

Olivier stared at her uncomprehendingly. '*Péro, no comprende, mi amor.* I don't understand. I like you. You like me. We are good together – *qué hay pasando? Hay algún otra?* You met somebody else?'

'No . . . no. Nothing like that.' Rianne blushed. 'I'm . . . thinking of taking some time off,' she said. It was true. 'I might go home for a while, I don't know.' The word 'home' had taken on new and troubling significance for her in the month since Riitho Modise had re-entered her life. At the thought of him, a chill ran through her. She was longing –

dying – to hear his voice. She drained her wine. 'Will you stay at yours tonight,' she said. It was not a question.

'*Está bien.*' He was fuming now. 'No problem. You do what you like. That's how you are.' He slammed down his glass and walked off abruptly.

It wasn't the end of it, Rianne thought, relieved, but at least it was the *beginning* of the end.

In Paris, Lebohang was watching Riitho like a hawk. Since they'd moved to the city, the Movement had provided them with two floors of an old office building. Riitho had been happy to convert the second floor into an open-plan home for himself, and two smaller apartments on the floor below, one for each bodyguard. They shared the same entrance, which made avoiding each other difficult. But for the most part it worked well.

Lebohang was more like an older, over-protective brother than a bodyguard and had been with Riitho almost all his life. They knew each other's moods, habits, likes and dislikes. Lebohang took the job of protecting Modise's son seriously, but he also understood Riitho's need for privacy and the occasional semblance of normal life. He did what he could to give the young man space when he needed it, and for that Riitho was grateful.

Khotso, the new bodyguard, was trickier: he was younger – Riitho and he were almost the same age – hot-headed and impatient. Lebohang often found himself the unwilling go-between when the two clashed. There was envy, Lebohang noticed. Khotso was often jealous. In Khotso's eyes, Riitho had it all: education, status, wealth. It was hard to place Riitho in conventional fiscal terms. He lacked for nothing. Quite apart from his salary as an architect, he had access to Movement funds whenever and wherever he pleased. It was one of the privileges he earned – there had never been an abuse of position, ever. His living expenses were assumed by the Movement, as were the incidentals – a car or two, foreign travel, hotels, the cost of protection ... and before that, the best education, the best opportunities. Riitho, without even thinking about it, had been given everything that the young radical, Khotso, had had to fight for. No English public-school education for him – not even a state-controlled Bantu education back home. In 1976, Khotso Moleke was fourteen, running in the Soweto streets when his class-mate Hector Petersen, whose image had been flashed around the world in seconds, was shot dead. At that time, Riitho Modise was at his desk in Malvern, head bent over Latin declensions. No wonder there was tension between them.

'Where are you going?' Khotso apprehended Riitho as he pulled on his coat.

'Out.' Riitho was curt. He needed to get outside the city for half a day and think. He hadn't phoned Rianne de Zoete, although he wanted to, desperately. It was something he'd learned from his father: when in doubt, wait; don't act; do nothing. For a while at least.

'Why are you making things so difficult?' Khotso complained. 'You should tell us where you're going. We can't let you just walk about, you know, no protection or nothing. It's our job, man.'

'I know it's your job. I just feel like being alone. Lebohang?' Riitho appealed to the older man. Get him off my case, his eyes signalled. Lebohang murmured to Khotso. Let him go. He'll be fine. It was a Saturday afternoon and the Secret Service guys hadn't been seen all day. Probably watching the football. Riitho wrapped a scarf round his neck and disappeared. Seconds later, they heard the screech of tyres as he roared off. Lebohang frowned. Something was definitely up. He'd been moody and withdrawn for days.

For Riitho, the problem was not just how to proceed, it was where and why. He'd done what he always did – he'd waited. He'd given himself a week to sit tight, think about what had happened and allow the next moves to surface. It was hard. He thought about her all the time. He knew there was someone in New York – the Calvin Klein model, Olivier Vasquéz. He'd seen the two of them in the press often enough. Pretty boy. Of no consequence. Rianne could – and would – walk away from that in a heartbeat. He'd known that from the minute they touched.

But that wasn't the question. It wasn't a matter of *if* they should go on, but *how*. And to answer that, he would have to take Lebohang into his confidence. Without his co-operation, it would be impossible. He couldn't bring himself to think of the consequences – what it *really* meant. All he knew at the moment was that he wanted to see her again. Soon. He nosed the car towards the Bois de Vincennes. His running shoes were in the boot. He would run – and think.

46

For the first time in almost as long as she could remember, Gabby was excited and it had nothing to do with Dominic. She sat in the small waiting room at Rights Watch UK, knees pressed neatly together. She had been asked to step outside the senior directors' office for a few moments while they conferred. There were framed posters on the wall depicting Rights Watch campaigns around the globe – Burma, East Timor, Haiti, USA, Argentina. Rights Watch was one of the world's most powerful organisations working on behalf of political prisoners, and she had just come out of a gruelling three-hour interview for a position as a junior lawyer/researcher.

She had come across an article in one of the Sunday papers about the organisation, an affiliated network of lawyers specialising in human-rights issues. With Amnesty International, they had recently made a proposal to the UN for the establishment of an international criminal court to which cases involving human-rights abuses could be brought. It would be a long, hard struggle to convince various governments around the world to sign up to the idea but it was a struggle to which they were committed. Gabby knew before she finished reading the article that this was what she wanted to do. To hell with tort, case, precedent, procedure! To hell with banking, tax and fiscal law! Six months after passing her final exam, she had applied for a job with them and was now awaiting their decision.

'Miss Francis?' Briony Stewart, one of the directors, had put her head round the door. Gabby stood up quickly. 'Do come in.'

'When can you start?' Peter Bensimon, one of the founding directors of the firm, asked. Gabby stared at him. She'd got the job? Yes, he nodded, smiling.

'Gosh, I don't know. Um . . . anytime – tomorrow?'

'Monday?' He laughed. 'We'll need a few days to sort out some office space for you – a desk and a computer and all that.'

'We'll introduce you to some of the other lawyers who're working on the same project,' said Briony Stewart. She looked at her watch. 'Well, it's almost five. Why don't I introduce you to a couple of people? Then, if you feel like it, you can wait around for half an hour or so and join us in the pub. Does that sound OK?'

'Yes, that sounds *great*,' Gabby said. She had warmed to Briony already. She shook hands with the three men and followed her downstairs.

Rights Watch UK was nothing like a conventional office. To begin with they were housed in an old two-storey warehouse, just off the Grays Inn Road. It wasn't the most amenable of areas: King's Cross was seedy, and prostitutes, drug-dealers and junkies haunted the surrounding streets. The offices were on Argyle Street, a side road leading away from Argyle Square, which was full of hotels where the prostitutes plied their trade. An odd place, she thought to herself, for a small group of dedicated, highly motivated people to be struggling on behalf of the world's most forgotten – and sometimes visible, too – prisoners, but Gabby had fallen in love with it from the word go.

She said hello to the three people she'd be working most closely with: Marwan Ahmat, a middle-aged Jordanian with an intense, serious face; Jennie Philipps, a lively young woman in her mid-thirties; and Ray Vardon-Green, a bookish, jowly young man, probably not much older than Gabby. They looked like the kind of people she'd known at Magdalen, earnest, intelligent men and women, working purposefully towards something other than the rapid accumulation of cash, which was what everyone on her law course had seemed obsessed with.

She sat at what – 'by Monday, I promise!' – would be her desk and tried not to stare at the books stacked on it. A surge of pleasure ran through her as she glanced around the room. There were probably twenty people working in the large, partitioned space. Each person had a desk, a filing cabinet, a computer and a shelf groaning under books, documents, files, papers, newspapers . . . it was chaotic. There was a table at the end of the room with a number of fax machines, some in seemingly endless motion, spewing long tongues of paper across the floor. She could hear English, French, Spanish and Arabic being spoken simultaneously. She hugged her knees. It was Thursday – four days before she could start.

'You'll initially be working with Marwan and Jennie on the Middle East sector,' Briony said to her, as they left the building. It was a short walk to McGlynn's, the company local. 'Mostly research, information-gathering and fact-checking – rather boring, I'm afraid.'

It had been so long since she'd had an intelligent conversation about anything, Gabby thought. After almost two years of indecision and grumbling, Dominic had finally started working for Lloyds of London, like his father, brother and cousins before him. She was bored silly with his talk of office politics – who'd been given a bigger desk, who had the better view, what the secretary looked like . . . what Alistair Campbell-*Jones* thought of Alistair Campbell-*Bingham* – too petty for words, although she took care not to show it. Despite his recent appointment at Lloyds, Dominic was getting worse, not better. These days, anything could set him off. And his bloody flat-mates . . . money, money, money and more money. It was all they could talk about. Two of them had gone into the 'city', whatever that was . . . between champagne breakfasts, champagne lunches and champagne brunches, there wasn't a huge amount Gabby could contribute to their discussions. She turned to Briony and Marwan eagerly. The discussion was about Palestine and the rising violence in the Gaza strip. For Gabby, it was pure bliss. Not only was she able to follow the conversation easily, she was actually able to take part.

'I've just been reading about the closure of the Palestine Information Office in Washington,' she said, savouring the moment. Marwan turned to her.

'Yes, it's bad news. Gaza is burning. The whole Middle East is burning,' Marwan said.

'When are you leaving?' she asked, sensing that he was someone from whom she could – and would – learn a great deal. She liked him immediately.

'Friday.' His accent was faint. He was a little shorter than she, a stocky, well-built man, maybe in his early forties, glossy black hair, dark eyes, a moustache. He was the only one among the men who wore a suit. It gave him an older, avuncular air.

'Is that where you're from?' she asked tentatively.

'Gaza?' He laughed mirthlessly. 'No, I'm one of the lucky ones.' Gabby looked at him enquiringly. 'I was born in Amman. My family are Palestinian but we hold Jordanian nationality.'

'Where did you study? Here? In England?'

Marwan made a faint 'tut', clicking the tip of his tongue against his teeth and nodded sharply, once. The gesture reminded her suddenly of someone. Instead of agreeing with her as the nod of the head intimated, he disagreed.

'Ah, no. Not at first. I studied at the American University in Beirut. Beautiful place. At least it was. Then I went to the United States. Then to France. And *then* I came here.' He smiled, rather sadly. Gabby stared at him.

That gesture, the 'tut' sound, the quick lift of the head . . . not the way Westerners would do it when they agreed with what you'd said, but the way . . . someone she knew did that, too. She started suddenly. It was Nael. They'd always laughed about it. It was his mother's gesture, he'd said. Southern types . . . his mother was Spanish or something. It was funny to see Marwan doing it. She made a mental note to call Nael. She missed him. They hadn't spoken in months. She'd promised to phone him back the last time he'd called and, of course, she hadn't. Dominic didn't like him – unfortunately, the feeling was mutual. She turned back to Marwan.

Almost three hours later, the group got up reluctantly. Luckily for Gabby, it was a short walk through Blooms-bury to her flat. She shook hands with everyone and thanked them for an enjoyable evening, especially Marwan. 'See you Monday,' she said, and walked a little awkwardly to the door. She hadn't wanted to sound *too* eager but, God, she'd enjoyed herself.

It was a cool night. The streets were almost deserted, except for the ever-present street-walkers, as she wandered down Wakefield Street and turned up Judd Street. It was the heart of the King's Cross Bangladeshi community. Men in long tunics and beards looked at her warily as she strolled home. Probably wondering if she was 'working', she thought, as she saw one man shrink away from an aggressive-looking girl. She walked past the Brunswick

Centre, huge and hulking in the dark, and crossed the road. She was almost home. She wondered if Lisa was in. Although they didn't share the same interests, she was dying to tell someone about her day. It was too late to call Nael, and Dominic suddenly didn't seem worth the effort.

Rianne was not looking her best, and she knew it. As she stood backstage at the New York shows, she fiddled nervously with the straps on her dress as she waited her turn to glide down the catwalk. Betsey, the make-up artist, had done her best to conceal the shadows that had formed under her eyes, but despite the layers of foundation and powder that she had smoothed onto her face, they still showed.

'You OK?' Betsey asked her, as she came off and sat down. She began brushing Rianne's hair and twisting it up into the spiked bun that all the models were wearing for the next set. 'You're not looking so hot.'

'I know,' Rianne said unhappily. 'I – I haven't been sleeping well.'

'Something up?' Betsey was concerned. In the three years she'd worked with Rianne, she'd never seen her so down.

'No, no. Just tired, I think.' Rianne was careful not to say too much. It had been over a month since she'd left Paris, and apart from a quick call almost a fortnight ago, she'd heard nothing from Riitho. He hadn't called, written, bleeped – nothing. She was sick with an emotion that was almost foreign to her: worry. She couldn't remember the last time she'd waited for someone to call or contact her. People came to her, not the other way round. She'd spent her whole life fending people off. Well, she was paying for it now. Now she had nothing to do *but* wait. He'd given her two instructions: get a beeper and install a separate line under another name in Mulberry Place. She was to fax both numbers through to him at the office on a plain piece of paper with his name at the top. Use a copy shop or the post office to send it, he'd instructed her, not from the house.

She'd done it almost immediately. And then nothing. She longed for someone – Gabby, Nathalie, Charmaine – to talk to. But she couldn't. She'd promised Riitho she wouldn't. She knew it was a promise she couldn't afford to break, ever. So she waited. And it was killing her.

As she was leaving the show Ross cornered her. 'You look dreadful,' she said, without preamble. 'Get some rest.' It was an order. She looked at Rianne closely. 'Are you all right?' Rianne looked away. What could she say? How could she explain?

'I'm OK. Just tired.'

'Well, go home and get some sleep. You look terrible.'

'I . . .' Rianne hesitated a fraction of a second.

Ross looked at her questioningly. 'What's the matter?' There was a moment's pause.

'Nothing,' Rianne said firmly.

'Ring me in the morning,' Ross said briskly, turning away.

Rianne watched her thread her way back through the crowd. Bullshit, she thought suddenly. It's all bullshit. She looked at the scene in front of her – hundreds of beautiful people, fawning over each other, wide, glittering smiles hiding what was really going on in their heads – how to get ahead, who was useful to whom – and for how long?

Life expectancy in this game was minimal. Rianne was only useful to Ross while her star was in the ascendant, whilst she was in demand. Rianne knew it. Ross knew it. The Lovell cancellation had introduced a different note into their conversations: uncertainty. Ross wasn't as sure of Rianne as she had been and that meant Rianne's well-being was no longer her only concern, not the way it had been in the beginning. Ross Carter had been around long enough to know that the best way to combat a star's waning appeal was to find another one. And she would. She was ruthless.

For Rianne, accustomed to everyone being interested in her simply because they had to be, it was a bitter realisation. Ross didn't care about her, certainly not in the way Rianne needed someone to care. Yes, she worried when Rianne wasn't looking her best, but not about the underlying reasons for it. Ross worried about the next contract, and the next. That was it. The truth was that Rianne was a commodity – people made money from her and that was what mattered. The truth hurt. For almost the first time in her life she wasn't OK and she wanted to tell someone about it. But she couldn't. She picked up her bag and walked out of the door.

A phone was ringing in the house as Rianne put her key into the lock. Her heart started to thump as she realised that the sound was coming from her room. It was her new private number. She flung down her bags and tore up the stairs, praying it wouldn't stop before she got there. She burst in and dived across the bed, hitting her arm on the headboard. 'Hello?' She was breathless. There was a faint 'beep', signalling a long-distance call.

'De Zoete.'

It was him. She closed her eyes and sank to the floor. 'Ree. Riitho.' Tears welled in her eyes. 'Riitho. Where are you? Are you OK?'

'I'm fine. You?'

'I'm – I'm OK. I've been . . . worried. Where are you?'

'Paris. I'm arriving in New York tomorrow evening. Take down this number.'

She yanked open her bedside drawer, fingers trembling. She could scarcely believe it. He was coming to New York. 'Got it.' She repeated it to him.

'Call it tomorrow morning, someone called Letsile will answer. Get the address from him – got that? Meet me there around 9 p.m. I'll wait for you outside the flat. Be there at nine. It'll be cold so don't keep me waiting.'

'I won't. I'll be there. How long are you staying – when do you—'

'Meet me there tomorrow,' he interrupted. 'We'll talk then.' He was suddenly quiet.

She could hear him breathing. 'I – I miss you,' she said, almost inaudibly.

'I know. Same here. I'll see you tomorrow.' The line went dead. She stared at the phone. After more than a month, she would see him the next day. She could scarcely breathe.

She saw him even before the cab had come to a halt in front of the apartment block. He was standing near the entrance, his face turned into the collar of his coat. Flinging a fifty-dollar bill at the taxi driver, she shoved the door open and hit the kerb running. She had been agonising for hours . . . how would it be? What would they say to each other? How would she begin? Driving uptown in the cab, she'd been a bundle of nerves. Suddenly, from *thinking* about seeing him every day for the past five weeks, she was actually on her way *to* seeing him . . . and she was scared.

In the event it was easy. The minute she saw him she knew exactly what to do. She ran straight from the taxi into his arms, almost knocking him over. He staggered, caught off-guard by the force with which she slammed into him. He caught hold of her, gripping her upper arms almost painfully. They stared at each other in the half-light of the entrance hall.

'Rianne.' He slipped a hand round the back of her neck and pulled her towards him, burying his face in her hair. Neither spoke. Rianne closed her eyes and breathed in the scent of him, already identifiable to her. 'Let's go.' He produced a key and opened the front door.

She looked around. They were in a large, rather grand hallway with chairs and sofas on one side of the room – she recognised the style, Art Deco – and a bank of elevators on the other. He held her by the wrist and pulled her into one. Third floor. They rode the short distance in silence, his fingers burning into her skin through the sleeve of the white shirt she'd put on, pulled off and put on again just before she left Mulberry Place. He opened a door somewhere down a long corridor and then they were inside a flat –

someone had been cooking not long before. It was dark inside. He bent down and switched on a table lamp. The room was suddenly illuminated. He straightened up slowly, his eyes never leaving her face.

'Just tell me, how long are you here for?' Rianne broke the silence. She had to know.

He smiled for the first time. 'A week.'

'A week?' She couldn't keep the smile out of her voice.

'A week. One week,' he said, coming towards her. He slipped his arms round her and she looked up at his face, then reached up and tugged gently at his glasses. She wanted to see him properly. He took them off and laid them on the shelf next to the door. She stared at his eyes – ebony black, with short, impossibly curled lashes, slightly slanted where they met the plane of his high cheekbones. His eyebrows were thick and dense, she ran a finger over one. He held her with one hand and caught her fingers with the other. Slowly, he turned her hand palm up and pressed it to his mouth. The tip of his tongue traced the folds between her thumb and index finger. Without question, it was the most erotic sensation she had ever experienced. Her breath quickened as he slid a hand down her back, under the waistband of her trousers and his fingers brushed the soft skin between her buttocks. She hadn't even taken off her coat. He lifted his head, shrugged off his coat and let it fall to the floor. She did the same. They looked at each other, then he took her by the wrist again and led her down the corridor.

'This first,' he said quietly, as he opened a bedroom door. 'We'll talk later. *D'accord?*' She nodded, and he kicked the door shut, then turned to her. In his face she saw everything – desire *and* pain, lust and anguish, fused equally. Everything. Possibilities – of what she could feel, what *he* could feel – suddenly lay between them. She could sense it in the way he ran a finger down the front of her shirt, lifting it by the tails and tugging it over her head. In the way he did the same, pulling his own sweater over his head in one swift, fluid movement, unbuttoning his trousers and letting them fall. He sat down on the edge of the bed and pulled her towards him, still standing so that he buried his head in the smooth skin of her stomach, his hands swiftly unfastening her own trousers and easing them over her hips. She trembled suddenly. He lifted his head from her navel where he had traced – again – the skin of her navel with the tip of his hot, wet tongue. He carefully slid the white silk panties down her legs. Watching her steadily, he laced his fingers in hers and lay back against the sheets. She slid on top of him. It was swift, it was perfect – afterwards, she would not remember. He shut his eyes. She watched his face, spellbound. He was lost, somewhere else, this young man who thrust his heat inside her, so far from home.

'Weren't you ever homesick?' she asked. They were lying side by side, barely touching.

'For what?' His eyes were closed, one arm raised above his head. She rolled onto her stomach to look at him.

'For South Africa. For home.' She said the word carefully, testing it on her tongue.

He was silent for a while. 'I never really knew it,' he said finally, his eyes still closed. 'I left when I was very young.'

'Why?' She was aware of her pulse quickening. Riitho was half asleep. It was hardly the time for a question like that, but she wanted to know.

He opened his eyes and looked at her quizzically. 'Why did *you* leave?' He parried her question.

'Me? I didn't leave, not really. I mean, I didn't *have* to. It was a choice.'

'Same here. Only it wasn't mine.'

'What do you mean?' She nuzzled her face under the crook of his arm.

He touched her hair absently. 'I mean, a lot of things that happen, they happen *to* me. I don't make them happen. It was decided.'

'Who decided?' She brushed her nose gently against the small whorls of his underarm hair.

'It was decided. Let's talk about this tomorrow, de Zoete. I'm shagged.'

She giggled, despite herself. She loved the way he spoke. A perfect mixture of economical seriousness and dry, sharp humour. His body burned steadily, a slow heat emanating from his sleek black skin that was like a pelt to her, a covering. She looked down at her own limbs in the half-light. The contrast was startling, unsettling. She closed her eyes. He pressed her head against his chest. They slept.

Gabby caught sight of herself in the mirror at the Dôme café on Upper Street. She blinked. She was having difficulty getting used to her new haircut. She touched the nape of her neck. It was very short. She'd had the same untidy, curly red hair for as long as she could remember, but so many things had changed about her recently. Her thick, ugly glasses had been replaced with a pair of frameless ones with delicate silver arms ... she still couldn't get over the transformation. Today she was wearing a cream ribbed sweater and a knee-length grey skirt. She looked like a stylishly elegant, intelligent young woman. Hard to believe it was her.

She smiled as Nael walked into the café. She saw him glance around, his eyes pass over her. She frowned, waving at him. Hadn't he recognised her? It hadn't been *that* long. 'Hey! Nael – over here!' She watched him turn back to her, do a double-take and walk over.

'Gabs! Shit, I didn't recognise you. You look so ... different.' He stared at her, momentarily confused.

'Oh, this! I've got a new haircut – I had it done ages ago.' Gabby put up a hand to it self-consciously. It wasn't strictly true. After a particularly gruelling morning spent combing through reports, she and Jennie had decided to walk up the hill to Islington and spend an afternoon in the pampering warmth of the salon. 'I can't get used to it myself.' She laughed nervously.

He frowned. Yes, the hair was different, but . . . there was something else. His eyes widened suddenly. 'Gabs . . . You're about half your size. What the heck happened to you? You're so thin!'

Gabby blushed. She couldn't get used to people calling her thin. In her own mind she was exactly the same as she'd always been – big confident exterior, and painfully shy inside. 'Oh, don't be daft. I lost a bit of weight last summer, that's all. I've just been working really hard – no time to eat and all that. How're you?' She was anxious to change the subject.

'I'm fine.' Nael took off his jacket, still shaking his head. 'I swear I didn't recognise you,' he said again, admiringly.

Gabby was still blushing. She wished he would stop staring at her. 'Enough!' she said, mock-stern. 'What about you? What's happening in your life? It's been too bloody long – and it's all my fault, I know. I'm sorry I never rang you back.'

'You still with you-know-who?' he asked, making a face.

Gabby smiled wryly. 'Sort of. I'll tell you more about it later. But come on, I want to hear what you're up to.' Gabby looked at him over the rim of her cup. She made a quick calculation. He'd have finished his master's degree at the LSE by now. 'What are you doing? Where are you working?'

'Actually, I'm not,' Nael said. He seemed almost embarrassed.

'Oh . . . I thought you'd have finished by now.'

'No, not that either.'

'What d'you mean?'

'I didn't finish. Change of plans.' Gabby frowned.

'What d'you mean you didn't finish? The course?'

'Yeah.'

'Why? I thought you loved it.' She was surprised. The

last time they'd met, almost a year ago, he couldn't stop talking about it. A master's degree in political theory.

'Yeah, well, it wasn't for me.' His eyes were bright.

He was being evasive. It wasn't like him. But before Gabby could ask further, he changed the subject again. 'And you? Tell me what you've been doing. Just leave out the bit about Dominic, unless you're dumping him, that is.'

'OK, OK.' Gabby smiled uncomfortably. She didn't want to think about Dominic right now. 'Well, let's talk about work, then. I've just found the best job in the whole world – really, it's amazing. I'm working with Rights Watch UK,' she said, glowing. 'I've been there almost six months and I'm working as a researcher. I'm with the Middle East team. I've been helping this other lawyer, a Palestinian, Marwan Ahmat. He's incredible, he – Nael, what's the matter?' She broke off suddenly. He had gone pale.

'Who did you say?'

'Marwan Ahmat. He's the principal lawyer. Why? D'you know him?' Gabby asked eagerly.

Nael took a gulp of his coffee, scalding his tongue. He shook his head vigorously. 'No. No, I don't.'

Gabby looked at him doubtfully. He was behaving most oddly.

'What did you say you were working on? What's your remit? Where do you file your reports?' He began firing questions at her.

Gabby frowned – what on earth was the matter with him? She described her job, what she did, who she talked to, what Marwan did, where he went – everything she could think of. Nael listened intently, sometimes breaking off to light a cigarette – a habit he must have acquired recently. She couldn't work it out. What was he so interested in? Was he looking for the same kind of job?

'God, no.' He wrinkled his nose. 'I couldn't work for anyone. I'm finished with all that.'

'What d'you mean "all that"?' She was puzzled.

'Oh, I don't know – I just don't want to work for anyone, not any more.'

'Why?' Gabby looked at him. 'Besides, it's not like I take orders from anyone . . . this is different. We're all in it, working together. It's completely different. It's not like working in some big law firm or something.'

'I know. It's not that. I – I can't explain it. I just don't have much faith in all that stuff.'

'What stuff? Nael, you're not making sense.' Gabby frowned.

'Aren't I? Sorry, Gabs . . . I'm just . . . Things don't seem to make sense to me any more.'

'What things?'

'You know . . . authority, the Establishment, those in the know. So-called.'

There was silence for a few minutes while Gabby struggled to understand him. 'Is that why you dropped out?' she asked eventually.

He smiled faintly. 'Spot on. You were always good at this sort of stuff, Gabs. Perceptive.'

She blushed. 'But you can't just do nothing, Nael. Why don't you want to work? Maybe not for someone like Rights Watch – but, you know, *do* something?'

He made a gesture. A faint 'tut'. A sharp lift of the head. Not a yes but a no. His gesture. Marwan's gesture. She stared at him. And then it came to her. 'Nael . . .' she said slowly, watching him – he couldn't meet her eyes. She was feeling her way carefully, instinctively. 'Tell me something. Your mother . . . ?' she said slowly. 'She's not Italian, or Spanish . . . or whatever it was you said. She's Palestinian, isn't she?' She held her breath. There was silence. Then he nodded, once, twice. She let out her breath.

'Spot on again.' He lit another cigarette.

'But why did you hide it? So what if she's Palestinian?' She was puzzled.

He raised his eyes. 'It's more complicated than that, Gabs,' he said quietly, blowing out a cloud of smoke.

'What d'you mean? Where is she? I thought she was here, in England.'

'She's in Ramallah, in administrative detention.' Gabby put a hand to her mouth. 'She's been there, off and on, for four years now.'

'Oh, Nael.' There didn't seem to be anything else to say.

'You've probably heard of her.' He lit another cigarette. 'Ahdaf Kilani.' Gabby stared at him in disbelief. Ahdaf Kilani? *Everyone* knew about her. The fiery academic-turned-politician, former dean of the Faculty of Humanities at Birzeit University. She'd been expelled from the university in the early eighties for refusing to condemn the PLO. She was a fearless critic of both the Israelis *and* the Jordanians. The Jordanians wanted her out. The Israelis wanted her dead or out, or both. She had been arrested and re-arrested, placed under house arrest, banned, gagged, censored, offered exile – but she refused to leave. She was one of Rights Watch and Amnesty's most visible prisoners. Marwan's time was almost wholly taken up by the Ahdaf Kilani campaign. She couldn't believe it. Ahdaf Kilani was Nael's *mother*?

'Shit.' There seemed even less to say. She took one of his cigarettes. She'd managed to kick the filthy habit, but she needed one now.

'Yup. So I know more about Rights Watch than you thought. I know Marwan. Yeah, we know him well. But it's difficult. It's difficult for my father. They were on the verge of splitting up the first time she was arrested. She'd only been out there for a couple of months. He and I were here, at home in Cambridge. But they both don't want me to go out there. She says it's the only thing that keeps her going, knowing I'm safe over here. She won't let me come to her, she just won't. But I can't stay here, Gabs. I'm going insane.'

His expression was one of pure pain. Gabby touched his arm. At that moment, she would have done anything for him. 'What are you going to do?' She was almost afraid to ask.

'I don't know. I've applied to work with the BBC World Service. There's a training programme starting in about six weeks' time for reporters.'

'What does your father think?'

'I don't care what he thinks. It's my life.'

Gabby leaned back in her chair. She pushed the tips of her fingers together. It was too much to take in. She looked out of the window at the crowds walking past in the early evening light, collars turned up against the cold, hands thrust in pockets. She sighed. 'Malvern seems like a million years away,' she said slowly. 'Everything was so much simpler back then.'

'No, it wasn't.' Nael smiled faintly. 'It just seemed that way. Things were just as complicated. Remember that thing with Rianne?' He gave a short laugh. 'It was all about that, too.'

'About what?' Gabby didn't follow him.

'Politics. That was why I couldn't be with her. No matter how much I wanted to. It was Ree. We were in the bathroom on the night of the ball just after we all got back and he was in a foul mood. I thought it was because he liked her himself.' He took a drag of his cigarette. 'I couldn't have been more wrong. He *hated* her. And I didn't understand it. I mean, he'd been with other white girls. But it wasn't that. He said to me – I remember the words exactly – "Just think . . . it'd be like you fucking Begin's daughter." I've never forgotten it. I knew exactly how he felt. That hatred. It can eat you up.'

Gabby picked up the salt cellar and twisted it slowly. 'I guess you're right. I never knew.'

'No.' He was quiet for a moment. 'D'you ever hear from her?'

'Yes, of course. We're still close. She's in New York. You've probably seen her face all over the place.'

Nael nodded. 'Funny. Ree's just left for New York. Let's

hope they don't bump into each other.' He stubbed out his cigarette.

'I doubt it. They move in pretty different circles. What's Ree doing these days?'

'He's an architect. He works for some big practice in Paris. He's doing well. We talk a lot too. He's amazing. He's the most disciplined person I've ever met. It's scary, sometimes.'

'He struck me as awfully arrogant,' Gabby said. 'I always felt so *silly* around him.'

'You weren't the only one. He *can* be arrogant. But he's brilliant. There's no one like him.'

'I guess so. I just never really knew him. Don't suppose I ever will. D'you think he'll go back too? To South Africa, I mean.'

'Yes, he will. He's his father's son, you know.'

'Like you're your mother's?' Gabby said softly. She understood what he was saying.

'Yeah. We understand each other.'

'Oh, Nael,' Gabby said again. She still couldn't quite believe that she was sitting in front of Ahdaf Kilani's son. Her only child.

'Na'el, actually.'

'What?'

'My name. It's not Neil, the way you pronounce it. That's what everyone calls me – it's what I call myself when I'm here – but it's Na'el – an Arabic name. You probably won't remember but you asked me about it once.'

Of course she remembered. She remembered practically everything they'd ever talked about. 'You said it was an old family name.'

'Yeah. I used to make up stories about it – the way you do. When I was a kid, I used to say there was an ancestor in the family from the Middle East, Na'el the Crusader. Don't laugh.'

'I'm not. You told me it was Welsh.'

'Yeah, well, it's not.'

Gabby looked across the table at him. He was wearing a dark blue V-neck jumper with a white T-shirt underneath. The frayed neck poked out and was sharp against the tan of his neck. His shoulders were broad and wide, his forearms covered in fine, dark brown hair. He wore a colourful, embroidered wristband – the deep colours had faded, in the sun or the wash, perhaps. He looked like the Nael she'd always known. The hair was a little longer maybe – it touched his shoulders, curling round the base of his neck – but it suited him. He was as boyishly handsome as ever. The eyes were the same . . . and his slow, sure smile. She realised, with a pang, that she was upset.

'Oh.' She blinked rapidly, afraid she was going to cry.

'What's the matter?'

'I – it's just – I—' To her horror, she felt tears beginning to well up in her eyes.

'Gabs? What's wrong?'

'I thought I *knew* you, Nael.'

'You do. You know me better than most people.' He looked puzzled.

'But I don't. Not any more. I don't even know your name. I don't know who you are. You were my friend, Nael . . . my best *friend*.'

'What are you talking about? I'm still your best friend – nothing's changed.'

'*Everything's* changed.' Her voice rose. 'I mean, first you tell me you're not half-Spanish—'

'I never said I was. That was your reading, not mine.'

'It doesn't matter,' Gabby said angrily. 'It doesn't make any difference. You could have said. You never contradicted me. And now you say, actually, you're half Palestinian *and* Ahdaf Kilani's son. It's a bit of a shock. And I'm just about managing to take all of that in and then you say, well, you're not Nael at all, you're Na-*whatever-it-is*. I just thought I *knew* you.' Tears were streaming down her cheeks. She wiped them away with the back of her hand, furiously.

'Hey, it's OK. Gabby, come on.' Nael pushed back his chair and slid into the one next to her. He covered her hand with his. 'I'm sorry, I didn't mean to upset you. You're the only person in the whole bloody world apart from Ree who knows this. I'm sorry. Really.'

'It's OK.' Gabby sniffed. 'I'm sorry, I didn't mean—'

'Don't be. It's my fault. I should have—'

'No, it's me being silly—'

'Gabs, will you stop apologising for me? *I'm* the one who should be sorry. I didn't mean to upset you. I wouldn't upset you for the world.' He leaned forward, putting his hand under her chin. For a second, one brief, absurd second, she thought he was about to kiss her. He didn't. Of course not. He touched her cheek gently and fished a napkin out of the holder on the table. 'Here.'

She took it, her hands shaking. 'Thanks.' She dabbed at her eyes, hoping the touch of mascara she'd put on wouldn't smear. Vanity. Some things never changed.

47

Charmaine was hopelessly bored. She'd been back in London almost six months and *there was nothing to do.* Nathalie was busy, busy, busy. Gabby was busy, busy, busy. Rianne was hardly ever in town. Her mother had a new boyfriend and, after the initial euphoria of Charmaine's return had worn off, she seemed inclined to spend her every waking hour with him. The friends she'd left behind had moved on. Thierry was back in Lyons, Nael was always away somewhere and, anyway, he was really Gabby's friend, not hers . . . it was boring. She couldn't understand it. She'd spent three years longing to come back, desperate to return and now that she was here there was nothing to do. Incomprehensible. But then, there were a lot of things Charmaine couldn't comprehend these days, starting with her own life. Here she was, twenty-two years old, with no qualifications to speak of (unless you counted a sideline in the supply and delivery of Class A recreational drugs), no money, no boyfriend, few friends – *and* she was still struggling to lose weight. She was back in Wilton Crescent, thanks to Rianne's unending generosity, but she was alone. She still owed Nathalie and Rianne heaps of money, which she could see no easy way of repaying, and, apart from a week's temping work, she'd pretty much done nothing since she got back. And everyone was miserable. All anyone could talk about was the impending recession. Recession, recession, recession. You switched on the TV – there it was. You turned on the radio, that's all they talked about. Newspapers? Same thing. What the hell *was* a recession anyway? Suddenly the phone rang.

'Charmaine?' It was Emily, her new friend from the gym. They'd met a few weeks previously while pounding the StairMaster. At least, Charmaine had been pounding it. Emily had barely broken a sweat. She was from Dublin, a budding actress, or, as she herself put it, a MAW. 'What's that?' Charmaine had asked. 'Model – Actress – Whatever,' Emily had laughed.

'Hi, Emily, what're you doing?' Charmaine was pleased to hear from her.

'Nothing much. I had a casting this morning – don't think I got the part. D'you feel like company?' Emily had been to Wilton Crescent a couple of times and loved the place. The fact that it belonged to Rianne de Zoete was an added and unexpected bonus. Knowing Rianne de Zoete, however marginally, could make all the difference between being a MAW and being a model. Or actress. Or whatever.

'Yeah! I'm bored out of my skull. Come over and let's make dinner.'

'I've got *just* the thing to fix the boredom. See you in an hour!' Emily hung up. She lived in Ladbroke Grove, on the top floor of a rather elegant Victorian terraced house. It wasn't quite the opulence and splendour of Knightsbridge, but it was trendy. Charmaine wondered how Emily, who never seemed to work, could afford it. Perhaps her parents were loaded. She never mentioned them. Some things about England hadn't changed, Charmaine thought, as she headed for the shower. It still didn't quite *do* to talk about money, where one got it, what one did with it. It made a change from LA.

Two hours later, Emily pulled a small plastic bag from the enormous tote she'd brought with her. Charmaine's stomach lurched. She couldn't. She *shouldn't*. She'd cleaned up her act. There was no way she was going back to *that*. She looked away as Emily leaned over the glass coffee table and divided the familiar white powder into four lines with the edge of her credit card. She rolled up a five-pound note and handed it to Charmaine.

'Come on, what're you waiting for?'

Charmaine shook her head. 'I don't – I used to . . . I can't, Emily. I *can't*.' She eyed the lines on the table with a mixture of fascination and dread.

'Come on, it's only a couple of lines. It's good stuff. Really.' Emily bent her head. Charmaine watched a line disappear. She swallowed. Her head was pounding, her palms felt clammy. 'Go on,' Emily proffered the rolled-up note.

Charmaine hesitated for a fraction of a second. Then she bent her head, the second line disappeared and she leaned back on her heels. Her first in almost a year. She waited for a few minutes as the familiar rushing sensation hit her brain.

'Whoa, you're a pro!' Emily smiled at her delightedly.

'Where . . .' she began, watching Emily demolish her share. So *that* was how she kept so slim.

'From friends . . .' Emily replied, knowing what Charmaine was about to ask. She had only the haziest details of Charmaine's past, but there was something about her that made Emily think she would be absolutely 'up for it', as she put it. She was right.

Charmaine had missed it, missed the buzz and the confidence cocaine gave her. She didn't miss the dealing, or the hassle, but she really, truly missed the highs. 'Got any more?' She giggled. She was beginning to feel *really* good.

'We can get some. What're you doing tonight?'

'Nothing. What did you have in mind?'

'Aha. Get your best gear out, gal. We're going to have some *fun*!'

A couple of hours later, Charmaine was ready. 'You look great!' Emily emerged from the bathroom, a towel tucked under her arms. Charmaine smiled at herself in the long mirror. Her hair had grown since she came back and it hung straight round her face, parted in the middle. She was wearing a figure-hugging red halter-neck dress with high-heeled black peep-toed shoes and a pair of large, silver hoop earrings. The StairMaster sessions were making *some* headway, though not as quickly as she'd hoped. She looked good enough to eat. She pirouetted for Emily and collapsed on the bed, giggling.

Emily had pulled a series of stunning clothes out of the huge bag she'd brought with her, and now she was deliberating over her outfit. She chose a simple black off-the-shoulder dress and fixed a black velvet choker round her slender neck. Her dark hair was gathered into a knot and piled high on her head.

'Where are we going?' Charmaine asked, looking at Emily enviously. Now *that* was what she called slim.

'You'll see. We're going to meet some friends of mine. They'll really like you.' Emily was vague, but there was something about the way she'd said it that made Charmaine nervous. A slight emphasis on the 'really'. Why wouldn't they like her? Charmaine hoped 'they' weren't a bunch of boring young trendies.

They clattered downstairs, checking their reflections one

last time in the hall mirror before stepping outside. It was a lovely evening, still just warm enough to go outside without a coat. Charmaine was excited. At last she was going somewhere! She was so glad she'd met Emily.

A cab screeched to a halt almost immediately. The driver had spotted them from across the street. Emily gave him an address in Mayfair and they clambered in. Charmaine failed to notice the look the driver gave them as he turned the cab.

The house they pulled up at was every bit as grand as Wilton Crescent, only bigger. Inside, however, it was another story: heavy carpeting, enormous chandeliers, ornate furniture and ghastly artwork. It looked like a bizarre film set. The butler seemed to know Emily and greeted them silently. Charmaine was apprehensive – it was all a bit odd. Very different from what she had imagined. The butler showed them into the drawing room on the first floor. It was incredibly opulent and utterly without taste. Emily looked at her . . . a little uneasily, Charmaine thought. They both sat down on one of the leopard-print sofas.

Suddenly a side door opened and a man walked in. 'Emily,' he smiled smoothly, 'how nice to see you.' He crossed the room to where the two girls were sitting. Charmaine stared at him. He was almost fifty! Short, slightly pudgy and almost bald. This was Emily's friend? Surely not.

Emily stood up gracefully and kissed him on both cheeks. 'James, may I introduce Charmaine?'

Charmaine struggled out of her seat. Her dress was still a *little* tight. James gave a funny little half-bow. '*Enchanté*, Mademoiselle,' he murmured, in badly pronounced French, lifting her hand to his lips. Charmaine suppressed the desire to giggle. It was all faintly ridiculous. James lowered her hand. 'Ladies, this way, please.' He ushered them towards the door.

'Who the hell is *he*?' Charmaine whispered to Emily, as they followed him. 'Where's the—'

'Ssh. You'll see in a minute. Just remember it's a grand for the evening, and you don't have to do anything you don't want to.'

Charmaine gaped at her, and Emily put her finger to her lips as James opened the door to a much bigger room. Two middle-aged men in suits were sitting opposite each other on large, comfortable-looking sofas, drinks in hand. They got up as James and the girls entered. Suddenly, Charmaine understood. She nearly turned and fled.

'Gentlemen,' James began his ridiculously formal routine again, 'may I introduce Charmaine and Emily?' He offered both girls a drink. Charmaine's head was spinning. A grand for an evening? She could certainly use the money . . . and Emily had said she didn't have to do anything she didn't want to. She looked carefully at them. They looked . . . all right. A bit paunchy, a bit grey, but basically OK. James handed her her martini on a glass tray with a line of coke and a dainty straw. Emily's head was already bent over her tray. Charmaine followed suit.

Ten minutes later, as the coke worked its magic, Charmaine felt better. Actually, they weren't that bad . . . they were rather entertaining. Terribly upper class. Jasper was a publisher, and Steven was 'in government', whatever that meant. Both men were old enough to be her father. She wondered how it worked, who 'went' with whom.

She was on her third line of coke and her second martini when Emily got up, Steven in tow, and walked towards the door. James escorted them out and looked expectantly at Charmaine. She was rather enjoying the look of anxious anticipation on Jasper's face. He was obviously dying to go wherever Emily had disappeared to.

Charmaine settled back into the sofa. She would make him wait. She uncrossed her legs slowly, watching Jasper squirm as he glimpsed her black lace panties. She parted her legs slightly and was rewarded with a furious blush. This, she thought, was rather fun.

'Would you like to see the rest of the house?' Jasper asked.

'Why not?' Charmaine said brightly. She stood up, smoothing her dress over her hips, her hands lingering for just a second too long on her thighs.

James appeared pleased as he opened the door for them. 'Ah, Mr Clifford and Emily are in the *Blue* Room,' he murmured to Jasper, as they passed into the hallway.

'How about the Master Bedroom?' Jasper said to Charmaine.

She followed him along the corridor until they reached a set of double doors. He flung them open and Charmaine stepped into an enormous room, complete with a four-poster bed and half a dozen armchairs. It was lit only by a bedside lamp and the sheets had been turned back. On the side table there was a tray with a jug of water and, Charmaine was delighted to see, a single white line with a straw. Jasper declined her offer and watched, somewhat amused, as she demolished it in a single snort. She sat carefully on the edge of the bed, wiping her nose daintily and looking at him expectantly as he removed his jacket.

'Take off your dress,' he said quietly. He settled himself in one of the armchairs near the bed. Charmaine paused as her brain responded to the coke, then lifted her arms and shrugged herself out of her red dress.

'Turn round.' Dressed only in her black lace bra, matching panties and high heels, she did as he requested. It wasn't so different from Flamingo, she thought, as she heard his sharp intake of breath. Here there was a lot more money and she was in much more comfortable surroundings, but the men were essentially the same: all powerful and arrogant in their suits but pathetic little boys when she exercised her sexual control.

'Bend over.' He made no move to touch her, just watched her from his chair. She rather liked being ordered around.

She heard him unbuckling his belt and removing his trousers.

'Spread your legs. No, don't turn round – keep your back to me. Bend over and lie on the bed. That's it.' Still he made no move to get up. Perhaps he was one of those men who liked to watch. She bent over, still with her legs spread and felt the cool silk of the bedspread against her cheek. He got up suddenly and stood behind her. She braced herself. She could feel his legs against her backside as he pushed her head into the bedspread. Then, he groaned, and she felt hot, sticky wetness hit the small of her back. He held her there for a second, then moved away. His semen spilled onto the bedspread. Was that it? Should she get up? She raised her head to look at him. He was putting on his trousers, looking for his belt.

'James will see you out. Thank you, Charmaine.' He put on his jacket. Before Charmaine had had a chance to straighten up, she heard him walk – almost run – to the double doors, and then he was gone. She stood up, used the bedspread to dry her back, then put on her dress, retrieved an earring, and was wondering what to do when she heard a gentle tap at the door. It was James. He held out an envelope and a glass of cold water, and told her that Emily would be waiting for her downstairs when she was ready. There was a fully stocked bathroom next door, if she cared to—

'Er, no, thank you. I'll be downstairs in a minute. Thank you, James.'

Charmaine took the envelope and waited until he had closed the doors. She tore it open. A thousand pounds in crisp new fifty-pound notes. She looked at them in disbelief. She hadn't even *slept* with him! She practically ran downstairs to find Emily. It was almost too good to be true.

PART FIVE

48

March 1989: Cape Town, South Africa

Lisette and Hennie were standing in her offices in downtown Cape Town. It was a clear, late autumn day in the southern hemisphere. Hennie finished speaking, his voice dying away as Lisette looked at her son's worried face and turned to face the windows. She looked out from the thirty-third floor across the marina to sea. From there, high above the city, it seemed as though the violence and uncertainty that had gripped the country in the past couple of years could not touch them. The skies were high, pale blue, gulls swooped inland, and wispy clouds drifted across the steel frame of the floor-to-ceiling plate-glass windows. It was beautiful – and deceptively calm.

In the distance she could just make out Robben Island, the offshore maximum-security prison where Mandela, Modise and the others were held. These were troubled times. P. W. Botha, the President, had just come out of hospital after a stroke and the country had been plunged into uncertainty. Violence was on the increase and the countrywide 'defiance campaign' of civil disobedience – an excuse, in Lisette's eyes, for blacks to indulge their primitive, ill-disciplined ways – was in full force.

Rumours were surfacing about the government holding talks with the banned political parties – Mandela's ANC and Modise's AFP. Lisette fervently hoped de Klerk, the new head of the National Party, would soon put paid to them and bring to bear the full weight of the law on the terrorists, either by hanging them or banishing them into exile. The whole thing was costing the country dearly. And now this. She turned back to Hennie. What was he saying? What money had disappeared?

'Disappeared how?' She crossed her arms. 'When? What are you talking about?'

'Well, this is the thing. It seems as though the bulk went when Uncle Marius did,' Hennie said slowly. 'But it's been going on for a while.'

'What do you mean?' There was a catch in her voice.

'Well, we don't know. One of two things. Either he knew about it . . . or he didn't.' Hennie was shaking his head slowly. How it had surfaced only now was beyond him.

Almost three billion rand had 'disappeared' from one of their company accounts over the past fourteen years. The withdrawals had been made through a Swiss account, to which only Marius had had access. Suddenly Lisette felt weak. She went to her desk, sat down and buried her head in her hands.

Hennie looked at her uncertainly. He'd never seen his mother so worried.

'Get Simon in here,' she said finally. 'No, don't call him, go and *get* him.' Her head was spinning.

Hennie ran out of the room and reappeared minutes later with a worried-looking Simon.

'Leave us for a moment, *skatjie*,' Lisette said. 'I need to talk to Simon alone.' Hennie left the room. Lisette could see that he wanted to know what was going on. After all, it was he who had brought the disturbing news to his mother, not Simon.

'What does it mean?' Lisette asked Simon, as soon as the door closed behind Hennie. 'What's going on?'

'We don't know, Lisette. We've got to find out who's taking the money. It's going to be difficult. If word of this gets out . . . The stock market is so volatile at the moment . . . It's not going to be easy.'

Gold shares were plummeting, driven downwards by the expense of mining operations in a country that was at war with itself. Labour costs were soaring. The unions were getting stronger by the day. And now, to top it all, there was talk in government circles of the 'inevitable', the release of Mandela and Modise and, God forbid, the legalisation of the banned political parties. Who knew where it would end. All of which would drive the price of gold down even further.

Lisette was silent. She remembered that evening, almost fifteen years ago, when Marius had stood in the dining room at Vergelegen. 'How long? How long can we go on getting away scot-free?' he had said. At the time, she had had no idea what he was talking about. She dug her nails into her palm. She was afraid.

'You'll need to go to Zurich, Simon, then London,' she said. 'I've got to stay here, find out what's happening, who's making the withdrawals. I can't trust anyone else. Will you do this for us?'

'Of course.' Simon nodded. 'I'll leave tomorrow morning. I'll think of something to tell the accountants. We'll find out what's happening, Lisette. Don't worry. We'll get to the bottom of it.' He touched her arm. 'I'll phone from Zurich.' He left the room, a worried frown on his face.

Lisette lit a cigarette. She inhaled quickly, trying to calm herself before she summoned Hennie. She felt better, knowing that Simon was taking care of things. It was good to have him around, someone she could rely on. She was so used to taking care of things by herself and it felt good to give up the responsibility to someone else. Another man. She smoothed her pale green silk dress over her still slender hips. She would brief Hennie, then take the rest of the afternoon off and drive home. She would go riding in the hills. She needed to get away from the city and think.

Hennie received the news with a frown. He was worried, but for selfish reasons: with his two uncles gone, Marius and Hendryk, it was to him that de Zoete Inc. should fall. His cousin Rianne hadn't been home since her last visit almost three years ago. She pretended she wasn't South African, he knew that. He was contemptuous of her reasons for leaving, but her absence worked to his advantage. With Rianne out of the way, Hendryk's sons, Piet and Coen, on a farm somewhere in the Orange Free State, and his sister Marika working with orphans or whatever the hell it was she did, Lisette relied almost entirely on him. Simon Kalen, capable and dedicated as he was, was not family. Hennie was, and would assume control one day of the vast business empire that Lisette had inherited. Someday de Zoete Inc. would he his. That was all he was waiting for. So he was afraid of what Simon would find: either Marius was dead, and someone had extracted the information about the account from him before he died . . . or Marius was alive. Neither prospect appealed to him. He began to chew the inside of his lips as he always did when he was worried.

49

Nathalie checked her reflection in the mirror. She looked good. She put on her lightweight tan leather jacket and decided against it. She was wearing a mossy green suede trouser suit with black brogues, a thick black leather belt and matching bag. She had lost weight in the past couple of months, not that she'd had much to lose. She looked older, more sophisticated. She smiled at herself, excited. She added a dash of lipstick, smoothed her hair and picked up her keys. Paul would be waiting for her at the gallery and she didn't want to be late.

She'd met him only a couple of months ago. He was an artist, a few years older than her, and apart from 'thinking', seemed to do little. He was handsome, witty, unbelievably popular . . . and broke. After men like Sacha and Marcus, it had come as a shock to Nathalie that there were men who were unable, and happily unprepared, to bear the cost of a relationship. Whenever she and Paul went out, he would cheerfully point the bill in her direction. That was what happened, Nathalie reasoned, when one pursued one's 'art' – and, besides, she had plenty of money. Why shouldn't she pay for things now and again? In fact, she liked the sense of power it gave her. She'd spent most of her working life persuading people to look beyond the petite, pretty façade and treat her like the strong, fiercely ambitious woman she felt herself to be and picking up the tabs every time they went out reinforced her image of herself.

It took ages to find the gallery. It was in Shoreditch, the up-and-coming art district, Paul had assured her. Nathalie had never been east of Liverpool Street and she'd certainly never heard of Hoxton Square. When she found it, she looked around doubtfully . . . didn't much look like an up-and-coming art district . . . all grubby industrial buildings and an unkempt square . . . but, if Paul said it was, it must be so. She locked her car, glanced at the address in her hand and hurried to the gallery, Ellingham Knight.

It was easy enough to spot. A crowd of young, good-looking people were standing on the steps of a large white building, all dressed in black. She stepped past a couple dressed head to toe in pleated Issey Miyake. For a bunch of broke, *un*gainfully employed people, Nathalie thought, as she scanned the entrance for Paul, they dressed well. She walked up the steps and through to the gallery. She spotted him almost immediately. He was standing next to an enormous white canvas with one – just the one, mind – black line drawn carefully down the middle. He had a glass of wine in each hand and was talking to a group of people who seemed to be hanging on his every word. Even the men.

'Paul.' Nathalie kissed him three times, as all artists seemed to do.

His eyes roamed over her appreciatively as he introduced

her to the group, none of whose names she could remember. In the sea of mourners, she felt rather conspicuous in her moss-green.

'You look absolutely *edible*,' he murmured in her ear.

Nathalie blushed. For all her tough exterior, she was still uncomfortable around anything sexual. She accepted a glass of white wine from a waiter and tried to follow the conversation between Paul and his assorted artist friends, but couldn't. Judging by the looks on their faces, he was saying something deep and meaningful. He loved an audience, she knew.

'Well, clearly,' he was saying, 'it's all about the search for existence . . .' Several people nodded knowingly. He carried on '. . . yes, the most *traumatic* loss . . . ', ' . . . a shedding, the way one might a skin . . .' The words floated above her head. She tried hard to look interested and knowledgeable, but *really* . . . it was bollocks. She had absolutely no idea what he was talking about. To her, most of the oversized, ridiculously overpriced canvases looked empty. How on earth was a green slash in the middle of sixteen square feet of grey supposed to signify a search for existence? She sipped her wine.

Paul grabbed her by the waist and propelled her from group to group until, almost hopping up and down with excitement, he introduced her to Josef, the artist behind several of the 'great' works. Josef looked her up and down – patronisingly dismissive, she thought. His eyes lingered for a minute on her shoes – wrong shoes, he seemed to be saying. She had to resist the temptation to stick a shoe out and kick him.

'She absolutely *adores* them,' Paul said, as he guided her and Josef across the room to stand in front of one of his 'works'.

Nathalie looked up at the canvas doubtfully. It was blank. Paul turned to Josef. 'She was just saying it would look fantastic in one of the stores.'

Nathalie looked at him sharply. She'd said nothing of the

sort. What was going on? Ah. She looked at the price tag: £3,500 – for *that*? What did he take her for? Then she smiled.

'Actually, no, I prefer that one.' She pointed to the enormous white canvas with the single black stripe. Five thousand. The two men stared at her. She moved away towards another one. Seven thousand. 'Or this, perhaps?' Josef and Paul were besides themselves. She stopped in front of an enormous red canvas. Ten thousand. 'Although . . .' Paul's face was a picture: pride, greed, desire . . . She was enjoying herself. She walked back to the first. 'I don't know. They're all so fantastic. Let me think about it. I need to picture where to hang them.'

Them? Nathalie watched with amusement as Josef revised his opinion of her. 'Not just a pretty face,' Paul whispered in her ear, as all three walked across the gallery floor.

'Is there a ladies' room?' Nathalie asked, downing her wine in one gulp.

'Down the hallway, to the left.' She had almost reached the toilets, still holding the empty glass, when she froze. A man was standing in front of an odd-looking sculpture with his back to her. She blinked. Oh, God. Oh, no. *Please* no. It couldn't be – just when everything was going so well. She stared at his back. It was him. There was no mistaking it. The height, his curly dark hair, the wide shoulders. The blood drained from her face. She stood rooted to the spot. The man turned slowly.

'Sacha.' Her glass crashed to the floor.

'Nathalie.' He didn't smile.

A waiter rushed up and started to pick up the broken glass. As if from a great distance, she heard a toilet flush, the sound of running water, and then the door opened. A slender young woman emerged, drying her hands on a paper napkin. She came up to Sacha and slid an arm round his waist. He still did not move.

'I – oh, God, I'm sorry,' Nathalie apologised, bending to help the waiter. She wanted nothing more than to run out of the gallery.

'Siena.' At last Sacha spoke. He put an arm round the young woman's shoulders. 'Let me introduce you. Nathalie Maréchal . . . Siena Ellingham.'

'Nilam, darling,' the young woman corrected him. Nathalie smiled weakly. Siena Ellingham-Nilam smiled back. 'He*llo*,' she said, and shook Nathalie's hand limply. *Very* English.

'Hi,' Nathalie replied tightly. There was a short silence. All three looked at each other.

'What brings you here?' Sacha broke it.

'Me? Oh, art's not my thing. It's my boyfriend – he's an artist.' Nathalie's voice shook. She looked around for Paul who was nowhere to be seen. She turned back to the couple. She searched for something to say. 'And you?' she asked. 'Do you know the artists?'

'Siena's the co-owner.' Sacha answered for his wife. 'Ellingham Knight.' Nathalie looked blank. 'The name of the gallery.' She nodded. Of course. There was another awkward silence.

Nathalie glanced around again. Where the hell was Paul? She *had* to get out of there. 'Well, it was very nice to meet you,' she said. 'And you – to see you, I mean,' she stammered to Sacha. 'I – my boyfriend – must be going . . .' She shook hands with Siena and offered her hand to Sacha. When he took it, an electric shock caught her in the pit of her stomach. She jerked away her hand, and almost knocked over a sculpture in her haste to get away.

She spotted Paul, still holding forth. She had to leave, she shouted over her shoulder. She'd forgotten a couple of things – she'd call him later. She ran down the steps, rushed across the street and crashed headlong into a cyclist.

'Nat . . . Nathalie . . . Nat . . . Can you hear me?' Nathalie could hear someone calling her from a long way off. She struggled to focus on the blurred face in front of her. Paul was peering anxiously at her. A group of people crowded around her as she lay on the ground. She struggled to sit up, aware of a throbbing in her temples and a dull ache in her right hand.

'Don't sit up, darling,' Paul chided her. 'Just lie back for a minute. Does it hurt anywhere?'

Nathalie nodded. What the hell had happened? She dimly remembered a cyclist, a flash of yellow and a bicycle crashing to the ground. She must have been knocked out.

'We'll have to call an ambulance,' Paul announced, to the crowd gathered on the street. 'I'd drive her to hospital myself but I've had too much to drink. Can someone call for an ambulance?'

'How badly is she hurt?' one of the gallery assistants asked, a minute later. 'They say it'll take half an hour!'

Paul swore.

'I'll take her.' It was Sacha's voice.

'Are you sure?' Paul sounded grateful.

Nathalie opened her mouth to protest – no *way* was she going to hospital with Sacha. She tried to sit up, but everything went black again. When she came round, she was being carried towards a black car, her head lolling against Sacha's chest. He lowered her into the passenger seat with Paul hovering attentively as she was strapped in. Then he got in and started the engine. 'I'll be back soon,' he told Siena and Paul. 'I'll take her to UCH and give you a call.'

'Thanks, man,' Paul said gratefully, slapping the roof of the car. 'I really appreciate it.'

'Not at all.' Sacha pulled away from the kerb. Nathalie kept her eyes firmly shut. They drove for a few minutes in silence.

'I'm really sorry,' Nathalie began. 'I've caused an awful lot of bother.'

'Nothing to be sorry about,' Sacha replied evenly. 'Still in pain?'

Nathalie's head was splitting, as was her wrist.

'Just lie still, we'll be there in a minute.' She closed her eyes.

An hour later, she was discharged from A&E at University College Hospital, her wrist bandaged and the headache receding, thanks to some strong painkillers. The junior doctor was cheerful. 'You were lucky,' he said. 'No broken bones, no stitches, just a sprained wrist and a headache. Wish all my cases were as easy. You'll need these.' He handed a small container of tablets to Sacha. 'They'll help her sleep it off. 'Bye now.'

Sacha pocketed the tablets. He turned to Nathalie. 'I'd better take you home,' he said. 'I'll drop you off and then I'll go back to the gallery. What's your boyfriend's name?'

'Paul,' Nathalie said faintly. She wanted to lie down.

'He'll have sobered up by now. He can bring your car back.' Sacha helped her through the doors. He touched her elbow. That electric charge again. She waited while he brought the car round and helped her in. She gave him the address, and was almost asleep by the time they arrived at her flat.

'I'll be fine, Sacha,' she said, as she eased herself out of the car. 'You don't need to see me in, honestly.' She wanted to crawl into her bed and block out the day's events.

'Give me your keys.' Sacha appeared not to have heard her protests. Meekly, she handed them over and they hobbled up the front steps. She hoped Gloria, the cleaner, had been in during the day. She had. At the sight of her luxuriously calm, tranquil flat, Nathalie was in tears again. She half-hopped, half-walked into the large living space with its bleached floorboards, muted grey walls and smoky, mushroom rugs. She was acutely conscious of Sacha behind her as she climbed the short flight of stairs to the mezzanine level and her bedroom.

'Get changed,' Sacha ordered, as he drew the heavy damask curtains. 'I'll get you some water and you can take one of these.' He pulled out the vial of tablets. She nodded, too tired to answer.

She opened a drawer awkwardly with her left hand and pulled out a pair of silk pyjamas. As Sacha's footsteps receded, she pulled off her clothes, as quickly as she could with one bandaged hand, and was fumbling with the buttons on her pyjama top when he came into the room.

'Here.' He put down the glass and briskly finished the job, then guided her to her huge antique French bed. She obediently stuck out her tongue as Sacha placed two small tablets in her mouth. There was an awkward moment when his fingers touched her tongue and Nathalie had to suppress the fierce urge to lick the tips of his fingers. He held the glass of water for her so that she could swallow the pills. Then he helped her into bed, drew the sheets over her and smoothed her pillow. She lay quietly for a moment, studying him beside her in the near-darkness through her lashes.

'Sacha,' she murmured drowsily. She wanted to thank him for his care, distant and efficient though it had been.

'Sshh. Go to sleep.' His voice was firm. Within minutes, the tablets had begun their work and she drifted off.

Nathalie arched her back as the sensations in her body intensified. Through layers of sleep and hazy, erotic dreams, she was melting slowly, deliciously. Her nipples were on fire: someone was stroking them. She moaned and turned over, pressing her stomach into the sheets and wiggling her toes. It felt so *good*. She could feel something soft, warm and wet trail its way between her shoulder blades, nibbling her skin. She lifted her arms above her head, grabbed the pillows as the wetness moved down her back. She was turned over, gently, slowly ... The trailing continued, over her stomach, below the waistband of her pyjamas, lower and lower. She arched her back again as she felt her pyjamas being eased off her, and raised her hips in breathless anticipation. Her whole body was on fire as the warmth spread between her legs and touched her, there – right *there*. She groaned, opening her legs wider, clutching the sheets as the stroking continued, soft and insistent. A hand reached up, rubbed her nipples lightly, first one, then the other. Her hips began to buck as the probing went deeper into her, hot and taut. She climaxed almost immediately, clamping her thighs around the intruder and shuddering as wave after wave of pleasure coursed through her body.

'Sacha,' she moaned softly, 'Sacha.' The stroking continued, over her hips, buttocks and down the backs of her legs, but lighter now, teasing. She smiled languorously in her half-sleep, rolled onto her back, her clenched fists relaxing. She could feel his breath on her face as she drifted off again, warm, secure. Her breathing calmed, her nipples softened, and the hot wetness between her thighs cooled. She slept.

Sacha looked at himself in the mirror. Nothing. His dark eyes stared back at him, blank. He could taste Nathalie on his lips. He bent over the sink and turned on the cold tap. He splashed the icy water over his face and lips. He gripped the edge of the sink. His body was swollen with desire. He breathed in deeply, ran a cold flannel over the back of his neck and straightened, still staring at his silent reflection. He turned off the tap and opened the door. Nathalie was fast asleep, no longer curled up in the foetal position she favoured but spread out across the bed. Her silk pyjamas were crumpled at the foot of the bed, where he'd pulled them off her with his teeth. He picked up his jacket and left.

Nathalie opened her eyes. She lay still, wondering where she was and why she was in bed. It was dark in her room. All of a sudden, the day's events flooded back, the gallery, the crash, the hospital . . . Sacha. A memory of something . . . It came back to her. She opened her eyes and looked around. There was no sign of him. Had she dreamed the whole thing? She could remember feeling him . . . She sat upright. She was half undressed. Her pyjama bottoms were crumpled at the foot of the bed. She was confused and disoriented. Her bandaged hand was no longer throbbing but her head still ached.

She swung her legs out of bed and got up gingerly. Where was Paul? She walked into her bathroom, washed her face with one hand and opened the medicine cabinet above the sink, looking for some aspirin. She found a packet, opened it awkwardly, and fished out the pills with her teeth. She bent down, cupped her good hand under the tap and swallowed a mouthful of water.

She looked at the small silver clock she kept on the bathroom sill. It was 10.15 p.m. She must have come out of the hospital at around three thirty . . . Did that mean she'd been asleep for six hours? She stared at her reflection in the mirror – a pale face with mascara smudged beneath her eyes. Her hair was dishevelled and she looked tired. She longed for a cup of tea.

She didn't notice the small white business card until she was curled up downstairs on the sofa, sipping hot camomile tea and wondering where the hell Paul was with her car. The card was poised on the edge of the walnut coffee table. Idly, she picked it up. 'Sacha Nilam', it read. 'Chartered Accountant'. It gave two telephone numbers and his office address. She leaned her head back against the sofa. So he *had* been here. And he'd left his card for a reason. She would call him in the morning.

A loud knock on the front door interrupted her thoughts. It was Paul, having sobered up enough to drive her car back. She let him in and allowed herself to be fussed over, but her mind was elsewhere. She was thinking about the next day.

'Hello, may I speak to Sacha Nilam, please?' Nathalie's throat was dry. It was ten thirty in the morning. She hoped it wasn't too early.

'Speaking.'

'Oh, Sacha, it's Nathalie. I just wanted to say thank you for taking me to the hospital and everything. It was very kind of you.'

'Not at all.' His voice was smooth. 'Are you feeling better?'

'Yes, much. The hand's still bandaged but it's nothing, really. I really appreciated your help,' Nathalie said, a little awkwardly. 'Perhaps I can take you out to lunch or something, to say thank you properly.'

'Sure. When?'

Nathalie was taken aback. 'Oh. Well, um, how about next week? Monday?'

'Sure.'

'I'll . . . er, call you on Monday morning. We could go somewhere close to your office.'

'Sure.' He was noncommittal.

'OK. Well, that's great. I'll see you on Monday.' Nathalie was flustered. She could never read Sacha. Sometimes he was distant, other times not. But maybe things were changing. They'd both grown up. Sacha was married. Nathalie winced. Well, if he didn't mention Siena, she wouldn't. And she started to think about what she would wear.

The following Monday, she was waiting outside the offices of Coopers Lyall Dearborn at one o'clock. She saw him come through the revolving doors and her heart beat a little faster. He was wearing a navy suit, a white shirt and an elegant, expensive-looking tie. His hair was swept off his face and he had on gold-rimmed spectacles. The suit did nothing to hide the powerful, athletic frame behind the City-gent mask. She could see the muscles in his thighs crease his trousers as he jogged down the steps towards her car.

'You got it back in one piece, then,' he said. It was a breezy day and Nathalie had the top down. Luckily it was an automatic and she could manoeuvre it without difficulty, even with her bandaged hand.

'Yes . . . It . . . I – thank goodness.' She was already flustered. She didn't like thinking about Paul in such close proximity to Sacha.

'So, where are you taking me?'

Sacha turned to look at her. She was wearing a scarf and her favourite sunglasses. Although he said nothing, she could tell by the way he narrowed his eyes that he liked what he saw.

'Well, it's such a nice day, I thought we could go out of London. It's not far.'

'Sounds good.'

She pulled into the traffic and headed east, out of the City. Forty minutes later, they drove into a small car park in a tiny Essex village near Braintree. Nathalie had been here with Paul a couple of months back, and had loved the family-run, out-of-the-way pub with its quintessentially English garden and its home-cooked food.

'This is very pretty,' Sacha commented, as they got out of the car. It was spring and the buds were just opening. They ate lunch on the patio, to the distant sound of farm animals. There were only two other couples in the place. To anyone looking, they were an ordinary, if exceptionally good-looking couple, he teasing her a little, she flirting. Nathalie had two glasses of wine, unusual for her but there was something about the afternoon, the sun coming out, her 'kidnapping' Sacha for lunch that made her feel reckless.

'How long have you got?' she asked. She hadn't looked at her watch but they'd been gone at least a couple of hours.

'Took the afternoon off,' Sacha said briefly. 'I had a

feeling this might take a while.' He set down his glass. 'And so did you.'

Nathalie said nothing. Her cheeks were flushed, a combination of the wine and Sacha's open flirtation. The image of what she thought had happened the previous week drifted into her mind. She felt slightly giddy. 'Sacha, I . . .'

'You know, you talk too much,' Sacha interrupted. 'I think I told you that once before.'

Nathalie's cheeks burned. It was true. And, if she remembered correctly, that admonition had been a prelude to something else, something that didn't require much talk. Was this an invitation?

'Follow me.' Sacha got up, and headed for the toilets. There was no one about. He opened the door marked 'Ladies' and beckoned to her. Giggling, she followed him in. It was empty. He locked the door, and kissed her hungrily, his mouth rough and demanding. Nathalie responded greedily, grabbing his hair with her good hand, her legs parting as his knee forced its way between them and his hands circled her waist. He picked her up easily and swung her round so that she was sitting on the washbasin ledge, facing him, her legs wrapped around his waist. He pushed up her skirt, then tore aside her underwear. His tongue was in her mouth as his fingers probed inside her. She felt him undo his jacket, then his belt, then his trousers – and then he was inside her, thrusting roughly, forcing her head back and covering her neck with hungry kisses. She came almost immediately, her head swimming and her hand throbbing as she held on to him.

'Nathalie . . . Nathalie . . .' He groaned as he thrust fiercely inside her. She could feel his excitement mount until, finally, with a harsh cry, he climaxed. Nathalie's head banged against the mirror so hard she thought it would crack. They clung together shaken and silent, panting. Finally, Sacha disengaged himself and Nathalie slid down dazed. There was an awkward silence.

'Wait a few minutes,' Sacha said, as he tucked his shirt

into his trousers. 'I'll use the gents' next door.' He slipped out.

Nathalie stared at her reflection in the mirror. There was a red welt on her cheek where Sacha had pressed his thumb into her mouth as he fucked her. Not made love to her. Fucked her. Yes, that was the correct expression. She pressed her head against the mirror. What was she doing? What was she agreeing to?

50

Rianne could tell from their blank expressions that Ross and Gina were not as enthusiastic about her 'return' as they should have been. Or, at least, as they had been over the telephone before they'd seen her. She was perched uncomfortably on the steel bar-stool at the fashionable TriBeCa Grill and tried to read between the lines of their polite chit-chat. She'd cut her hair – Ross didn't like it. She'd lost weight – Gina didn't like it. She'd stopped smoking – *Riitho* didn't like it – which was making her edgy. She felt as though she'd spent the past couple of months reshaping herself to fit others' needs and she was tired of it. She turned back to Ross. 'What?' She hadn't been paying attention.

'Your hair, who did it?'

'What does it matter? You don't like it.'

'No. It's the wrong colour for you.' Ross was blunt.

Rianne sighed. How could she explain to them that she'd changed her hair to make it easier and safer to meet Riitho? Or that she spent so much of her time just waiting for him to call that she'd lost track of time and her appetite. 'I just felt like something different. That's all. I've had the same haircut since I was about thirteen.'

'Well, change it back.'

Rianne sighed. She'd almost forgotten how much she

hated this aspect of her job. All that standing around, just waiting to be scrutinised, prodded, pulled, pinched, shaped. Now, more than ever, she was uncomfortable about the way she made a living. Sitting around or walking endlessly up and down catwalks for obscene amounts of money. She'd tried telling Riitho what she felt. It wasn't that she'd developed a conscience, she told him earnestly, it was more that she was embarrassed in front of him about her choices and the small range of options with which her expensive education had left her.

'You're not stupid, Rianne. Not by a long shot. You make stupid choices because you think you are, but you're not.' She didn't understand him. The frustration she felt in him was not at her, it was with her. Make better choices, he seemed to be saying. You've made one already. She smiled suddenly.

She watched Ross and Gina exchange a glance. She lifted her glass. Let them. She didn't care. That was the thing they'd never understood. She'd never cared.

Riitho looked again at the brief in front of him. He took off his glasses and pinched the bridge of his nose. He glanced at his watch. It was almost eleven. He'd been at his desk since nine that morning. He picked up the papers again. The project had only just come into the office and Jean Neumann had put it on his desk. The Senegalese National Museum. It was much bigger than anything he'd handled before but he knew why Jean had passed it to him: it was his chance to show what he could do that others couldn't. Despite his exhaustion, his stomach tightened with excitement. It was the opportunity he'd been waiting for. He wanted to tell Rianne. He couldn't remember where she was – London? New York? She was having a hard time at Face!, he knew. Her booker kept sending her on wild-goose chases: she'd turn up at assignments and be sent back again, not quite what they were looking for, little too this or a little too that – she couldn't understand it. Was she losing her looks? Riitho did his best to calm her down. No, of course not, but fashion was a notoriously fickle business. Today's look was over almost as soon as it came out. The smart ones got in and left at the right time, moved on to something else. 'Like what?' Rianne asked crossly – and a touch apprehensively.

'I don't know. Find something else to do, Rianne. This can't last for ever.' It was easy for him to say, he knew. He'd never suffered a lack of direction. His problem was the opposite: too much direction, too much focus. She sometimes wondered about him – buried under all the expectations there had to be something he wanted to do, something he wanted for himself. But if there was, he never said. He seemed to love what he did with a passion that took her breath away. She wouldn't admit it – no, never – but she envied him. Yes, she envied him his choices.

He closed the dossier and picked up his jacket. He would try calling her from the phone box at the end of the street. He walked to the windows and peeked through the blinds. No one about.

'*Bonne nuit*,' he called to the two final-year students who were working *en charette* at the practice. It was a form of slave labour: they were called in for competitions and worked half to death for little money but tons of 'experience', as the practice called it. Fortunately, the allure of working for the mercurial Neumann was sufficiently strong to attract an endless stream of ambitious young things.

Riitho smiled to himself as he walked down the stairs. It wasn't so long ago that he'd been one of them. He checked the street. It was still empty. He slipped into the phone booth and dialled the number. The phone rang and rang in the empty flat he had never seen. He sighed, and hung up. As strong as he had learned to be about their situation, it wasn't easy. He walked back to his car.

As he pulled out of the street, he saw the familiar headlights of the two BOSS agents behind him. So they were watching him, after all.

51

From the moment she walked into the empty apartment, Gabby knew she wanted it. 'I'll take it.' She smiled at the realtor who had accompanied her.

'Great!' The young woman snapped her file shut. 'You'll just love it here.'

Gabby nodded. She'd seen more apartments in the past week than she had in her whole life. This one was a little out of the way, about an hour's subway ride from her new offices on 42nd Street, but she loved it. Situated next to the lovely wooded Cloisters in the Washington Heights neighbourhood, she'd felt at home almost as soon as they'd pulled up outside. It was a large, turn-of-the-century apartment block with an internal courtyard and a wonderful shabbily grand entrance hall. The rent was outrageous – almost half of her new salary. Everyone at the UN had warned her that New York was a great posting but it didn't come cheap. 'So, what do we do now?' she asked. Things worked differently in America. Everything was so much more formal.

'We'll go back to the office, fill out the paperwork. You'll need to get me a cashier's check and get your insurance. We'll sort it all out. Then I give you the keys, you get in a cab – and move in!'

Gabby walked through the apartment once more. It was a two-bedroomed, almost split-level flat with parquet flooring, nice high ceilings and a lovely view out of the back windows onto the gorge for which the area was named. Although it was only June, it was already hot and she was relieved to feel a breeze wafting through the empty rooms. She would have to buy some furniture – apart from the cooker, fridge and some empty shelving, there wasn't a thing in the place. Luckily her new job came with a relocation allowance. Maybe there was a Habitat or something similar nearby. Yes, yes, the realtor nodded. She'd give Gabby a list.

A week later Gabby lay back on the sofa cushions, thrilled. The apartment was transformed and she'd done it on a shoestring. The sitting room was dark green – Hunter green, the man in the shop called it – with white skirting-boards and ceiling. She'd managed to buy a large blue sofa, a dining-table and four chairs, an old leather armchair, a bed, a desk, and several lamps at a discount furniture shop just down the road. The salespeople had barely spoken English and Gabby's Spanish wasn't the best, but they'd managed.

Washington Heights, once a prosperous middle-class Jewish neighbourhood had been slowly squeezed by Spanish Harlem. One by one, the doctors, psychiatrists and academics, no matter how liberal their politics, had moved out and the Dominicans and Puerto Ricans had moved in. Now in place of the dry-cleaners and kosher bakeries, there were small corner shops selling *arroz*, *timbáles* and *café con leche*. It was perfect. It reminded her of London. She got up and went to the kitchen, plugged in the automatic coffee machine – no one seemed to have electric kettles in the States – and gazed out of the window. It was her first Saturday morning in the new apartment. She made some coffee and went back into the living room. She put her feet up on the table and eyed the pile of reports waiting for her. She could scarcely believe where she was, what she was doing, how her life had turned out. It had been the most incredible year.

It had started off badly with the New Year's Eve party. She, Dominic and a group of his friends had gone up to Edinburgh for Hogmanay. Someone in the group had a distant Scots relative, reason enough to claim Edinburgh as the place to see in the New Year. Gabby hadn't wanted to go: Jennie, Marwan and a couple of the others at Rights Watch were going to Paris for a couple of days and she had wanted to join them. But she didn't want to risk making a scene, and both Jennie and Marwan were taking their partners – she couldn't imagine Dominic in their company for longer than an hour. At least *he* didn't have to worry about her fitting in with his friends – she fitted in with everyone. So, she told them regretfully that she couldn't come, a prior arrangement, Dominic's parents . . .

The drive up to Edinburgh hadn't been too bad. She, Dominic and his friend Giles had borrowed a car from Giles's mother and they'd left early in the morning. Gabby was quiet, thinking about the others making their way by ferry and train to Paris. She'd only been to Paris once, on a school trip. Rianne was supposed to be there too, although she was being rather cagey about her New Year's Eve plans. Gabby wondered if she'd met someone. It had been a bit of a surprise, her leaving Olivier – she'd done it rather abruptly. Still, it had been over a year, and although she was photographed every other week coming out of a restaurant, going into the theatre, doing whatever it was that highly paid supermodels did, there didn't seem to be anyone else on the scene. It would have been nice to meet up with her, introduce Rianne to the group. They all knew she and Gabby were close – it was a bit of an office joke. Serious, intensely political Gabby, best friends with Rianne de Zoete who was hardly the most politically sophisticated spokesperson her country had ever produced.

'Gabby. You're not listening.' Dominic turned round. She was sitting in the back seat, watching the landscape unfold in the winter morning. It was snowing in Cumbria. She followed the curve of the motorway, stretching out like a black ribbon in front of them, lost in her thoughts. The hills were bleak, windswept and desolate. The setting was rather appropriate. 'Gabby?' Dominic said again.

'What? Sorry, I wasn't listening.'

He looked cross. He hated her not paying attention to him. 'I *said*, where's the road map?'

'The road map? I don't know. I didn't have it,' she said flustered.

'I gave it to you.'

'No, I brought the bags out to the car, like you told me to. I didn't have the map,' she insisted.

'For God's sake, Gabby, can't you just take care of one simple bloody task? I gave you the map. Jesus.' He turned back to Giles, who was driving. 'Unbelievable. She'd lose her fucking mind if it wasn't for me.'

In the back seat, Gabby flushed. She hated scenes like this, especially in front of Giles. Besides, it wasn't even remotely true. Half the time *he* was the one who'd be lost if she didn't organise things. She tried to regain her composure, but she was upset. It had started out reasonably well. Giles wasn't one of the worst friends. In fact, he was OK. He was quieter than the rest of the group, someone who seemed content to watch and listen rather than join in. It was calming to be around him sometimes. She'd been relieved to hear they'd be travelling up with him. She'd been thinking about how much she would rather be with Jennie and Marwan but, an hour or so into the trip, she'd started to relax. Giles had asked a couple of questions about her job, about the things she did, which was somewhat unusual for one of Dominic's friends. She'd answered his questions then, worried that she was taking up too much of his attention, she had relaxed into the back seat and dropped off. Now the fragile peace was ruined. Over a bloody map. Couldn't they just pull off the motorway and buy another?

They were staying in Gilmore Place, in a lovely large flat that belonged to the friend of a friend of someone else. The occupants had opted for Marbella at New Year and the six had the place to themselves: Gabby and Dominic, and four other men, his friends, Giles, Jude, Magnus and Tim – all insurance brokers. There were three bedrooms: Gabby and Dominic had one, Jude and Magnus shared the second double room, Tim was in the single and Giles in the living room. They had brought vast quantities of beer and they spent the first evening glued to the television, drinking steadily. Gabby was bored. She went to bed.

She woke up on New Year's Eve, wishing desperately that she was somewhere else. Dominic wasn't there. She didn't remember him coming to bed. Perhaps they'd gone out. She stumbled out of bed and slid her feet into the woollen slippers she liked so much, which Dominic pulled a face at every time he stayed over. It was cold in the flat. She pulled back the curtains. It was a typically overcast winter's day. She shivered and looked around for her dressing-gown, put it on and padded outside. The doors to all the rooms were wide open. She wandered into the sitting room. There were beer cans lying over the floor and the remains of the Chinese takeaway she remembered them ordering just before she went to bed. They'd stayed up watching some silly video – wrestling or something equally daft. She bent down automatically and began picking up the cans. She had almost finished setting the room to rights when there was a loud rap at the front door. She looked at her watch. It was only nine o'clock.

'Hello?' she asked, trying to squint through the spy-hole. Dominic and the others had keys, she knew.

'Gabby, hi – it's me, Giles. Forgot the key, sorry.'

'Oh, hi,' Gabby said, and opened the door. 'Where's everyone else?' she asked. He looked rather the worse for wear.

'They're still at Jill's. They're having breakfast.'

'Jill?' Gabby was alarmed. Who was Jill?

'She's Magnus's friend from university. She's got a flat up in Tayview.'

'Oh.'

'Yeah, don't worry,' he said quickly. 'She's just a mate. They'll be back after lunch. Dom said to tell you.' He looked at the floor.

She knew he was lying.

He struggled to unwrap his scarf. His blond hair was

sticking up on end and his face was already covered in stubble.

'Right. OK. Well, I was just making some tea. D'you want some?' Gabby was brisk. She didn't want his pity.

'Yeah, that would be great. I'm going to take a shower. D'you have any aspirins, Gabby?'

She liked the way he was always so polite to her. It made a change from being yelled at by Dominic. 'In my bag. Hang on, I'll get you some.'

'You've always got everything, haven't you?' he said, following her into the room. 'Doesn't matter what it is, you've got the answer for it. You're the most organised person I know. Thanks.' He held out his hand and Gabby shook a couple of pills into his palm. 'Except the map,' he added, and grinned.

'Yeah.' She smiled ruefully. 'Still, we got here, didn't we?' She turned to slip the pill bottle back into her weekend bag. And that was when it happened.

She heard him move and then, suddenly, his arms slid round her from behind. She froze. He held her tightly, his face nuzzling against her neck. He turned her slowly so that they faced each other. She couldn't see his expression. It was still quite dark in the bedroom. He slid her dressing-gown off her shoulders and slipped his hands under her pyjama top. He was breathing fast, unevenly.

Gabby was petrified. As if in a dream, she watched herself slip her hands under his sweater, feeling the roughness of hair under her fingers. He pulled her down onto the bed, drew back the covers and they climbed under the duvet. Suddenly, they were both naked.

Gabby closed her eyes. Dominic was the only man she'd ever been with. It wasn't possible that another could want her. She'd hung on to Dominic because, deep down, she thought he was all she would ever have. And being with him was better than being alone.

Giles's hand was on her belly, then lower, between her legs. And then he was on top of her, blotting out the pale morning light as his lips found hers and he drew her tongue into his mouth. She felt herself arching up towards him. Everything was happening so fast – she felt the muscles in his stomach tremble as she slid her hand down to help him, and then he was inside her, moving against her, his hands covering her face. She felt an incredible rush of something inside her and then they exploded, violently, together. She caught her breath, tears coming to her eyes with the sheer force of her climax. There was silence. She could hear him breathing fast beside her.

'Gabby.' His voice was hoarse. 'I'm sorry – I don't know what – I shouldn't have—'

'No. It's OK, Giles. Honestly.' Gabby looked at him under her lashes. He was nice. That was all she could say. She was calm. She turned to him. 'Thank you.'

'What for?' He sounded surprised.

'For this. For everything.' She lay still for a few minutes. Just as he was dropping off to sleep, she got up. He mumbled something. 'Go to sleep,' she murmured softly. 'I won't be here when you get up, Giles, but thank you.'

'You're welcome,' he muttered.

A couple of hours later as the train pulled out of Waverley Station, Gabby leaned back in her seat and closed her eyes. She'd packed her things, left a note for Dominic and called Rianne. It was too late to get to Paris in time for the New Year celebrations but she'd made a reservation for a flight the following morning. She didn't know where Marwan, Jennie and the others were staying but suddenly it didn't matter. What mattered was that it was over, her and Dominic. Her brief encounter with Giles had been a moment of madness, but enough to break the spell. She looked out at the landscape she'd stared at through a veil of tears the previous day. She felt like crying now – but this time with relief.

She spent a week in Paris with Rianne and got back to

dozens of messages on the answering-machine from Dominic. She erased every one. Funny, she thought, as she scrawled 'return to sender' across yet another letter, she'd always thought she was the desperate one. She returned to work the following week, a new woman.

Jennie was delighted. 'None of us could work it out,' she said at lunch-time, munching a celery stick.

'I couldn't either. It was like . . . being in a kind of trance. I don't know what happened. I just snapped out of it.'

Jennie said nothing. It was obvious what had happened. Sweet Gabby. It was one of the strangest things about her. There were few other people who were as sharp as she was. Sitting there, at her desk, the corner of her mouth tucked in concentration, chewing the end of her pencil, she was the one everyone turned to for the last word. Nothing escaped her, not a single detail. She remembered names, dates, places . . . if someone had been arrested, where and when. She handled the highest-level cases, was trusted with the most sensitive information . . . and then she went home to Dominic.

'I bet he's all over you now,' Jennie said, reaching for more celery.

'Yeah. But it's too late for that. I never want to hear from him again. Ever.'

'Good on you. Now, where's that report on Ras-el-Ein?'

'On my desk. I have made the right decision, haven't I?' she asked.

Jennie nodded decisively. 'Absolutely.'

She hadn't seen Giles again, but she didn't need to. She threw herself into her work, amazed at how good it felt to be free of Dominic, free of the pressure of thinking about him twenty-four hours a day, seven days a week. She felt as though an enormous weight had been lifted off her shoulders. It was almost too good to be true. She went to work every day marvelling at how lucky she was and how alive she felt. And then, just as things were settling down into a steady, if intense, routine, an offer had landed on her desk out of the blue. She'd been recommended for a post at the United Nations Transition Assistance Group. They were looking for a lawyer with a background in human rights and emergency-relief development. One of the international observers she'd met on her last trip to Gaza had mentioned her name. She did nothing for a couple of weeks, said little about it. Jennie and Marwan were encouraging, even a little envious, but it was to Peter Bensimon that she eventually went, worried about his reaction.

'Of course you must take it,' he said to her gently. 'It's a wonderful opportunity. We'll miss you like hell, of course, but you should go. We work closely with the UN in any case, you know that. It's not like our paths won't cross again soon.' Gabby was overcome with emotion. It felt like leaving a family.

She took a week's holiday at the end of May and went to Porto with Nathalie and Charmaine. Rianne couldn't join them – she had to be somewhere else – Gabby couldn't remember where. They promised to meet up in New York as soon as Gabby had settled in.

Rianne had told them she was trying to buy a flat in London. She'd cut back on her bookings, only working when she felt like it. It was driving Ross Carter insane but there was precious little she could do about it. Somehow, Rianne always got what she wanted. Even if she was no longer the top girl at Face!, there was something about who and what she was that kept her in the public eye. She'd made the transition from supermodel to celebrity almost unnoticed.

A bar of late-morning sunlight fell across Gabby's face. She opened her eyes. She must have drifted off. She swung her legs off the divan and heaved the pile of papers towards her. She was UNTAG's assistant regional representative in southern Africa, covering Namibia, Botswana, Angola and South Africa. It was an enormous job, with responsibilities greater than any she'd ever had before. With a staff of 8,000, including 4,500 military personnel, 1,500 police and 2,000 civilians, the work – in so far as Gabby had been able to judge – was intense, stimulating and exhausting.

Her brief was to help the special representative in the area to ensure that all hostile acts in Namibia and adjoining Angola had ended; that the occupying South African troops were returned to base and ultimately withdrawn from Namibian territory; that refugees were permitted to return, that South African apartheid-based laws were repealed, and law and order impartially maintained. The road to independence had been rocky, and although things appeared to be heading in the right direction, it had not always been the case.

From her research and the briefings she'd had over the past few weeks, Gabby had gleaned a history of the country. She knew the Germans had been the first Europeans to move in, although their claim to the territory was quickly challenged by the British, and that the South Africans had taken possession of the territory in the aftermath of the First World War.

The name de Zoete cropped up again and again. The family had played an important role in the occupation of the territory, buying the enormous Oranjemund – Orange Mouth – diamond mine in the early 1940s and using it as a market-balancing mine, varying its output to control world diamond prices. Was there nowhere they hadn't been? Gabby wondered.

She was now preparing for her first trip to Windhoek in a couple of weeks' time. UNTAG was seeking to open operations the following month and she'd been given the special project of co-ordinating the various organisations that were springing up to help Namibians cope with the transition from freedom-fighters to government-in-waiting. It was an important task. Namibia was the dress-rehearsal for what was going to happen in South Africa. Everyone knew it. It was only a matter of time.

She worked her way through the reports until midnight when she could no longer keep her eyes open. Then she looked at the ashtray on the floor in alarm. She'd smoked almost an entire packet – within days of arriving in New York, she'd broken her resolution to stop smoking. She emptied the ashtray into the bin. Exhausted, but completely satisfied she'd done a thorough job, she crawled into bed.

52

He woke at the first ring. It was the red telephone beside his desk – only Justin had the number. He grabbed the receiver. Two minutes later he replaced it, his hand shaking. He was to meet Justin at the end of the Santa Monica pier in an hour's time. He couldn't fucking believe it. He jumped out of bed and ran towards the shower. After two years' silence, he finally had a new command.

It was chilly, even in LA. Bruce pulled his flimsy windcheater tight and scanned the faces coming towards him. Justin was over an hour late. He reached into his pocket for a packet of Luckys, but as he bent his head to light the cigarette, he saw the thin, unmistakable figure coming towards him. He turned to face the sea, remembering what he had been told about meeting in public. True to form, Justin walked up to the railings and asked him for a light.

'Café across the street – Borzo's. Meet me in the men's in half an hour.' He nodded thanks for the light and disappeared.

Bruce was washing his hands when Justin came into the men's room. He scanned the room and slid a set of car keys towards him.

'There's a white sedan parked outside on a meter,' he said. 'The directions are in the glove compartment. Meet us there as soon as you can.' Bruce took the key. This was more complicated than any set of arrangements he'd followed before – something must be afoot. He dried his hands and walked out, looking for the car.

An hour later, somewhere in the hills above Encino, he found the house. He parked a couple of streets away, as he'd been told, and walked up the driveway. The door opened before he reached it. A young black man looked at him for a second, without smiling, then stood aside to let him pass.

'Eastman.' Justin was standing by the window. 'Come in. Shut that door behind you.' Bruce looked around warily. There were several young black men in the room, who looked at him with little interest. One said something in a language he didn't recognise.

'We've got a small job for you, Eastman,' Justin began. 'It's not complicated. I need you to be in Paris this weekend. Call this number – it's a London number. You'll get instructions from them. After that, things may go quiet for a while but you'll hear from us. Got it?'

Bruce took the scrap of paper from Justin and nodded. A couple of the men in the room were talking quietly in their language to one another. He nodded again. 'Got it.' He looked at the number, folded the scrap carefully and held out his hand. 'I'll be in touch,' he said confidently. Justin ignored his hand, nodded quickly and stood up.

'OK. We'll be waiting to hear from you. You'll have to find your own way back to Santa Monica.' Bruce followed Justin to the door, wondering what the hell the whole thing was about. The other men didn't glance up as he left.

How was he supposed to get to Santa Monica? he wondered, as he began the long walk down the hill. He'd never been anywhere by public transport in LA. Did buses even come to Encino? To his surprise, he found a bus stop almost at the next corner. As he got onto the crowded bus, it occurred to him that the rich homes of the San Fernando Valley were exactly like those of Sandton, Johannesburg – and the same maids and gardeners who rode the combi buses to work there rode the CTA network in LA. His was the only white face in a sea of Hispanic and black workers. Sometimes, he thought wryly, you had to travel to see what was under your nose.

'Nothing.' Simon Kalen looked at Lisette, defeated. 'Still can't get a thing out of them. No information, no access, no records – nothing.' Lisette reached across her mahogany desk for another cigarette. 'All we know is that the withdrawals have been regular. Once every six months, like clockwork, almost as soon as Marius went missing.'

'What do *you* think?' She tapped the ash nervously.

'Lisette, there's only one thing to think. He must have set this up before he died. I don't know what it means. The last withdrawal was made in January of this year. That's a total of almost three billion rand. I just don't understand it. Why? What for?'

Lisette looked at her hands. She was worried. She had always had doubts about Marius's death. She'd said nothing to anyone, but over the years a number of odd little things had happened. Like the time she'd come home to Vergelegen, six weeks after he'd gone, to find something missing from the wing he'd shared with Céline and Rianne: a heavy, tortoiseshell antique hairbrush that had sat on Céline's dressing-table. She remembered seeing it after he'd gone, when she was wondering whether to pack up the master bedroom or to leave everything as Marius had left it, hoping he would somehow, miraculously, turn up. And about three years later, she'd noticed that the silver-framed picture of Céline and Rianne that had stood on his desk in his carefully maintained empty office was missing. Small things, personal things . . . things that would have no value to anyone except Marius. She'd put it down to the servants as she always did when confronted with domestic issues she couldn't explain, and left it at that. But the doubts remained, niggling, persistent. And now they returned. Three billion rand was a lot of money, far more than

Marius could spend on his own. She knew her brother – he was not a lavish man. No, this was for something else.

A fragment of a conversation she'd had at a dinner almost six months previously popped into her mind. She'd been seated next to Piet Odendaal, the chairman of the Johannesburg Chamber of Mines, and they had been discussing the strikes. What was it he'd said? Something about money . . . about *funds*. 'Where were they getting the funds?' he'd said. Not only to support the miners during the strike, but to train them. Men were being smuggled abroad – to Moscow, Libya, Algeria – for political training, then slipping back into the country to spread their propaganda. Lisette believed she knew.

'Simon, I need to trust you,' Lisette said suddenly. She clenched her fists.

'You know you can.'

'What I'm about to say,' she said slowly, 'mustn't be repeated. Ever.' Lisette looked at him. 'It *was* Marius. I think he's been making the withdrawals ever since he disappeared.' She blew a cloud of smoke towards him.

'What do you mean? You think he's—'

'Yes.' She let out a deep sigh. 'Yes, I do. Don't ask me why, but I do.'

'But . . . where is he? Why the disappearance? What's going on, Lisette?' Simon had blanched.

'How much is left in the account?'

'Impossible to say. It's linked to so many of our other holdings. When our shares do well, funds are automatically diverted. Marius set it up that way. At the time I'd no idea why, but he was insistent. It's the only account that no one else has access to.'

'There's no way of stopping the withdrawals?'

'No. Not unless we – you – go bankrupt, and *that* won't happen. And that's the odd thing. Three billion rand is a hell of a lot of money, but it could have been much, much worse. No one's noticed it for years. I suppose it shows how well we're doing,' Simon gave a wry smile, 'but it doesn't make a lot of sense.'

'Oh, I think it does,' Lisette murmured, eyes narrowed.

'What do you mean?'

'*Ag*, nothing. I need time to think about this, Simon.' Lisette got up from behind her desk. 'I'll call you over the weekend.' She stood up. Their meeting was over. He touched her shoulder briefly, indicating his support, and left the room.

Lisette walked over to the windows. Something was happening, she could feel it. She knew from her government contacts that things were falling apart, that the old order was about to crumble. The mood in the country had changed yet again but this time it was more sinister, more aggressive. Some of her servants had left suddenly, after years of employ. People were afraid to go out at night: whole areas of Johannesburg were off-limits after dark. White areas. White suburbs. Suburbs that used to be safe. And in the countryside there were deaths, break-ins, even *rapes*. The country seemed to be on the brink of an abyss, shaking alternately with fear and rage.

And it wasn't only *in* the country. She'd had the most disturbing piece of news a month or so ago: Rianne had been seen somewhere, she couldn't remember where, in the company of a young black man. The friend who'd passed on the gossip had heard it from someone else. They'd been spotted coming out of a hotel together, and although they'd immediately gone separate ways, the friend recounted, it had been obvious that they'd been *together*. Once they left the country, she'd confided to Lisette, it was so difficult. All the good breeding and upbringing, gone to waste. Lisette had resisted the urge to slap the woman. How dare she? Rianne had always been a troublesome child, so headstrong and wilful. Could it be that she'd inherited her father's madness? She put the thought firmly out of her head. Probably a fellow model, she reasoned. Although they certainly weren't used *here*, she'd seen plenty of black male models in European and American magazines. Some were handsome, she was forced to admit. An image of a young black man, staring haughtily from a magazine cover appeared before her eyes. She frowned. Modise – it had been his son, an engineer or an architect. He'd been on the cover of *Time*, or was it *Newsweek*? Stunning-looking. She shook her head. What on earth was she thinking about? She glanced at her watch. She'd been standing there for over an hour and she was flying to Johannesburg that evening. She dreaded it. That city, much more so than Cape Town, was *consumed* by the madness. Dirty, unpredictable, hostile and dangerous. She picked up the phone.

Three things were happening in Charmaine's life. She was losing weight, making money and making friends, sort of in that order. She was loving it. It was nine months since Emily had introduced her to James. Twice, sometimes three times a week, she and Emily would spend an evening – never a night – at the house in North Row, Mayfair. Her earnings were never less than two thousand a week. She was living in Wilton Crescent, rent-free. She went to the gym, shopped or lay sprawled in front of the TV.

In nine months she'd never met a bad guy, had never been asked to do anything she didn't want to. Most of the time she rather enjoyed it. There was something about watching those slightly pathetic, poor-little-rich men suddenly able to act on their secret fantasies – men who could only dream about screwing girls like Charmaine and Emily and who had to pay through the nose for it – that Charmaine enjoyed. She revelled in the sense of power and strength that came from watching them drool over her, their weakness exposed as she peeled off her clothes for them. At first she'd thought them just like the Flamingo men – desperate, sad creatures. Now she realised they were not. Flamingo men had nothing: no money, no power, no class. These men had everything – wives, families, power, wealth, you name it. And they wanted *her*.

Charmaine looked through the racks of bras with

interest. She was in U/d 3 and she was impressed. She couldn't imagine Nathalie designing or wearing most of the stuff on display – too damn *risqué* for prim Nathalie – but *she* loved it. She chose a delicate black lace bra with tiny red roses and matching panties. There was a simple black silk teddy that went with the combination and she picked that up as well. A pair of high-heeled mules with a single velvet red rose . . . and, *voilà*, her 'outfit' was complete. In the corner there was a cream bustier with matching thong and garter – and then she saw a schoolgirl-style bra and knickers set to team with a short grey skirt and white shirt. She knew exactly who would enjoy *that*.

Ten minutes later, her purchases were in pink and white striped bags, individually wrapped in light tissue paper with scented 'sprinkles' thrown in. She popped into Debenhams to pick up some skin cream and body lotion, added a few bottles of fragrance to her enormous collection and took a cab home. She was meeting someone new this evening. Someone special, James had said, just flown into London.

She outlined her mouth with the new Chanel lipstick and stood back to admire the result. She looked great. Dark eye make-up, a full, plum-red mouth, her skin lightly dusted with silver powder. The only thing bothering her was her nose. It had been running for several days now and there was a faint but discernible redness around the nostrils. She thought she might be getting a cold but hadn't developed any further symptoms. It hurt when she sniffed. She added a dash of concealer to hide the redness and resolved to cut down on her consumption of cocaine. Perhaps it was all the snorting that was leading to problems. But first, just a teeny line to prepare her for the evening ahead. She was about to meet Mr Special, as James had been referring to him all week – she needed to look and feel the part.

'Charmaine,' he said quietly, looking at her appraisingly. Charmaine stared at him. She'd seen him before, some-where, she was sure. He smiled smoothly. 'Charmed, I'm sure. Now, tell me that's not your real name.'

Charmaine's mind was racing. He *was* rather special. He was good-looking, to begin with, which, in her line of business, was unusual. Tall, over six feet, and well built. He was probably in his late forties and carried an air of unmistakable wealth, power and confidence. He was dressed conservatively, but stylishly. She noticed the label on his jacket as he handed it to the butler. Adolfo Dominguez – she'd seen the shop on Regent Street. And she'd heard his voice before. But *where*?

She knew not to ask too many questions, especially in the beginning. She'd learned from Emily that the best deal, the safest and easiest, was to find a 'regular', a guy you saw once or twice a week, every week, who knew what he liked and, more importantly, knew that *you* knew it. And you had to work at finding him – he had to want you enough to keep asking for you. If Mr Special was to be that man, Charmaine thought, as he held out his hand, she was in luck. So she lowered her eyes and took his hand.

'You can call me what you want. *Anything* you want.' She noted the flicker of recognition in his eyes. He understood what she meant. He stood back as James opened the door to the drawing room for them. Charmaine walked ahead: her fuchsia silk dress was slit from the shoulder almost to her buttocks and, she knew, showed off her tanned back to perfection. For the first time since she'd started 'working', she felt a stab of excitement.

53

Nathalie was sleeping badly, and it showed. In the past few weeks, she'd almost gone round the bend. It was six months since she'd met Sacha again – six months of hell, and their affair, if it could be termed such, was taking its toll on her. She'd all but stopped functioning, except when he was around. Luckily for her, she had a team of capable assistants and designers and, for the time being at least, U/d ran itself. She attended meetings, checked merchandise, approved advertising, went over designs, but her mind was elsewhere. She waited by the phone day and night, carried a bleeper to which only Sacha knew the number, and made herself available no matter when he called or why.

He *seemed* to need her. He called or came to her flat at odd hours – in the middle of the day, late at night, sometimes early in the morning. She supposed these were the hours when he could get away. He never spoke about Siena. Nathalie would lie in bed at night, willing the phone to ring or the door to open, chain-smoking and watching television listlessly until the early hours of the morning.

Sometimes she would fall asleep on the couch, a half-empty wine glass beside her. Then, without warning, the front door would open, and she would wake up just in time to see him remove his jacket or his shirt. He would slide into bed or come to where she was lying on the couch, make love to her quietly and intensely, without words. Then he would leave. It was sex, no more than that.

It was just past midnight. Nathalie drained her wine. She didn't think he would show up now. It had been over a week since his last visit and she'd heard nothing from him. It was the longest he'd been gone in the past few months, and she was worried.

In contrast to her inner turmoil, her flat and her immediate surroundings were immaculate. Thanks to Gloria, who came twice a week, everything was dusted, polished, gleaming. Suddenly tears were flowing, thick and fast. She crouched on the white sheepskin rug and sobbed uncontrollably. These were supposed to be the best times of her life. She was in control of a successful business, her designs and boutiques were expanding to critical and commercial acclaim; she was healthy, attractive . . . and miserable. She was afraid to leave the house or the office for fear of missing Sacha, missing his call or a late-night visit. She hardly ate, hardly slept. She thought about him constantly, trying to analyse his behaviour, his attitude, his intentions. They hardly spoke to one another but in her head Nathalie made up conversations between them. She couldn't remember a time when she didn't think about him or wonder what he was doing.

She drove herself crazy imagining what he was doing at different times of the day, where he was, who he might be talking to . . . and what he did in his 'other' life, with his 'other' wife. She had even taken to calling him at the office and hanging up as soon as she heard his voice on the line. She didn't have his home number or nothing would have stopped her calling him there, too.

There were days when she thought she would explode. This can't be love, she thought. It's not supposed to be like this. She would dream about walking away – of not answering her phone or changing her locks. She would fantasise about taking control of her life again, about going out without agonising as soon as she turned the corner that she might have *just* missed him. But somehow, each and every time she would catch sight of his strong, capable hands, his dark, shining eyes, she melted. His voice, with its faint unplaceable accent, the way the muscles in his forearm rippled as he opened a bottle of wine or reached over to hit her alarm clock – these tiny fragments of his overwhelmingly physical presence undid her resolve. She was hooked.

She was still curled up on the rug, sobbing, when she heard the front door open. She got up quickly and wiped her eyes. He was here.

'Hi,' he said, as he opened the door. 'Were you . . . asleep?'

'No, just . . . reading,' she lied.

'Nathalie . . .' he began hesitantly. Her heart started to pound. He seemed unusually nervous. Nathalie looked at him, alarmed. What was he going to say?

'This . . . *thing* . . .' he began again. Nathalie closed her eyes: she had seen it coming. 'Nat, it's been going on for a while . . . and I can't do it any more.' Tears were streaming down her face again. She made no effort to stop them. 'We can't go on. I'm sorry to have to tell you like this, but . . . something's happened. Siena's pregnant. I need to stop.'

There was silence in the room as they faced each other. Nathalie tried to speak but couldn't find the words. Slowly, she turned away from him, her arms wrapped tightly across her stomach. She walked over to one of the sofas and sank into it. Sacha was standing in the doorway. 'Well,' she whispered slowly, 'that makes two of us.'

Her last period had been over two months ago. She had put it down to stress, then anxiety. Now she knew why. She didn't need to confirm it. Sacha's eyes widened briefly, then dimmed. She knew he would walk away. She hadn't planned on telling him, let alone like this, but it had slipped out.

'What are you going to do?' he asked, his voice expressionless.

'I don't know.' Nathalie stared at the carpet. The silence in the room was thundering.

Then, as quickly and quietly as he had entered the room, Sacha put the keys on the side table and left. Nathalie sat immobile, pain, hurt and fear flitting alternately across her face. An hour passed, and another. Finally, just before dawn, she made some decisions. She would have the baby. She would not see Sacha again and he would never see the child. But it would be hers. She had something that no one, not even her mother, had managed to keep – *her* little part of Sacha. If she couldn't have him the way she wanted, the way she'd hoped to, then she would have him by this means.

54

In a small log cabin buried deep in the midwinter snow, close to the tiny village of Ringebu in central Norway, Marius Tertius de Zoete opened his eyes and focused, as he had done every morning for the past eleven years, on the silver-framed picture of his beloved wife and daughter. He stared for a moment at the image of Céline, twenty-nine years old for ever, standing in the gardens at Vergelegen, with the laughing six-year-old Rianne in her arms. His eyes dimmed and the room lurched.

He blinked. This was no time to start getting sentimental. It was a time to focus. The next few months would be the most important of his life, the reason why everything had been sacrificed. He got out of bed, his mind racing ahead to the day's meeting. He looked outside the window as he walked to the small kitchen to make his coffee. Everything was still, silent, white. The nearest cottage was almost half a mile away, hidden by the snow-covered birches and half buried by the short blue shadows that the wintry sun threw over the landscape.

Cup in hand, he looked out of the dining-room window. It had begun to snow lightly. It was so different from where he had grown up, amid the earth-coloured and ochre hills of the eastern Transvaal. It was different, too, from the sunny open skies of the Western Cape where he'd taken Céline, and where he'd imagined spending the rest of his life. And different, too, from the life that had been planned for him. By the time Marius, the first-born son and heir, was eighteen, de Zoete Inc. was one of the most powerful players in the global precious-metals market and one of the largest privately owned companies in the world. At his father's funeral, government ministers, French aristocrats and the heads of rival mining conglomerates had sat together, drinking South Africa's finest wines and quietly marvelling at the distance – in geographical and cultural terms – that the ambitious young man from a tiny *shtetl* in the Ukraine had come. And how well his first son, Marius, had turned out, a credit to his mother and father.

But appearances could be deceptive. The signs were there, had anyone cared to read them. Somewhere along the way to making yet more money, becoming yet more powerful, more profitable, Marius had changed. Perhaps it was the years spent in England. Perhaps it was his wife, the foreigner, with her foreigner's perceptions and mistrust of their South African 'way of life'. Who knows how these things unfold. Whatever it was, something in him changed. For the first time, just before Anton finally handed over formal control of the companies to his son, Marius began to ask questions, potentially dangerous questions about their operations, about the way the black workers were treated, about the conditions in their country that made such treatment not only possible but preferable. He wondered at the competitive advantage South Africa held over other gold- and diamond-producing countries, the system of labour – *slave* labour – that kept production costs down and profits high. Céline knew about his confusion and it was to her that he had turned. But she could not provide him with answers that made sense to him, or the means to act on his questions.

In secret, then, far removed from the world of board-room meetings and corporate dinners, he began to seek out others who shared his concerns. Although there were precious few among the privileged white class – Afrikaners and Englishmen – who reacted as Marius had, there were educated, politically savvy young Africans who were prepared to risk everything by slowly and gently leading the few whites like Marius towards a more concrete expression of their doubts. Marius's political education began long after his formal one had ended. This time, unlike his triumphant period in England, he was not in charge. But his passion and his hunger for understanding surprised both him and his would-be educators. The organisation behind the young African men whom he met in townships and rural community halls knew they were on to something special in Marius de Zoete. It was not only his position within the country, his business and political contacts, it was something more. As Livingstone Modise's right-hand man, Moses Chikwe, had remarked, sometimes revolutionaries are born, not made. The future they planned – Marius included – was indeed nothing short of revolution.

And then, out of the blue, things had changed again. Céline, his beautiful, precious Céline, drowned in the family pool on a sunny Wednesday afternoon like any other. There was no explanation for it, no answer that the doctors or the coroner's office could provide. He had come home from a meeting, ostensibly in Johannesburg but in reality some thirty miles to the south of the city, in the desperate township of Katlehong. He saw the ambulances and police cars as soon as he turned into the long driveway that led to the secluded family home. He ordered Solomon, the driver, to stop the car and ran towards the front door, pushing past police and paramedics. He could hear Poppie crying, deep, heaving sobs, and saw her pressing Rianne's face into her apron, shielding the child's eyes from the body on the drawing-room floor, wrapped in the standard-issue black bag that Marius had seen countless times in the townships and on the mines – but never in the affluent white suburbs and never in his own home. It was his wife now lying inside it.

In the end, his wealth, the power and the privilege it afforded him, had counted for nothing, absolutely nothing. Céline was dead; he could not protect her. That afternoon, that ordinary, warm, April afternoon, everything changed. It was all over, finished, *klaar*. Afterwards, Marius couldn't go back to that life, the meetings, the deals, the dinners and new business ventures. Nothing and no one, not even Rianne, his darling little girl, could bring him back or coax him out of the murderous rage that descended upon him after he had buried his wife and faced her accusing parents.

Marie-Hélène and Claude de Ribain blamed him, he knew. What they didn't know was that he already blamed himself. He should have been with her, there in the pool, not thirty miles away, playing at being a revolutionary while she struggled for breath in the water. Well, if there was one thing he would do no longer, it was play. He chose to disappear.

He walked out on all of it. Rianne, he knew, would be safe with his sister, Lisette. She would love and care for the child as her own. Rianne would be better off with Lisette and her family. He no longer had a family. He was about to betray them all, betray everything they had worked for and everything they stood for. Better to let the child escape now, while she had no choice. Let her think him dead. After all, like all revolutionaries and terrorists, in one sense he already was.

He took a sip of coffee, scalding his tongue. He was in a reflective mood. He glanced again at the picture of his family. Maybe, just *maybe*, if the negotiations could be pulled through, it would not have been for nothing. He breathed deeply and fished around for his spectacles. There was much work to be done.

55

Riitho walked out of the aircraft at Kotoka International Airport, Accra, and breathed deeply. The damp, humid air enveloped him totally. It was like walking into a soft, damp cocoon. Ghana. Africa. He smiled. It was good to be back. Next to him, Lebohang whistled, uncharacteristically cheerful. He, too, was glad to be back on African soil. Although he never complained, he had been away from home for over twenty years, the vast majority of those spent shadowing Riitho – following him, never participating. Riitho knew that there was a wife and children somewhere in Soweto, but apart from the two occasions when Lebohang had been smuggled in 'underground', he hadn't seen them for most of their lives. Yet he never complained. His loyalty to Riitho's father, and to the cause, was unswerving. He knew everything – or almost everything – there was to know about Riitho. He had watched his young charge grow to manhood, had watched from a discreet distance the friends and relationships along the way. Even this last one – the longest one – and the most dangerous. He now knew who she was. At first, he and Khotso assumed she was just another one of the beautiful young white girls who seemed to fall for Riitho with alarming regularity. No one special. Neither man was the type to read women's magazines. But one day Lebohang had overheard her talking and had detected the unmistakable trace of South Africa in her voice. He had done a little searching. He didn't have to search very hard. He saw her face one morning on the cover of *Paris Match*. He was appalled. Rianne de Zoete? Lisette de Zoete-Koestler's *niece*? He was agitated. For the first time, he was unsure what to do. Riitho showed no signs of tiring of this girl, as he usually did. If anything, as the months went by, it appeared stronger, deeper. So Lebohang just watched carefully and waited. It was his job to protect Riitho, not betray him.

'*Nkosi sikelele iAfrika.* Good to be home, eh?' he said to Riitho, as they walked down the rickety steps together. Riitho nodded. They crossed the tarmac to the arrivals hall. The night air was dense with the sound of crickets, people cheering to incoming relatives and friends from the balcony above, and the whirring of the aircraft engines as the BA flight prepared to head back to Europe almost immediately. He breathed in again, deeply. It was the closest air to freedom.

Two days later Rianne's first impression, as she walked out of the aircraft and onto the steps, was that she'd walked into a sauna. She gasped as the evening air hit her, hot, thick and wet, and by the time she'd got half-way down, she was dripping with sweat. She tried not to stare at her fellow passengers. She had never been so close to so many Africans before. She followed the half-bare back of a woman who descended the stairs gingerly in front of her. She was dark, the same smooth darkness of Riitho's skin. The indent of her spine, framed by two perfectly rounded shoulder blades followed the cut of her brilliantly coloured dress, ending just below the small of the back and disappearing into the tightly wrapped skirt. A head-dress made of the same material was swathed around her head – beneath it, two enormous gold hoops flashed under the headlamps of the waiting bus.

Rianne was conscious of the other passengers staring at her, a single white girl among the families and businessmen getting onto the bus. So this was what it felt like. She had never been aware of her own colour before. Never. To be white in Europe or America was to be invisible, colourless. Even in South Africa there was a public deference accorded her at all times . . . blacks moved out of her way to let her pass. Here, it was the opposite. People shoved and pushed, cut in front of her, trod on her foot. To be white here was to be marked, singled out. She felt it in their glances, even in their smiles. The immigration official, a young soldier, looked at her French passport curiously.

'De Zoete. How do you say that?' he asked, unsmiling. Place of birth: Paris, France.

'Yes, just like that,' she said, smiling. 'That's correct.' The West African accent was different from the English the blacks at home spoke. Less formal, without the hardened Afrikaans inflection. She liked it.

'And the purpose of your visit?' She smiled again. She liked the way he said it. Per-poss.

'Holiday.'

'Have a nice time. *Akwaaba*. Welcome to Ghana.' He handed her passport over. She walked through the crowded arrivals hall, avoiding the jostling, shouting mass of people as they waited for their luggage to arrive off the ancient conveyor belt. She left the air-conditioned comfort of the terminal building and, again, was swallowed up by the hot, damp night. She looked down at the piece of paper in her hand. The Golden Tulip Hotel. Room 124.

'Taxi, madam, taxi?' She was immediately surrounded by what seemed like a hundred men, jostling for her attention.

A soldier stood by, holding a long cane. He watched the men with narrowed eyes. If any came too close, he shouted something in their language and swished the cane around. It was a crude, but effective system. She was led away by one young man, amid jeers and envious laughter from his colleagues. A white tourist. That meant a good fare and a generous tip. He led her to the most beaten-up taxi she had ever seen. It had originally been . . . a Fiat? It now sported a Mercedes star on the bonnet and BMW wheels. There was even an old Peugeot marque on the boot. She smiled, despite the heat, and settled into the back. The seats were covered with plastic and her shirt stuck to it.

'Now, now, madam. We go reach now now.' She looked at him, confused. What was he saying? She looked at the dashboard. There was a sign painted onto it. *In God's Time*. He started the engine with a roar and they trundled out of the parking area. God's time indeed. The little car could barely do 30 m.p.h. Luckily, the hotel was only a ten-minute drive away. The driver was overcome with the five-dollar tip. It was more than he would make all week.

She grabbed her carry-on bag from the boot and practically ran into the hotel reception area. A minute later, she had the key to room 124 and she hurried past the swimming pool, lit up eerily at night. She found the room easily. She rapped once, hard, just as he'd instructed her. The door opened at once. He was there. He pulled her into the room and kicked the door shut.

In the hired Jeep, driving towards Cape Coast, Rianne lolled against Riitho as he drove. They had been together almost a week – the longest they'd ever spent together – and she couldn't get enough of him. It was desperately hot. Every so often he turned his eyes from his fierce contemplation of the landscape and looked at her, his expression unreadable.

As they approached Elmina, a fine salty mist enveloped the castle, thrown up by the pounding waves against the rocks at the base of the fortress. She swallowed. From the guidebook she had read that the castle, the point of departure for slaves leaving for the Americas, had been built by the Portuguese, won and lost by the British, the Danes, the French and, finally, after independence, was maintained by the Ghanaian government. She found it hard to believe that the horrors of the slave trade could have taken place in such a setting – clear blue sea, sandy beaches, coconut and palm trees. Every so often a cool sea breeze wafted in from the ocean, providing a moment's respite from the unrelenting heat.

They left the car in the hotel car park and continued to the castle on foot. It was a weekday and there were few tourists around. The town was sprawled around the castle walls. It was crowded with fishermen and their boats, market women, in strikingly patterned cloth, walked amongst the boats, children and goats balancing their wares on enormous platters on their heads. She watched them, awed.

The women were different from the African women Rianne had grown up with – not a Poppie to be seen among them. Loud, brash, confident, there was none of the automatic deference accorded a white – a *madam* – at home. No one moved to make way for her, murmuring 'Sorry, missus, sorry', as she walked, apologising for brushing past, coming close . . . just for *being* there. Here she was like anyone else. She watched two women pass each other, going in opposite directions, and suddenly stop.

A tray of tiny, dried fish balanced precariously on the head of one; a pyramid of tomatoes and small, plump green peppers on the other's. They stood together in the street, exchanging greetings and confidences under the swaying weight of their loads, glancing at Riitho and Rianne. African Americans – the husband, at least, coming 'back' to Africa to discover his roots. Poor fools. They laughed together in their language and parted.

Rianne could feel a trickle of sweat slowly make its way between her breasts to her stomach. They crossed the ford that separated the fortress from the town and stood in front of the massive stone walls. Riitho walked ahead, alone, over the drawbridge and through the enormous wrought-iron gate. She followed him cautiously. Inside, the recent refurbishments were evident. Freshly painted signs showed the way to 'Male Quarters' and 'Female Quarters', 'Officers' Mess', 'Slavemasters' Dining Quarters', and so on.

It was quiet inside the grassy courtyard, the thick, mouldy white walls rising vertically around them. A guide hurried up, anxious to appear helpful and welcoming. Riitho declined the offer of a tour, preferring to wander alone, his black notebook in hand. He moved off, Rianne following. He stopped frequently, to draw something or make a note. He offered no explanations but she was fascinated by the way he observed the physical presence of the castle, recording it in astonishing detail. He showed her how to make what he called a 'section' through some of the spaces they walked through, revealing a hidden way of seeing the world behind the walls, doors, windows and spaces they inhabited. He stopped at one point in front of an unusual narrow gap in the thick walls. Not a doorway, not exactly a window, it led almost directly down to a series of rough-cut steps and the beach. He stood in front of it, touching the walls, measuring the opening with the span of his hand. She wondered what it was. He shook his head; he didn't know.

Almost an hour later, tired by the heat and the emotion

of wandering around this graveyard of slaves, traders and colonisers, they walked up the steps to the bookshop. The same guide doubled as the assistant and as Rianne browsed through books that she, with all her privileged education, had never heard of, Riitho pulled out his sketchbook and asked the guide about the gap he had seen.

'Well, that one . . . it's for the slaves, you see,' the guide explained, eager to show his knowledge and understanding of that period in his country's past. Riitho looked puzzled. 'You know, it's for the *measurement*.'

'Measurement of what?'

'For the slaves. If they can pass through, then they can go to the ships. If not, then they have to wait. It's for the numbers . . . you know. So many on the ship, so they have to be a bit *thin*.' The guide was patient. Many visitors were shocked by this crude fact.

'They have to be able to pass through the wall?' Riitho frowned.

'Yes, yes . . . through the wall.' The guide smiled sympathetically. 'Those times . . . ter-rible. Ter-rible.'

Riitho nodded, his mouth tightening. Rianne recognised the expression: a tense concentration, a retreat into himself, something that set him apart from her. She feared it, was inexplicably drawn to it. She knew he would be quiet for the rest of the day. She knew, too, that later the tension generated by their visit to the castle would spill over into his lovemaking. That he would tell her with his body the things he couldn't put into words.

56

A week later Gabby was in London having lunch with Rianne, a pile of purchases shoved under the table. They'd met to go shopping that morning. Gabby was on her way to a meeting in Geneva and she'd rung Rianne from New

York for last-minute wardrobe advice. They'd spent a thoroughly enjoyable morning looking for clothes and catching up on each other's news. Nathalie's baby was due any day. She had split up with Paul almost as soon as she'd found out she was pregnant.

Gabby couldn't quite understand it – yes, it was true he'd been a bit dull, and obviously something of a sponger, but still, raising a child alone was no joke. For a while, back then, Nathalie had seemed so happy, but she'd become secretive too, always disappearing at weekends, reluctant to say where she'd been. They'd all assumed that things were working out between her and Paul. But then she'd told them she was pregnant and that she'd ended it with him. They were all worried about this but Nathalie was adamant. No contact, no support. It was her child – she would manage alone. She and Charmaine had bought a pram together, and they'd all arranged to meet at Rianne's later that afternoon. It was the first time the four of them had been together in ages even though Charmaine was still living rent-free in Wilton Crescent and showed no signs of wanting to move out.

Rianne was browner than usual – she'd obviously been somewhere hot, Gabby mused. She looked better than she had in months: her eyes were shining, her face was clear, and she'd even put on a little weight.

'But what do you actually *do*?' Rianne looked at Gabby across the restaurant table.

'Well, different things.' She took a sip of wine. 'I write reports, I do research, I travel. I'm working on the UN Declaration for Women's Reproductive Rights at the moment. Boring legal stuff, mostly. Is that what you mean?'

'It sounds so . . . *proper*.'

'Proper?'

'Yeah. It sounds real – a proper job. I envy you.'

Gabby was puzzled. 'You must be kidding. You're the one with the glamorous life, Rianne.'

'It's not. It's anything but.'

'So why d'you do it?'

'I can't think of anything else to do. I've never done anything else.'

'What would you like to do?'

'I don't know.'

'Well, that's half the problem. Before you can make a change, you need to figure out what you'd like to change *to*.' Gabby wasn't overly sympathetic.

'Did you always know you wanted to do this?' Rianne played with the stem of her wine glass.

'What? Law? Human rights?' Gabby was quiet for a minute. She knew Rianne well enough to grasp that the conversation was unlikely to be about her, Gabby, and whether she was happy in her work. It was much more likely to be about Rianne and how she was unhappy in hers. She couldn't quite work out why. Rianne seemed made for the kind of life she led. What was she trying to say? That she wanted another one? 'What's brought this on?' she asked.

Rianne pushed another plum tomato covered in balsamic vinegar around her plate. 'Nothing.' She broke off the end of a crostini and nibbled it. 'Do you ever hear from anyone at St Anne's?' she asked.

'Like who?' Gabby was surprised. Apart from Nathalie and Charmaine, Rianne had never expressed the slightest interest in anyone at school.

'Oh, I don't know. Becky? Or that Nigerian girl – what was her name? Jumoke.'

Gabby laughed. 'Last I heard from Matthie – which was ages ago, by the way – Becky had married a farmer and Jumoke went into medicine. She's probably a doctor by now. Why?'

'Oh, no reason,' Rianne mumbled, toying with her wine. 'Just curious. How about the boys?' she asked. 'You're still in touch with Nael, right?'

'Yes. He's in Bosnia.' She saw Rianne's puzzled look. She

probably didn't know where Bosnia was. She gave the briefest of explanations. Rianne followed, her eyes narrowed slightly.

'There – you see?' Rianne said. 'Everyone's doing *some*thing.'

'I'm surprised you haven't asked about your archenemy,' Gabby said.

Rianne's face was suddenly unusually tight. 'Who d'you mean?'

'Ree Modise. Who else?' Gabby grinned. Then she noticed that her friend had gone pale under her tan. 'You're not still . . .'

'Gabby. Can I trust you with something?' Rianne's voice was urgent. 'Something huge.'

'Of course you can. You know that. What is it?'

Rianne was silent for a few moments. 'I love him,' she said simply, without elaboration.

Gabby looked at her in amazement. 'What?' she spluttered. 'What're you talking about?'

'Ree. Riitho. We've been . . . oh, Christ, this is so difficult. We're together.'

Gabby hadn't been so shocked since Nael had told her who his mother was. 'What are you talking about? What d'you mean?'

'We're seeing each other.'

'Since when?'

'It's been a couple of years, now,' Rianne said slowly.

Gabby stared at her. 'Two *years*? You've got to be kidding.' She couldn't believe her ears. Riitho Modise? 'And you've never said a *thing*?'

'I couldn't. Gabs, you're the only person in the whole world, apart from his bodyguard, who knows. I can't tell anyone. If he knew I'd told you, he'd go mad.'

'Jesus, Rianne.' Gabby blinked. Rianne looked close to tears. She reached across the table and squeezed her hand. 'Where . . . ?'

'In Paris.' Rianne drew a deep breath. Just telling

someone else had made her feel better. Someone else to share the burden with. She began to tell her how it had happened.

Gabby sat opposite, propping her chin up on her elbows, her mouth still agape. 'Unbelievable,' she said, when Rianne had finished. 'It's unbelievable. I can't believe this was happening to you and you never said a word. How *could* you? How did you keep it to yourself? I'd have been shouting it from the rooftops!'

'It's been hard. But he's so careful. It's more from his side. What his people would do if they found out. I don't think mine would care, frankly.'

'Don't bet on it.' During her time at UNTAG Gabby had been amazed at the hostility provoked by the name de Zoete, even in Namibia where they owned plutonium and uranium mines. Did Rianne know that Lisette and Hennie now went everywhere with State police protection? Hennie was rarely seen these days without his entourage of bodyguards and secret servicemen. The threats against the family were coming thick and fast, from all corners of the political spectrum, left and right. 'When was the last time you went home?' she asked.

'To South Africa? Three years ago. When Uncle Hendryk died. It somehow doesn't feel . . . right. Until Riitho can.'

Gabby couldn't get over it. This wasn't the same Rianne who had walked into St Anne's eight years ago – it wasn't the same Rianne who'd walked into the restaurant half an hour before.

'It's changed, Rianne,' Gabby said carefully. She had been to Johannesburg on her last visit for UNTAG a couple of months previously. 'It's not only Ree's people you have to watch out for. It's yours.'

'What do you mean?'

'When was the last time you spoke to Lisette?'

'A month ago. Why? What's happened?'

'Nothing yet. But there's been all sorts of threats, even death threats, against the family – against Hennie. Ever

436

since Vlakfontein.' Rianne frowned. *Vlakfontein.* That word again. 'There's a breakaway faction, the Transvaal People's Republic – the TVR – they're holding your family up as a shining example of what Afrikaners can achieve. You're the only non-Jewish one of the Big Six.' Rianne looked puzzled. 'The big mining firms,' Gabby explained.

Rianne shook her head. They *were* Jewish, her grandfather was Jewish, Rianne told her. Her uncle Hendryk was buried in Evanside, the Jewish cemetery.

'Well, maybe, but it's not universally acknowledged,' Gabby said. Rianne was staring at her. 'But if word gets out about this you could be in real trouble, Rianne. Those people are fanatics. They're insane.'

Later that afternoon Rianne mulled over what Gabby had told her. Riitho had said almost the same thing a week ago. Only it wasn't extremist Afrikaners he'd been talking about, it was black separatists. They wanted to rid South Africa of every last white. Dangers seemed to be coming at them from every corner, thick and fast. Riitho was back in Paris. They were to meet at the end of the month. He'd managed to rent a small flat in the north of the city, near Buttes-Chaumont, completely off the radar for paparazzi and supermodels. There was a safe phone in it and the only other person who knew of its existence was Lebohang. Now Gabby knew of it. It was safe enough: Gabby would never tell another soul. Rianne was sure of it.

Rianne propped herself up on one elbow and looked at Riitho lying next to her. Should she tell him now? Or later? He opened his eyes and looked at her. He reached up, took a handful of her hair and twisted it, watching it fall like liquid gold through his hands. She knew he was not as fascinated by their differences as she was, but he did like her hair. He pulled a thick strand of it across his eyes, inhaling the scent. Coconuts, and cigarette smoke. They'd eaten dinner at a tiny couscous restaurant across the park from them. The air was thick with smoke. At least she'd given cigarettes up.

'Riitho . . .' she began hesitantly. He looked at her. When she wanted to tell him something important, she always began that way.

'Mmm?' He let his hand slide down her neck, coming to rest against the hollow of her throat. His thumb caressed her. She watched his other hand reach round and cup a breast, stroke the hardening nipple, watching her lazily as her breath quickened. 'Mmm?' he asked again, smiling as she closed her eyes.

'Nothing.'

'Nothing?' He continued stroking, increasing the pressure ever so slightly. She stretched languorously – like a cat, he'd told her once – and gave in to the exquisitely sweet sensations. He took her hand and pressed it against himself. He was hard again. 'Sure?' he asked her as he found his way between her thighs. She didn't answer. He entered her slowly, wondering again and again as he brought them both to a shuddering, gasping climax, just what it was about her that made him lose all sense of control. When he was near her, when he touched her, all he wanted was to be inside her. She told him once, after he'd made her come a second, and a third time . . . that it was what she believed. He tilted his head, not following her. 'Making love,' she said. 'I read it somewhere. *It's the only place we can make that's not just a place to stay.*' He nodded slowly. She was right, wherever she'd read it.

'Ree . . .' she began again, an hour later. This time he really was asleep. She nudged him, her face against his chest. 'Riitho. Wake up. I need to tell you something.'

'What?' He opened an eye cautiously.

'Don't be angry. Promise?' She was fiddling with her hair.

'Promise.'

'No, I mean it. Really promise.'

'De Zoete, how can I promise when I don't know what you're talking about?' He opened both eyes.

She cleared her throat. 'I . . . I told someone.'

'Told someone what?' His voice rumbled deep in his chest.

She propped herself up and looked at him. 'About us.'

He was silent for a moment. Then he rolled away from her and sat up. She looked at his back, at the firm, sculpted muscles that she knew by heart through her fingertips. He was holding on to the edge of the bed – his biceps were straining, as if he was trying to contain something.

'Who?' His voice was cold.

'Gabby. I had to. I'm sorry – I just had to.' She looked at his back nervously. In two years she'd never seen him so angry. The memory of Serendipity's came back to her.

He swung his legs out of bed, walked through to the bathroom and slammed the door. Rianne lay still. She heard the shower being turned on. Five minutes later he walked out, a towel round his waist. He said nothing to her as he began to dress.

'Riitho – I—' Tears were welling in her eyes.

'Don't say another word.' He finished buttoning his shirt, pulled on his jacket and left the room. Moments later, she heard the front door slam and he was gone. Just like that.

He came back. Almost four hours later. He walked into the flat, threw the keys onto the table and got straight into the bed where she was still lying curled up as he'd left her. He didn't even take off his jacket, just lay on top of her, fully clothed, pressing his head into her neck. He smelled faintly of cigarette smoke and rum. She began to sob.

'I'm sorry.' His voice was muffled against her skin. 'I'm sorry.'

'I shouldn't have . . .' she said, through her tears. 'I don't know why . . .'

'Ssh. It's OK.' He tasted the salty trail that the tears had left on her cheek. 'I understand. I'm sorry. I shouldn't have reacted the way I did.'

She was silent, her arms around him, her body stirring in deep breaths beneath his. He rolled to one side, still holding her tightly. He sensed trouble ahead.

57

When the baby slipped free of her, screaming for all it was worth, Nathalie struggled to sit up, putting the heel of her palm on her trembling stomach. The midwife held her hand and wiped her sweaty forehead as the doctors cut the cord and immediately took the infant to weigh it. She strained to see – what was it? A boy or a girl? She'd refused the doctor's attempts during her pregnancy to tell her, caring only that it was healthy and strong.

'It's a boy,' the Scots midwife told her. 'A healthy, bouncing boy. Seven pounds! Not bad for someone as wee as yourself!' Nathalie leaned back against the pillows, crying with relief. There was a minute's wait as the doctor weighed the squalling baby and then, suddenly, wrapped in soft white cotton, he was in her arms. 'I've finally met you,' Nathalie whispered to him, as his little fists waved and his mouth opened to yet another deafening scream. That was what it felt like. Nine months of waiting to meet someone. She was slightly dazed. The combination of gas-and-air, pain and anticipation had almost knocked her out. She held him to her, and looked in wonderment at his tight, dusky pink face, the shock of jet black hair. The baby was hers, but he had come out favouring Sacha, in his image alone.

Jenny, Philippe's wife, was waiting with Annelise, their three-year-old daughter, and Cordelia in Nathalie's hospital room. Annelise kept running to the door to check if Auntie Nathalie was coming.

'Mummy, she's here!' she shouted, as she saw Nathalie being wheeled down the corridor towards her. Jenny and Cordelia jumped up.

'Annelise, come here – that's it, you hold the door open,' Jenny said, as Cordelia turned down the bedclothes. The room was filled with flowers – Cordelia had remembered what it had been like giving birth to her two children on her own. Not even a card, even though she'd at least had a husband, unlike her daughter. She'd only met the baby's father, Paul, once, and hadn't thought much of him – but it was so rare to see Nathalie with someone that she'd just been thankful. She often wondered what was wrong with her. She was so *driven* – she didn't seem to feel the need to make time for men, or a family, or any of the other things that most young women wanted. But now all that had changed. Nathalie was a mother.

The orderlies wheeled her in. The baby was nursing at her breast, swaddled in one of the cotton shawls that Cordelia had bought. None of that starchy hospital rubbish for her precious second grandchild.

'Darling,' Cordelia said, smiling through a sudden rush of tears. The orderlies were helping Nathalie into bed. 'Oh, *Schatz*, look at you.'

'Mama, could you . . .' Nathalie pushed at the covers with her legs.

Cordelia and Jenny bustled about, plumping the pillows, helping her to settle. Annelise hung back shyly.

'It's a boy?' Jenny said.

Nathalie nodded. She drew the shawl away from the baby's head, and there was a moment's silence.

Cordelia took in the thick black hair, the faintly Oriental eyes . . . the olive hue of the skin, and gasped. She stared at the baby, her eyes widening. She turned to look at her daughter.

Don't. Nathalie's eyes were hard. Don't say a single fucking *thing*.

58

It was London Fashion Week, and Rianne was beside herself with excitement, not just about the week-long programme of fashion shows and parties but because Riitho, unbelievably, was to be in London at the same time. She was booked with the avant-garde London designers and, for the first time in ages, was looking forward to the shows. Steven Fairley, the latest Bright Young Thing to hit the London scene, had had an afternoon-long rehearsal with the models the day before and she loved his ideas for the catwalk, the music, flowers, lights. She was in an exceptionally good mood, burning with an inner light – no one knew why, of course, and that made it all the more special. She walked about, knowing that at the end of the first hectic night, she would check into the Hilton on Park Lane under an assumed name and he would do the same. Then they'd meet. It was wonderful, carrying around the thrill of anticipation in her all day. The designers looked at her and took notice. Other models sneered. The glow of delicious tension in her couldn't be faked, not at any price.

She came off the catwalk at the end of Fairley's show to thunderous applause. The outfits, long, slithering trails of black silk, outrageous feathered hats and delicate figure-hugging evening dresses, had gone down a storm. He was beside himself with delight and insisted on walking back out to the crowds with her. She was *his* model, *his* creation, the clothes had been made for her.

Rianne was impatient to get away, but the press were determined to get their money's worth. Fairley came backstage and implored her to keep on the last outfit she'd modelled – a bizarre concoction of white silk and tartan tweed, complete with bustle and riding boots. Laughing, Rianne shook her head, no she had to go. She had to meet someone.

'Absolutely *not*,' Fairley said, grabbing her by the hand and dragging her out of the dressing area. Meet a friend? Was she kidding? This was London Fashion Week and he and she were *stars*. This was his moment, and hers – no way was she going to miss it. A few carefully planted pictures of her in his outfits in the tabloids the next morning would translate nicely into pounds and pence. 'I won't hear of it, darling!' he shouted above the din.

The Chelsea warehouse where the fashion shows were held had been turned into a glittering party hall with thousands of just opening red roses dipped in glitter hanging from the ceiling, along with ruby-red candles throwing flickering light over the industrial walls. It had been Fairley's idea – *never* use a nightclub or a restaurant for a party, my dear, we don't want to compete with its own tired image. Do something different! Transform the space! It worked.

Someone thrust a cocktail glass into her hand and, before she could protest, she was swept into the crowd. And it was enjoyable. She saw people she hadn't seen for ages – models she'd worked with in the past, a rock star or two, photographers who raised their glasses in appreciation of her 'return' to the fold.

It was almost midnight before she could extract herself from the throng. Fairley had long since disappeared into the crowd and she slipped into the dressing rooms and took off his outrageous outfit. She glanced at her watch. Riitho had been guest of honour at a charity ball at the Dorchester that evening. He'd promised to be back in his hotel room by ten. She was two hours late! She pulled on her black jeans and her leather coat and picked up her bag.

She waited for a taxi and directed him towards the Park Lane Hilton. Traffic was bad – Saturday night, an' all that, the driver said – and it took ages to get through Knights-bridge and into Park Lane. On impulse, she stopped the cab, jumped out, and walked up to the Dorchester. Men in black tie were emerging onto the street or standing in the foyer, ball guests, she supposed. She remembered him saying it had been arranged by the Labour Party Anti-Apartheid Committee. Politicians and Labour Party figures would be there, he'd said, as well as the more politically inclined members of the London arts and architecture world. Not her crowd. She recognised one or two faces but no one recognised her. With her hair pulled back and the theatrical make-up scrubbed off, she looked like many of the beautiful women who routinely went in and out of the hotels on Park Lane. She pushed her way through the crowd – the party was still in full swing.

She saw him immediately. But she wasn't prepared for what she saw. He was dancing with someone, a pretty young black girl, laughing at something she said. He bent his head – she was much shorter than he was – she didn't wait to see the rest. Jealousy had caught Rianne by surprise, tearing straight through her, making her knees wobble. She turned and walked out, ignoring the photographer who snapped her.

She ran, down Park Lane, her eyes burning. She collected her keys from Reception and ran up the twelve flights of stairs, ignoring the lift. She opened the door to her room, slammed it behind her and flung herself onto the bed, trying to shake the image of Riitho's head bending towards the girl's. She couldn't recall ever feeling so threatened or afraid. Who was she? How did he know her? What was he doing with her? He'd never done anything like it before. Then again, they never went anywhere together. How would she know? She was so angry she couldn't even cry. Her breathing was ragged – she felt as though she couldn't get enough air into her lungs. She was *seething*.

Half an hour later, there was a light tap at the door. She ignored it. She heard his voice. 'Rianne? It's me. Open up.'

'Go away,' she said loudly, her heart hammering. Her mouth was dry.

'Rianne? What's the matter?'

She could picture him frowning. 'Go away. Fuck off.' She

walked over to the door and put her hand against it. She peered through the peephole. He was standing in his tuxedo. He looked angry.

'What are you playing at?' He was glaring at the door.

'Leave me alone.' She leaned her head against the door. It thudded suddenly as he slammed his hand against it and she jumped back in alarm.

'De Zoete, I swear to God, if you don't open this fucking door I'll break it down.'

She stared at it, and turned the lock. He burst into the room. 'Just leave me alone,' she shouted, as he slammed the door.

'What's the matter?' he asked her, his brow furrowed. 'Something's upset you?'

'Are you kidding?'

'What?' He looked genuinely puzzled.

'Don't "what" me!' Her voice was tight with rage.

'De Zoete, I can't read your mind. What is it? Tell me.'

'Well, I can read *yours*.'

'Meaning?'

'You *know* what I mean! Don't pretend you don't know what I'm talking about. I *saw* you.'

'Saw *what*? What is this about?'

'I saw you with that girl – you were dancing with her.' She couldn't bring herself to say it. That black girl.

'Thandi? Thandi Dyani?'

'I don't know *who* she is. I don't *care* who she is. I came to look for you and I saw you kiss her – don't lie to me!'

'Rianne, you're out of your mind. I didn't kiss anyone. That's Thandi Dyani – Dyani's daughter. I've known her since I was a kid.'

'But you were *holding* her,' Rianne hissed at him.

'It was a fucking waltz, Rianne. Of course I had to hold her.' He started to laugh, and moved towards her.

'Don't laugh at me – don't you dare laugh at me. *Don't!*'

'Hey, come on – calm down. There's nothing going on with anyone. Come here. Come—' He moved towards her again. '*Ouch!*' She had hit him, catching him off-guard. Her fist landed on his shoulder. He grabbed her arm easily. '*Stop* it. What's the matter with you? Are you crazy?'

'Why don't you just say it?' she sobbed.

'Say what?'

'That you prefer—' She couldn't say it. They faced each other. He was breathing fast. He let go of her arm and moved away, yanking at his bow-tie.

He ran a hand over his face. 'You're way out of line, de Zoete.' He was dangerously quiet.

'I don't give a shit. I just want the truth.' She glared at him.

'The truth? You want the truth?' He grabbed her arm again and dragged her to the window. He was angry now – angrier even than she was. 'Listen to me. I'm only going to say this once. Get this into your head. I don't prefer anything. It's never been about that.' He looked her straight in the eyes. 'You see the rest of the world out there?' He drew back the curtains. 'Well, that's the world we don't have to deal with right now. We ignore it, we can afford to. But have you *any* idea what's going to happen when this gets out? Everyone else out there is going to make it about *that*. You *don't*.' He let go of her abruptly and walked away. She stared after him.

He sat down on the edge of the bed, his face in his hands. She swallowed hard. Moments passed. He raised his head. 'Come here.' He beckoned to her. She walked over, unsteadily. She stood in front of him. He looked at her, shaking his head slowly. Her make-up was smudged, her hair was dishevelled. He thought her beautiful. He pulled her down onto the bed.

Much later, he rolled onto his side to look at her, propping himself on one elbow. Her face was covered with her hair – she'd let it grow again and it lay like a thick, gold blanket over her cheek. He traced the outline of her eyes, swollen with tears. 'You know, we have to figure out how to talk about things like this. I don't mean don't get angry, but we have to deal with it. You have to talk to me.'

'You have to talk to me as well.'

'I think I do.'

'Without getting mad.'

'I don't. I'm not.' He was quiet for a moment. 'Am I?'

'Sometimes. Sometimes I'm – afraid to bring it up.'

'Why?'

'I don't know ... it's difficult. Sometimes I think it doesn't matter that I'm white and you're black. You're just you, Riitho, like I'm just me. I don't think about it.'

'Come on, de Zoete, you can't be that naïve. Everyone else notices. It's pretty hard to miss.'

'I know, I know – but it's different for you.'

'Why? Why's it different for me? Why do you keep saying that?'

'Because it *is*. You're the ones ... with the power. It's your time that's coming.'

'What d'you mean? At home?'

'No, not just there.' She turned into the space hollowed out by his arm. Her voice was muffled. 'When I first met you, at St Anne's, it was different then. *I* was different. I didn't know anything else. I didn't know how to *be* anyone else once I'd left there – South Africa, I mean.' She was struggling for words. 'That's the problem, you see. For whites, for people like me – we don't know anything else. We don't know how to *be* anything else. If you stay in South Africa, it's fine – well, it *was* fine. But once you go outside, once you leave, you see that it's just a lie. Life isn't like that anywhere else. Nothing fits – all the things they tell you, about the way the world is, the way they'd *like* it to be – that's the thing, you see. It's all about what they'd like, the people who planned it, nothing to do with what's real, how things *really* are. So when you leave, that's when you realise you've been living in a lie. You *are* only half the story. You're only half alive. There's another half – the missing half – the half we never saw back there.' She fell silent, and he stroked her head. He was listening warily. 'You're the other half,' she continued, after a while. 'You make everything whole. For me.' He made a movement with his hand, a warning.

'Be careful, Rianne. I'm not here to save you.'

'I know that.'

'I mean it.'

'I know.'

But she didn't. Not really. He saw that. Whatever else she said, she was treading water, now, waiting for something, some sign from him that would show her what to do, how to be. He said nothing. The question of how to continue lay between them, unanswered. It lay heavily in the air.

59

Three months later, in London, Charmaine was enjoying herself. Mr Special had turned out to be as good as his name. Apart from his gifts, fine wine and sexual expertise, she liked him. He was different from all the men – boys – she'd been with before. There was a maturity about him to which she responded without thinking about it. When she made him laugh, or smile – or better yet, when she excited him – she loved watching his reaction. She wanted his approval.

She lowered her head to his lap. Within seconds, he had climaxed, brought to the edge, she knew, by the way she raised her eyes to meet his as she ran her tongue round the tip of his cock and pushed her full breasts into his thighs.

There was a moment's silence. 'I'm afraid I'll have to cut it short, today, sweetheart,' he told her.

Charmaine looked up at him, pouting.

He smiled regretfully. 'A million things to do. I'll arrange another meeting with James.' Like most of the men who used Charmaine's 'services', there was no question she wouldn't be available. James would see to that.

Charmaine was pleased that he'd seemed to enjoy what she'd done to him, but disappointed too. 'Shame,' she said teasingly, as she straightened up. She enjoyed watching his eyes travel over her.

'I just got into town,' he said, as he reached for his tie and jacket. 'I'll set up something for tomorrow or the weekend.'

Charmaine stood with her back to him in her black lace thong. She leaned forward to push her breasts into her bra, and heard his sharp intake of breath. 'You're beautiful, you know that?' He stood up and pushed his body into hers from behind. 'Beautiful,' he repeated, cupping her breasts. 'I'll be back later on tonight. Wait for me.'

Charmaine gave a mock-salute. He reached for his trousers.

He'd had to rush back to the flat he'd borrowed for the weekend and change his trousers – he'd spotted a large stain on the crotch. His first thought, when he opened the door to the unmistakably feminine scent of perfume and cigarettes, was that Rianne must be using it temporarily. Lisette hadn't said anything but he knew her niece lived a somewhat peripatetic life. He called out, as he placed the keys on the side table and looked around the hallway, but there was no answer.

The place smelled strangely familiar. How odd. It was the scent Charmaine used. He was mildly irritated that Rianne was in town. He'd been thinking of bringing Charmaine here for the weekend. He walked through the flat, hauling his suitcase behind him. Rianne was probably using the master bedroom, he thought, so he went into one of the guest rooms. The bed was made and there were flowers on the bedside table. Lisette must have told the housekeeper he was coming.

He began to unpack, mentally running through how he

was going to break the news to her. The withdrawals were increasing, both in amount and frequency. Something was definitely up – in the past month, almost R350 million had gone. He'd been back to Zurich twice in the past two months and the result was always the same: no way of tracing what was happening. Herr Schmidt at UMB, one of the discreet, anonymous banks that de Zoete (Pty) Ltd had been using for decades, was apologetic, but firm. He could say nothing. Whoever had set up the account knew what he was doing.

An hour later, he put down the phone and leaned back into the sofa. Lisette had taken the news rather well, considering. He was to come back to Cape Town at the end of the week. He glanced at his watch: nine fifteen. Just enough time to take a shower and get something to eat before he called James again. It really was a pity that Rianne was around. He'd have liked to put Charmaine in a cab with nothing on, just a coat. He looked at his watch again. He ought to call Stella and the kids. He was just about to reach for the phone again when he heard someone come in. Rianne.

He straightened his tie and stood up. It was ages since he'd seen her, although her face was familiar enough. There were precious few South African celebrities who had made it on the international circuit. Back home hardly a day went by when he didn't see her image on the cover of a magazine. He heard her heels click-clack on the hallway floor and walked forward, smiling, to greet her. When she came into the room, he stared at her, open-mouthed. It wasn't Rianne, it was Charmaine.

'What the . . .' He recovered himself. 'Who the hell gave you this address? How did—'

'Excuse me, I *live* here.'

'The hell you do. Do you know whose home this is?'

'Of course I do. It's my best friend's. Rianne de Zoete.'

'Eh? Your *what*?'

'My friend. Rianne de Zoete.'

'Jesus,' said Simon Kalen, and sat down suddenly on the sofa.

Charmaine remained standing. 'You still haven't told me what you're doing here,' she said.

Simon looked up at her. Then it dawned on him. Of course. Sans Soucis. She'd come with Rianne, one of the group of friends from that school Rianne had been sent to. He'd always had a strange feeling he'd seen her before. That made her how old? Oh, Christ. Did Rianne know what she was doing for a living?

'I'm an old friend of the family,' he said smoothly, praying she wouldn't recognise him. He had to get rid of her – fast. He looked at her, standing in the doorway, staring open-mouthed at him, still in the long silk dress she had been wearing that afternoon. She looked good enough to ... He thought fast. 'Does Rianne – er, know what you—'

'Do? Oh, God, no. And you mustn't tell her, please.' He saw fear in her eyes. And shame.

'Of course not.' His mind was racing. So, she had a secret to keep as well. Well, that changed things. 'Is Rianne staying here?'

'No, she's got her own flat. I moved in when I came back from the States. Her aunt Lisette said it was OK.' She was worried, he could tell.

'Oh, I'm sure it's fine. I was just wondering ... So it's just you here, on your own?'

'Yeah, except for Dinah. She comes in in the mornings to clean up and stuff.' Charmaine was frowning, but then her eyes widened, and Simon saw that suddenly she'd placed him. She looked away. 'So ... you won't ... say anything?' she asked, her voice low.

'Not if you won't.' He smiled at her now. 'Come here.' He patted the space beside him, and she moved towards him.

In the early hours of the morning, the bedside phone rang.

Simon reached out an arm and picked it up groggily. Charmaine didn't stir.

It was Lisette. He lay there listening to her instructions, Charmaine's leg resting gently against his cock. As he talked, he felt himself begin to harden again. He turned his attention back to Lisette. She was upset – couldn't sleep. Was Marius alive? And if so, where was he? Simon listened quietly, sliding a hand up Charmaine's warm thigh. It excited him beyond belief to be playing with her at the same time as he talked to Lisette. The fact that the women knew each other – if only distantly – made it even more pleasurable, almost unbearably so. It was like possessing them both at once.

Charmaine woke sleepily and he pushed her head downwards. What pleasure to feel her hot mouth engulf him as he comforted Lisette. She was so good at it, too. His climax was exquisite. He put down the phone and pulled her into his arms. He looked at his watch: 5.23 a.m. Plenty of time.

In the rented flat in Buttes-Chaumont, Riitho was agitated. It was almost six and Rianne still hadn't shown up. He'd been waiting for her for two hours. It had been over two months since they'd seen each other and her last-minute Paris booking couldn't have been better timed. He missed her dreadfully. But where was she? She was supposed to have been there hours ago. He paced up and down the living room, his mind racing, a cold knot of fear in his stomach.

Who could he call? He knew from his own sources that the situation at home was in danger of fragmenting. There were too many competing factions, too many demands to satisfy. De Klerk was not the man to hold things together. He was weak. Around him, a kind of power vacuum was forming – and that was the most dangerous thing of all, everyone rushing to fill it.

Lebohang had murmured to him at the beginning of the

week that he thought it was too risky, him and Rianne staying in the flat at Buttes-Chaumont together. There were rumours, nothing proven yet, that the breakaway group who called themselves the Azania People's Liberation Movement were planning something, no one was sure what, but the de Zoete name had come up. Lebohang didn't know whether it referred to Rianne or to her cousin, Hennie de Zoete-Koestler – a hated figure on the political landscape – or even her aunt, Lisette, who was possibly the most hated woman in the country. Getting at either Hennie or his mother would be difficult: both had round-the-clock protection. But Rianne was another matter. '*Ipheji namabinisi*. Warn her.' Lebohang felt the two of them took far too many risks. Renting the flat had been one. Lebohang thought it was madness. It was impossible for him to join them there because it was too small – there was nowhere for him to stay, discreetly or otherwise. But Riitho was adamant. They needed somewhere where they could be alone. Well, Lebohang understood that. Everyone needed that – even he sometimes. But never for a whole night and never without making sure Khotso or, lately, Moses was covering for him. It was murder trying to explain to them where Riitho disappeared to once, sometimes twice a month. Please. *Ungathathi ama'chance*. Don't take risks.

Riitho had nodded impatiently. He didn't like talking about Rianne to Lebohang. It was bad enough that he'd figured out who she was. He felt like he was doing something wrong, fraternising with the enemy, not that Lebohang had ever said anything. The closest he'd made to a comment was to say she was beautiful. If you liked that sort of thing. Riitho hadn't spoken to him for days afterwards.

He looked out of the window. It was quiet in the street outside. No one ever came up here. It was an elegant, slightly shabby neighbourhood and it suited them perfectly. You could spot a car waiting anywhere on the street. It wasn't an easy place for anyone watching them to hide.

That was why he'd chosen it. He looked at his watch again: 7.13. He'd have to phone someone. Might as well start with Lebohang.

Ten minutes later, he put down the phone, his heart hammering. Lebohang was on his way over. He'd be there in half an hour.

It was already dark when Rianne left the YSL showrooms. She walked quickly down rue Rambuteau, wrapping her coat round her and twisting her hair up into a knot on top of her head. She reached the Champs- Élysées. It was easier to get a taxi from there. She'd refused a car the receptionist had offered – she didn't want anyone at YSL to know where she was going. It was almost Christmas, and the lights shimmered in the rain, sending rivers of red and gold light cascading onto the dark surface of the damp streets. She looked at her watch. Almost four. She was late. She'd told Riitho she'd be there at four and it would take her the best part of an hour to cross the city. She looked at the taxi rank. It was empty. Then she searched the oncoming traffic. A black car pulled up in front of her, the door opening before it had come to a standstill. Someone got out and turned in her direction. She looked past him to the car ahead. Was that a taxi? The man was walking towards her, blocking her view. She tried to move round him, but he held out his hand. 'Rianne?'

She looked at him in surprise. 'Bruce Eastman?' He was the last person she'd expected to see. 'What are *you* doing here?'

She was just about to take his hand when she heard a car pull up, the scuffle of shoes and voices right behind her. She turned. Two young black men were standing in front of her. She took a step backwards – they were a little too close for comfort. Suddenly one lunged forward and grabbed her elbow.

Before she could scream, a gloved hand went over her mouth, the second man opened the car door and she was shoved, face down, into the back seat, banging her head painfully. She felt the cold steel of a gun against her cheek. The doors slammed, and she was screaming as the car powered away, swerving wildly as the driver cut across several lanes of traffic. She felt, rather than saw, the hand coming towards her, smelled a crisp, sharp odour then everything went blank.

The murmur of voices filtered through her sleep, and she stirred, still drowsy, struggling to open her eyes. Her head was thudding. Sharp bolts of pain shot through her head. She tasted fear in her mouth, thick and tight, and sat up. There was a concentration of pain around her eyebrow – her fingers touched the edge of a cut.

It was almost pitch dark. In the distance, beyond the closed door, she could still hear the voices – men arguing. Where was she? What had happened? Bruce . . . She remembered being surprised to see him in Paris – then she had been pushed, someone grabbing her hair viciously, hitting her head as she fell against the seat—

There was a sudden noise outside the door. She froze. A man entered the room and switched on the light. They stared at each other for what seemed like ages. She had never seen him – she was sure of it. His eyes flicked over her with a contempt she found hard to bear.

'*Kom*.' His voice was loud, filling the bleak room. 'Get up.' Her legs trembled as she slid from the bed. In his hand he carried a gun: she couldn't take her eyes off it as he gestured her through the doorway in front of him.

'No. No police.' Lebohang was firm. 'If she's been kidnapped, they'll kill her. They don't care.' He blew a cloud of smoke out of the corner of his mouth. He and Riitho were standing in the living room. 'We wait. A couple of days, no more. Someone will get in touch. But once this gets in the papers, man, it will be difficult.'

'Who's taken her? What are the possibilities?' Riitho's mouth was dry with fear.

'Hard to say. APM, maybe. Bunch of radicals there. Maybe APLM – maybe Dixie's men?'

'Jesus.' There were so many factions, so many splinter groups. 'Who do we have on the inside?'

'Khotso knows some of the guys . . . Dhladhla and the others from Turfloop.' Riitho nodded. The notorious Pretoria jail had housed many freedom fighters, from all factions. Khotso must have connections, some who went back over the years from before the various splits had occurred, forcing everyone to take sides.

'He knows?'

'Khotso? About her?' Lebohang shook his head. 'No, man. Not about her. No one knows.' He was silent for a while. 'Maybe that's better. In a way.'

'How so?'

'Well, if we ask about her, about what's happened, it's OK. No one will make the connection. Problem is, if it's government people, they mustn't know about it. No way. About you and her, man. Weakens us. It weakens your father. He can't go into negotiations with a question like this hanging over him. It's suicide. For him.'

Riitho winced. In all the time they'd been together, it was the one thing he could not bring himself to think about. How his father would view their relationship. When Rianne had attempted to talk to him – once – he'd cut her off swiftly. 'Don't go there,' he'd warned her. 'Just don't.' He didn't know how he felt about it himself.

'When?' He was impatient. 'When will they get back to us?' If Khotso had contacts, let him push them now.

Lebohang looked at his watch. 'Soon. Those guys'll start working on it tonight. I'll go home – call me if you hear anything at all. I'll be back tomorrow morning.' Lebohang looked at Riitho's tense face. 'Take it easy, *Bra*,' he said, and put a hand on his shoulder.

Take it easy? How could he? He couldn't stay there alone

all night. He *had* to talk to someone. He watched Lebohang push open the gate and disappear into the dark. He walked over to the phone. His hands were shaking as he dialled.

Gabby's plane landed in Paris at exactly 9 a.m. By eleven she was standing outside the flat. She could hardly believe she'd made the flight. Riitho had rung at three the previous afternoon with the dreadful news. He'd needed to talk to someone, and the only person in the world who knew of their situation was Gabby. It had been her idea to fly out to Paris – he'd protested . . . no, there was no need. 'Are you kidding?' was Gabby's answer. 'I'll be there in the morning.' And she was.

It was bitterly cold. She paid the taxi driver and hurried up the steps. Riitho was standing at the window. He buzzed her in and was waiting at the top of the stairs. They embraced in the doorway – he looked as though he hadn't slept.

'Ree.' She hugged him again. Somehow, the fact that they hadn't seen each other for years didn't matter.

'Gabby, come in.' He led the way into the sitting room. 'Would you like some coffee? Juice?' Gabby stared at him. Coffee was the last thing on her mind. 'Don't give in to it,' he said, apparently reading her mind. 'Panic isn't useful in these situations.'

'How can you be so calm?' Gabby said, bewildered. She watched him walk over to the tiny kitchenette and light the stove.

'I'm not,' he answered, measuring coffee beans. 'Believe me. But if there's one thing I've learned from my father it's not to panic.'

'What's the situation? Have you heard anything?'

'Nothing yet. My bodyguards are asking around. They have . . . contacts. It depends who it is.' He looked at his hands. 'There are so many complications. I don't need to spell them out, Gabby. You, of all people, will understand.'

Gabby wondered how much he knew of what she did.

Again, he seemed to have read her thoughts. 'And yes, I know what you do. Whatever contacts you have . . . anyone you can think of . . .'

Gabby wasn't sure what she could do to help – not until they knew more.

The downstairs buzzer sounded, and Riitho walked over to the intercom. It was Lebohang, who nodded to her as he entered the room. If he was surprised to see her, he made no sign. Gabby remembered him from Malvern. He looked almost the same – a little older, perhaps, and more tired than when she'd last seen him. He walked over to the dining table and briefly touched Riitho's shoulder. He lifted his eyebrows questioningly.

'She's OK. We can talk in front of her,' Riitho said.

'Well, the news isn't good,' Lebohang said, and hung his jacket on the back of his chair. Gabby swallowed. His gun, in its holster, was strapped across his chest.

Riitho stiffened. A muscle in his jaw clenched and unclenched. 'We had some news last night but I wanted to check it out before coming over. Khotso found it out. He thinks it's a breakaway faction of the Azania People's Liberation Movement. They called themselves the Azania People's Organisation – the APO. They're under the command of a coloured guy from Cape Town, Justin Groenewald. It seems they're looking for a place at the negotiating table. They were expelled from the APLM a couple of years ago – we're not sure why.'

Riitho said nothing, his eyes unreadable.

'Who are they? What sort of power base do they hold?' Gabby asked.

Lebohang looked surprised at the question.

'I work with the UN,' Gabby said. 'I'm a human-rights lawyer.' Lebohang nodded slowly, pulling the sides of his mouth down. She knew what she was talking about, then.

'Unclear.' Lebohang addressed them both. 'There was a whole group of coloureds from District Six. We don't know what happened. They'd started out with the New National

458

Party but something went wrong, we're not sure what. Some of the old ones, they didn't like the younger guys and that was it. They left. But the blacks didn't want them in the ANC. Too bitter. Too much to prove. They ran into trouble with Dyani and Chikama. A month later, there was a vote and they were out. Expelled.'

'And these are the guys you think have taken Rianne? What does she have to do with anything?'

'She's a bargaining tool.' Lebohang spoke. 'They're going to try to force the government and his father's hand – the APP's hand. She's well known, she's Koestler's niece – they want to show they can get at anyone, anytime. She doesn't even live in South Africa. No one is out of their reach. It's their way of showing off.'

'Will they . . . hurt her?' Gabby was almost too afraid to ask.

'It depends,' Lebohang said.

'On what?'

'On how desperate they get.'

Rianne lay rigid in the narrow bed, listening to the voices in the other room. Her hand kept going to the back of her neck. She'd almost passed out with fear when he pushed her into the seat by the kitchen table and brought a knife to her throat. He'd grabbed a fistful of hair and sawed at it until a long rope lay on the table between them. Then he had shoved her back into this room and locked the door.

She could hear shouting again. She sat very still in the dark, straining to hear what was being said. They were speaking a mixture of Afrikaans, Zulu and English. She caught references to herself, to Hennie . . . to Mandela and Modise, de Klerk . . . even her father. She couldn't make sense of it. They switched languages too often for her to follow properly. Her hands were shaking. How many times had Riitho told her to be careful? She'd shrugged it off. She had been so ignorant, she saw that now. As usual, he had seen the dangers she couldn't – or wouldn't – recognise. His face flashed before her and her eyes flooded with tears.

The phone rang, shattering the silence. Riitho jumped up, every muscle in his body tense. It was Khotso. He passed the phone to Lebohang, who listened for a few minutes, replaced the receiver and turned to them. 'It's the APO. They took her last night, from the centre of town. They're holding her somewhere in Paris.' He reached for his jacket and checked the clip on his gun. 'Amateurs. They don't know what they're doing. It'll be easy to find them. Let's go.' Riitho was already on his feet, grabbing his coat and scarf.

Gabby looked at them, bewildered, then grabbed her coat and followed them. Riitho and Lebohang were clattering down the stairs. Lebohang stopped at the front door and put out a restraining hand to Riitho and Gabby, who were close on his heels. Years of discipline and training made him check the street outside before he sprinted towards the black BMW that was parked there. 'You drive,' he shouted to Riitho, and tossed the keys across the roof of the car.

'Let's get Khotso first,' Lebohang went on, as Riitho swung the powerful car onto the main boulevard, 'then head for Sarcelles. You know Dumi's place?' Riitho winced. He'd last seen Dumi on his first date with Rianne. At the thought of her, his stomach tightened. Where was she? He knew she was alive – there had been no ransom demand, no contact. They probably had a day or two at most to locate her.

They stopped by the Marais to pick up Khotso. He was waiting outside the flat, half hidden in the doorway. He jumped in, nodded briefly to Gabby. The atmosphere in the car was tense and no one spoke. In the back seat beside her Khotso pulled out a handgun, slotted in a clip and pulled back the safety catch.

Gabby swallowed. She turned back to look out of the

window at Paris flying past. At St Denis, Riitho pulled off the *périphérique* and headed north. They passed through shabby, industrial suburbs until finally he pulled up outside a rundown housing estate and killed the engine. All three men got out and Gabby followed. They walked towards one of the entrances.

A man was waiting for them. He led them into the estate. There were several young black men standing in the corridor, none of whom glanced at her. They were led into someone's flat. A young woman, a baby on her hip, looked up as they crowded into the tiny hallway. She let them into the sitting room. She was a pretty girl, with smooth, dark skin and long braids that swung this way and that as she addressed the men, the baby beginning to whimper in protest at the noise they brought with them. She was flirtatiously sulky, her mulberry-painted lips pouting as she went about the room, bringing glasses, opening a whisky bottle, hugging the crying child. The men left the room and crowded into the tiny kitchen. The door closed. Gabby and the girl with the baby were alone in the sitting room.

Gabby looked around her. The girl ignored her tentative smile. The smoked-glass coffee table was already groaning under the weight of books, magazines, yesterday's newspapers and the leftover glasses from the previous night's visitors. An old sofa, the cushions permanently hollowed with the indentations of continuous occupation, as one backside gave way immediately to another, stood across the room. Gabby had never been in a home quite like this before. There was the dining room 'suite' – the shiny-topped table with its six chairs, one missing an arm; the flowered carpet and matching wallpaper; the hi-fi equipment; the coffee table doubling up as a desk; two uncomfortably upright armchairs still in their plastic covering, and delicately crocheted antimacassars – standard items, available from any budget furniture store. Every square inch of space was used and re-used – the piles of newspapers on the floor served as rugs; the dining table was both storage and dining surface. Pictures of Mandela, Modise, Gandhi, Mao, Nkrumah – she recognised each one in turn – adorned the walls. It was indeed a living room – in another, deeper sense of the term – the territory in which the inhabitants lived, a symbolic space of the society they worked together to overthrow.

The kitchen door opened and the men came out, still arguing among themselves in their own language, even Riitho. Gabby looked at him. He was calm, focused, absolutely sure of himself, completely at home in the extraordinary situation in which they found themselves. She had never seen him like this. She understood immediately what Rianne was drawn to: it wasn't just that he was handsome or clever or sexy, or any of the rather ordinary criteria by which women of her age and class judged the men they met. No, there was something else about him, something magnetic. When he was around, he pulled you into his orbit . . .

It was power – that was it. He was powerful in a forceful, almost theatrical sense. It radiated from him. It was there in every gesture, every word. Gabby had never seen his father. An old picture, taken some three or four years before the Rivonia trial, had survived censorship – it was the same one on the wall. Gabby glanced at it, looking for resemblances in the proud, watchful face of the young man before her. It was hard to say. The same steady gaze, the tense, square jaw, the tight, high cheekbones. But the man in the picture looked African, whatever Gabby understood by that: the old-fashioned haircut, the 'proper' European suit with the thin black tie. And Ree . . . well, he looked . . . what? He looked like Ree. He was at ease in her middle-class, middle-English, middle-European world as she was. There was something different about him, even from the bodyguards and the men who now surrounded him, fingering their guns with nervous tension. They had something of the look of Modise Senior about them, a peculiar, old-fashioned reserve, perhaps. Riitho, despite the fact that he spoke the language seemingly as fluently as they did, did not have it. He was – what? Twenty-five? Twenty-six? She compared him to some of the men she knew in their twenties. Dominic? Giles? The comparison was not possible.

The men sat down, thigh to thigh, on the sofa, in the armchairs, on the floor. The room was filled with their talk – in French, sometimes in English, mostly in their own language. Plumes of cigarette smoke drifted upwards, curling round the bare lightbulb that hung over the low table and cast an eerie circle of light around them. Drinks were poured, men wandered in and out. Two young women came in and beckoned to the girl with the baby. She left, waving the air in front of her vigorously and wrinkling her nose. The smoke. The baby.

The phone rang, breaking into the voices – someone got up. For Gabby, struggling to follow the conversation with her rudimentary French, the sensation was one of total immersion in a language, gathering and place in which everything was strange to her. Yet despite the tension there was comfort in being with these men – safety in their presence. Voices rose and fell around her, the smell of cooking wafted in as someone opened the door to the kitchen to fetch more glasses, ice, a bottle of water.

'No, Kanji? *C'est vrai?*'

'For ten years I've been telling them . . .'

'*Ag*, man . . .'

'Look, those guys? They don't feel for *any* body, nobody. I'm *telling* you, man. *Nobody.*'

'*Prends pas* . . .' She sat back, observing the dialogue, not taking part.

An hour passed. The women brought food – chicken, rice, something that looked like dried porridge, a gravy made with tomatoes. The men ate quietly, their fingers expertly moulding the porridge-like mass into little balls, dipping them into the gravy, breaking off a piece of chicken. No one used a knife and fork. One or two smiled a little at Gabby's attempts to eat with her fingers. Riitho came over and sat on the floor beside her to show her how to mould a ball of 'pap', as he called it, how to make a little indentation in the centre with the thumb and how to scoop the gravy into it. She made another attempt and gave up, acknowledging defeat. Riitho called to the girl, and a knife and fork appeared. Everyone grinned.

Another hour passed. And another. The men were quiet now. Everyone was waiting. One or two dozed. Gabby looked at her watch: 4.05 a.m. They had been there almost six hours. She was tired and her leg ached from where she'd been sitting on it. Riitho was deep in conversation with Lebohang and a man who had come in late.

The phone rang again. Dumi jumped up. There was a terse conversation. He turned to Riitho. They'd found her: 2 rue d'Alençon. Montparnasse. Some white boy had rented a flat some months previously. He'd brought the keys to a house in Barbès. One of Khotso's 'boys' had been visiting at the time. They were pretty sure she was there.

'*Masihambe*. Let's go.' Lebohang gave the order.

The men pulled on their coats. Gabby stood up.

Riitho shook his head almost imperceptibly. He was carrying a handgun, she noticed, similar to the one Khotso had loaded in the car. 'Gabby, you stay here. It's not safe for you to come.'

'No. I'm coming with you,' Gabby put a hand on his arm.

He covered it briefly with his own and squeezed her fingers. 'No. It's not safe. I mean it, Gabby. You stay here.'

The girl looked on, faintly sneering. Did she think that Gabby was his? She sat on the sofa and the men left the room, one by one. Seconds later, she heard the cars pull away, fast. She stared at the whisky bottle and the glasses that the girl had laid out, opened the bottle and poured herself a measure. It was the longest night she'd ever lived through.

In that moment – the sound of hammering, the scrape of

chairs, the staccato burst of someone shouting – Rianne's eyes flew open. She was awake in an instant. She lay in the dark, her heart pounding with fear. Another shout and then, *crack*! A sharp, metallic sound – and a thud. There was a short burst of gunfire and a woman's screams. She slid off the bed and under it, terrified.

The door opened and a man burst in. She heard him stop – the shuffle of his feet across the wooden floor and then, suddenly, he was above her.

'Get up, get up – come on, man, quick!' he hissed.

She'd never seen him in her life before: a short black man with a straggly beard and a woollen hat pulled down over his eyebrows. 'Rianne, get up. Let's go! *Masihambe!*' He thrust out a hand and pulled her up. 'Riitho sent me. He's outside.' She stumbled after him.

They burst through the doors and she glimpsed a body slumped across the kitchen table, and the angry face of a light-skinned young man with a gun to his temple. Then she was hauled up the basement steps and thrust into the waiting car.

A man was at the wheel, his face hidden by his collar. Several men jumped in beside her, there was the slam of car doors all around them and the sound of racing footsteps, another short burst of gunfire and, in the distance, the wail of a police siren. Everyone was shouting in Xhosa.

With a screech of tyres, the cars pulled away from the kerb and raced towards the main road. Rianne was crying with fear and shock. She'd banged her knee and cut her foot – there hadn't been time to put on her shoes or grab her coat.

The car stopped at a red light. The man at the wheel looked into the rear-view mirror and caught her eye. It was Riitho. He stared at her as long as the lights would allow, then gunned the engine, heading back to Sarcelles. It had taken them just under six hours to find her and seven minutes to get her out. Three were dead and a seething Justin Groenewald was left behind.

PART SIX

60

December 1990: Paris

Rianne could hear police sirens screaming as the cars sped in the opposite direction, melting into the early morning traffic on the *périphérique*. She lay against someone – she didn't know whom – shaking hysterically. The man put a blanket over her and said something to Riitho. They were speaking Xhosa and she couldn't understand his response. She buried her face in the blanket. The drive seemed to go on for ever. Everyone was talking, but not to her. The car stopped. She heard the door open and someone else get in – the man next to her moved up to make room. Then someone got out – she heard Riitho talking, fast, urgent. There was the slam of the door and the engine started again. The man next to her – Lebohang, she'd recognised his voice at last – said something. Avenue Foch – they were taking her home? She struggled to sit upright but Lebohang's arm restrained her. 'It's OK. Lie still. You've been hurt.'

'Rianne, *calmes-toi*,' Riitho said. '*Nous serons là dans quelques instants*.' She slumped back in the seat.

A couple of hours later, Riitho closed the bedroom door and walked into the kitchen to talk to an alarmed Aïcha. Lebohang and Dlamini, the new bodyguard, were in the sitting room. They were waiting for the detectives to show up. The story was out, if not yet to the press. The High Command had been notified. Riitho had done the right thing. It was unfortunate, his ... involvement, but they would deal with that later. Riitho had felt the hairs rise on the back of his neck. *Unfortunate*. What did that mean? But there was no time to dwell on it. They had to deal with the current situation. He would receive full support, Dyani promised him, including lawyers to help him handle the police. Negotiations were at their most delicate stage and nothing could be allowed to disturb that. Dyani's voice, on the line from Stockholm, was quiet, authoritative.

The doorbell rang. It was Benet and Kouao, the APP lawyers. Aïcha showed them into the sitting room. Riitho joined them and, together, the five men sat, listening for the bell.

Riitho waited until the lawyers and the police started talking in earnest. He knew a deal would be struck. The lawyers would give a certain amount of information in exchange for immunity from questioning – he'd seen it before. He excused himself and went to the bedroom where Rianne was sleeping. The sedatives were wearing off – she turned her head drowsily as he opened the door.

'Hey,' he said softly, and sat on the edge of the bed. She opened her eyes slowly, struggling to focus. 'You OK?' he touched her cheek. The doctor had washed and dressed the cut on her forehead – it had looked worse than it was. No, she didn't need stitches. He stroked her hair. A lock was missing from the back of her head. He could see where they'd simply taken a knife and cut. He supposed he should be grateful it was just hair they'd cut off. He looked at her. She was slipping in and out of sleep.

'Wh-what time is it?' she asked, her voice hoarse.

'Almost noon. Don't worry about the time. I want you to get some sleep.' She closed her eyes. The pills hadn't quite worn off. She slipped back down again. Riitho watched her for a moment or two then left.

He opened the door to the drawing room, where the men were still talking, and closed it, leaning against it. He watched Kouao under the pressure of their questions skilfully manoeuvre the conversation back to his advantage. His voice was smooth, rapid. Detective Kassel and his men were drawn into his net. He commanded them – this matter went high, very high ... *yees* ... very high indeed. He lapsed into English from time to time. It was his game and he was good at it.

Kassel was convinced: there would be a press statement later that afternoon. She'd been mugged walking back to Avenue Foch late in the evening. Her bag and her watch had been taken. She'd suffered a nasty cut above the eye where one of the muggers had hit her. A lesson to all young women. If it could happen in St Germain-des-Prés, it could happen anywhere. Kouao and Benet showed the police to the door.

Of course, as Riitho said to Lebohang later that evening, *if you want to make God laugh, tell him your plans*. Lebohang laughed shortly. By mid-afternoon, somehow, the story had leaked and the press showed up outside the apartment. The curtains were drawn, the shutters closed. Riitho had been given strict instructions: no one was to talk. While the story that she'd been mugged might hold – at least for a while – she could not afford to be connected to the APP. Not yet. They were days away from reaching a settlement with de Klerk. It *had* to be kept quiet until then. No one could afford to be weakened by the news that Modise's son and de Zoete's daughter were connected. It would lead to all sorts of questions about de Zoete. The news of his involvement with the APP might cause the talks to collapse and no one could afford that.

In Stockholm, in Oslo, in Johannesburg, everyone waited, praying Groenewald would hold his counsel. They were *so* close.

In Paris, Aïcha was sent out to buy food for the four of them. On the evening news Rianne's face flashed up: the victim of a suspicious attack. They had arrested a South

African man after an incident in the south of the city, which had left three other South Africans dead. Police were treating it as a mugging, although there were questions about the connection between the attack and her status as the daughter of South Africa's richest and most influential family. The chief of police made a statement.

Rianne lay in the darkened room, holding Riitho's hand.

The following morning, a further piece of information emerged. A junior receptionist at YSL had been reported saying a man had called on the day of the mugging asking for Rianne de Zoete, *oui*, by name. The receptionist's face appeared the following day in *Le Figaro*. The man arrested in connection with the mugging had been named as Justin Groenewald. Sources in South Africa confirmed that he was the leader of a breakaway faction of Livingstone Modise's APLM party. In another curious twist, Modise's son, the architect Riitho Modise, was living in Paris. He was not available for comment. He had not been seen at the practice where he worked since the night of the mugging. No connection had been established between the good-looking, charismatic young man and the supermodel – but wasn't it time to consider the role of France in sheltering radicals from all corners of the world? In Stockholm, Dyani instructed Riitho to sit tight and ride it out.

At the end of the week, almost simultaneously, two major stories broke. One, coming initially from Reuters but picked up immediately by press agencies around the world, confirmed the news that everyone had been waiting for: a deal had been struck between de Klerk, Mandela and Modise. The impasse had been broken: the world's longest-serving political prisoners were to be freed. A formal announcement would be made the next day in the South African Parliament. For the first time in almost thirty years, their pictures and words could appear in newspapers and on television screens around the world. It was an incredible moment.

The second occurred in Paris. The prime suspect in the de

Zoete kidnapping case – which was what it had now become – Justin Groenewald, had made a statement. Riitho Modise's personal bodyguards were among those who had shot and killed three of the APO men. Yes, he could confirm the relationship between the girl they had taken and Livingstone Modise's son. His organisation had been watching them for months.

Groenewald's announcement dominated the headlines for the rest of that week. Rianne de Zoete. Riitho Modise. Their photographs were on the cover of almost every newspaper or magazine. That there appeared to be no pictures of them together, save a shot that showed them walking out of a hotel in mid-town Manhattan taken some years earlier, added to the drama and sense of intrigue. *How* had they kept it secret?

In London, Nathalie and Charmaine stared at the *Evening Standard* in disbelief.

In Johannesburg, Lisette de Zoete-Koestler put down the *Evening Star* and thought she was going to be sick.

From Victor Verster prison in the Cape, Livingstone Modise rang his son. Riitho took the call, blood rushing to his temples at the sound of his father's voice. Modise had asked de Klerk not to release them immediately but in a week's time. Both he and Mandela needed time to prepare their families and their organisations for their release. De Klerk had reluctantly agreed. Riitho was to fly back to South Africa with his sister for the first time in over twenty years. De Zoete's daughter would go to Oslo the following morning. The Movement would take care of it from there. It was the only time his father referred to Rianne in their twenty-minute conversation. De Zoete's daughter. When Riitho put the phone down, he knew what had happened. Their fathers had come to claim them both.

61

Rianne walked down Frognerveien, a long, winding street in one of the most fashionable parts of Oslo. The streets were still covered with snow, the blackened bark of the birches silhouetted against the bleached landscape. She pulled a map out of her pocket. Tidemansgate. Eckerbergsgate. There it was.

She turned up the small street. The houses were large, almost stately, with beautiful gardens, old stone walls and snow-covered trees. She dug her hands into her pockets and continued walking. Number thirty-five. It was an elegant old townhouse, white, with painted grey shutters and gabled slate roof. She paused outside the gate, for a moment, as though she were considering whether to turn and run. She blew her nose, squared her shoulders, and pushed the gate open. She walked up the garden path to the front door.

It opened before she reached it. Her heart was thumping – she could feel and hear it in her head. As she walked into the hallway, she felt a tremendous sweep of expectation, exhilaration. As she often did when faced with something so *huge* she could scarcely believe it, she felt herself slipping away to watch herself, as if from far away. The words circled in her mind. Her father was alive. It had been over a week since Riitho had told her and she still couldn't believe it. Her heart was in her throat as she turned to the two heavily armed Norwegians who were guarding the entrance.

'Miss de Zoete? He'll be down in a minute,' one said, hoisting his gun onto his shoulder.

Rianne tried to recall her father's face. It came back to her in snatches – Marius seen through the eyes of a six-year-old, an eight-year-old. She remembered the smell of him, yes . . . the prickle of his stubble as he bent to kiss her goodnight. He was hard to recall: she'd lived for so long without memories, pushing them away, that all she could summon now, when it mattered so much, was a *feeling*, not a memory exactly – the sense of him, not the detail.

Her pulse was racing. He would be in front of her any minute now. What would she say? How should she *be*? But it all happened so quickly.

Someone cleared his throat above her. She looked up at the landing on the first floor. A man was slowly descending the sweep of the staircase. Tall, much thinner than she remembered – a shock of almost white hair falling over his face. He reached the bottom and walked towards her. They stared at each other.

'Papa.' Rianne's voice caught in her throat.

'Rianne.' He clasped her forearm. A clasp, not a caress.

62

History in the making. After more than three hundred years minority white rule in South Africa was coming to an end. True to his word at the bargaining table, de Klerk began the systematic dismantling of many of the apartheid laws – the Group Area Act, which had confined people to different areas, both urban and rural, according to race, the segregated public spaces, amenities, beaches, buses. People of all races were now free to use the same restaurants, libraries, public transport, and the restrictions on political gatherings were eased. In one swoop at the dramatic opening speech in Parliament, he lifted the bans on all thirty-odd political parties in South Africa, including the South African Communist Party, Mandela's ANC and Modise's APP. Political prisoners across the country were freed and the State of Emergency that had been in force for almost two years was partially lifted. The world's press descended on the small town of Paarl, the site of the prison from which the two men were scheduled to walk the next day.

For Riitho, sitting in the first-class lounge at Heathrow waiting for the girl – woman – who was his sister to join them on the London–Cape Town leg of their journey home, it was a strange and emotional time. It seemed everybody wanted their little piece of the world's most famous political family. That they were strikingly good-looking, intelligent and articulate people in their own right only served to feed the frenzy. He waited with George and Chinbe, the new bodyguards, his stomach churning as they waited for Mpho and her own bodyguards to arrive. He hadn't seen her in almost twenty years – a single, brief meeting, when he was eight and she twelve, on her way to the US. Theirs was not a close relationship – in fact, it was barely a relationship at all. Too much time had passed, the distances between them were too great. She too had left their home and everything they'd ever known to cross the continent at night and emerge into the cold light of northern Europe a week later. Where Riitho had gone to Geneva with Jo Kotane and his wife, both members of the APP's inner circle in exile, Mpho had gone to Norway, to suburban Oslo and the home of Toril and Per Sommer, who had known Modise and his wife, Njeri, when Toril had worked for the Red Cross in South Africa and who had offered to take the children, should it ever come to that. The placement had not been successful: for Mpho, already traumatised by the loss of her family, the all-white, strange environment had been too much. Riitho had been too young to understand what had happened. Apart from that one, awkward meeting between them, they did not contact each other.

Now, as Mpho and her bodyguards followed the BA ground crew member who led them the back way across the terminal to avoid photographers, the tall, strong and handsome young woman, with the fantastic dreadlocks and the cocky attitude of a young Ali, was thinking only of two things: the journey ahead and how she would like to strangle her brother.

Home. She had no idea how she felt about it. Her life was complete in the US. She had a beautiful apartment in downtown Boston, an on-off boyfriend, two cats and a goldfish, her work and her three girlfriends. She had great prospects as a junior professor at Harvard. What was she giving up to go 'home'? She had no idea how long she would be there. No one had said. And what did she know about South Africa? Her father had long since ceased to be the warm, sometimes funny man who came into her room late at night, smelling faintly of cigarette smoke and always, always preoccupied. He had become an image, a father in name only. Almost as soon as he was arrested for the third and last time, he was gone. He belonged then, as he did now, to the Cause, not to her and Riitho.

She was happy he was out of jail, of course. But no one knew of the guilt she had carried with her: everywhere, at all times . . . it was her shadow. How could she enjoy life with him locked away? How could she laugh, swim, read, travel when he could not? When his first phone call came she had stood in the kitchen in her underwear, in tears. She was ecstatic. But she was angry too. No one had asked them how they felt about leaving, or whether they wanted to go. There hadn't been time to say goodbye to the twins, or even their mother. They had been bundled into the back seat of a car . . . a last, desperate wave, and they were gone. They took nothing with them. Nothing at all. Everything simply disappeared. A week after they had arrived in Europe, Riitho had disappeared too and, with him, Mpho's last link with her past. After that, everything she'd done she'd done alone.

She thought for a moment about Riitho. She was angry with him. Oh, she was angry. She was furious at the stories that had dominated the headlines in the US for the past week. 'The New South Africa'. 'Faces of the Future'. 'The

Rainbow Nation'. How *could* he? With *Rianne de Zoete*? That silly little slut? While Mpho had learned to hide her feelings about most white people under a reasonably pleasant façade, that was a line she would never cross.

'Right,' the BA woman said, on reaching a set of double doors. 'You go in through there and I'll go round the side to distract them. You'll have to make a run for it. There's a couple of metres before you reach the first-class doors. Good luck,' she said briskly and watched Mpho and the two men exit through the door. As she pushed her way through the other door, the sound of clicking cameras and shouts from the press hacks assaulted her like the sound of stampeding beasts. Out of the corner of her eye she could see the door close behind them. She turned to face the disappointed press.

Mpho marched through the first-class lounge as if she owned it. People turned to look at her but she paused for no one. There he was. His face was already familiar to her from the newspapers of the previous week. Even the *People* magazine she'd picked up in-flight had had their faces on the cover. He was frowning at her, pointing at his watch. She couldn't believe it. After twenty years, he was scolding her for being late! Jerry, her bodyguard, recognised the familiar tightening of her mouth and laid a restraining hand on her arm. The ground staff, relieved she'd made it in time, hurried brother and sister through another set of back doors. They were delivered directly to the plane. A few disgruntled hacks using ridiculously long lenses, captured them disappearing into the first-class cabin. Within hours, newspapers around the world were receiving the first prints. It didn't look as though Rianne de Zoete was with him. So where was she?

63

The crowds at Cape Town International Airport were not there to see Riitho or Mpho Modise, specifically. Few, if any, knew they were on the arriving BA flight. The crowds were there to meet everyone and anyone. Planeloads of returning exiles had been arriving at the country's three main airports for weeks now, and the crowds gathering to greet the returnees grew larger. Many of those who made the trek to the airport each day did not know anyone among the returning faces – it was enough to be there, to show one's support for the Movement and the unstoppable changes it had wrought. Each new flight brought with it the same desperately expectant faces as they emerged from the depths of the arrivals hall into the full glare of the waiting masses. There were screams, tears of joy, shrieks of laughter as this one or that one was recognised – Is that *you*, Johnny? Look! It's Johnny, everybody, *Johnny* – and discharged into the bear-hugs of the welcoming parties of relatives, friends, political colleagues . . . everyone, even those who had found themselves on opposite sides of the political divide. It was euphoric.

For Riitho and Mpho, met at the aircraft by a sleek black Mercedes and powered away immediately from the thronging crowds, theirs was not the shrieking embrace that signalled the arrival home; they were whisked through the night to Bishopsgate, one of the affluent white suburbs of the city where Njeri and the two youngest children had been staying for the past week. Riitho and Mpho had hardly spoken on the flight. Mpho was still too angry at what she considered to be a betrayal of the worst kind. How he could have slunk around the globe with that white bitch, knowing who she was and what she stood for, when their father was in jail as a result of their greed and support for the regime that had kept him there – it was beyond her. What was he thinking?

To Riitho, listening with half an ear to her thinly disguised contempt with barely suppressed anger on his part, she had it all wrong. His tough-talking, brash sister, with those ridiculous dreadlocks – she understood nothing. Despite her impressive academic credentials, her grasp of the complexities of the situation was weak. Very weak. He noticed the bodyguards exchanging glances. He caught the murmur – they were behaving like spoilt children . . . spoilt *white* children. The irony wasn't lost on him.

They swept into the driveway at the home of the archbishop to whom the Modise family had been entrusted and where they would spend the night before going to the jail next morning. It was a beautiful, spacious house, nestling in the purple shade of an enormous lilac jacaranda tree. Outside the gates, a number of policemen kept the press photographers at bay. There was the blinding light of a dozen flashbulbs as the gates opened and the car swept through. Riitho and Mpho sat impassively, each trying not to think about the moment when they and Njeri, whom they could no longer accurately remember, would meet. The car drew up beside an elegant veranda with two stone lions on either side of the wide, sweeping steps. The garden – although it was too dark to see it properly – fell away from them to the left of the car. Riitho could smell the evening scent of orange trees and something else . . . something sweet and fragrant . . . frangipani? It was unfamiliar – those were not the childhood scents of Soweto.

And then there was a shriek from inside the house and, before either of them could react, Njeri Modise ran full tilt down the steps to her children, clasping each one possessively to her in turn. The bodyguards looked away discreetly. Lebohang felt an unusual moistness behind his own eyes. He would have to wait until the morning, until they were driven to Soweto to see Mpho and Riitho's *gogo*, their grandmother, before he would see his own wife and children.

There was complete silence: even the noise of the crickets

had faded into the darkness. Held tightly by Njeri, Riitho and Mpho climbed the steps and went into the house.

In London, Gabby was glued to the television. The day everyone had been waiting for – the release of the world's most famous political prisoners – had arrived. The news crews had begun the coverage at dawn. The two men were to walk out of Victor Verster prison on the outskirts of Paarl in the Western Cape – together. The press – domestic and international – were besides themselves in a frenzy to get the best stories, the best photos, the best details. Nothing was too trivial or intimate to be reported. In the week prior to the release, the eyes of the world were permanently trained on this pretty, if unremarkable, spot.

'Thank God for the BBC,' Gabby murmured to Nathalie, grinning at Nael as they sat in Nathalie's flat in London watching the news. She looked at him and smiled. He was now one of the BBC's war correspondents, flying from one disaster zone to another. Hardly a week went by without his face appearing on television. His contacts – both his and those provided by his mother – his instinct for going after the truth until he felt he'd uncovered it and his photogenic looks had made his rise from relatively unknown print journalist to successful reporter one of the most rapid in recent years. Nael's voice – his calm, measured *English* voice – describing events, talking to people . . . ordinary people, just like those you'd meet in Cheltenham or Nottingham, going about their daily business . . . a trip to the shops, stopping at the hairdressers . . . taking the kids to school. With his unusual name . . . the way he slipped into Arabic or French during interviews and refused to allow the BBC to dub him so that you saw him as both Arab *and* British, Eastern as well as Western. He had a way of making *that* context seem just like *your* context . . . and then suddenly, they weren't just 'a lost cause' – the connection had been made. Cynical, but it worked. People were suddenly a lot more willing to acknowledge the complexities of the situation than they had been before Nael Kilani-Hughes started commentating. Gabby grinned at him again. It was great to see him. He was on a week's leave and it was perfect that he was there.

She turned back to the TV. Almost everyone in London had gone Mandela–Modise mad. Trafalgar Square, which had been home to the longest-running anti-apartheid demonstration, was transformed into a gigantic street party. From Oxford Circus to the Embankment, little black, green, gold flags were fluttering in the weak sunshine and thousands of people had descended on South Africa House. For so long it had been the symbol to the British nation of South Africa's long and dirty war. Today, it was the site of celebrations.

To Micha, now beginning to take his first, tottering steps, the early morning celebrations in his house were pure bliss. He was passed around from adult to adult – it was impossible to take hold of his sturdy, chubby little body without squeezing him and planting kisses on his fat little cheeks. As long as his mother was within eyeshot, he was ecstatic. Nathalie looked at him, sighing half in despair. After the morning's excitement, she would never get him off to sleep.

'Coffee anyone?' It was Nael. *Na'el*. Nathalie and Charmaine were unable to deal with *that* change – they continued to pronounce it the way they always had.

Nathalie looked up at him. She was also really pleased he was here with them. Although he and Gabby had been in touch since they'd all left Malvern, she and Charmaine hadn't seen him for ages. And he was now on TV! It was like having a celebrity in the house. She'd had to yank Charmaine aside and tell her to stop gaping at him – at least when Gabby was around. Even if the others couldn't see it, Nathalie could tell that Gabby had feelings for him. It was written all over her face. And who wouldn't? Not only was he divine-looking – his curly hair had grown long now and he wore it pulled back into a pony-tail – he was so *nice*. Every time you passed him you had to control the urge to pull his hair out of its band and— She stopped suddenly. That was *quite* enough. She'd been berating Charmaine all morning for staring at him.

She wondered why Nael and Gabby hadn't hit it off in that way. Gabby looked fantastic these days. It was almost impossible to recognise in her the overweight, ungainly girl she'd been at St Anne's: she was elegant and sophisticated, yet underneath she was the same kind, caring Gabby she'd always been. Of them all, she led the most interesting life, no doubt about it. She was always being sent to exotic and dangerous locations around the world, laptop and briefing notes in hand. She was on first-name terms with half-a-dozen government ministers and at least as many heads of state. Much more interesting than *my* life, Nathalie thought, with a wry smile. Not that she'd change it for the world. She looked at her son who was trying to walk over Charmaine's face and thought her heart would burst.

Just then, Gabby gave a shout from the other end of the room where she sat transfixed.

'Come on! They're coming out! Look!'

Everyone scrambled over, including Micha. He was put out that the focus of attention had suddenly shifted away from him.

'God, what a crowd,' Charmaine said, looking at the sea of faces that lined the streets of Paarl. Somewhere, buried in the crowds, was Riitho. Nael and Gabby lay on their stomachs on the floor in front of the TV, their legs waving together as the excitement levels, palpable even at this distance, mounted. It was two o'clock in London, three in South Africa. The moment when the two men would walk out of the prison gates after twenty-seven years – in the case of Mandela; Modise had followed him onto Robben Island four years later – was fast approaching. Yet nothing appeared to be happening behind the prison gates.

'Weird place to have a prison,' Charmaine remarked, flopping onto the sofa. 'Looks more like someone's country home.'

'It's an open—'

'It's a model—' Gabby and Nael spoke at once. They looked at each other and laughed. Nael deferred to Gabby – southern Africa was her province, after all.

Gabby explained that Victor Verster was an open prison, a half-way stage between jail and freedom, chosen so that the negotiations and discussions between Mandela, Modise and the government could be held in privacy and comfort. Nathalie and Charmaine listened, impressed. Everyone turned back to the TV.

Nael nudged Gabby with his foot. Nicely done, he mouthed. She blushed, looking intently at the screen. The scene had shifted to Cape Town where several hundred thousand supporters were waiting at the Grand Parade. The quiet, murmuring voice of the BBC commentator made some inane comment about the face of the new South Africa – *Modise's son, the well-known architect . . . and although she was absent from the celebrations, his partner . . . the glamorous South African supermodel, Rianne de Zoete . . . recent revelations about the nature of her father's involvement in the independence struggle . . . a fitting tribute, this relationship between the two scions of South Africa's troubled history . . . and perhaps the brightest hope for its future . . .* He droned on and on.

Gabby smiled, a private, wistful smile. She, out of all of them present, was the only one who had seen Riitho in that light. Since the kidnap attempt, which had still not been fully and publicly explained, she had a deepened respect and sympathy for Riitho and the risks he had taken in allowing – yes, that was the right word – the relationship between himself and Rianne to develop. She knew, too, that today was only the beginning. For Rianne, the return of her father and the revelation of his contributions over the past sixteen years were a mixed blessing. The distance between the public perception of the man who inspired love and hate in almost equal amounts and her need to acknowledge that her own life had been profoundly changed by his willingness to give her up, as she understood it, was enormous. And painful. It was something she would have to come to terms with. And for Riitho, grappling with a thousand emotions and the single, urgent question – *who am I?* – what Gabby would have termed an *existential* question, the realisation that his own life was no longer his own was only now beginning to come to him, slowly. The next phase of his life would indeed be different. For now he had to learn what it meant to be Modise's son.

Twelve thousand miles away, in Victor Verster prison, both men were restless. The telephone inside the cottage where Mandela had lived for the past two years rang continuously. Between the government officials, members of the ANC and APP and high-powered journalists, there was barely a second when it lay silent on the mahogany desk. Mandela's wife Winnie chatted to Njeri – their children and, in the Mandelas' case, grandchildren, were waiting at City Hall. Modise had been brought from his cottage further to the rear of the prison estate. The atmosphere was emotional. Mandela embraced his jailers. But there was no time for farewells – the crowd outside the prison gates was impatient. Helicopters carrying TV crews, journalists and photographers were circling overhead.

At a quarter to four, the men stood shoulder to shoulder with their wives and the doors of the cottage opened. The cars were waiting, with the motorcade that would escort them to the gates of the prison property. They were to stop a few hundred feet from the gate so that they could be filmed walking towards freedom.

Charmaine was still sprawled on the sofa. As pleasant as it was to look at Nael lying on the floor in front of her, she missed Simon. And she was more than a little confused.

He'd gone back to Cape Town in December, just after the news of the relationship between Rianne and Riitho had become public. He'd given her a diamond necklace when he left. He'd hidden it under the pillow, a bit cheesy, but it *was* beautiful. And expensive. She'd had it valued. But apart from that, and one phone call in the middle of January, she'd heard nothing from him. No wonder she was eyeing Nael . . . she was bored again.

Her friendship with Emily was also waning. She was tired of Emily's *faux*-sophistication, her weary seen-it-all, done-it-all cynicism. Sometimes Charmaine wondered why Emily was even in the game – she kept saying it wasn't the money, or the glamorous lifestyle, or even the men. She could walk away from it any day. So why don't you? Charmaine thought, half a dozen times a week. Plus she was high all the time. Charmaine instinctively put a hand to her nose. Thank goodness it had stopped bleeding every day. Somehow she always managed to pull herself back from the brink of *total* destruction.

Bruce walked past the news-stand on Hollywood and Devine *en route* to his ritual early morning coffee and pancakes at Denny's. He saw the picture of Rianne and Riitho in the *New York Times* and bought a copy, tucked it under his arm and half jogged down the street – it was raining and a little chilly. He found his seat by the window, ordered his breakfast from the inanely cheerful waitress and settled down.

He opened the paper. Another fantastic shot of them, and a caption: 'The New South Africa'. He closed it with a snap. He wasn't sure he could bear to read about them. It. The New South Africa. He felt a fool – Justin had played him like a puppet. In the aftermath of the bungled kidnap attempt, Bruce could only stand by and watch in horror as the plan unravelled. He'd had no idea Justin was acting on his own. All along, he'd thought he'd been playing his part in the revolution, doing his bit for the Movement, and he'd been played. Justin was languishing in some Parisian jail, three of the others were dead, the entire group discredited. Today, South Africa was taking her first step to freedom, and he was hiding out in an LA coffee shop, worrying.

Should he go to the police with what he knew, or to the Movement? On the one hand, he longed to go home and explain what he'd thought he'd been doing these past ten years or so – surely that deserved some consideration? – but on the other, he feared their reaction. How could he have been so gullible? Back home, he'd been just another white boy playing at being a revolutionary. Here, he was just another casualty of freedom. He stared out of the window at the Angelinos hurrying past, their *double-decaf-hold-the-foam-lattes* in hand. Life was so simple for them. A place in the sun that was theirs. They had no idea.

Rianne watched the celebrations on TV in the beautiful villa on Eckerbergsgate. Marius had gone out, she had no idea where. The events of the past month were too much for her to cope with – the kidnap, the rescue, the days of waiting in the apartment on Avenue Foch, and then the news that she was to go to Oslo. *She was to go.* Said who? Riitho had broken the news to her: Marius was there.

Rianne looked at him in disbelief. 'What are you talking about? My father's dead, you *know* he is.' Her voice rose.

Riitho didn't know the full story, he told her, just bits of it. Marius had been working for the APP. He'd had to fake his own disappearance. Her father and his were working on the same side. He looked at her, worried. She was shaking her head slowly, in disbelief.

'Then it's OK? About us, I mean – everything's OK?' She was hesitant. He saw with a sense of wonderment that the news of her father had been subsumed immediately by her worry over *them*, their situation. He reached out and took her hand. 'No ... Rianne, this is going to be ... complicated.'

'Why? What d'you mean? Why's it complicated?' She

recognised the hesitation in his voice. 'It's good, isn't it? That he's working with you?'

'Rianne, listen, it's not that simple. Go to Oslo. See him. I have to go home—'

'You're going without me? You're leaving me?'

'I'm not leaving you. Don't be silly. You have to see your father and I have to see mine. We'll meet in South Africa. I need time to sort this out between us.'

'Between who?'

'My family and me.' Riitho wouldn't say any more. He tried to put his arms around her.

She shook him off. 'I know what's going to happen. The minute you get back, they'll say you shouldn't have – they'll say we shouldn't—' She stared at him, daring him to tell her it wasn't so.

He held her, stroking her hair, his lips pressing against the sticking plaster on her forehead. 'No, it won't be like that. You don't know my father. It'll be fine.'

She moved into his arms, wanting to believe him, *willing* herself to believe him. She wanted him to make love to her, now – *now*. She was leaving the next morning, it might be weeks before they saw each other again. He gently removed her hand. *Sssh*. She needed to rest, not make love. She was feverish. Her forehead was damp with sweat. She began to cry. He pulled her back into his arms and did as she asked.

Afterwards she lay beside him, examining his hands, her fingers tracing the blunt ridge of his nails, holding his hand against her hot, damp face. As it always did after love-making, his body burned, heat emanating steadily from him, drawing her slowly into its warmth. She held his hand against her, and she was afraid.

She was right, she saw that now. The next morning everything happened so fast. The car came for her at eight. She was covered from almost head to toe in a long coat, scarf, sunglasses. Riitho had packed a few things for her and came over to where she was standing by the window.

'I don't want to go,' she said, close to tears again.

'Sssh.' He wrapped his arms round her from behind, resting his chin against her shoulder. In the window, she could see their reflection. She tried to catch the image, catch hold of how she saw him, looking at her, but it slipped away. She couldn't hold on to things at the moment, too much had happened. Too much was about to happen.

There was a tap at the door. Time to go. He kissed her, hard. 'Don't worry, de Zoete. I've got us covered.' Another tap at the door. The press were beginning to arrive. *Let's go.* And then she left.

They bundled her out of the house, pushing aside the reporters and photographers and running with her to the car at the kerb. The driver was skilful. Within half an hour he'd lost the few motorbikes that followed them. When she pulled up outside the terminal at Charles de Gaulle, no one recognised her. Within minutes, she was inside the departures lounge and on her way to the aircraft.

Now, watching his unbearably beautiful face on the TV screen, listening to the voice of the commentator describing her, describing *them*, she began to cry again. Mandela and Modise had finished their speeches to the thousands below them at the Grand Parade. The camera panned across the crowds and came to rest on the two women standing beside their men – Winnie Mandela and Njeri Modise. Rianne saw with a painful shock how like his mother Riitho was. Riitho stood to one side in the entrance at City Hall as, one by one, the faithful followed their leaders. His face was a public one, assumed for the thousands of reporters and cameramen who had been stalking him for the past few weeks. Rianne looked at the image, his face flattened by the pixels on the television screen and tried to grab hold of it before the camera moved away.

What was going to happen to them? She slipped from the couch and lay curled in a ball on the floor, sobbing. She was still there when Marius finally came home.

64

It was almost midnight when Nathalie closed the door on Gabby and Nael and stifled a yawn. They were going to a party somewhere in Hammersmith – some of Gabby's London contacts. Nathalie wondered where they got the energy. She slid the bolt on the door. The living room was an unholy mess but at least Gloria would be in the next day. Upstairs on the mezzanine, Micha was sleeping soundly, thank God, his little tummy filled to bursting with the last bottle that she had somehow managed to give him. Charmaine had disappeared earlier in the evening – she had a date, plans for the evening, she was vague.

Nathalie switched off the lights downstairs, quietly picking up Micha's toys and bits and pieces of clothing. She wondered what Rianne and Riitho were doing at that moment. What a life. She shook her head, smiling a little to herself. Not that she wanted it. With Micha, hers was finally complete.

Gabby and Nael flagged down a cab almost as soon as they stepped through the gate onto Fulham Road. The driver was West Indian but didn't seem to share their sense of joy at Mandela and Modise's release. No matter. They were both drunk on excitement, as well as champagne. Gabby told the driver where they wanted to go – 'Just off Hammersmith Broadway,' she said, 'as fast as you can.'

When they arrived the party was in full swing. They could hear laughter from half-way down the street. Gabby rang the doorbell and they were dragged inside to cries and cheers of welcome. They inched their way up the narrow staircase, Gabby stopping every other minute to kiss, hug or grasp someone by the arm – she seemed to know everyone. Everyone who was anyone in the anti-apartheid movement was there – campaigners from Trafalgar Square, including some who'd been camped outside South Africa

House for more than ten years, human-rights lawyers, voluntary-sector and charity workers, VSO, Amnesty International, Rights Watch. Nael recognised Marwan Ahmat and a group of others he'd met in Palestine – blacks, whites, Jews, Arabs. Everyone was there, celebrating wildly. A victory for South Africa was a victory for them all: one step closer to ending global imperial rule.

He watched Gabby disappear into the crowd of well-wishers and old colleagues, some of whom she hadn't seen since her move to New York. He looked on as they hugged and held her tight, grabbed her by the hand, kissed her. They were thrilled she was there, celebrating with them. There was no doubt about it, Gabrielle Francis was *loved*. He was oddly disturbed by the sight of so many men coming up to his Gabby and pulling her away. His Gabby . . .

He found a corner of the room and stood by, watching the celebrations around him, feeling oddly out of place. He turned to the young black man draped in ANC colours standing next to him. 'Got a cigarette, mate?' He needed one. The music was suddenly turned up, and he wandered out of the room and up the stairs. There was a small study at the top, just as noisy, but empty. He leaned against the radiator and looked down into the street. More people were arriving. He glanced at his watch. Two in the morning.

Gabby appeared in the doorway in front of him, two bottles of beer in her hands. She laughed at him above the noise – he bent forwards. What?

'Escaping?' she said, passing him a bottle.

He took a swig. Then it hit him. He loved her. He'd always loved her. She was the most brilliant person he'd ever known. She brought out the best in him – in everyone.

'Let's go,' he said, finishing his bottle.

'Now?'

'Now.' They walked down the stairs, not pausing to say goodbye, then in the direction of the Broadway, not saying anything. Nael found them a cab and they clambered in. Wilton Crescent? She nodded.

He rested his head against hers. Gabby was aware of his hand, just lying there, next to hers. His fingers brushed hers – or was it the other way around? In the darkened space of the cab, their hands lay loosely entwined, a natural extension of the excitement and pleasure the evening had brought. Gabby turned to him dreamily. Their lips met – and held.

'This it?' The cab driver turned. They broke apart, Nael swearing softly. He pushed a note into the driver's hand, opened the door. He helped Gabby out and they stood for a second in front of the door, looking at each other, not speaking. For her, the night had a surreal quality to it. The kiss – the touch? – in the taxi was simply the confirmation of something she'd always felt for Nael. From her school-girl textbook fantasies all the way through her troubled relationship with Dominic and even Giles, who had released her from the nightmare. It had always been about Nael. Always.

He watched her wriggle out of her jeans and slip off her silk blouse. She stood in front of the dressing-table mirror, clad only in her black bra and panties, her pearly white skin reflected in the dim light. He came up behind her, putting his brown arm round her waist, staring at the image of them in the mirror. He eased the bra straps off her shoulders and slid them down her arms. Gabby stood very still. With one hand, he unhooked her bra and watched her face as the bra fell away and she was almost naked in front of him. She watched as he brought the other hand up, touching first one nipple, then the other. His hand moved across her stomach, further down ... 'Nael,' she whispered, to the reflection in front of her. His hand did not stop. He stroked the slippery flesh beneath the fingers of one hand, caressed her nipples with the other. Through half-closed eyes, they watched as he brought her to one trembling climax after another.

Charmaine woke suddenly. She'd heard a noise – someone had cried out. She looked at her watch. It was nearly 10 a.m. She swung her legs out of bed, put on her slippers and opened the door. Gabby was staying at Wilton Crescent. She padded down the long corridor to the guest rooms.

'Gabs?' She pushed the door open just in time to glimpse a pair of tanned buttocks disappearing under the duvet. She stopped dead in her tracks. Gabby's scarlet face appeared over the top of the duvet. 'Oh, shit! Sorry, Gabs,' Charmaine mumbled. Backing away. She was as embarrassed as hell. *Gabby?* And who did the buttocks belong to?

'Hi, Charmaine,' Nael said drily, his face suddenly appearing beside Gabby's.

Charmaine's mouth fell open.

'Close your mouth – and the door, please,' Gabby instructed her.

Charmaine turned immediately and fled back down the corridor. Gabby turned to Nael. 'Sorry about that. She should have knocked.' Nael grinned. He didn't mind.

'No worries. She'd better get used to it. To me, I mean.' He reached for Gabby again. It was noon before they fell into a deep, exhausted sleep.

'It's *happened*,' Charmaine hissed at her down the telephone, looking over her shoulder.

'What's happened?' Nathalie asked, looking anxiously over her shoulder at Micha, sitting perilously on the second step. He looked triumphantly at his mother.

'Gabby. And Nael. Here. In *bed*.' Charmaine was at her dramatic best.

'What? Now?'

'Yes! I walked in on them this morning. Well, almost. I only saw his bum.'

'Charmaine! Oh, Micha – no, don't!' Nathalie was

distracted. 'I'll call you later!' She slammed the phone down and reached for him, catching him before he fell.

Charmaine walked into the dining room. It wasn't fair. Everyone got what they wanted, except her. First of all, Riitho and Rianne – unbelievable, they'd been sworn enemies. Then there was Nathalie and Sacha – well, he wasn't exactly *hers* but at least she had Micha. It had taken Nathalie ages to admit the truth about Micha's father but Gabby had seen Sacha once in a bar with Nathalie and had known immediately that Micha wasn't Paul's child. He was Sacha's. Nathalie had reluctantly told them the truth.

Now Gabby and Nael. Everyone had paired off neatly with everyone else. That left her. Why hadn't Simon called her? She had no way of contacting him, that was the problem. Somehow, whenever she asked, he forgot to give her a number or told her he'd contact her – better that way. He didn't want to alarm his wife unnecessarily. He was working things out, putting everything in place for when he would leave. And it would be soon, he promised. She pulled open one of the drawers in the elegant little telephone table. A black book nestled among the papers and telephone directories. She pulled it out. It was leatherbound with discreet gold-embossed lettering: *Addresses*. She opened it and flicked rapidly through the pages. Bingo! Simon Kalen. She picked up the phone and dialled.

'Hello?' A woman answered on the third ring. A polite, well-mannered voice.

'Could I speak to Simon, please?' Charmaine didn't bother to give his last name. Let him wriggle out of it.

'Can I ask who's calling?' the woman asked, her voice suddenly wary.

'Charmaine.'

There was silence for a moment. Charmaine could hear the woman breathing steadily. 'Just a minute,' she said.

Charmaine heard the phone being put down, heard the clack of heels across a floor and a door open. There was silence. A minute passed. Then another. Someone fumbled with the receiver.

'Hello?' Simon's voice was clipped.

'Where are you? Why haven't you called me?' Charmaine whined. There was a short silence.

'Fine, thanks for calling. I'll get back to you in about an hour to confirm. Thank you, Charmaine.' And the line went dead.

Charmaine stared at the receiver in her hand. Well, she'd had some sort of response. He would call back in an hour, she knew he would.

In his beautiful home in Hout Bay, Simon Kalen put down the phone. Stella had come into the living room to find him watching the reruns of yesterday's events, eating the last piece of grilled kingclip and draining his lunch-time wine. 'Phone,' she'd said curtly. 'Overseas call. Some girl called Charmaine.'

He'd stared at her, aghast, then controlled himself. Stella had no idea who Charmaine was – she could be anyone, a new secretary at Regency Wharf. The idea came to him suddenly. 'Oh, yes, that's the new girl Lisette hired. Thanks.' He got up, the hair under his arms prickling. He took the phone, and conveyed to Charmaine that he would call her back. Now he pulled on his jacket and gathered up his keys. He had to rush to the office, he called to a silent Stella. An emergency.

'Don't you *ever* call me again,' he said angrily to Charmaine, an hour later. 'Have you gone mad?'

'I missed you,' Charmaine said tearfully. 'I haven't heard from you in weeks.'

'That's not the point. You pull that number one more time and I swear I'll—' He stopped. He'd what? Tell Lisette she was turning tricks in Wilton Crescent? Charmaine would implicate him. He took a deep breath, trying to calm himself. 'All right. I should have called. I've been busy. I'm back in London in a fortnight's time, OK?' Actually, he missed her too. The prostitutes he picked up occasionally at the Waterfront had none of Charmaine's charm – or skill. 'All right?' he repeated. 'I'll see you then.'

'You all right?' Gabby had walked into the dining room. Charmaine started.

'Yeah, I'm fine.' She wiped her face.

'You sure?' Gabby asked, peering at her.

'Yeah, yeah. Sorry about this morning,' Charmaine said, changing the subject.

It worked. Gabby turned bright red. 'Oh, that . . .'

'Yeah, *that*. It's great, isn't it?'

'No, yes – it *is* great. I mean, I'm—'

'Just about the best lay I've ever had,' Nael finished the sentence for her as he walked into the room. He bent to kiss her face.

Charmaine was laughing, and clapped her hands. 'Come on, breakfast! Let's celebrate! This is brilliant! Just brilliant!' Her earlier pangs of jealousy were forgotten. Just looking at Nael's face – and Gabby's – it was brilliant. She'd never seen two people more suited to each other – and it looked like they knew it too now. 'Champagne brunch?' she asked.

65

Marius de Zoete and his daughter flew into the country a full ten days after the celebrations. Rianne sat stiffly beside him. She was still reeling from the conversation they'd had that morning as they left for the airport. She'd been so afraid of the reaction from Riitho's family she'd failed to understand what she might meet from hers, from *him*. Marius was gentle but firm. He knew how much the young man meant to her, he could see that, but the obstacles were too great. No relationship would survive under the kind of pressure they would be exposed to. He didn't want to see her get hurt.

'How can you say that?' Rianne looked at him angrily.

'Because I can. I know what it's like, *skatjie*. Trust me. That's no life for anyone.'

'I don't understand what you're talking about. What life? Riitho has his own life – he can do what he likes.'

'That's where you're wrong, Rianne. It's not his any more. His father, his people, they'll want certain . . . things from him. I'm not saying he doesn't love you, I'm sure he does. I'm sure you love him. But this is different. There will be pressures on him. I just don't want to see you hurt.'

'How can *you* say that? You don't know the first thing about him!'

'I know more than you think I do, *skatjie*. Believe me, this is a bad idea.'

'Why?' she demanded. 'You're wrong. You're completely wrong. You don't know him.' There was silence. He stared at her, a sad look in his eyes, and she turned away. He was hurting her. 'What's wrong with him? Why don't you like him?'

'It's got nothing to do with that, my darling. I do like him. Of course it's not that. I just don't want to see you get hurt. I care about you.'

'It's because he's black, isn't it?' A look of dread passed between them. 'Isn't it? Why don't you just admit it?'

'Rianne, you're being ridiculous. It's nothing to do with that. I care about you and I don't want to see you get hurt.'

'*You?* What do *you* care about me?' Marius knew what was coming. He tried to reach out and hold her, but she wrenched away her hand. 'You're just *jealous*!' she shouted. 'You're just jealous that I—'

'Rianne. Don't,' he said quietly. She stopped. They stared at each other. He spoke first. 'I know what you're thinking, that I gave up any right to tell you what to do when I left. I know that. But understand this. I know what he's going through. Don't make him choose between you. Walk away. You'll find someone else.' And with that Marius himself walked off, leaving Rianne standing in the middle of the dining room, the bodyguards in the hallway looking away as discreetly as they could.

She was floored. Her own father! How could he have said that? How could he tell her to walk away? Marius was wrong. Riitho wasn't like that, he wouldn't buckle under the pressure, no matter how great. He'd said it to her himself. *I've got us covered.* All she had to do was follow him there. And wait.

They were met at Jan Smuts by an unsmiling young black man at the aircraft door. A few people glanced curiously as they were escorted off the plane by the two young men who had sat in the row behind them, not speaking, for the duration of the flight. One or two of the businessmen had recognised him as Marius de Zoete, and the young woman as his daughter. You know, the one who . . . Newspapers rustled, a few heads turned. But the presence of the two bodyguards and the attentive flight attendants prevented any exchange, pleasant or otherwise.

A black BMW was waiting for them when they emerged from the VIP lounge. The driver took them straight to Houghton, to the home of a white lawyer whom Marius had met in the Germiston township, Katlehong, many years before. An Afrikaner, like Marius, who had 'turned'. Their sixteen-year-old daughter simply gaped at Rianne – evidently, she couldn't believe that *Rianne de Zoete* was sitting there, in *her* kitchen. Was it really true that . . . her mother frowned.

It was an emotional homecoming for Marius. He and Theo de Vries sat late into the night, talking. Rianne was exhausted. To the disappointment of both mother and daughter she excused herself as soon as she could and went to bed. She wanted to call Riitho but she had no idea where he was. Their situation had undertaken a bizarre circle:

from not being able to call or see each other for fear of being found out, to the whole world wanting to see them together, and then to being unable to see each other. She undressed slowly, thinking of the day ahead.

They would go early in the morning to Bryanston, to Lisette's. He had left a message with Poppie to let her know they were coming. Marius was taking her back there to stay, he said. It would be best for her. It wasn't clear yet what his role would be. He would be in talks with Modise and the government over the next few months. He didn't even know if he'd be in the country. She couldn't stay with him. He would take her back to Lisette, just for now. She would have to make up her own mind about what she wanted to do. She was a grown woman, now.

She was dreading seeing Lisette and her cousins again. She and Riitho had been living in a kind of cocoon, she realised with a shock. They'd been together for four years and the only person other than themselves whom they'd had to deal with was Gabby. Lebohang was different. They'd been so blind: the strength of opposition had caught her unawares. She was afraid and not only because she feared her cousins' reaction. If she wasn't with him, who was she? Her father's voice broke in on her thoughts. She jumped. 'What?'

'Nervous?' he repeated.

She shook her head. Liar. Of course she was nervous. She looked straight ahead. Perhaps it wouldn't be as bad as she feared. Marius was with her. She'd changed. The whole country had changed. Perhaps even *they* might have changed.

They had not.

Poppie opened the door to them, her face streaked with tears. She fell upon Rianne, hugging her and crying. Rianne hugged her back, seized with an urge to tell Poppie how she'd changed, tell her about Riitho and what he meant. But Poppie turned to Marius. They embraced, the tall man bending down to hug the woman. Rianne noticed, with a shock, the grey hairs at Poppie's temples, covered only partially by her *doek*.

Poppie led them through to the living room where the remaining members of the de Zoete family were seated – Lisette, Hennie, Marika. A young man hovered in the next room. From the glances Marika gave him, Rianne understood him to be hers. She turned to face her family. The anger in Lisette's face was palpable – she could have touched it. As was the hatred in Hennie's. It was only Marika, sitting to one side, who seemed pleased to see her, even if she did look on the verge of tears.

The air was thick with tension. Hennie looked contemptuously at Rianne and Marius, his handsome face now twisted with rage. There was silence. Rianne held her father's hand. The gentle pressure of his fingers guarded her against bursting into tears.

'So . . . you're back.' Lisette spoke first. She glanced at Marius, then Rianne. 'And I suppose you're looking for a family reunion.' She reached for a cigarette.

Marius looked at her a little sadly. 'I'm not looking for anything, Lisette. I brought Rianne home.'

'This is not her home.' Hennie spoke quietly. His light blue eyes flicked over her insolently. '*Geen kaffir-boeties hier.*' No nigger-lovers here.

'Hennie!' Marika gasped.

Rianne looked straight at him, her eyes glistening with anger. She opened her mouth but Marius spoke first.

'You have no right,' he said slowly, deliberately, 'no right to judge her. None at all.'

Lisette stood up suddenly, a cigarette in her trembling hand. She jabbed at the air. 'He has every right,' she said, her voice rising. 'More right than you, Marius. You have no rights at all. None, d'you hear me? *Hoekom*, Marius? *Ek kan nie verstaan nie. Hoekom?*' Why, Marius? I don't understand it. Why? She sounded close to tears.

'I don't expect you to understand, Lisette. We've always followed different paths.' Marius did not answer her in

Afrikaans. He wouldn't be drawn. 'I didn't come here to discuss those, or to talk about the differences between us. They are clear enough, don't you think? No, I brought my daughter home to see you, as a sign of respect—'

'Respect?' Hennie broke in. 'If you had any respect you'd hide, you nigger-loving thief. Go back to where you came from. You're not wanted here. *Voetsek*.'

Voetsek. It was what you'd say to a stray dog. Fuck off, get lost.

'Hennie!' Marika jumped to her feet. 'Don't say such things. It isn't true.'

'Ah, but it is.' Marius turned to his niece. A strange smile played around his lips.

Rianne looked at him. She was so proud of him. She thought her heart would burst. Hennie's face was purple, his fists clenched. She had never seen such hatred. It was he who had lost his dignity and self-respect, not Marius.

'Then get out. You have no shame, Marius, none – either of you.' Lisette turned to her niece. 'If you have no love for your family, or your country, get out.' Lisette's face was white. 'Leave this house!'

'No, Lisette.' Marius's voice was firm. 'You misunderstand. On the contrary, I am ashamed. But of you, not of myself or Rianne. I would be ashamed of myself only if I had done what you do, which is nothing. It's what you've always done, what you will continue to do, regardless. I would be guilty of *not* loving my family – or my country – if I had continued *to do nothing*. Do you understand that? I will not do *nothing*.'

Lisette stood stock still. It was as if she couldn't hear him, could not understand the language in which he had spoken. They stared at each other, brother and sister, the same flesh and blood . . . the old order against the new.

'Get out of my house, Marius,' she said slowly, clearly. 'Get *out*. You are dead to me. *Dead*.' Marika started crying again. Marius made to touch Lisette, a gentle, almost languid touch. She recoiled.

Rianne looked away. It was the same gesture she had made, ten years earlier, when a man she had no reason to fear or despise had reached out to touch her. She moved towards Marius. If he was going, so was she. He shook his head. This was her home. She was to stay here. Where he was headed there was no place for a beautiful, spoilt daughter, no matter who she'd fallen for. He walked out without looking back.

66

Riitho came downstairs early, before anyone else was up. Or so he thought. He'd slept badly. The noise surrounding the house in Houghton was almost as bad as it had been in Cape Town, that first night after his father's release. Outside, he knew, there were dozens of reporters from all round the world wanting not only to photograph Livingstone, but him as well, possibly even Rianne de Zoete. Although she wasn't there.

Since he'd been back, no one apart from Mpho had mentioned her. It was a far cry from the scenario they'd both left behind. Then, the coverage of their relationship had competed with the news of the impending release. In some of the tabloids, Mandela and Modise had taken a back seat to the glamorous couple the world couldn't get enough of. Rich, beautiful, famous . . . a whiff of political intrigue . . . a kidnap and a shadowy rescue . . . he was black, she was white . . . The story had all the right ingredients. It was turning into a soap opera. He was sick of it.

But, in a curious way, the silence surrounding her was a blessing. It gave him the time he desperately needed to think. The change in his life since his father's release could not have been more dramatic – or sudden. A plunge from one kind of existence, lived partially in shadow, to another, played out in the full public glare. He was used to media interest, nothing new there, but this was intense. And while the public appetite for news of her continued to mount, the silence inside his family grew correspondingly louder. He knew her father was back – he'd heard his name in passing, the day before. But nothing about her. She had disappeared, along with his old way of life, and there was no one who he could ask.

He barely saw his father. Since their arrival at the house in Houghton a week before he'd seen him twice, maybe three times. Njeri was always there – she kept the four children to her, jealously possessive. But Riitho was awkward even with her. It would have seemed . . . he didn't know . . . inappropriate?

He pushed open the door to the dining room and rolled his eyes. Mpho sat alone, reading the morning papers, a cup of coffee at her side. She looked up as he entered. There was a short, embarrassed silence. He caught a glimpse of the cover story. There it was again. The same damn picture of them coming out of the Sanderson Hotel in Manhattan. They weren't even holding hands. Mpho turned over the paper deliberately slowly. Contempt was written all over her face. He felt anger rise in him, spreading like a stain across his face. Her bangles clacked as she raised the mug to her lips. 'Sleep well?' she murmured.

'Fine,' he said shortly.

He was about to say something about the article, bring her name up, when the kitchen door opened and Njeri came in, smiling at them. 'Something to eat?' she asked Riitho, hugging him to her.

He was uncomfortable. It wasn't easy, going from nothing to this. He'd lived alone for more than twenty years. The idea of a mother – or a father – was not only alien to him, it was painful. Unlike a few of the boys back in Malvern, say, who'd lost one parent, or maybe even both, Riitho hadn't *lost* his: they were still alive, his father in jail, his mother under house arrest. Over there. What he'd lost was the memory of them, the tactile sense of what his mother felt and smelled like. Although Njeri had dutifully written to them both over all those years in exile, and included photographs of their younger brother and sister, the letters had meant little to him – no way to connect the wooden, politely smiling faces in the photograph to any memory . . . of anything. Hugging her now was like hugging a stranger. Mother. Father. Sister. Brother. In the bodily sense of the word, he had nothing to hold on to.

'No, I'm OK,' he said stiffly. He didn't care for the mealie-pap that she'd prepared each morning since they'd arrived.

'What's the matter?' Mpho asked. 'Pap not good enough for you? Oh, I forgot – you probably don't eat breakfast. They don't, do they? The models and tramps you hang out with.'

'Mpho!' Njeri said sharply. 'That's enough.' She had sensed immediately the tension between them, even on the first day. She sighed. She was worried about Riitho. She and Livingstone hadn't had time to talk about it, about this girl, de Zoete . . . Of course she'd seen the papers, and she knew who the family was. Mpho had told her she was a model, something like that. Someone who made a lot of money doing very little. What did someone like her need with more money? She wasn't even beautiful – all that tangled hair and showing off her body like that. Mpho hadn't said it outright but, those girls, what kind of life did they lead? And what did she want with her son? He wasn't just anyone, you know. He wasn't someone to be grateful because you, a pretty little white girl, suddenly discovered that . . . well, she didn't want to think about that, actually.

But the fact that Riitho seemed to want *her* worried Njeri. She knew he thought about her – she could see it in his eyes, the way he stared into space, or the way he jumped ever so slightly when the telephone rang. She hadn't had time or the opportunity to talk seriously about it with

Livingstone but they would have to, soon. They had other plans for Riitho. Plans that did not include a white girl with no qualities to speak of – it didn't matter what her father had done for the Movement.

There was a struggle going on between Riitho and Mpho, Njeri realised. They'd only been together a week and already they looked as though they'd like to strangle each other at times. They were strangers. They even spoke differently, Mpho, with her hip, black American slang and Riitho with those . . . how did the press call it? Plums? In his mouth. Njeri had never been to Britain or the United States. She could only imagine where her children had been almost all their lives from the TV or the few films she'd seen. Britain, with its rain and red buses and gentlemen in bowler hats – she couldn't picture Riitho there. He'd sent a few pictures, of course, in the beginning. And Lebohang had kept the family up to date. But she could see nothing in the quiet face of the little boy in the cap and shorts, his knees pressed together neatly, that meant anything to her. Later, as the years passed, she looked at the latest picture – the handsome, tightly controlled face that stared out in front of Big Ben or the Eiffel Tower – and was distressed. He looked lost, his eyes vacant. It was not possible to know what he was thinking, ever.

A week passed, and then another. Riitho, accompanying his father as he flew around the country, felt himself sinking under the combined weight of his parents' expectations – and, through them, the Party's.

One evening, almost a month after they'd been back, Livingstone called them into the study. Just the three of them – Njeri, Riitho, Mpho – no bodyguards, not even Lebohang. The twins were with relatives in Durban. He closed the door and walked across the room slowly, his hands clasped behind his back. He waited until they were all seated. Then he began to speak. When he had finished, there was silence. Livingstone cleared his throat.

'It's the right thing to do, Papa,' Mpho said.

Riitho looked at her thoughtfully. He wasn't so sure. For the two parties to merge was one thing. For the new party to retain the ANC name was another thing altogether. As Livingstone explained it, no matter how integrated the senior executive, the fact that the APP was about to give up its identity to be subsumed into the larger organisation might be perceived as a sell-out, a capitulation – maybe even a betrayal. Logic was one thing, political affiliation another altogether.

'The rank and file members,' Riitho said, 'how will they see it?'

Livingstone nodded approvingly. His daughter was quick to approve, quick to take offence, like her mother. Riitho was slower, more analytical. He took his time, weighed the options, seldom thought aloud. People mistook the silence for reticence, lack of interest. They thought him arrogant and unconcerned. Sometimes they read it as strength. Although he hardly knew the young man sitting next to him, in another sense he knew him well. He was like himself. A cliché, but true. He considered the question. 'It's a risk. The junior cadres, they may not come with me. With us.'

'And if they don't?' Njeri and Mpho spoke at once.

'Well, the Party will split. We've discussed this. It's a risk but we think it's worth taking. We have to put the country's needs before the Party's pride.'

'It's expedient.' Riitho looked at his father. Both men nodded. Expedient, yes. A betrayal . . . maybe. A risk, certainly. But it was expedient. Mandela needed Modise, just as Modise needed him. At the upcoming NEC meeting in Lusaka, the heads of both parties would announce the merger. After nearly sixty years, the ANC and APP would put aside their differences and come together as one. Mandela would take over the presidency from the ailing Oliver Tambo, Modise would act as his deputy. With the combined weight of the two largest black political parties in the country, the National Party would not have a hope of winning the vote at the election everyone knew was coming. The timing was right. They would not get a second chance.

Outside the tight inner circle of APP leaders, no one knew, least of all de Klerk, of the political bombshell that they were about to drop. It was the most dangerous moment of Modise's political career. But, as his son had articulated, it was expedient. That was what mattered.

Livingstone took Njeri's hand. It was an unusual gesture. A public display of affection between them was not their way. The merging of the two parties would be announced in a week's time at the ANC national executive committee meeting in Lusaka. Riitho was to accompany his father. Mpho would remain with Njeri. There was much to be done.

Riitho walked upstairs slowly to the room he'd chosen on the third floor of the enormous house. It had previously been the lawyer's study, tucked under the eaves of the colonial-style house. It was ironic, he thought, as he pushed open the door and surveyed the quiet, airy room with something akin to pleasure, that the imperial architectural ideology was now occupied by those it had sought to exclude.

Thinking about it he experienced a sudden wave of longing – and loss. Would he ever go back? To Paris and the life he had so carefully constructed for himself? Architecture, for him, had been no accident. It wasn't only the physical edifice he was building . . . it was a place, not for his clients, but for himself. Every idea that became a sketch then a drawing, then eventually a building was, for him, a way of realising a future over which he had no control. His profession was a way of recuperating that control. He had told Rianne as much. Things happen *to* me. He thought about her. It had been a month since he'd seen or spoken to her. She was out there somewhere and she was silent. He was having difficulty believing she'd ever existed.

He walked over to the bed and lay down, his hands behind his head, staring up through the skylight at the brilliant blue Transvaal sky above him. His mind drifted back to the conversation in the study, their father's announcement. He and Mandela would join forces. Mandela as president, Modise as his deputy. Then the ANC was assured a victory at the polls. It was a smart and politically expedient thing to do. In saying that, Riitho had unconsciously given his father the blessing he sought. And it hadn't been a surprise: he had thought it would happen. The only issue had been one of timing.

The questions flowed through his mind, thick and fast. What did it mean for them? How would their lives change? He was to accompany Livingstone to Lusaka. Why? For what? He would become the son of the vice-president of South Africa. It was a role he had never thought about. His identity, as a man, as a person, was so intimately tied up with being the son of one of the world's most famous prisoners. It was the mark of distinction, the thing that people whispered about when he walked into a room, the thing on everyone's lips, even if it remained unsaid. It was who he *was*. Who would he be now? What would it be like as the son of someone who led the country? Could he go back to his old life? And, the biggest question of all, Rianne.

She seemed so far away from him now. He recognised the tactics: the family were slowly silencing her. No one mentioned her. Inside the circles in which he now moved, she had ceased to exist. It was understood that whatever indiscretions had taken place outside, now that he'd come home there were different, more urgent issues to consider. Like who *he* was. Who *she* was. As far as everyone else was concerned, who they had been, for each other, all those years . . . that simply melted, vanished. It was, as Lebohang said – all in the past. Finished. He turned over onto his stomach, his face pressed against the pillow. The realisation that he was, now, *in reality*, the thing he had never been – his father's son – was only just beginning to come to him, slowly. He closed his eyes and tried to picture her. What was happening to her? Was it the same with her people? Would he ever see her again? The worst thing was, he wasn't sure he wanted to. His life had experienced a rupture, entered a new cycle, one for which he felt he had been preparing all his life. Rianne seemed now to belong to the old life, which was slowly but irrevocably slipping away. To go to her now, to bring her into his new self – he didn't know if he should, or could.

Alone in the living room in Bryanston, Rianne again watched the news on TV. Marius had disappeared, and she had no idea what to do next. She did not know how to contact Riitho and, worse than that, was afraid he wouldn't want her to anyway. It was as if everything between them had faded to nothing. She'd been afraid of this. In Paris, as he tried to calm her fears, she'd been so afraid. He was now with his people, and she ought to be with hers. No matter what he had said, no matter how often he had reassured her, she had known that he, too, was changing . . . and that the changes would not include her.

She didn't know how she was going to cope. For the first time in her life, she wanted someone so badly she thought she would die. Panic, fear and loss rose in her and she felt as though she were drowning. She could go back to London or New York – but should she? Was that what he wanted? Did he mean her to disappear from his life? And if he did want that, why didn't he have the guts to tell her? Why was he torturing her like this? She began to cry, tears rolling silently down her cheeks. Poppie walked by and shook her head slowly, sadly.

Rianne watched the press conference with the sound on mute. There was Mandela, with Modise next to him. The camera panned round the room. There were several

Africans in military uniform, important-looking people. She reached for the remote control. The commentator murmured their names ... Mugabe, Kaunda, Masire ... Livingstone Modise ... Riitho Modise. She sat bolt upright. He was *there*! The camera landed on him for a second, then moved away. She sat staring at the screen. He was in Lusaka? Where the hell was that?

Twenty minutes later she had her answer. The delegation were staying at the Congress Carlton, in downtown Lusaka, Zambia. Thank God for Gabby. She hadn't minded being woken in the middle of the night. She called the hotel and left a message for Riitho Modise. The receptionist would see that he got it. She sat at home all day, sure that at any moment the phone would ring and it would be him. She lay on the sofa and thought about him, the sound of his voice, his calm, steady presence.

The atmosphere in the house was tense. Lisette was away often, on business. Hennie was hardly ever there. He did something important in the army, according to Poppie. From the sneer on his face every time Rianne encountered him, it was clear what he thought of her. But all she cared about was hearing from Riitho. As the days became weeks, she escaped to her room at every opportunity. Why didn't he call? It was worse than it had been in the beginning. She felt him all around her, everywhere she turned. It was the last thing she thought of before she went to sleep and the first thing that came to her when she awoke. Call. *Please* call.

From Lusaka, Riitho went with them to Dar es Salaam. An estimated half a million people met them in the streets of the Tanzanian capital. Nyerere, his father's political mentor, embraced each member of the delegation, including Riitho. He had taken on an unofficial presence at the talks, standing next to Livingstone, a good head taller than his father, his quiet, thoughtful presence a constant reminder of just how far the organisations had come – look at their children. The world they would inherit was a far cry from the one they had pledged to destroy.

But some among the delegates looked at Riitho suspiciously, too. Could he be trusted? Look at that business with the de Zoete girl. The whole affair could have cost them dearly. Never mind what her father had done, *she* was Lisette de Zoete-Koestler's niece. Even if she *was* good-looking. Some of the older men, remembering what the long, lonely years of exile had been like ... perhaps something deeper, a buried memory of the comfort they might have found, out there in some of the coldest cities of the world ... they shook their heads, almost fondly. 'Leave him alone,' they murmured. 'It's over now. Finished. He's back, helping out in whatever way he can. He's paid the price of exile many times over. A credit to his father. And to his people.'

To Riitho, listening with half an ear to the snatches of conversation, the weeks passed in a blur. From Dar they flew across the country, bearing south-west towards Namibia. Riitho looked out of the window of the private 747 loaned to them by Kenneth Kaunda, the Zambian president, and watched his country unfold, mile after mile. The pilot, the first black commercial pilot any of the men had ever seen, pointed out the landmarks as they flew. They fell silent as they looked on the territory they had spent years preparing soldiers to infiltrate, many of them from maps only with no real memory of the terrain – they had been in exile too long. Now they looked on it for real. They headed across the northern tip of the country, across Pietersburg in the northern Transvaal, across the southern tip of Botswana, Gaborone, the capital and then across the desert, the Kalahari. They could see the national parks and game reserves, a burst of green in the dry, reddened land. And then it was the mountain ranges, the Karas and Zaris, before they came in to land at Windhoek airport.

As the convoy drove, motorcycles screaming and sirens wailing, into the small, pretty capital, Riitho felt something dissolve in him, a lightening of the pressure inside his head. He did not speak a word of the many languages that he'd heard since he and Livingstone took off from Johannesburg airport. He was as much a stranger among the people and countries they visited as he would have been in London, or Boston, or Singapore. He watched his father being embraced by one leader after another. Many of the men who met them at the various airports had served time with Mandela and Modise, back on the island. Theirs was a reunion of brothers, in the African sense of the word. Some had shared cells for years.

They were humbling moments for Riitho. There was so much about himself he did not know. He understood now the sense of release he had felt coming away from the airport. It was his sense of himself that had claimed him, just as his father had, a few months before.

By the time they landed at Jan Smuts, six weeks later, he could hardly recognise himself. They had flown almost twenty thousand miles, visited twelve countries and addressed more than three million people. By some unspoken, tacit agreement, he found that the fuss surrounding his entry into South Africa had been forgotten. The question on everyone's lips was no longer about Rianne de Zoete. It was about him. What was he going to do? Would he take up a position in the new party? As the jubilant group walked through the doors of the airport terminal into the blaze of cameras and reporters, Riitho was silent. He slid into the back seat of one of the waiting cars. Lebohang was at the wheel. Their eyes met. He nodded silently. It was good to be home.

67

Charmaine was in a fever of anticipation. Simon had rung that morning from Johannesburg – he would be in London the following day. She snapped out of her boredom and began the preparations for his visit. A stop at the hairdresser's, a quick manicure and pedicure, a bikini wax. Sad cow, she thought, lying in the bath later that evening. Nothing to do but dress up for Daddy. She sat bolt upright. Christ, where had *that* thought come from? She hadn't thought about her father in . . . well, for ever. She lay back in the bath, disturbed by what her own imagination had thrown up. But she was excited. She'd asked Dinah to give the whole place a spring clean and order flowers for every room. Dinah had raised an eyebrow.

Simon waited until he'd heard the door to Dinah's flat close. Then he took off his coat and loosened his tie. Charmaine was all soft and sweet-smelling. She was wearing a particularly pretty dress, stockings, heels – the works. It felt good to know she'd made an effort. He couldn't remember the last time Stella had dressed up for him.

He sat down on the couch and beckoned to her. She came over, smiling that naughty, secret smile of hers. He patted the space beside him but she shook her head. She knelt down in front of him on the pale sheepskin rug, nestling her body between his knees. He sighed luxuriously, leaned back and closed his eyes. She was amazing – she knew exactly what made a man feel good. He opened his eyes to watch as her red-tipped fingers went to work on his belt, unzipping his trousers as she gazed up at him with those wonderfully large blue eyes. She took him in her mouth – he was immediately hard. Within seconds, she'd brought him to the brink. Neither heard the kitchen door open behind them, or saw Dinah's horrified face as she closed it again.

'Did you miss me?' Charmaine snuggled up to him afterwards on the couch.

'Sure,' he said easily, looking at his watch above her head. He had a meeting in about an hour.

'Really?' she asked, raising her head. She frowned. He wasn't even looking at her – he was looking at his watch. 'Really?' she repeated.

'Yes, I did. Charmaine, I have to go. You're sitting on my jacket.' She shifted her rump. 'I'll be back this evening. Probably late. Don't wait up for me. I'll wake you up – *he*'ll wake you up.' He pointed to his now limp cock and grinned.

Charmaine pouted.

He zipped himself up and got to his feet. He was running late.

He hailed a cab just outside Harrods. He felt refreshed, relaxed. Charmaine's early morning ministrations had done the trick. He was off to a meeting with the first prospective tenants at the just-completed Regency Wharf and he was feeling good. As the cab pulled out into the morning traffic on Old Brompton Road, he thought back to his meeting with Lisette at the beginning of the week.

'I want to pull back from the mines,' she had said to him. They were sitting in her office in Cape Town. He stared at her, shocked. Only days before she'd made it abundantly clear that she was still in control of the company, despite Marius's dramatic return. He might be back in South Africa but there was no way she would tolerate his presence at de Zoete Inc. Unfortunately, the decision wasn't hers to make: Marius was determined to bring black shareholders on board. Lisette had recognised this was a battle she could not fight. 'I'm handing over most of the day-to-day running to Hennie,' she continued.

Simon was silent, not quite able to believe what she was saying. What did it mean for him? 'But . . .' he began cautiously. She couldn't give it up. She'd worked too hard.

'I know. We've worked hard over the past sixteen years,

Simon, but things are changing here . . . and not for the better. But I'm tired of fighting. If Marius wants to hand over control to the blacks,' she said resignedly, 'then so be it. I want to concentrate on other things.'

'Regency Wharf?'

'Exactly.' She looked at him directly. 'Are you with me on this?'

'Absolutely.' There was no hesitation.

'Good.' She got up from her desk, walked towards the elegant mahogany sideboard, opened the doors and took out two crystal champagne glasses, then buzzed through to Sabine in the adjacent office. A couple of minutes later, a chilled bottle of champagne was brought through.

'Thank you, Simon,' she said, and offered him a glass. 'You've been magnificent through this . . . ordeal. I know I don't often say it, but thank you. Your loyalty has meant a lot to me. It still does.'

Simon felt warmth spread through him. He raised his glass. 'To you, Lisette. You're simply the most *wonderful* person I know.' He blushed. He sounded like a schoolboy.

She raised her own glass. 'To a new direction,' she said, taking a sip.

'A better one,' he echoed. 'Regency Wharf. What needs doing?'

'A couple of things,' Lisette said, eager to get on with business. KdZK London had been handling the final stages of construction, she said. The topping-out ceremony of the tower had been held with that rather nice minister, Michael Portillo – a vast improvement on his predecessor. Lisette looked forward to spending an afternoon or an evening in his company. The previous Environment Minister had been a dreadful bore . . . she couldn't even remember his name. The press coverage at the party afterwards had been favourable. The entire Regency Wharf project was a particular favourite of the British Prime Minister, John Major – as it had been his predecessor's, Margaret Thatcher. She and Lisette got on exceedingly well together: two driven and ambitious women in almost exclusively male-dominated arenas. Lisette was also of the opinion that Thatcher shared many of Lisette's concerns about the situation in South Africa. She loathed the unions, whether they were black or white. She also seemed to be one of the few world leaders prepared to speak out *against* sanctions. All of which endeared her to Lisette.

Lisette leaned forward. 'Something's bothering me,' she said. 'I've heard rumours that the government are expecting KdZK to contribute major amounts to the Underground, the Jubilee Line Extension, as the price for granting assent. They haven't got the money and they expect we will.'

'What makes you think that?' he asked.

'Just a feeling. They know they'll have us over a barrel – we'll be the biggest developers in the area. We've got too much invested already to let the project go belly-up if any of the components fail. And transport's going to be the weak link, I promise you. You've seen the Docklands Light Railway?' Simon nodded. She was right. 'No way is that going to be able to handle the numbers of people coming in every day. And if we can see that, believe me, the people we're looking for as tenants can.' She drained her glass. 'That's why we, as the ones with the most to lose, have to be most careful.'

'What do you have in mind?' Simon knew Lisette never brought up a problem unless she had a pretty good idea of a solution.

'Well, I want to make a deal. With the British government. We lend them the money – not as KdZK, that would be a conflict of interest. We need to form another company, one that doesn't *appear* connected to us in any way, in exchange for shares in the transport network. Public private partnerships. PPP. They're all the rage in the US but they haven't caught on yet in the UK. The British don't know what they're missing. Private money, public services, but with private profits. We can't lose.'

Simon began to smile. Lisette was formidable.

'Go to London this weekend,' she said. 'Scout around. I want you to do two things. Look for tenants, and find out what's being said about the transport network in government circles. I don't care how you do it.'

Simon nodded, finishing the last of his champagne. He loved working with Lisette. For Lisette. She made things happen. If she wanted to hand over the mines and the headaches that that particular sector of the economy generated, especially now, in this political climate, fine. Let Marius deal with his beloved blacks. Lisette had chosen to work with Simon. That suited him just fine.

'This it, guv?' the taxi driver asked.

Simon looked up at the rather shabby steel-and-glass building. First International Bank of Boston. He had a meeting with an old contact – someone he'd met on safari in Kruger Park years before, an American on an extended honeymoon-holiday with his third wife. He was now the CEO of the Boston-based bank who were looking to move headquarters, or so he'd heard. Simon had just the thing.

It was almost midnight by the time the cab dropped Simon at Wilton Crescent and he made his way rather drunkenly up the steps. It had been a productive evening, although he'd had difficulty keeping up with Bill Myers and his fifth wife. They seemed to inhale alcohol, not drink it. They'd had just over four bottles of wine between the three of them and much as he would have loved to wake the lovely Charmaine he wasn't sure how effective he'd be. Alcohol always impaired his performance – or, at least, that was what Stella used to claim. It had been a long time since she'd made *any* kind of comment on his performance.

He walked unsteadily into the living room. Charmaine was sitting in one of the leather chairs, clad in nothing but a pair of his boxer shorts. He felt something stir in his trousers. Perhaps he wasn't as drunk as he'd thought.

'How did you get into ... James and his little group?'

Simon asked her, an hour later. She was lying in the crook of his arm, almost asleep.

'Through Emily.'

'But why? You were at that school with Rianne – did you go to college?'

'No, I went to LA after school. My boyfriend took me out there. Jerk. I don't know what happened to him – he might still be there.'

'Did you work?'

'Sort of. I sold drugs.' Charmaine giggled.

'Eh?' He was startled.

'Mmm. Me and Baz – that was my ex – split up, and then I went into business with a guy I met in a supermarket. Except we got caught. Well, I got caught. Drew ran away. I don't know what happened to him either.'

'You mean—'

'Only for four days. Then Nathalie came and got me. She was at Sans Soucis too – with brown hair.'

'I remember her. So that's when you came back to Britain?'

'Yeah. I still owe Rianne tons of money – she and Nat paid my lawyer's fees. I don't know how to pay them back.' She sounded glum.

'How much?' he asked her, enjoying the feel of her breasts against his arm.

'Oh, loads.'

'How much?'

'Well, almost ten thousand pounds, counting the plane ticket.'

'But didn't you earn reasonably well at . . . James's?'

'Yeah, but me and Em just seemed to spend it all. On coke.'

'Ah.'

'Anyway, I'll pay them back one day. And it's not like they're desperate for the money.'

'Pay them back tomorrow.' His voice was calm.

'How?' Charmaine laughed. 'I've got about twenty

pounds in my purse and not a lot in the bank. I've hardly been to James since I met you.'

'I'll loan you the money.'

'You?'

'Yes. If I'd been seeing you at James's, it would have cost me close to that by now.'

'You don't have to do that. I like you.'

Charmaine's voice was muffled against his chest. He wondered if she was embarrassed. 'Charmaine,' he said, nudging her face away from him. He felt a wetness near his left nipple. Was she crying? 'It'll be a loan,' he said.

'But how will I ever pay *you* back?' She sniffed.

'You will. Don't worry, I won't ask for the money. But I will ask for your help. OK?'

'But what can *I* do?'

'Oh, I can think of lots of things,' he said, smiling in the darkness.

That evening, as he'd staggered to the door, Bill Myers had accompanied him, leaving his wife to clear the table. 'If you're ever interested in having some *real* fun,' Bill had leered at him, tapping the side of his nose conspiratorially, 'lemme know. I know a coupla nice gals.'

Simon had nodded jovially. I bet you do, he'd thought. But you probably don't know half as many as I do.

Or half as good, he added now, looking at Charmaine's short blonde hair against his tanned chest. He stroked her head, letting his hands run over her deliciously soft breasts. He felt his penis stiffen again. Just thinking about paying Charmaine to service someone else turned him on.

68

'Why not?' Nael looked at Gabby. They were sitting in a café in Hampstead. They'd just been for a bracing walk across the Heath. It was Sunday, and Gabby was due to leave for New York the following morning.

'But—'

'But what?'

'Well, isn't London easier?'

'In terms of what?'

'It's closer.'

'To what?'

'I don't know – your work, Palestine, your mother.'

'There are direct flights to everywhere in the world from JFK, Gabs,' Nael said gently. 'If that's your only concern—'

'It is. I'd love you to come,' Gabby said shyly. 'I mean it. I just don't want you to regret it.'

'Gabby, it's taken me ten years to realise that the person I've always wanted to be with has always been with me – I just didn't see it. No regrets. At least, not for me.'

Gabby reached across the table for his hand. Nael wanted to move to New York with her. She couldn't quite believe that in a little under a month, when he was back from his latest trip, he'd catch a flight to JFK, she'd go to the airport and pick him up, they'd go back to her place, and he'd be there for a whole fortnight, until his next assignment. She pursed her lips, trying desperately not to show him *just* how pleased she was.

Rianne studied the face in front of her in the mirror. Her dark brown eyes stared back at her, flat, expressionless. She applied mascara to the outer lashes with a shaking hand. It took her almost half an hour to put on her 'face', transforming herself from the wan, listless person she'd been for the past two months into something even vaguely approximating her modelling days. She drew the lipstick over her lips, pressing them carefully together to blot off the excess shine.

She looked at herself. She looked OK. She had finally snapped. She'd been here for almost three months. In that time, not a word. Not a single, fucking word. She'd run the gamut of emotions from worry to fear, anger, hurt and back again. She no longer jumped every time the phone rang or every time the guard announced a visitor. She no longer sat in front of the TV wondering if and where she'd see him next. She was angry now.

Last Thursday, she'd picked up the *Weekly Mail* and seen her face on the cover. *Modise and de Zoete – It's Over!* She'd read the article, her hands shaking, the print blurred by her tears of anger. For the second time in her life she read an interview with him that suddenly changed everything for her. He'd declined to answer the questions about them. They were spending some time apart. They'd see.

Inside the house at Bryanston, Rianne had refused to answer the phone. She knew what would happen next. A round of 'he said, she said' articles . . . her pain and hurt made public. No. He'd done the one thing she was sure he would never do . . . he'd moved on. Without her. Well, she was moving on too. She was nearing thirty. She had plenty of money. She could do whatever the hell she liked. She knew she couldn't stay in Bryanston . . . buried under the weight of the things that couldn't be said, in that house.

Marika had fled back to Cape Town almost immediately. It was as if she couldn't bear to look at Rianne. The hypocrite. She was full of herself and her 'good works', using her money to buy credibility amongst the liberal white class she so admired. All that crap about how cool it was when Ree Modise was at her school, how great he was, how great his father was . . . it was bullshit. Thinking about them from a safe distance was one thing, Rianne saw that now.

For most of her family – and, she supposed, the friends with whom she no longer had any contact – Rianne had crossed the line that none of them were willing to cross. Loving them from a distance . . . that was safe. *Sleeping* with them . . . oh, no. Too much. Too dangerous. Lisette was icily polite. They didn't talk about him, or about Marius or about anything. She was gone more than she was at home, thank God. She was in Cape Town most of the time. She and that idiot Uncle Simon. He'd hardly said a word to her the one time he'd come round to the house. Just looked at her as if she had leprosy or something.

She heard the cuckoo clock in the hallway chime 7 p.m. She started. She looked at herself again in the mirror. She was nervous. She'd made up her mind, yes . . . she was leaving South Africa. This time for good. But before she went, she wanted to see him, one last time.

She knew he would be at the Carlton Hyatt that evening. She'd managed to get an invitation through someone Gabby knew. Good old Gabby. She glanced at her watch again. She'd better get a move on. She grabbed a handful of hair and piled it loosely on top of her head, securing the careless twist with a butterfly grip. She fastened a black glass and diamond necklace around her neck – nothing else – and stood up. She smoothed the long black dress over her curves. It followed the contours of her body until it reached her knees, flaring out gently before settling around her feet. She bent down to fasten the straps on her sandals. She heard the door open. She straightened up. Hennie stood in the doorway.

'Can't you knock? Asshole.' Rianne glared at him in the mirror angrily. He looked her up and down with his usual arrogant insolence. She turned around. 'What do you want?' He made her nervous. He'd been making her nervous ever since she arrived. He was always creeping around, coming up to her silently, his light blue eyes on her as she walked across the room, went for a swim, picked up the car keys to escape the house. He made her feel sick. She couldn't believe she'd ever thought herself in love with him. 'What? What do you want?' she asked again. He smiled, a horrible, mocking smile.

'So . . . where to, Rianne?' His voice was cold.

'None of your fucking business.'

'No?' He walked into the room, closing the door behind him. Rianne swallowed. Lisette wasn't in . . . she'd heard her go out earlier that evening. Poppie was somewhere in the kitchen. She stopped. She was being ridiculous. He was her *cousin*, for Christ's sake.

'Just leave me alone.' She turned her back on him and walked over to the bed, bending to collect her clutch purse.

In a second he was behind her, his hands sliding over her waist, pulling her roughly towards him. She panicked, twisting round and stumbling at the same time. He gripped her arm, and she opened her mouth to scream, but his hand went under her jaw, hard. He bent his head. She felt his tongue slide into her mouth as his hand groped her breast under the thin silk of her dress. She struggled furiously with him, jerking her knee towards his groin. She tried to hit him with her free hand.

He released her suddenly, pushing her away, and she fell, gasping, onto the bed. His breathing was fast and ragged. 'Don't worry, cousin. I wouldn't *dream* of touching what he already has.' He walked out of the room, slamming the door behind him.

Rianne lay on the bed, shaking. She was stunned, not only by what he'd done but the way he'd done it. He *hated* her. The look of disgust on his face was worse than the look he'd given Marius when they'd first arrived. She felt sick. How could they hate her so? She pulled herself up and sat on the edge of the bed, shaking. Her jaw ached where he'd grabbed her. Her mouth felt thick and dirty. She got up, wobbling in her sandals, and looked at herself in the mirror. Sure enough, there was a reddened welt across the side of her mouth, her lipstick was smeared, her cheeks red with rage.

She was leaving in two days. She already had her tickets. She would wash her face and go down to the Carlton. She hadn't come this far to let Hennie ruin the only chance she might ever have of reaching closure.

The ballroom at the Carlton had been transformed for the first ANC fund-raising dinner to court the white business community. The hall was decked out in gold, green and black banners. Huge sashes of gold satin swathed the curtains and the doors that led out to the hotel gardens. The hotel staff, black and white, worked together to transform the rather dull, corporate interior into something worthy of a dinner where businessmen and their wives had paid the equivalent of a year's salary for most of the country's black population for the chance to sit amongst the black elite. By six o'clock that evening, it was almost complete. The first guests were due to start arriving at eight. Joachim Pieterse and his staff looked around them with pride. He was pleased. He asked four of the girls to finish off by bringing out the enormous flower arrangements . . . lilies, sunflowers, dark green palm fronds . . . he hadn't been able to find black flowers, exactly, but the florists had sent over some beautiful, dark purple tulips. The girls moved quickly about the room, adding a tulip or two to the displays, placing the vases just so. The lilies immediately released their fragrance into the late autumn air.

Riitho walked in ahead of the rest of the family. He couldn't be bothered with the photographers and the reporters who persistently asked the same question – *Rianne de Zoete. Can you confirm your relationship is . . .* he brushed them arrogantly aside. They sloped off. Modise and the rest of his family were far more obliging . . . they posed for photographs with Mandela and his family before entering the hall to thunderous applause. Many of the guests had already arrived and were seated at the linen-covered tables that dotted the room. At the far end of the room was the head table – like boarding school, Riitho thought to himself with a small smile – where Mandela and Modise and their two families would sit. The chairman of the South African Board of Mines was there, although many of the individual mining firms were not. Marius de Zoete was there . . . Riitho noticed him with a sudden jolt. His eyes quickly scanned the room . . . no, of course not.

She wouldn't have been invited. He turned to look at his mother and father walking in. Njeri looked wonderful. She wore a traditional West African *kaba*, in black and red, a pair of simple diamonds peeping out from underneath that elaborate headdress. Even Mpho looked stunning. Her bloody hair had been tucked away under a similar wrap – she looked elegant, absolutely regal. The twins looked delighted in their stiff new tuxedos. They smiled shyly at everyone. They too were growing into their new roles. He felt a sudden surge of pleasure . . . things were beginning to fall into place. He waited until everyone had reached the table. He pulled out a chair for his mother and then one for Mpho. She smiled back at him. They were finally relaxing with each other. The first few cracks in the ice. Njeri noticed, and was thankful. The waiters hovered at their elbows. The dinner was scheduled to start at eight. It was almost time.

He saw her seconds before she saw him. He was watching the PR staff who had organised the dinner dart in and out of the room as they made last-minute adjustments to the seating arrangements before the first speech. She walked straight into his line of vision. His heart missed a beat. There was a sudden lull in the conversation – several people turned their heads as she swept past.

Jesus. She was making straight for his table. Riitho scraped back his chair and stood up. Njeri looked at him, evidently puzzled. They were just about to start. Mandela was fumbling for his spectacles. She heard Mpho swearing to her left and turned her head. Across the hall, Marius saw her too and rose.

'Cover for me,' Riitho hissed to his sister, as he left the dais. He strode across the floor. He saw Marius out of the corner of his eye, moving towards her. A photographer jumped to his feet, camera ready. Marius motioned to him to step back – *I've got her*. Around them, conversation buzzed. Look, isn't that – what's she doing? Is she drunk? Oh, my God – it is! *Look!* Someone gasped.

Marius grabbed her by the upper arm, swung her around and walked her through the hall to the exit. At the tables closest to the doors, everyone watched them, mouths agape.

Riitho spotted a door to his left, behind the potted palms. He slipped out before the photographer or anyone else noticed – everyone was too busy staring at the main doors. He walked down the corridor towards the reception area. He saw Marius come out of a side room. He waited for a second, until he'd passed out of view, and quickly walked over. He opened the door.

Rianne was sitting at one of the tables, her head in her hands. She lifted her head. They stared at each other without speaking.

Rianne's heart was thumping. She stood up, facing him. She couldn't believe he was standing in front of her, looking at her as if he was angry with her. *He* was angry?

He spoke first. 'What the hell are you doing here?' He was breathing fast. 'What do you want?'

'What do *I* want?' She was furious now.

'What did you come here for?'

'What else was I supposed to do?' she yelled. 'I've been waiting for three months, Riitho! *Three months!* I'm leaving the day after tomorrow. I'm going back to the States. You haven't called me – you haven't tried to get in touch! What the hell did you expect me to do?' She looked away. She couldn't bear it. She couldn't bear to look at him. He looked the same, exactly the same, nothing had changed, nothing about him was different. He was every-thing she'd ever wanted. Why had it come to this? She turned her back on him, wrapping her arms round herself. She heard him clear his throat.

'Rianne.' His voice was quiet. He lifted his shoulders, unable to speak. Then he opened his mouth, and hesitated. She knew what was coming and wanted to block her ears against the sound. 'I'm sorry,' he said. 'Jesus, Rianne, I'm sorry. I can't do this any more. *We* can't.'

'We? *We?* There is no "we", Riitho. You've made that clear.' He was silent. She drew a deep breath. It was hard to recognise the man standing in front of her, not wanting to meet her eyes, as the man she'd loved for the past four years – before that, even, as only she knew. He didn't want her. Like her father, he'd made his choice. She wondered at that – just what it was that made men like Marius and Livingstone – and now Riitho – make such choices. She picked up her bag and walked out the room. She had what she came for. Closure.

He stood still for a moment after she'd gone, breathing deeply. He pulled out a chair and sat down at the conference table, burying his head in his hands. Seeing her . . . everything came rushing back. Malvern, Paris, London, New York. Each precious moment they'd spent together. Before he'd seen her, he'd been sure – as sure as he could be – that it was better for both of them to end it. The pressure he was under, the pressures she would face – and, even worse, the pressures the two of them would face in the immediate future – would undo them. That was what he feared. South Africa wasn't ready for them – the world wasn't.

Theirs wasn't a simple love story, that had always been the problem – both of them represented too much. There were always other people in their relationship, standing between them, behind them – his father, his country, her father, her way of life. Everyone had made it abundantly clear that he couldn't sustain a relationship with her and one with his family. The distances he'd travelled since he got back, the things he'd seen . . . Rianne de Zoete wasn't part of that landscape. And he was. Of that he had been sure.

Had he done the right thing? He got up and walked to the window. He could hear the faint sound of applause coming from the ballroom – Mandela must have finished his speech. That was the world he belonged to now. Christ,

Rianne . . . He closed his eyes. She was beautiful, desirable, sexy, all the things he'd seen in her when she first came to him, in Paris. But there was more. She fascinated him, like he did her. On the surface, they represented the antithesis of each other: she, the rich, protected child of white privilege; he the product of oppression. White/black; rich/poor; powerful/powerless. A set of simple equations. But that was only the surface. In the beginning that was what had drawn her in. She wanted to know more, to see things below the surface, the things that had been hidden from her all her life. That was why she'd come. And that, in a curious way, was why he'd let her in.

He was touched by her vulnerability, she who should never have been vulnerable, not before him. And they recognised a part of themselves in each other. He knew both worlds intimately – the world she believed him to come from, and hers. He was more comfortable in her world than she was – she saw that in him, and was drawn to it. When she came to him in his office, she'd come openly, offering herself. There was no edge at which they might have *met* one another and considered the risks. No, she had just walked straight in. She was fascinated by him, by his sameness and by his difference.

She complained there were boundaries in him she could not cross but it was the sense that there was more, that he could give her more that kept her there, waiting for him to show her the way. He'd told her, time and again, 'I'm not here to save you, Rianne.' She claimed she knew, and understood, but she didn't. She was only half alive without him, that was what she said. He knew she meant it.

And yet . . . for all his confidence, there were moments sometimes, being back here, when his doubts threatened to undo him. Their relationship was special in that it shouldn't have happened, not between *them*. He had thought that *being* with her crossed all the lines. But of course it wasn't enough.

He had done what he had to. That was how he'd have to look at it. But, Christ, it hurt.

Rianne left the hotel blinded by tears. She ignored the concern on the doorman's face and hurried to her car. She was humiliated and hurt beyond belief. She sped back to Bryanston with one thought on her mind: it was time to leave South Africa, and all the pain it contained, and start again somewhere else. She had no real idea where she would go, just that she had to get away. She put her foot down. If she was lucky, Lisette would be at home. She would talk to her about money. She had a vague notion that she was due to inherit some on or around her thirtieth birthday. It was time to take charge of her life. Then she would go to Gabby, and on to New York. A step at a time. She would take it from there.

Unfortunately, her first steps were not as smooth as she'd hoped. Lisette *was* home when she arrived but their encounter left Rianne reeling. Her first question to her aunt was met with a cold stare. 'How much money do I have?' Rianne asked.

'What do you mean?' Lisette regarded her niece coolly.

'Exactly what I said. How much do I have?'

'That depends.'

'On what?'

'On what you want to do with it.'

'Bullshit. I'm over twenty-one. I can do what I like with it.' Rianne was equally cool.

Lisette got up and lit a cigarette. She blew the smoke out slowly. 'That's where you're wrong,' she said.

Rianne looked at her uncertainly. 'What d'you mean?'

'That you don't come into any inheritance without my approval. It's one of the stipulations of your trust. You should check these things, Rianne.' Lisette inspected her nails. 'In fact, I think you'll find that one of the conditions of your continuing to draw upon your trust is my approval. Now that all this,' she waved a red-tipped hand in the air dismissively, 'is out in the open, I'm no longer sure I can give it.' Rianne's eyes flashed. 'I want your word, Rianne.'

'On what?'

'I want your word that this – affair with Modise is over, that you've come to your senses, that you're sorry for the disgrace you've brought upon us—'

'Go to hell.' Rianne got up, her cheeks flaming.

'Rianne!' 'Don't you *dare*—'

'What? Talk to you like that? Who do you think you are? I'll see who I please when I please – it has nothing to do with you. Nothing!'

'It has everything to do with us! How *dare* you? How dare you bring such shame on us? After everything we've done for you!'

'*You?* What the fuck did you ever do for me?' Rianne shouted. 'Don't talk to me about shame. You don't know the meaning of the word! I don't ever want to see you again.'

Lisette's cigarette shook in her hand. 'Fine. Walk out, just like your father did. When you can't face the truth, you run. Well, let's see how far you get, you spoilt brat. You could have had everything – we've done everything we could for you. Bad blood. Just like your mother. I should have known.'

Thank God she already had a return ticket to New York, she thought, flinging clothes furiously into her enormous suitcase. She had no idea what to do next. She was still unable to understand or appreciate exactly what the exchange with Lisette had meant. Was she to be cut off? But it was Marius's money, surely. All she had to do was ring him. He would sort it out, give her whatever she wanted.

But something stopped her. Pride? Perhaps. She remembered that he, too, had warned her away from Riitho. She couldn't bear to go crying to him now. She'd been so sure of Riitho, of the strength of their relationship. How could she now crawl to Marius and admit he had been right, Riitho had given her up, made his own choices that didn't include her. She couldn't.

She'd have to find another way. She had some money in her bank account in New York, she knew that. She had her credit cards. She still had money from her modelling days – although she had no idea how much. She couldn't believe she was so naïve about money. She had an accountant, provided by Lisette, of course. In fact, everything she'd done or possessed had been provided by Lisette – her schooling, her career, her homes. Well, that had to stop. It was terrifying – in one swift swoop, she'd lost everything. Well, almost everything. If they thought she would simply crumple up and die, they were wrong. She was made of sterner stuff. She would show them. And him.

69

Charmaine looked at Simon. What did he mean? He reached across the restaurant table and covered her hand with his. 'Nothing unpleasant, my darling,' he said smoothly. 'Just . . . like you did at James's. I want to make a good impression on Bill. He could be one of our key clients.'

'You mean *your* clients,' she said, biting her lip. Somehow, when he'd talked about them being together, this wasn't quite what she'd had in mind.

'No, no, *ours*. We could work *together*, you see. As well as *be* together.' He sipped his wine and refilled her glass.

Charmaine liked the sound of that better. 'So I'd be like . . . a spy or something?' She asked, her eyes lighting up.

'Yes, exactly. An industrial spy. I find the clients, you get as much information out of them as you can and we use it to our best advantage. Ours. Yours and mine.'

'And Lisette? Where does she come into it?' Charmaine wasn't stupid.

'Nowhere,' he said. 'This is a private arrangement between you and me. Of course, the information will help everyone out, including Lisette. But you and I will set up something separate. Like the thousand pounds I gave you. And I'll buy you a flat and a car, if you want one. We'll be business partners. As well as . . . other things.'

Charmaine nodded eagerly. It was the 'other things' she was interested in. He'd all but said he would leave Stella as soon as he could organise things. Perhaps this latest idea was part of the plot. And he'd been as good as his word about the money. It had been so easy. He had telephoned the transfer through that morning. Money and sex. Sex and power. In Charmaine's head, the three were fused. She nodded again, taking a large gulp of wine. The truth was, not only did she find it financially gratifying, it was erotic too.

She slipped her foot out of its high-heeled black pump and slid it up his thigh. He choked on his wine. She smiled and turned to look at the other diners in the fancy Knightsbridge restaurant. She wanted to live like this always, she thought. A handsome older man, a beautiful flat, money in the bank and nothing particular to do, except make herself more beautiful, more desirable . . . indispensable. She stroked his penis with her toes, slowly, deliberately. He was breathing hard. It was easy, so easy.

This time, too, he kept his word. He was off to a meeting in New York at the end of the week so they had to move quickly, he said, a couple of days later. It was early morning. Charmaine was still in bed. He was dressed, ready for the day's meetings. He opened his briefcase and tossed a number of estate agents' brochures at her. 'Choose something,' he said. 'Something nice.'

'But what about the costs?' she asked, enjoying the speed

at which he moved. She loved men who made things happen.

'Don't worry about that. Find something you like. Don't go overboard but, remember, that's where you'll be ... entertaining a lot of the time. I'm sure you'll manage.' He kissed her and picked up his briefcase. 'I'll be back some time after dinner.'

Charmaine heard the front door shut behind him, stretched her arms above her head and yawned. What should she wear? There was the pink suit, the fake Chanel one with white piping and gold buttons. Too dressy. The brown trouser suit with the matching chiffon blouse? Too dull. Her grey tweed trousers? With her cashmere sweater cardigan thing that belted at the waist? That would do. It was classy but not too dressy, stylish without being overly trendy. She might have to get a new pair of shoes – maybe a pair of those high-heeled boots everyone was wearing. She jumped out of bed and headed for the bathroom. It was almost nine o'clock. She could hear Dinah in the kitchen making coffee and warming some croissants. She stretched again, grinning. Not only did she want to live like this for ever, she was beginning to realise that she could.

'Yes?' The young man sitting behind the desk at the estate agent's was slow to catch on to the importance of Charmaine's visit. At first glance she seemed like a nice, pretty, but unexceptional young woman. But her too-new Louis Vuitton bag and the squeaky patent boots seemed a *little* out of place in this elegant part of Kensington.

'I phoned earlier?' Charmaine said, smiling prettily and taking a seat opposite him. He nodded, trying to recall their conversation. 'I'd like to look at the flat on De Vere Gardens,' she prompted, blue eyes shining.

He was all ears now. 'Oh, right. Yes, of course.' The beautiful two-bedroomed flat at the south end of the street was one of the more elegant and expensive ones on their books. His face took on its most obsequious aspect. 'Would you like to view it straight away, madam?'

'Yes, please,' she said, holding out a hand. He took it, his commission reflected in his firm grip.

Charmaine followed him out of the office onto Kensington High Street. She'd seen three other flats that morning but this was the closest to the shops – and *what* shops. She was in love with the mixture of boutiques, grand old department stores, shoe shops, restaurants – and, of course, her favourite shop in the whole world, Harvey Nichols. She hoped the flat would be everything the brochure said it was. They hopped into a cab for the five-minute ride to the property.

'Oh, gosh, it's really pretty,' Charmaine breathed, as the young man showed her the sitting room and adjacent dining nook.

The owners were leaving for the Far East and wanted a quick sale, so the flat had been freshly painted and decorated. All the prospective client had to do was move their personal effects in: everything else, right down to the towels, was in the sale. She surveyed the sitting room. The walls were a deep red, cream window surrounds and ceilings. The floor throughout was covered with that ultra-fashionable coir carpeting, giving the whole place a calm, sophisticated feel. The furniture was elegant and comfortable, including a beautiful antique coffee table on which vases of perfectly trimmed red roses sat, perfuming the air. There were deep red and gold cushions scattered throughout and a large bowl of rosy apples on the teak dining table completed the picture of domestic sophistication and bliss.

Charmaine walked through to the main bedroom – off-white walls, little navy-blue headboard lights recessed into the wall above the wrought-iron bed – it was divine. The bathroom was gorgeous: soft, sandstone floor and an elegant old-fashioned bathtub. How much was it again?

She pursed her lips: £205,000. It sounded like an awful lot of money.

'Yes, we've had several viewers this week. It'll go pretty soon, I think,' the agent said.

Charmaine thought quickly. 'We'll take it. My ... partner will be in later this afternoon. Yes, it's lovely.' She peeked into the sitting room one last time. She could just picture herself lying on the light grey sofa or bringing a glass of wine from the spotless little kitchen through to the dining table, pulling out one of the chairs, reaching behind Simon to put her arms round him as dinner simmered in the oven. Not that she would cook, of course, but the picture of domestic bliss was a heady one. She clapped her hands excitedly. Douglas, the estate agent, smiled. He preferred women clients. They seemed to have a talent for projecting themselves into the spaces he showed them ... the men would um and ah forever ... women saw themselves cooking in the kitchen, entertaining in the dining room, making love in the bedroom ... and the deal was done. As he locked up the flat, he hoped this one's 'partner', whoever he was, would come good. He'd been stung a couple of times lately by young girls who'd simply got carried away, going way over the budget set by their respective sugar daddies, as he called them, and he'd watched his commission disappear down the drain.

'Thank you, thank you, *thank* you,' Charmaine nibbled on him, kissing him everywhere, her lips making a soft trail across his chin, his nose, his eyes.

He grabbed her by the hair. 'Show me,' he ordered her, pushing her head between his legs. He held on to her, tightly, as he thrust roughly in and out of her mouth. She gagged. This wasn't the passive, almost lazy manner he favoured. This was rude, crude. She choked as he came. Tears sprang to her eyes as she spluttered and coughed. He was still gripping her hair, she tried to twist away but his thighs held her.

'Ow! You're hurting me, Simon – *ow!*' she yelped, pushing at him ineffectually.

He stared at her for a second. Then he let her go. 'Sorry,' he said, smiling. 'Got a little carried away there. You do that to me, you know – drive me over the top.' He pulled her back into his arms and stroked her head. 'Sorry, my darling. You'd make Jesus lose control,' he said, wincing. Christ, he was corny. But Charmaine seemed mollified. He knew she loved any reference to her sexual power. You could do almost anything to her, then tell her it was her own fault because she was too beautiful, too sexy, too good at it, and she'd melt. What on earth had happened to her in her childhood to make her so pathetically insecure? She'd obviously been round the block a bit. She could have done anything, but she'd become a whore. Mind you, it wasn't as if Rianne had turned out any better. Look at her. All that beauty and money and class and what was *she* doing? Fucking *kaffirs*. He felt sick at the thought.

70

How could she describe it? It was as if the earth had suddenly shifted underneath her, whilst she was still standing. As if the temperature around her had dropped, without warning. As if the space around her had closed, trapping her with only the pain for company. She was drowning. In the safety of Gabby's flat in New York, she thought she would never surface. Oh, there were ways to describe it, words . . . endless, useless words. Words were easy. It was the rest that was hard. To say she missed him – she had never before known what that meant. His powerful presence she'd felt within the first two seconds of meeting him . . . the presence that had been with her since Paris and stayed with her ever since . . . it was suddenly gone, dropped out, disappeared. She was lost without it. The heat he brought with him, not just the heat of his body but of his concentration, the thing that had held her magnetised for so long . . . it was gone and in its place there was nothing but the cold blast of fear. She talked and Gabby listened.

In the end it wasn't Riitho who saved her but Gabby. It wasn't just that Gabby knew more about her relationship with Riitho than anyone else, it was that she *understood*. She'd always understood – right from the beginning. For Rianne, falling in love with Riitho had defined her: her life fell neatly – if not easily – into two distinct halves – before him and after him. She'd thought the after meant for ever in the same way that knowing him had changed her, for ever. Now, he was gone. What was she supposed to do?

'I'm scared, Gabby. I can't be without him – I keep seeing his face—' She stopped.

'I know. It's going to be rough, Rianne. I can't defend him – you're *my* friend and I care about what's happening to you, not him, but it can't have been easy for him either.'

'He promised it wouldn't happen. He *promised* me.' Rianne started to cry again.

Gabby reached out for her hand. 'What are you going to do?' she asked her, trying to get Rianne to focus on what lay ahead. 'Will you stay in New York?'

'I can't go back to that, Gabs.'

Gabby sighed. 'What else d'you want to do?'

Rianne stared at her. There it was again. The question Rianne had been hearing all her life. What would she like to do? What was she planning to do? She had no idea of the answer. Somehow being with Riitho, waiting with him for things to happen *to* him, as he had said they always did, the question had been answered without her even noticing. Do? She didn't have to do anything. *Being* was enough. Being with him.

'I don't know – I don't know anything any more.'

Gabby looked at her. She knew what Rianne meant but that was part of the problem, surely. Rianne didn't have to do anything. When the chips were down, as they were now, she had nothing to hold on to: no real job, at least not in the sense that Gabby understood it; no home that hadn't been provided for her by someone else; no man, now that Riitho was gone. Rianne wasn't cut out for this. What had happened was a tragedy, and Rianne had no tools to deal with it, which was strange, given the losses she'd sustained in her life.

How could you teach someone to survive? You pointed them in the right direction and hoped they'd swim, not sink. Waving, not drowning. That was what she wanted to see Rianne doing. Waving from a safe shore. Rianne wouldn't understand the idea that there might be more important things in life than individual happiness. It was ironic because that was what her father had done: he had given her up for something greater than himself – yet he couldn't explain to her why he'd done it. Rianne thought it was hypocrisy or, worse, racism that had prompted him to declare Riitho was not right for her. Gabby saw it differently. Marius knew his daughter. She was not the wife for someone like Riitho.

She tried to imagine what she would do if Nael left her. She would be terrified. And she understood something of what Rianne was going through. But her life wouldn't be *over*, not in the way Rianne now viewed hers. Perhaps that was at the root of the problem. For someone so blessed, Rianne was curiously insubstantial. She had drifted into almost everything she'd ever done. Coming to England, her modelling career, going back to South Africa and returning to New York. She'd always allowed others to shape and suggest the direction of her life. The one thing she'd taken control of, catching that plane to Paris to see Riitho, she couldn't explain. She'd simply gone . . . thought about it the way she'd thought about catching a train to London, one Saturday afternoon . . . she was bored . . . she didn't think about it, she just did it and waited to see what would happen. After that, everything had fallen into place. She'd allowed herself to be directed by Riitho and *his* cause, the events that shaped *his* life, not hers. She'd continued modelling half-heartedly, but it was more to fill the time when she couldn't be with him than from any desire to be someone other than what he made her. *Might* make her – and that was part of it, too. It was an easy trap to fall into, mistaking a lack of self-direction for an expression of love. Many women did, especially those who had fallen for men whose causes – political or otherwise – offered a glimpse of an existence whose meaning *seemed* greater than that of their own.

Gabby sometimes felt that way about Nael. She thought back to the conversation in the café in London when he told her who he really was or, at least, who he thought himself to be. If she was honest with herself, her distress had been laced with envy. As Nael became Na'el, he had assumed another, more symbolic identity, he moved away from her, ahead of her – out of her ordinary, desperately *English* orbit. He had something she could never have; he was someone she could never be. It was part of who he was and it was part of who Riitho was – the thing that drew so many to him. He had told Rianne that he wasn't there to save her. She must know how to save herself. He was right.

Gabby got up from the table and walked to the window. It was almost summer. The light outside the apartment was sharp and warm, the city was sloughing off the spring. She lit a cigarette. She tried not to smoke when Nael was around but Rianne had smoked almost non-stop since she'd arrived. She spoke softly, as much for herself as for Rianne. Their friendship was slipping a gear, deepening. She could say things to her now that she wouldn't normally have said. To anyone. 'It's part of the attraction, isn't it? The difference – not just the colour difference, the race thing, but that they're something we're not . . . and never will be.'

Rianne looked at her, struggling to understand what she meant. Gabby turned round. It wasn't quite like that with Nael, she said, but it amounted to the same thing. On the surface, you didn't really see it, not like she did with Riitho. Nael's *distance* from her – that was how she would put it, his distance, not his difference – was hidden, beneath the surface . . . not something to be seen, touched or felt. And sometimes that confused her. It was like being with two people, simultaneously. When he spoke to his mother on the phone, in Arabic, or when she saw him on TV, speaking to people, his *keffiyah* around his head, he was a stranger to her. And then when she was with him again, listening to the voice she'd known since forever, she couldn't reconcile the two. He confused her. She could say that, to Rianne. Not to him. It was only when they made love, when he was at his most open and unguarded, she saw she possessed them both, the stranger and the person she'd always known – the things he kept apart in himself, always. It was . . . erotic? Could she admit to that? She blushed suddenly. Rianne nodded through her tears. Gabby was right. She was exactly right. Of course. She put into words what Rianne couldn't. 'If you want him back, Rianne, you'll have to fight for him.' She stubbed out her cigarette. Rianne looked up at her.

'What do you mean? How?' she asked, her voice breaking.

'Exactly as he said. You have to find yourself. When you meet him again, you have to know who *you* are. He's finding out who he is. As painful as it sounds, he was absolutely right.'

'You're wrong, Gabby,' Rianne said thickly. 'He's gone – he said it. He's made his choice. It's over.'

'Maybe.' It was all Gabby would say.

It was harder than she'd ever thought possible. Nothing went right – from the moment she walked into the bank on Fifth Avenue and learned that she had less than five thousand dollars in her checking account and just under the same amount in her savings account. Ten thousand dollars for all that work. She stared in disbelief at the bank manager. 'Are you sure?' she asked nervously. Ten thousand dollars? What had she done with all her money? She inspected the balance sheet again. She ought to contact her accountant – but she couldn't remember who he was. 'Er, this may sound strange,' she began, 'but I need to talk to my accountants. You wouldn't happen to have that information, would you?'

'Information?'

'Who they are.'

'Oh, yes, of course.' He was used to beautiful women – wives, mainly – not having a clue about their finances. 'If you'd like to come this way?' He led her into a private office. At least she was still with Behrends, the private bank Ross Carter had introduced her to. They knew how to treat their customers.

Within half an hour, she had the telephone number and address and a thick file containing her bank statements over the past four years. Maybe Gabby would have some suggestions about what to do next. She needed to find work, that much was clear. She would ring Ross in the morning.

But Ross was less than pleased to hear from her. After the kidnap Rianne hadn't bothered to contact Face!, even to let them know that she was all right – and it had been from a fitting at YSL that she was snatched. Gina had had to scrabble around for a replacement – the show had to go on. And then months of silence! Rianne was *not* flavour of the month and Ross didn't see why she should pretend otherwise.

Rianne spent a painfully humiliating fifteen minutes on the other end of the phone as Ross explained calmly why she wasn't taking her back. Rianne was getting on and there were hundreds of beautiful young girls coming up through the ranks now, all desperate for the chances Rianne had been given – and had thrown away. She was welcome to try her luck elsewhere but, really, Ross was looking for someone much more . . . professional. Someone who needed the job. *I need it,* Rianne wanted to scream at her. *I need it now! Give me another chance* – but she couldn't.

Gabby was sympathetic but not alarmed. Rianne would never be penniless, nor would she ever not have somewhere to live. Not while Gabby was still alive. This – *punishment,* as Rianne called it – perhaps it wasn't such a bad thing, you never knew, it might – just *might* – be the making of her. She listened and waited and watched.

'You've got ten thousand dollars, Rianne. That's a heck of a lot more than most people have. You've got to figure out how to spend it. Wait until you've been to a couple of agencies. If you get taken on by someone else, go out and get an apartment. Not before. You need to *plan*, not just *react*.'

Rianne looked at Gabby in awe. She was so focused and organised and calm, and all the things Rianne wasn't. Suddenly she felt very small. She had so much to learn.

On the other side of the Atlantic, Charmaine was having second thoughts about the whole Mata Hari business. At first, it had been fun. She'd paid back Nathalie and Rianne, and moved out of Wilton Crescent into the Kensington flat. Now, though, she paced the sitting room nervously. She wanted to show everyone her new place but she didn't know how to explain it. They would think it a little odd, her being given this gorgeous place by a boyfriend who was never there. Gabby was in New York most of the time, thank God, although she was due to come round in twenty minutes. She was in London on her way to Geneva and she'd promised to call in. The buzzer sounded.

'Jesus,' Gabby said, as she walked into the hallway and peeped into the sitting room. 'Charmaine, it's beautiful, but how can you afford it?' She was puzzled. Charmaine *still* didn't have a job.

'Simon bought it for me,' Charmaine said, slightly defensively, Gabby thought.

'Simon?' Gabby had never heard of him. She stared at Charmaine.

'He's my boyfriend, haven't I introduced you?' Charmaine said gaily.

'Er, no, you haven't.' Gabby looked at her sharply. Another dodgy boyfriend? She'd ask Nathalie. It was difficult keeping up with the twists and turns in Charmaine's life, especially from so far away. She walked through the flat. The bedroom disturbed her – all that velvet and silk, black sheets on the bed. She wrinkled her nose. It looked like a parody of a brothel. She noticed a long silk cord wrapped around the wrought-iron headboard. She made a mental note to call Nathalie the minute she left Charmaine's.

Charmaine was in high spirits. She gabbled on about Simon and some project he was doing. Regency Wharf – it was the tallest building in Europe, they were going to make tons of money, they were investing in the transport infrastructure.

Gabby was amused. Since when had Charmaine ever been interested in transport infrastructure? When she started babbling on about PPPs, Gabby interrupted her: 'What d'you mean? What's a PPP?'

'Oh, it's something . . . like when you get money from the government.' Charmaine was hopelessly vague.

'Public private partnerships?' Gabby looked at her.

'Yes, that's it! Mr Dorland – Mike – was talking about them the other night.' Charmaine had gone bright red.

'Mike Dorland? The Environment Minister?' Gabby was alarmed. What on earth was Charmaine doing in Mike Dorland's company? Or, more worryingly, what was *he* doing in hers?

'Yes, he's a friend of Simon's. We all went for – er, dinner the other night.'

Gabby had known Charmaine almost all her life and could tell when she was lying. 'Char, who is this Simon?' she asked, sitting down in one of the cream easy chairs.

Charmaine fiddled with her necklace – a rather elaborate gold and diamond affair. It wasn't quite her. 'He's . . . in the City,' she said evasively. 'He's a banker.'

'He lives here? With you?'

'No, not exactly.'

'He's not married, is he?' Gabby asked gently. Charmaine didn't answer. Gabby touched her arm. 'Oh, Charmaine, what does he say? That he'll leave his wife?' She felt so sorry for Charmaine, trying to appear so sophisticated and grown-up but, underneath it all, looking so desperate.

'I know he will, just as soon as—'

'As what?'

'Well, it takes *time*, Gabby. These things take time to organise.'

'Char . . .' Gabby began. Charmaine looked away, and she fell silent. Charmaine had a faraway look in her eyes that Gabby hadn't seen before. She was worried about her. This 'relationship' wasn't like the others Charmaine had been in. This guy, whoever he was . . . there was something not quite right about the set-up. And it wasn't just that he was a married man making all the usual empty promises to an infatuated bit-on-the-side. No, there was something more . . . sinister about it.

Charmaine was drifting, it was true. She saw the look of concern – and exasperation – in Gabby's eyes and cringed. She hated appearing silly and desperate in front of anyone, especially Gabby. She'd always felt so silly around her. Gabby always had everything under control, always. Her difficulties with Dominic and her battles with her weight were completely lost on Charmaine. Gabby always gave practical, sensible, caring advice . . . as far as Charmaine was concerned, that meant she had everything in order. Job, money, man . . . everything was perfect in Gabby's life. Her own life, on the other hand . . . well, it was falling apart. Just thinking about what she was going through made her feel sick. How could she tell anyone what was happening? No one would believe her. She could scarcely believe it herself. She thought about the awful events of the previous week and shuddered.

It was a Wednesday evening. Simon was in town for a week. He'd asked her to wear something special for dinner that evening – they were going to meet Mike Dorland, the Environment Minister who was tipped to become the new minister for transport. Simon wanted some answers about the government's estimates on the cost and timescale of extending the Jubilee Line to North Greenwich. He and Lisette had set up the ancillary company – Zeus Investments Ltd, with head offices in Jersey and the Cayman Islands ... difficult to trace back to them. What they needed to know was how much of a sweetener to drop the government's way. If Charmaine couldn't get it out of him through conversation, she knew what to do next. There was a hidden video camera in the bookshelf across from the bed. She only had to press the switch as she entered the room. It was wired up to a bedside light. Even if the unsuspecting gentleman requested that the light was turned off, the camera would continue rolling. There was already enough evidence on tape to implicate half a dozen cabinet ministers and influential businessmen.

Charmaine dressed carefully that evening – something long and clingy. She sprayed herself liberally with perfume, took a few quick puffs on a joint, then headed out to hail a cab. She was feeling a little tired.

By the time she got there the restaurant was full. She handed her silk shawl and bag to the attendant and was led through to the private booth at the rear of the room where Simon and Dorland were sitting, a nearly empty wine bottle between them.

Simon looked at her appreciatively, she noticed, as she came over in a cloud of expensive-smelling perfume and full cleavage; Mike Dorland too. He was a short, podgy man with pale, stubby fingers who talked non-stop, mostly about himself. It was almost midnight by the time he got up to go to the toilets.

Charmaine rolled her eyes at Simon. '*Yuk!*' she whispered. 'He's *awful*! Don't tell me I have to—'

'Yes, you do, my darling girl,' Simon said, sliding a hand up her thigh. 'He's pretty drunk – he probably won't be up to much anyway.'

She nodded impatiently. She wanted to go home, get him into bed and get the whole thing over and done with. She could feel Simon's finger probing her and she clamped her legs together. He pulled his hand away just as Mike came back from the toilets, his belly wobbling over his trousers.

The cab dropped them outside the flat. Charmaine walked ahead of the two men, swinging her hips as provocatively as she could. The thought of having to touch, have sex – do *anything* – with the sweating Mr Dorland was making her feel ill. She would have to do a line or two before she could get her head round the idea. They walked upstairs, Dorland a little unsteadily. He'd had far too much to drink, he kept mumbling, his eyes fixated on Charmaine's rear.

Inside, she dimmed the lights in the sitting room, made both men a drink and excused herself for a minute or two.

In the bathroom, she opened the medicine cabinet, pulled out the little plastic bag in which she kept her weekly stash, then expertly cut and drew a line. She wiped her nose, checked herself in the mirror and added a touch of lipstick. She shrugged out of her dress, dusted her naked body with golden powder and walked into the bedroom. She switched on the camera, opened her underwear drawer, selected a red lacy thong and wriggled into it. She checked her reflection in the mirror one more time – beautiful, who could resist her? – and walked out into the living room.

Dorland couldn't keep his podgy hands off her arse as she led him into the bedroom. She lay back on the bed, her arms raised above her head as she tried not to look at his pale, blubbery body. *Ugh*. She wished he would hurry up.

She smiled at him encouragingly, her moves exquisitely timed and practised. She knew the drill.

Dorland humped away on top of her. Of course he'd asked for the lights to be switched off – there was only the dim glow of the scented candle she kept on the window-sill to light the room. She knew it was enough to film by: they'd tested it many times before. She heard the bedroom door open. The idiot, she thought. Simon wasn't supposed to come in until they'd finished. Dorland was too busy grunting and groaning to notice.

She felt Simon sit down on the bed and heard him say something to her. Then she felt a hand slide up her leg, and another grope her breast. Dorland giggled as he slid out of her, and Simon prepared to take his place. It was obviously an arrangement between them. She wanted to cry. She lay there passively as the two men took it in turns to satisfy themselves with her. It was horrible. She'd never felt so cheap in her life.

'I'd better go,' Gabby was saying. 'I'm meeting Nathalie in about ten minutes.'

Charmaine snapped back to the present. 'So soon?' She pulled a face.

'I know, it's only a flying visit. I'll come again on my way back from Geneva. Are you sure everything's OK?'

'Yeah, I'm just a bit bored. Not much to do.'

Gabby picked up her bag and gave Charmaine a hug.

'Come and visit us in New York,' she said. 'Nael'll be over in about a month's time. We're looking for somewhere bigger.'

Charmaine marvelled at how easily everything had fallen into place for Gabby. It was hard to believe sometimes. When she thought back to St Anne's . . . Funny how it had turned out.

Gabby nipped into the phone box at the end of Charmaine's road and dialled Nathalie's number. Nathalie answered immediately. 'What're you doing? Can I come over?' Gabby asked.

'Oh, please! *Yes!* I'm dying for some adult conversation!' In the background, Gabby could hear Micha hollering. 'Jump in a cab – I'll share the cost with you. The tube'll take for ever.'

Gabby hung up. She probably earned more than Nathalie now but old habits died hard. She supposed it hadn't been all that long ago that she'd been the perpetually broke student among them. She thought again of Charmaine, and winced. Perhaps Nathalie could think of something for her to do. She needed something that wasn't connected to a man.

'Gabs!' Nathalie flung open the door. She was covered with flour. Micha. She shrugged, half embarrassed. Gabby grinned. Nathalie looked so . . . *happy*. Her normally neat kitchen was ankle-deep in flour and sugar, with Micha's little handprints everywhere. He was sitting in the middle of the floor, gurgling to himself in delight.

'What on earth have you been doing?'

'Baking,' Nathalie said drily. 'Or trying to. He seems to prefer it raw.' Gabby bent down and picked up the wriggling child. He looked nonplussed for a second then let out an ear-splitting yell. Nathalie took him from her. As soon as he was in his mother's arms, he stopped, his enormous black eyes trembling with tears.

Gabby laughed at him. 'Poser,' she said, and pinched his nose gently.

'How's Charmaine?' Nathalie asked.

'She's OK,' Gabby said, wondering whether to bring up the subject of Simon. Nathalie looked as though she had her hands full without having to worry about Charmaine.

'Did you meet her boyfriend?' Nathalie asked, as though she'd read Gabby's mind.

'No. Have you?'

'No. He bought her the flat, did you know that?'

Nathalie pulled a tray of buns out of the oven with one hand while she held Micha with the other.

'Yes. What does he do?'

'I don't know. She's always going on about Regency Wharf – he's one of the developers or something. Did you know that's the development Lisette's doing?'

'Yes, I read about it. She was working on it when we were at Sans Soucis. Who was the guy she was in partnership with? He was there too.'

'At Sans Soucis?'

'Yeah. What was his name?'

'Simon Kalen. That's Lisette's company . . . Kalen de Zoete Koestler. KdZK. Why?' Nathalie looked puzzled.

'Isn't that the name of Charmaine's boyfriend?'

'Simon? Yes . . . but no, it can't be, don't be ridiculous. Simon Kalen's *old*.'

'Well, how many young men can afford a flat like hers? Oh, God, I hope it's not.'

'No, she'd have said. It's impossible – she'd be the same age as his daughter!' Nathalie put Micha down. The two watched him stumble across the floor towards Gabby. He'd obviously decided she was safe. He clung to her legs unsteadily as he looked up at her. Gabby smiled at him. He was the spitting image of his father – she had only seen him once, that time in the bar in Chelsea, but he was hard to forget. She looked at Nathalie. 'Have you heard from him?' she asked quietly.

Nathalie shook her head. 'Nope. And I won't. He doesn't know about it. Or him.'

'Is that fair?' Gabby asked gently.

Nathalie shrugged. 'Is it fair? Or unfair? I don't care. He gave me nothing, Gabs, nothing but heartache. I don't care what's fair to him.'

Gabby picked Micha up.

'But it's hard on my mother,' Nathalie added suddenly. Gabby looked at her questioningly. 'She lost his child – remember?'

Gabby nodded slowly. God, what had happened to them all? She thought of Charmaine and the mysterious Simon. Rianne and Riitho – the kidnap, the collapse of their relationship. Nathalie and her struggle with Sacha, the knowledge of his affair with her mother. It was all so complicated. When she thought about it, she and Nael were about the most straightforward couple in the world. She looked at her watch. They were meeting in just over an hour. A surge of love ran through her. Nael was moving to New York soon. They would spend a fortnight together looking for a bigger place in which they would start their lives together. He wanted to wake up next to her in a place that belonged to both of them. She couldn't wait.

71

It wasn't glamorous and it certainly wasn't fun. It was bloody hard work. At first she'd been reluctant. 'Catalogue work? Me?' She'd stared at the agency manager in disbelief. I'm Rianne de Zoete, she wanted to say. I do editorial and runway modelling, not fucking catalogues. But she bit her tongue. It had been almost a month of walking up and down Manhattan, on almost a hundred go-sees. She didn't know what had happened – had Ross Carter put the word out that Rianne de Zoete wasn't to be trusted? She couldn't find any other explanation for the cold shoulder she received from just about everyone who was anyone in the business. Ford, Storm, Models 1, she'd tried them all. She was too tall, too thin, too fat, too old, too well known, her time was over. She'd have to start at the beginning again if she wanted anything in modelling. Where was that, exactly?

'Catalogues, honey.' The manager leaned back in his swivel chair. 'Good money, regular work. Nothing to turn up your pretty little nose at. When can you start?'

Rianne looked at him and shuddered. Eight thousand dollars was all she had left. 'Now?'

'Good girl.' Bertie Muñoz knew he was on to a winner. She was good-looking enough ... a little tired-looking, perhaps and her face was drawn, but she had the right ingredients. A little on the thin side ... he didn't particularly care for these skinny girls with their jutting bones but, hey ... he had a Marshall Fields catalogue shoot coming up and she fitted the bill. Tall and blonde. That was what was required. He didn't mind she was nearly thirty. 'The shoot's in Newark,' he said getting up heavily from his desk. He handed her a piece of paper.

Rianne took it. Newark, New Jersey. It was a far cry from the Caribbean. She folded it and put it into her bag. Ignoring his look of approval as she stood up, she walked out of his office.

It paid the bills. That was all she could say about it. The work was undemanding, dull. No teams of hairdressers and make-up artists, personal dressers, the press. This was the graft end of modelling. Three or four girls sharing the same stylist, cups of bad coffee on tap, and Bertie Muñoz on his cellphone, organising the next job. She worked for Marshall Fields, Hudsons, Macy's. Muñoz wasn't fussy and neither was she. She was determined to find and make her own way.

The other girls, knowing who she was – or who she had been – were a little wary of her. They couldn't quite understand what she was doing among them. Rianne kept to herself. As the weeks slowly turned to months since her return to New York, she had discovered something – that it was easy to disappear from oneself, to slip out of sight. She was living far below the radar of her earlier life – no parties, visits, phone calls, days at the spa. Apart from Gabby, there was no one around her who knew her from before. She found and rented a small studio apartment on the East Side. It was almost the same size as her bathroom in Bryanston, the smallest space she had ever lived in. She was alone. She wanted it that way. She shuddered when she thought of Lisette and Hennie, or Olivier and Bruce, and the life she'd lived before in Mulberry Place or Wilton Crescent or any of the homes Lisette had provided for her.

It was only when her thoughts turned to Riitho that she experienced pain. Hot, horrible, searing pain that threatened to rip her apart. Walk into it, Gabby had advised. Don't block it away like you usually do. Walk into it and out the other side. She did just that, lying in tears in her bed in the early morning as she tried to picture him . . . what was he doing, where was he? Was it possible to hurt this much? Still? She lay in bed and found no answers.

'Well, where do *you* fancy?' Nael asked, reaching across the table for the jam.

Gabby got up, came across and kissed him hard. It was early September. He'd been in New York for a week and she loved having him at home with her. 'I don't know. Suppose it ought to be somewhere that's easy to get to from the airport. I'm beginning to find this area a drag.' She refilled her coffee cup.

'That's 'cos you fly business class, my dear,' Nael said drily. It was a joke between them. The BBC were more likely to pay for the kinds of flights that came into Newark, New Jersey, than JFK, New York City. Gabby, as a *bona fide* UN employee . . . Hell, she was entitled to all sorts of perks, he claimed, his head in her lap as they watched the news. Business-class air travel, limo service to and from the airport, a grocery-delivery service, free dry-cleaning, and an Anglo-Palestinian lover on demand. No wonder the UN never managed to solve a crisis – they were too busy making sure their employees were looked after. War correspondents, on the other hand, he continued, absent-mindedly caressing the inside of her arm with his thumb, now they *really* had it tough.

'Oh, yeah?' Gabby looked down at him, his hazel eyes

half-hidden by his lashes. He was nut-brown – he'd spent a week in the scorching sun in Dubai before coming to New York. He and a group of hacks, as he called them, the young reporters, photographers and cameramen who chased wars and famines, strikes and political clashes across the globe, had decided on the spur of the moment to take a break in one of Dubai's glittering hotels, drink a couple of beers and look at women. 'And did you?' she asked him, gently biting his earlobe.

'What?'

'Look at women.'

'Course not. What d'you take me for?' She could feel him smiling into her stomach.

'Liar.'

'OK. One or two.'

'And?'

'And what?' His voice was muffled.

'How do they compare?'

'To you?'

'Mmm.'

'Well, there *was* one . . .' he turned and squinted up at her face. It was unusually tight. 'Hey . . . I'm joking . . . I'm only joking, Gabs.' He opened both eyes. She was smiling, but only faintly. He touched her cheek, propping himself up on one elbow so that his face was almost level with hers. 'I love you,' he said, looking at her intently. She blushed, half-turning away. He nuzzled at her face with his own, his lips soft against hers. 'I mean it. I love *you*.' He lowered his head, burying his face in her stomach again. 'Well?' he asked, his lips tracing a pattern across her skin. Gabby blinked. She'd been daydreaming. 'How about Brooklyn? It's cheaper,' she offered.

'Sounds good to me. Will you look while I'm gone?'

'Yep. When are you going again?'

'You know when I'm going – Friday.' He grinned.

Gabby nodded. Friday. Four whole days away. At the moment, things couldn't possibly get any better.

She was wrong. On Thursday evening, they walked down Fort Washington Parkway to Patchouli's, Gabby's favourite neighbourhood restaurant. He was leaving early in the morning and she was dreading having to say goodbye. He ordered a bottle of wine and reached across the table to take her hand. 'Cheer up,' he said. 'I'm back in a month. It'll go by quickly.'

'I know. And I'll be really busy. I'm supposed to be in Geneva next week. It just feels like a really long time.'

He reached into his jacket pocket. 'I thought I'd get you something, you know, to remember me by.' He held something in his closed fist.

Gabby pulled a face. 'Don't say that, it sounds terrible. Like you won't be back or something.' She laughed, trying to make a joke of it.

'Well, now's not the time to bring it up but things are tense at the moment. But I don't want to talk about that. Here.' He opened his hand towards her.

Gabby froze. In the centre of his palm was a little square black box. She swallowed.

'Go on, take it. Open it.'

She took it from him, her fingers trembling. Her eyes filled suddenly with tears. She opened it. It was a single diamond set in a band of white gold. She stared at it, not quite able to believe it. Things like this didn't happen to girls like her. She slipped the ring out of its velvet band and tried it on. It was a perfect fit.

'I had to nick one of your other rings,' Nael said. 'But I wasn't sure which finger you wore it on – the one with the blue stone. I kept staring at your hands last week but you didn't put it on. D'you like it?'

'It's perfect,' Gabby said, with a catch in her voice.

'Will you?' His voice was suddenly quiet.

'Yes. Yes, I will.'

Some time in the night, just before dawn, she awoke. She lay still for a moment, feeling Nael breathing beside her.

She switched on the bedside lamp and watched him cautiously. He didn't stir. She drew out her hand from under the sheet and stared at the ring in the soft light, watching it glow and sparkle.

Nael was asleep, as always, on his stomach, one arm flung over her legs. His breathing was deep and even. It was a warm night and she'd turned off the air-conditioning as soon as they got into bed. She hated sleeping with it on – she'd wake in the morning, frozen, then step outside into the heat, dripping with sweat. No wonder half of her office had colds. He was naked, his buttocks and legs covered by the loose cotton sheet that was draped over them. She traced the contours of his body with her eyes, taking in the tanned muscular back, the light sprinkling of freckles and dark moles on his shoulders; the patch of lighter brown hair under his arms; the sharp cut of his biceps and the darker brown hair that covered his forearms. His hair was free of its pony-tail and lay curling around his neck. The sun had bleached the ends – they were almost golden. His cheek rested on the pillow – she could see the dark shadow of a beard under his olive skin. She followed the curve of his lips, the flat plane of his cheekbones, the thick, dark lashes. There was a tiny mole just below the corner of his left eye. She stared at it, as though seeing it for the first time.

She looked down at the diamond flashing on her finger. Nael and the ring . . . two unconnected entities, beautiful, sensual and desirable in their own way. And yet they *were* connected, through her. In a way, she had possession of them both. She rolled the phrase around in her mouth. Had possession. To have possession. To be possessed. A fragment of a Borges poem came to her: 'The useless dawn finds me in a deserted street corner: I have outlived the night.' She frowned. How did it continue? 'What can I hold you with?' That was it. Well, he held her now.

She slid the hand bearing the ring down his back and switched off the light with the other one. He mumbled in his sleep, turning over to bring her into the circle of his arms. Even in sleep she never had to ask to be let in, to push, to knock. He drew her in, right from the start.

At times she had to pinch herself to make sure she was awake – and that the past few months had really happened. She'd just moved into their new apartment in Park Slope, Brooklyn, a block away from Prospect Park in one direction and the pretty cafés and shops on Third Avenue in the other. It was a brownstone, a typical Brooklyn building with a lovely bay window at the front. She'd hung a wind chime on the fire-escape stairs at the rear of the apartment. Nael was in Kuwait City, covering the aftermath of the Gulf War. He'd be back in New York in a month. Plenty of time to get settled into your new job, he'd said.

She looked at the computer screen. 'Violence against women devastates lives,' she'd written. 'It fractures communities and destroys families. Domestic violence, rape, harmful traditional practices and other forms of gender-based violence are obstacles to achieving gender equality in every nation.' She tapped her pencil against her teeth. Not bad.

She loved her new job. She was a human-rights adviser to UNIFEM, the women's fund at the UN that provided financial support and technical assistance to programmes around the world that had promoted women's rights since 1979. She had a small office on the fifteenth floor of the building on 45th Street, with a team of dedicated, committed and tough workers, mostly women, who lived and breathed their jobs. She had to support and advise the sixteen regional programme directors who were spread in countries across the world and came together in New York twice a year. Their target was to shift public perception of violence against women and girls as a predominantly women's issue and turn it into a key human-rights one.

She'd been told when she took on the job that she had to be prepared for a lot of travelling, to Europe, Africa, Asia, Latin and South America. She was young, she was eminently capable, and no, she assured the panel, she had no family ties. Not yet. It was ironic. None of the men on the panel had noticed their bias. So far, she'd been to Geneva twice, and once to Nairobi. In New York, she spent her days in meetings. When she went home, there were reports to write. She'd never written so many in her life. She hadn't been long enough in the UN system to know that this was usual: they made progress, yes, but they also wrote an awful lot of reports.

72

Nathalie sat in the waiting room, holding the letter from Joseph Stern. He was her business accountant and had asked to see her. She'd left Micha with Charmaine – again. She hoped he would be all right.

'Nathalie.' Joseph Stern opened the door to the waiting room and beckoned her in. He looked serious but, then, he always did. He ushered her into his office, offered coffee – no? Perhaps some water? No? 'Fine. Well, let's get started. Might as well get down to business.' He pulled open a number of files and placed a spreadsheet before her. She looked at the figures, and gulped.

An hour later, her head reeling, she walked out of the offices and straight into the chaos of the King's Road. She was oblivious to the morning shoppers, her hands thrust into the pockets of her raincoat. U/d was in trouble. All four stores. They were over-extended – a downward turn in sales, recession, luxury market the hardest hit. He'd drawn up a series of reports: 'Sales Analyses'; 'Forecasting Trends'; 'Retail Decline'. She shuddered. They sounded like terminal diseases.

The scary thing was, she hadn't noticed it happen. Even when he was talking, she'd been staring at his mouth, watching it open and close, open and close . . . a cough here, a hand to the mouth there . . . she wasn't listening. It was only when he'd said her home was at risk that she'd sat up, startled. Yes, he explained briskly. Her stepfather, Clive, had used the house as partial collateral against the business. Standard procedure, particularly as the business had been doing so well. But things were different now.

'If you'll allow me,' he coughed discreetly and prised one of the files out of Nathalie's grasp, 'in here, you'll find a modest plan . . . an outline, if you like, a few suggestions. We may have to consider a . . . budget,' he continued delicately. 'Just until the market swings round again. Although, I must say, it's looking rather glum.'

Nathalie blinked. A budget?

He pushed another file across the desk and flicked it open. 'Personal Expenditure'. She stared at it. Christ, had she really spent that much this month? She looked up at him. He nodded. Her mouth tightened. She thanked Joseph Stern as firmly as she could and hurried out of his offices.

'Can I come round this evening?' she asked Philippe from a phone booth on the King's Road, her voice breaking.

'Of course. What's the matter?'

'I'll – I'll tell you then,' she said, sniffing back a tear.

'Nothing's happened to Micha, has it?'

She heard the concern in his voice. 'No – nothing like that. I'll see you later. Eight-ish?'

'Yes, of course. Come earlier if you want and bring him along. He can sleep in Annelise's room. She'll be over the moon.'

Jenny lumbered about the kitchen, bringing things to the table, stopping to chat, planting a kiss on Philippe's head. She was eight months pregnant with their third child and glowing. Pregnancy suited her. Nathalie had been sick almost every day of hers. She watched the two of them, so perfectly in tune with each other, and felt a lump in her throat.

'So, what's going on?' Philippe said, pouring them both a glass of wine. Jenny looked ruefully at her fizzy water.

'It's the business.' To Nathalie's horror, tears welled in her eyes.

'Hey!' Philippe jumped up and put an arm round her. 'Is it that bad?'

'Yes.' Nathalie nodded. 'I had a meeting with Stern this morning. He said I had to go on a – a budget!' She felt incredibly weak and silly.

Philippe hugged her. 'Come on, everyone's on a budget these days – even the rich. There's a recession on, Nat, hadn't you realised?'

'Not really.' She sobbed. 'I just don't have time to go into the shops any more, I don't have time to read the papers, I don't—' She broke off to wail louder.

Philippe looked at Jenny. Nathalie was on the verge of hysteria. He squeezed her shoulders, hard. 'Nat, it'll be all right. Come on, don't worry. Show me the reports later on and we'll figure something out. A rescue package. Come on.' Nathalie clung to him. She hadn't realised how tired she was, or how drained she felt. She hadn't cried in months. There just hadn't been time. Philippe let her cry, holding her gently and signalling to his wife. A drink. Get her a drink. A strong one. Eventually, her sobs began to lessen and her shoulders stopped shaking. She really was exhausted. She hiccupped.

'Th-thanks,' she said, her voice shaking as Philippe handed her the whisky. He pushed a box of tissues towards her. 'I – I really needed that.'

'You should have come to me earlier, Nat,' he admonished her gently. She blew her nose.

'I didn't realise that it was so serious. I haven't had time to think.'

'It's tough,' Jenny said sympathetically. 'I mean, I'm not working or anything and I've still got a nanny five days a week.'

'But you've got two,' Nathalie protested. 'I've only got Micha. I can't understand it – why can't I cope?'

'I've got Philippe,' Jenny said quietly. 'It's not about having one or two or even three.' She pointed to her swollen belly. 'It's about having someone to lean on.'

'Don't you dare lean on me, not with that weight behind you,' Philippe joked, trying to lighten the air. Jenny pulled a face at him. Nathalie watched them enviously.

'I guess so,' Nathalie said slowly. 'But . . . it's not an option for me.'

'Maybe not with Sacha,' Jenny said slowly, not looking at Philippe. She knew his name was dangerous territory in this family. 'But have you thought about seeing anyone else. Not for support, necessarily, but just . . .'

'Me? In this state?' Nathalie almost laughed.

'You need help,' Jenny said firmly. 'Nanny help. I'm going to call Deirdre tomorrow, see if she knows anyone. She's brilliant.'

'I don't know if I could.' Nathalie hesitated.

'You have to, you've got no choice. You've got to let him live,' Philippe said gently. 'He's the most precious thing in your life – he always will be – but you can't watch over him day and night. He has to learn to get by without you from time to time. It's healthy. All children need that.' Nathalie was silent. She looked at her brother. She knew he was right.

'Come on, let's eat,' Jenny broke in. She could see Nathalie had been persuaded. It would take her a while to get used to the idea, that was all. It was such a pity Cordelia wasn't able to help. She'd been brilliant with both Annelise and Jacques but she couldn't bring herself to look at Micha. Understandable. But still a great pity.

Nathalie picked up her whisky and drained it. She felt the fiery liquid burn through her, and realised she was hungry. She hadn't eaten all day.

'Stay the night,' Philippe said, walking back into the kitchen. He'd been to check on the children. 'Micha's fast asleep. Annelise can't take her eyes off him. She wants to know why he's got such curly hair and she doesn't. It's apparently all the rage among four-year-olds.'

Nathalie smiled. Things were so simple at that age.

A few days later, Nathalie opened the door to a pleasant-looking middle-aged lady with sensible shoes and a large handbag.

'Hello.' The woman held out her hand. 'I'm June Hargreaves. Jenny Maréchal asked me to drop by.' Nathalie nodded eagerly. She liked her immediately.

'Hi, I'm Nathalie, Jenny's sister-in-law.' There was a shriek. Micha hated his mother's attention being elsewhere. June Hargreaves stepped inside. Nathalie was torn between wanting to pick him up and appearing firm, capable of withstanding the aural assault.

June took over. 'Let me help,' she said. She put down her bag, put on the kettle, picked up the screaming Micha and popped some biscuits onto a plate. Micha stopped crying, the kettle whistled and, before Nathalie could blink, she was sitting down at her own kitchen table with a cup of tea in front of her and a contented-looking Micha eyeing her from June's lap. She was dazed. And that was only the beginning.

Two weeks later, she walked into the house to find Micha picking up his own toys and putting them into one of the large wicker baskets that June had bought. 'They keep the place looking tidy,' she'd said, and laughed. Nathalie did a double-take. Micha? Putting things *away*? He was a little over a year old! She'd thought they couldn't do anything until they were . . . three? Four?

'Oh, no.' June smiled at her. 'They can start any time. It's just a matter of training.' Micha chortled happily. 'All about boundaries,' June said, putting on her coat. 'You'll see.'

Nathalie picked up her son and kissed him. She turned to

June. 'I don't know how to thank you,' she said. 'It's made such a difference.'

'My dear, you're running a hugely successful company, Mrs Maréchal tells me. That's your job. This is mine, helping you to do yours. Now,' she said briskly, pulling out her umbrella, 'still raining, I see?' Nathalie's coat was soaked, and she nodded, laughing. June Hargreaves was Mary Poppins. 'I'll see you tomorrow. 'Bye, you little rascal.'

Nathalie looked at the kitchen. June had laid out her supper and Micha's: three little Tupperware boxes and the table was already set. With things at home settled down, she could concentrate on the other thing – her dying business empire and what to do about it.

Nathalie and Philippe studied the spreadsheets in front of them. He chewed his inner lip in concentration; she frowned. Every once in a while he raised his eyes and stole a look at her. His little sister. She had her reading glasses on, the ones she hated, and her hair was pulled back into an untidy pony-tail. Her red pen flew across the papers, adding, crossing out, subtracting, totalling. They passed the calculator back and forth between them, pausing only to refill their coffee mugs.

Finally, after scoring through a set of numbers for the last time, she pushed away the sheet and put down her pen. 'That's it,' she said softly. 'We're pretty damned near the edge.'

Philippe's calculations had told him much the same thing. He was amazed at how fast she worked. He'd been an accountant for almost five years but Nathalie, as far as he was aware, knew next to nothing about accounting and here she was, slicing through spreadsheets like a pro.

'There's nothing for it, Nat,' he said slowly. 'You're going to have to close down. Cut your losses and clear out. We'll need to get you out of the leases on the properties, that's the first issue. The monthly payments are crippling. I'll phone Clive tomorrow morning. Someone from his office can help us. You're near to the end of your lease agreements on the other two so it's only the Notting Hill one that you really have to worry about – there's a couple more years on that one. Then you'll need to consider selling the stock. It's possible, just possible, that you'll recoup some of the losses that way. We'll cancel any remaining orders. Lim Soon will be disappointed but that's the way it is. You'll need to pay them out, of course—'

'Philippe. No,' Nathalie interrupted. 'No.'

'What d'you mean?' He looked up at her, puzzled.

'I'm not closing down.' Nathalie was firm.

'Nat,' he said gently, 'it's just not going to work. You're close to bankruptcy. You can't continue haemorrhaging money like this. It's just not worth it.'

'Philippe, I built U/d from nothing after a conversation at dinner. We all did. We can't just let it go under. So the economy's not doing well. So what? We can't turn tail at the least hiccup and bail out. We can't.'

'It's not a hiccup, Nat. It's serious. Things are changing, the whole country's in recession. No one knows when the recovery's going to hit, or when things will turn round.'

'Isn't that what they taught you at uni?' Nathalie asked, getting up from the dining table. 'You told me once. What goes around comes around? Swings and roundabouts?'

'Yes, but—'

'No buts. I'll wait it out. It might take a while, I don't kid myself it'll happen overnight, but it will happen. I got into this when I didn't know what I was getting into – none of us did, we were so young. I've learned a lot since then, things have happened to us – I've had a child. I'm thinking about Micha now, too. I'm not quitting. We can adapt, scale down, whatever. But we don't quit. *I* don't. Now, where are those leases? Which shop d'you think I should keep on?'

'Nat . . .' Philippe began. Phew, his sister was made of strong stuff.

'Philippe, just give me your professional advice. Notting Hill? Islington?'

'Islington's cheaper,' Philippe said finally.

'But Notting Hill's nicer.'

'And you're still within your current lease.'

'Then that's what I'll do. I'll call a meeting with the designers tomorrow morning. We're going in for a new look – utilitarian, no frills, no fuss, pared-down. Black and white undies, maybe a bit of grey. Back to basics. Isn't that what Major called it?'

'Yeah, well, *that* campaign went down like a lead balloon. I'm not sure that's the example you want to follow.'

'This isn't a campaign, darling. Just knickers.'

'Hmm.' He looked at his sister. She was a fighter, not a quitter. He felt ashamed of himself. She had more backbone than anyone he'd ever met. He watched her gather up the spreadsheets and get up.

'A small toast.' She opened the fridge and pulled out a bottle of wine. She handed him a corkscrew.

'A toast,' he agreed. 'Good on you, Nat. I think you're mad to sit it out . . . but, hell, stranger things have happened. You might just win.'

'I will. Cheers.'

Nathalie studied the young man across the table from her. *Dr* Eric Harris. He was a friend of Jenny's and, by happy coincidence, was also Micha's paediatrician. He was nice. Medium height, medium build, short blond hair, blue eyes that crinkled at the corners, even when he wasn't smiling. He was about as different from Sacha as anyone could be.

'What would you like to drink?' he asked, looking at the menu. He'd brought her to a trendy Japanese restaurant, somewhere in Soho. She knew he'd thought long and hard about where to take her – she could tell by the way he kept glancing nervously at her to see if she liked the place, and she didn't have the heart to tell him she hated sushi. She lowered her eyes to the menu.

'Saké?' she hazarded a guess. It sounded nice and strong.

'Good choice. I'll join you.' Eric sounded relieved.

Nathalie went back to studying him over the top of the menu card. She was cautiously pleased. After almost a month of constant nagging on Jenny's part, she'd finally agreed to go on a date – *just a date, mind!* she told Jenny a dozen times – and she was glad she'd come. He was easy to talk to. He seemed genuinely interested in her, asking her about the business, about Micha, about how she coped. It had been ages since anyone had asked her how she coped – with anything – and it felt good. She smiled at him and tried to turn the conversation to him, asking him about *his* job, things *he* liked to do.

They had almost finished with their plates of sushi and assorted delicacies that Nathalie could only guess at when she heard someone call her name from behind her. It sounded like – it couldn't be – it was! Charmaine.

'Nathalie?'

'Charmaine?' Nathalie twisted round to get a better look. Charmaine had just walked in – with a middle-aged man.

'Oh . . . *shit*.' Charmaine's mouth dropped open. There was a sudden awkward silence. Nathalie's eyes widened. She recognised the man . . . where had she seen him before . . . she almost choked on her last piece of raw salmon and sticky rice. It wasn't . . . it *couldn't* be . . . yes, it was! Simon. Rianne's Uncle Simon. She couldn't remember his last name. What on earth was he doing here, in London – and with Charmaine? Charmaine was blushing. Nathalie scraped back her chair and got up to kiss her. There was another awkward silence.

'Nat, this is Simon,' she said reluctantly. Nathalie shook hands with him and turned to introduce Eric.

'I believe we've met before,' she said to Simon frostily, as the two men were introduced. Charmaine looked as though she wished the floor would open up and swallow her. Nathalie groaned silently. Gabby was right – he was her boyfriend. But how? And why? Simon and Charmaine excused themselves and went off in search of their table.

Eric's puzzled eyes were on her as she sat down again. 'A friend of yours?' he asked.

'Yes, my best friend,' Nathalie replied automatically. She watched Charmaine squeeze between two tables – what the hell was she wearing? A black dress that was slit almost all the way up her legs. She could see the flash of suspender belt and sheer stockings as Charmaine sat down. She looked like . . . a tart.

'And her boyfriend?'

Nathalie paused for a moment. 'Um, he's Rianne's uncle.'

'Rianne?'

'Oh . . . she's my best friend too.' She took a sip of saké. 'Just wait till Gabby hears about this,' she said, half to herself.

'And who's Gabby?' Eric asked, beginning to smile.

'She's my – our other best friend.' Nathalie knew this was sounding silly. 'She lives in New York.' She giggled.

'How many best friends have you got?' Eric said, laughing.

'Three, actually. There's four of us. We were all at school together. Oh, I suppose it sounds a bit girly.'

'No, not at all,' Eric replied untruthfully. 'What do they all do now?'

'Well, Charmaine doesn't really do anything. She was in LA . . . for some time.' Nathalie thought it best to gloss over that one. She didn't know what Eric would make of Charmaine's colourful past. 'And Gabby lives in New York. She's a human-rights lawyer. She works for the UN. She's fantastic, you'd really like her. And then there's

Rianne. Rianne de Zoete. She's a model. She's also in New York at the moment.'

'Not the one who used to go out with Riitho Modise?'

'Yes! D'you know him?'

'No, not really . . . but I know someone who used to. One of my friends at UCL hung out with him. He was a bit of a playboy. All the nurses fancied him. Nice guy, though,' he added hastily, at Nathalie's slight frown.

'Yes, he's lovely. A bit frightening. He was at the boys' school near ours. I never really knew him.'

'Well, your friend – your *best* friend,' he smiled, correcting himself, 'she's certainly beautiful. Always thought it was a shame they broke up. They seemed really well matched.'

'They were.' Nathalie wondered how Rianne was doing. The last time they'd spoken she'd heard something new in Rianne's voice: determination. She hoped she was all right. She looked at Eric, who caught her eye and smiled. She blushed.

Across the restaurant, Charmaine looked enviously at Nathalie. She and Eric looked like any other couple. He was teasing her and she could see from the way Nathalie fiddled with her hair that she was enjoying it. She looked nervously at Simon and wondered where all of this was headed. He hardly ever spoke about them being together any more – properly together, that was. He didn't talk about leaving Stella or coming to London for good, or her coming to Cape Town. All he talked about were the deals they were putting through, and Charmaine was no longer confident that she was any part of the 'they' he talked about.

He'd got the information he wanted out of Dorland. Apparently it had been easy – a couple of stills from the video and he'd blurted out everything he knew, and more. Whatever he had told Simon, it had apparently been worth it. She was dreading the evening ahead. Lately, at night, he had talked for hours. He never wanted to make love to her: he seemed to have lost the taste – and the knack – for it, preferring to lie back and let her do all the work.

He had the British by the balls, he claimed. They wouldn't know what hit them. KdZK were going to be the biggest, most powerful developers the world had ever seen. He'd cut her allowance in half, claiming she spent far too much money. It was all Charmaine could do to stay awake. Perhaps he noticed her boredom: lately he'd been telling her all kinds of things she was sure he oughtn't to tell anyone. It was a pity she couldn't remember afterwards what he'd said. She'd starting smoking heavily again – a joint in the morning, a couple in the afternoon, several in the evening and one before bed. It stopped her dwelling on her situation. And it was cheaper than coke.

He had some kind of power-fixation, and now it wasn't enough to give him a blow-job. No, he had to force her to do it and she had to pretend not to want to. He'd grab her by the hair, push her head down, slap her about the face – nothing too hard, mind – with his erect penis, then push it down her throat, making her gag, and pulling her hair sharply if he felt her teeth. It was horrible. And even worse, lately he'd taken to demanding sex – or his version of its equivalent – in the strangest of places: in the hallway at home, listening for people coming down the stairs; in the back of a cab with the driver looking at them in his mirror, knowing exactly what she was doing. He'd leave an enormous tip as he got out . . . and then wink.

The other day at dinner in a fancy restaurant in South Kensington, he'd excused himself from the table and half-dragged her with him to the toilets. Luckily there was no one about. He pushed open one of the stalls and hurriedly pulled her in, pushing her head down in that now all-too-familiar gesture of his – she was sure her heels were sticking out from under the half-door. She had heard the outside door open, then a gasp, then someone giggling as she furiously sucked him. He came almost immediately. Nauseating. But how was she going to get out of it? What else could she do? It was eerily like LA all over again.

She turned her attention back to him. He was staring at her. 'What?'

'Follow me.' He got up, throwing his napkin onto the table. She sighed. Jesus Christ. Not again.

Eric and Nathalie stood up to leave. Charmaine and Simon were nowhere to be seen. They threaded their way through the diners and emerged into the cool night air, then walked down the street to his car in companionable silence. He made no move to touch her, although Nathalie found – to her surprise – that she *wanted* to feel his arm at her side or even the touch of his fingers against hers. She hadn't felt this way about anyone in a long, long time.

'D'you want to go straight back?' he asked her, as he started the engine.

It was as if he'd read her thoughts. Nathalie peered at her watch. 'Oh, I . . . well, I'm not much fun in a nightclub.' She laughed to cover her embarrassment. 'I feel too old for that. You . . . would you – you could come for some coffee at my place,' she said, in a rush. 'Micha's at my brother's. Not that it matters, I mean . . . you know . . .' She was flustered.

'Yes, I'd like that very much.' He smiled at her.

She blushed again. What was wrong with her? She was worse than Gabby.

'Beautiful flat,' he commented, as she opened the door. Without Micha the flat seemed eerily quiet. She led the way into the sitting room, conscious of Eric behind her. His eyes followed her as she slipped off her coat and shoes and walked in her stockings into the kitchen. She fished out two mugs, then changed her mind and took out wine glasses and a bottle. She came back into the sitting room to find him sitting on his heels, looking through her records and CDs.

'Good taste in music, too,' he said, holding a CD aloft. 'May I?' Nathalie nodded and set the glasses down. Anita Baker's full, sensuous voice filled the room. She poured the wine and sat on the soft white sofa, her feet tucked under her, not sure what to do with her hands, her eyes . . . her thoughts.

Eric confused her, she wasn't sure why. With him, the butterflies in her stomach weren't the jittery, ice-cold tremors that ran through her every time Sacha turned up or she heard his voice. And they weren't the I-barely-notice-you feelings she'd had with Marcus, or the don't-come-too-close feeling she'd had with Paul. It was something in-between. Eric was familiar – the things he said, his humour, even the way he looked. Typically English, about as unlike Sacha as . . . Marcus had been. And yet not. She was aware of him in a way she hadn't been aware of anyone since . . . well, since Sacha. She *felt* his presence, beside her, around her. Looking at the nape of his neck, at the thick, dark hair that sprang up from beneath the V of his jumper or the pale underside of his wrist, she was moved to touch him.

Eric settled himself next to her, not touching her, and picked up his glass. 'Great evening,' he said. She blushed yet again. 'You're lovely when you blush.' Nathalie went even pinker. 'Is it me, or do most men make you blush?' He said it with a smile, teasing her.

'No, I don't normally go this red.' She found her voice at the same time as she found her wine glass. She took a large sip.

'Ah, so it's just me.'

'No . . . yes . . . no.'

'By that you mean yes. Yes?'

'No.' They burst out laughing. And then it was easy.

He remembered to set the alarm clock – he was the doctor

on rotation that weekend. 'You can sleep until midday,' he whispered into her neck.

'I don't normally,' she whispered back, kissing his.

She felt him smile. 'You seem to be doing an awful lot of out-of-the-ordinary things this evening. Miss Maréchal. What's normal, then?'

'Well, this isn't.'

'How about this?' She giggled. Eric was so easy. And for that she was grateful.

73

In Johannesburg, Riitho found it wasn't getting any easier. He thought about her constantly, threads of memory holding her together in his mind. The experience of loss, of missing someone, was alien to him: he had left his family twenty years earlier without a backward glance. He had spent most of his young adulthood making sure no one ever came close enough for him to miss them. Now he was paying for it. The threads unravelled, she slipped away. Livingstone saw and was worried. He spoke to Riitho one evening – it was rare for them to be alone. Njeri did not know what had passed between them, father and son. Neither said.

That evening, the longest – and only – conversation they'd ever had that touched on such personal matters, Riitho outlined his ideas about his future and, for the first time, Livingstone listened. They did not speak about Rianne, both guessing intuitively that it was not a subject to be exhumed, not yet. Riitho needed time – time to get used to it, time to get over it. Livingstone had spent his life waiting for time to pass. He was patient. He hoped his son would heal. They spoke instead about Riitho's political future, about what he would do with and for his father. He knew the plans he held were different from the ones

Livingstone had for him. Rianne was one thing; to give up his future to be consumed by the organisation was another. He didn't want to sit at a desk in an office, waiting for the chance to join the ANC's proposed Ministry of Housing in three years' time, worried that everyone would assume he was there under his father's influence. He'd been thinking since he got back, he said quietly, looking at his father. Livingstone nodded.

'Well, I know everyone says there isn't one but there *is* a black middle class here – anyone can see that. They've got money and taste – and power. Some of them were in exile, in London and New York, and now that they're back, they need architects, designers – people like them who know about both worlds, here and there. That's what I know how to do.' Livingstone looked thoughtfully at his son. 'I've talked to a few people,' Riitho continued, 'there's lots of work, if I want it. Embassies, housing, public buildings. There are almost no black architects here. Let me make my mark – my *own* mark.'

Livingstone was silent.

'I've done what you wanted,' Riitho said quietly. 'I gave her up. Let me do this.'

Livingstone looked at his son. He was right. Of course he was right.

Riitho phoned two friends in London, both of whom had studied with him at the Bartlett. Adrian Marshall – Aido to his mates – and Rahesh Malik. Listen, he had an idea. How did they feel about coming out to Jo'burg? Forming a partnership? Aido and Rahesh needed no persuading. They were there within weeks. Modise Marshall Malik. They made an interesting trio: Aido, the big, burly Mancunian with a heart of gold and an unusual passion for old Land Rovers; Rahesh, the drop-dead-handsome, disorganised genius of their postgraduate years; and Riitho, good-looking, cool and *so* well connected. The New South

Africa, people called them: black, white, Indian – they were bound to be successful.

They found premises in a disused brewery on Isipingo Street in Yeoville. They spent a month cleaning out the cavernous space – for the three of them, coming from the cramped working conditions of London and Paris, the vast, open warehouse was luxury. They kept the renovations to a minimum, preferring to leave the patchy, distressed paint-work and emphasise the raw, urban feel of the industrial space it had once been. They installed high-tech lighting, glass-topped desks, sisal carpeting, and thought it looked fantastic.

Njeri and Mpho thought it looked unfinished, as if they couldn't afford a proper office. Why can't you paint the walls? And what's this grass on the floor?

'It's *supposed* to look like that,' Riitho explained patiently.

Rahesh and Aido suppressed their laughter.

He found that some days were better than others. When, after a hard day of discussions and arguments in the office over the direction of a particular project, the three went out for a beer, he could almost be persuaded to believe it *would* get better. That he wouldn't miss her as much, that he might even get over her, as unlikely as it seemed. Rahesh and Aido were more than willing to restore him to his 'bad-boy ways', as Rahesh put it. But Rahesh was concerned, and told him so. This new, brooding, intense Riitho was *not* the person he'd last seen jumping out of a bathroom window at a party in Chelsea because not one but *three* of his girlfriends had turned up. He remembered a very different Riitho – the one who had dragged *him* to parties in obscure London suburbs and, more often than not, abandoned him to the Trafalgar Square night bus as he made off with the hostess and, occasionally, her friends. Sometimes Rahesh wasn't sure quite what to do with this Riitho when he suddenly went quiet in the middle of a conversation, with the familiar look of loss in his jet-black eyes. 'Have another beer, mate. Look, the girl by the bar –

she's checking you, I promise . . .' That was Rahesh's way of dealing with him. Aido, in his calm, unhurried way, said nothing. Just slapped him on the shoulder occasionally to let him know. He knew, he cared . . . but a 'chin-up' slap on the shoulder would just about be the extent of any conversation they could possibly have on the subject. Not a man of many words, Aido.

Riitho saw that they cared, and was grateful. For the most part, it worked. The practice was new, but already busy. As everyone had predicted, the media lapped them up, and they had plenty of work. At home, Livingstone was away so much, he barely saw him. Mpho had found a job – or a calling, as his mother joked – with some of the grassroots activists who worked in the townships and was also out most days. Njeri was alone in the enormous new house in Houghton – or as alone as she could be with the relatives, bodyguards, state security and a steady stream of visitors and foreign journalists who showed up each morning. From berating him almost every day, she'd suddenly gone quiet on the subject of Rianne de Zoete. And that worried him. Not only was it totally out of character for Njeri, he had the feeling it was dangerous. He viewed her with caution. It didn't take long to find out what she was up to. Or, perhaps more accurately, *who*.

Her Royal Highness Princess Moshidishi Madadeni Sifopamhene Motsame. Shidi to her friends. She was the ninth daughter of King Motsame, the Zulu monarch and the largest thorn in the ANC's side. Riitho knew the history. The tensions between the almost exclusively Zulu Inkatha supporters and the ANC were not new – the reasons were historical as well as political – but in the run-up to independence, there had been violence. Mandela and Modise had reason to worry: the country was bleeding to death, poised on the verge of civil strife. They were under pressure to suspend the armed struggle, something they had refused to do until steps had been taken towards the negotiation of power. It was a controversial issue within the

Movement. Modise and Marius de Zoete were among those who thought suspension was political and ideological suicide, but they were in the minority. Those in favour argued that it was the only way forward: they had to suspend the armed struggle to create the right climate for moving the talks forward. In June de Klerk lifted the State of Emergency, and in August, the ANC and the government signed the Pretoria Minute. They all hoped that the violence would end.

But it did not.

From the sidelines, Njeri watched the journey towards independence lurch dangerously back and forth between success and failure – and made her decision. She despaired of them ever reaching a political settlement to the violence and mistrust, even if Livingstone didn't. She was subtle. More than six months of freedom and five thousand dead, she pointed out to him at breakfast one morning. The ANC was being derailed in its attempt to move from an illegal, underground liberation movement into a legal democratically elected political party. He raised his eyebrows. She was telling him what he already knew?

'No,' she insisted. 'I want you to listen. Something else is needed. An alliance of a different sort.' Njeri was no fool. European kings and queens had done it for centuries – African royalty, too, come to that, Sobhuza and Shaka. It was one way of bringing together that which could not be joined. Moshidishi Madadeni Sifopamhene Motsame. She was young, educated ... and royal. With his daughter married into the opposition, Motsame would have no option but to call off hostilities.

After dinner one evening Livingstone looked up from the papers he was studying. 'What are you playing at?' he asked her irritably. 'You're trying to be a match-maker?'

'What do you want?' she asked, her lips pursing. Livingstone sighed. His women. 'Don't tell me now you approve of that ... de Zoete girl.' She glared at him. 'I didn't sit down and watch you taken away from me for twenty-four years for him to come back and take up with her.' Her eyes flashed. 'I didn't join the struggle and sacrifice *everything* so that *he* could come back and dance with white girls. Neither did *you*.'

Livingstone said nothing. Njeri could be stubborn. Oh, twenty-four years apart had done little to change *that*. She snorted, moving away from him in exasperation. Fine. Faced with such opposition from her men she would simply step up her efforts. She went on the offensive.

Riitho saw through her campaign immediately. At first he did nothing. He didn't respond. He knew exactly what she was doing and it angered him beyond belief. He refused to co-operate or confront her. It was not their way. No, their war was a silent one, which saw Riitho retreat even further into his work at the office and renew his resolve to move out of the spacious home on Briar's Avenue into something of his own. Mpho, of course, was on her mother's side. Rahesh and Aido looked on, not sure of the strength of Riitho's objections. His relationship with Rianne de Zoete had been over for ages, or so he said.

'She's cute,' Rahesh said, one morning, as the three were working together.

'So?' Riitho was curt. He was bent over a model with a scalpel in one hand. He hacked away at the cardboard angrily.

'I'm just saying . . .' Rahesh began, as Riitho destroyed the base they'd spent two hours building.

'What?' Riitho looked as though he were about to wreck the model too.

'Well, I don't know. It could be worse,' Rahesh said, a little lamely.

'How?'

'She could be ugly.' In Rahesh's eyes at least, the far greater tragedy.

Aido looked up from his drawing-board. Uncharacteristically, he offered an opinion. 'Yeah, short *and* fat.' He fell silent again.

Riitho looked at them, annoyed. 'Jesus, you two, is that all you care about?'

'No, of course not. We're not *that* shallow. But it *could* be worse. Really. At least she looks OK.' Rahesh sounded as though he was pleading.

Riitho said nothing. He couldn't believe his family was doing this. Shidi Motsame was everything Rianne wasn't. Unexceptional. Pretty, not beautiful, not too tall, not too short. Not too clever, not too quiet. Demure, respectful, polite. She was polite, too. Politely pretty, politely educated, politely feminine.

It had nothing to do with race, as Mpho accused him. Shidi just wasn't his type of woman. They had nothing in common. He didn't find her in the least bit attractive or interesting, or even friendly. She was cold and stiff, and she'd never heard of Mies van der Rohe. Neither had Rianne, he thought quickly, guiltily. But Rianne was a quick learner. She picked things up, just as he'd picked things up about her world. And at least she had one. He'd only met Shidi twice and on both occasions he'd been bored out of his skull and irritated by the effort of trying to make conversation. He certainly wasn't looking forward to the coming weekend. Njeri had organised a garden party and Shidi was the guest of honour. There was no way for him to avoid it.

74

'My sister says you've just come back from the US.'

It was a brilliant summer afternoon. The sunlight streamed in through the trees, like molten honey, slipping through the openings in the enormous marquee that had been erected for the occasion. In the far distance, a faint rumbling could be heard: the threat of a summer storm. Riitho was standing with Moshidishi Motsame under the approving eye of Njeri and several well-dressed women who had come with the royal group. He ignored his mother and tried to concentrate on getting a response from the young woman standing next to him.

'Yes.' Shidi Motsame was shy. Riitho Modise was very different from the men she knew, especially the way he spoke. If you closed your eyes, you'd think he was white.

'Whereabouts?'

'Sorry?'

'Where were you? What part of the States?'

'Oh. Boston.'

'Pretty town.'

'Yes.' There was another silence. Riitho wondered what to say next. He looked across the garden. Aido was ambling towards them, two bottles of beer in his hands. He stopped beside them and passed Riitho a bottle.

'Thirst's a killer . . .'

'. . . in this hot, dry climate.' Riitho finished the sentence for him with a laugh. He took a swig. It had been their catchphrase on their three-week, self-directed safari around southern Africa. Aido had driven the entire six thousand miles semi-drunk. He turned to Aido and picked up the thread of a conversation they'd been having in the office. Aido made a he-can't-help-it face at Shidi and the two men launched in. Shidi smiled politely, distantly.

She wasn't accustomed to socialising with white people, not the way Riitho Modise was. The three of them – the white man, the Indian and Riitho – were like a family, always doing things together, talking fast, laughing. She found it strange and difficult. Plus the fact that she didn't speak their language well. Riitho preferred to use English or, even worse, French. She didn't understand half of what they were saying, and certainly not the jokes. She took a cautious sip of lemonade and looked around the garden for someone else to talk to. She could see Mrs Modise glaring furiously in their direction. Oh, well, she'd tried to talk to him. He just wasn't interested.

Riitho glared at Njeri. They were standing in the kitchen. 'But what's wrong with her?' Njeri almost wailed.

'Nothing. She's fine. I just don't need you to organise my life for me.' Riitho's face was closed.

'I'm not organising your *life*,' Njeri said. 'All I asked was that you be nice to her, talk to her—'

'I did talk to her. She's got nothing to say.'

'Oh, you! You are so – you make me *so* cross, Riitho.' Njeri banged her fists on the kitchen counter top.

'Why?' Riitho asked mildly. He knew he was goading her but she was driving him insane with this silly game.

'Don't take that tone with me,' Njeri said furiously. 'I will not—' She broke off. 'Where are you going?'

'Out. Away. I've had enough of this. You talk to Shidi if she's so damned interesting.' Riitho walked quickly out of the kitchen before his mother could say another word. It was rude of him, he knew. In their culture, you didn't do things like that.

He signalled to Lebohang, ignoring the looks that passed between the well-dressed women and Njeri. 'Let's get out of here,' he said.

He and Lebohang walked towards the car. The driveway looked like the forecourt of a Mercedes dealership. They got into the BMW and quickly pulled out of the driveway. 'Where to?' Lebohang asked him, heading for the M1 freeway.

'I don't know. Anywhere. Away from here.'

'Mama C's?' Lebohang mentioned a shebeen bar in Mamelodi, the Pretoria township. Riitho nodded. Anywhere.

He was quiet as Lebohang joined the traffic heading north out of the city. They drove past the defunct mine dumps, ghostly yellow mounds rising to form a chain around the northern suburbs. The air was warm, the threat of rain hung somewhere in the distance, settled close to the horizon like a darkening bruise on the vast, open plane of the sky.

The landscape that unfolded before his eyes as they drove north was painful to him. At times it didn't seem possible that she wasn't with him, that she was gone. It didn't seem possible to have shared such closeness ... and then, nothing. A terrible hostile loneliness, burned out of the intimacy they had once shared, swept over him. Everything he did conspired to remind him of her, of them together – even the things he didn't do, the places he hadn't been, places *they* hadn't been. She would have travelled through the same landscape, he knew. She'd been everywhere in this country, which was as unfamiliar to him as it was dear. He remembered her talking about Shaka's Beach, far in the south, telling him how they'd gone snorkelling and scuba diving at Sodwana Bay. She'd been as far north as Kosi Bay, just before the border with Mozambique, she told him once, hiking through the coastal forest. She knew almost every inch of the country – the white country, he had reminded her. He knew that the images he carried with him, the townships, the squalor, the Bantustans, the prison where his father had been kept, were different from hers.

He thought back to his life in London and Paris. It was as if he'd taken a giant leap back in time. It was the thing his parents didn't seem to understand: that it was as hard for him to be here with them now as it had been to leave all those years ago. To survive outside, away from them, he'd had to cut himself off, develop a protective skin so that things didn't get to him. Not for him the luxury of *real* feeling. He reacted to emotion the way he once heard someone describe how people with depression sometimes avoided music – something about it unlocking all the things they struggled to suppress. Well, it was like that for him: he couldn't imagine ever getting close enough to anyone to lose control. But that was before he had met Rianne. It had taken a while, but she had penetrated the shell and lodged herself firmly inside. He'd have given *anything* to be near her again.

PART SEVEN

75

April 1993: New York

There was a rainbow, a slow, radiant strip of colour, then one of those unexpected spring showers that burst above the Manhattan skyscrapers and pour out of the sky, hitting the surface of the roads with a hiss, mingling with the steam rising out of the manholes as soon as it touches the ground.

Rianne ran down Prince Street, dodging the puddles, an open newspaper held above her head. She turned into Mercer Street, dancing her way across the pot-holes in the road. She opened the door at Space Unlimited, her favourite coffee shop/art gallery, and shook the rain from her coat. It was almost empty.

She put her briefcase on a table and looked around for Simi, the owner. She was here for a meeting, representing Nina Lindberg, the Midwestern photographer, winner of the Jesse Hemmens Prize for Landscape Photography; grandmother; believer in acupuncture and alternative medicine; friend, mentor and employer who had just arrived in New York City and was looking for openings. Nina was also one of the most talented people Rianne had ever met. She'd been working for her for six months and she loved it.

After a year spent in the most mundane and awful jobs – everything from catalogue modelling and secretarial work to working in a florist's – she'd finally stumbled on something she enjoyed. She'd started out as a lowly assistant, lugging Nina's equipment around, looking for studio space, calling galleries, making bookings, organising shows, but she had soon begun to take on other tasks, doing the things Nina disliked and was hopeless at – the publicity and promotional 'stuff', as she called it – and soon Nina couldn't imagine how she'd ever coped without her. Rianne was smart and she was tough, and although she didn't know much about the art business, it wasn't – as she said – a million miles away from fashion which she knew so well. Same flighty, mercurial people, same fragile egos and bullshit.

'I can't pay much,' Nina had said to her, as soon as the interview started, 'just the basics but I can offer you a percentage of any sales.'

Rianne wasn't doing it for the money. As long as she made enough to cover her bills and not dip too much into her fragile savings, she was fine. Nina had never heard of Rianne de Zoete although . . . she was South African? Wasn't she related to the mining family? Related, yes, Rianne told her, but not financially. She was on her own. Nina respected that.

'Hi, Rianne.' Simi spotted her and walked over. They shook hands and sat down. It had been Rianne's idea to approach Space Unlimited. There was something about the easy, everyday atmosphere of the neighbourhood gallery that appealed to her. And Nina's photographs, sensual, enormous pictures of the land from the air, were perfect for the space. She began pulling out scaled-down versions of the prints.

'We thought we'd call it "Taking Measure",' she explained to Simi, 'starting with the smallest-scale at the entrance – maybe these ones here – then moving out.' She had even done a rough plan – which Riitho had taught her to do – of the gallery and indicated which prints should go where. She picked up an image – a clutch of rape fields, taken from the air. The earth appeared as an abstract painting instead of a series of ploughed fields in the depths of Middle America. 'Amazing, isn't she?' she murmured.

Nina Lindberg had found out at the age of fifty-two that

her husband had spent most of their hard-earned savings on new clothes and jewellery for his secretary, with whom he'd had an affair, and had taken up photography as a way of dealing with her pain. She flew around the country in a small Cessna, her Hasselblads and Nikons at the ready, taking the most incredible photographs of the land in which they all lived but never saw. 'Taking Measure'. Taking stock. If Nina could do it, so could Rianne. It was a thought from which she took comfort almost every day.

Simi and she walked around the gallery discussing logistics. The opening would be held in a fortnight's time. Within an hour Rianne had everything sewn up and moved on to her next meeting. She glanced at her watch. She also had a date – of sorts – that evening, her first in over a year. A quick visit to the hairdresser wouldn't hurt. She looked up at the sky. It had stopped pouring. She headed for the subway.

76

Charmaine popped open the little packet and took out her pill. She placed it under her tongue, reached for the glass of water and swallowed. Four pills later, she was done. She rinsed the glass and put it carefully on the draining rack.

Half an hour later, she pulled on her coat and collected her keys. She locked the front door and began to walk down the stairs. Half-way, she stopped. Had she remembered to lock the front door? She hurried back up the stairs. She had. She was out of breath. She turned and went down. She looked at her watch. It was 9.13 a.m. and she was a little late. She worried that she would miss the bus.

She worried about lots of things these days – about being late, or leaving the flat unlocked, or forgetting to brush her hair, small things, silly things. Luckily, just as she rounded the corner, the bus swam into view.

She jumped on and found a seat, her heart beating faster than normal. She tried to calm down. She wouldn't be late. Today everything was under control. She turned to look out of the window, smiling at no one and nothing. She began to feel better. She got off at her stop, walked carefully down the road until she came to number fifty-four. She rang the bell.

Sylvia opened the door almost immediately. 'Just go straight up, won't you?' she said, closing the door behind her. 'I'll be there in a second. It takes me a little longer.'

Charmaine went up the stairs to the consulting room at the top of the house.

'So, how are you today?' Sylvia asked her gently. She nodded encouragingly as Charmaine carefully went through her week. 'Good,' she said, 'it sounds all right.'

Charmaine nodded. The pills were helping. She ran her fingers surreptitiously over the scars on the inside of her wrists. They were healing. She relaxed, little by little. Sylvia's gentle questioning, her warmth – it was easy to talk to her. When they had finished, fifty minutes later, she was still calm. She stood up, buttoned her coat and walked down the stairs. She said goodbye to Sylvia, then opened the front door and stepped out onto the pavement.

It was an unusually clear, bright spring morning. The sky was blue and her breath scrolled out frostily before her as she walked down the road. She could see the brick walls, the brightly coloured front doors up and down the street, but at the same time she couldn't. It was as if there was a thin, gauzy veil between her and the world outside. She waited patiently for the bus. When it came she dropped the exact fare into the driver's palm and took her ticket. The whole outing had taken just over a couple of hours.

When she got back to the flat Nathalie was waiting for her. She was four months pregnant and 'sick as a dog', she remarked cheerfully. She gave Charmaine a quick hug, then made them a cup of tea.

'How're you feeling?' she asked.

Charmaine nodded cautiously. 'OK. Fine.' Nathalie looked at her closely. She was worried about the effects of the pills. Since coming out of hospital, Charmaine had been awfully subdued.

'What d'you feel like doing?' Nathalie asked, biting the edge off a KitKat. 'Shall we go for a walk? Or to a film?'

Anything. Charmaine didn't mind. She didn't like being alone but she didn't mind what she did. Most evenings she went round to Nathalie's, sometimes staying over when she felt too tired to walk back to her own flat. She visited her mother on Sundays but the silences in the Pimlico flat upset her. Mary Hunter was filled with despair over Charmaine. She blamed herself, she blamed Charmaine, she blamed Simon, she blamed everyone. Staying at Nathalie's was better. Eric, Nathalie's husband, was lovely. He was a doctor – he knew when to stop probing for answers she couldn't give. And Micha . . . Charmaine adored him. He was always climbing onto her lap for a wet kiss or a hug. That helped. He called her Auntie Shammie. It was the one thing Cordelia had instilled in her daughter: friends of one's parents were *not* to be addressed as 'Jane' or 'Bob' but as *Auntie* Jane or *Uncle* Bob. It was good for the children: it helped keep the boundaries clear.

'I know,' Nathalie said suddenly. 'How long has it been since you went shopping, Char?'

Charmaine frowned slightly. She couldn't remember. Her sense of time had gone all weird. Some things she could remember easily – they popped in and out of her head all day long. Things she didn't want to remember, too. Important things were hard to hold on to. Take the past two years, she couldn't *really* remember what had happened when. She couldn't remember if it was the Christmas before last or this one that she'd gone skiing with Simon and his three friends who turned out to be clients. Or if it was last summer that they'd been walking down Kensington High Street and she'd walked off the edge of the pavement and into the path of an oncoming car. She didn't know why she'd done it. She had seen the car coming fast and just stepped off the kerb. An idiot passer-by had grabbed her at the last second and thrown her to the ground. Simon just thought she'd been careless. He had barely spoken to her for the rest of his visit.

'Well?' Nathalie said gently.

Charmaine was staring into space. 'What?'

'Shopping . . . would you like to?'

'Yes. That would be nice.'

Nathalie bit her lip. 'Shall I get your coat?' she asked her.

Charmaine got up to take the cups to the kitchen. For the second time that day she washed them, rinsing them carefully and putting them on the rack to dry. She looked around the kitchen. It was all in order. She followed Nathalie down the stairs.

She fingered the dress that Nathalie had pulled out. It was pretty – dark blue background with small silver flowers and thin satin straps. A party dress. What party?

'Are you OK in there?' she heard Nathalie call.

'I'm just putting it on,' Charmaine lied. She looked at it again. Then she put down her bag and stared at her reflection in the mirror. Everything looked OK. She was wearing a pair of jeans, a black woollen sweater, flat black shoes. She seemed fine, normal. She looked at her arms. The same . . . like everyone else's. Until you reached the wrists. She sat down on the little ledge. She pulled up a sleeve, past her elbow. Slowly, she rotated her arm until it was turned, palm-up, to face her. She looked at the reddened, puckered skin at the wrist. She closed her eyes.

Even afterwards, after she'd rung Nathalie in panic and Nathalie had called an ambulance and it had come screaming up the street to fetch her, blue light flashing, even then, she couldn't say *why* she'd done it. It was easy enough to see how – the knife she used for slicing onions lay on the floor of the bedroom, covered with blood and bits of her skin. One of the ambulance men had picked it up and washed it before Nathalie arrived. What could she say? How had it happened? She really didn't know.

She had tried to piece together the string of events for the doctor who admitted her but she couldn't. It seemed as if she'd been feeling that way – yes, suicidal, if that was what he wanted to call it – for months. For ever. She couldn't remember a time when she hadn't fell like this. *Like what?*

She heard his voice from far away. She rolled over, turning her face into the pillow. He pulled up a chair and sat at her bedside, his pad open in front of him, his pen poised to make a case history out of her fragmented story. *Like what?* She shrugged. Like . . . nothing. She just felt empty. She'd woken up as usual, long before dawn.

How long have you been waking up early? A while. *And what do you do when you wake up?* Nothing. Think. Try to go back to sleep. *And do you?* Sometimes. *What do you think about?* Nothing. Everything. *What happened this morning?* She looked at her wrists. She couldn't remember. She'd woken up . . . yes. She remembered waking up early. It was cold. She went into the kitchen to turn up the thermostat. It was still dark. She switched on the light so she could see the dial properly. That was when she saw the knife. She picked it up. She wasn't really intending to do anything . . . just picked it up. It was lying there. She ran a finger along the blade – it was sharp. She pressed her finger into it. It punctured the skin, almost easily. Her finger bled. She didn't really remember what happened next – she was sitting down on the edge of the bed. She'd left the light on in the kitchen . . . she remembered that.

She didn't know why she'd pressed the knife into the skin at the base of her palm . . . first the right hand, then the left. She made a kind of rhythm out of it, pressing hard on this side, a little harder on that side, back and forth. Blood trickled down her hands. It didn't hurt, not really. She just kept on pressing the knife into her flesh. But then it started dripping onto her pyjamas, so she took them off. By then there was a lot of blood and she couldn't stop. She went to the bathroom and washed her hands. When they were clean she started pressing again. And then there was a lot of blood, it covered the carpet, and she washed her hands but it didn't stop – there was blood everywhere, on the bed, on the carpet, on her body. She panicked. And that was when she called Nathalie.

Were you alone? Yes . . . my boyfriend doesn't live here. *Where does he live?* In South Africa. *How often do you see him?* Not very often. *How often?* This year . . . just once. *When was that?* Um, about three months ago. *How often are you in contact with him?* Not very often. *How often? When was the last time you spoke to him?* Um, three months ago. *But he is your boyfriend?* Yes . . . yes, I think so. *You think so?* I guess so. *Does he love you? Care about you?* I suppose so. *What does he do?* He's a businessman. *How long have you been seeing each other?* About three years . . . no, four. *And he's never lived with you? He's always lived abroad?* Yes. *And you don't want to live out there with him?* No, I can't. We . . . can't. *Why not?* He's married. *Oh. And how do you feel about that?* I don't know. *Does he have children?* Yes. *How old are they?* I don't know . . . a bit younger than me, I guess. *Where are your parents?* Who? *Your parents . . . your mother and father?* Oh, my mother's here. In London. I never knew my father. He left when I was small. *I see.*

For a moment there was silence. Then the psychiatrist wrote out a prescription and called Nathalie into the room. He recommended counselling, gave Nathalie a card with the prescription he'd written. She was to start right away. Her wrists had been stitched, there would be scars. He had diagnosed clinical depression. But with the right drugs and counselling, there was no reason why she shouldn't make a full recovery. It would take time, but she ought to come through it. 'Do see the counsellor, Charmaine,' he said to her, as they got up to leave. 'I'm sure you'll benefit enormously.'

Whatever. She had turned her head into the pillow again. She was tired, very tired. She didn't hear him leave.

'Char?' came Nathalie's voice. 'Are you all right in there?' She tweaked the changing-room curtains.

Charmaine started. The dress was still lying in her lap. 'Yes. I'm fine.' She got up slowly. The dress. Put it on. She unbuckled her belt.

77

Gabby looked at Nael. Rwanda? She wasn't even sure where it was. 'When?' she asked, trying not to show her annoyance.

'Tonight. Behrends wants me to fly out tomorrow morning with a French crew. It means catching the six o'clock flight.' Nael ran a hand through his hair. He knew she'd be upset. He'd been thinking all morning of how to tell her he was leaving just three days after he'd arrived.

'What's happening in Rwanda?'

'Not sure. It seems the president's plane was shot down last night. There's talk of mass killings. Trouble's been brewing for months.' Nael looked worried.

'Is it . . . ?' Gabby could barely bring herself to say it.

'Safe?' He looked her squarely in the eyes. 'No better or worse than anywhere I've been before.'

It was getting harder. Each time he went away now her heart was in her mouth.

'Hey,' he said gently. 'It probably sounds worse than it is. You know Behrends. I'll be back in a month.'

He was wrong. It wasn't over in a month. It was three months before he got back to New York and to the Park Slope brownstone. And when he did come back, he couldn't speak. Gabby met him at the airport, her heart in her mouth, Rwanda was now on everyone's lips. Thanks to reporters like Nael and the hundreds of others who had stayed, the world knew what was happening – even if it looked the other way. She was afraid for him – and afraid of what he had seen. She'd watched his dispatches, she'd scrutinised his face on the screen, trying to read between the mask of the professional correspondent and the ordinary, human response to the genocide taking place around him. She couldn't. She watched him walk through the barrier at JFK and emerge, dazed, into the sweltering heat of midsummer.

'Nael.' She waved.

He turned at the sound of his name. He saw her and gave a brief, unhappy smile. 'Gabs.'

He came up to her, dropped his bag and put his arms round her. He buried his face in her neck, and she held him tightly. 'Let's go,' she whispered against his neck. He nodded. He seemed not to want to let her go. She steered him towards the car. 'Is that all you've got?' She looked at his bag. It wasn't the one he'd left with. He opened the boot and slung it in.

'I burned it. I burned everything. The smell.' She nodded slowly and started the car. He slid a hand across to rest on her knee as she drove. He needed to touch her, he said, to remind himself. They drove home in silence.

'I'd forgotten what this place looked like,' he said, as they parked outside the apartment.

'Missed it, have you?'

He nodded slowly, as if to himself. 'Gabs,' he said suddenly, turning to her, 'what are you doing for the rest of the week?'

'Working. Why?'

'Let's go somewhere – just the two of us. Somewhere warm . . . a beach. I need to get away.' She was worried by the note of desperation she heard in his voice. Something in him had changed.

'Sure. Where d'you want to go?'

'I don't know . . . California? I've never been.'

'Me neither. San Francisco?'

'Let's start there and drive north. I need to be somewhere clean . . . and to see something beautiful.'

She saw there were tears in his eyes. She came to him, put her arms round him. 'We'll go tomorrow. I'll book the tickets tonight. Come.' She held open the door. Percy the cat curled himself around Nael's ankles, purring excitedly. He *liked* Nael, who paid him lots of attention. Not like Gabby: a quick stroke as she left for work in the morning and sometimes, if he was lucky, a scratch under the chin as she sat and read on the big red sofa.

She felt his tears on her again that night as they made love. He stayed inside her, even after he was spent, his weight resting slackly against her body. On his face there was a salty wetness – she traced the line of his cheek with her tongue. He didn't speak, just lay against her, the swollen head of his penis in her, still. In the darkness she stroked the face she knew so well, felt the furry sweep of his lashes now wet with tears, her fingers curling around the short hair at the nape of his neck. His whole body was tense, poised.

'Go to sleep,' she whispered. 'Don't say anything, not now. Not yet. Talk to me when you're ready.' She felt him sigh. The tension began to leave him, slowly.

At last he slid off her, his body leaving hers, wetness on the thigh and then he was next to her, shielding his face with his arm. She slipped an arm through his. 'Tomorrow. The day after. When you're ready.' He nodded heavily. He didn't think he could bring himself to talk about what he'd seen.

By the time they pulled into the driveway at the Dancing Coyote Lodge the following evening, it was hard to believe that Kigali or Goma or Gitarama had ever existed. Looking out over the undulating hills of Point Reyes and the immense, muscular swell of the ocean, Nael felt the images that had lodged themselves right there, on the inside of his eyelids, so that he saw them, awake or asleep, slowly begin to dissolve.

He lit a cigarette – he'd started smoking again. He sometimes thought it was the only thing that had kept him sane during his descent into hell. That and the occasional beer – even wine. They'd come across an abandoned wine cellar once, in one of the deserted hotels in Kigali. He, two reporters from the Associated Press and the BBC camera-men had steadily drunk their way through the hotel's supply of fine red wines, night after night. There had been no hangover. In that place, you went from deep sleep to fully awake, alert, in a blink.

He offered one to Gabby. She took it silently. They smoked in companionable silence. She was the perfect person to be with – he thought. A human being who wasn't tainted in the way he'd come to understand. Someone who was content to sit with him, her warm body touching him somewhere, anywhere. He needed that. The silence and the softness of her touch. He made love to her often, like it had been at the beginning. He was unprepared for the surge of feeling that came over him each time he entered her, her clear eyes on his, her hand on his back, steady and sure. He couldn't speak. She didn't ask.

He held her hand, the left hand with its diamond ring. He rubbed his thumb against its sharp, angular head. Three years. It had been three years since he'd asked her to marry him. Yet they hadn't. He was always away on assignment, she was busy, busy, busy. They'd made plans – oh yes, big plans – where would they have it? A small ceremony, just family and friends ... in New York? In London? In Ramallah? They'd even considered Cancún, one of those bloody awful wedding-honeymoon-holiday-of-a-lifetime combinations. But there were always other things to consider. His mother in detention – again, his father ill. And Gabby's parents. She seldom spoke about them, seldom *to* them. He shrugged. So what? It wasn't like Gabby had anything to prove to anyone. She was climbing slowly but steadily towards the top of her game. She had integrity . . . shit, she *was* integrity. Who cared if her father had none? Nael knew all about weak fathers.

He twisted the ring. 'Gabs, why don't we? Right now, just the two of us?'

'Why don't we what?' She rested her head on his shoulder. Her hair was long now. A strand fell across his sleeve.

'Get married. We could drive across the border to Reno. Or Vegas. It takes four hours, maybe five. We could leave right now.' She raised her head and looked out over the sea. It was calm in the early morning breeze. Above them, gulls circled endlessly, cawing in their strange, almost human-sounding voices. She turned to him. There were tears in her eyes.

'Yes. Why not?' He stroked the edge of her eye gently, wiping the unshed tear with his finger. He stubbed out his cigarette. 'Come on, let's go before we change our minds, either of us.' He got to his feet.

'What'll we wear?' Gabby smiled, nervously. She looked down at herself: khaki shorts, a white T-shirt. Her hair fell in loose curls around her face – she hadn't washed it since they'd been swimming the night before. She hadn't brought very much with her, certainly nothing to get married in. Nael looked at her and then at himself – faded blue jeans, hacked off at the knee, a Cambridge University dark blue T-shirt, and he needed a shave. They laughed. 'Let's stop by one of those outlet malls on the way. We'll find something. We can book into a hotel when we get to Vegas. Shall we check out?' Then he answered himself. 'No, we can drive back tomorrow morning.'

'Nael, we're going to spend the whole holiday driving,' she protested, laughing.

'So? I'll drive – don't mind.'

'OK.' She looked at him uncertainly.

He grabbed her arm, pulled her towards him. 'I love you.' He said it slowly, separating the words. I. Love. You.

'Me too, *habibi*,' she whispered back. 'Let's go. What do we need?'

'Drivers' licences, I think. I read somewhere that's all you have to bring with you. They even provide the witnesses. And a credit card, of course. Can't get married without one of those.' He laughed again.

'Let's do it. We can tell them on the way down that we'll be back tomorrow.' She picked up the car keys and her bag. They were going to get married. When they came back the next day, she'd be Mrs Nael Kilani-Hughes. Well, she wouldn't. There was no way she would change her name, he knew that. But . . . a *wife*? My *husband*. She tried it out on her tongue, silently. Husband. She liked the sound of it. Even if she couldn't quite believe it.

'*Sure.*' The girl behind the reception desk at the Holiday Inn smiled at them. She was incredibly friendly. 'No problem.' *Praw*-blem, she pronounced it. Gabby peered at her mouth. She wondered, not for the first time, how it was that Americans seemed to have so many more teeth than anyone else. Perfectly straight, perfectly white. She tore away her eyes from the poor girl's mouth. 'We cater for all kinds of tastes, all kinds of budgets. We have many different types of ceremony – indoor, outdoor, themed, traditional. What kind of money did ya wanna spend?' She continued smoothly. She knew her pitch.

Nael looked at Gabby. Help. Gabby lifted her shoulders. 'Three hundred dollars?' she hazarded.

She and Nael turned back to Goldilocks.

'Sure!' Her smile widened even further. 'Indoor or outdoor? We have a real nice Gazebo Package.' Nael resisted the temptation to snort with laughter. Oh dear. This wasn't how he pictured it.

Gabby nodded. That sounded fine. The girl bent down,

selected a brochure and slid it across the counter to them. *Las Vegas Gazebo Weddings.*

Gabby gulped. It was like buying a car.

'Package Three would be just about right for you guys,' the girl said, sliding an impossibly long nail down the page. 'There.' Her red-tipped talon tapped the spot. Nael and Gabby quickly read the description.

Have Your Own Private Wedding Ceremony held Outdoors in this Beautiful Gazebo. This Wedding includes:
· Minister
· Use of the Gazebo
· Wedding Music (You may bring your own CD)
· Stretch limousine service to and from your hotel/home
· Complimentary make-up and hair (bride only)
· A commemorative photo in an acrylic frame
· Postcards (3)
· 'Just Married' bumper sticker.

You will be picked up in a Stretch Limousine at your hotel/home. You are then off to your Once in a Life-time™ Wedding. This wedding requires a $55 deposit with the balance (plus tax) being paid the day of the wedding. Call us to reserve your Once in a Lifetime™ Wedding. Call today!

'Is that a genuine patent?' Nael asked Goldilocks, sliding the brochure back across the shiny marble counter top.

'Huh?' She looked confused, her smile fading momentarily. She was wary of the English guests. They always asked the *weirdest* questions.

'Don't listen to him.' Gabby smiled. 'This is fine. We'll take it.' Goldilocks smiled back, her confidence restored. 'What do we need?' Gabby asked her, briskly. 'A marriage licence?'

'You can get them twenty-four hours a day from the Clark County Marriage Bureau on Third Street. Here, I'll show y'all on the map. It costs fifty dollars, cash only, no checks or credit cards, you don't need a blood test and it takes about fifteen minutes.' She paused for breath. 'Y'all been married before?' They shook their heads. 'That's fine. The State of Nevada doesn't require you to present divorce papers. Y'all over eighteen?' They giggled, then nodded. 'OK. That's it. When would you like to get married?'

'Today? Is that possible?' Gabby said.

'No problem. Lemme just call and check.' Five minutes later, everything was done. A hairdresser – a *beautician* was what Goldilocks called her – would come to their room at six-thirty that evening with a selection of dresses and beauty products. The wedding was scheduled for eight. It was a five-minute ride from the hotel. It would take about twenty minutes, ten minutes for photos, and they'd be back in time for the Honeymoon Dinner. They looked at each other. Gabby had never wanted to giggle so badly in her life. She just about made it back to the elevator before she exploded.

Gabby came out of the elevator into the lobby. Nael watched her put up a hand self-consciously to touch the flower she'd tucked behind an ear. She looked lovely. He saw several men glance at her as she walked across the marble floor towards the bar. She still hadn't seen him. She slid onto one of the leather bar-stools, the long loose folds of her dress draping around her legs. Her skin was very white. Against the fake-bronze tans and bleached hair around her, she stood out, porcelain . . . and real. He watched her order a drink – something on ice, he could see the liquid catch the light as she raised the glass and drained it in one go. She was nervous. He got up from where he was sitting across the room and walked towards the bar. 'Ready?' He slipped onto the stool beside hers. 'You look . . . beautiful,' he said, touching the orchid Mary-Jo had persuaded her to wear.

'Not so bad yourself, Mr Kilani-Hughes,' she said, and slipped a whisky-coated ice-cube into her mouth.

'Come on, *hamoudi*.' My love. 'Let's go.' He helped her off the stool. They walked out into the searing dry heat. The stretch limousine was indeed waiting. The driver leaped out – another row of perfect, pearly teeth – and then they were off.

Half an hour later they were standing on the patio at the Imperial Palace Hotel in whose grounds the gazebo stood. The couple in front of them had almost finished making their vows. Nael turned his head to look at her. She was calm, her breasts rising and falling gently in her fuchsia dress. He touched her elbow lightly. There was a faint smattering of applause. The couple turned and walked back down the rather worn red carpet that led almost directly to the hotel bar.

Nael squeezed her arm. They moved forwards.

'Religious or civil?' The minister smiled.

'Religious.'

'Civil.' They spoke together.

The minister laughed. He was an enormous man, with a thick black beard and a deep baritone voice. The spitting image of every black preacher she'd ever seen on TV, thought Gabby. 'How's about I do a little of both?' he offered. They turned to each other and smiled. America. Anything you wanted, any which way.

'Dear Father, dear friends,' he began. 'We are gathered . . .' Gabby thought fleetingly of her parents, of Rianne, Nathalie and Charmaine, of Nael's mother and father. Tears of joy prickled at the back of her eyes, and there was a lump in her throat. When Nael slipped onto her finger the ring he'd bought in the hotel shop just minutes before they left, she choked back a sob. Then he kissed her briefly, hard, and the minister and the hired witnesses shook their hands. His arm was in hers as they walked out into the dying evening light. They were married.

They followed the red carpet into the bar. Nael seemed unable to contain his happiness. 'What would you like, Mrs Kilani-Hughes?' he asked.

'A whisky, please, sir. Double.' Gabby gigled.

'Y'all just got married?' the bartender asked.

'Yep,' Nael said.

'And you want a whisky? Not champagne?'

'Well, I don't know.' Nael looked at the bottle he held up. 'I'll have to ask the missus.' He turned to Gabby. His wife.

78

Dr Marshall had been right. Charmaine did begin to recover. One morning she woke up long after the sun had come up. She lay in bed, watching the curtains sway in the breeze. She glanced at the radio beside her. It was 8.17. She was a little shocked. She couldn't remember the last time she'd slept through the night.

Without thinking she reached out and pressed the 'on' switch. It was Capital FM. Sound flooded the room – music. When had she last listened to music of her own accord? She couldn't remember. She looked around the room. There were flowers on the dressing-table. Who had put them there? The light caught the bottles of perfume . . . perfume? When was the last time she'd smelled perfume, a scent . . . anything?

She drew back the covers gingerly and slipped out of bed. The wooden floor was warm under her feet. She walked over to the dressing-table and the small vase of red and pink roses. Nathalie must have done it. Or Gloria, Nathalie's cleaner. Nathalie sent her over to clean Charmaine's flat once a week. Not that it needed it. Charmaine kept the place very neat and tidy. It was as if she was trying to keep the same hold on her own emotions, everything neat, everything tidy, everything locked away.

The only place she felt safe enough to step outside the boundaries she'd imposed on her thoughts was Sylvia's. There she felt safe. She picked up one of the bottles, turning it over in her hands. It was full, heavy. She peered at the label. Christalle. Chanel. She frowned. She didn't recognise it. She prised off the square black lid and sniffed cautiously at the silver nozzle. Nothing. She squirted a little on the back of her hand and lifted it cautiously to her nose.

In the next instant a wave of emotion rolled through her, shocking her with its intensity – she felt as though her heart would burst. She dropped the bottle and stumbled backwards, sat down heavily on the bed. The urge to weep swept over her, and tears burned her eyes. She lay down and cried, gasping for air, groaning with anger, which flowed through her, hot and thick, curling around the inner corners of her mind, skilfully seeking out the images and memories she'd stuffed away.

Simon, bending over her, slapping her face with – *that*. The four men laughing at her as she struggled to please them. She wept. Slut, whore, bitch. His face looking down at her, handcuffs ready. She offered him her hands, her face averted. Kylie's voice was warbling happily over the airwaves. She stuffed a fist into her mouth and wept.

When she walked into the room at the top of the stairs the following Wednesday, Sylvia knew. There was an alertness, an edginess to Charmaine that she hadn't seen before.

'How are you?' she asked carefully.

Charmaine fiddled with the threads on the arm of the chair. 'OK.' There was a short silence. 'I'm ... I don't know ... I can't understand it ... It's— I feel—' She stopped, unable to find the words.

'Yes?' Sylvia's voice was gentle, but firm.

'Angry?' Charmaine looked at her doubtfully. Sylvia smiled ruefully. Good. At last.

'At?'

'At . . . him,' she said, letting out a deep breath. 'I don't know why, but I am.'

'You should be. You've been angry with yourself for too long.'

'No, I haven't been *angry* . . . I've been . . . well, I don't know – unhappy?'

'Depression is often repressed anger, Charmaine. What we can't express outwardly, at others, we turn on ourselves. You've been hurting yourself, not him. You've been punishing the wrong person.' Charmaine's eyes were suddenly brimming with tears.

Sylvia slid a box of tissues towards her.

At last.

And that had been the beginning. After that, each day was a little better. By September, she was sitting on the grass bathed in the late-summer sun in Waterlow Park just next to Eric's new practice with Nathalie, Eric and Micha, eating an egg sandwich and looking for all the world like a normal, healthy, happy young woman. The scars on her wrists were fading – you had to look quite hard to see the twisted flesh on either side. And the scars inside were healing. Dr Marshall had warned her not to come off the pills . . . another year or so. They wanted to flush out any lingering signs of the disease. And once she'd come to accept it as a disease, not a sign of weakness or stupidity, her pathetic inability to get it right, to take control of her life, well, it was easier.

She lay on the grass with Micha, watching Eric and Nathalie. Nathalie was huge – she was due almost any day now. Eric lay on his back, one hand on his wife's burgeoning belly, the other across his eyes. A wasp flew overhead. It was warm. Charmaine pulled Micha onto her own stomach. He wriggled to make himself comfortable. He couldn't sleep on Mummy's tummy, he told her seriously. His baby sister was in there. He might *hurt* her. Charmaine stroked his head.

A few days later she was seated purposefully at the kitchen table, flicking through the newspapers. She chewed the side of her nail absently. Same old stuff – secretarial work, receptionist, bar staff, hairdressers . . . she thumbed her way down the page. Nothing appealed. She looked up, sighing. She was determined to do *something*. She just didn't know what. One thing she had learned from over a year of therapy, she told Nathalie briskly: if she didn't have something to occupy her, at least temporarily, she slid. Into anything and anyone. At her last session, Sylvia had said, 'Occupy your mind, find something you enjoy doing. Get a job, enrol on a course.' She was full of advice. Charmaine turned back to the paper.

'How about this one?' She underscored the advertisement with her forefinger. ' "Receptionist wanted. Busy lifestyle magazine. No experience necessary. Knowledge of fashion and interiors a plus".' She looked at Nathalie.

'Give them a ring. It can't hurt. God, is that the time?' she asked, looking at her watch. 'I'd better get going.' She picked up her bag and car keys, and got heavily to her feet. Let me know what they sound like.'

Charmaine nodded absently. Her mind was busy. She was already thinking about what to wear for the interview and whether or not she could persuade Mary to part with some cash. She would need something new. Something trendy. It was a style magazine, after all – she needed to show she had some. She waved at Nathalie and reached for the phone.

As soon as she walked into the offices on Farringdon Road she knew that she wanted the job – and that she would get it. *LifeStyle* was exactly where she wanted to be. Even the reception desk was a statement. Charmaine could picture herself sitting there, her hair swinging glossily as she answered the phone or chatted to the beautiful people who worked there. She looked around the entrance foyer in delight. It was a new magazine, a new concept. 'Fashion +interiors+travel+glamour=*LifeStyle*.' A simple formula and it seemed to be working. Circulation was rising, the advertising revenue was pouring in – it was all going according to plan.

She excused herself before her interview and slipped into the glass and chrome ladies' with its wall-to-wall mirrors and black slate floors. She looked at her reflection in the mirror – she looked good, better than she had in ages. Her eyes had regained their sparkle, her hair was shiny and her face was open, clear. It was hard to believe everything she'd been through in the past year. Things were different now: she'd touched rock bottom and she was swimming steadily towards the surface. Nearly there. She wanted this job badly. She touched up her lipstick, then went out and walked upstairs.

'Well, when can you start?' Tyson Berkeley looked across the mahogany desk at the pretty, sparkly young woman before him. He turned to Cameron, his art director, on one side, and Suzi, his editor-at-large on the other. Charmaine looked and sounded perfect. Just the right combination of public-school girl – convent, perhaps? – and style queen. She was wearing a long caramel skirt with black fishnet tights, a red, fitted V-neck jumper and a short denim jacket. Not much jewellery and a pair of those new shoes. Campers. Just arrived in the shops from the Continent. Obviously kept abreast of things. Just what they wanted.

'Monday?' Charmaine said. That would give her three shopping days to get herself organised. She could see from everyone around her that people here were serious about style. Take Tyson Berkeley, the man sitting opposite her. Good-looking, stylish, tasteful. A pair of thick, black-framed glasses, hair flopping casually over his eyes, a pinstriped jacket and dark green velvet trousers – velvet? When was the last time she'd seen a man in velvet? A pale yellow shirt and no tie. Suzi, sitting next to him, was no less dramatic. A shirt and skirt in two different Paisley patterns with sheer tights, Adidas trainers – *trainers?* – and her hair in two plaits. She looked more like an art student than the editor of what seemed to be a large, successful magazine.

'Monday it is.' Tyson stood up. He shook Charmaine's hand. 'Great. Welcome to *LifeStyle*.'

Charmaine smiled at him. She'd broken the surface now. She was treading water comfortably. She followed Suzi downstairs to meet the rest of the 'team'. Nice people. Charmaine immediately felt at home.

79

'Here,' Nina handed over one of the cameras to Rianne. 'Ain't she a *beaut*?' Her enthusiasm was infectious. Rianne took it nervously. It was heavy. She turned it in her hands. 'It's a Leica. Took me ages to find one,' Nina said. 'Look through the viewfinder – go on. It's fantastic.' Rianne lifted it to her eye the way she'd seen Nina do a hundred times, and peered through. She was right. It was a wide-angle lens – it distorted the world around her in a strange, beautiful way.

'It's great,' she agreed. 'Is there film inside?'

'Yeah, I loaded it this morning. Take some pictures. Whatever you like. Here, take some of me. Did you see those hideous portraits the photographer from the *New York Times* took?'

Rianne laughed, then swung the camera round, enjoying the weight of it in her hands and focused on Nina's face. She clicked the shutter. Once, twice, winding on the film as she'd seen Nina do. She took a few more. Nina was sitting with her head bent, absorbed in the task of sorting through her films. Sunlight filtered in through the blinds, creating a soft halo of light around her grey head . . . she snapped again. She handed the camera back to her. 'Waste of a roll of film,' she laughed.

Nina smiled and shook her head. Rianne had a much better eye than she gave herself credit for. She'd seen her discussing prints – cropping and framing a particular picture to foreground particular qualities with gallery owners – she had good aesthetic judgement. She just didn't realise it.

Rianne turned to her diary. She checked off a few dates – they were looking for a new gallery – and picked up the phone. She watched Nina pack away the cameras and lenses. It was . . . nice, she thought, holding the camera, framing a view and shooting the way Nina did. She'd enjoyed it. Made a change from holding a phone or a diary. She'd enjoyed looking at Nina's face through the lens too – an unusual face, square, almost mannish. She'd tried to capture the way Nina held her head, slightly away from her body, her chin thrust forward, aggressively. She wondered how the pictures would turn out.

To her surprise, they were good. 'Look,' Nina said to her, tossing over the contact sheet a week later. 'I like that one. That's just about the best photo I've ever seen of myself.'

Rianne looked up from where she was organising Nina's slides and hopped to take the sheet. She looked at the photos Nina had circled. She was right. They were good. The one Nina liked was an unusual portrait, slightly off-centre but nicely composed with the sunlight capturing fine details in the air-dust, smoke. It was a beautiful portrait of a woman absorbed in her own world, caught mid-creation. Perhaps she did have an eye. 'Good, isn't it?' Nina confirmed.

Rianne put the contact sheet down, embarrassed, and

went back to labelling and filing. That was what *she* got paid to do. Nina was the photographer, the artist. Not her.

But a couple of days later as she was collecting a new lens from Zlatek's, the second-hand camera shop where Nina bought most of her equipment, she spotted an elegant old Nikon sitting on the shelf. She stared at it. How much did he want for it, she asked the old man standing behind the counter.

'Three hundred and twenty-five dollars. A bargain,' Tomás Zlatek said.

Rianne hesitated. Should she? Could she? She picked it up. It was nice and heavy. She looked through the viewfinder. It wasn't as unusual a lens as the Leica had but she liked it. She bought it. Even if she only used it to take pictures of Nina and Gabby, it would be fun. Something to do while she waited. For what, she couldn't say.

She took the bag from him with a mixture of embarrassment and trepidation – and a funny sense of having just done the right thing. She practically ran all the way home.

She took to it like . . . like a duck to water, Nina laughed at her delightedly. The first time she came into the studio bearing a sheaf of contact sheets, Nina knew she'd just lost the best assistant she'd ever had. She took one look at the images Rianne held shyly in front of her and smiled in defeat. Very different from her own style, she noted – thank God – and not exactly her taste: she had little time for humans, she explained a thousand times a day to whoever would listen, preferring the vast and powerful beauty of natural landscapes, but Rianne had a way with her subjects. She held the prints to the light – they were edgy, slightly off-key portraits of ordinary people – the Korean butchers at the end of her street, two elderly Greek grandmothers, meeting in a café for coffee and pastries, a young girl waiting at the bus stop, her face a study in longing and anticipation. None of them knew they'd been photographed. How Rianne had managed it, Nina couldn't tell.

What she could tell was that they were good. Ordinary people made extraordinary by her eye.

'These are good, Rianne. Truly.'

'You think so?' Rianne couldn't hide her delight.

'I do. They're great. I told you, you have an eye. *The* eye. You should do some more.' Rianne took the sheets from her and stowed them carefully away in the little black portfolio she'd bought. She was trying hard not to smile but damn . . . it felt good! Someone – Nina – praising her for something she'd *done*, as opposed to something she *was*. It felt better than good – it was fantastic.

80

Nael opened the door quietly, hoping he wouldn't wake his sleeping wife. He'd just flown in from Kampala – an unexpected week-long break. It was just after dawn and New York was still, unbelievably, asleep. It was cold in the apartment, especially after the tropical heat he'd just been in. He put down his case and bent down to scratch a delighted Percy. Ssh, he mimed to the purring cat. You'll wake her up. He took off his jacket and boots and walked in his socks across the sitting room to the bedroom.

Gabby was fast asleep. He could hear her breathing, see the top of her auburn head sticking out from underneath the white duvet. He paused in the doorway, watching her for a moment. Then stripped off the rest of his clothes in the corridor and, before she had time to rise to the surface of consciousness, slid naked into bed beside her. A surprise wake-up.

It wasn't the wisest move. Gabby almost leaped out of her skin. 'You – *idiot*!' she yelled, when she'd calmed down enough to be able to speak.

'It was meant to be a surprise.' He was taken aback by her response.

Gabby sat up with the duvet clutched to her chest. 'A *surprise*? You nearly frightened me to *death*. What are you doing here? You didn't tell me you were coming.'

'I had a week's break,' Nael said, his own temper rising. 'Jesus, Gabby, I thought you'd be pleased to see me.'

'I am, it's just – I mean, I was fast asleep. I'd no *idea* who was in the bed. I thought it was a burglar,' Gabby said, and tears spilled down her cheeks.

Nael looked at her in alarm. Gabby? Crying? 'Hey, hey . . .' he said, pulling her close to him. 'Sorry, I didn't— Gabs, come on . . . come here.' She sniffed back her tears and moved into the circle of his arms. 'Ssh.' He wiped away her tears and drew her down beside him, wondering at the sudden storm of emotion. It was not like her at all. Soon his caresses turned to something else, and Gabby stopped crying, pleasure coming to her slowly, wrung from her by his touch.

He woke, a few hours later, to the sound of someone retching. He heard the toilet flush and the sound of water in the sink. Gabby came through the door looking pale.

'What's the matter?' he asked, propping himself up on his elbow.

Gabby hugged her stomach. 'I don't know. I must have eaten something. I felt sick yesterday, too.'

'Come back to bed. You've been working too hard. If I'm not here—'

'I get eight hours of uninterrupted sleep.' Gabby smiled faintly as she climbed back into bed. 'I don't work the hours you seem to think I do,' she murmured, still holding her stomach.

'Sure you don't,' Nael mumbled against her neck. He was tired. The flight from Kampala to New York hadn't been as straightforward as it sounded. More like Kampala –Cairo–Frankfurt–New York. He dozed.

The next morning, Gabby was sick again. She felt too ill to go into the office and, besides, it was wonderful having Nael home. By the evening she'd perked up enough to go out, have a glass of wine and win an argument with him on the finer points of UN bureaucracy.

Their lovemaking that night was an extension of their conversation and made all the more pleasurable by the knowledge that they had another four days together. But on the morning of the third day, she woke up with the now familiar taste in her mouth and her stomach in upheaval. He stumbled after her into the bathroom and held her head as she vomited. When she pulled her head from the bowl, wiping her mouth with the back of her hand, he stared at her – it clicked.

'God, what's wrong with me?' she groaned, getting to her feet. 'That's four days in a row. What on earth did I eat?' She bent over the wash-basin.

'What's wrong with you?' Nael frowned, then half smiled. 'Don't you know?'

'What are you grinning at? I feel like *shit*.'

'Gabby.' Nael began to laugh. 'I don't believe you. How can you not know?'

'Know what?'

'You're pregnant, you idiot.'

There was a sudden silence in the small bathroom. Gabby's eyes caught his in the mirror above the wash-basin. She stood very still. The word, his intuition – of course he was right. His face was in the mirror behind hers. She looked at herself, at him. He returned her gaze. She slid a hand under the waistband of her pyjamas to touch her stomach. Nothing. Everything. She, who had mothered everyone all her life, to become a mother. The thought terrified her. She was unable to move or tear her eyes from the image of the two of them standing stock still in the early morning light.

'It'll be fine, Gabs, you'll see,' he whispered. 'You'll be brilliant.'

Somehow, from somewhere, she never knew how *he* knew, how he always seemed to know, Nael had understood what she was unable to say. His arms were round her before she'd had time to register his movement.

When he left at the end of the week, she was just getting used to the idea. She hadn't told anyone and had made him swear not to. The day after he left she closed her office door and lifted her sweater. She stared at the pale skin of her belly – nothing to be seen. She looked at her desk, piled high as usual with books, reports, stacks of paper – how was she going to find time to be a mother? She gazed at her bookshelves. She was now so closely involved in women's issues – from women's rights firstly as human beings protected by the umbrella of the UN Charter that she had been involved in writing, to their own, gender-specific rights – reproductive, sexual, familial.

During the day in her office she wrote about the issues, attended meetings, helped draft the documents. At night she went home and stared at herself in the mirror on the back of the bathroom door. She didn't know how to articulate it to herself but the balance she'd been seeking all her life – between the personal and the professional, or the political, as Nael would say – had been achieved.

Finding Nael, shaking off the ghost of Dominic, had been one triumph: discovering she was about to become a mother was another. With this, she was closing the gap between her own unhappy childhood and the promise of what she could give to a child of her own. She stared at herself again, and again. It would be another three months before Nael was back. By then, she thought, she would have changed completely.

81

Charmaine was in her element. It was almost impossible to reconcile the confident, smiling receptionist at 119 Farringdon Road with the girl who'd been admitted to A&E at Kensington and Chelsea and who had sat listlessly on the edge of the bed as the resident psychiatrist examined her.

Every morning, as she selected her outfit for the day, or applied mascara to her lashes, or walked along Kensington High Street to the tube station, she marvelled at how far she'd come in such a short time. The job wasn't terribly demanding: she answered the phones, booked appointments, made tea, ensured that the flowers on the glass table were fresh and that the leather and chrome chairs – by Le Corbusier, she learned – were perfectly aligned. She was *LifeStyle*'s resident hostess – and she loved it. She learned to tell a Barcelona chair from a Corbusier *chaise-longue*, an Eileen Gray from a Robin Day, who Charles and Ray referred to and how to make a floral display out of a bag of grey pebbles and a single palm frond. After a month, people in the office were wondering how they'd managed without her.

And if sometimes, just occasionally, her smiles seemed a little *wide* in relation to the event taking place, that was just Charmaine. Slightly over the top. And she'd been through a lot, it was rumoured. Tania, one of the style managers, had become friends with her and had seen the tell-tale scars on her wrists. It didn't take long for the whole shocking story to emerge between gulps of coffee in the café downstairs. A survivor. That was how Tania described her. Everyone liked her, especially the men.

'Um, d'you think . . . could I use . . . could you show me the bathroom, please?' Charmaine looked up into a tanned face, with sunglasses and dark hair, and gulped. The accent was Australian, or New Zealand – she could never tell the difference – and belonged to a good-looking bicycle courier in skin-tight black cycling gear and orange-tinted wraparound sunglasses. He was holding a large package addressed to Tyson.

'Yes, of course. Down the stairs, on the left.' She smiled her prettiest smile and watched as the most glorious pair of thighs and buttocks moved across the foyer and disappeared down the stairs. She was still smiling when he came back five minutes later.

'Thanks. Sorry about that – it's so damn cold outside. Plus I've been drinking this all day.' He held up an empty Evian bottle. Her stomach lurched. He was gorgeous. He'd pushed the glasses up onto his forehead – lovely, green eyes, thick lashes . . . the stubble of a beard. Wow.

'Not at all.' She stared at him for a second. She'd lost her voice. 'Um, who are you . . . do you . . . ?'

'Need to drop this off? Yeah.' He laughed. 'Tyson Berkeley?'

'That's right. You can leave it with me.' Charmaine reached across the counter. There was a tiny spark as she took the package and her fingertips touched his hands.

'It's heavy,' he said, and helped her to set it down.

'Yes. Well, er . . . thanks.' She remained standing.

'OK. Well, see you around.' Just before he reached the door, he stopped. 'Shit – you're supposed to sign for it. I clean forgot. Here,' he handed over a clipboard, 'just sign there, print your name and your phone number. That's the most important thing.'

'Home or work?' Charmaine was flirting shamelessly and enjoying it. It was ages since she'd done anything like it. A couple of years, to be precise.

'Home number, please.' He grinned. She arched an eyebrow and wrote it down. 'See you . . . Charmaine.' He smiled, looking at her signature.

'That would be nice,' she said. She sat down again, crossing her legs carefully. She was well aware of the glass counter. She waved at him as he got onto his bike and cycled down the road. She picked up the phone. She had to tell Nathalie.

He didn't ring that evening, or the next. By the end of the week, the bubble had burst. She'd skipped the usual Friday-evening drinks at the Eagle across the road from the offices – a weekly ritual for the staff at *LifeStyle* – and had gone straight home, dejected. How could he not have called? Had she written the number down wrong? She felt herself sinking. These were the dramatic highs and lows Sylvia had warned her about. She tried to take hold of herself before despair overwhelmed her. It was frightening. She hadn't felt so shaky in months. She slid off the couch and sat on the floor, bawling like an infant. She was crying so hard that at first she didn't hear the phone ringing. When she did, she practically broke her neck leaping over the couch to get at it.

'Hello?' She sounded breathless and nasal. She tried to wipe her nose on the back of her hand.

'Is this . . . hi, are you Charmaine?' An electric shock ran straight through her, all the way to her toes. She had never experienced such relief. 'Yes . . . this is Charmaine.'

'Hi, um, dunno if you remember me. I'm the courier – I came into your offices on Monday?'

His voice was gorgeous, just the way she remembered. 'Oh, yeah, I remember. How're you?' She tried hard to sound calm.

'Fine. Great. You?'

'Fine,' she lied, rubbing her eyes furiously with her free hand.

'Well, good.' There was a short silence. 'Um,' he continued. He sounded rather nervous. Charmaine liked that. 'Thing is, I was wondering . . . if you'd like to . . . if you've nothing else planned, that is . . . would you like to go out? To the movies or something? Or dinner?'

'Er, yeah, that'd be nice. When were you thinking?'

'Oh, well – tomorrow? Or is that a bit soon?'

'No, no. Tomorrow's fine, actually. I'm free. For once,' she added hastily. Didn't want him to think she sat at home on Saturday nights.

'Great. So, where can we meet? Where d'you live? I mean, what's easiest for you? I don't know London that well. Yet.'

He was at pains not to sound too pushy. Charmaine recognised it. 'How about Soho?' Lots of cinemas and bars.

'Yeah, that's fine. D'you know Ed's Diner on Old Compton Street?'

'Yes. Shall I meet you there?'

'Great – seven o'clock? We can walk down to Leicester Square. Cool. So . . .'

'See you tomorrow.'

'Yeah. See you, Charmaine.' As she put the phone down, she realised she didn't even know his name. Thank God she only had to wait a day to find out.

'Hi.' He was waiting for her outside as she walked up, seven minutes late. Well, she'd been hanging around outside Foyles for fifteen. Minimum five minutes late, Nathalie had instructed her.

'Hi.' She gave him a stellar smile. Out of his courier's uniform, he looked even better. He bent down to kiss her on each cheek. She put up a hand to her face. His stubble was prickly.

'You look really nice,' he said.

Charmaine turned pink. 'You too,' she said. They stood grinning at each other for a moment. Then she remembered. 'D'you know something?' she began, as they started walking towards Shaftesbury Avenue.

'What?' He seemed to be trying to decide whether or not to offer her his arm.

'I don't even know your name!' She giggled.

He hit the side of his head with his palm. 'It's Jess. I should've said.'

'Jess. Short for . . .'

'Jocelyn. But no one ever calls me that,' he added quickly.

'Jess what?'

'Dalton. And you?'

'Charmaine Hunter.'

'Well, Ms Charmaine Hunter, it's very nice to meet you. Even if the first time was with a full bladder.' He laughed.

'Nice to meet you, Mr Dalton,' Charmaine replied. Jess

Dalton. Charmaine Dalton. Her mind was racing ahead. Slow down, she told herself. You've only just met him!

'What d'you feel like seeing?'

'I don't know. What do *you* feel like seeing?'

'I don't know either.'

'Well, shall we have a drink while we decide?'

'Good idea, Ms Hunter.' He smiled down at her. They were standing outside a place that looked like a bar. 'Shall we?' He led her inside.

'I'm in love,' Charmaine said, to her reflection in the mirror as she checked her lipstick. Completely, totally, horribly, helplessly in *love*. Jess Dalton was the nicest, sweetest, funniest man she had met – ever. Ever, ever, ever. She pressed her lips together – a little too much gloss – and ran back upstairs. Jess was sitting exactly where she'd left him, watching her walk across the room. She felt rather self-conscious as she came up to him, aware of his eyes on her. She slid into the seat next to him. Their thighs were touching – it felt lovely and warm to be sitting so close to someone, wondering what was going to happen next.

'Had enough?' he asked. She considered the question. Enough of what? Sitting in a crowded bar with cigarette smoke and cheap perfume wafting through the air, having to shout to be heard? Maybe. Sitting next to Jess Dalton, staring into those dark green eyes, catching the faint scent of his aftershave as he moved his head, the feel of his leg against hers? Most definitely not.

'You?' She avoided the question.

He ran a hand through his hair, pushing it out of his eyes. 'Depends. Of this place, yeah. But not of you.'

Charmaine almost passed out with pleasure. She couldn't quite believe it. Jess Dalton had the script absolutely right. She'd sat next to him all evening, enraptured. He was from Australia – she'd got that right – a place called South Yarra, a suburb of Melbourne, he told her. He was an exchange student of anthropology at SOAS – whatever that was –

he'd been in London for three months and his job as a courier was a way to kill three birds with one stone: keep fit, earn some money and see the city. Charmaine thought he was lovely.

'I'm sure he is, Char,' Nathalie said, three weeks later. Charmaine could hear her struggling to balance her two-month-old baby girl and the phone. 'But keep your head, won't you? Are you still taking the pills?'

'Sylvia said I shouldn't stop, not just yet. But it's not the pills making me happy, Nat, it's *him*. Jess. You've got to meet him, you really must. Then you'll see. It's not just me. He's perfect. He really is.'

'Yes, well. When are you seeing him next?'

'Tonight. He's coming round for dinner.'

'Well, don't do anything . . . rash, will you?'

'*Nat!* Listen to you – you sound like my mother!' Charmaine protested. She was more than a little flustered. She'd spent the whole morning cleaning the flat, paying particular attention to her bedroom. She'd dusted, swept, polished and perfumed the place to death. There wasn't a surface in the tiny bedroom that hadn't been touched in her efforts to present the most seductive environment she could think of. She'd even doused the sheets with something called – she craned her neck round to read the label – Sleep Tight – perfumed water that you sprinkled on your pillows to get a better night's sleep. Not that she was thinking about sleeping, *per se*. She said goodbye to Nathalie. It was four o'clock. He'd be there at seven thirty. Time to start the dinner preparations.

She opened a bottle of wine. Dr Marshall had warned her that Prozac and alcohol weren't the best combination and that she ought to exercise restraint but, hell, she was nervous. And she didn't want it to show.

'Wow.' Jess stared at her. Charmaine was standing in the

doorway of her flat, leaning against the jamb, one arm stretched above her head. She was wearing possibly the tightest dress he'd ever seen on anyone.

'Hi.' She smiled at him. It had taken her two hours to decide what to wear. She'd spilled the contents of her wardrobe across the bed, hopping from one outfit to another before settling on a sleek black silk dress with a plunging sweetheart neckline and a wide, shiny belt. It was a little dressy for a stay-at-home dinner but she was determined to show Jess what he – so far, anyway – was missing.

He'd been the perfect gentleman. He kissed her, of course, long, slow kisses that she simply couldn't get enough of. He held her arm, nibbled her ear, and once or twice his hands had brushed across her nipples but then . . . nothing. She wasn't used to this. The men Charmaine had gone out with previously had been only too quick to go from hello to bed. This 'getting to know you', as Jess called it, was disconcerting. That, and her mood swings. If anything, they were getting worse. The highs were more intense than she'd ever known them, and the corresponding lows were almost as bad as . . . well, back then. If he was ten minutes late for a date or half an hour late with a call, she fell to pieces, convinced it was over, convinced her life was over. Nathalie could only stand by and watch anxiously. Charmaine was right about one thing – Jess really was nice. She'd met him the week before and warmed to him immediately. She really hoped it would work out. Charmaine deserved it.

'I wouldn't give a Castlemaine four . . .' he murmured, as he kissed her.

Charmaine giggled.

'Four?'

'Not sure. I got distracted half-way through. You smell great, too.'

'D'you want to come in or are you going to stand in the

hallway all evening?' she smiled at him over her shoulder. Provocatively, she hoped. She bumped into the coat-stand. Oops, she'd better watch herself – the wine had gone straight to her head.

'Oh, in, definitely.' Jess closed the door behind him. 'Australia's finest,' he said, putting a wrapped bottle on the kitchen counter. 'Nice place,' he added, looking around. 'You live by yourself?'

'Yes. I've been here almost two years.'

'How d'you afford it? If you don't mind me asking,' he said quickly. 'London's so bloody expensive.'

'Mmm. A . . . friend bought it for me. A long time ago.'

'Wow, some friend.'

'More like an uncle, really.'

'Oh.'

'Glass of wine?' Charmaine handed one to him, then walked over to the stereo and pushed the 'on' button with a red-painted toe.

The day he found out about it, Charmaine had left her pills on the kitchen counter, by accident. She'd been so careful. She never left them out, ever. Now that Jess stayed over at hers two, three times a week, she was especially careful. She knew he was puzzled by her sometimes – she could tell from the way he looked at her sharply when she laughed too loudly or cried at the cinema, or when a discussion threatened to spill over into an argument and she became almost hysterical with fear that he might disappear. Jess didn't get it. At such times she seemed so out of character it was like watching someone else. He said nothing, but he worried. One night, when he was showing her what he meant when he said she was beautiful from head to toe starting at her fingertips, he ran his tongue across the inside of her wrist and felt something just before she snatched away her hand. It took a week but he managed to sneak a look at her wrists – yes, the tell-tale razor line, a thin pinkish scar. Oh dear. He had no idea what she'd been through but her wrists had been under a knife, that much was clear.

When he came across the little orange tube of pills marked 'Fluoxetine – to be taken once daily', he was even more worried. Epilepsy? He asked someone at college the next day. Prozac. Charmaine was on anti-depressants. And did that explain where she went every Wednesday morning?

'It was a long time ago,' Charmaine said tearfully. She had a sick feeling in the pit of her stomach. This was the part where he'd look at her and mumble something about having to go home. And that would be it.

'How long ago, Char?' His voice was soft. So were his hands on her shoulders. Charmaine looked at him, tears falling. She knew it. He was aiming for the gentle goodbye, then . . . the kind, concerned, friendly brush-off.

'Last year,' Charmaine was crying now. 'And I'm fine, now, really I am.'

'I know you are. I'm just . . . you know, worried about you. It's nothing to be ashamed of, you came through it.'

Charmaine stiffened. What was he saying?

He pulled her closer. His lips were warm against her forehead. 'Come on, you don't need to be upset.'

'I . . .'

'You don't have to talk about it, sweetheart. Not if you don't want to.' Jess continued his gentle stroking, running his hand through her hair.

Charmaine was confused. He didn't seem to be getting ready to leave. In fact, he was settling himself more comfortably in her bed, stretching his legs and crossing them at the ankle. She allowed herself to sink just a little into the warmth of his arms and turn her wet face against his chest. It was almost midnight. She lay there, breathing in the smell of him, feeling the comforting weight of his

hand at the nape of her neck, rubbing softly and rhythmic-
ally until she fell asleep.

And when in the morning they awoke before dawn, he
made love to her with an intensity that told her he wasn't
going anywhere, not just yet, and she felt something give
inside her, something warm and good – the last piece of the
jigsaw falling firmly into place. He turned his sleepy green
eyes towards hers and she knew, in that ridiculously happy,
silly way, that everything was going to be all right.

82

Nael was getting anxious. It had been days since he'd
managed to secure an outside line to call New York. Gabby
had just over a month to go and he wanted to be with her
when it happened. The last time he'd seen her, almost five
weeks ago, she'd been huge – tired, uncomfortable, and
tearful. He'd wanted to help but didn't know how. He felt
in the way. Rianne was with her, fussing and clucking
around like a mother hen. He was glad. She'd been
fantastic with Gabby – who would have thought it?

He smiled to himself when he thought about Rianne. The
childish crush had disappeared, along with his flared jeans
and Soft Cell records. It was Gabby who preoccupied him
now. He'd promised to be back in a month, and he'd
already broken that promise. He was back in Kigali,
following the RPF forces as they moved through the
deserted landscape of the country's interior. At times it was
almost impossible to reconcile the surreal nature of his two
lives – the domestic comfort of Brooklyn, and the numbing
destruction he was witness to, day after day in Central
Africa. One evening, Paul Kagame, the RPF commander,
had addressed his troops and the gathered foreign press. It
was an important occasion: Kagame was not fond of the
international media and rarely allowed himself to be filmed.

Nael struggled to follow the story but his mind was elsewhere. Many of the reporters with him were already fathers, and from them, he gleaned little comfort. It was hard for them too to witness the dead bodies of children, many of the same age as the ones they'd left behind in St Albans, Edinburgh, Brussels and Lyons. Sometimes their professional response slipped and he came upon them, crying silently as the cameras rolled. Sometimes, too, a jet overhead trailed a faint plume of smoke – South African Airways, on its way to Europe or America. He would squint up at the sky, longing to be on board.

Gabby was at her desk, eating an apple and reading through a sheaf of papers, when she felt the first sharp twinge. She frowned. She still had five weeks to go. It was a dull cramp, rather like a period pain. She was used to the odd sharp jolt when the baby kicked but this was different. Half an hour later, the spasms were more intense. She moved uncomfortably in her chair. It was 8 a.m. and Janice, her new secretary, wasn't yet in. She tried to concentrate. By eight thirty she knew something was happening. She called her obstetrician, who told her not to worry and to time the contractions. When they'd reached every half-hour, she was to call back. They would get things ready at the hospital. Yes, she was going into labour. And then, without warning, something went wrong.

The ambulance ride from 45th Street to Mercy General Hospital took about twenty minutes. She was dimly aware of a pain in her lower back and an intense ringing sound in her ears. Her head was heavy. She couldn't remember clearly what had happened. She had seen blood on her dress and her chair. She remembered shouting for Janice, somebody – anybody. She'd tried calling Nael at the hotel in Kigali but she couldn't get through. Then she called Dr Fineberg and then there was panic and the ambulance, the men pounding through the office, putting her into the wheelchair, something sharp going into her arm. After that it all became blurred.

The paramedics rushed her through the hospital doors. She thought it was all a bit like *ER* – doctors in green overalls shouting, nurses in blue rushing around. She heard their words drift over her . . . *pre-eclampsia, her veins are shutting down* . . . She kept trying to open her mouth and form the questions that were racing through her head but it wouldn't co-operate. Nothing but a low moan came out. The last thing she could recall was the anaesthetist bending over her, asking her whether she'd eaten anything that morning. She heard his voice slipping away, his words freezing in the air around her and then . . . nothing.

When she next opened her eyes, she couldn't work out where she was or why she was lying in a room with bright lights overhead and a TV playing soundlessly in a corner. There was a dull ache in her lower abdomen. She closed her eyes. The next time she opened them several people were standing around her bed. 'Gabrielle? Can you hear us, Gabrielle?' one was saying.

Gabby moved her head. 'Gabby. Not Gabrielle.' It suddenly seemed important.

The man in the green coat nodded. 'You've had an emergency C-section, Gabby. Can you understand me?'

Gabby blinked. Of course – the baby. The *baby*! 'Where's the . . . my baby?'

'Your baby's doing fine. She's a little small, about a month early. She's in ICU.' It was one of the other doctors who spoke.

Gabby sank back against the pillows, exhausted. She began to cry. A nurse took her hand and squeezed it. 'You'll be fine, honey,' she said soothingly. 'We'll give you something for the pain and let you sleep for a bit. You've had a pretty big operation. We'll take you to see her when you're a bit stronger.'

Gabby said nothing, tears rolling down her cheeks. She

was supposed to be sitting up in bed with her baby in her arms, her husband by her side. Where was Nael?

He came. Three days late. He walked into the hospital room to find Gabby sitting by herself doing something to her breasts – *milking* them? – and crying. The exhaustion and pain on her face made him wince. He couldn't believe it had happened without him, that he hadn't got there in time. She put the contraption down and buried her face in his chest. 'They said I have to do that,' she sobbed, 'otherwise it'll dry up – the milk.'

'Sssh. It's OK, Gabs. Where's the baby? Is it OK?'

'She. It's a she. She's fine. She's in an incubator but you can't go in there – not until the nurses come. Nael, it wasn't supposed to be like this – I didn't—' She choked on her tears.

He squeezed her shoulders. He felt like an absolute shit. Poor Gabby. He kissed her salty cheeks. 'Sssh. It's going to be fine. Everything's going to be OK.' She clutched him, tears and milk running in almost equal amounts now onto his shirt. The door opened and one of the nurses poked her head into the room.

'Hi, there. You must be the father.' Nael felt still slightly dazed. Him – a father? 'I'm Cindy. Your wife's going to be fine. She's a little sore – it's kinda upsetting, you know. But the little girl is doing just fine. Would you like to see her?' Nael nodded. 'Go ahead – Betsy'll let you in. I'll just help Gabrielle get all cleaned up. Come on, honey, let's get you bathed. Did Dr Fineberg tell you? She'll be coming out of ICU tonight.'

Nael stared at the tiny, red creature with thick dark brown hair wrapped in white cotton in the incubator and thought, like millions of men before him, that he had never seen anything so special, so beautiful. She was awesome. He was in love from the second he set eyes on her. He turned to look at Betsy. She smiled and nodded. She'd seen it all before. The miracle of birth. She'd watched hundreds of men come in here, take one look and be smitten. Nael turned back. She was perfect. More than perfect. Her features blurred in front of him.

He was indulgent – what shall we call her? You choose. Yasmeen. Yasmeen Kilani-Hughes. They both looked at the little red face, now sleeping in well-fed bliss. Gabby was amazed at how naturally the whole thing had come to her – how to hold her, feed her, talk to her. She, who had only sketchy memories of her own, largely absent mother, had discovered a secret well of ability within herself – instinct was what they called it, she supposed. She bent her head to kiss the smooth delicate, pale brown forehead of her daughter. Yasmeen was dark, like her father.

As Nael watched his wife hold his daughter in her arms, her red curls falling over their faces, he realised that things for him would never be the same. The danger and adrenalin-filled intensity of the life he knew away from them would no longer be his. He had something to protect now. At all costs and above all else. He stared at them. This, in the end, was what it was all about.

PART EIGHT

'What shall we look like, when that sunrise comes?'
Mongane Wally Serote

83

October 1994: London

London. Damp, chilly and gloomy. October had rolled in, wet leaves and early dusk, marking the end of summer. Rianne walked down Regent Street, her portfolio in hand, towards Piccadilly Circus. Despite the weather, she was radiant. Bryson Mowbray, one of the hippest galleries in the city had just signed her to do a solo show – her first. They *loved* her work, Sally Bryson had said so.

It had taken over a year to put together a collection of prints she felt confident enough about, then get on a plane to London and walk into Sally Bryson's office with little more than her name, her portfolio and a recommendation from Nina Lindberg. Not that a recommendation from Nina was anything to sniff at – on the contrary. She'd been taken upstairs to meet the legendary gallery owner almost immediately. As the prints were spread out across Sally's enormous oak table, she began to relax.

'So . . . you got fed up with modelling?' Sally asked, as she inspected the black and white prints. Her mind was already racing ahead. The young woman standing in front of her was a transition of the best kind – from in front of the camera to behind it. Rianne de Zoete. Fame, fortune, tragedy, talent. Lovely. And a great by-line. 'Time for a change?' She peered at Rianne over her glasses.

'Er, yes.'

'And how long have you been doing this?'

'Well, I've been helping Nina for a couple of years. Not as a photographer,' she added quickly. 'This . . . this has just been a hobby, really.'

'Well, they're excellent. Have you a title?'

'Er, no, not yet.'

'Get one.'

Rianne blinked. She'd been away from England for a while. It took time to get used to the clipped British efficiency.

' "Snapshots"?'

'God, no.' Sally cocked her head to one side and waited for something to come to her. It did. ' "Dispatches",' she said firmly.

' "Dispatches"?'

'Mmm. They're quite unusual. Mixture of art and reportage.' Sally brought together two heavily bejewelled hands and pushed the fingers against each other. 'Good. When?'

'When?' Rianne was struggling to keep up.

'A show. When?'

'Oh. Well, any time.' She couldn't believe it was happening so fast.

'March?' Sally consulted a large calendar on the wall behind her. 'That gives us five months to get it ready. Small show, it'll run for a month. We'll hold it in the front gallery – the one you come into off the street. I'll put you in touch with Gideon Crowther. He's in charge of organising our shows. The two of you can talk about layout, frames, that sort of stuff.' She sat down in her leather swivel chair and picked up the phone – Rianne recognised the gesture: it was pure Ross Carter. The two women were at the top of their respective careers, both ambitious and driven with the same attitude: being successful was about getting *other* people to do the work. Sally was Ross, and this time Rianne wasn't going to fuck it up. She gathered her prints and slid them back into her portfolio. She left Sally a London number –

she was staying with Nathalie and her growing brood – and shook hands firmly.

She crossed the road at Hamley's, trying to avoid the hordes of harassed-looking parents and ecstatic children streaming in and out. She was on her way to Nathalie's to see Charmaine, just back from three weeks in Australia visiting Jess's parents. She had *news* for them, she'd yelled down the phone line from Melbourne the week before. *Big* news! Sitting in the kitchen in Rianne's apartment in Washington Heights, Gabby and Rianne had looked at each other and grinned. They knew exactly what it was. Rianne was going to London in a week's time. It wasn't possible for Gabby, struggling to balance the demands of her job with Yasmeen, to go with her. Nael was in line for a job at CNN, which would mean moving permanently to New York – the only reason he'd even *considered* it, he told Gabby sternly. She didn't care. She wanted him home with her and the baby. When that happened, perhaps the three of them could fly over. In the meantime, she'd laden Rianne with gifts to take with her.

'This is ridiculous.' Rianne laughed, as they struggled to shut her suitcases. 'She hasn't even told us she's pregnant.'

'Come on, they're already married. What other news could it be?' Gabby puffed, as she battled with the zips. She laughed, remembering the wedding. A mad, rushed service at the Chelsea Town Hall with Charmaine in red, and Mary Hunter looking bemused, but pleased. Charmaine had finally done the right thing. And Jess *seemed* very nice . . .

'I know. But aren't you supposed to wait until the third month, or something?'

'*You* might. Not Charmaine.' Gabby said firmly. 'And, besides, she might be past the third month. Who knows?'

Rianne was quiet for a moment. Gabby's innocuous comment had hit home, hard. '*You* might.' Not bloody likely. The three men she'd dated recently were certainly not candidates for fatherhood. Not that she was anywhere near being a candidate for motherhood.

'What's wrong?' Gabby looked up from her position on the floor, then put out a hand and touched her. Neither said anything.

It was three years since Rianne had walked out of her old life, three years since she'd seen or heard from him. What was amazing to her wasn't the pain it caused, it was the intensity. Three years. One would have thought it might lessen. It hadn't. Sometimes, she told Gabby, she felt as if someone or something had reached down inside her and ripped her apart, reconstructing her in her own image, yes, but with the pieces rearranged. On the outside she looked the same, a bit thinner, a bit older, hair short, not long – but on the inside, there was no resemblance to the person she'd been. Funny, really. In their time together, it was Riitho who'd been struggling to come to terms with his identity, not she. And in the end that was what had torn them apart – who *he* was, not who *she* was. She would have followed him anywhere, been anyone, done anything. She wanted only to be with him. But it wasn't enough for him. He complained that she didn't understand what he was forced to go through now, who he was being forced to become. It was different for her, he claimed. She was so secure in her rich, protected white world, she didn't have to try. Well, she'd lost that world. Despite his reading of her, she'd lost it all.

Yet somehow, God alone knew how, she had survived. And far from drowning, she'd learned to swim. 'Waving, not drowning,' as Gabby liked to remind her. It was a line from Gabby's favourite poem – Rianne hadn't wanted to know the rest.

'Hey,' Gabby said again, nudging her. 'Come on, let's grab something to eat before Yassie wakes up.'

Rianne shook her head briskly from side to side. An old trick to clear it. 'OK. What d'you fancy? Leftover Chinese? A salad?' She peered at the contents of her fridge.

'Anything. That's the thing with breastfeeding – you get ravenous. I'll never lose the weight I gained at this rate.' Gabby looked ruefully at her breasts.

'Gabs, you just gave birth!' Rianne protested.

'Four months ago. Don't worry, I'll get rid of it. I wouldn't go back to being fat. *Ever.*'

Just then, as if on cue, Gabby's daughter woke up and yelled. Gabby joked that she went from sleep to starving in a heartbeat. Rianne watched as she picked her up and settled on the sofa. Within seconds Yasmeen's wails had stopped.

'*Rianne!*' Charmaine shrieked, as she saw her friend turn the corner. She was sitting in the kitchen bay window of Nathalie's beautiful new Hampstead home.

'Char, ssh! You'll wake Anna.' Nathalie frowned. Bloody Charmaine. It had taken her hours to put Anna down. Charmaine was clueless about children . . . well, she'd learn soon enough. It had taken Charmaine all of two seconds to blurt out the news as soon as she was in the front door.

'Sorry,' Charmaine mouthed guiltily. She scrambled off the window-seat and ran down the flight of stairs to the front door. It was over a year since she'd seen Rianne or Gabby – and it was such a shame Gabby couldn't be with them. 'You look *amazing*!' she yelled, as Rianne walked in.

Anna had joined in. Nathalie made a face at Charmaine and went upstairs to fetch her thirteen-month-old daughter.

'And *you*!' Rianne said.

Charmaine had put on a little weight since the last time they'd met and she looked good for it, she knew. Three weeks in the Australian sun had given her a healthy glow – she was relaxed, happy, content. Stronger too.

'You'll *never* guess,' Charmaine began excitedly. Rianne feigned surprise. It was Charmaine's big secret. 'I'm *pregnant*!' she announced triumphantly.

'*No!*' Rianne began to laugh.

Charmaine looked at her suspiciously. 'Did Nathalie tell you?'

'No, of course not. We – me and Gabs – we kind of guessed.' She gave Charmaine a hug. 'Gabs is heartbroken she can't be here – she sent loads of things and *I* lugged them all the way across the bloody Atlantic. Come on, let's open them. Where's Nat?'

It took them three hours to plough through the gifts, books and baby advice that Gabby had sent, between attending to Anna and listening to Micha when he came back from school.

Rianne lay back on the coffee-coloured rug and watched them. She'd fished out her camera and, amid cries of protest, had taken almost a roll of film, contemplating domestic bliss – a postcard-perfect image of two young women in their prime, surrounded by children and loved ones. Charmaine glowed with the special, earthy sensuality that sometimes comes to women in the early stages of pregnancy, before the morning sickness, nausea and tears. Rianne enjoyed looking at them all through the dispassionate lens of her camera, seeking out the unusual in the scene in front of her.

Despite its rather austere elegance, Nathalie's house was warm and comfortable on the cold autumn evening. Eric was at work, and Nathalie had taken the afternoon off from her normally punishing work schedule. Things were finally turning round for U/d, after three lean years. She'd been right to hang on: women were treating U/d as an old friend, a brand that had been around for a while, something you could trust. Unlike so many of the businesses that had gone belly-up during the recession, U/d had hung in there. Now the loyalty her customers had displayed was paying off. Nathalie was in a good position: all she had to do, she had told Rianne and Charmaine, was update her lease and her look, and shift the collections back to something *slightly* more glamorous, *slightly* more sexy.

'So, where's Jess?' Rianne asked Charmaine. She couldn't believe she was the only one who'd not set eyes on him. Even Gabby had met him – he'd passed through New York the previous spring on his way to a conference. Rianne had been with Nina in New Orleans, and Gabby and Nael had taken Jess to dinner. They *loved* him. Rianne was tired of being the only one who didn't know how special, wonderful, beautiful, etc., he was.

'He'll be here any minute,' Charmaine promised.

'He'd better be,' Nathalie said drily. 'I've booked a babysitter – we're all going out. It'll be my first night out in . . . God, I don't know how long. Get used to this, Char,' she added. 'No more late nights for you, my sweet. No sex either,' she added, laughing at Charmaine's sceptical face.

'Maybe that's what happened to you,' Charmaine said primly, 'it won't happen to me and Jess.'

'Hmm. Talk to me in a year's time,' was all Nathalie would say.

'Char,' Rianne said suddenly. She wanted to say something to her while it was just the three of them. Charmaine looked up from *Dr Spock's Guide to Child-Rearing: The Updated Version*. 'I'm . . . we're so glad for you. Really.'

Charmaine looked at them, her eyes momentarily bright. 'Don't. I can't thank *you* enough,' she said hoarsely. 'I can't tell you what your support has meant to me.'

'Don't be silly, Char, we're friends. That's what we're for.'

'Well, not many friends would've done what you did for me.'

'Oh, Char, just seeing you here, hearing your news – I can't believe it. It's great.'

'Yeah – it's turned out OK, hasn't it? For all of us, I mean.' Charmaine looked at Nathalie, holding her second child. 'But what about you? Don't you want . . . ?' She gestured in Nathalie's direction.

'Er, yes . . . yes, of course I do. Just not right now.' Rianne could feel her face turning red. How could she explain that seeing Nathalie and Eric filled her with envy? That seeing Gabby and Nael together – the longing cut straight through her? That despite all her efforts to stop loving him, she couldn't? She stood up abruptly. 'Loo. Back in a moment.' She ignored Charmaine's puzzled look and ran down the corridor.

She slid the bolt on the door and stared at herself in the mirror. She turned on the taps and splashed cold water over her face, feeling it mingle with her tears. She drew a deep breath. And another. She stood still for several minutes, waiting for the pain in her head to pass. She tried not to think about him. It was hard to see Charmaine so happy and Nathalie bathed in domestic bliss. They'd all found themselves – and happiness too. She was back to being the outsider, the odd one out. In New York, she was so disciplined – she refused to allow herself to think about him. Most of the time it worked. She avoided the reminders of her previous life – that was how she thought of it – every day. She had a different life, now. A life without him. She splashed a little more water on her face to cool her burning cheeks.

Just as she emerged, the doorbell rang. From the cries of welcome, she guessed correctly that Jess had arrived. She steeled herself for the picture of happiness she was about to encounter and went downstairs to meet the latest addition to the group. For once, she thought, as she shook his hand, Charmaine was not only right, she was lucky.

84

It was almost nine o'clock in Johannesburg at the end of a long, tiring day. Riitho was alone in the office, finishing a set of drawings. He walked over to the cupboard in the tiny kitchen and poured himself a small glass of whisky, neat – the way he liked it. He swallowed, feeling it burn the back of his throat, smooth and strong. He glanced at his watch. He'd eaten nothing all day. He picked up his car keys – he'd stop by Aido's place and see if he could be persuaded to come out. He was just reaching for his jacket when the phone rang. He picked it up, wondering who would be calling at this hour.

'Ree. It's Nael.'

'Nael?' It was the most welcome surprise. 'Where are you, man? Christ, it's good to hear you!'

'I'm here in Jo'burg, believe it or not. Carlton Centre.'

'I'll be right over. How long're you in town?'

'Two days. I'm on my way back to New York. Couldn't get a flight from Kampala so we came south.'

'Stay where you are. Meet you in the bar?'

'You got it.'

'What're you drinking?' Nael asked, as he came into the bar. He'd been held up trying to put a call through to Gabby.

Riitho held up a tumbler of whisky and ice. 'Join me? It's my second. What a day.'

Nael nodded, smiling broadly. 'Good to see you, Ree. You're looking well.'

It was true. He looked sleeker and fitter than ever. In his trademark black sweater and slacks, he looked more like a well-tuned athlete than an architect living on coffee, whisky and little sleep.

'And you. Oh, congratulations, by the way.' Riitho smiled at him.

'On?'

'The baby. You sent me a card, remember?'

'You mean Gabby sent it. You know me – I don't call, I don't write . . .'

'Yeah, well, I'm not much better.' They clinked glasses.

It had been almost two years since they'd last seen each other. In the background, a pianist played something light, banal. The bar was full of fat businessmen in dark suits and loud ties, drinking away the strain of deals done clandestinely before 'the whole country goes to pot'. There were those in the white business community who viewed independence differently from those who had fought for it. Soft, tinkling music, perfumed air. It was a far cry from the noisy bars they'd hung out at the last few times they'd met.

'So, what's new?' Nael turned to him.

'*Ag*, nothing much. Work, life – you know the score.'

'How's the practice?'

'It's doing well. Lots of work.' He took a sip. 'We won a couple of competitions last month – enough to last us the next year or so. We've been lucky. We can't complain.'

'And the other stuff?'

'What d'you mean?'

'Life . . . women . . . Anyone special?'

'No.' Riitho paused. He picked up his glass, watched the golden liquid spill against the ice as he twirled it in his hands. 'Nothing.'

'Come on – *you*?' Nael laughed, taking a sip of his own drink. He looked at Riitho expectantly.

'No, there's no one.' His face burned. It was like being back at school, him and Nael, discussing an evening's activities. 'And you? You and Gabby, you're happy?' he asked.

'Yes, we are.' Nael was suddenly quiet. 'She's the best thing that ever happened to me.'

'You're lucky. You don't know how lucky. I wish—' He stopped.

'What?' Nael was staring at him. There was something in his voice. Riitho sounded almost . . . envious?

'*Ag*, nothing. I'm happy for you, that's all,' Riitho said quickly. He was surprised at himself. Nael's obvious joy had unsettled him. He wasn't used to talking about himself, not like this. It had been a long time since he'd talked – properly – to anyone.

'No . . . what were you going to say? You wish . . .' Nael's voice was gentle.

There was a long silence. Riitho turned the glass round and round in his hands. He sighed. 'I don't know. Christ, Nael, it just gets harder.'

'What does?'

'Being without her.'

'Who?'

'Rianne.'

'Ah.' There didn't seem to be much else to say.

85

Charmaine was late for her doctor's appointment. She raced along Oxford Street, battling with the wind and rain, cursing herself for the hour she'd spent – and the small fortune – in Baby Gap. Jess would kill her, she thought, when the credit-card bill came in. The trip to Melbourne had just about cleaned them out. His junior lecturer's salary wasn't enough to keep them in the luxury Charmaine enjoyed.

She'd given up *LifeStyle* as soon as she found out she was pregnant. Jess had been baffled – most of the girls he knew back home worked until their waters broke, but Charmaine didn't see it that way. Neither did her mother. The pair spent hours in the little flat poring over baby books, baby clothes, baby this-that-and-the-other. The flat, too, had been a major bone of contention. Jess didn't want to live in her flat – understandably, he pointed out to a sulking Charmaine. He hadn't probed but it was clear that the man who'd bought it wasn't an uncle – at least, not in the conventional sense. He didn't care what she'd done before he met her, or what she'd done to deserve the flat, but he was damned if he was going to profit from it too. So they sold it – or Charmaine sold it – and he'd been adamant. Put the money somewhere you can't touch it, he'd told her. He knew her almost better than she knew herself, she thought ruefully. So she did – and now she had a tidy sum sitting in an account in trust for the darling baby they were going to have.

But on days like this, when she wandered from one shop to another, she wished she could get her hands on a bit of it – just a bit. Those little dresses with pink ribbons, she couldn't resist them. She was already thinking about how to soften the blow of her small – *tiny*, really – spending spree . . . Jess couldn't stay mad at her for long. Not in her present state. She swore as someone bumped into her, again. She was five months pregnant with a sizeable bump and struggling through the crowds with three huge carrier bags plus an oversized handbag was no mean feat. No one moved aside for her, no one took any notice of her. Pigs, she thought, as she twisted and turned.

She glanced at her watch. It was almost four – she was over an hour late. A crowd of Japanese tourists was coming towards her, arms linked, cameras pointing in every direction. She stepped into the road to avoid them, forgetting to look behind her. And then everything seemed to happen at once.

There was a terrific shout, a long, screaming sound coming from far away, like a breath being exhaled – hands grasped at her and she felt something, a blow, a deafening roar, and then the back of her head hitting the ground, hard. The world around her froze. She could see people's faces, turning towards her in shock and horror. She tried to say something, grab hold of the hands that were moving towards her, but her arms felt so heavy, she couldn't hold on. She could hear shouts, a woman held her head, someone else grasped her hand – she could hear crying, someone screaming. A wave of black nausea and pain ran through her, making her gasp and turn. Something was pinning her to the ground. She struggled against it, feeling rather than hearing the sound of her heart pumping, the blood rushing through her ears. And a siren – she could hear its wail. She tried to turn her head to look but found she couldn't move. There were tears . . . She felt them slide down her face into her mouth – she was gasping for breath.

And then, suddenly, when she felt she couldn't stand the noise another second, there was silence. Soft, warm silence. Fatigue spread through her, pouring from behind her eyes, down her neck, stopping in the hollow of her throat and spilling over her chest. She felt herself slide . . . It started to cover her, fill her. She tried to cry out but her mouth was full. She could taste something thick and warm, the sweetness of peace, at the back of her throat. An unbearable, cloying sweetness . . . a lightness of being . . . an unbearable lightness of being. That was Kundera's phrase. She felt herself smiling. *Damn. Who would have thought it?* she spoke to herself alone, testing the words on her tongue. *Kundera. Didn't even know I knew his name.*

86

'Will you get it?' The doorbell rang. Nathalie looked up at Rianne from her position on the floor. She had almost managed to get Anna to sleep. 'It's probably Charmaine. She's back early.'

Rianne jumped up and ran down the short flight of stairs. She could see two figures through the opaque glass of the front door – two men. She opened the door.

Her first thought when she saw the two policemen was that she'd parked the hire car illegally. Nathalie was always going on about parking in London. How 'dangerous' it was. She smiled, already culpable. The men didn't smile back.

'Ms Maréchal?' one asked.

Rianne's heart began to beat faster. 'No, I'm a friend of hers. She's upstairs. What's happened?'

'May we come in?' the elder of the two policemen said, taking off his cap.

Rianne nodded, a cold, hollow feeling in her stomach.

'Who is it?' Nathalie called, from the dining room.

'It's the police.' Rianne cleared her throat. 'They want to speak to you.'

'Ms Maréchal?' the policeman asked, looking up. Nathalie had appeared at the top of the stairs, a sleeping Anna in her arms.

'Yes, I'm Nathalie Maréchal. What's wrong?'

'We're terribly sorry to bring you such news.' The younger one spoke. 'Do you have somewhere to sit?'

'Tell me what's happened.' Nathalie rushed down the stairs and Rianne took Anna from her. The baby woke and began to cry. The policeman's words, when they did come, were almost drowned by her wails.

'Charmaine?' Rianne repeated, staring at the policeman. 'That's impossible. She was just here. She went shopping this morning.'

'Miss, I'm awfully sorry. It must be a terrible shock. Your friend's address was the only contact detail we found on the . . . on her.'

'No, no . . .' Rianne's voice caught in her throat.

Nathalie clung to Rianne's arm, her face white and wide-eyed with shock. 'No,' she echoed. 'Please. *Please* no.'

'Did – does Mrs Dalton have any living relatives? A husband? Parents?' the policeman asked. He had been through similar scenes a hundred times before. Shock, denial, tears, sometimes rage. Each time was as painful as the last. He motioned to the junior officer. Get her a drink. Quick.

Nathalie had doubled up on the floor.

Rianne was still holding the crying baby. All she could do was stare into the abyss that had opened up in front of her. Céline, Marius, Riitho. Everyone she loved was taken from her. She hadn't realised how much she had loved Charmaine until she was gone.

It was a blustery late-autumn day. Rain fell intermittently, bursting out of the sky and briefly soaking the funeral party. Rianne, Nathalie and Gabby wound their way through the small cemetery to a gash in the earth where a grave had been prepared – a raw, open scar in the lush green lawn. Nathalie was sobbing, but Gabby was silent.

Rianne watched the clouds overhead becoming darker and heavier with unshed rain. She tried to focus on what was happening in front of her. The men were releasing the coffin, lowering it awkwardly between them until it rested beside the hole in the earth. She watched Mary Hunter lean into Jess's father, pushing her head into the folds of his jacket, while she held on to Jess. There was a moment's wait.

The men struggled to lower the coffin. Then it was done – the coffin rested securely on the earth at the bottom of the grave. There was absolute silence, nothing but the sound of the wind in the trees. Everything held its breath. The skies opened again – a brief, intense shower and then it was over. The vicar read something – none of them could have said afterwards what it was. They were still in shock, stunned by the tragedy.

In the car on the way back to London, Gabby held Yasmeen in her arms and watched the autumn landscape slide past the window, her mind wandering. Charmaine was gone? It wasn't possible. At High Wycombe, the ploughed earth and dark fields gave way to semi-industrial suburbs. She followed the silvery tongue of the river as it ran alongside the road, disappearing into stagnant pools alongside clumps of dark trees whose names she had forgotten. The greenery lurched and blurred before her eyes.

87

They each reacted differently. Unusually for her, Gabby clung to Nael, as if she was afraid he would disappear if she let him out of her sight. With the circumstances of his job, it was difficult. He cancelled first one assignment, then another as Gabby's tears threatened to become hysterical. She couldn't believe how much she missed Charmaine. Her death didn't seem *right* – not for all the usual reasons but because it was Charmaine. She was life itself: she'd disregarded the rules that the others, even Rianne, followed. It didn't seem possible – or fair – that she was the one from whom it had been taken.

In that time Nael was there for her, as he'd said he would be always. He watched her, took care of Yasmeen, cancelled his assignments and bore her anger. For better or worse, he told her, stroking her head as she lay in bed on the mornings when she couldn't get up. This is worse. It will get better. Gabby held his hand and was grateful.

Alone at home in London, Nathalie was racked with guilt. She hadn't told anyone – she would never tell anyone, ever – but for the tiniest fraction of a second, a split second after the policeman had said Charmaine's name, relief had flowed through her that it wasn't Eric. A second later, she almost fainted, both with the shock of the news and revulsion at herself for thinking, for even *daring* to think ... *thank God, thank God it's not Eric*. She was still in shock, as they all were, but hers was laced with guilt. She did what she had to, each day – took Micha to school, looked after Anna, went to the shops but her mind was elsewhere. Charmaine.

In some ways, she was grateful for the way Jess leaned on her in the weeks and months following the accident. He had made it through the funeral – his parents had flown out from Australia almost immediately – but it was clear to everyone present that he couldn't – and shouldn't – be left alone. He'd stayed with Nathalie and Eric for a few days after his parents had left, just until he'd sorted out what he wanted to do. Charmaine, he told Nathalie, had been his reason for living in London. Now that she was ... He couldn't bring himself to say it.

Nathalie and he spent long hours together, in the weeks that followed, sometimes with Eric, sometimes with only Anna for company. In those conversations, he had revealed a happier, more stable Charmaine, someone with plans for the future and a deep love for the friends who had helped her get there. Things she wouldn't have said to Nathalie or the others. Things that made Nathalie feel worse. But, like Gabby, Nathalie had the support of a husband, and in her sadness she wasn't alone. Having Jess and Eric with her helped. Eric knew from a source of professional experience that the shock and disbelief would eventually give way. And the guilt. He knew, even if she didn't say it, what she'd been thinking. He could see it in her eyes.

Rianne had no one. Alone in her flat in New York, she thought about Charmaine and what her friendship had meant. The four had been together for so long now. It was thirteen years since St Anne's, and it had been Charmaine who had been the first to extend a hand to her. She thought back to their first, awkward outing – Serendipity's – and then, of course, seeing Riitho. She stood at the kitchen window, looking out at the tiny patch of sky her view afforded her, and listened to the sounds of the street traffic. Standing there in the cool spring air, she experienced a double sense of loss – the loss of a sister as well as a friend. She loved Charmaine like a sister. They were all like sisters. Rianne was closer to them than she was to anyone else in the world. She'd been with them so long – with their thoughts and faces and conversations in her mind, even when they weren't around – that she'd almost forgotten to think about them. Gabby, Nathalie, Charmaine. They were just there, in the way family were often 'just' there.

Except Charmaine was no longer there. But, she thought, her loss wasn't hers alone: it was everyone's. It made the pain just that bit more bearable. It also made the pain of losing Riitho just that bit worse. What if something happened to him? Not being with him was one thing – but to think she would never be, that the possibility could never exist? She hadn't realised how much she still thought about him, 'talked' to him in her head . . . considered him. He was part of her. He always would be. She closed the window abruptly and waited for the thought to pass.

88

Riitho switched off the computer and stared out of the window. It was almost ten-thirty in the evening. He took off his glasses, moved aside the yellow detail paper and cardboard models that cluttered his desk and pinched the bridge of his nose. He could hear Rahesh and Aido arguing in the boardroom – they were working on a competition, which, if they won it, would catapult the practice into the big league. They'd been living in their offices for the past ten days and tempers were short. He looked at the sketches in front of him. His mind kept wandering back to the shocking phone call. Nael had called to tell him about Charmaine Hunter. Not that Riitho could remember her well – he'd hardly known her. But Gabby was devastated. As was Rianne. It had been the most horrible accident, Nael said. No one could believe it. Gabby was only just beginning to regain her normal, even-tempered balance.

He rubbed his eyes and picked up his glasses again. He stared at the phone. At that moment, he wanted nothing more than to talk to her, tell her he'd heard from Nael, that he was sorry for her – their – loss. His hand went to the receiver. He paused. Unbelievable as it seemed to him, even after so long, he didn't know her number. He sat staring at the phone, unable to think for the images that were crowding his mind. Rianne: her face a mask of rage and pain, as he'd seen her last. Rianne as he'd seen her first – the haughty arrogance. The look on her face when she'd walked into his offices in Paris, the delight as she followed him around Vaux-le-Vicomte that evening, the touch of her lips as he kissed her for the first time. He put his face in his hands, breathing deeply. He was trembling.

89

A month later Gabby was lying on the sofa in their apartment, arguing mildly with Nael. 'We can't do that to her. Or to him,' she said, shifting Yasmeen's position.

'Well, she won't come if we tell her. Neither will he.'

'Nael, I can't do that to her.'

'Well, how else are we going to do it?'

'I know. I . . . just *can't*. Not after what's happened.'

'But you've said it yourself – she's not over him.'

'So?'

'Well, maybe it'll be a good thing – either help her get over him, or—'

'Or what?'

'I don't know. He's not over her, either.'

'Nael, don't be silly. You can't play God.'

'I'm not. I'm just—'

'Just what? It's not up to us. It's up to them.'

'I know it is. I'm just suggesting they need . . . a helping hand.'

'Come on, Nael. A helping hand? What are you – Oprah? Be serious.' Gabby smiled faintly.

'I *am*. It's the only way.'

'Well, I don't think it's a good idea.' Gabby got up and

walked into the kitchen. It was supper-time, when Yasmeen struggled to put as much food as possible on the walls, floor, table, bib, her mother, anywhere but into her mouth. Nael watched them, amused. Gabby didn't think it was a good idea. But she hadn't said no.

Rianne lay in the bath looking at her legs sliding in and out of the water. She was paler than she had been in ages. She'd come back from London where 'Dispatches' had just opened – a month later than planned, for personal reasons, she'd explained to Sally Bryson. The show was dedicated to Charmaine and one of the last-minute additions to the photographs was the last shot she had taken of her friend lying on the sheepskin rug in Nathalie's living room, her hair spread out behind her, her face turned in a slow, sexy smile towards the camera. That was how Rianne liked to remember her – at peace with herself. She'd sent Jess a framed print and he'd written to thank her. She could read his tears in the letter.

She looked at the little silver clock on the shelf above the bath. Eleven a.m. The christening was at two. Reluctantly, she got out of the bath, wrapped herself in an enormous towel and padded into the bedroom. She dried herself slowly, thinking about what to wear. She opened her wardrobe door. It was a far cry from the vast, walk-in space she'd had at Lisette's, she thought, as she flicked through the hangers. That was something else that had been pared down over the past few years. She'd had too much stuff. Now everything she owned fitted neatly into the one-bedroom apartment: her clothes filled the wardrobe and no more. That was it.

She pulled out a floor-length ivory silk skirt and a long cashmere cardigan and laid them on the bed. Yes. With a pair of black leather boots and a wide, silver belt. It took her moments to find underwear, tights and earrings, then she was blow-drying her hair and putting the finishing touches to her make-up. She looked at herself in the mirror

– a quick, faint smile, she looked fine. She grabbed her bag, the present she'd bought for her goddaughter, and closed the front door behind her.

Riitho stood in the vestibule of the church, breathing deeply. His heart was thudding, a slow, heavy pulse that measured the minutes as they ticked by. He twisted the silver ring he wore on his index finger. He couldn't quite believe he had come. It was Nael's idea. In the small, dimly lit space, he was alone with his thoughts for the first time in nearly a week.

Nael had persuaded him to fly back to New York with him – he'd been on assignment in Johannesburg for a fortnight. Yasmeen was about to be christened – against Nael's wishes, his friend had said, smiling ruefully, it was Gabby who insisted – and he had only agreed to go along with it if Riitho would consent to be her godfather. Put like that, Riitho could hardly refuse. It wasn't until they were half-way across the Atlantic that Nael mentioned the other thing. The other reason he'd asked Riitho. It had taken all of Riitho's strength to remain seated. Not that he'd had many alternatives, Nael pointed out. Wasn't really any place to go. Not at thirty-nine thousand feet.

By the time they landed at JFK, Riitho was sufficiently calm to shrug the matter off. *No big deal. She's moved on. So have I.* He failed to notice the look that passed between Nael and his wife.

Now, five minutes before she was due to arrive at the church, he realised he'd had it all wrong. It was a big deal. A *huge* deal. He twisted the ring again and looked out into the street. And then he saw her. Exactly as it had been the last time they met, he saw her first. She stepped out of the cab – tall, graceful . . . beautiful. Exactly as he remembered her. He watched her pay the driver, shake her hair in the way he knew so well and turn towards the entrance of the church. Gabby was waiting to tell her he was there before she saw him and bolted.

Nael walked up to him, his daughter in his arms. 'You OK?' he asked.

'Yeah. Fine.'

'Priest's just gone down to meet them. We'll start in a couple of minutes. You sure you're OK?'

'Yeah. Come on, let's go.' Riitho's heart was thumping.

In the dim light of the entrance, he moved out of the shadows to face her. In that moment, the blood rushed to his head, he struggled with himself to speak. 'De Zoete.' The lapse was swift and unchecked. He held his breath.

Rianne closed her eyes against the unbearable sweep of longing that the sound of his voice had exhumed. Gabby and Nael moved away discreetly.

'Riitho.'

They stared at each other for a moment, neither wanting to speak. He bent forward to kiss her on each cheek. His hands were firm on her arms. She moved back a step. He saw, and winced. There was a great tension between them, a rush of memory, pain, anger.

Before they could speak, there was a discreet cough behind them. All four turned. The priest had arrived. He shook hands with them, welcoming them to his church. He strode in front, his snowy-white surplice billowing behind him as he led them towards the pulpit. It was dim and quiet inside: through the stained-glass windows, shafts of tinted light fell on the empty pews. They stopped briefly as Father O'Leary ran through the order of the service.

Rianne didn't trust herself to look at Riitho and concentrated fiercely on the floor instead. Gabby and Nael looked nervously from one to the other – Nael cursed himself. Riitho looked as unhappy as Rianne did. He could have kicked himself for being so insensitive.

Fortunately for all of them, Yasmeen began to cry, loudly . . . in between trying to comfort her and listening to the priest's words, the rest of the ceremony passed in a blur.

*

Afterwards, as they stood on the steps waiting for the car that would take them back to Gabby and Nael's, Rianne roused herself from the frozen, dreamlike state into which she'd slipped to steal a look at the man standing next to her. She couldn't quite believe he was there – memories of what had happened the last time they met ran through her like liquid fire. He'd left her in the conference room at the hotel. He'd spelled it out to her – no more, over, finished. He'd given her up, turned away, done all the things he said he never would. At the time, she'd thought she would die.

Day after day, waiting by the phone, the pressure in her chest rising to choke her. She watched him talk to the priest, make a joke, turn to Nael. She watched him laugh – his whole face lit up by the same high-wattage smile. She had to resist the ridiculous urge – absurd how *that* hadn't changed – to slip her hand into his, stand a little closer to his heat. He looked the same – a little older, perhaps, the body beneath the black coat broader. She noticed the way the sweater he wore stretched across his biceps and hung loosely over the planes of his flat, hard stomach. He caught her looking at him and she blushed. It was happening again: she was being drawn in. That old, familiar sense of watching herself came back to her.

From far away she watched herself talking to Gabby, turning to Nael to answer a question, holding Yasmeen. And always, always, Riitho's eyes on her. She was conscious of him beside her as he held out his arms for the baby.

Ten minutes later, in the cab, she was conscious of the curve of his thigh next to hers, his arm resting on the back of the seat, his voice. The conversation rose and fell around her. Locked in her own private world with her own private struggle, she turned to stare out of the window.

The brownstones and churches fell away as the cab sped up Flatbush Avenue. To be so close to him was more than she could bear. Riitho was polite, but distracted, a distant look in his eyes. Rianne took it for indifference – and was angered by it. It made her all the more determined not to let him any closer.

Later that afternoon Riitho watched from the window as Gabby and Rianne headed back into Manhattan. He watched her twist her hair and throw it over her shoulder, then fasten her seat-belt. The afternoon had been a terrible strain.

Despite his calm exterior – everything under control, always – his mind was in turmoil. He had known the minute he saw her again that he wanted her – desperately. If anything, the years of absence had made it sharper, more acute. As he watched them drive away, he was aware of the wishes of his family sloughing off him. He couldn't recall a single reason why he shouldn't be with her. All the opposition, the fuss, the pressure. It was extraordinary. Next to the intensity that surrounded Rianne, it dissolved, into nothing. Nothing.

90

When the phone rang later that evening, Rianne knew it was him. She knew that if she didn't pick it up he would never ring again. He knew she was there, watching, waiting. She knew that about him, as he did about her. She hesitated, then picked up the receiver. This time, she spoke before he did.

'Riitho.'

'Meet me. Will you?'

She arrived in the lobby of the hotel on Mercer Street, her heart in her mouth. Why had she agreed to meet him? What could he have to say to her? Or she to him? It was asking for trouble. But how could she have refused? It was like playing with fire. She'd once told him she couldn't live without the heat he brought, and it was true. She remembered something he'd read to her, long ago. He'd opened a novel and traced the words with his fingers: 'Nobody told me love was warm. Such warmth – I seemed to remember it, it seemed like something forgotten by me since I was born. All the fires are here, and the warmth of my mother's bed long ago and the deep heat of the sun.' She'd gone out the very next day and bought it. She still had it. Reading it reminded her of what she'd lost. And now she was contemplating a return to that heat – only to have it snatched from her again, as she was sure it would be.

She looked around the elegant space with its black leather seating and exotic plants but couldn't see him. Anger rose in her. Damn him! He was making her wait. They hadn't even met yet and he was already playing games with her. By the time she sat down on one of the sofas, she was fuming. She ordered a drink, something to calm her nerves. Two minutes later, a flirtatious waiter brought the whisky sour. She sipped it slowly. She would give him five minutes. No more.

'Hey.' He had come up behind her chair. She almost choked and turned, angry with herself now. She'd practised slipping behind her cool, aloof mask and, in two seconds, she'd already blown it.

'Hi,' she said tightly.

He sat down opposite her and didn't pretend not to study her. 'You look great.'

She was wearing a long, black silk dress and a soft lambswool coat. 'Thanks,' she said shortly. She looked at him. He looked at her. There was a sudden silence between them.

The waiter glided back.

'What're you drinking?' Riitho asked, looking at the half-empty tumbler.

'Whisky sour,' the waiter replied for her. 'Best in Manhattan.'

'Sounds good.' Riitho nodded. The waiter left. They sat back, silence falling between them again. A minute later, his drink arrived.

'So . . .' Riitho leaned forward to pick up his glass. The urgency that had made him lift the phone that evening left him suddenly. Evaporated. Rianne de Zoete was sitting in front of him and he had all the time in the world. 'So,' he repeated, his jet-black eyes looking straight into hers, 'Nael tells me you're a photographer?' He leaned back in his seat, watching her.

'No . . . well, yes . . . sort of,' Rianne said, thawing just a little. Under the heat of his gaze . . . it was hard to remain cold. And, she realised, she wanted to tell him what she'd done, who she'd managed to become. It was important to tell him. She knew why. 'I've just had a show in London.'

' "Dispatches". Nael told me. It's great – a whole different side to you.' He sounded genuine.

Rianne nodded slowly. *There are many sides to me you don't know*, she wanted to say, but couldn't. She took a sip of her drink. 'And I hear from Gabby you're doing really well – in the practice, I mean.'

'Yeah, we've just won a competition. There's three of us . . . I have two partners.'

There was a short silence. Rianne raised her eyes to his. 'Any other partners?' she asked.

He toyed with his glass. 'No. You?' Rianne shook her head slowly, looking away. He smiled faintly. 'What? No one? That's hard to believe.'

'You said that the first time we met. Remember?' She turned her gaze on him.

'Yes, I do. What's stopping you?'

Rianne seemed about to speak, then drew a deep breath and raised her eyes to his. He saw the lids fall, in a self-conscious gesture, then open again, looking at him fully. The irises of her eyes were wide and dark – he had the sensation of looking into her, not just at her. Her lips parted – he could see the tip of her tongue resting against her teeth as she considered the question. She let out a breath and then she spoke. 'You,' she said simply, without a trace of coquetry.

There was a great silence between them. He looked at his hands, at the glass he was holding. Then, very carefully, he set it down on the steel-and-glass table. 'Come.' He matched her directness. She was aware of warmth spreading through her, not unlike the whisky warmth. It began at the back of her throat and slowly slid its way down, spreading like a stain through her body. He stood up, holding out his hand. She took it and they walked past the front desk into the elevator. He pushed a button, they stepped inside and went up.

The doors opened and they walked out into the corridor. He turned to her. 'De Zoete,' he began, the key to his room in his hand. She looked down at it, then at him. 'This . . . is going to change everything, you know that?' She nodded. He took her hand and they walked down the corridor. He stopped outside a door and then, suddenly, it closed behind her and she was in his arms, her head pressed tightly to his chest.

She breathed in the familiar scent of him, wrapping her arms round him, the feel of him flooding her senses. Her body had associations of its own with the solid feel of him in her arms. She began to move against him.

'Rianne,' he said thickly, against her ear, 'I . . . This is . . .' She put a finger to his lips. Stop. Stop talking. She reached forward and their lips met. His were soft – she felt the warmth of his tongue, the gentle tug on her lower lip as he drew it into his mouth. She closed her eyes. Riitho. There was nothing and no one like him.

Some time later, he couldn't say when, he opened his eyes, feeling the goose-bumps on her skin soften as her breathing slowed. She lay against him, her hair spread across his arm, stirring under the rhythm of her breath. He turned to look at her. *You are the most precious thing in the world to me.* He didn't know if he'd said it aloud.

EPILOGUE

May 1996: Johannesburg, South Africa

Rianne stands in front of the mirror. She is alone in the room, with nothing to distract her except the sound of her own breathing. She slides the thin strap of her dress over one shoulder and fastens it, her fingers shaking very slightly. She can hear her heart thudding, the sound is loud in her ears. She looks at herself: poised, perfectly calm. The pale silk dress sits well on her, fitted tight across the bodice, falling in a simple line to the ground. A band of tiny pale yellow roses secures her hair and, in her hand, a matching bouquet. She can hear footsteps outside the door, and the sound of voices. Njeri is scolding Riitho – in their language that she still cannot understand. Mpho's voice – in English – his bow-tie isn't quite right. She smiles to herself. Two years. It's taken them two years to win his family's approval – and trust. She thinks for a minute: that's been their story all along. Waiting. It's fifteen years since they first met. She is not the same person, and neither is he. She can hear her father coming up the stairs. He's saying something to Njeri. She hears a suppressed giggle and the door opens.

Marius enters the bedroom closing the door quickly behind him, following Njeri's cross words to her son: 'You're not supposed to see her . . .' Her voice trails off as the door closes. Rianne turns to him.

'You look beautiful,' Marius says, smiling. She blushes. In front of him, his daughter waits nervously. She blurs in front of his eyes, suddenly – she is so like her mother.

'Ready?' he asks, his voice suddenly hoarse. She nods. He offers his arm.

She takes one last look at herself in the mirror. Outside the house, she knows, the photographers will be waiting, hundreds of cameras pointed at them like weapons. It's the wedding – and the story – of the decade in South Africa. And elsewhere. From Houghton it's a short ride to the elegant stone church on Jeppe Street where the archbishop will marry them. She smooths her hands over her dress and over her stomach, lingering there, just for a second. It's her secret, no one knows. Not even Riitho. She squares her shoulders.

Marius opens the door. Riitho is standing there, much to Njeri's annoyance. 'This one,' she says, in a half-aside to his sister, 'he doesn't listen.'

Riitho still isn't listening. He watches her walk out of the room on Marius's arm. It's the same for him as it's always been. Everything and nothing. She was wrong: this isn't just a place to stay. This is it. Everything and nothing. He smiles and takes her hand.